Alpha Wolf

More by Brooke Shaffer

The Timekeeper Chronicles

The Chivalrous Welshman
Time to Kill
Tick Tock
Windup
Stopwatch
Free Time
Leap Second
Imminence (Summer 2022)

The Hands of Time
In the Hands of the Enemy
The Hands Pulling the Strings
The Hand Holding the Knife (Winter 2023)

The Lone Wolf
Wolf Pack
Alpha Wolf
Lone Wolf (Spring 2023)

Singles
Of Saints and Sinners
Chasing the White Bear (Winter 2022)

Alpha Wolf
Book Two of The Lone Wolf
The Timekeeper Chronicles

Brooke Shaffer

Black Bear Publishing

Published in Michigan by Black Bear Publishing.

ISBN:
 Hardcover: 978-1-953113-19-1
 Softcover: 978-1-953113-20-7
 eBook: 978-1-953113-21-4

For George, who always knew the way to Peace

Words and Phrases

Adahnesagi'a | He is conjuring/witching (Cherokee)

Aiawa | Slur against an Ayvwiya

Agi'a | He is setting it down (Cherokee)

Aki | (my) Father (Choctaw)

Ale | And (Cherokee)

Atsakta | Choctaw (Cherokee)

Atsvstdi | Light (Cherokee)

Chagga | Slur against a Chahta

Chahta | Choctaw (Choctaw)

Chalakki | Cherokee (Choctaw)

Chishke | (your) Mother (Choctaw)

Galohisdi | Doorway (Cherokee)

Galo'ondiha | He is picking it up (Cherokee)

Galo'ondiha ale Agi'a | Gravity

Gayalvnga | It is sticking to it; it is attached to it; Magnetism (Cherokee)

Guka | Mom (Lenape)

Hitsa | (your) Father (Krydik)

Hoda | (your) Brother (Krydik)

Humi | (your) Grandmother (Krydik)

Ikilish | English, British (Choctaw)

Ishki | (his) Mother (Choctaw)

Kanchi | Sellout, an Indian who is "too white" (Choctaw)

Ki | (his) Father (Choctaw)

Miliki | American (Choctaw)

Nishab | Slur against an Anishinaabek

Nocha | Dad (Lenape)

Oceti Sakowin | Sioux Nations (Sioux)

Okla inla hopoyuksa | Savage foreigners (Choctaw)

Sashki | (my) Mother (Choctaw)

Tibafa | Hollowed-out, cave-like depression in the side of a hill (Choctaw)

Tsitsa | (my) Dad, Daddy (Krydik)

Tsitsi | (my) Mom, Mommy (Krydik)

Tsituta | (my) Grandfather (Krydik)
Udilegv'i | Hot (Cherokee)
Udilegv'i ale Uhyvtsa | Thermodynamics
Uhnvyvgi | Noise, sound (Cherokee)
Uhyvtsa | Cold (Cherokee)
V-e | Yes (Krydik)
Vv | Yes (Cherokee)
Wado | Thank you (Cherokee)

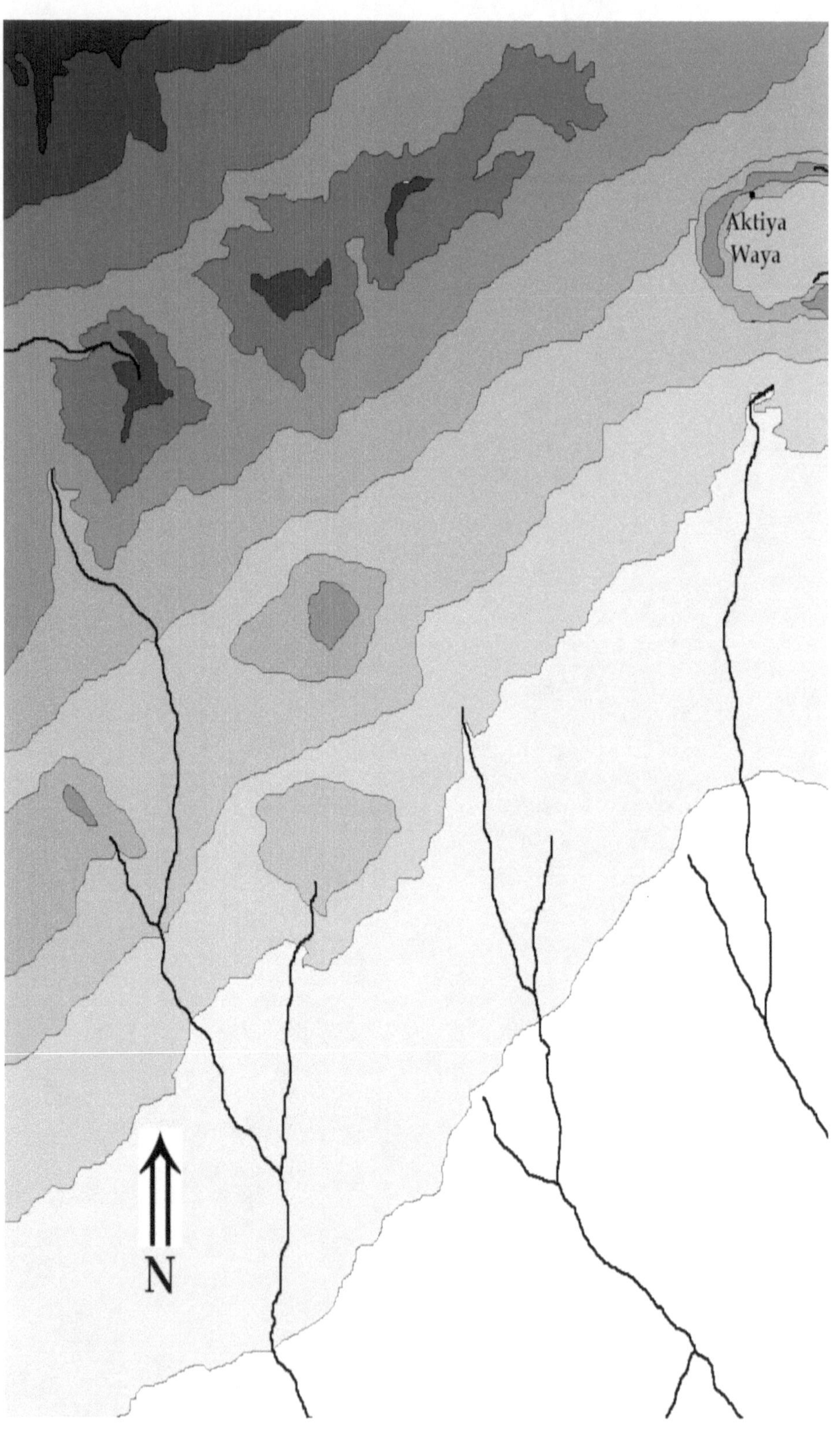

Aktiya
Waya
N

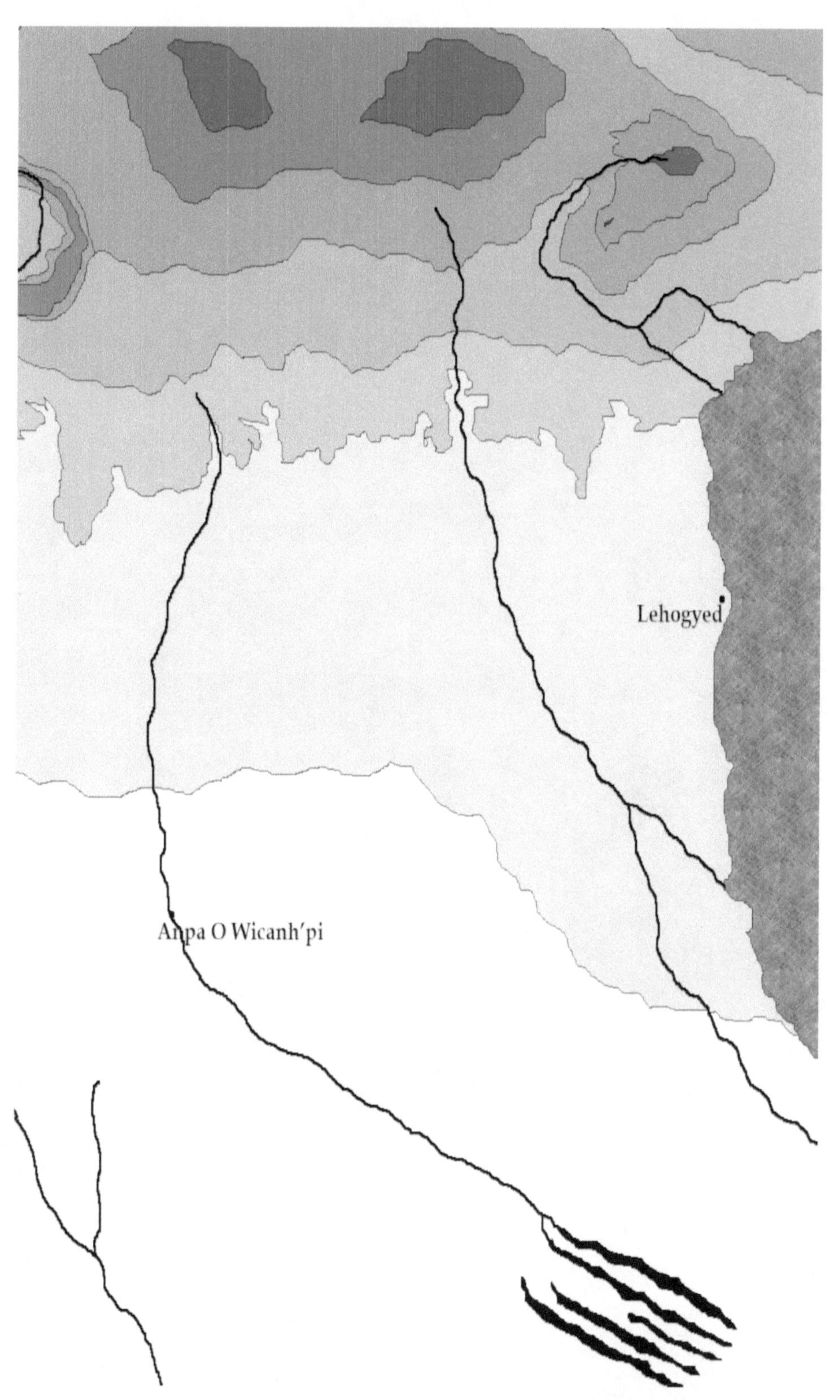

Lehogyed
Anpa O Wicanh'pi

Achaffa Tushafa

Waiting

The first time Roland heard of Aktiya Waya, he'd been huddled in a small camp somewhere in what the white men called Missouri, waiting for the supply wagons to meet them so they could cross the river. His people were not the only ones being moved west, and he often listened in on the stories from the others over the campfires, the stories helping the people to ignore the demands of their stomachs for a little while.

Roland was not his name, or not his real name. His mother said that it was the name his father gave him, made it easier for him and his people to pronounce. Roland didn't know what was so difficult about Ola Achukma, except that it wasn't an English name. His mother's language didn't even have that funny "rr" sound.

But that didn't matter anymore, or so said his family. They were going to new lands now. Western lands where they could live however they wanted, just as their ancestors had. The people had made a lot of concessions to the new United States, had many disagreements, but this would solve their problems. They would move west into lands set aside just for them, and they wouldn't be bothered anymore.

Well, it wasn't just them. Other people were leaving, too, going to their own lands. There were Chaḷakki, too, and others on different roads, all heading west.

It was the Chaḷakki who spoke of Aktiya Waya. They tried to speak of it in hushed tones, as if they did not wish for anyone else to hear about it, as though very many people understood their language anyway. But Roland's father had spent a great deal of time among many nations and learned their languages before meeting and marrying his mother. He'd taught Roland many of the languages in hopes that he would one day use such talents to foster peace and understanding.

For the time being, he used it to eavesdrop on others, listen to their stories.

Aktiya Waya certainly sounded like a wonderful place. There was plenty of game, vast wilderness, many friendly people. There was no war in Aktiya Waya, no hostile people to raid and steal and pillage. Children could play without fear, and women could forage without looking over their shoulders. Men could test their strength against nature, the storms and the beasts.

But the Chaḷakki also said that Aktiya Waya was free from the white-skinned people, and they often spat the name. Finally Roland got up the courage to ask his mother why they disliked the Americans so.

"The Chaḷakki were treated very badly by the Ikilish and the Miliki," she said, taking him on her lap and wrapping him with the blanket. "Grudges are very hard to forget."

"Aki was Miliki and he never treated us bad," Roland said.

"No, he was very good to us." His mother sighed sadly. "He was very...very good to us." She nodded. "But not everyone is like that. Some people in this world are very bad and very mean. It was those people who mistreated the Chaḷakki and make them resentful."

"Why don't they go to Aktiya Waya, then?"

She grinned. "Oh, my love. Chaḷakki stories, nothing more. The same way we have our stories that we like to tell. Stories of old times and far away places."

"Are they as far away as Jerusalem and Judea, like in Aki's Bible?"

"Farther, my love. Much, much farther."

Roland leaned against his mother and shivered once. "Sashke, do you miss Aki?"

His mother sniffed and took an even breath. She rested her head on his chin. "Yes, Ola, I do. I wish he were here with us right now."

So did Roland. He missed his father, missed climbing into his lap at night to read from the Bible. He liked the stories. He liked listening to Jesus heal the sick people and feed the hungry. If He were here now, He might have been able to make this miserable trip a little more bearable. He could provide blankets and medicine, and he could multiply the people's meager rations. But Jesus wasn't around anymore, Aki said, not like that. Now He was with the people in spirit. One day He would return in the flesh, and Roland should always be ready for such a day, but for the time being they had only His promises and his commands to live by.

"Love God with everything you are," Ki told him, "and He will provide for you. But, interestingly enough, that is not the only command Jesus gave. In fact, the second one He said was equal to it. Love others as yourself. If you love others and make peace between them that they might love each other, then there will be harmony among men."

Roland's father had been as much missionary as diplomat, but he was well-loved by all the peoples he came into contact with. He'd been so well-loved, in fact, that multiple peoples almost went to war over who got to adopt him as one of their own. But, with his calm demeanor and bright spirit, John Aberdeen made peace between these arguing peoples.

Looking around at the groups huddled against the cold, Roland wondered what his father would do or say now, or if they would even be moving west. In his last days, Roland's father had opposed the removal. It was not a relocation, it was a removal. And when the states wanted more land, they would remove the Indians again. And again and again until there was nothing left of the indigenous population; surely the land could not go on forever. They should learn to live together, two people in the same room, rather than forcing out the current occupants over minor disagreements.

But for as beloved as he was among men, John Aberdeen was not rich, nor did he come from an especially influential family, and his voice was small enough to be drowned out with little protest. As a peacemaker, he could not very well call for violent opposition, and those who could peacefully oppose the measures would not, for they were the ones who wanted them: farmers looking for land, developers looking for land, tradesmen looking for resources, politicians looking for land and influence.

"Never give in to violence, Roland," Ki said, spending his last days abed, terribly ill and burning with fever. Later in life, Roland would wonder if he somehow knew that his wife and child would be forced to move west with the rest of them. God knew he'd fought the sickness with every ounce of strength he had. "Never give in to it. Violence is a dangerous, hungry beast that will consume you as much as those you are fighting, and in the end, no one really wins."

"Even Jesus drove the moneychangers out of His temple," Ishki chided, bringing him some cool water to drink. "Why shouldn't we take back our land?" She went on before he could get the breath to respond. "The land is the product of the Creator. It is His home. We would be cleansing the land of such monsters and disease that these okla inla hopoyuksa have brought."

"Would you drive me out as well?" Ki wondered, a light in his eye flickering to life, one he got when he teased his wife.

"You respect our land, our people, our way of life. They don't."

"And some of your own people call you too white, even a kanchi. They don't like the Bible that I carry or the skin that I wear. Yet they will be in the same position if they are moved. And the western peoples may decide to defend themselves."

"And then what?"

Ki took a labored breath. "I don't know. I don't have the answers. I wish I did."

Ishki replaced the rag on his forehead. "Neither do I."

"I've tried to make a safe, peaceful world for Roland and Priscilla and Evan, but I don't know that I've done a good job of it."

"You have. I know you have. And they will carry the flame of peace, just as you have taught them."

Roland jolted awake. Once he realized he was cuddled up with his mother under a threadbare blanket, he yawned, did a small stretch, being careful not to open the blanket, and tried to ignore his stomach.

Priscilla was the first to succumb to the disease. Roland remembered his sister as being terribly pale, her blue eyes almost glowing before they were closed. Evan was next, a few days later. One day the toddler was wailing because of the fever and the pain, and the next day he wasn't. Then Roland fell ill, and the next morning his father had died.

Sometimes, Roland wondered if his father had not despaired to lose all his children, and so gave up before he had to listen to the news of another child gone. Other times, he wondered if his father hadn't given up his life to save his last child, his firstborn. But it was a terrible time, and between the grief and the illness, his mother herself had worried terribly whether she should lose her entire family—again—to this beast. First it had taken her mother and father and three brothers, and now it was taking her husband and children. She wailed and pleaded as Roland lay abed. Whether it was her prayers or his father's sacrifice, no one really knew, but Roland had recovered.

Now it was just the two of them on this road west.

He looked around at the camp. Was this peace? Shivering in the cold, hungry bellies growling, looked after by men with guns though they did not appear to be faring much better. Or was this simply waiting to die?

Roland clutched his father's Bible to his chest. He wanted to open it, but that would mean opening his blanket to the cold. He also worried that the others would see it and try to steal it from him, rip out the pages and feed their puny fires.

It wasn't just the stories that Roland cherished now, but his father's handwriting, underlining verses, writing down cross-references, and jotting down notes and minor commentary.

He buried his head under the blanket, his mother quick to close up the hole, and peeked at a random page. There were several verses underlined here.

"but whosoever will be great among you, let him be your minister; And whosoever will be chief among you, let him be your servants: Even as the Son of man came not to be ministered unto, but to minister, and to give his life a ransom for many."

Matthew 20:26-28, Roland saw. There was another verse on the next page.

"And all things, whatsoever ye shall ask in prayer, believing, ye shall receive."

Matthew 21:22, one of Ki's favorites, and one he prayed often before traveling to another place, whether he'd been there a hundred times or not at all. He always asked for wisdom and the words to speak to bring truth and peace.

Roland now asked only for warmth and a bit of food. He didn't need much. He wasn't asking for a castle or a great feast. Even a good campfire with dry wood and a woodcock on a spit would do. Something. Anything. Even the dogs got the crumbs that fell from the master's table. That was in the Bible somewhere, he knew.

The sun came out that day, taking the edge off the chill so Roland dared to leave the warmth and safety of his mother's blanket. He found a couple other children around his age to play with, running around and tagging each other, or else playing hide-and-seek. Their parents got together in something like light-hearted conversation, and even the elders looked on fondly.

For a while, one could almost believe that things were almost normal.

A couple of soldiers came around with the day's rations. A cup of corn, half a cup of coffee grounds, a pinch of salt, a slice of hard bread, and a couple cups of water. Once the soldiers were gone, the children ran back to their parents for a meager meal.

Roland did not like the coffee; he thought it was far too bitter. But over the last few days, he'd come to tolerate it as a flavor his mother mixed in with the corn as she added a bit of water to soften it up and set it over their tiny fire to warm. He got most of the corn, while she sat there with her cup of coffee. She ate the last little bit of corn at the bottom of the tin cup, the stuff that mixed with the burned coffee grounds that Roland absolutely refused to eat.

A few of the older women had gone out once to see if they might forage for something, anything, amid the frost and snow. The best they could come up with were a few shriveled leaves, a handful of grasses, and a couple handfuls of pine needles from a small tree. Had they found more, the soldiers might have been persuaded to look the other way when they left camp, but with such a meager offering, they had been forbidden from leaving camp again. Couldn't have them running off back to Mississippi.

"It's better back home," Roland said, taking a small drink of water. "Why can't we go back?"

"Because we're moving west," his mother told him, and not for the first time. "We have to go."

"Why? Kintushi and his family stayed."

"Yes, but they wanted United States citizenship, and they were able to get it."

"Why couldn't we?"

His mother hummed a bit. "It's better this way, Ola Achukma. I know it doesn't seem like it now, but it will be better where we're going. We won't be United States citizens. We will be our own sovereign nation."

"What does sovereign mean?"

"It means we can make our own laws, our own rules, and no one can tell us otherwise. And the United States can't tell us what to do, either."

Roland stared at the water in his cup. "Would Aki have come, if he were still alive? He was a United States citizen." His mother faltered, and he pressed harder. "If he had wanted to stay, would we be back home?"

His mother hesitated and hummed again. "Oh, my love. There is so much you don't understand."

"But I do understand!" Roland insisted, standing and spilling his water. "Aki isn't here and you want to run away and you hate the Miliki and you want to take me away, too! What if I want to be a United States citizen?!"

"Hush, child," a nearby elder commanded, his words augmented by the disapproving stares of the rest of the elders around the fire. "Hush up and sit down. Listen to your mother."

Roland sat in a heap and grabbed his cup. There was still a bit of water left in the bottom which he reluctantly drank.

"Yes," his mother said after a moment. "If he were still alive, we might not be here. But he is gone. Our family is here now. All of us, the

Chahta, together."

"What about Grandmother Sara?" Roland mumbled, trying not to cry. "Or Uncle Robert?"

"Come now, you know better than that. You know they never liked us. They barely tolerated your father."

"But why? Why is this happening?" Roland felt hot tears roll down his cheeks.

His mother took an even breath. "Because some men want something that we have, and we are powerless to stop them from taking it."

"Why?"

"Because they have the weapons to kill us, the laws to silence us, and the numbers to overrun us."

Roland looked longingly at the Chalạkki, huddled around their fire, and imagined their stories of Aktiya Waya. Vast landscapes, no enemies, and no white men. He glanced at himself, his skin and hair very much like his mother's. He should very much like to see Aktiya Waya. But it was as his mother said. Only a story.

He stood and wandered off as if to relieve himself, heading down the bank of the river and sitting in a tibafa, a hollowed-out, almost cave-like depression in the bank. It was colder here, the wind coming across the river unabated, stinging his face with icy spray from the froth. The boat wasn't so far away. It was ready to go, but the supply wagons were late, perhaps hindered by their own fair share of foul weather. Or perhaps they'd been attacked. Ishki said they were powerless and had no weapons, but that didn't stop some from fighting back. But they were always defeated, in the end.

Ki had spoken of peace and warned against violence. Yet he had not held this removal in especially high regard. Would he have made this trek as quietly as the rest of them? Would he have gone back to Washington City to talk to the president and ask to not be moved? If their family had been allowed to stay, what would he have done about the rest that had to go? Could he have stopped all of them from leaving?

He was so confused. What did the other peoples think about this?

The Chalạkki were terribly bitter and resentful, yet they went along with it. Ki had once said that before the Revolution, the Chalạkki were a mighty and feared people. Then the British had burned more than half of their land and villages, and they'd never recovered. All they had left was their resentment, it seemed. Their resentment and their stories.

But what about the others? Why did they meekly surrender?

Was this what peace looked like? Ki had talked about turning the other cheek, but Roland would admit to feeling more like the man beaten and left in a ditch, to be ignored by the priests and helped only by a good Samaritan. Where was their good Samaritan? Who was going to come to them in their desperation and their squalor, to bind up their wounds, feed them, and make things right? Did such people even exist, or was it all like Aktiya Waya, just a story? Was it real, or simply something to use as a teaching moment?

Roland wiped away a few more tears. He wanted Ki. Ki would know what to say and what to do. He wouldn't make them leave. Or if he did, at least he would be there with them.

He wiped some spray from his face and eyes. Behind him, up the river toward the camp, he heard a commotion. Turning, he peeked over the lip of his tibafa.

A dozen wagons and another dozen horses lumbered from the road into town, stopping near the docks. Men were shouting and pointing, and those from the camp were meandering their way over to them.

Roland climbed out of his hole and ran over, pushing through the crowd, looking for his mother amid the sea of dull gray blankets. He reached the front of the crowd before he found his mother and almost ran into a soldier carrying a large sack.

"Get back, brat!" the man snapped, shoving Roland back with his boot.

Roland got up and scampered behind the nearest person, hoping no one had seen it, knowing everyone had.

"It's about time," one man was saying. He was a big man with a fat belly, a coat too small to cover it well, and a large hat with a feather. "We were only a few days away from having to cut rations again."

"Yeah, well, the bureaucrats chose a shit time to start moving these people," another man, this one not quite as big but taller and having equally insufficient clothing and an equally large hat, though without the feather. "We lost two wagons to weather and roads. Some of the load we could redistribute, but..."

"So, what you just left it out in the woods?" the fat man demanded.

"Am I an imbecile?" the tall man growled. "No, we didn't leave it out in the woods. We sent a couple men to the nearest town to fetch the blacksmith and a few others. We ended up trading some of the supplies for repairs to the rest of our train and shoes for a couple horses." He continued before the fat man could protest. "If we hadn't, we would have lost even more. Then we would have had to leave supplies out in the woods."

The fat man was greatly displeased by the news, Roland could tell.

"Fine," he said at last. He tossed some papers haphazardly to the ground. "Since these cargo lists are no longer accurate, why don't we just see what you've brought us and make a new list?"

"Sir?" a third man, hardly more than a teenager, who had been standing quietly off to the side, interrupted meekly. "The redskins?"

"What about them?" the fat man grumbled.

"Shall we give them more rations? Or at least distribute some of these blankets and coats?"

"I would recommend the blankets and coats at least," the tall man agreed. "Looking at the sky, there is some severe weather coming in tonight."

"I know how to read the weather!" the fat man snapped.

As if to make a point of it, he turned south and west and looked at the clouds rolling across the horizon, squinting his eyes against the wind. He mumbled a few things to himself, his large audience waiting expectantly.

"Peterson!" he barked at the third man. "Come with me to get an accurate count of these supplies. Goldsmith, I want you to oversee the loading of these supplies onto the barge."

"Sir?" a fourth man, perhaps Goldsmith, inquired.

"If we wait for the weather, we'll be stranded here for days going through supplies that are already scarce and not getting any better. I want to start moving people across within the next two hours!"

"Is that wise?" the tall man wondered. "Surely the river is far too rough to attempt such a crossing. And multiple crossings at that."

"We're going to cross," the fat man decided. "We cross now, then even if we have to be stranded, we'll be stranded on the side that lets us move quickly once the weather clears up." He lowered his voice so that only the closest of listeners could hear. "And if a few of these damned redskins die in the process, then so what? More rations for the rest of them, right?"

His companions, including the tall man, looked visibly displeased by the statement, but no one, not even the "redskins" said a word about it.

"As a matter of fact," the fat man went on, "let's get some of these men to help." He pointed. "You, you, you, and you. Go with Goldsmith and start loading the barge. Do a good job and your women and children get to be on the first trip across. Peterson, you're with me."

The young man, Peterson, followed the fat man and the tall man. The men whom the fat man had named approached the man called Goldsmith who began directing them to unload the horses. The rest of the audience, seeing that there would be no rations, and cautiously optimistic at the prospect of moving again, dispersed back to their fires.

Roland stuck around, lingering for a moment before sneaking around and falling in behind Peterson. It was a minute before the young man noticed him.

"What are you doing here? Get lost," he said.

His tone said he didn't really mean it, not maliciously, Roland decided.

"Sacks of cornmeal," the tall man said, rummaging around in the first wagon. "One, two, three, four, five…"

"Will this last us all the way to where we're going?" Roland asked, keeping his voice and trying to stay out of line of sight of the fat man.

Peterson made marks as the tall man spoke, and it was a moment before he sighed and answered, "That's the hope."

"What if it doesn't?"

As soon as an item was counted in a wagon, it was moved off and taken to the barge.

"Sacks of coffee," the tall man began. "One, two, three…"

"I don't know," Peterson said, clearly distracted. "I guess that's where you come in?"

"Me?" Roland wondered.

"Your people. You forage and live off the land, don't you?"

Roland looked toward the people huddled around the fires. Their skin was dark, their hair was black, but their clothes were nearly the same as what the Miliki wore. They lived in similar houses. They tended crops and had animals and slaves.

"Um, I guess," he replied.

"Then you'll just have to forage for a little while," Peterson told him.

Roland thought of the shriveled leaves and pine needles. "What are we supposed to forage? It's winter and nothing's growing."

"It's warmer, where you're going. At least I'm told it is. There'll be something there, I'm sure."

"You mean you've never been there?"

"Me? No, of course not, are you mad?" The young man turned to face him. "You think I want to go west? There's savages out there that are ten times more fearsome than you lot. No, thank you." He turned back to the wagon and made some more marks.

Roland glanced west, across the river. The clouds seemed just a bit darker than before, he thought. "Who's out there?"

"Sioux, Pueblo, Apache. Comanche are downright possessed from what I'm told, absolute devils."

"How will we defend ourselves?"

Peterson gave him a look. "How am I supposed to know? Listen, I'm just a bookkeeper. I make sure all the accounts are in order, make sure the supplies are properly accounted for. I don't know anything about what's supposed to happen once you get where you're going. That'll be up to you."

"Because we'll be a sovereign nation," Roland stated, using his mother's words.

"Yeah, sure, whatever." More marks on the page.

"Then where will you go?"

"I don't know, probably back to Boston."

"Boston? That's so far away!"

"No, this is so far away. My employer back in Boston asked if I wanted to come out here to help with the removal. He said it would bolster my reputation and my credibility, and give me a chance to see the West. Said there'd be extra pay in it for me, too, which is the real reason I'm out here."

"Oh. But—"

"Matthew!" the fat man snapped suddenly.

The tall man was just climbing out the wagon, all the supplies apparently accounted for.

"Get that redskin out of here before he steals something!" the fat man ordered.

"He's just talking to me, sir," Peterson protested. "He's not stealing nothing. Hell, he can't even read."

"Yes, I can!" Roland piped up.

"I don't care! I don't want him near the supplies!" The fat man lumbered over, making shooing motions as though trying to frighten a dog. "Go on! Get out of here! Go sit with the rest of your people and wait for your turn to cross!"

Roland ran off, dodging other men as they took the supplies from the wagon to the boat. The men who looked like him gave him sympathetic glances, while the white-skinned men pretended as though they hadn't seen or heard anything.

He found his mother who readily gathered him up in the blanket.

"Where have you been, my love?" she asked. "I saw you in the crowd, but then you didn't come back to the fire."

He told her about following around the young bookkeeper and recounted their conversation as best he could remember.

"If the West is so dangerous, why would they come out here in the first place?" he asked.

"I don't know," his mother sighed, in that way she did when she might have actually known and had an answer, or even just an opinion, but was too tired to continue a conversation about it.

"And why would they send us out here if there are so many bad people around?" he went on. "If we can't stop the Miliki, how can we stop the Sioux or the Pueblo or the Apache? He said that the Comanche were possessed!"

His mother chuckled. "Oh, child. The Miliki call us frightening, savage redskins, but have you ever seen us raise a hand or be violent toward these men?"

"No."

"Do you think that it could be the same way with the other people, the Comanche included?"

"I don't know."

"I think you do." She shifted him on her lap.

"But if we're not savages like they say we are, then why are they moving us? Why can't we live together, like Aki said?"

His mother hesitated, then answered, in that special way, "I don't know."

"But—"

"Hush, Ola. You heard the big man. As soon as the supplies are on the boat, we're going to start crossing. We need to listen so we know when to gather our things and put out the fire."

It was an excuse, and they both knew it. They didn't have anything that couldn't be grabbed in one instance, just the blanket, which remained perpetually around Ishki's shoulders, and a shoulder bag that carried their two cups, some small utensils, and a few beaded artifacts from his mother's family. Roland used to have a small toy, given to him by a well-meaning preacher's wife when they started out, but that had been lost many days ago. He hardly even missed it, or remembered it existed.

As the thought of moving on percolated in the minds of the people, and as the distant horizon started to look less and less friendly, a few more men volunteered to move supplies onto the boat while the women started gathering people into groups to make the crossing. While they tended to stay to their own tribes, Roland noticed that there was still plenty of cooperation.

Was this peace? This helping of strangers? A stranger from another tribe held a Chahta infant while his mother gathered up her other two children and their meager possessions. Roland glanced over at the barge where light- and dark-skinned men loaded crates and barrels with little complaint to or about each other. Did the Miliki think they were helping the Indians by moving them? What if that help made things worse?

If this was peace, then, why didn't they help each other back home, without having to leave? Who needed help, and why wasn't it given? Roland didn't think they'd needed help; they'd had a home, good land, healthy animals, and a few slaves whom they'd treated with some manner of decency. Perhaps, then, it was the Miliki who'd needed help in some way. But if that was the case, why the removal?

The call came up for the first group to board the boat.

Instantly, there was debate. The older men and women didn't trust the boat, or the men operating it, and yet the weather and the river would only worsen as storms rolled through. Similarly, what if they couldn't all make the crossing before dark and got separated?

The fat man yelled at them to hurry up and get on the boat.

Finally people started boarding, a thoroughly mixed group, having in common only a sense of fear and the courage to brave the first crossing. Roland and his mother were not among them.

"The next one," she promised.

The boat pushed off from the dock and bobbed away from safety. It would be a long time before they knew the fate of those passengers, but Roland's mother was not willing to lose their spot on the next crossing.

They waited. Roland's mother talked to others around them who also wished to ensure their spot on the second crossing, but Roland himself quickly grew bored. He started to wander away, thinking his mother wasn't paying attention, when suddenly she grabbed his hand.

"Come when I call for you, Ola Achukma," she told him seriously. "I don't want to be separated from you. Come when I call."

"I will," he promised.

She let him go, and he ran off, back to the fires. There was only one topic of conversation now, and that was the crossing. It seemed that those who were not actively waiting for the boat, like his mother, were rather staunchly against crossing that day.

"The wild winds whisper danger and misfortune," one elder grumbled. "Even the Miliki say so!"

"What happens if we become separated?" a woman wondered, sitting with her husband and their two young children.

"What if something happens to the boat and we have not all crossed?" someone else asked grimly.

It was not a pleasant thought to consider, so Roland sought out more enjoyable company. He found some children who were playing a short distance away and joined them. He recognized them as Chalakki.

"The boat's coming back across!" one said.

They'd drawn two lines in the snow, evidently the river. One of the children used a piece of bark to simulate the boat while the other children used rocks for people. Roland grabbed a small rock of his own and squatted down on one side of the river.

"Everyone get onboard!" the boat-driver ordered, the piece of bark touching the line of the bank. "We have to make the crossing before the storm hits!"

Roland and the other three children on their side of the river put their rocks on the piece of bark.

"Now we're going to the other side. We have to hurry!"

Halfway across, the boat-driver stopped and started wiggling the bark. "Oh no! The river is too strong! The storm is here! We can't make it!"

"That's all right," one of the Chalakki children said. "We'll just go to Aktiya Waya—" She and the other Chalakki children ran to a sapling only a few paces away. "—and come back." They ran back to the safe side of the river, successfully crossed.

"That's not fair!" Roland protested. "What am I supposed to do?"

The girl shrugged. "You can't come with us, so you'll just have to drown."

"Sogwili, you can't say that," one of the boys, perhaps the oldest of the group, said. "Yvgidahi says we have to help as many of our people as possible."

"But he's not our people, he's Atsakta."

"Yvgidahi says we're all one people now."

"That's what Yvgidahi says, but that's not what everyone says."

"Who's Yvgidahi?" Roland asked, feeling rather disheartened.

"He's the skiagvsta of Aktiya Waya."

Another boy, around the same age as the girl, hit her in the back of the head. "Mom and Dad said not to tell outsiders about Aktiya Waya!"

"It's a real place?" Roland wondered. "I listen to your stories at night."

Now they all stared at him.

"How can you? Your Atsakta," the oldest boy stated.

"Goliga hingo'i." (I understand your tongue.) "Is it true, then? Is it a place with no enemies and large mountains and forests and much game?"

Instead of answering, the oldest boy asked, "How did you learn our tongue?"

"My father taught me."

"Your father was Ayvwiya?"

Roland felt the blood rush to his ears. "Well, no. He was American."

Now it was the girl who spoke. "Well, Aktiya Waya is a place where there are no white-skins, so even if it was real, you couldn't go there."

Roland was glad the other children chose that time to walk away so they didn't see him standing there fighting tears. Finally he could take it no longer and he took off, running back to his mother who was still waiting. He clung to her like a child half his age, burying his face in her skirts, startling her.

"Ola, is everything all right?" she asked, kneeling down. "What's wrong?"

He didn't say anything, just wiped his face on his sleeves and turned toward the river. "Is the boat back yet?"

"No, not yet."

"When will it be here?"

"I imagine it's reached the other side by now. Then the people have to get off, and then they have to move the supplies. You still have time to play."

"I don't want to play."

"Well then, stay here. Just don't go wandering off too far where you can't hear me."

He did not reply, just pulled the blanket closer around himself until he was completely hidden. His mother continued her conversation with whoever was standing next to her.

He hated those kids. He hated Chalạkki kids.

Roland looked at his hands, then up at his mother's hands where she held the blanket close. Their skin looked the same. Why had the kids called him a white-skin? He used the blanket to wipe his eyes.

The boat couldn't return soon enough as far as Roland was concerned, but then they had to wait even longer so the men could load the supplies first. As soon as people were allowed, Roland was dragging his mother by the hand.

"Slow down, Ola," she told him. "What's gotten into you?"

"I want to get across the river, and I want to see our new home," he said, still pouting a bit.

His mother said something to the person she'd been speaking to, but Roland didn't hear it. He didn't care. When they were finally settled, squatting low on a surface that was suddenly no longer stable, he looked around for the Chalạkki children. He didn't see them. That was fine. They could go to their stupid Aktiya Waya. He was going to a new home. There the Chahta would be a sovereign nation and they could do whatever they wanted. They didn't need Aktiya Waya.

It was clear from the start that some were better suited for the river than others, or perhaps it was just the way they were sitting, or the ferocity of the winds.

Roland was fine when they were tethered to the dock, although the jolt and occasional bump against the wood left much to be desired. He had one hand on his mother and one hand on a nearby rope.

Suddenly, that didn't matter anymore. The lines were loosed and the boat began floating away from the dock. It was not so bad at first, and he dared to hope that things might be all right. This illusion was shattered as they reached open river. Nothing Roland grabbed could keep him steady as his side of the boat heaved high, then dipped low, a spray of water dribbling over the side and soaking him. Then the boat heaved high again, and he found himself looking down at water. This time, when the boat dipped low, it also turned a bit, the rear kicking out as a sudden surge of water slammed into it.

Roland was too paralyzed with fear to give much thought to his stomach, but there were others who seemed to be unable to consider anything else. One man who was older but not quite an elder let go of his hold on the boat in order to hold his stomach, and he pitched to the floor at the next heave. One of the women gripped the side of the boat so she could vomit over the side, heedless of the water splashing her in the face and soaking her entirely, clear to her skin.

Few were unaffected in some way. Few were not praying for it to end. Even those who did not appear to be struggling with nausea looked unhappy.

What if they tipped over? What if they went in the water? Would anyone rescue them? Could anyone hope to swim against such strong currents? Even if they did make it to shore, would they survive as the wind and cold froze them where they lay? Roland startled as another wash of water soaked his back and a gust of wind slapped his face. He picked his head up as someone vomited, his intent to do so over the side, but a sudden loss of footing saw him fall back into the boat and unable to control himself as he heaved.

A weak cry went up that the other side of the river was just ahead. About half the people looked up. Some sighed with hope and relief, others didn't seem to understand what they saw. All that mattered was the present moment and the overwhelming misery of the trip across the river.

"We're almost there, Sashki," Roland said.

"All right," his mother replied evenly.

He looked at her. She sat as still as she could manage on the rocking boat. Her face was pale, her eyes closed. The blanket was soaked but she did not seem to notice. All her concentration seemed to be taken by simply sitting upright.

They neared the far shore. Roland could not see much, but he could tell that they had passed the worst of the river's current. The heaving was not so wild, the sudden strike of a wave or current not so severe. Some of the more mildly affected passengers stopped vomiting and were able to collect themselves, while a few remained curled up and whimpering.

Not a few people jumped as the white men began calling to each other. Soon a mooring line was hurled through the air. Roland stood and stumbled to the front of the boat. They were not terribly off course, for the lines were able to be seized by those on the docks, but it was a tremendous physical effort to pull the boat back against the current in order to tether it to the dock.

Only when the side of the boat bumped against the dock did Roland's mother open her eyes. He went to her.

"We're here, Sashki!" he said. "We made it!"

"So we have," she said, her voice tight. She straightened her legs and stood slowly. "Are you all right, Ola?"

"I'm fine."

It was more than he could say for most of the passengers. Most of the children appeared to have been unaffected while the elders looked near to death for their pale faces and inability to move.

"Help the elders," his mother ordered, pushing him gently toward one old man who was lying in his own vomit and shaking tremendously. "I'll find us a spot in the camp."

Roland did so obediently, helping the elders disembark even as the white men yelled at them to hurry. They had to unload bile cargo and then go back for the rest of the people. They didn't have all day. Couldn't they see the storm was moving in quick? A few of the Miliki started unloading the cargo anyway, pushing past the sickly passengers with crates and barrels and nearly knocking an old man into the water as he unsteadily stepped onto the dock.

Once the elders had been assisted to the camp, Roland ran off to find his mother. In spite of the trip across the river, with the influx of supplies, morale was lifted.

The fires were not much bigger than they had been on the east side of the river, but with the new supplies, they were afforded a little more corn, a little more coffee, even a potato and a small cut of salt pork. The Miliki had to cut the pork for them as all knives and scissors had been confiscated at the start of the journey. This was not to say that some people did not have one or two hidden in packs or in secret pockets in their clothes, but they were not going to show them off just now.

"Eat, Ola," Roland's mother said, taking the food off the fire. She gave him the salt pork, most of the potato, and most of the corn. Once again, she used the coffee as a sort of gravy, though he noticed she tried to avoid giving him too many of the gritty grounds.

"You have to eat, too, Sashki," he told her.

"I am, child. But you are the future. You will be the one to make our new nation successful. Eat."

He did so obediently. With the fear from the river now wholly abated, he scarfed down the food greedily while his mother ate more slowly, more thoughtfully.

"How long until we reach our new home?" he wondered.

"I don't know," his mother answered. "A few days. A few weeks. Depends on the weather, I suppose. I don't know that we'll be able to travel tomorrow, if the storm is as bad as I think it's going to be."

"How are we going to protect ourselves?" He glanced at their tiny tent, wondering if it would hold up against the wind.

"We'll make it," his mother told him. She shivered once and pulled her still-wet blanket closer around her. After a moment, she made a gesture and he went and sat with her, pulling the blanket tight around him.

"What do you think Aki would say if he were here right now?" he wondered.

His mother sighed, rested her chin on his head for a long moment, then answered. "I think he would open up his Bible and find a story to read, to pass the time and set our minds on other things."

Roland reached for her shoulder sack and looked inside for Ki's Bible. He found it, greatly distressed when he saw it had gotten wet.

"Don't worry," his mother said. "It's only the outer edge of the pages and a bit of this corner." She showed him. "It will be dry soon enough. It's not the first time this Bible has gotten wet, you know. And I think you know the stories well enough to fill in any gaps."

This pleased the child greatly, and he waited eagerly as his mother carefully flipped through the pages to find a story.

Pàke Nischa

Decisions

It was perhaps the first day that really made her think of spring. The snow had been melting, the sun had been shining, and the temperature had been rising, but there was something about this day that really made her believe that spring was officially here. Maybe it was the lack of icy sharpness in the morning air, or the way the sunlight hit the melting icicles at the window. Whatever it was, it was a good sign of a good day ahead.

Nendawagan slowly got out of bed so as not to disturb her sister beside her and tiptoed through the tiny stone house, mindful of her parents who were still sleeping in their room about ten feet away. It was late in the morning, far later than anyone normally slept, but the meeting had gone late last night, and few had left happy. The strain of it saw her father straight to bed with hardly a bite to eat.

She pushed aside the heavy leather curtain that served as a door and stepped out of the house. Once outside, she no longer tiptoed but walked freely to the communal pool.

Some years ago, perhaps twenty years or so after the settling of Aktiya Waya, the men had engineered a water collection system, gathering the snowmelt as it dripped down the mountainside and channeling it into a great stone pool near the townhouse. A small bit was diverted into a second pool inside the townhouse, a sectioned off area where only the priests could go. Any overflow was channeled back out of the cave and into the crop fields. With the arrival of spring, the pool was filling up fast, and Nendawagan had no qualms about filling her buckets to the rim to take back home.

There was talk about reworking the channeling system and making it so that it ran to each house which would have its own reservoir. Then the people, most notably the women, would not have to make the trek to the communal pool for water. It was an intriguing idea, and some of the young men had taken to the rooftops to try and work out the details, but with the communal pool firmly in place and working well, such ideas were set aside for the moment in favor of more pressing matters.

By the time Nendawagan returned home, her sister Popokus was awake and quietly preparing cornmeal for bread. There was two years between them, Nendawagan being forty-five years and Popokus forty-three, but because of their use of sorceries, neither one looked more than twenty. Their brothers, all younger, were all married, some with children of their own, but the girls were content to wait and stay at home a while to help their parents.

"Do you think Simaquon will come today?" Nendawagan asked quietly, elbowing her sister.

"I wish he would," Popokus sighed. "I had hoped so, a month ago, but with all this news from the Old Land, I think he's forgotten about me."

"He hasn't forgotten about you. He's trying to think of a way to impress you."

"You think so?"

"Of course. What if he went to the Old Land and brought something back for you? Wouldn't that get your attention?"

"I suppose so. But do you think there will be an expedition to the Old Land?"

Nendawagan frowned. "Hard to say. I think so because it affects many peoples. A lot of people here still have family in the Old Land."

Popokus appeared uncertain. "You want to go with them? If they do travel to the Old Land, I mean?"

"Of course I do."

"Nenda, why do you want to get so wrapped up in political affairs?"

"I don't want to...it just happens. It's like a trap I keep walking into."

"Why?"

"I don't know. It intrigues me. How people get along or why they don't, and how mere words can alter the landscape of an area or the history and future of different people."

"You're forgetting one thing," a sleepy voice said.

Both girls looked up as their father emerged from his room, their mother close behind.

"Did we wake you?" Popokus asked fearfully. "We're sorry."

Their father, Yvgidahi, shook his head. "I've been awake for some time." He looked at Nendawagan. "You're forgetting a major part of politics. Power and control. Land and resources are good, but what it comes down to is power over people. How else should a man acquire land except that he either convinces or forces someone else to give it up? What shall a leader call himself if no one listens to his commands?"

"But power itself is not evil," Nendawagan stated. "It was the uku who directed the construction of the water channeling system."

"You are correct. Perhaps, then, it is the lack of wisdom and understanding that causes men to abuse power. And such a fault can be found in anyone, even ourselves."

"Yvgidahi, the sun has only just risen," their mother, Mesim, said firmly, taking the cornmeal from Popokus. "Please turn your mind to other things and leave politics for the meeting tonight." She looked at her younger daughter. "Do you expect Simaquon to come today? He seemed very interested in you last night, except for all the bustling and arguing."

Having longer lives helped to relieve some of the pressure of finding a husband and having a family as soon as possible. Nendawagan had heard innumerable stories from those from the Old Land about the various courting customs and the importance of having a family. Her mother had often stressed this point, saying that just because they had longer lives did not mean they were indestructible or immune to all illness. What if something should happen to her sons while they were out hunting? What if one of her daughters should be injured in the fields and contract an infection? Thankfully, this brewing courtship between Simaquon and Popokus had her full attention so she didn't fret over Nendawagan's interest in politics.

"You know, if Simaquon doesn't come today, I happen to know

Chilita has been looking your way, too," Yvgidahi mentioned casually, splashing his face with water at the basin.

"A chagga?" Mesim hissed. "You would entrust our daughters to one of those?"

Yvgidahi sighed. "We've talked about this. This is Aktiya Waya. We are all one people here. All one pack."

"Is everyone so interested in such things?" She went on before he could speak. "Don't think I didn't notice how you turned away any and all Iroquois suitors. Your people hold deep grudges against them still."

"My people," he echoed. "Your people. Those people. Please, I want to make us one people. Why couldn't we be? I mean, look at us."

It was an old argument, one that was had every time there was some hubbub in the Old Land.

Nendawagan's mother, a Lenape of the Old Land, had been part of a group called Moravians, trekking toward a place called the Ohio Valley. They'd been beset by nameless warriors. Some had been kidnapped. Her mother had been injured, presumed dead, and so left behind. It was either pure luck or divine intervention that brought the Aktiya Waya scouts to their location. They rescued the living, including Mesim. She'd lived in Aktiya Waya ever since.

Having breakfast appeared to smooth some ruffled feathers and calm the brewing storm. They didn't eat much, their family. Her father credited it to the sorceries they used, that they were nourished by the spirits and maintained by them so that they lived much longer lives. Her father had been born almost eighty years ago, yet he appeared no more than forty. And yet, they were still mortal, and they did need to eat occasionally. The stress of leadership, especially the recent meetings, certainly made it necessary for her father. Regardless of the need to eat, or lack thereof, food was a way of adjusting one's mood for the better.

"I expect I'll be in the townhouse much of the day," Yvgidahi stated. "Tonight's meeting begins at twilight, as usual."

"Twilight" for them meant when the sun came around and started to set, shining somewhat indirectly into the cave. Crystals and pieces of glass had been hung from the water collection trough in order to catch the sun and officially proclaim twilight and the start of important public meetings. Speckles of light would dance over the cave walls and ceiling for a short time, and it was almost a magical experience.

"Do you expect much progress will be made?" Mesim wondered honestly. "The men were near to blows last night."

"We can only hope. Now that everyone has made known his frustrations, maybe they'll be more willing to listen."

Nendawagan heard her mother mutter something about "that's what happens when you try to force too many people to live together" but if her father heard it, he did not react. She herself stayed silent, glancing at Popokus who looked just as uneasy.

When breakfast was finished, Yvgidahi departed for the townhouse while the women started cleaning up.

"I expect you both out in the fields helping today," Mesim said.

"Clearing snow?" Popokus questioned.

"The men want to build a second water system," Nendawagan told her. "This one would collect more snowmelt and hold it so that when summer comes and the river gets low, we will have a more ready supply of water for the fields that aren't directly on the river."

Her little sister thought about this for a moment and finally nodded.

So it was that after they were done cleaning, the three women left the stone house, heading for the fields. Their house was near the townhouse which was situated just off-center in the cave. This far back, the winter snows did not reach them. Toward the mouth of the cave, whatever ancient civilization had occupied this place in the past had chipped away at the stone so any accumulated snow ran down the slope and not into the cave. It, too, was supposed to be made part of this new irrigation system.

Nendawagan paused and put a hand up at the lip of the cave. She looked out over the valley. Their particular town, situated in the cave, was part of a great bowl. But it wasn't just any ordinary bowl. The Sacred Wolf guarded them, curling her body around the people. The cave where the town rested was situated in the rise that constituted her belly, a mother protector. Her tail curled around to the right, to the west, where it almost touched her nose, a small gap providing easy passage out of the bowl to the south. A river ran down the slope to the east, over her shoulder and along her chest and front legs, disappearing into her mouth. The people had been told long ago that the river must always feed the wolf for the wolf to protect them.

This, then, was the point of contention over the proposed irrigation system. The snowmelt fed the river for the spring flooding. If they diverted that snowmelt, what would it do to the river? And would their hoarding of water be seen as selfish and faithless? Could they only be causing more problems for themselves in the future?

The men were already out, standing on a rise where rock met grass. Those who were merely there to help clear snow or offer minor insight waited for instruction.

The system which fed the communal pool was made of wood. The tree it came from had a natural resistance to rot owing to its sap. If one were to study the hollowed logs, he would find that the wood itself was coated in a hard resin, the crystallized sap. This waterproofing sap was used for many things, and, as the first system was still in place and working very well after fifty years or more, no one saw a reason to not use the same idea for the new system.

One such log lay on the ground before the men as they spoke and pointed here and there. Many springtimes had been spent in studying the rise and fall of the land, the movement of the water, and the placement of the crop fields. Those who had been tasked with this endeavor were confident in their plans, but few wanted to have to move such a large, complex system if something was off. With the onset of spring and the snowmelt already coming in, now was the time to do rough tests of the system.

Normally it was the men who did all the heavy lifting in the fields, but Mesim and her daughters were wanted for a different reason. The sorceries beget an ability called Udilegv'i ale Uhyvtsa, Hot and Cold. As with many things, hot and cold had to be kept in balance. A person who invoked one or the other for too long ran the risk of injuring himself.

For example, as Nendawagan and her sister and mother invoked

Udilegv'i in order to melt the snow, feathering the snow with only the lightest touch of their palms and watching it melt, it stole the heat from their bodies and the surrounding area. They did not melt the snow, then, as a great fiery force, but more as a gentle summer breeze.

They melted the snow for a good twenty yards down the slope and perhaps ten feet on either side where the logs were to rest. Several logs, hard with crystallized sap, were laid down. The project supervisors came down, looked, thought, studied, thought some more, then gave more instructions.

When Nendawagan and Popokus became chilled from melting the snow, Mesim, looking a bit chilled herself but not admitting to it, sent them home and called for others with similar talents. The sisters happily retreated to the safety and warmth of the cave.

"Simaquon was out there, did you see?" Popokus said, trying to still chattering teeth.

"Yes, I saw," Nendawagan told her, "but only because I saw you looking at him more than what you were doing."

Popokus blushed. "I think he saw me."

"Of course he did."

"But suppose it doesn't work out? What will I do then?"

Nendawagan rolled her eyes. "Why wouldn't it work out? Guka likes him. I like him."

"I don't think Nocha likes him, though."

"Of course he does. Why wouldn't Nocha like Simaquon?"

Popokus hesitated. "I think Nocha would greatly prefer that I married someone not from Guka's people. Or maybe even his own. I think he believes that if I married another, like Chilita, then it would somehow make us all one people."

Nendawagan frowned. "It would certainly show some good will."

"Yes, but, Nenda, there are so many peoples here, how shall we make ourselves one? How shall we say to one people, 'we will keep your tradition,' and turn around and say to another people, 'you must give up yours'?"

"Why should we tell anyone that they must give up their

traditions?"

"What if one of those traditions involved killing others? Shall there be murder in Aktiya Waya over a tradition?"

"But murder is wrong," Nendawagan stated.

"Not if it's a tradition," Popokus said. "For them, it may be salvation."

Nendawagan took an even breath. "There has been talk..."

After a long moment, Popokus said, "The Comanche."

Nendawagan nodded. "Yes."

Her little sister put a sympathetic arm around her. "We are the first generation native to this...experiment. We may have to find our own way and be the people our parents wish us to be."

"Maybe, but in order to do so, we would need the help and cooperation of the entire native generations." At her sister's look, she clarified, "Our nieces and nephews are the second generation of this experiment, and they are nearly grown." She went on before Popokus could speak. "Let us wait and see what happens with the current troubles in the Old Land."

Popokus nodded. "Agreed. Things do always seem to get worse when there is trouble in the Old Land." She grinned and giggled. "It's funny to call it such."

"Yes, it means different things to us versus our parents."

They reached their home and ducked inside, adding a small log to the fire. The smoke rose into a hole in the ceiling and vanished. The old civilization had solved the problem of smoke by boring tunnels into the ceiling and directing the smoke out through holes underneath ledges that did not become packed with snow.

The women settled in, grabbing some bead or leather work, talking and carrying on. It wasn't long before their mother joined them, shivering against the cold, the heat she'd lost to Udilegv'i ale Uhyvtsa. She breathed a sigh of relief when she saw the fire was stoked, and Nendawagan moved so her mother could sit closer to the warmth.

"Guka," Popokus began. "What if things with Simaquon don't work out?"

"I don't see why they wouldn't," Mesim said, puzzled. "At least, I don't believe it would be for any error on your part."

"But what if it didn't, for whatever reason? And what if Chilita came calling instead?"

"Chilita—"

"—was born in Aktiya Waya just like we were. He's never been to the Old Land, just as we have not. Even Simaquon is of the first generation born here."

Mesim huffed and gave both her daughters a look. "I see where this is going. And I suspect that you both conspired against me in this hypothetical."

"Why should you and Nocha be permitted to marry, and Chilita and I not?" Popokus asked directly. At their mother's look, she went on, "I've heard the stories of the Old Lands, how the different peoples would kidnap men, women, and children from neighboring peoples in order to replenish warriors or simply bring new blood into their families. Why should Aktiya Waya be any different?"

"It's a matter of assimilation," Mesim said.

"Assimilation into what?" Nendawagan inquired. "Nocha's people were the first ones to resettle in Aktiya Waya. Shall we do everything by the way of his people?"

"Many things are. Even this place, Aktiya Waya, comes from his people's language."

"And yet the most common language spoken is English, from a people who, it has been made clear, is not welcome here."

Mesim was visibly uncomfortable, but her annoyed gaze was fixed on Nendawagan. Finally she said, "You know, perhaps you should go to the Old Land, assuming there will be such an excursion."

"You think so?"

"I do. Perhaps if you witness the chaos of the Old Land, the despair and the pain and the suffering, then you will understand."

Nendawagan nodded. "Very well. I will go."

Not much later, when the glass and crystals cast dancing starlight across the ceiling and walls of the cave, Nendawagan headed purposefully to the townhouse.

The townhouse itself was of good size, oblong, with enough room for five hundred people, perhaps more if they packed in and discarded use of seating. A small section on the north side was walled off, its use reserved only for the priests. A great fire burned in the center of the townhouse, with chairs set up for the skiagvsta and the uku and their advisors, the women's council, and the priests. Bench seats were arranged for elders who could not stand for long periods. Everyone else in attendance either sat on blankets, brought their own seating, or was forced to stand. The altar rested before the fire, incense prepared and simply awaiting a priest to light it to pray and begin the meeting.

It was already well and full of people, few of them in what one might consider a good mood. A good night's sleep and a bit of food had evidently helped to calm things, but Nendawagan could already see that things could spiral out of control very quickly.

Her father looked like he hadn't slept at all and had been arguing quite a bit already throughout the morning. Nendawagan knew who it was who was challenging him, too. Utsonadi was her father's greatest opponent. Her father said that was why he'd been chosen as an advisor.

Nowhere was the divide of the people more evident than at these meetings, and it went beyond simple politics. Governance was done in the tradition of the Aniyvwiya, her father's people. Those who were not Aniyvwiya still carried some trepidation and even resentment, appearing displeased and uncomfortable in the meetings.

Once the skiagvsta, the uku, the advisors, the women's council, and the elders were seated, the priests appeared, lighting the incense and saying a prayer before permitting the meeting to begin. The head priest handed the speaking pipe to Yvgidahi who was the skiagvsta. Nendawagan watched her father light the contents of the pipe, take a long drag, and release a large cloud of smoke around himself.

"News has come from the travelers," he began slowly. "The river crossing was successful, if treacherous, and they continue their journey west."

There were some sighs of relief among those gathered. Previous news had been grim, that the travelers had been stranded at the river with few supplies and food running low. Such had been the point of contention at the last meeting. With that out of the way, Nendawagan thought the rest of the night might pass relatively smoothly.

"There seem to be other western journeys planned for the spring as well, though along different routes."

"Who is being moved?" one of the elders inquired.

Yvgidahi hesitated for only a moment. "Everyone, the same as before." He continued as murmuring swept through the crowd. "As before, some will be permitted to stay in the United States and be given citizenship. Others will be moved west to establish sovereign nations."

"Sovereign nations," Utsonadi grumbled.

Now it begins, Nendawagan thought, sighing internally.

"Our peoples were sovereign before the white men came!" the antagonistic advisor said, already jumping into his rage. "Shall the United States give our people something they already had? Or did they steal it? Why should we suffer the demands of a thief?"

"Who is suffering?" Dagsi, another advisor, inquired. "We are safely here in Aktiya Waya. It is no secret that we are a safe haven."

"The citizenship to the United States is a choice," Yvgidahi cut in calmly. "Just as flight to Aktiya Waya is a choice. Some may wish it, others may not."

"But the western removal is not a choice," Utsonadi said. "We must either help our people flee, or we must help them fight."

Now Yvgidahi's tone turned icy. "We already fought." He took another drag on the pipe. "And we lost."

"Flee, then," a third advisor, Adahi, said. He was the most soft-spoken of the advisors. There was some relationship between Adahi and her father, Nendawagan knew, but her father refused to speak of it beyond what was known. He went on, "We should bring the people here."

"Which people?" Utsonadi challenged. "Ours are not the only ones being removed." Nendawagan did not miss the ripple of indignation from those who were not Aniyvwiya. "Shall we also bring the Creek? You slaughtered plenty of them as a young man, didn't you? Or what about the Iroquois, who slaughtered our people? How about the

Choctaw? The Sioux?" He turned his gaze to look directly at Yvgidahi. "With our people and others pushing west, shall we have compassion on those who are being forced into smaller territories themselves? The Navajo? The Apache? How about the Comanche? Let us bring wounded Comanche warriors here and see how they fare, or how we do."

"Enough," Yvgidahi said, fixing Utsonadi in a stare until the large warrior sat down. Then he looked at those gathered and took another drag on the pipe. "Our people fled to Aktiya Waya to avoid extinction and live in peace. Over the years, we have taken in others who wished the same. Itsa'ti was no different in Gvnagadoga's day."

"Gvnagadoga is dead and Itsa'ti is fallen," Tsisgwaya, the fourth and oldest advisor, stated. "We must ensure that Aktiya Waya does not succumb to the same fate."

Yvgidahi shifted position. "And what fate is that, exactly?"

"A canoe can only hold so many men before it sinks. This bowl is vast, but not infinite. We cannot save everyone."

"Shall we abandon our persecuted brethren to the cold and snow and whims of a tyrannical foreign government?"

"I didn't say we shouldn't help, but—"

"We should also consider that there may be those who are fine with it," Adahi interjected. "There may be those who want to go west and settle new lands."

"Does that make them any different from the white men, then?" Utsonadi threw in. "And again I ask, shall we then have compassion for the western peoples who find themselves pressed into smaller lands? How many people shall we bring here? How many peoples shall we bring?"

"There is land beyond the bowl," Yvgidahi said. "With exception of the first excursion when my brother and I came to this place many moons ago, we have hardly set foot outside the bowl but for minor hunting excursions into the forest."

"Shall we then divide our peoples, as we once were?" Dagsi asked. "Shall the Aniyvwiya remain in Aktiya Waya and send the Iroquois out to find their own land, and the Choctaw and the Creek and all others?

We would be fighting each other within a decade."

"The Aniyvwiya had many towns scattered throughout the mountains, but we were all one people."

"But we are not, not in that way."

Dahlsgewi, the fifth advisor, spoke up then, saying, "We should keep our discussion focused on the travelers. Those of our people who go west with those being removed will expect an answer and a course of action."

"To which 'our people' are you referring?" Yvgidahi inquired casually. "The Aniyvwiya in general, the Aniyvwiya from Aktiya Waya, or simply those from Aktiya Waya?" He puffed on the pipe once more.

With the advisors momentarily tripped up, the rest of the audience was blessed with a bit of silence.

"We have no reason to believe the United States government will honor their agreement and simply let any of the removed peoples be," Yvgidahi continued. "Those of us from the Old Land, especially before the Revolution, we remember well the deceptions. It began with the British, but the Americans are proving no more honest in this regard. However, it will be honored for the time being, just long enough to soothe the wounds of the journey and make the people compliant enough to give in again in the future.

"In that time, I would expect each people to establish their government and councils. They are the ones who speak on behalf of the people of the Old Land. As Adahi has stated, we must consider that some may be more accepting of the new life and wish to stay there."

"We are separating ourselves from the Old Land, then?" Tvdisdi, the sixth advisor, wondered.

"We have been separate for a very long time, I think," Yvgidahi told him. "Aganstata and Atagulkalu remained as the leaders of the Aniyvwiya after our departure. It seems to be more the case that our governance was the incidental one. I can no more tell the people of the Old Land to fight or not fight than they can tell us to hunt here or there."

"You would then abandon our people?" Utsonadi demanded hotly.

"Shall we fight for those who do not wish to be saved?" Yvgidahi shot back. "Where is the fight? Where is the war? There are no more battlefields except the courtroom."

"Where the laws shall always favor the white men. Where the laws proclaim these removals both necessary and righteous."

"Those who stayed behind agreed to live as such."

"By force!"

"Those who left do so as free men who seek to reestablish themselves as a sovereign nation."

"But for how long? And when the white men have worn them down, eroded their will and their spirit, will we fight for them then, or shall we turn our backs?"

Dahlsgewi cleared his throat. "Before we get to that point in the future, we should address the problems of the present." He shifted in his seat. "The Old Land is now well within winter, which is hardly the best time to try and establish a new village, never mind trying to do so in a strange and hostile land. Meanwhile, we are just coming into spring."

Dagsi nodded. "It is not unreasonable to suggest we help the most unfortunate, the worst affected by the removal: elders, women, and children."

"It should also be considered," Tvdisdi cut in, "that some here may want to go back."

He paused to let that sink in, and Nendawagan saw her father look around at those gathered.

Nendawagan knew of precious few people who had left Aktiya Waya with the intent of resettling in the Old Land. Most often, those who did so were warriors who had been terribly injured but wished to return to the fight, preferring to die in the Old Land among their ancestors. She knew of only a couple families who returned simply to be among their own people, back when Aktiya Waya was almost entirely Aniyvwiya.

"We have never stopped people from returning to the Old Land," Yvgidahi said simply after a moment of contemplation, shifting position in his chair. "For most, Aktiya Waya is the most logical answer, a safe haven."

"Our peoples were at war before the white men came," Adahi stated. "Shall we end up the same way again?"

Yvgidahi regarded Adahi for a long moment. "You agree with Utsonadi, then?"

"It is not unreasonable for us to have rules that people must abide by if they wish to stay here," Tvdisdi said. "This is our home now, and if they wish to stay here, then..."

"What rules shall we make, then?" Yvgidahi asked of him. "Shall we designate one language to use? Shall we punish an elder for not using this language even if he has never heard it in all his life?"

"The Aniyvwiya were here first," Utsonadi began.

"We were not here first," Yvgidahi said severely. "These ruins belonged to a people who existed long before us, so long ago that not even their ghosts remain. No, we were not first."

"And how many of those ancient rites do we observe?" Tsisgwaya wondered casually. "We were the first ones here. The Aniyvwiya. We have had compassion on many people who suffered terrible fates at the hands of the Anigilisi, some even worse than we did. But if we are to be any better than the savages who drove us here, we must establish rules and laws and determine what actions to take in order to ensure peace. And any who wish to live here must abide by such rules. Otherwise, they may take their grievances and their violence back to those whom they will fight. Only then may we consider ourselves one people."

"People are more than the rules they follow," Utsonadi said, unimpressed. "It is their history, their heritage, their ancestors. It is their families, their sons and daughters and the things they teach them."

"So then tell me, Utsonadi," Yvgidahi began, very matter-of-fact. "To which people do my children belong? Hm? The Aniyvwiya and the Lenape are matrilineal, so by those rights they are Lenape. However, Mesim forsook her traditions when she became a Moravian, and she has never indicated to me that she has renounced such vows. By those actions, my children are Aniyvwiya." He went on before Utsonadi could speak. "And what of my grandchildren? Some have Lenape mothers, others Aniyvwiya, others Choctaw or even Chickasaw. Shall I cherish any of them any differently?"

"Not everyone is as comfortable as you with this intermixing," the hotheaded warrior growled.

"There is also the matter of the sorceries," Dagsi threw in.

"And the Book," Tvdisdi mentioned.

Yvgidahi sighed, and Nendawagan mirrored him. Not everyone was comfortable with the sorceries either, inasmuch as it appeared anyone could learn them with great proficiency. To say nothing of the Book, which her father had hoped would have been long forgotten by now.

"The Book has not been consulted in fifty years," Yvgidahi said, quieting the murmur of the crowd. "As for the sorceries, what shall I say about this gift my brother gave to the people? Why should it not be this thing that brings us together as one people and defines us?"

"Because some just wish to live in peace, in their own way, as they always have," Adahi told him. "This just happens to be their best option."

"Well sometimes things change!" Yvgidahi snapped in a rare flash of anger. "Sometimes the world changes. Shall we revert back to a time when we knew nothing, simply because our earliest ancestors knew nothing? Shall we go back to killing animals with rocks and forsake the snare? Whether the people choose to remain in the Old Land or come to Aktiya Waya, some things will have to change. We offer them a chance at safety, but that does not mean that we can bring all our old problems with us. Shall the Cherokee and the Iroquois here go to war simply because that is the way it was in the Old Land? Or shall we work together in this new land?" He stood. "That is the choice that faces everyone here, and anyone who comes to Aktiya Waya seeking refuge. This village is not a place to savor hatred and nurse grudges while basking in safety. It is a place to put those grudges aside. Any man who seeks to exploit our kindness and the bounty of our land will be sent back to the Old Land, never to return." He sat down again. "It is not a law that we must like each other, but we do have to live together. As of right now, I declare us to be one people."

"And what shall we call ourselves?" Utsonadi asked snidely. "How shall we introduce ourselves to our brothers and elders when we go to them on their trail of misery and tears?"

Yvgidahi gave him a look. "I don't know. Seeing how purity and identity seem to be your biggest bone of contention, why don't you come up with something? Not here, not tonight, but give it some thought."

Nendawagan could feel the loathing come off of Utsonadi toward her father, but Yvgidahi had already moved on.

"Now then, with that out of the way, we should begin preparations to receive refugees from the trail as well as any settlements the people of the Old Land may have tentatively established."

"This is only the first removal," Tsisgwaya said. "No doubt there will be many more to come."

Yvgidahi nodded and puffed on the pipe. "Agreed. What is our housing situation?"

"Two uninhabitable," Dahlsgewi stated, "due to some damage taken over the winter. Otherwise, we have approximately sixty-five unoccupied residences. I imagine that some people may be able to move in with relatives."

"The people are being removed in far greater numbers than that," Tvdisdi said. "Before, we have helped some here, some there. An operation of this scale, we'll be overrun."

"We can't save everyone," Adahi said quietly, deliberately not looking at Yvgidahi as he spoke.

"Not everyone wants to be saved," Yvgidahi said evasively, deliberately not looking at Adahi. "But Tvdisdi has the right of it, that the people are being removed in greater numbers than we are prepared to handle, even if only a fraction agree to come here."

"Perhaps we should limit our rescues," Utsonadi suggested.

"And who, pray tell, would you bring?"

"Only those who remember the old ways that we wish to preserve. It does no good to bring one of our people over who has adapted so well he has become a white man in everything but skin color."

There was not a little support for his idea from those gathered.

"Elders, then," Yvgidahi stated calmly, taking another drag and blowing out a cloud of blue smoke.

"And children," Utsonadi added. "That we may save them from the terrible burden of ignorance of themselves, and the lost dreams that their parents willfully gave up."

It was Adahi who spoke up now, giving Utsonadi a look. "You fled here with the rest of us rather than stay and fight."

Utsonadi scoffed but could not refute him.

Yvgidahi turned to his seventh advisor. "Ihya, you've been quiet so far. Is there anything you wish to say?"

Ihya had been nearly an elder when he made the crossing eighty or so years ago. He'd learned some of the sorceries in order to help the people in the early years of Aktiya Waya. While he had not used them for some time, his years had been lengthened and he now appeared quite ancient with wrinkled skin that reminded Nendawagan of coarse, gravelly sand in the river bottom, and stark white hair like fresh snow that reached his knees when braided.

"Compassion and love are great virtues, but beware the enemies who do not share your sentiments, nor your goals," the old man croaked. "And do not scorn those whose eyes are closed only by lack of knowledge and experience. We were all naive children once, and sometimes the greatest lessons come from the simplest of understanding and the most honest of curiosity."

The elder rarely gave straight commands, instead preferring to give advice to think about for a while before acting on it. It could be infuriating at times, when more direct answers might be desired, but he never spoke just to hear his own voice. Some said he was already walking with the spirits and dispensing their advice, and it was up to men and the priests to interpret it.

After a moment, when Ihya said nothing more, Yvgidahi nodded as if making a decision. "We will send a party to the Old Land, to assess conditions and see who we might bring. I suspect we may be sending numerous smaller parties to do the actual moving of people, so we should form some tentative groups who should be ready at a moment's notice."

"I will go and assess the people now," Utsonadi interjected. "I will determine who may be brought back to Aktiya Waya."

"Your party will assess and determine," Yvgidahi corrected coarsely. "And you must look across all peoples, not merely the Aniyvwiya. In fact, I want your party to be made up of at least one member of each of the peoples you expect to encounter."

"How shall I do that? We are all one people now, you said it yourself. And I do not expect to find any members of Aktiya Waya in such desolate conditions as to—"

"Shut—up. You know what I mean, and I expect you to do as I have asked."

The large warrior met Yvgidahi's cold stare. Finally he dipped his head stiffly. "Of course. I will do as you have asked."

Nendawagan pushed her way forward. "I will go with one of the smaller groups."

Her father faltered slightly. "You?"

She was no stranger to political discussion at home or in other, private conversation, outside the townhouse, and everyone knew she had an opinion on things. But it was forbidden for women not on the women's council to speak, a fact she was quickly reminded of as several of those of prominence told her to sit down.

She did so, if only to save her father the embarrassment of having spoken out of turn. It was actually Tsisgwaya who saved her.

"If children are to be a priority, it would be useful to send women," he stated. "We have sent women and children in the past in order to blend in."

"We have sent families in the past," Tvdisdi said. "The women can't go alone, it's too dangerous, and it wouldn't be proper to go out with another woman's husband, or any eligible young man."

Yvgidahi puffed on the pipe. "She has brothers, you know." He shifted in his seat. "Moskimus, my oldest son, he will lead one of these smaller groups." He nodded to Moskimus, somewhere in the crowd

Nendawagan could not see. He looked at her. "And Nendawagan will go with him." Back at Moskimus. "Take three others with you, either your own family or your brothers."

Moskimus assured him he would.

There were seven groups in all ready to go, depending on Utsonadi's findings.

"This does not solve the problem of the sorceries, however," Dahlsgewi stated.

"I didn't realize the sorceries were a problem," Yvgidahi said, already exasperated from an old argument.

"If we are going to bring a large influx of refugees here, are we expected to teach them the sorceries?" Utsonadi inquired. "You remembered the old arguments as much as I do."

"I do remember them, thank you. Who shall we teach? Who wants to learn? What are we expected to do with these sorceries? No doubt some may want to take the sorceries back to the Old Land in order to fight back against the white men."

"And?"

Yvgidahi hesitated. "The sorceries were given to us as a means of protection. It saved us from near-extinction when the white men came. Yes, I remember the arguments. But in the same way that we cannot revert to our old infighting, so we cannot simply use the sorceries as a tool of war. A hammer has a use, and it can be used to kill. So, too, do the sorceries. We should view it as a tool first, and a weapon second. Am I not correct in observing its use in the construction of the new irrigation system? So it shall be. Some will be more proficient in it than others, in the same way some are better carpenters, better hunters, better tenders, and so on. Yes, it may be our defining feature that sets us apart and unifies us. That does not make it a weapon, nor us bloodthirsty monsters intent on war."

It was the calmest discussion they'd had about the sorceries in quite a long time, Nendawagan reflected, and it relieved a burden she hadn't realized she'd been carrying.

At the mention of the new irrigation system, Yvgidahi passed the pipe to Gokhos, the uku of Aktiya Waya.

In the Old Land, her father had told her, the skiagvsta was the leader in matters of war, and the uku was the leader in manners of peace and daily living. With no wars to fight in Aktiya Waya, the skiagvsta now oversaw all goings-on between them and the Old Land, and the uku took charge of daily life within Aktiya Waya, such as overseeing the new irrigation system. Gokhos would also be in charge of ensuring there was enough housing for any refugees they brought back.

Discussion of the concerns of Aktiya Waya was a much more placid affair, and Nendawagan was hopeful that they might actually get some rest tonight without having to look over their shoulders on the short walk home. Indeed, when the meeting was finally over, Nendawagan was able to speak to Moskimus outside the townhouse in pleasant conversation.

"You embarrassed Nocha, you know," Moskimus tsked.

"I know," Nendawagan sighed. "But I knew that if I didn't speak up there, then I was never going to get a chance."

"Why do you want to go to the Old Land?"

"Guka seems to think I need to. And I want to, besides."

"All the tales of misery and suffering, Utsonadi lamenting how most of the people are white in everything but their skin color, none of that deters you?"

"Until I see it for myself, it's all just stories to me, Mosk. The same way that we used to tell each other stories about the people who used to live in Aktiya Waya countless generations ago."

"But you can stay here and help get the refugees settled and achieve the same thing."

"No, I can't. Please, Mosk. It's just something I need to do."

Her brother sighed and shook his head. "Just like you, Nenda. Well, it might be a day or two, but you should be prepared when I call you to leave."

"Come by tomorrow morning and tell me what I need to bring."

He agreed and they went their separate ways.

Her father remained in the townhouse and would be there for some time yet, Nendawagan knew, and she returned home to find only her mother was there.

"I know," Nendawagan said before Mesim could speak. "I know I embarrassed Nocha."

"Well, at least I don't have to tell you about it," her mother said pointedly.

"You said to get involved."

"You didn't have to be rude about it. In case you have not been paying attention, your father is in a rather precarious position. And this fiasco with the removal and the refugees is not helping."

"You don't think his declaration of being a single people will hold up?"

"It might, if he can convince the refugees to agree to it. But then how will that make the long-term residents feel? Really, it should have been the other way around. We should already be one people before the refugees come." She huffed a sigh. "Too late for that now, I suppose."

Nendawagan did not say anything to that. Instead, she looked around and asked, "Where's Popokus?"

"Last I saw, she was speaking to Simaquon."

"Oh really?"

But her mother's tone suggested she was not interested in changing the subject.

"The women's council was unusually quiet tonight," Nendawagan sighed, tearing a chunk of bread off what was leftover from the morning loaf.

"They made their opinions well known last night," Mesim stated. "They do not want to see any child made an orphan because of unnecessary violence or foolish, hasty decisions. The hardship of the removal is no doubt making orphans of many children, to say nothing of Utsonadi's point of the loss of heritage they are no doubt experiencing."

"You agree with him, then? Does he intend to steal those children away from their mothers, then?"

Her mother gave her a look. "He is only going to assess and determine who is best suited to come here. You will be the one actually stealing them away."

Nendawagan blinked. She hadn't though of it quite like that. Perhaps she could ask Utsonadi if she could join him. No, he wouldn't do that. He was gruff and hard-nosed, and he wouldn't want her with his team for the simple fact that she was Yvgidahi's daughter, not even considering how improper it would be given that she was not related to anyone else in his party.

Before either of them could say more, Popokus walked in the house. Or, more accurately, she glided into the house and did a few joyful dance steps.

"So, Simaquon lives," Nendawagan teased.

"He lives in my head and my heart," Popokus giggled. "He is going to be in one of the parties to the Old Land, and he has promised to bring me back something marvelous!"

"The Old Land is covered in snow and we are intending to visit the heart of despair and desolation of the people there. What marvelous thing could he possibly bring you?"

Her little sister stopped and considered this for a long moment, brows furrowed. Finally she shrugged. "I don't know, but I'm sure it will be lovely all the same."

With her sister's light-hearted attitude and gushing over Simaquon, conversation was arbitrarily steered far away from politics. This was assuming that either Nendawagan or Mesim could get a word in edgewise. Mostly it was Popokus talking all about her beloved and how much she adored him.

It wasn't much later when Yvgidahi returned, looking far better than he had the previous night. Nendawagan approached him sheepishly as he sat down at the table.

"I'm sorry for embarrassing you," she said humbly. "I know I spoke out of turn."

"You do not need to apologize to me," he told her. "I understand. But I appreciate that you are cognizant of it, for others were not so understanding. I had to tell the others that you wished to make a statement as a kind of proxy for the women's council, knowing that those of the council, as well as Gokhos and myself, have sworn ourselves to remain in Aktiya Waya during our service and not travel to the Old Land."

"And they believed it?"

"Unlikely, but it has placated them for the time being." He stood. "But please, be on your best behavior while you're in the Old Land. Listen to your brothers and do what they tell you."

Nendawagan nodded. "I will, Nocha. I promise."

Tuchena Tushafa

Snowstorm

Indian Land it was called, at least to their faces. Behind their backs, late at night, when the white men thought everyone was asleep, Roland heard them call it Oklahoma.

That should have been the first clue that the United States had no real intention of letting the Indians govern their own affairs as a "sovereign nation." They should have known that the Americans were always going to come for them eventually. Send the Indians ahead to settle the land, establish farms and towns. Later on, when the United States needed more land, they would just remove the Indians again—assuming they hadn't perished by some other means—and move into these established places.

These were the grumblings of the adults and the elders, and Roland absorbed it all.

The relief and hope that the supply wagons had given the people before they crossed the river quickly dwindled. The weather grew worse, as did the condition of their clothes and tents, those who were lucky enough to have them.

Their progress slowed until they were at a standstill. The snow closed in around them and pneumonia spread within them. It was hard to blame the white men when they suffered just as much, complained just as much.

Was this peace? Roland wondered as he and his mother huddled in a stuffy tent with fifteen other people, the wind beating at them mercilessly, whispering through the thin threads of the canvas, while the snow piled up outside. They had no fire, for they had no fuel. They ate their dinner cold, those who could eat anyway; they were all ill to some degree, and some simply lay down, moaning, coughing, and wheezing. At least a few would not be breathing by morning, he knew.

He could hear the sickness in his mother's chest as he huddled with her under the blanket. She did not complain. She did not say much of anything as she simply sat with her eyes closed, perhaps laid down or leaned against someone to sleep a bit.

There was little to do, sitting there in the tent, except listen to the storm. For a while, there had been some light to read by, but with no fire and no lanterns, his chance to read and escape was limited.

He'd thought to read happy stories from Ki's Bible. Stories about Jesus healing the sick, and especially about raising Lazarus from the dead. He'd thought these stories might encourage the people. Few of them reacted at all, and those who did simply made snide remarks and told him to stop reading. He did not close the Bible, simply stopped reading aloud.

Before he knew it, he was yawning, and yet it didn't feel as though the day was over. The storm raged on with no sign of letting up. He wondered how much snow would be around the tent in the morning. What if they were buried?

Roland had once heard stories of a people who lived far, far to the north, beyond the reach of greenery where there was only snow, beyond the reach of even the sun, where it was dark for months at a time. These people hunted great whales and enormous reindeer the size of bears. He'd imagined these people to be very frightening indeed. Now he wondered whether they would not be meeting such people at the end of this snowy journey. Were they out there even now, stalking through the snow? Were they as fearsome as the bedeviled Comanche?

Somewhere in the back of his mind, he knew it was foolish. His father had once shown him a map of North America. He'd taken some of Ishki's sewing pins and marked where the different peoples lived. The Comanche were west, where they were heading. The people of the ice lived far, far north.

And yet, with the snow swirling about the tent, it was easy to imagine them out there.

He sighed, which turned into a yawn, and lay down beside his mother. If there was any good news, it was that the snow seemed to have piled up enough that it actually sealed the gap around the edge of the tent so no more wind or snow could blow through. He coughed several times in the thick, humid air as he tried to get comfortable. He could breathe if he sat up, but he was just too tired. And yet, when he lay down and started coughing or couldn't breathe, he didn't sleep anyway.

At some point he must have slept, for he dreamed of snow giants hunting enormous reindeer and monstrous whales. Roland had never seen a whale, except for illustrations, and he imagined them to be very large indeed. He wondered if perhaps a whale was the great fish that swallowed Jonah. He had seen many small fish, and many big fish, too, but none of them had been able to eat him, and he was yet a child. But if whales were the prey of the northern giants, then maybe they were big enough to prey on smaller men.

He jolted awake from a particularly strenuous bout of coughing. His chest hurt and his throat was starting to feel raw. It was entirely dark out now, and he couldn't see a thing.

All around him in the tent, people were coughing and wheezing, most of them in a sleepy daze. The wind had died down some, but as Roland sat up, he could feel where the sheer volume of snow was pressing against the sides of the tent, bowing the canvas and the poles. He tried to press back, tried to offload the snow, but with limited success. What if the tent should collapse? What if they should be buried here?

The thought was frightening, but his fear was momentarily ignored as he began another bout of coughing. It felt worse than before. He could hardly catch his breath. He tried to lie down, but he couldn't breathe and only coughed more. There wasn't much room to sit up comfortably, and it opened an uncomfortable gap in the blanket, but it was the only position that let him find anything remotely close to comfort, at least enough to sleep.

He did not know how much more sleep he got, though he knew he must have gotten some, for he knew he dreamed again. He dreamed of better days, when Ki was with him, when his brother and sister were alive and they would play together. He dreamed of the friends he had left behind. Some had been Americans. Some had been Chahta who elected to stay behind, either become American citizens or take their chances with the government anyway.

Roland longed for his father, and he prayed that his mother would not leave him, too, on this treacherous journey. What would he do, where would he go, without her? He knew some of the other Chahta who were traveling with them, but he didn't want them. He wanted Ishki.

Unlike other mornings, no one came to rouse them and tell them to hurry up and get ready to move. As Roland slowly woke with the dawn, he discovered that they were indeed well buried by the snow. The tent canvas bowed so that anyone sleeping near the edge was weighted down. He was only one of three who were awake, and he was arguably the most lively. This was of some significance considering he only wanted to go back to sleep in order to forget his illness.

He could not hear much outside the tent, though he could tell there was some movement. He heard a bit of yelling and the crunch of boots through crisp, fresh snow. He heard muffled, muttered cursing as someone passed near to their tent. The person passed by and all was quiet once more.

After a short while, someone returned, and they brought more with them. There was some grumbling, a bit of growling, a barked order, and then there was the distinct sound of shovels cracking through the snow. The tent canvas wobbled, and the noise woke some of those still sleeping, including Roland's mother.

"Ola, what's happening?" she murmured.

"The tent is buried in the snow," he told her, yawning. "The men are digging us out."

She did not seem to care one way or the other as she managed a weak sigh, coughed profusely, and laid her head back down. Roland leaned against her, listening to the scrape of shovels in the snow, watching as the light grew brighter through the canvas as the snow was removed.

Suddenly there was the sound of ripping canvas and a cold wind blasted into the tent as a shovel punctured through the side. One man cursed righteously and his fellows also berated him for it.

If anyone had still been sleeping, the cold wind jolted them awake, though there were more coughs than protests at the sudden interruption. But then, this also meant that anyone who still appeared to be sleeping was more likely dead.

"Looks like four," one man said, pushing his head through the hole the shovel had torn. "Maybe five. One I'm not so sure."

"Well, if it ain't dead now, it will be soon enough," another man outside grumbled.

"Are we leaving?" someone asked weakly.

"No, not yet," the first man said, sounding a bit disappointed. "Still got more tents to dig out. But if you get up, get around, and get your rations, then you'll be ready to go when we do get moving."

No one looked excited at the prospect of going anywhere, Roland included. He wasn't even all that excited for breakfast. His stomach grumbled, but coughing made his middle hurt, and he really didn't feel like eating.

His mother sighed and sat up. She looked terrible, Roland thought, but she got herself upright and situated, shifting the blanket and pulling him inside for just a moment. He could feel her fever. He knew he had one, too. Yet he cherished her presence more than he despised the uncomfortable warmth.

"Ola," she murmured, sounding very much asleep still, "why don't you go fetch our rations? Maybe they'll be more sympathetic to a child."

He highly doubted it, but he was in no mood to argue. There were plenty of children about, and they got the same thing the adults did: not much. Actually, he was one of the more privileged children, as he still had good clothing. Some of the children had started out the trek with little more than a sheet covering them, and most had perished.

Even so, his clothes felt wholly inadequate for trudging through snow. A few paths had been shoveled, and there were more tracks where simple use had worn a usable trail. His shoes still filled with snow, freezing his feet. He wrapped his arms tight around himself and shivered as he joined the ration line.

"Here you are," the soldier said, his gruff voice less threatening today because of the cold.

"I need another for my mother," Roland told him.

"She'll have to come and get it herself. They're called rations for a reason; no one gets any extra."

"Please, sir, she can't come out."

"Well then I don't expect she'll be needing the rations here shortly, eh? More for the rest of you then. Now move along. Next!"

Someone shoved Roland in the back and it was all he could do to stay upright and not drop his meager rations. He stumbled a short distance away and stared at the corn, coffee, and a single turnip. He didn't like coffee. There wasn't even any bread to go around, or much of anything else. He didn't want to be stuck with the coffee.

He trudged his way back to his tent.

An elder had once told him that if a man were to resort to begging, then he ought not refuse any kindness offered to him. Roland didn't want the coffee. He didn't want to beg. He felt as though something had been taken from him, but he could not say what. The word "dignity" came to mind, though he was unsure exactly what that word meant. It felt fitting nonetheless, a word his father would have used. Dignity.

Dignity and peace. Roland looked around but could find little of either in the current scene.

He climbed back into the tent and huddled in the blanket with his mother. She seemed a bit more lively now, enough to get a tiny fire going in order to boil water. The warmth brought more life to those in the tent, and something like comfort soothed the worst of Roland's unease. He didn't like the coffee, but his mother used it to bring some flavor to the corn and the turnip.

They ate in between bouts of coughing. Finally, when they were done, his mother gave him a gentle nudge toward the opening in the tent.

"Go, Ola," she said hoarsely. "You don't have to stay here with me.

Go play outside with the other children."

"Sashki, I'm tired. I don't want to play," he murmured.

She sighed, coughed, but accepted him into the blanket.

He got a bit of sleep, or he thought he did, though it was frequently interrupted by coughing and general malaise. He wasn't entirely certain of the meaning of that word either, but he'd heard it used often enough when someone felt wholly unwell.

At one point, when he woke in one of his coughing fits, he was blinded by the sun glaring into the tent. A minute or two later, there was shouting from outside. The soldiers expected to be leaving within the hour.

Roland weaseled his way out of the blanket, trying not to disturb his mother, and poked his head out of the tent. It felt somewhat warm out, certainly warmer than it had been when he woke up earlier that morning. The snow was just warm enough to melt, when it became wet and heavy. But the sun was a welcome sight, even as he erupted into a terrible bout of coughing.

He found himself doubled over in pain. His stomach did not hurt, and he did not feel nauseous, but he was unsure whether he was about to give up his rationed breakfast.

When he looked out of the tent once more, a shadow passed over him, and he looked up to see an unfamiliar man. Roland knew the faces of most of the soldiers and guides, and he knew fairly well the faces and names of the Indians traveling with them. This man was completely new. More than that, he looked healthy and well-fed, with gleaming skin, glossy hair, and clothes that were more reminisce of the old ways, cut of leather and stitched with sinew.

"Siyo, ayohli," he greeted softly, squatting down in front of him. (Hello, child.) Chalakki, then.

"Siyo," Roland replied in kind, unable to manage more than that before he had to cough again.

The man looked concerned. "Tsvtsvga?" (Are you sick?)

Roland nodded. "Ale agitsi." (And my mother.)

"Tsadoda?" (Your father?)

Roland shook his head.

"What's your name?"

"Ola Achukma."

The man's expression turned confused. "That's not an Ayvwiya name."

Roland shrugged weakly. "My father taught me. My mother is Chahta."

"Choctaw. I see." He shifted his stance. "My name is Nimenees."

"That's not Ayvwiya either."

He grinned. "No, it's not."

"It's Lenape."

"Very good. You know a lot."

"My father taught me," Roland murmured, only a moment before he burst again into coughing.

Nimenees frowned. "Your mother is also this ill?"

Roland nodded, not looking at the man who seemed a bit distressed, his expression like that of one who is trying to come up with a plan quickly and unsure how to go about it.

"Ola Achukma—"

"Most here call me Roland."

"Well, I will call you Ola Achukma, for that is your name. And where is your home?"

Roland shrugged again. "It used to be in Mississippi. Then we had to move. They tell us we're going to Indian Land to be a sovereign nation, but I don't know where or what that is."

"I see." Nimenees frowned, clearly displeased. "And is this what you want to do?"

"I want to go home. I want Aki to be alive again, to tell me stories and read to me. But I know he's not coming back, and the only thing we can do now is go to Indian Land."

"What if there were another option? What if you could go someplace else?"

Roland looked at him. "You mean like Aktiya Waya?"

Nimenees raised a brow. "How do you know of Aktiya Waya?"

Roland looked away. "Some of the other children were talking about it. They said I couldn't go there."

"Why is that?"

"I'm not Chaḷakki, and Aki was an American. 'No white-skins allowed,' they said."

Nimeness made an "ah" sound and nodded slowly. "Well, it's not quite like that. It's true there are no British or Americans there, but there are Choctaw and Lenape and others. And there are mixed-bloods, too. We're all one people in Aktiya Waya."

"So it is real," Roland stated. "And there is peace and wild game and everything wonderful?"

He was already coughing by the last few words, and by the time he was done, he was making a wretched, hollow sound in his chest, and his throat was raw.

"There is medicine in Aktiya Waya also," Nimenees said. "Would you and your mother like to go there?"

Roland could only nod.

"All right. Is it just you and your mother? Do you have any brothers or sisters?"

He shook his head.

Nimenees' expression softened. "I'm sorry to hear that." He stood. "Our people are simply scouting right now, counting how many we need to prepare for."

"When will you return?" Roland asked, suddenly alarmed.

"Tomorrow, maybe the next day at the latest." The man squatted down again, then fished something out of his bag and pressed it into Roland's hand. "Stay strong, Ola Achukma. We're coming for you. We'll bring you and your mother to Aktiya Waya."

Then he stood and was gone. Roland watched after him, noting that there were several others roaming around the camp, just as healthy and well-fed.

He uncurled his hands and saw that Nimenees had given him several strips of jerky and a bit of dried fruit. Roland dove back into the tent and tunneled his way into his mother's blanket, devouring the food.

The soldiers came around again, telling everyone to get packed up and ready to move.

Few people had any real possessions to gather, and fewer still had any motivation to get up and around. Roland managed to rouse his mother and get her ready to go before the soldiers came around and started hitting people to make them move. She had roused some, but she was as ill as anyone else. Roland briefly wondered if he shouldn't have given his mother some of the fruit and jerky, too. It would have made her happy, and maybe it would have made her stronger.

They started out much later than they wanted to. As slow as the people were moving, the soldiers and guides were not much better. Many of them were ill also, and those who weren't were forced to pick up the extra work, all of this on top of temperamental horses displeased with the snow and wagons that were in rather critical need of repair.

Roland watched a man die that day. He was an old man and terribly frail. He'd started out on a horse, but the horse had been butchered many days ago for meat. Since then, he'd hobbled along on unsteady legs, helped as much as possible by his family. Then, like many others, he fell ill. Some had thought he'd perished in the night, but he'd gotten up and around and stumbled along with the rest of them.

The old man was shuffling along with the rest of them, old limbs likely numb from the cold. Some of the people had given up their blankets to wrap around his shoulders, but it wasn't enough. He simply went to his knees, wailed something into the wind, then pitched forward and did not move anymore.

The blankets were taken from him, and the only burial he got was to pile snow over him and leave him where he lay. One woman, maybe his daughter, managed to shed a few tears, but there was no time for mourning, and their plight muted any further emotion.

It was not the first time Roland had seen someone die on this trip. It was just the first time he found he didn't care. He didn't care, and he didn't question. Death simply was. It just was. And nothing could change it.

He looked around, the line of people, horses, and wagons seemingly endless, and yet so much smaller than what it had been. Would more die today? Tonight? Tomorrow? How many of them would reach their new homes?

He thought of Nimenees and the others who claimed to be from Aktiya Waya. Were they going to rescue everyone and take them to Aktiya Waya? And why take them there, and not to the new Indian Land where they could be sovereign nations? Although, peace and plentiful game did sound very nice.

Roland didn't really know what he expected or wanted. He wanted food. He wanted to not be ill. He wanted his mother to not be ill. He wanted to go back to a time when he lived happily with his family, his father and mother and brother and sister. He looked at his mother, wondering if he wouldn't lose her as well.

How were the people from Aktiya Waya going to find them? His encounter with Nimenees seemed incidental at best. What if Roland hadn't been peeking out of the tent when the man came by? What if he hadn't known the man's language?

From Ki and Ki's Bible, Roland believed in God. But as he looked around at the sick, starving travelers, he had a hard time considering His goodness. What good was going to come from this? Were the Americans right about their manifest destiny, that God gave them the land? But if God were giving this land to those who believed in Him, why were Roland and his mother forced to move as well?

He had little desire or willpower to wrestle with such questions. Maybe it was God's will that they should go to Aktiya Waya. Maybe there he would understand peace. Maybe he would learn how to make and spread peace beyond Aktiya Waya, bring it back to the Indians and the Americans.

But it all felt so far away, and the pain in his chest and throat and the cramps in his stomach were of more immediate concern. He was uncertain whether the pain in his stomach came from hunger or because the jerky and fruit had been too much. He glanced at his mother, wondering if she knew what he'd done.

His mother was as absent as the rest of them, her gaze fixed on something far in the distance, a hope just over the horizon that could be seen but not touched. Like the rest of them, her feet were soaked from the melting snow, but she seemed not to notice. Roland's feet had been soaked since he first stepped out of the tent, and he barely felt the cold anymore. He remembered his father saying something once that such a thing was not a good sign, but there was nothing anyone could do about it out here on the trail.

Their heading was almost exclusively south, and while the snow remained constant under their feet, the air remained warm enough to melt it. If it kept up, Roland overheard one hopeful soldier say, then it should be almost completely melted by morning.

That soldier was the only hopeful one of the group, and his optimism did not reach beyond one or two people.

Several more people died that day, or they fell behind and were left to die.

As Roland plodded along beside his mother, his chest felt tight and his throat felt raw, even bloody. He tried to eat melting snow to relieve the pain, but while it offered minimal comfort to his throat, it only made his chest feel worse.

With the sun halfway below the horizon, they made camp. It was cold again, enough to freeze melted snow back into ice, but there was no rain or snow from the sky to chill them. The people packed into tents. Roland didn't know which was worse, the cold that froze his chest, or the humidity that congested it. But he liked the feeling on his skin and how he didn't have to huddle for meager warmth in a threadbare blanket.

A count was taken. More had perished during the day, and certainly more would pass on in the night. It was just the way things worked out anymore on the trail. Roland looked to his mother for comfort as other mothers wailed over lost children, and children wailed for lost parents. Some of these desperate parents ended up adopting the orphaned children, forming new families that had no guarantee of survival.

Other relationships were formed, too, among the teenagers. It had been more prevalent at the start of the journey, when the weather was warm and there was still hope to be had. Roland might have expected it to taper off—and it did, some—but it seemed as though the interactions were had, not from love, but desperation. Of course, Roland was old enough to know what was happening, but he just couldn't imagine doing it while it was so cold, or with dozens of people around. He didn't even like going out to pee in the cold, and he certainly didn't want anyone looking.

Nightly rations were handed out. Roland ate only because he knew he needed to, but it was hard as he suddenly and involuntarily erupted into spasmodic coughing, sometimes spraying his food and drink, and other times choking on it which only caused him to cough harder. Two children died this way as their coughing lodged their food in their throats so they suffocated.

"Sashki," he said as they lay down together.

"Yes, my love," his mother sighed, sounding very tired.

"Do we have to go to Indian Land?"

She sighed again. "Oh, Ola, you know we've talked about this before. You know we can't go back."

"But do we have to go to Indian Land?"

"What other choice do we have?"

"What about Aktiya Waya?"

His mother coughed and let out a weak breath. "Oh, Ola. Stories only. And Chalakki stories at that."

"What if it was real, though?"

She managed a weak smile by the light of the dying fire. "If it were real, I think it would be very nice to go there."

He pressed close to her. "We'll go there, Sashki. We'll go to Aktiya Waya. I know we will."

His mother ran a hand through his hair. "Of course, Ola Achukma. I'm sure we will."

The morning brought wails of loss. Children, elderly, the ill and injured. Their bodies were taken away, the soldiers being kind enough to rough up some shallow graves for them in the semi-frozen ground.

Ishki was able to get up and around to collect her rations that morning, and Roland wondered if perhaps she were feeling better now. Maybe she would be one of the lucky ones to survive the sickness. He glanced toward the edge of camp where the shallow graves were.

Most of the snow had melted overnight, leaving everything soaked. Roland's feet were again terribly wet, but at least they weren't frozen.

He wondered if Nimenees would come back for them today. He would like that very much. He would like it even more if Nimenees came right now to take them to Aktiya Waya.

Roland did not want to walk. He did not want to see others die. He did not like the unfamiliar landscape and the strange sounds at night. He did not like the food, especially the coffee. He did not want to sleep in a small tent under a threadbare blanket with too many people crowding around.

But no one asked what he wanted, and soon they were packing up again.

"Feels like a storm wants to come together," one of their guides, the tall man from the river, commented, peering at the distant horizon. "We'll have to move quickly, cover as much ground as possible."

"Come on," another man scoffed. "Move quickly? We've been moving slower and slower every day. The only reason we're moving as fast as we are is because the weakest are dying on the road."

"If we don't hurry, there won't be anyone to deliver to the Indian Lands," the tall man said.

The second man shrugged. "Won't bother me none. I don't like these injuns."

"Yeah, well, it's not these injuns I'm worried about. Any of these western savages catch us out here and decide to try something, we'll be sitting ducks. Surprised they haven't tried something already."

"Have you seen this lot? We don't have anything worth taking and wasting gunpowder on. Even the people aren't much to look at."

"No, but our scalps are pretty valuable to them still."

Roland retreated to the safety of his mother. He was miserable enough without being reminded of the western peoples. From what he'd heard, the Apache and Navajo were somewhat reasonable, but all accounts agreed that the Comanche were the real threat. Roland could only hope that the Comanche had been moved far away where they wouldn't want to attack them even if they could reach them. He looked at the guns the white men had and wondered if it would be enough.

Then they were moving. The lack of snow helped, but the uncertainty of the horizon certainly put a damper on things. It did little to make anyone move faster. Few could even if they wanted to. By now, most blisters had hardened into callouses, but it did nothing to ease aching joints.

Was this peace? Roland looked around. Indian, American, mixed-blood, all looked sullen and miserable under the gray sky. If anyone was being favored, it was those who drove the wagons and the few who were on horseback. Roland would have very much liked to ride on the wagon, but anyone who tried to set children or elders on a wagon were yelled at and even beaten, accused of theft. Only the wagon driver and the shotgun rider were permitted on the wagons, no one else.

So they walked. Even the soldiers who walked were little different from the rest of them.

The wind kicked up harder. Roland heard one of the white men comment that it was good that it had snowed and that the snow had melted, else they would be eating either dust of snowflakes about now.

And still the weather grew worse, until there was virtually no progress to be made. The people were weak and unable to overcome the force of the wind. Words were lost as orders were shouted, probably to make camp and shelter in place. The line came to a halt and the strongest men began scrambling to break out the tents.

One tent was lost as it was ripped from the hands of the men attempting to unfold the canvas. Another man grabbed a horse and rode off after it.

It began to hail, sharp, stinging ice pellets hammering down from the sky. Roland huddled down in the safety of the blanket his mother held up, unable to keep a tight seal and defend her head from the hail at the same time.

One tent popped up. Then two. The people rushed to these tents, packing in even tighter than they had the night before. Those who were left out huddled around outside these tents anyway until another popped up, and it was a mad rush to lay claim to even a tiny space.

Another tent popped up. Roland leapt from the safety of his mother's blanket and ran to it, sliding inside and claiming a space before doubling over in violent coughing. More people pushed inside the tent. Then more. Then more. Until it seemed as though no more room could be found.

"Sashki!" he called, unable to move, unable to breathe. He weakly pushed against whoever was pushing on him. "Please...my mother...she's coming..."

He coughed again but managed to wriggle up through the bodies to peer dimly over the heads of those gathered.

"Sashki?" he wondered.

His mother was nowhere to be seen.

Suddenly fearful, he tried to get out of the tent, make his way toward the opening, but to no avail. He was too small, and there were just too many bodies in the tent for him to move.

After a while, when more tents had been erected, including the one that had been taken by the wind, the people were able to clear out and make things more accommodating. Roland was able to breathe, or breathe as best he could between coughs. He still did not see his mother, but it was too dark to see well in the tent and too stormy to go outside and look.

Fear gripped Roland as he found himself in a tent full of strangers, many of them not even his own people. He didn't even have Ki's Bible for comfort, for that was in the bag his mother carried. He might have cried if he'd had the strength, but coughing robbed him of that. He felt very alone in that moment that was eternity.

There was little room to lie down, and Roland curled up in a ball, wishing to make himself small. He did not know why, exactly, except that it somehow made him feel safe, as if he could pretend that his mother might be close by. He tried to tell himself that the person whose back was pressed against his was his mother, but to little effect.

The hail continued for over an hour before finally tapering off to pouring rain. There was a hole in the floor canvas of the tent and water started to seep in. Roland could feel it, but no one made any mention of it. What could they do about it at this point? He couldn't even inch away from it.

Through it all was the wind, a thunderous noise that beat against the little tent so that Roland feared it might take flight and carry them all with it. There was a bit of actual thunder and several flashes of lightning. Then the hail returned for a short time, followed by a slightly gentler rain.

Few got any real sleep that night, Roland included. He wondered if Nimenees had forgotten about him. Perhaps he and the others had been delayed themselves because of the storm.

He wondered how they intended to travel to Aktiya Waya. Would they really have to walk there? Roland was tired of walking. He wished for a horse, or a wagon, or even someone to carry him.

He finally fell asleep and dreamed of riding on horseback to Aktiya Waya. In the dream, the landscape was lush, green forest at the height of summer. He dreamed of the woods around the home their family had lived in before the illness. Ki rode beside him, pointing to various plants and explaining what they were. Ishki, Evan, and Priscilla rode behind them, talking and laughing.

The dream made his heart so sick that he woke himself up from it. He quietly sat up.

It was fully dark now in the tent, but the roar and ferocity of the storm had moved on, leaving only a steady rain. The floor canvas was terribly wet, but all around, the people had somehow found sleep and dreams of their own.

Roland managed to sneak through the tent to the flap and slipped outside. The sky was still dark and full of clouds, making it impossible to judge how far off the dawn lingered. But there was still the rain and a chill in the air, and Roland hurried off to find somewhere to relieve himself.

When he returned to the camp, he saw several people out and about, carefully walking around the tents. As he drew nearer, Roland was able to pick out the old style of clothing.

He did not see Nimenees, nor could he say he recognized the others by the light of their lanterns, but so far the only people who had looked and acted healthy and whole had been those claiming to be from Aktiya Waya.

They were moving from tent to tent, bringing out several people from each one. Roland ran to join them.

"What are you doing here?" one of the men from Aktiya Waya wondered.

"Nimenees said he would take me and my mother to Aktiya Waya," Roland told him.

The men sighed. One of them asked, "Where is your mother?"

Roland looked around. "I don't know. We got separated in the storm when they were setting up tents and—" He broke off into a bout of coughing.

"Sali, help him find his mother," the man said.

Sali was a woman of about thirty years. She took Roland by the hand, and they began looking in the tents. When they opened the flap of a tent, the chill wind brought most people to wakefulness. At each one, Roland would poke his head in and ask, "Sashki?"

Ishki was the term for "mother," so it was not uncommon for several women to look up, sometimes just out of curiosity at the sound of a child's voice. Each time, Sali would ask him, "Do you see your mother?" If he did not, they moved on.

"You're Choctaw, aren't you?" she asked kindly as they made for the sixth tent.

Roland could only nod, coughing as he opened the tent flap and looked in.

"Sashki?" he wondered, growing more disheartened with every rejection.

A few people looked up. Then one woman said, "Ola Achukma?"

"Sashki!" Roland cried.

He heard her half-sigh, half-sob of relief. He saw the vague outline of an arm stretch toward him in the darkness. "Oh, Ola, come here!"

"Sashki, you have to come here. Now!"

"My love, it's dark, and we're both tired."

"Please, you have to come."

With a sigh and a cough, his mother finally relented, perhaps out of curiosity only that her son insisted on going out in the middle of the night. She ducked out of the tent and looked at Sali.

"Are you the one who brought him here?" she asked. "I thank you. We got separated when the tents were being set up."

"He told me," Sali replied gently. "But he is right; we have to go now."

"Wherever are we going in this light? And who are you? I don't recognize you, and you look well-fed."

Sali grinned shyly. "My name is Sali, and we are going to Aktiya Waya."

Roland's mother scoffed and looked at him. "Oh, Ola, really? You've been listening to stories again, and now someone is intent on—"

"They're not merely stories," Sali said gently. "Please, come with me. Just a few minutes, and we will show you that it is real."

"Who is 'we'?"

"My husband, father, and brothers."

Roland couldn't figure out why his mother was so against this. Sure, he could understand why she didn't want to go out in the dark and cold, but why should she hesitate about fleeing to Aktiya Waya?

At the last moment, she relented, though she walked several steps behind Sali and kept her head on a swivel. She hesitated only once, when they returned to the larger group, but then she relaxed, took Roland's hand, and kept him close.

There were six from Aktiya Waya and about thirty from the camp. It was almost entirely elders and children, though there were a few women, too, and a great majority of them were Chalakki.

"These are the last," Sali told the others.

"Choctaw," one of the camp elders stated.

"One of us now," one of the young men stated. He added quickly, "If they choose to stay."

"You really expect to go to Aktiya Waya?" Roland's mother asked skeptically.

"Of course we do. It's where we're from."

Another of the men addressed the group at large. "We will go to the edge of camp here, near the trees. When we are there, we will open the door to Aktiya Waya. Please go through as quickly as possible. It will be uncomfortable. Some of you may lose consciousness. Please be assured that you are safe. When we arrive, find a place to sit. Food and water will be brought to you."

Roland found this all very exciting, and he still didn't understand his mother's hesitation. Even now, she looked ready to return to the tent, but what was waiting for them there? Cold and starvation, the same as always. Even this far-fetched hope seemed like a better alternative she was willing to try.

Their group made it past the camp sentries without issue, and they made their way only a short distance to a cluster of trees. Once everyone was accounted for, one of the men spoke, reminding them to be swift, do not balk at discomfort, and there was assured safety on the other side.

Suddenly, it was as though a door burst open before their eyes. Roland jumped and his mother might have shrieked a little if her throat were not so raw, so the best she could do was a gasp and a strangled squeak.

There was no frame, no depth to this opening that stood before them now, yet there was clearly a passageway to another place. It appeared to be made of stone, and a warm fire burned hot and bright.

Roland did not understand the magic behind this incredible feat, but the people from Aktiya Waya were unfazed, and the young men began assisting the elders, each man having one elder on each arm, showing them how to cross and bolstering their courage. Then the young men returned to assist more elders.

Once the first few got going, the rest eagerly followed. They could feel the warmth from this other place, smell food they had not smelled since they started this awful journey.

"Come on, Sashki!" Roland said excitedly, pulling his mother toward the doorway.

She held back. When he looked at her, her eyes were enormous and afraid, an animal that has spotted something and is trying to decide whether to run.

On the other side of the door, more people had appeared to get the elderly situated. Some had indeed passed out and were being maneuvered onto blankets and given pillows. The rest were also given blankets and pillows, and more well-fed people started handing out cups which were filled with water from a pitcher.

The elders were all through, as were the children, orphans, apparently. All that left were the women, with and without children.

"Quickly, please!" Sali said. She stood the side of the doorway. Her voice was strained, face slick with sweat, hair plastered to her face and neck. Was she the one responsible for the doorway? Was she some kind of witch? Roland knew only a tinge of fear, and then it passed.

Finally his mother gave in. Roland was unprepared for her to pick him up and then bull through the doorway, fear and hope crashing together.

Roland had loved wrestling with Ki and Evan. The favorite move for the larger competitor was always to sit on the smaller, making it the least favorite move for the smaller opponent. Ki wasn't a big man, but he was big enough to make it hard for Roland to breathe when he decided to use that little maneuver.

That was how it felt, passing through the doorway, and Roland was sure his illness wasn't making it any more pleasant. He blacked out momentarily, coming to when he felt himself being taken from his mother's grasp. He wriggled, but a comforting female voice told him, "Sh, it's all right. Just getting you situated is all."

He rubbed his eyes, bringing things back into focus. His mother was asleep on a blanket, and he was maneuvered onto another blanket right next to her. A kind-eyed older woman gave him a pillow.

"There you are, little one. And here's a cup for you, and another for your mother when she wakes up."

She handed him one tin cup and set the second beside his mother. Then she moved off to tend to the others who were still crossing.

Another woman, no older than fourteen, came around with a pitcher of water. She filled both tin cups without a word and hurried away.

The last of the camp refugees made it through the doorway and the rescuers from Aktiya Waya crossed through, Sali being the last. The doorway shut like a cloth falling to the ground. The view of the trees and the trail vanished and the chill dissipated in only a few moments.

Curious, Roland stood and went over to where the doorway had been. There was nothing. Nothing but stone. He turned as he heard his mother stir, and he went to her.

Before he could say anything to her, there was the sound of heavy footsteps and a large man entered the building.

"Hello," he greeted, looking over the refugees. "My name is Yvgidahi. Welcome to Aktiya Waya."

Pàke Newo

Incorporation

Nendawagan was part of the group that made up the food for the refugees, and she and the others moved about the townhouse to serve the food about halfway into her father's speech.

They were a sorry lot.

Utsonvdi had taken his men to survey the camp and those who stumbled along it. Their report was not what one would call promising, and it was decided that if a rescue attempt was to be made, they would have to do it soon. Sickness was rampant, the weather was getting worse, and there was no way that the people would survive.

Nendawagan had gone with her brothers the first day and rescued fifty people, most of them women and children. The elders were dying on the trail faster than they could be rescued, and even then, most refused to go. At least if they died in the Old Lands, they would join the ancient ancestors in familiar lands and skies, not these new skies filled with new spirits.

She'd been horrified by what she'd seen, though she thought she had managed herself well. At least, none of her brothers had said anything to the contrary. But even if she could have gone back the second day, she would not have.

Instead, she now served food to the new refugees. Many were too ill to take much, but they were happy to have bread, nuts, vegetables, and a strip of jerky.

"There is plentiful hunting in the forest outside the bowl," her father was saying, still speaking to the refugees, "and we are just coming into spring, which will no doubt tempt the animals. As you might imagine, in addition to the customary deer, turkey, bear, and others, there are some unfamiliar creatures here. Our warriors will show them to you and explain. Similarly, there is much forage both within the bowl and outside, and our women and elders will educate you on what we have."

Every chance he got, her father said "we," "us," and "our," trying to solidify the idea that they were one people. He made it clear that if anyone did not wish to live with these new neighbors, then he was free to return to the Old Land. But there were rules in Aktiya Waya, and they were to be civilized inhabitants.

Nendawagan finished the first round of food and left the townhouse to fill the water pitchers at the communal pool.

"They look even worse than the group from yesterday," Popokus observed mildly beside her. "I didn't think that was possible."

"I didn't either. I didn't think things could be so bad until I went with Moskimus." Nendawagan screwed up her face as she filled another pitcher. "I didn't understand how one people could be so cruel to another. Popokus, they don't have good blankets or good tents. Some of the children don't even have clothes. Almost no one has shoes. And they eat so little, it's a wonder they have the strength to walk to relieve themselves, never mind travel great distances." She went on, "I don't understand how people can do this to themselves, or their own kind, either. The white men were not in much better shape. Why would people allow themselves to be subjected to such a thing?"

She thought her sister looked a bit distressed at her musings. Finally she shrugged, set aside another filled pitcher, and said, "I don't know, Nenda. Why do people do anything except that they think it will bring them happiness and make things better?"

They gathered the water pitchers and returned to the townhouse, making the rounds to fill the tin cups. Many of the people drank greedily, having far more enthusiasm for water than food at the moment. Her father was still speaking, now explaining some of the things people could expect to experience in Aktiya Waya.

"Coming into spring, there will be more and more sun shining into the cave in the morning and evening," he was saying. "However, the cave remains fairly dim through the majority of the day. This is not always a blessing if you choose to remain here through the summer as the south sun can make the cave hot and there is no wind to keep you cool. Some summer residences are built outside the cave for anyone to use.

"We ask that you do not enter the communal pool. You may draw water from it as you need, but we wish to keep it clean. If you desire a swim, there is a pond down in the valley where you may do so."

Talking about normal things like drawing water and bathing seemed to breathe some life back into the refugees. As Nendawagan made a second round of food, the people appeared to relax. They no longer acted like dogs, suspicious of others and hoarding food. They took the offered food with a polite "thank you," partook like civilized men and women, and shared what they did not eat.

After another round of water, Nendawagan's job was basically done until her father called on her to assist people in finding a new home. She filled all the pitchers again, just to have something to do for the moment.

Galv'na, an older woman, was also drawing water at the pool. She was part of the women's council and the one in charge of assessing any and all illnesses of the refugees.

"You look unhappy," Nendawagan observed, filling a pitcher.

"We waited too long," Galv'na said, her voice tight. "Most all of them have pneumonia, and that's the least of their worries." She frowned. "If we had rescued them sooner, or if we had even intervened and stopped this from happening at all—"

"We don't know what would have happened. For all we know, things could be a lot worse."

"Worse than this?!" the old woman hissed, gesturing toward the townhouse. "Most of those in there would be dead in a week if we hadn't rescued them, and I don't know that some still might not be. As for those still in the Old Lands, still there in the cold with no protection..." She shook her head. "There is no Indian Land. There will be no 'sovereign nations.' The white men are going to keep marching the people around and around in circles until they all drop dead! This is murder, Nendawagan. Murder disguised as charity. And you can tell your father I said that."

"And then what?" Nendawagan challenged. "What do you want us to do? Shall we go back and kill all the white men? There are always more. And they are in a better position than the people."

Galv'na huffed but did not back down. "I don't know, but we need to make a decision before there are no people left to save. If we are to be a safe haven for resting warriors, then we ought to be training our warriors to fight and take back what is ours."

"We are a safe haven for people to live in peace."

"Which people? Because as long as we continue to take in refugees from the Old Land, there will always be a divide. Aktiya Waya and the Old Land. Native and grafted. Old and new. Cherokee and Lenape. As long as we continue to bring in those who would remind us of our differences, we will never overcome those differences."

"You want to seal us off?" Nendawagan questioned.

"If we want to be our own people, we have to be our own people with our own identity. Who are we, and how do we know that's who we are? These are the decisions that your generation will have to make, Nenda. Yours, your nieces and nephews, all those who were born here, with no interference from those from the Old Land. You will be the ones to decide whether Aktiya Waya thrives or crumbles into nothing better than what we left."

Nendawagan nodded. "I understand. But consider, too, that if you wish for the young people to make good decisions in order to build this better, unified life, then the elders must also give encouragement and set an example of it."

Galv'na gave her a look. "Your attitude is going to get you in trouble one day, Nendawagan. Is it any wonder no suitors have come asking after you?"

Nendawagan winced at that, grabbed her pitchers, and walked away.

Her father was just wrapping up his speech when she entered the townhouse and dropped off the pitchers. A few stayed in the townhouse for general use, but the rest would be picked up by their owners once the refugees were gone and settling into their new homes.

"If you would now be so kind," her father said, "please divide up into groups, those you would intend to live with in a home. The homes may not be what you are accustomed to, but they can sleep seven or eight people well."

The refugees, who had been relaxing and settling in, suddenly seemed uncertain about the prospect of moving. Probably they could have all closed their eyes and fallen asleep right there by the fire. Nendawagan didn't blame them. She still wasn't certain how half of them were alive, never mind moving and traveling.

The people got themselves sorted out. Few had any single units comprised of seven or eight people, and some chose to stick together in odd, mismatched groups. Perhaps they had made friends on the trail, comrades in misery.

"My daughters," Yvgidahi introduced, gesturing to them, "Nendawagan and Popokus will take you to our available homes. You may choose whichever one you please, and you may ask them any questions you may have. I only wish to remind you that we are a peaceful place, and we do not want to see any fighting. If there are problems, please bring it before the council."

And just like that, Nendawagan and Popokus were left to take the refugees, about thirty of them, to their new homes.

Thirty refugees, but there were so many more left behind, Nendawagan knew. If they were in as bad a shape as they looked and as Galv'na proclaimed, there wouldn't be too many left to save in the near future. They should have brought more. Fifty. Sixty. A hundred. More. They had the room. Aktiya Waya had the housing. They were coming into spring and summer, which meant food would be plentiful and people could find their place here.

Or was it as Galv'na had said, and they couldn't allow so many people in who would not or could not assimilate? And assimilate into what? They didn't even have a name for their supposedly unified people.

In spite of her father encouraging the people to ask questions, most of them looked like they just wanted to get some sleep. Many of the children were already asleep in their mother's arms, the mothers looking strained as if they could hardly lift a needle, never mind a heavy child. Some of the people, as soon as Nendawagan or her sister pointed out that a home was available, walked right in without a second thought.

Once all the refugees were deposited into their new homes, Nendawagan returned with her sister to their home. Their mother was already there, adding wood to tide the fire for the night. It wasn't long before their father joined them.

"I think that went well," he observed, sounding rather hopeful.

"Will there be more tomorrow?" Nendawagan inquired.

"We have to save as many as we can. I knew it was bad. All the reports said so. But to bring them here and to see how bad they look, how crushed they are in spirit, knowing that there are hundreds or thousands more in the same predicament..."

"We can't bring them all here," Mesim told him.

"The land can sustain them a hundred times over."

"The land can, but can we? They're grateful now because they've been rescued from death. What happens when they've recovered and old grudges make themselves known again?"

"We've laid the ground rules. Now we have to enforce them. There will be no infighting. We are one people."

"And there were never clan feuds among the Aniyvwiya?"

Nendawagan saw her father hesitate, but with a certain expression he had when considering a new idea that's just formulated in his mind. He nodded once. "Of course there were. But we were always Aniyvwiya. Now we are...a new people."

That was as far as the argument got that evening, and everyone was able to retire to bed more or less in peace.

The following morning, Nendawagan was up early, going door-to-door to check on the refugees. As Galv'na had predicted, some had died in the night, in spite of any food or medicine they'd been given. The families often didn't know what to do with them. They could not bury their deceased in the Old Land, but they were equally unsure about burying them in this new, foreign land. But they couldn't just let them lie there, cold and disrespected, and they themselves had to get up and get moving.

They were weary and ill, Nendawagan knew, but there was also a certain determination about them that put her a bit in awe of them, that they did not, could not sit back lazily upon their weakened state. They were determined to keep going. Or perhaps she was romanticizing it in her mind. They had been harshly conditioned to keep going, no matter the cost to their bodies and souls. They needed rest.

Her father and two of her brothers had gone out early to catch game for the refugees. They walked with her and delivered the carcasses, gutted and still warm, to the homes.

"It's been a long time since I've seen such a plump rabbit," one woman commented, nearly in tears as she took the rabbit and began preparing it with a knife Moskimus also provided her, as a replacement for the one the white men had confiscated.

The rabbit was hardly plump, at least to Nendawagan's eyes, for it had used up most of its winter fat stores.

If anyone seemed to bounce back swiftly, it was the children. They were happy to sleep in as long as they pleased, in a place that was warm and dry. They were happy to have water and food. They were happy that they didn't have to march along a cold road, following only a promise and an order.

The children of Aktiya Waya followed Nendawagan and the others at a distance, not interfering until the adults had moved on. Then they would run up to the house to see if there were any children about and ask if they wanted to play.

Nendawagan slapped a palm on the outside of a home, sort of like a knock, saying, "Good morning."

"Come in," a woman said.

The homes could comfortably sleep eight, but as Nendawagan and her father and brothers entered, the space got smaller very quickly.

"We're here to check on you," Yvgidahi said. "We've brought game for you, and some tools. Has anyone here walked on the night?"

"Not this night, but my father Daniel is very ill," another woman said. "He may not last another night."

"Galv'na will come around with medicine and clothing," Nendawagan promised.

"Understand that you are not confined here," her father went on. "You are not our prisoners, but our guests. If you wish to move about, you are free to do so."

"Do you intend to send us back, once we are well and clothed again?" a third woman inquired.

"If that is what you want, we can arrange it. Otherwise, you may consider yourselves people of Aktiya Waya."

"How did we get here?" the first woman asked. A young boy slept with his head in her lap. "What is this place? You are all Cherokee."

"Not all," Moskimus said at the same time Yvgidahi replied, "No, we are all of Aktiya Waya now."

"Please, sir, with your sons you speak Chalakki. You look like Chalakki. You are Chalakki."

Nendawagan saw her father consider his words carefully. "We were Cherokee. And I can no more stop speaking it as my mother tongue, or erase my childhood memories among the Cherokee, than you can erase who you are or were. It is true, Aktiya Waya began as a Cherokee settlement. But there is more than that here now. Which people are you from?"

"Chahta. Choctaw."

He nodded once. "Yes, there are residents who were once Choctaw as well. If it makes you more comfortable, my daughter—" He gestured to her. "—could introduce you to them later."

For a moment, Nendawagan was afraid the woman would insist on being taken and introduced to them right then. After a moment, however, she simply nodded and silently agreed.

After inquiring about any further immediate needs of the people in the home, Nendawagan and the others moved on.

Once everyone had been taken care of, her father and brothers headed to the townhouse to discuss things, and Nendawagan fell in with Galv'na, making secondary rounds of clothing and medicine. Few people had arrived with shoes, and even those who had, had suffered from terrible sores. Many suffered frostbite to some degree. Almost all of them had pneumonia, some quite severely, and many had other illnesses and infections on top of that.

Seeing to the refugees took most of the morning, part of the afternoon, and virtually all of Nendawagan's will. She hated to see the people in such wretched shape, and she was glad that they were getting help, but there was a part of her that burned with righteous fury that they were in such shape to begin with.

She had little energy to do anything about it, however, and she returned home to hopefully make some tea for herself. After a full day of helping others and watching them eat, well, it stirred her to want to at least drink something, and perhaps a cup of tea would help to calm her nerves and focus her mind.

Her father and brothers, and likely the rest of the council, were still at the townhouse, and she could not interrupt their meetings, but she could wait for her father at home.

Her mother and sister were not home either; they were busy at another home, making the clothes to give to the refugees. Nendawagan figured she should probably join them, but not before she got her tea.

Mesim and Popokus returned first, followed shortly by Yvgidahi.

"How was the meeting?" Nendawagan asked.

"Between the two rescues, we have determined that, as of this morning after the burials, we have thirteen elders, sixteen women of marrying age, two young men who are crippled, four boys who are nearly men, and twenty children."

"Fifty-five? That's all?"

"What do you mean, that's all?"

"Nocha, we rescued eighty people. There are hundreds of people being forced to march and leave their homes. More are dying every day! We can't just leave them."

"Nenda, our resources are only so great," her father said. "Few of the refugees will be able to support themselves in the very near future, unless some of the women decide to marry. Some may be taught to snare small game or fish, but the few cannot supply for the many."

"There are men on the trail."

"Few of whom are educated in the old ways. All of those people are old or gone now. The young men were raised to be white, to be American, in hopes of just keeping their land. Now that it has been taken from them, they don't even have their heritage to preserve."

"There must be something more we can do. They can't all be..." Nendawagan trailed off before she said the hateful slur.

"Can't all be what?" her father prompted knowingly.

"They can't all be apple Indians." Red on the outside, white on the inside.

"I'm sure there are some very knowledgeable young men on the trail; it may be the only reason they're surviving. But we can't conduct interviews on everyone. And if we were to explain what we're doing, if they think that we hold them in such disregard, they may come to see us as enemies. Then we are no longer trying to rescue their women and children, but steal them."

"If they are that different, though, if they are that white, and that far removed from the old ways, wouldn't they see it that way anyway?"

Her father sighed and did not answer that. Instead, he said, "Yes. They are dying on the trail. As we have seen, sometimes even rescue comes too late. It will only get worse. It has been decided that we will not attempt any more rescues at this time. We need to see and understand what we're doing here and now, with these few refugees, before we take on a much larger project."

"But there may not be any larger, future projects if the people are only being marched to their deaths!" Nendawagan blurted.

"There will be," Yvgidahi cut in sternly, "because there are a great many Indians still in North America. This is only the beginning, Nenda. Believe me, the Americans will not stop with this. There will be more to save in the future. But we have to be smart about it. Furthermore, if there is in fact an end to this, if there is truly an Indian Land where the people will be permitted to settle, however temporarily, the settlement that they build will show us who remembers and observes the old ways."

Nendawagan thought of all the people she had seen in the camp, too many people huddled in too few tents, too little clothing for too cold weather. Children without parents, mothers losing their children, knowledge and wisdom dying with the elders in unforgiving, unfamiliar lands. She wiped tears from her eyes. "It's not fair."

"You're right," her father said gently. "It's not. We are very fortunate to have found this place. We live very peaceful, very...robust lives here. Your anger is not unwarranted, and your compassion is not shameful. But you have to think of us, too. We have this prosperity for a reason. That reason must be remembered, respected, and retained."

"I know." She huffed. "Why didn't Nathan and Andrew rescue more people? In the Book, it says that there are ruins far to the south. I can't imagine that there are not other lost civilizations, ancient ruins, somewhere on this world."

"It took years to establish this settlement. More than just homes and water, we had to learn new moons, new stars, new seasons, new game, new forage. The conditions were right. I don't know why they didn't move more people, but I don't think the people on the trail would be so successful today; you saw them yourself."

She nodded sullenly and took another drink of tea; it was quickly growing cold. Finally she sighed and stood. "I promised one of the women I would take her to meet the Choctaw. Or former Choctaw. I should probably do that."

Her father's look was impossible to determine as she stood and left the house.

Nendawagan remembered when she was a teenager, breaking into womanhood. There was a period where her mind felt as though a curtain were being pulled back, great mysteries revealed, and she realized, to her astonishment, that other people and an entire world existed beyond her and her family. Of course she'd known and seen the people of Aktiya Waya, participated in daily life, but it was a sort of spiritual awakening as she came to understand her place among the people, see how everything was interconnected.

That web was a terribly tangled one, if the council and the politics could be believed. Now she felt as though she were having a similar revelation as they talked about the refugees and as she interacted with them. She was realizing, again, much to her amazement, that other people and an entire world existed beyond her and her comfortable life. It was as if Aktiya Waya was only half of a drawing, half of a portrait of her people. Now she was seeing that there was another half, and it still existed in the Old Land.

She had a drawing like that, somewhere in the house. She'd wished to draw both woman and wolf, life-givers and caretakers of the people. The image in her mind was grand and beautiful, the charcoal scratching on the leather hide, less so, and it remained unfinished.

She reached the house where she believed the Choctaw woman to be. Not many of the adults had moved, but of the five children she'd seen, four of them were out, perhaps playing with the Aktiya Waya children.

"Do you still want to meet the Choctaw residents?" Nendawagan asked politely.

The woman nodded, got to her feet, and her son followed. He looked a bit pale, and his cough sounded terrible, but she remembered how it had sounded the night before and was thankful Galv'na's medicine seemed to be working.

"What's your name?" Nendawagan inquired as they left the house.

"Fichik Lukoli," the woman replied.

"I'm sorry, I don't know your language."

"It means 'constellation' in English, but many of them called me Francis, just because it was easier to say." Pause. "And you? What did your father call you?"

"Nendawagan. It means 'torch.' "

"That's not Chalakki."

"No, my mother was Lenape."

She could feel the woman's gaze. Scrutiny, confusion, exhaustion. Finally she said, "Then it is possible to live in peace."

"Of course." Nendawagan hoped she could convey enough hope to cover up her uncertainty.

"Aki liked peace," the boy said.

"Who's Aki?"

"His father, John," Fichik Lukoli sighed. "He died not long before we had to leave."

"If he hadn't, we wouldn't have had to leave," the boy went on. "Aki was a diplomat. He would have gone to Washington City and talked to the president and told him that we weren't going to leave."

Nendawagan looked at the woman who was clearly embarrassed as she looked around to see who might have heard.

"His father was American?" Nendawagan asked.

"Yes," the woman answered, her dejected posture suggesting she expected to be returned to the trail because of it.

Nendawagan paused in their walk and knelt in front of the little boy. He might have been as young as six for as thin and ill as he looked, but he could have been as old as twelve once he got properly fed and recovered. "What's your name?"

"Ola Achukma, but most call me Roland." He coughed weakly.

"Well, Ola Achukma, you say your father liked peace?" He nodded. "Good. Because we like peace, too. You'll be more than welcome here."

Her words seemed to have a calming effect on the boy's mother as Nendawagan stood and continued walking through the village.

"Have you been here long?" Fichik Lukoli wondered.

Nendawagan grinned. "I was born here, as were my sister and all my brothers and all my nieces and nephews."

"I heard the Chaląkki talking about Aktiya Waya at night, around the fires," Ola Achukma said. "They said that the Chaląkki fought against the white men and lost, but they weren't defeated. They vanished into fire and shadow, promising to return one day and avenge the people."

Nendawagan laughed. "Well, it didn't happen quite like that, but it's the story the elders tell in order to delight the children."

"Well, it delighted him enough that he insisted we follow strangers into the darkness in order to come to this fabled place," his mother said, managing a small smile. "We had nothing to look forward to, not really, so we came."

"You speak Cherokee, then?"

"His father taught him many languages." Fichik Lukoli sighed again. "He really believed in peace, in unification. He really believed the white men and the Indians of all nations could live together as one." She shook her head. "I just don't know if that's possible."

"Aktiya Waya must offer some proof of that?" Nendawagan stated. "If there has been any mistreatment—"

"No, not at all. But then, those of us from the trail have been here less than a full day. We are in no condition to even argue, much less fight. I have not seen enough of life here to say for certain. But for the moment, it is very kind of you to offer us shelter."

Nendawagan frowned but said, "Of course. You are free to stay or go, as my father has stated."

Before either could stay more, Nendawagan spotted one of the Choctaw residents and waved her over, a middle-aged woman with a toddler grandchild in tow. Fichik Lukoli wasted no time in going to her and attempting to strike up conversation. There seemed to be some disconnect and distress between them, but Fichik Lukoli paid Nendawagan no further mind, and the two Choctaw women moved off, still speaking.

Nendawagan watched them leave, then turned and headed back home. It was growing dark, and a crisp wind suggested overnight snow. The men were coming in for the night, looking tired and not the most pleased. There was some hangup with the secondary irrigation system, and now there were new refugees to deal with. Few would have anything to do with that, but it was the knowledge that there was something else going on that warranted great and careful attention.

She returned home where there seemed to be some great commotion about. A sweet smell wafted from the house, and many dozens or hundreds of strips of meat had been hung to cure outside the door. She didn't even get to ask what it was, for Popokus was more than happy to enlighten her just as soon as she walked in.

"Simaquon came by!" her sister gushed. "And he brought gifts!"

Nendawagan couldn't help but smile. "I see. What sort of gifts?"

"You were right! He brought back things from the Old Land, things few can speak of, or even name."

Popokus grabbed her hand and dragged her into the room they shared where a number of items were laid out. Nendawagan was able to identify many of them as generic things, such as feathers or necklaces and such, though she was not able to identify the specific animal or materials.

"He brought meat, too, which Guka is cooking," Popokus said.

Nendawagan nodded, breathing in the sweet smell.

"Simaquon said it was from an animal called a...a goschgosch, a hog."

"A hog? What's that?"

"He described it as an animal with hooves, but it is very short, only about this tall." She put a hand to her knee. "But he says that they are very big, extremely round, and they're pink in color. If I hadn't seen it with my own eyes, I wouldn't have believed such a thing as a pink animal! They also have tails that curl, and ears that flop over. And they have snouts which they use to root around in the dirt."

"In the dirt? What do they eat, worms?"

"Simaquon says they eat roots and plants. The white men keep them as livestock to butcher."

Nendawagan gave her a look. "You mean he stole it?"

"Of course he did, from the white men. He said he was very sneaky about it, too."

"Does Nocha know?"

"Of course he does. He thought it was quite amusing."

Nendawagan turned to leave the room, but Popokus grabbed her arm. "Nenda, don't. Nocha knows. And I think you've exhausted him enough for the time being with your obsession over politics and the Old Land and the refugees and everything else. He needs to rest and think of other things."

She hesitated, but finally agreed and turned back to the treasure trove. "I guess you're right. What is the rest of this, then?"

"These are feathers from a bird called a red-tailed hawk. And these are from a bird called a woodpecker. They beat their beaks against the bark of a tree to drill into it and find bugs."

"And what is this?" Nendawagan picked up the smallest bird she had ever seen, with wings like lace and a beak like a needle, but with gloriously iridescent feathers.

"That's called a hummingbird," Popokus answered. "Simaquon said he found it dead, but thought it was pretty and brought it back, more to inquire about finding and bringing more to Aktiya Waya, to introduce to the land here."

"It is very pretty."

"Nocha says they fly very fast and bathe in the petals of flowers after it rains."

Nendawagan grinned. "We should definitely bring some here."

Popokus picked up several pieces of jewelry. "These rocks are called pearls. Simaquon doesn't know much about them, other than they are very rare and very valuable."

"What about these?" Nendawagan picked up another necklace with three large beads in the middle. "These look like very large glass beads."

"No, not at all. Those are gemstones. He said this one is a ruby—" She pointed to the red one in the middle. "This blue one is a sapphire, and the green one is an emerald."

"They're very nice."

Popokus giggled. "Father said that they're all very expensive, and Simaquon must have robbed a king to acquire them."

"Did he?"

"He wouldn't say."

"Did he at least leave something for them, or offer to trade?"

"He didn't say anything about it. But, come on, Nenda, he went through all that trouble...for me!"

"And...?" Nendawagan wondered.

"And what?"

"Did you accept? Did he officially ask to marry you? Come on, Popo, you've only been dreaming of this for a year, if not longer!"

Her sister blushed and looked away shyly. "Guka says that tomorrow, we should invite everyone to dinner in the townhouse; she will cook up all the hog meat to serve. And I will wear the pretty jewelry and the feathers and everything else, and I should walk around and show it off. And when people ask what the meat is, where it came from, who provided it, and where I got my pretty jewelry, then I will tell them that Simaquon gave it to me for our engagement."

"Oh, that sounds fantastic! Then everyone will know you are engaged and that you are the luckiest woman in Aktiya Waya with the most thoughtful husband!"

Popokus grinned and blushed even harder. "Oh, Nenda, I'm just so happy!"

"And I'm happy for you," Nendawagan told her. "Really, I am. You're going to be married!"

"Yes, but..." Now her sister seemed uncertain. "What if I can't have children?"

Nendawagan hesitated. "Popokus, I—"

"You know the sorceries affect us like that. I haven't had a blood in almost fourteen years. It's why some men forbid their wives and daughters from learning the sorceries, and why some men refuse to use it themselves."

"I know. Maybe you'll just have to stop using them for a while. Maybe you can use the sorceries to help yourself."

"Help myself how?"

"You can Touch, can't you? You know how your body works. See if you can't force it."

"But I don't want to make things worse."

"How can you make things worse?"

Popokus hesitated. Then, "I guess you're right. But that will be something for later, I think."

Nendawagan nodded and tried to get back in a cheerful mood. "Yes. Later. Right now, we have your engagement party to plan."

Popokus waved a hand. "Please, you know Guka has had such things planned since our brothers started getting married before we did."

"That's right I did," their mother said from the next room.

The sisters were laughing as they joined their parents for a dinner of seasoned hog meat. It was very sweet, Nendawagan thought, and extremely juicy, the fat rendering as perfectly as any meat she'd ever prepared.

"Perhaps we shall bring hogs to Aktiya Waya as well as hummingbirds," Yvgidahi mused, savoring the meat.

"We keep no livestock beyond our horses," Mesim reminded him. "Everything else was either abandoned as the white man's ways, or turned loose to become feral."

Yvgidahi shrugged. "We need not keep hogs as livestock. The sheep may have perished, but the goats and the cows have survived, running free to the more southern plains."

"But do we really need to bring them here? There are plenty of animals indigenous to the area, without us bringing more."

"If the hog were as beautiful as the hummingbird, which you so loved, too, would you feel the same way?"

Yvgidahi gave his wife a tender look. Nendawagan glanced at her sister, thinking about how Simaquon would be looking at Popokus in such a way.

The following day, Nendawagan was again up early, this time going from house to house, inviting everyone to her sister's feast of engagement. Few had any clue what this was, as far as a village affair, for it had always been done largely only between the two families being joined. Even so, a good number of people agreed to attend, if only to investigate this hog meat Nendawagan spoke of. Some of the elders from the Old Land knew what it was, as well as a few who had been to the Old Land, and even they remembered it as something delicious.

There would not be enough for everyone to have a full meal of the hog meat, but they could try a bite of it at least. Otherwise, Yvgidahi and Moskimus went out to take a few deer to supplement the meat, and Mesim and Popokus were gathering what forage they could find before returning to the house to properly adorn the newly-engaged daughter.

Nendawagan also made sure to invite the refugees. They were

thrilled by the prospect, and happy to celebrate good news. A few were still very ill and unable to attend, but those who were able promised to be there.

The townhouse was abuzz with excitement as dozens of people prepared for the event. Most of them were Nendawagan's brother's wives and mothers-in-law. The rest were the women's council and the priests. The couple would receive a formal blessing on their engagement, and a date would be divined for the wedding ceremony.

It was not unusual for the smell of cooking meat to permeate the air in the cave, but this was a different meat. This was hog meat, and the new smell brought many curious noses as the day wore on.

Nendawagan had been told on several occasions that the white men from the Old Land had a certain obsession with time. They marked out their days according to precise hours and minutes and even seconds, and one was expected to keep time with all vigilance. If a man promised to do a thing at a specific hour, he was expected to do this thing at this specific hour, if not before.

Their people were not so rigid, and their days were kept by the movement of the sun: morning, noon, evening, and night. The crystals were used to tell twilight for council meetings, the cycles of the moon were diligently observed, and the priests had ways of divining perfect sun, when the sun was directly overhead, and perfect moon, when the moon was in the same spot, but on any given day, there was only a vague inclination toward time, at the behest of one's best judgment.

So it was that when the sun came around toward evening and the crystals at the mouth of the cave exploded into thousands of tiny stars, people started showing up to the townhouse, expecting to get something to eat and find out just what the party was all about.

It was Simaquon's father and brothers who made cuts of the deer meat, and his mother and female relatives who served the forage and other non-meat items. Mesim was the one solely in charge of distributing the hog meat.

Nendawagan got herself a plate of food and sat down. Simaquon strutted about, adorned in feathers and bone armor, a cage of antlers protecting his shoulders and making him look bigger. He had his bow on his back, freshly oiled. Across the room, Popokus dazzled all in her new jewelry. She even had a red, patterned cloth made of something called silk, which was soft and fine, and she had it wrapped and tied around one shoulder. Not a few women took notice of her.

"So what are they saying?" Nendawagan asked when her sister finally made it around to her.

"Who?" Popokus asked innocently.

"Anyone. The women over there."

Her sister giggled. "The older women talk about how their husbands never lavished on them like that, and the younger ones seem to have set higher standards for their suitors."

"Yes, I can see some of the young men looking very...unsettled. Uncertain is the word I should use."

Popokus grinned hugely and meandered away.

Nendawagan finished her food and was just about ready to stand up when someone sat next to her. It was one of the refugee women. She still looked markedly thin in the face, and her hair was brittle, but being able to freshen up, wear new, proper clothes, and attend a great feast made her appear hopeful again.

"Is this how things are done here?" she wondered, still seeming to be a fish out of water.

"I suppose so, yes," Nendawagan answered. Truthfully, this was the first celebration of its kind. Other warriors who went to the Old Land sometimes managed to bring back a trinket or two, but Simaquon was the first to offer such grand treasures to a woman he wished to woo. She shifted position to face the woman. "Why do you ask?"

"It's a marvelous party," the woman said, grinning and looking around. Her expression turned serious as she looked Nendawagan in the eye. "My betrothed, he still walks the cold road. No doubt he fears what has happened to me. Please. Will the warriors return to retrieve him?"

Nendawagan hesitated. "I don't know. Our resources are limited here."

"He's an excellent hunter," the woman said quickly. "He can also fish very well."

"I'm sure he can, but…" She hesitated again. Then, "Let me ask my father tonight. What is his name?"

"Usgwado, but his English name is Matthew Whiteford."

Nendawagan nodded, hoping her face remained neutral. "I will ask my father and see what he is willing to do."

The woman thanked her profusely, then stood and went to speak to another group of women, all of them refugees. They looked frail in their new dresses, clothing seemingly meant for more robust women. Did they all have fiances waiting for them?

Later that evening, once Mesim had retired from her hog meat delegation and Popokus had finally been convinced to return home, Nendawagan brought up the subject to her father before he, too, could slip away to sleep.

"Bring a young man here?" he wondered.

"The woman says he knows how to hunt and fish," Nendawagan said. "If our greatest concern is resources and how we will care for the refugees, why not bring those who can provide? And if they are betrothed, then surely they still intend to get married and they will have a family here."

Her father took an even breath and let it out slowly. "You are correct —"

"Then what are we waiting for?"

"We can't go back for just one man. Practical reasons aside, I don't think you would allow it. But as it has already been decided, we cannot overwhelm ourselves."

"The people on the trail are dying, Nocha," Nendawagan said. "Some of them die even with Galv'na's help. Maybe we have reached a point where it is too late for the very young and very old." She hated herself for saying so. "Maybe this time we should rescue those who are healthy and have a fighting chance. Rescue the young men who can contribute."

"Contribute what? Nenda, we've been over this. Many of them can't contribute. Maybe this woman's betrothed is a rare exception, but most of them have forgotten their people, forgotten the old ways."

"Then we can teach them! We can give them a life and a purpose again!"

But her father appeared to have made up his mind. "No. Or rather, not yet. Let the people settle, let them build. Those who survive and observe the old ways, to them we will extend an invitation to come to Aktiya Waya. If the woman's betrothed is everything she says he is, then what is a few more moons to wait?"

Nendawagan had words in her chest, but she dared not let them pass her lips. She did not need to embarrass her father, and certainly not on the tail of an otherwise joyous occasion. She looked around the townhouse, relieved when she could not spy the woman who had spoken to her. Nendawagan wasn't sure how she could tell the woman her father had refused, or the reason why.

"I know you want to help everyone," her father said gently. "I know you want to save everyone. One day you will learn that such a thing is not possible. Even my brother had to sacrifice himself in order to save just a handful of our people."

"I know," Nendawagan sighed.

"Why don't you go on home? I think Popokus may need some help getting to sleep."

Nendawagan laughed. "You just want me to be the pot into which she pours her words so that you may sleep peacefully."

Her father grinned. "You know me so well. Go on, then."

Nendawagan returned home, heart heavy.

Talhapi Tushafa

Distant Dream

The day was hot, and the game seemed to be smarter than they were about finding shelter, Ola Achukma thought, bringing his hand up to shield his eyes from the sun. Really he wanted nothing more than to return to Aktiya Waya and jump in the pond at the bottom of the bowl, near the wolf's mouth. But he was becoming a man now, and he had responsibilities; he couldn't indulge in every childish whim anymore.

South of Aktiya Waya, about three days' hard ride, was a vast swath of open plains, an ocean of green as tall, luscious grasses waved in the wind, large bunches of tiny wildflowers forming the foam. In the far, far distance, you could just make out the pale gray rise of hills, not quite mountains like Aktiya Waya, but great hills nonetheless.

Ola Achukma felt his heart skip a beat. He hated this place. He didn't like feeling so open and exposed; there may not have been other peoples to war against, but that did not mean there were not predators. Furthermore, he didn't like being so exposed to the sun and its merciless heat. There were a few scraggly, twiggy trees that more closely resembled large bushes, but they had left the forest proper in the late afternoon the previous day.

But most of all, he hated this place because it reminded him too much of the Trail. The stark horror had faded over the years, so that it sometimes felt like little more than a distant dream, a nightmare that clung to his subconscious. And yet, it was places like this that brought it roaring back to life.

He recalled the first time he'd been brought here, when he was about thirteen, going on his first real long distance hunt. They left the forest in the night under the dim light of a crescent moon, and he had thought nothing of their surroundings then. In the morning, when the sun rose and he saw only the openness, he'd broken down, shrieking like a madman and bawling like an infant.

Many of the refugees were that way, those who made such a journey, anyway. Those who had been children on the Trail were the worst. But Ola Achukma had learned to deal with it, push it aside, and carry on with his task.

All the same, he tried to focus on the distant hills as much as possible, and remind himself that there were no white men here.

"There's nothing here," Unitsiya said distastefully, looking around at the same empty plains. "Let's check the rivers, see if anything has gone there to drink."

While the idea was sound, Ola Achukma could see that they were all thinking more about getting water for themselves and their horses, rather than chasing down any game that they happened upon at the river.

At the height of summer, the river was only about waist-deep, and no more than twelve feet across at the widest point. Close observation of the landscape showed where the spring flood depth reached almost ten feet and about sixty feet wide.

There were a few more respectable trees in this area and innumerable animal tracks coming and going from the bank and across the river. Ola Achukma recognized deer tracks, as well as the tracks of dozens of animals of all shapes and sizes that did not exist in the Old Land. But for all the tracks, there did not appear to be an animal in sight.

Disheartened, the hunters dismounted, and both man and beast went into the water.

The chill was a surprise, but a welcome relief, and Ola Achukma got down on his knees, then his seat, immersing himself to his chin. Then he took a breath and went under. He stayed there as long as he could, feeling the current change as the others had similar ideas. When he could hold his breath no longer, he broke the surface and pushed his hair out of his face.

Everything just felt better after that, he thought, and as the others poked their heads back up above the water, he could see they were thinking the same thing.

Lapish was the last to come up, although his emergence was not so calm as the rest. He was a couple years younger than Ola Achukma, and quite a bit more immature. For instance, he thought it would be great fun to pull himself along the bottom of the shallow river and pop up behind his horse which stood in the river, drinking peacefully and nibbling on grasses. What he expected the horse to do, no one quite knew, least of all Lapish who suddenly found himself fighting for his life to dodge spooky, wild hooves and climb out of the river. This may have been better accomplished if he and his horse had chosen opposite banks to climb onto, but when the horse broke onto the bank and found itself being chased by the scary thing that popped out of the river, it did the only thing it knew how to do: kick. Then it ran off.

Ola Achukma was the last to reach Lapish as the others dragged him out of the river where he'd landed.

"Stupid child!" Okchanlush hissed, slapping Lapish in the face both out of spite and to rouse the boy who was limp and groaning. He slapped him a second time. "Wake up! Can you speak?!"

Lapish managed to move one arm, but when he went to move the other, he gasped. That movement evidently caused him more pain, and soon enough he was contorted in several unnatural ways, gnashing his teeth, shrieking and weeping at the same time.

"Stupid fool!" Okchanlush said again, this time striking Lapish in a spot on his ribcage which was broken, causing the young man to cry out, though it tapered off to blubbering sobs. "Now we have to return to Aktiya Waya for a stupid mistake, and we don't even have any game to show for it!"

"I'm sorry," Lapish babbled in between sobs and sniffs.

"He didn't mean anything by it," Unitsiya said calmly, returning from his horse with a pack of supplies for just such an emergency. All the same, he was less than gentle when it came to positioning Lapish in order to bind his wounds.

"Maybe not, but the boy doesn't think!" Okchanlush growled. He looked at Lapish. "What did you think would happen?"

But Lapish was not paying attention, instead groaning loudly as Unitsiya probed his wounds, finally frowning and shifting position. "The bones will have to be set by a skilled doctor. I am not proficient enough in the sorceries to do it here."

"You mean we will all have to—"

"We don't all have to return," Unitsiya interrupted. "We can send one back with him."

"And deny a hunter a chance to take game back to his family because this—"

"There is plenty of game between here and Aktiya Waya. It will just be smaller game, not part of the drive."

"But—"

Unitsiya stood and faced Okchanlush. "I am the one in charge of this outing. I will decide what we do. And unless you want to be the one to take Lapish back to Aktiya Waya and so forfeit your chance to go on this drive, I suggest you stop talking, chagga."

Okchanlush took offense to the name, but said nothing more. Unitsiya looked around at the rest of them.

"Ola Achukma, go find his horse, bring it back. Shikak, you'll take Lapish back to Aktiya Waya."

Shikak was the same age as Lapish, but more soft-spoken, more mature, and less likely to disobey orders. Even so, the boy looked sullen at being told to go home and abandon the hunt.

Ola Achukma grabbed his mount and went to look for Lapish's horse. It hadn't run far, for it was still within sight of the rest of the horses, but with this little incident, it was far more difficult to catch and convince to return to the river. By the time Ola Achukma did return to the others, skittish horse in tow, Lapish had received a good scolding from all the older hunters, and Shikak was ready to go as well.

He handed off the horse to Unitsiya, and Okchanlush roughly pushed Lapish onto the horse's back. Neither teenager said a word as they turned and started up the bank and started riding back the way they had come. Ola Achukma could only imagine the pain Lapish was in with his broken ribs, rumbling along on a bony horse. He deliberately turned his gaze from them back to the group.

Despite Yvgidahi's best efforts, the people were still very divided according to their ancestral peoples. There were ten who had started out, four Chahta, two Aniyvwiya, two Seminole, an Iroquois, and a Lenape. The Seminole had taken some offense to something the first night they were out and had turned back. Now they had lost Lapish and Shikak who were both Chahta. Would there be any left to even make this a proper drive, or would they all be forced to compromise with maybe one deer and a handful of small game?

Unitsiya sighed but nodded in agreement. There was a bluff just downstream that would provide some protection from the wind, and here they made camp, hastily pitching tents and gathering dead wood from the bushy trees to start a fire.

"With any luck, we won't run into the Oceti Sakowin tomorrow," Ashagi grumbled, to the disgruntled agreement of the rest.

The Oceti Sakowin, or Sioux nations, were one of the more recent additions to Aktiya Waya, and perhaps the one most regretted by Yvgidahi. There weren't many of them—only forty had been saved, with only twelve men who might be considered warriors—but they were a terrible force in the open plains, and they took every opportunity they got to go on such game drives.

Ashagi himself was the Iroquois in their group, although his mother had been an Anishinaabek woman, taken as a prize in a raid. She named her firstborn son after her own customs. He had been but a child when the war in the Old Land came, when the British turned on their allies, the same war that Yvgidahi had fought in. He had been rescued along with four others when the British burned his village.

He was perhaps the one Ola Achukma got along with the best on this trip, for he understood how it was to be of mixed parentage from the Old Land, especially when at least one of the sides was hated by the Aniyvwiya, whatever Yvgidahi claimed.

"These plains are plenty big enough for us to have our own space," Unitsiya said, though his words sounded hollow, rehearsed, as if he couldn't quite convince himself, never mind anyone else. "And if we do run into them, there is no reason we shouldn't help each other."

"Of course," Okchanlush said sarcastically. "All one people, right, aiawa?"

Unitsiya did not react to the name the way Okchanlush had, but his expression was still annoyed.

It was tempting to go out in the cooling darkness and see if anything came tiptoeing around the river in the evening, but they didn't dare. For one, it was too easy to lose track of one's prey and the camp when the blood ran hot and the light ran out. For two, there were plenty of predators lurking in the darkness also, and the hunters did not need to become the hunted.

The hunters nibbled on some corn instead, taking the dry mash and adding some river water to it in a small cup to soften it. This, too, reminded Ola Achukma of the Trail. The first time he had come out, he had refused to eat in such a way. This resolve lasted only a few days before he decided that the hunger was a worse memory.

Somehow, doing these things—coming out to the plains, eating softened cornmeal in a cup—helped to ease the pain in his mind, as if he were telling himself that it was all right, these things were not evil by themselves.

What, then, was evil? What had been evil about the Trail? Sickness? Death? Uncommon among the Aktiya Waya inhabitants, but not unknown. Intentions? Motivations? How could one fight such things?

Ola Achukma had learned to keep his more philosophical leanings to himself. Many such things no longer mattered now, not in the way they had when he was a child. Although, living in a place where the leader proclaimed harmony among the peoples, yet it was not so, he still found himself pondering the meaning and institution of peace. Certainly it did not exist in their camp.

Sometimes he wondered if such a thing existed at all, or if it were merely an idea, an aspiration to keep a man going in his darkest moments, but having no tangible application.

He was getting to an age and status now where he would have a voice in the meetings, but seeing how few people even brought up the topic, he wondered how it would be received. Yvgidahi would like it, yes, but would anyone else?

"Do you really think we'll meet the Oceti Sakowin tomorrow?" Ola Achukma asked of Ashagi quietly, trying not to disturb the others in their conversation, or argument, whatever one wanted to call it.

"I don't know," Ashagi admitted. "I hope not."

"Why do they stay if they are ungrateful? If they wish to conduct war, why do they not return to the Old Land?"

"Because that isn't a war they can win. Here, they can, if they've a mind for it."

"Why, though? The Apache and the Navajo were grateful enough, and they're more than happy to live in Aktiya Waya and assimilate into the people."

"Five families total, all of them coming from hard times and sickness, hardly a large group with many warriors. As it is, I'm glad Yvgidahi saw the wisdom in forbidding the retrieval of the Comanche."

"Your people never interacted with them, though, did they?"

"Maybe not, but there are some cultures out there that are just wholly incompatible with our own."

"Why, though? If they could see the vast lands, the plentiful game, and—"

But Ashagi was shaking his head. "You don't understand, Ola. Peace is your mindset. This is how you are. It is the core, the essence of your very being, your very soul. Most are this way, I truly believe; you just have it more than most. But not everyone is this way. You see land to be explored. The Comanche see land to be taken. War and conquest and raiding is their mindset, in the same way that peace is yours."

Ola Achukma shook his head. "But is it? If it's about resources, then we need only to—"

"Why does Okchanlush fight with Unitsiya? Why the fight earlier over Lapish? Lapish could have been dying—he could be dead now, for all we know, if he bled internally. We had the means to bind his wounds and return him to Aktiya Waya. Lesser wounds can be healed by the sorceries. So why fight?"

After a moment of quiet dread, Ola Achukma answered, "Power."

"Yes." Ashagi finished off his food. "You are too kind to understand such things, I think, and still very young. Have you begun learning the sorceries?"

Ola Achukma nodded. "Yes, just this year."

The Iroquois grinned and put a hand on his shoulder. "Good. Maybe you will have a chance to use them tomorrow, hm?"

"On the game, not the Oceti Sakowin."

"That would be preferable. The last thing we need is to return to Aktiya Waya and explain to Yvgidahi that we've managed to start the first war here on Hlohi."

Hlohi was what they called the land, the island they were on. Ola Achukma had a disjointed memory of a white man calling such a thing a "planet," but he couldn't remember the context of the conversation.

"There will be no wars," Unitsiya butted in from across the fire. "If we happen to run into the Oceti Sakowin tomorrow, we will greet and interact with them respectfully."

Even Ola Achukma could see he was merely repeating Yvgidahi's orders, and not voicing his own beliefs.

It was a half moon, enough to make out general features in the landscape and spy the horses where they were staked out, but not so good for navigation beyond going to the river and back.

They did not have tents, but rather something more akin to a wind- and rain-block. They slept on the blankets they sat on when they rode their horses, picking bundles of grass to put under the blankets to form a sort of pillow. Ola Achukma would not say it was not a tad uncomfortable, but he was accustomed to it. They all were.

Memories of his bed and his childhood home were even more distant than his memories of the Trail, and sometimes it felt as though it hadn't happened at all except as a dream. Then he would remember Ki, and he would know that it had all been real. But Ki was gone, as was Priscilla and Evan. This was his life now, spent sleeping under the stars in the southern plains, hunting for food for himself, his mother, his stepfather Chilita, and his infant brother Apushi.

He put a hand on his pack by his side. Perhaps the most firm reminder that his old life had been real was Ki's Bible. He hadn't realized the hatred it would garner, and several times someone had sought to destroy it. Even Chilita had not been the most accepting of the artifact, though he tolerated it for the sake of his wife, Ola Achukma's mother.

While no one had made mention of it for several moons now, perhaps believing it destroyed or a topic too old to care about anymore—hardly—Ola Achukma always brought it with him when he went out, just to make sure nothing happened to it while he was away. He didn't know what he would do if he lost the only remaining possession from Ki.

He fell asleep with his hand on the Bible, and he woke up the same way.

Unitsiya was quietly waking everyone, his face barely visible in the early morning gloom. Ola Achukma stifled a yawn as he sat up, stretched, then picked himself up off the ground and joined the rest.

"There are tsuyoniyvgi downstream, maybe twenty or so," Unitsiya said softly. "If we can drive them along the river and keep them there, we can cut their legs out from under them and try to drown them."

It would have been easier with the ten men they'd started out with. As it was, Ola Achukma was going to be running the right flank with only Okchanlush. Two more would be on the left flank, and two more behind. Each man had a bow with arrows and a club, but the senior hunters, such as Unitsiya and Okchanlush, had steel swords from the Old Land as well.

They went out to their horses who were dozing in the tall grass. A couple snorted and protested being woken up and roused for hard work, but none of them made enough noise to make the hunters worried. Ola Achukma knew how the horses felt as he stretched one more time, strangled a yawn, then jumped on his horse's back. His horse yawned, then snorted and pawed once, but was otherwise responsive.

Ola Achukma glanced once at Ashagi, tasked with the rear, then at Okchanlush, his partner for this drive. He wasn't quite sure what

Okchanlush thought of him. He seemed to be in a perpetually grumpy mood when they were out in the field, yet when they were in Aktiya Waya, he was typically very pleasant. The man was not lazy by any stretch of the imagination, but he just seemed to loathe leaving the bowl for longer than a day. And yet, he had reportedly volunteered for this drive with some enthusiasm.

"You know what you're doing?" Okchanlush murmured as they navigated their horses to the other side of the river.

"I've done the right flank before," Ola Achukma said.

"With only two people?"

"Well, no."

The senior hunter grinned in the muted light. "Take the rear right flank position. Ashagi and Espan will keep the herd moving forward. You keep them from running off to the right, and Dagki will do the same on the left. Unitsiya and I will cut them down."

Ola Achukma nodded and murmured assent. He knew his role, but it would be more difficult with only six of them. He felt for his club, reached for his bow and arrows.

"Only take shots you are confident in," Okchanlush said. "There is no need to waste arrows, and you don't need to fall off your horse into the path of many tsuyoniyvgi, or worse, Ashagi or Espan."

He nodded again, in full agreement. He had no desire to end up like Lapish.

They brought their horses around and got into position, waiting for Unitsiya's signal. Ola Achukma's heart was thudding in his chest. After many days of simple riding and baking in the hot sun, he was ready for some action.

He gasped as fire suddenly flared from Unitsiya's position, the warrior striking flint and lighting a torch. He let out a war whoop, turned his horse, and began a thunderous charge down the river. Ola Achukma felt wretchedly slow as he turned his mount and kicked hard, lurching forward and pounding after Okchanlush, whooping and hollering.

From a distance, tsuyoniyvgi were very much like deer in

appearance, although they had a spread of antlers that was easily three times their body length, with hundreds of spindly spikes sticking out in every direction, very much like large thorns. If they ever made their way into the forest, these spikes often picked up many leaves and brambles, make it look even more like a bush atop their heads. When a man spotted a large cluster of bushes that appeared to be moving in the tall grass, he could be assured that he was in the presence of a herd of tsuyoniyvgi.

Even now, as the sun prepared to squint over the horizon, Ola Achukma saw the bushes bouncing over the top of the grass, like a leaf that floats along a river's current. As the hunters neared, the bushes rose from the depths, and small, beady eyes and long noses peered at them, eyes slitted against the rising sun which burst from behind the riders with a long stretch of shadow.

It didn't take long for the tsuyoniyvgi to issue a warbled warning cry, turn tail, and flee. They were tan-gray in color with a white belly and a black stripe along their backs to a rather long tail. Male animals had a bushy black mane about their neck and shoulders

A single tsuyoniyvgi, or a herd with sufficient openness in which to run, could easily outrun a horse before a hunter could get within even bow distance. But when they got packed in together, their enormous antler spreads clacking against each other and even becoming locked together, they were just as easily overtaken. Ola Achukma soon found himself galloping alongside the herd, Okchanlush nearly in front of them.

The older hunter swung his sword and his club, holding onto and steering his horse with only his legs. One tsuyoniyvgi went down from a strike, dragging a second one down with it, their antlers tangled together. In the rear, Ashagi rode by and struck the second one with his club, killing it.

Okchanlush struck again, slicing the legs out from under a large male tsuyoniyvgi. The creature made a ghastly sound as it went down, tumbling and rolling directly in front of Ola Achukma and then getting tangled under his horse's hooves. His horse whinnied in surprise, throwing its hooves everywhere to try and shake it off. Its front left leg punched through a number of smaller spines, the main branches lashing the beast in place.

The horse panicked and broke from the formation, veering away, still trying to get rid of the dead animal clutching its leg. Ola Achukma was merely an inconvenience on its back as he bounced along, trying to hang on and maybe rein in his steed.

In a moment of clarity that seemed to stretch out for a while, Ola Achukma became aware of himself, and he was struck by the revelation that his fear wasn't helping things.

One of the first things anyone learned from the sorceries was Touch, reaching inside oneself and being fully aware of himself in both mind and body. It could also be used on others. It aided in the diagnosis of injuries and ailments, when a doctor did not have to guess or hypothesize. It was how Unitsiya had known Lapish's injuries were too great for mere field medicine.

Its use was not limited to people, but animals as well. Such a feat was both easier and harder on animals, in fact. Easier, because their minds were simple. Harder, because men had to hold back his more useless baggage when using Touch on an animal.

Ola Achukma took a breath and Touched his horse. He knew very well that the thing on the horse's leg was not dangerous; trying to run with it still attached was more dangerous by far. But he could not convey such complex thoughts to a horse and expect it to understand. Instead, all he could do was try to convey a sense of safety, the danger was past. Safety, the danger is past, he willed.

Eventually, the horse began to slow. The gallop tapered off into a high trot, and the tsuyoniyvgi, now little more than battered and tattered meat scattered across the plains, came off the horse's leg. The horse made a noise, tossed its head, did a dance, and finally slowed to a walk. It circled back to sniff the remains, decided it was indeed not a threat, then went about grazing.

Ola Achukma breathed a sigh of relief and all but fell off his mount. He slid down, stumbled a few steps, and collapsed in the grass, breathing heavily. He'd done it. He'd survived. He'd managed to use Touch, and he'd survived.

As he sat up, he heard the thunder of more hooves, and he looked up to see the rest of the party riding hard toward him. As he stood, they reined in, and Okchanlush was jumping off his horse before it had even stopped.

"Are you all right?" he demanded.

"I'm fine," Ola Achukma replied. "Just a little...anxious."

"You're not hurt, are you?" Unitsiya asked.

"No, no. A little winded is all."

"And your horse?"

He went over to his horse, still picking out the choicest grasses with its lips. The sharp spikes on the antlers had scratched the beast's leg deeply, and it was still bleeding heavily, but when he again used Touch and gently explored the depth of the wound, he found it not as bad as it looked. As long as they didn't do any more hard riding, it would be fine for the ride home. He reported as much to the others.

"How many tsuyoniyvgi did we get?" he asked of Unitsiya.

"Fourteen. Might have been fifteen, but..." Unitsiya looked at the ugly mess that was the remains of the animal on the horse's leg. "I don't expect much meat will be salvaged from this. We may cure it for ourselves for the ride back, but that's all it's good for at this point."

"We should retrieve the others," Okchanlush said, "before anything else gets to them first."

No one disagreed.

"Ola Achukma, see to your horse." Unitsiya tossed him the bag of supplies. "Then come meet us."

The five of them turned and started back to the drive area while Ola Achukma tended to his horse, grabbing the reins and taking it to the river where he washed the wounds.

"Seems all of us refugees are making fools of ourselves on this trip," he told the horse. "As long as Ashagi doesn't do anything foolish, he may redeem us. But I know those like Unitsiya and Okchanlush, those who were born here, they don't think too highly of us."

The horse took a drink of water, then lifted its head to sniff where he was working on its leg. It sneezed mucous in his hair, then turned its attention to the grasses on the bank.

"But then, even though they were born here, Unitsiya and Okchanlush don't think too highly of each other, either. I don't understand where all of these groups intersect. Does Unitsiya think less of refugee Aniyvwiya even though they're his own people? And does he like them more or less than Okchanlush who's Chahta, but was born in Aktiya Waya?" He shook his head. "I don't understand."

He took the horse out of the water. While the leg dried a bit, he did what he could for the remains of the tsiyoniyvgi. As Unitsiya had said, there wasn't much to save as far as meat, but the antlers were always useful. Once he got these fastened to the horse's pack, he bandaged the leg, then climbed on and started back toward the others.

"Welcome back," Ashagi greeted, looking up from where he worked on a kill, a pile of guts beside him. "All is well, then?"

Ola Achukma nodded wordlessly and dismounted, sending his horse to graze with the others.

Once each carcass was gutted, it was dragged to the river and thrown in so the cold water could clean it out more and help keep the flies away while they worked on the rest. Ola Achukma was good with a knife, and he knew his way around a carcass, but he was still nowhere near as skilled as the others in processing so many large carcasses so quickly. He was only able to finish one while the rest got two or three done in the same amount of time.

"Well then," Unitsiya said, "why don't we start a fire, make use of some of the remains from Ola Achukma's tsuyoniyvgi, and then we'll set out for home."

They'd only just struck flint when the sound of new hooves grabbed their attention. Looking downstream, they saw half a dozen riders, galloping hard in their direction.

"Oceti Sakowin," Okchanlush said lowly as the riders drew close enough to be recognized.

It had never been difficult to tell who the Oceti Sakowin were in

Aktiya Waya. They had never really assimilated into the white man's culture, not to the degree that the eastern peoples had, and were still fiercely protective of their ways.

Despite being alone and, supposedly, among friends on Hlohi, the Oceti Sakowin warriors were painted and dressed for war, as were their horses. Ola Achukma wondered what would happen if they truly had come to attack. Would there truly be a war here? Who would be blamed? How would it be stopped?

The Oceti Sakowin did not attack, although they did not rein in their horses until they were in the middle of the camp the rest of them had set up. One of the horses scattered the kindling they'd just been about to light.

"Can we help you?" Unitsiya asked irritably.

"We were coming to ask you the same thing," the Oceti Sakowin leader said. "We were on patrol along the river and noticed much blood in the water."

"On patrol?" Okchanlush echoed. "Patrol against what? Or who?"

"Anyone who would encroach upon our land. As you are doing now."

"What land?" Ashagi wondered. "There are no territories to be won here. We're all one people."

"Yes, that is what your leader Yvgidahi proclaims, but I've seen little evidence of the unity he espouses. Therefore, in order to avoid the chaos and dilution of culture and character that we possess, we claim all rights to the plains land. This is our land, this is our territory."

Unitsiya folded his arms, his posture and expression unimpressed. "And when did this happen? We only just left Aktiya Waya a few days ago, and I don't recall news of any defection."

"Then you've not been paying attention."

A second Oceti Sakowin warrior grinned. "You aiawa don't see anything that isn't obvious. This has been coming for some time."

"If Yvgidahi wants to force the issue, he is welcome to speak to our chieftain," the first went on. "We're running patrols frequently." He turned his horse. "But I understand that you didn't know. So even though this is—" He gestured to the dead animals in the water. "—by rights, stealing, I'm willing to forgive it this one time, on the understanding that it will not happen again."

"You can't do that," Unitsiya said lamely.

"We already have," the second warrior chuckled.

"Return to Yvgidahi," repeated the first. "Tell him of what has transpired. I would be willing to bet that he already knows and is worrying endlessly over what to do about it."

If they had hoped that the Oceti Sakowin would leave them to their task and go about their patrol, they were sorely disappointed. If they had hoped that the Oceti Sakowin would have at least helped them secure the carcasses for travel, this, too, proved to be a disappointment. Ola Achukma tried to ignore them, but he couldn't help sneaking glances here and there. The six warriors had them surrounded, sitting on their horses and just watching them as they worked as hurriedly as they could.

When the last of their haul was secured and they were all mounted, the first Oceti Sakowin warrior spoke again, addressing Unitsiya.

"Don't stop to make camp until you have left our land."

"We won't make it in time," Unitsiya said, "and it's too dangerous to travel at night in this way."

"That's not our problem. You shouldn't have come onto our land."

"We didn't know it was your land," Ashagi said. "And anyway, if you hadn't decided to stake a claim and divide us, destroying everything we could have been and making us little better than what we were in the Old Land—"

"I tire of your words, nishab," the first warrior said loudly, inclining his head toward the sky. "So please, shut up." He looked back at Unitsiya. "Get out of our territory. And tell Yvgidahi what we have said."

They didn't seem to have much of a choice. Six against six was fair enough in numbers, but Ola Achukma was hardly a seasoned warrior, and his horse was still injured. They did have the advantage of the sorceries, of which Unitsiya and Okchanlush were modestly proficient, but who wanted to be responsible for igniting a war?

Ola Achukma did not have to imagine the Oceti Sakowin laughing at their backs as they retreated and started across the plains; they made that abundantly clear, laughing loud enough to be heard back in Aktiya Waya it seemed.

Of course, the Oceti Sakowin did not simply trust them to leave the plains on their good word, but they followed at a distance. Every time Ola Achukma looked back, there they were, just close enough to be discerned as warriors on the horizon.

The day was hot again, and Ola Achukma longed for the shade of the trees. The Oceti Sakowin could have their stupid plains; he certainly wasn't interested in them.

He was still trying to process everything that had happened. Suddenly, in this land of peace and plenty, a line had been drawn. A line that divided them. He was not permitted on one side of the line, and they were not permitted on the other. Something had been cut off, severed, and he didn't know what to make of it.

He thought of the Trail, and all the talk of going to a new land where they would be a sovereign nation, where they could do as they wished with no one to tell them otherwise. Except they'd had to displace other peoples to achieve these ends. Here, there were no such peoples to displace; certainly there was plenty of land in other directions for them to move about. Why shouldn't the Oceti Sakowin be permitted to live how they wanted? This was how they chose to live, and who were they to dictate to them otherwise?

Was this what peace looked like? He still considered this question from time to time, and suddenly it seemed to be very relevant to the situation.

Was sovereignty the same as peace? Was independence the same as peace? If not, would forcing the return of the Oceti Sakowin to Aktiya Waya somehow produce peace? But if the Oceti Sakowin could not live as they wished, if they lost, as they said, their culture and character, could peace be too high of a price?

They moved as swiftly as they could, but their load was large, and his horse was still wounded. Their slowed pace left too much time for thinking. He recalled the earlier incident, when he'd been bouncing along on a panicked horse, how long each moment had seemed. Now they seemed even longer than that.

By the time the sun touched the horizon, the forest was at least visible in the far distance, though it was near midnight before they reached the treeline. The Oceti Sakowin warriors had galloped up to them to physically enforce their exit from the plains. No words were exchanged, friendly or otherwise, though there were plenty of looks all around.

The Oceti Sakowin remained at the tree line for Ola Achukma knew not how long. He did not want to look back, did not dare to.

They continued on a short while, just to be sure, finally making camp when it seemed to be near dawn. No fire was built, no food was consumed. Blankets were laid out, and they slept where they found room.

Ola Achukma slept as well as could be expected, but he found himself waking up initially confused as to why they were in the forest and not still on the plains. It all came back to him in a rush as he sat up.

"So it all really happened," Ashagi said, his expression saying he was experiencing the same thing.

"We should go back," Okchanlush grumbled. "Teach them a lesson."

Unitsiya shook his head. "We can't." He went on before Okchanlush could protest. "I'm not saying I don't want to myself, but this is bigger than me and you. This could actually lead to true conflict."

"Why, because the Oceti Sakowin have established themselves and not allowed themselves to be trodden underfoot by aiawa?"

"Do you want them to come to Aktiya Waya, to raid and pillage and steal your wife and children?" Unitsiya hissed hotly. "Because that is where this is going to lead if we don't do something."

"He's right," Ashagi said. "We need to take this to Yvgidahi and the council."

"That bastard back there said Yvgidahi already knows by now. Why don't we wait and intercept them? Or get the jump on—"

"No," Unitsiya stated firmly. "We return to Aktiya Waya as

planned. If nothing else, we need to get this meat back to the people."

"We may run into Lapish and Shikak, too," Ola Achukma offered.

"Agreed, we can pick them up as well."

No one was really enthusiastic about the idea, but it was all they could do at this point.

After a meager meal, they mounted their horses and were on their way once more.

They did in fact catch up to Lapish and Shikak that evening. At some point, Shikak had fashioned a litter for Lapish to be pulled behind a horse, rather than try to ride. He did not look much more comfortable, lying on the crude implement and bumping along on the hard ground, but at least he was not in danger of falling off his horse and hurting himself more. The young teenagers looked thrilled by the number of tsuyoniyvgi, but became disheartened when Unitsiya relayed their encounter with the Oceti Sakowin.

"We must return to Aktiya Waya with all haste," the senior hunter told Lapish and Shikak, and Ola Achukma knew exactly what he meant to do. "Take your packs. We must take your horses and ride swiftly to warn Yvgidahi."

There was nothing else to be done. As soon as the teenagers removed their personal packs, Unitsiya and Okchanlush mounted their horses, kicked them to a trot, and bounced off up the trail, leaving the rest of them to plod along.

"Come on, then," Ashagi said, taking charge. "They may be riding ahead, but that doesn't mean we can loaf about, and we can still cover some distance before nightfall."

They nudged their horses and continued on at a far slower pace. They made it a few more miles before Ashagi bade them stop and make camp. He attended to Lapish while the rest of them gathered wood for a fire and pitched a tent.

"What do you think the Oceti Sakowin actually want?" Ola Achukma wondered, giving voice to the question running around all their heads.

"Nothing good," Ashagi said, ignoring a gasp of pain from Lapish as he probed. "And it will only get worse if Yvgidahi does not do something decisive about it."

"Wouldn't that only antagonize them, provoke them to war?" Shikak asked.

"If we don't do something, they'll walk all over us, take more and more for themselves because they know they will not be stopped."

"But there is plenty of land out there. They wouldn't have to do anything to us."

"There is plenty of land now, yet they feel the need to stake out a claim." Ashagi went on before anyone could speak. "I don't know. I don't understand it either. We will leave matters to Yvgidahi and the council. Our task now is to deliver this meat to the people."

Ola Achukma studied him. "Shall we tell our families that this may be the last tsuyoniyvgi they eat for quite a while?"

All eyes went to Ashagi who hesitated before answering, "No. We don't need to alarm them. Besides, it's not as though tsuyoniyvgi is a great delicacy. We will carry on as normal."

This was easier said than done, and Ola Achukma doubted anyone got much sleep that night. If it wasn't the events of the day, it was Lapish's whimpering and moaning as he struggled to get comfortable. Finally, when the sky was light enough to see by, they packed up and continued on.

It was not difficult to believe that Unitsiya and Okchanlush reached Aktiya Waya days ahead of them, but it was still a bit of a disappointment to find that Yvgidahi and a dozen or so others had already departed. Ola Achukma had hoped to accompany them, seeing how he had been part of the hunting party who'd been confronted. But then, he was barely a man, hardly the seasoned hunter or warrior that the others were. At the very least, he had hoped that there might be a few nights' worth of meetings as the council decided what to do, just so he could know what was going on, what the plan was, what to expect. His mother and her husband would know, but he still wanted to be there.

Each tsuyoniyvgi was divided in two along the spine. One half went to one of the hunting party or their family, and the other went to a family in need, most often a widow with children. One whole tsuyoniyvgi was reserved for the priests and elders, to be divided as they deemed fit. The hides were given to the women's council to make blankets and clothing for the most in need.

Ola Achukma's mother was more than delighted when he brought his half a tsuyoniyvgi in the house, and she immediately went to work on it.

"How many did you kill?" his mother asked, somewhat ignorant of how the larger game drives worked.

"I was able to get one," he admitted shyly. "Unfortunately, my horse spooked and ran away from the drive after that."

"Then you were not there when the Oceti Sakowin attacked?"

He gave her a look. "Attacked?"

His mother blinked. "Well, that's what they're saying. The Oceti Sakowin attacked your hunting party. Lapish was injured. They've since claimed the plains as their own."

"Who told you this?"

"Okchanlush and Unitsiya said this at the meeting," Chilita said behind him, emerging from the room he and his wife shared. "They rode hard into Aktiya Waya, demanded a meeting immediately. They said that you had been out hunting, as planned, and a war party of six or more Oceti Sakowin attacked. Lapish was terribly wounded, and your horse sustained some injury as well. They said they had delivered you all to safety, then rode ahead to warn us that the Oceti Sakowin were camped in the plains and possibly planning an attack."

Ola Achukma's eyes must have been as big as the moon, but he didn't care. He opened his mouth but no words came out for a long moment. Finally he blinked, shook his head, and said, "No! No, that's not what happened at all! They're lying!"

"Why would they do such a thing?" his mother wondered innocently, looking back and forth between her son and her husband.

"You're sure about this?" Chilita asked. "It's no small thing to accuse such senior hunters and warriors of lying."

"Absolutely sure!" Ola Achukma said loudly, practically shouting.

He stormed out of the house and started running, making for Ashagi's house. The dwelling was empty, and he went out in search of his friend.

As he rounded a corner, he collided with another person. He stumbled back a step, reaching for a wall to catch himself, rubbing his forehead.

"Ow," he mumbled. "Are you all right?"

When he looked up, he saw it was Nendawagan, Yvgidahi's oldest child. She, too, was rubbing her forehead. She nodded and straightened, letting her arms drop to her sides. "Yes, I'm fine. You?"

He made as if to put his hands on her shoulders, reconsidered, and let his hands drop. "When Unitsiya and Okchanlush came back to Aktiya Waya, what did they tell your father? What did they tell Yvgidahi?"

She blinked. "They said that you had all gone out hunting and the Oceti Sakowin attacked. They severely injured Lapish, wounded your horse as well and—"

"They lied," Ola Achukma cut in. "We weren't attacked. Lapish had an accident with his horse, and my horse got tangled up in tsuyoniyvgi antlers. Yes, the Oceti Sakowin lay claim to the plains now, but they never laid a hand on us."

Nendawagan stared at him, her gaze flitting back and forth. Then, "If what you're saying is true, then my father and a dozen warriors are riding into the plains to start a pointless war."

"We have to stop them. Do you know where Ashagi is?"

"Still tending to Lapish, I think, in the townhouse."

He gave her a wisp of thanks and turned to head in that direction. He sucked in a breath as he felt a tug at the air around him. He saw people around him come to a standstill, except for Nendawagan who came up behind him.

"What are you doing?" he asked.

She grabbed his arm and they continued heading toward the townhouse, saying, "Conjuring Time. I can't hold onto it forever, but we can't waste even a moment. We have to catch up to my father before he reaches the plains."

"What do you mean 'we'? You can't go; it's too dangerous."

"I'm the only one who has the skill in the Time sorceries and can speak to my father about the matter." She stopped, faced him, and added, "If you go alone, or even with Ashagi, it will only be seen as a warrior's feud. It is difficult and disrespectful to accuse someone of their status of this kind of treachery. But he'll listen to me. And I will Conjure Time so that we reach them even faster." She huffed a sigh. "I don't know why they would have lied, except they knew they had the time to do so."

Ola Achukma nodded. "We have to stop them."

They continued on to the townhouse, Nendawagan still speaking. "Who else was with you in your group? Tell me everything that actually happened."

Pàke Kwëtash

Settlement

The sun was warm, but the wind whipping through her hair as they galloped along burned her skin and made it difficult to see. Ashagi and another warrior, Nohdatsi, who had also been on the hunt, were in the lead, and Ola Achukma was beside her. Shikak brought up the rear, and the thundering of hooves crashing upon the ground was all they heard for many miles.

Nendawagan tried to work through it in her mind, even as she also tried to keep intense focus on her conjuring, slowing Time around them so they could move faster still.

Why would Unitsiya and Okchanlush lie like this? What did anyone have to gain by starting a war? And it wouldn't be so much a war as a slaughter. The Oceti Sakowin were impressive warriors, but there couldn't be more than a dozen, maybe two if they included all their inexperienced boys.

It didn't seem to fit with their personalities, either. Okchanlush was a bit forceful and could intimidate someone if he really wanted to, but Unitsiya was fairly level-headed, if stubborn once his mind was made up. Furthermore, neither of them was particularly fond of the other, their relationship strictly business with no room for casual comradery.

And that wasn't even considering the Oceti Sakowin. A few dozen, rescued from the Old Land, the same story that most of the refugees had. But rather than being grateful and trying to work for peace, they had become obstinate, ungrateful, even hostile. Yvgidahi had been prepared to send them back to the Old Land. Then they'd disappeared. Now they knew where. But why stake a claim and make threats?

Something was missing here, Nendawagan thought. She just didn't know what.

Using the sorceries for any great length of time was liable to cause headaches, in addition to any other side effects. Nendawagan ceased conjuring after a while, not wishing to debilitate herself to the point of being useless. They didn't know how far ahead the others were, or what they would find. She needed to be ready for anything as much as the rest of them.

Actually, her greatest fear was that her father had the same idea and was conjuring himself and his group, and he was far more skilled than she. What if they were already too late?

No, she couldn't think of that. If she was going to chase shadows and fret and worry, she could have stayed home and stayed out of the way of the men. Looking at them, they seemed a little bewildered by the experience with the sorceries. Ashagi and Nohdatsi had some knowledge, but Ola Achukma had only just begun learning, and Shikak was only aware of the sorceries from watching others use them.

Nendawagan, her sister, their mother, they used the sorceries for more mundane tasks. They used Touch to interact with the animals, to tell if they were sick or wounded, and even check on pregnancies. They could also use Touch on plants, to check their health and vigor. Time was sometimes invoked for cooking, or to tend to many tasks at once. Sometimes it was used to corral unruly children. There were other abilities as well, some of them becoming so mundane she couldn't think of them right off-hand.

But the men, she knew, used the sorceries for other purposes. If they wanted to, they could conjure Time, slow everything around them, and kill an animal with barely a need for stealth. This was rarely invoked for such a thing, for it was considered dishonest and disrespectful to the animal. But it was used in combat, and Nendawagan had watched the young men wrestle, both sides conjuring Time and trying to gain an advantage over the other. Most of the men also used Touch, and it was often used in conjunction with Time to heal relatively minor wounds. The priests and other skilled healers could do just about anything, including drive away disease.

She eyed the metal bracelets the men wore. They were a special type of metal, magnetic. All of their weapons also sported this metal in some way. When a man invoked Gayalvnga, the metal activated, more powerfully than normal, and he could call the weapon to him from a short distance. The women did this, too, though normally it was used for cooking and cleaning, being able to call a utensil without having to actually go and retrieve it.

Her father had never really told of his time in the war in the Old Land, not more than short, pointed, relevant anecdotes to augment an argument or add to a discussion, and she sometimes wondered what a true battle would look like if both sides were capable of these sorceries. As it was, the only reason the Anigilisi had beaten the Aniyvwiya was because of their use of fire. Fire was the most difficult thing to control, and many agreed that it could not be done.

As they sat around their campfire that night, Nendawagan wondered what power fire held that it could render such astounding sorceries useless. She considered probing the fire, perhaps using a stick as a medium for Touch, then decided against it. It was an experiment for another day, after this matter with the Oceti Sakowin had been taken care of.

If not for the uncertain terrain, Nendawagan might have suggested Conjuring Time for each other, condensing an entire night of rest into only moments. One could not conjure sorceries while unconscious, so such a feat would have to be done back and forth; she could conjure for the others, and then Ashagi or Nohdatsi could conjure for her. But the darkness was too unpredictable, too dangerous for the horses; they would have to wait for daybreak.

She could have used Atsvstdi, or tried to. It was one of the more finicky sorceries, trying to bend light. When standing still, it was possible, to use available light and make it brighter or dimmer, and there were other interesting things that could be achieved with its use. But it was difficult to master, and even more so from horseback. No, she needed rest anyway. They would start again in the morning.

Just as soon as they were awake and could see each other across the way, the five of them were again on horseback, riding as hard as they dared. Nendawagan waited until the light was better before conjuring, bringing the sun to a standstill in the sky.

They slowed only once in order to get something to eat and rest the horses, stopping alongside a brook.

"You're sure we're still going the right way?" Nohdatsi asked of Ashagi.

Ashagi nodded. "It's the fastest route, and a dozen warriors on a mission leave a pretty obvious trail."

"How so?" Nendawagan wondered.

The senior hunter pointed. "You see those broken twigs there, and the way there are many green leaves on the ground? And hoof prints from hard riding, ten horses or more."

"Can you say how old this trail is?"

"The leaves are green, but the ends of these broken twigs are dry. I would say yesterday, last night at the latest."

She shook her head. "We're moving too slow. We have to intercept them before they reach the plains."

"We can't do that if our horses collapse from exhaustion," Nohdatsi pointed out. "And Hitguttit would never forgive us if we told him that we killed six of the horses."

"Would you rather sacrifice these boys—" She gestured to Ola Achukma and Shikak. "—in a stupid, pointless war?"

Nohdatsi opened his mouth, then closed it and shook his head.

Still they did not resume their ride right away. Nendawagan told herself to be patient, that she needed strength as much as the rest of them, but it was terribly difficult. When Ashagi finally suggested they continue, she was halfway on her horse's back before he finished speaking. If not for his expertise in tracking, she might have been the first one out.

Indeed, she and Nohdatsi traded places, so that she was in front with Ashagi, and Nohdatsi rode beside Ola Achukma. Shikak remained in the rear.

She was tired from conjuring, and it didn't take an experienced rider to know the horses were growing fatigued as well. Her conjuring was nowhere near as strong and rigid as before, and their pace was somewhere between a trot and a gallop.

They stopped a little earlier that evening than the previous night. Nendawagan had a terrible headache, though she tried not to let on how much it bothered her. The horses were grateful for water and the chance to graze a bit on the thick undergrowth.

"The broken branches are wet," Ashagi reported, returning from a brief mission to scout ahead and determine their trajectory in the morning.

"What does that mean?" Nendawagan wondered, lazily Touching herself and feeling the pain in her brain, trying to quell the aching.

"It means the sap is still running; they're not far ahead. If we start out at first light, we may catch them by midday."

That would be a welcome thing, she thought. She was entirely unfamiliar with the forest and the plains, except for what the hunters reported, but even she suspected that they were closer to the plains than anyone really felt comfortable with.

"Get some sleep," Ashagi said, turning over a log in the fire before lying down on his blanket. "We need to start as early as possible tomorrow."

Morning came far too soon, and Nendawagan felt terribly slow and unprepared. Her head still ached some, and she really didn't want to conjure. Truly, this was the most intense conjuring she'd done in a very long time. Only the thought of preventing a war kept her going and made her continue to conjure against her better judgment.

"There they are!"

Ola Achukma's voice jolted her from her stupor. She'd simply shut down everything except the conjuring and whatever muscles she needed to stay situated on her horse. Now she came alive again, losing the conjuring and looking around. Her head was beating harder than any drum she'd ever heard, and she wished for nothing more than to sleep.

The forest had begun thinning some as they neared the plains, and up ahead she could make out a dozen horses.

Their group started shouting and whooping, trying to get their attention. Nendawagan did not have the energy, and indeed she thought they might have been heard all the way to the fabled Oceti Sakowin settlement.

At last, someone dared to look back. There was shouting, yelling, confusion, and finally Yvgidahi's group began to slow. It was probably half a mile before everyone finally came to a stop, and for a long moment, the only sound to be heard was the heavy breathing and snorting of the horses.

"What's going on?" Yvgidahi demanded finally, looking at the five riders who had joined them. His gaze settled on Ashagi. "Why are you here? What's happened?"

"Yvgidahi, this entire expedition is based on a lie," Ashagi said levelly.

"What are you talking about?"

"The Oceti Sakowin never attacked us. They confronted us, but there was no attack. Lapish had an accident with his horse. Ola Achukma's horse got tangled in the tsuyoniyvgi's antlers."

Nendawagan watched as her father considered this, studying Ashagi, glancing at Ola Achukma and the others, and finally settling on her.

"And why have you come?" he asked.

"To conjure Time," she answered calmly. "So we could intercept you before you made a terrible mistake."

Her father turned around to look at his group. Some appeared dubious, a few entirely disbelieving. Finally he said, "Unitsiya. Okchanlush."

The two men nosed their horses forward to stand beside him. Yvgidahi looked at them with a stern gaze.

"We are within half a day of reaching the plains," he stated evenly. "When we get there, what are we going to find?" When the accused did not answer, he went on, "You would have me believe that we are at risk for imminent attack so that we may attack them first. And in doing so, it would spark a war, at best. At worst, it would become a massacre." He shook his head. "Why have you done this?"

Still neither man spoke. Yvgidahi frowned deeply.

"This greatly disturbs me," he continued. He looked at Ashagi. "My thanks to you, for coming to us."

"Are we returning home, then?" one of Yvgidahi's warriors wondered.

Yvgidahi shook his head. "No. We've come this far. And whether or not the Oceti Sakowin are planning to attack—" He gave Unitsiya and Okchanlush a look. "—they have still defected, and they have staked claim to land and challenged me. I intend to find out exactly what is going on."

He turned his horse around, his apparent intent a much calmer walk. One of his warriors spoke up. "Do you intend for the woman to accompany us? We still don't know the Oceti Sakowin's intentions."

Yvgidahi glanced back at Nendawagan, a certain light in his eyes. "If she is strong enough to conjure five riders over several days, I do not worry for her in a fight. Besides, she may have some sway with the Oceti Sakowin women, to convince them to return to Aktiya Waya and not sacrifice their sons in a needless war."

Nendawagan might have been able to take more pride in his words and confidence in her had she been feeling better, but for the moment, the best she could do was a tired nod.

With that, he nudged his horse forward, and the group, now nearly twenty strong, started off. Unitsiya and Okchanlush suddenly found themselves under heavy escort as everyone tried to silently ascertain their motives.

Nendawagan could see that Ashagi, Nohdatsi, and the others from the hunting party wanted to speak to their guarded comrades, but they didn't dare. And yet she knew the question that was going through their minds, for she was thinking it, too: Why did they lie, knowing that they would be found out so easily? What did they think would happen when Ashagi and the others heard the story? Had they simply expected that those who could expose them would arrive too late? Had her conjuring truly prevented a war?

No longer needing to conjure, and moving at a far more agreeable pace, she was able to recover most of her wits by the evening. They could have made it to the plains, easily, for they could smell the grass and feel the wind through the sparse undergrowth, but her father had decided against it, citing the possibility of ambush. So they settled in for the night, making do with only the two tents the interceptor party had brought and keeping their fires small.

"Ashagi, Nendawagan, come here," Yvgidahi ordered, sitting down near one of the fires.

The two glanced at each other before going over to meet him.

"We are going to speak to the Oceti Sakowin tomorrow," her father began slowly. "And I need as much information as possible before a peaceful meeting turns into a bloodbath, and that's assuming we can have a peaceful meeting in the first place. Ashagi, tell me everything that happened on the hunt."

The young warrior did so, explaining their trek out, their poor fortune in the heat, Lapish's foolish stunt that saw him trampled by his horse, the drive that resulted in Ola Achukma's horse being mildly injured, the confrontation with the Oceti Sakowin, and returning to the forest.

"Unitsiya and Okchanlush had us trade horses, said they wanted to ride ahead to inform you as soon as possible of what had happened," he concluded. "Otherwise, our journey was uneventful. When we arrived back in Aktiya Waya, we learned that you had already left with a dozen men."

Now Yvgidahi looked at Nendawagan. "And how did you get mixed up in this?"

"I ran into Ola Achukma in town. He wanted to know where you were. I explained what had happened, and he adamantly insisted that it was a lie, that almost none of it had happened. So we went to the townhouse and found Ashagi and Lapish who agreed with him. We decided that we couldn't let you run into a war over a lie, so we grabbed Nohdatsi and Shikak and I conjured us here."

Her father nodded. "And you did it well, I think." He frowned and looked at Unitsiya and Okchanlush still under guard at a different fire.

"But why? What does anyone gain by starting a war? Ashagi, did either of them ever mention anything about the Oceti Sakowin on the trip out?"

Ashagi shrugged. "Some comments were made about how the plains were better suited for the Oceti Sakowin, and how they did well on the drives. Certainly none of us wanted to run into them while we were out."

"They have had a hard time adjusting to life in Aktiya Waya," Yvgidahi mused. "I thought it had more to do with the mountainous terrain. I thought they might adapt. But everyone who comes here knows that they either adapt to live with us or they get sent back to the Old Land."

"You can make all the rules you want, Nocha, but you cannot change men's hearts," Nendawagan told him, hoping she didn't come across as rude.

He sighed. "You have the right of it, I will not deny. But there is being unable to solve a minor dispute, and then there is starting a war. I don't understand." He straightened a leg. "But, I think, we will find out soon enough, once we meet with the Oceti Sakowin."

"Do you think it will be peaceful?" Ashagi wondered.

"We're going to find out, aren't we?"

It was not the most comforting thing to hear, but it was the best they could hope for, given the circumstances.

Nendawagan stayed close to her father, as she was the only female in the group, and he her only relative. Even so, she often found herself staring at Unitsiya and Okchanlush across the camp, wondering what had caused this. What were they thinking? What did they—what did anyone have to gain by fabricating a battle in order to incite a war?

She thought of Lapish. He'd wanted to come, too. Even if it meant admitting his only foolish mistake, he wanted to stop Yvgidahi and the others as well. But no one would allow him to go. Even with the skilled priests using the sorceries of Heal and Touch, as well as Time to knit wounded flesh back together and condense the healing time to only a few days, he still needed rest. Shikak would attest to his wounds, as would Ashagi. Ola Achukma would attest to his horse becoming scratched by the sharp antlers.

She looked at each of them in turn, her gaze settling on Ola Achukma. If there was any young man her father admired, it was him. He rarely said anything at meetings, and she hadn't interacted with him, really, between the time he was rescued and today, and yet his temperament was calm, his mindset fixed on philosophy. At one meeting, a few years ago when he'd first earned his voice, he'd posed a question in relation to some dispute that was up for debate. She did not remember the question exactly, but it had to do with peace and disputes between neighbors, and it so puzzled and frustrated the advisors that they had cut the meeting short, right then and there.

Since then, her father had taken an interest in the boy, and, when possible, intentionally suggested he join mixed hunting groups, such as this fateful group. Perhaps he hoped the boy would be able to mediate and make peace among feuding party members. Nendawagan was uncertain how successful this was, except, maybe, he had finally found his real voice.

Yvgidahi set two guards on Unitsiya and Okchanlush and two more for the camp itself, in case the Oceti Sakowin decided to expand their territory a little in the night. Nendawagan knew the men were strong and would not hesitate to defend the camp—although she heard Ola Achukma mention something about it being more difficult to harm a brother, suggesting they were not the brothers her father proclaimed them to be—but she would also not deny that she laid her head down that night with a tingle of trepidation.

Other than a couple of trips to the Old Land, now many years past, this was the first time she'd left the safety of the bowl, left the watchful eye of the Sacred Wolf. She was a woman alone in the wilderness, and there was every chance that there could be battle in the next day or two. Would she be killed? Taken as a prize? She found herself having mixed feelings. Fear, that it might happen, that she could die or lose her father. Fear, that she might be separated from her family. Relief, that she had no husband or children waiting for her dubious return. Sadness, that she'd never married or had children.

Her dreams were dark, but she woke to fresh air, a warm breeze, and beautiful colors painted across the sky. It was enough to lighten her mood just a bit and ease the worst of the fear.

Unitsiya and Okchanlush had not run away in the night, and still they did not speak.

They packed up camp quickly and moved on, the plains well within reach. They did not even all make it into the tall grass before riders appeared over a rise. They appeared at a walk, but when they spotted the large group, kicked into a gallop.

Nendawagan felt her heart race. Were they just trying to cover ground quickly? Did they truly intend to attack? She could see the men fingering their weapons, apparently having similar thoughts.

"Be calm," her father said, his voice tight. "Don't give them an excuse."

Then the incoming riders slowed to a trot, and Nendawagan let out a breath. There were four of them, and she recognized all of them as warriors who had been wounded and sick when brought to Aktiya Waya.

"That was fast," one of the Oceti Sakowin commented, his tone and posture mocking.

"S'ungina," Yvgidahi greeted, trying to remain amiable. "I was told that you wished to speak with me."

S'ungina grinned. "With you, yes. And it would not surprise that you might bring one or two with you as witnesses. But this is quite the entourage. One might mistake it for being a war party."

"Except for the woman," another warrior, Hinhan, said, his tone impossible to judge though it made Nendawagan not a little uncomfortable.

"Something of a misunderstanding," Yvgidahi told them, "in which it would be unfortunate if you had any involvement."

"That sounds almost like a threat," S'ungina commented. "Perhaps we should go where the odds would be more in our favor."

"You claim to have established a village. I'd like to see it."

Surprisingly, the warriors agreed. Nendawagan glanced around at their own group. If it came to a fight, the Oceti Sakowin would surely have the greater numbers, if only by a small margin. But they had also more recently come from war and desperation. Her father and the rest of them were strong and powerful in their own way, but they had not needed to go to battle for quite some time. What did that mean for them, then? She glanced at Hinhan and caught him staring at her. She looked away.

At a hard ride, the village was a full day away, and they arrived just as the sun vanished below the horizon. It was not a very big village. At most, there were forty Oceti Sakowin, including a tiny baby that couldn't have been more than a few days old. They appeared to be doing well, at least, Nendawagan thought. There was food over the fires and pelts being stretched on racks. Their tall, stick and skin homes, which they called tipis, appeared sound and stable against the wind.

But there was something else in the village, and it came even from the teenagers, boys and girls: hostility. A glare from an elder, a dirty look from a woman with a toddler, the brandishing of weapons by the men.

S'ungina ordered a halt and a dismount. The Oceti Sakowin horses were taken by friends and family. Those from the intruding party were reluctantly seen to, mothers sending their young children to collect them and take them to graze.

"Who is your leader, then?" Yvgidahi asked. "If it were you, we could have spoken at the edge of the forest."

"Or perhaps I wanted my brothers by my side, in case you decided to attack while you had the advantage," S'ungina stated. He held Yvgidahi's gaze for a long moment, before smirking. "But you're right. I am not the leader here. Hoka is our chieftain."

"Hoka," her father huffed. "I might have known."

"You may choose three to bring with you to speak with him. The rest will remain outside."

Yvgidahi studied the warrior for a long moment. Then, without breaking his gaze, "Ashagi, Gvtvgi'a, Nendawagan."

"You want the woman with you?" Hinhan sneered.

"She will act as the women's council. Surely you have your own?"

It shut him up, anyway. Nendawagan watched as her father pulled aside another warrior and whispered something to him, perhaps telling him to keep an eye on Unitsiya and Okchanlush. Even she did not miss the look from S'ungina, the silent question of why they were not being asked. But then, neither was Utsonadi asked. She briefly wondered at the wisdom of having the three of them together.

"This way," S'ungina said stiffly, turning and making for a tipi, easily twice the size of the rest, decorated rather liberally with feathers of all colors and sizes, as well as long strings of bone beads and woven horsehair.

Inside was a small fire, where four men sat perfectly at ease. S'ungina joined them as they rose to meet their visitors.

"Yvgidahi," the middle man greeted. He was an older man, not quite an elder, but on the falling side of his hill. He was dressed rather modestly, really, in a plain pair of pants, plain moccasins, and bare chest, though he wore a decorated belt around one shoulder.

"Hoka," Yvgidahi acknowledged.

"You bring no gifts, and many warriors. One might think you were here to attack. If not for the woman, I might order my warriors to strike you down this instant."

"Then she does both of us a service."

Hoka sat first and the rest followed. "So then, why are you here? Is the so-called peacemaker of Aktiya Waya really so upset that a small group has defected?"

Yvgidahi took an even breath. "What do you know of the incident some days ago, when your warriors chased my hunters out of the plains after a drive?"

The Oceti Sakowin leader blinked. "I know that your hunters were driving game. My warriors intercepted them and told them to leave. They were even generous enough to let them keep their kill."

"Then you deny attacking them."

"This is outrageous!" one of the other men, a young man no more than twenty, said, standing suddenly.

"Sit down, child, and shut up," Yvgidahi said. Hoka's expression echoed his annoyance. "I am not accusing anyone of anything, I am simply trying to understand something." He went on before anyone could speak. "Two of my hunters came riding back to Aktiya Waya, claiming they'd been attacked and that your warriors were already on their way to attack. I set out with a dozen of my best to meet this force." He gestured to Nendawagan and Ashagi. "Then the rest of the hunters, as well as my daughter, show up and explain that this was not the case. So far, the most common story that I have heard is that your warriors intercepted my hunters and cut their game drive short."

"If that is what happened, then so be it, for I was not there," Hoka said, though his tone suggested true surprise by the news. "But although I will not deny that we have staked our claim to this territory and we will defend it, for I assumed this was the reason you came, even I am not so foolish as to believe we could face off against you and your warriors." He shifted position. "Which of your people proclaimed this lie?"

"Unitsiya and Okchanlush."

"Hm." Hoka and his men nodded. "This does not come as a surprise, except, perhaps, that they concocted this scheme together." He glanced at Ashagi, then at Nendawagan. "And it seems as though we have you to thank for preventing a tragedy. We could never have stood up to your warrior prowess, to say nothing of your witching."

Another of the men, this one truly an elder, grunted in agreement and muttered something in their tongue which Nendawagan did not understand.

Her father shifted position. "Is that what this is about, then? Tell me, Hoka, why did you leave? If it is war you seek, there are plenty to be had in the Old Land. Otherwise, there is no reason for it here."

"Our decision to leave was not about attacking you or establishing territory or conquest. It was about protecting ourselves from you." Hoka looked away and opened his mouth, struggling to find words. "This...sorcery, this conjuring, it is not natural. Wakhan Thanka made the universe, and I will not say that we are ungrateful to find this land of peace. But we must ask ourselves, is this a land of peace for men, or the sanctuary of gods? What you are capable of doing..." He leaned back and shook his head. "It is not something we can rightly partake in, but neither is it something we can defend against."

"Hoka..." S'ungina murmured.

Hoka put up a hand, not looking at the young warrior. "Your willingness to rescue us at all, and your wisdom to listen to counsel and call off an attack has earned you this explanation." He hesitated. "We are not the only ones. There are many who are afraid."

"Many of the Aniyvwiya were afraid when the sorceries were first shown to us," Yvgidahi acknowledged. "Even I questioned my own brother."

"Yes, but what need do we have of the sorceries here? What wars have we?"

"The sorceries are not only a weapon of war, but also a tool. Galo'ondiha ale Agi'a, to lift heavy objects. Touch, to heal wounds. I admit, I am not well-versed in your traditional ways, but are not relationships with the spirits of the greatest endeavor? Is not the concept of all being connected—"

"Connection," Hoka interrupted. "Singularity. Unity. One with all. The sorceries are a means of power and control and dominance."

"Is using the sorceries for the construction of irrigation systems evil, then? Or the healing of the sick and wounded?"

"In the same way that you may heal a man's lungs, so you may also crush them," the elder said now. "What terrible weapon it is to be able to reach within a man's body and destroy him so. Even among your own people, this is witching."

"We will not tolerate it," Hoka said. "And we are not the only ones. The Western peoples you have rescued, the Navajo, the Apache, the Pueblo, they see it as devilry akin to the evils of the Comanche, to say nothing of the persecution from the white men."

"What are you saying?" Yvgidahi wondered.

"We agreed to leave first," S'ungina cut in. "We were the largest people and the best suited for battle if you decided to come after us to force us to return."

"And if there was no war, then the others—the Navajo, the Apache, the Pueblo—they would all follow."

"Exactly," the chieftain confirmed. "And any others who wished to have no dealings with the sorceries."

Yvgidahi shook his head. "We've never forced anyone to learn or use the sorceries. We've never threatened anyone. I have always believed the public meetings to be productive—"

"The council is all Cherokee, with exception of Gokhos," S'ungina stated bluntly. "And there is plenty of animosity to go around, whatever you claim. Did you think Unitsiya and Okchanlush would not use the sorceries to kill every Oceti Sakowin he saw? Would you have refrained from its use?"

Yvgidahi took an even breath. Then, "No. But that does not mean that you could not learn."

"We cannot," Hoka said firmly. "We will not. Now it is up to you to decide whether your sorceries truly are merely a tool, or a weapon of war. And how it will be used." He shook his head sadly. "We stake our claim to the plains, but we know our defenses are weak. Their strength depends upon the honor of those from Aktiya Waya."

Nendawagan felt a weight settle over her, and she knew her father felt it doubly so. She considered conjuring Time, if only to give herself a moment to process everything that was going on. Then she considered present company and their expressly stated opinions, and she refrained.

"Please, Hoka," her father said, more gently now. "Even if you wish nothing to do with the sorceries, do not separate yourselves from us so absolutely. One day, your children will not remember this exchange. They will not remember the Old Land. They will know nothing of this, and they will become fearful and paranoid of the sorcerers living in Aktiya Waya. There will be blood. And war. And everything that we hope to achieve will be forever lost."

Nendawagan could see there was some disagreement among the Oceti Sakowin men over this, but only Hoka spoke.

"Yes," the older man said slowly. "This thought has crossed my mind as well. It has also been of great concern to us how few of us there are. I am the only leader here, when there ought to be at least four, if not seven. But not all the peoples are here."

"We can send you home," Yvgidahi offered. "Or there is certainly enough bloodshed in the Old Land to bring more here."

Ashagi made a sound and shifted position but said nothing.

Hoka shook his head. "No. No, I do not believe we would fare so well if such a thing were done, either sending us there or bringing more. Besides, adding more of one people or another..." He sighed. "Yvgidahi, I understand that you are old, but you still act very naive at times. If you cannot bring peace to one hundred men, how shall you bring peace to a thousand? Or more? Aktiya Waya has its own troubles, but you will find that we are not one of them. All we ask is to be left in peace, a sanctuary for those who wish nothing to do with the sorceries."

"We have never forced anyone to learn or use the sorceries," Yvgidahi repeated. "In spite of the terrible events that nearly happened today, we are not a threat to you. I ask that you do not separate yourselves from us. Even I know that you are accustomed to large families, large villages, and a large nation. You are but forty here, at most. Let us remain friendly, as a whole people."

For a long moment, no one said anything. Only Hoka looked any bit thoughtful or interested in what her father had to say, Nendawagan thought. The rest seemed annoyed and disinterested, though thankfully not hostile.

"Stay in our village this night, in the tents you have brought," Hoka said finally, much to the dismay of his men. "In the morning, send half of your warriors home. Then we will speak again."

Yvgidahi dipped his head once. "Thank you."

They gave appropriate deference to Hoka and the others as they departed the tipi.

As soon as they emerged, the remaining warriors breathed a sigh of relief and swarmed them.

"We will stay here tonight," he told them. He did not mention sending half of them home, but for the moment, it put them at ease.

The men went off to pitch their small tents; Nendawagan wondered if Hoka knew they had not brought much, and what he could be implying. If there was any good news, it was that the night remained warm, and there was no rain, nor even a single cloud, on the horizon. Before Nendawagan could join them, her father put a hand on her shoulder.

"I want you to go with them in the morning," he said.

"But my place is here," she protested. "Without me, you would have been attacked, to say nothing off—!"

"And your purpose has been served. If Hoka means treachery, he will do so in the night, and even then, he knows he is no match for the sorceries. I don't suspect he will try anything."

"But—"

"Return to Aktiya Waya. Help your mother as you have always done. I will return once we have come to an agreement here."

Nendawagan opened her mouth but, at her father's look, could only sigh and nod. "V-e, Nocha."

He patted her shoulder and moved off to speak to the warriors. She left them to it and meandered about the village a bit, noting that the residents were not overly fond of her presence.

She knew most all of them, just from helping them when they first made their escape to Aktiya Waya. What was it that changed their opinions so readily? Were they truly afraid of the sorceries? Had they escaped to Aktiya Waya only because they believed it to have been their final chance at life? Did they simply believe they were choosing the lesser of two evils by remaining on Hlohi rather than return to the Old Land?

No one spoke to her, and she did not attempt conversation. Feeling very uncomfortable, she made for the tiny camp the warriors had set up. Her father, Unitsiya, Okchanlush, and a couple others were not present, but the rest were either cooking over the small fire or engaging in exceptional boasting contests which often turned into wrestling matches.

Someone offered her a bowl of hominy, and she readily accepted.

"Thank you," the man said.

She looked up and found it was Ola Achukma. She blinked and

grinned awkwardly. "You gave me the soup."

He grinned and looked away for a moment, then at the ground. "No, I mean, thank you." He looked at her. "For believing me, and for getting us here quickly so we could stop the war."

Nendawagan nodded. "You were the one brave enough to call out the lie."

"Ashagi or Lapish or any of the others would have done the same, once they heard what had been said."

"Would they? Do you think Lapish would have turned down the opportunity to make himself look better, attacked and injured by enemy warriors, rather than a fool who got trampled by his horse? Or Shikak, who had to be sent back with him, meek and empty-handed? Or Ashagi or Nohdatsi who would have to explain to their families why there was so little meat brought back?"

The teenager blinked. "Yes, but..." He shifted position. "This is bigger than that. This is war."

Nendawagan frowned and studied her soup. "My father says that in the Old Land, young men would travel hundreds of miles to kill an enemy and bring back spoils to impress a girl."

"That sounds...a bit excessive."

She looked around to see if there might be other prying eyes or listening ears. She lowered her voice. "My father thinks that the animosity between the peoples of Aktiya Waya persists because the men need to feel important and set themselves apart. The only iron they have to sharpen their knives is each other." She looked at him. "Is that true?"

Ola Achukma frowned and did not meet her gaze. "Aki—my father, he always told us to never give in to violence, to strive to be a peacemaker." He shifted uncomfortably. "But I would be lying if I did not say that a part of me wished for battle today. Some days, the tension in Aktiya Waya feels too great to bear. I feel as though I tread on sharp rocks; I must step carefully lest I get cut too deeply. Sometimes...I do wish to just...settle it. Like the wolves in a pack, I wish to establish my place, to know for certain where everyone stands and what is expected because of it."

She nodded. "Believe it or not, I understand. While I have always enjoyed the lengthened life the sorceries have given me, there is a part of me that...desires restraint. Or at least a boundary. A limit of some form."

"A challenge," Ola Achukma said. "Something to overcome."

"Yes, that's it. A challenge. Not that helping refugees isn't a puzzle, and politics is certainly a challenge to overcome, but I suppose I also wish for a challenge in my life."

"You aren't married, then?"

"No, I'm not, although my mother wishes I were, so I could give her even more grandchildren."

"Well, according to my mother, marriage is a challenge all by itself."

Nendawagan laughed. "Yes, I suppose it is. And I know all about children, too. Between caring for my brothers when they were young, and watching my nieces and nephews." She sighed and ate some soup. "I guess I don't know what I want, really."

Ola Achukma nodded, hastily spooning some hominy into his mouth as if trying to avoid speaking.

"You did well, Ola Achukma," Nendawagan said.

"I suppose that's all I can try to do," he said into his soup. He shifted position. "I still carry my father's Bible."

"Really?"

He nodded. "It's all I have left of Aki, and I like the stories."

"Do you still believe in them?"

He looked at something across the camp. "I don't know. I have no reason not to, I suppose. What's so bad about a Man healing the sick and feeding the hungry?"

"You know if someone were to find it—"

"I know. That's why I always keep it with me." He shifted his elbow to guard his satchel.

Nendawagan frowned as they returned to their own soup and their own thoughts, the other warriors still bragging of themselves and wrestling in the dirt.

Shall we say to one people, "we will keep your traditions" and to another, "you must give up yours"? Nendawagan mused silently. She conjured Time so she could study Ola Achukma freely, his elbow still tight against his satchel which had never left him, even when he lay down to sleep. Now she knew why. Why should he live in fear that someone should destroy his most precious possession?

It was perhaps the hardest lesson for any child to learn, that other people existed, and they were not like you. It was an extraordinary thing to consider, that not everyone observed the same rituals and prayers, and somehow, they survived, whereas your own parents and priests conveyed the utmost importance of those rituals. It was the beginning of true thinking, of free will, that most basic of questions: Why?

She ceased conjuring and looked about the village, that single word racing through her mind. Why?

This bothered her all the way to sleep and haunted her dreams. The following morning, when her father divided his warriors—not mentioning that it had been Hoka's will that he should do so—Nendawagan waited patiently upon her horse while the warriors made every argument to stay. She did not blame them, and part of her wished to make her own arguments. But she was not a warrior. Similarly, she was not only part of the group, but she was his daughter, his own flesh and blood. For her to challenge him would be terribly disrespectful and embarrass him not only in front of his own warriors, but the Oceti Sakowin as well. Nothing good would come from ensuing negotiations.

Shikak and Ola Achukma were among those being sent back.

"It's not fair," Shikak lamented once they were out of earshot of the village. "First I am sent to escort Lapish back home, and now I am sent home from negotiations which could turn to battle at any moment!"

"Hush, child," someone said, at the same time someone else said, "You will have another chance. There will be more hunting trips."

"Yes, but what about battle? We hear stories of great battles and great exploits all the time from the elders, yet we will never experience such a thing for ourselves! Ola Achukma, Lapish, and I, we will be nothing if Yvgidahi has his way!"

"Why do you wish to kill?" Nendawagan asked before anyone else could speak.

The silence that settled over them did not last as long as she might have hoped.

"I wish to prove myself and take spoils," Shikak said.

"Are the beasts not enough of a challenge?" she questioned.

"A beast is not a man, and wrestling produces no prize, no plunder."

"And what sort of plunder do you wish to take? If we were to turn around now and attack the Oceti Sakowin village, what would you take? What do they have that is so important that you would kill a man for it?"

He evaded the question, instead saying, "The elders talk of blood rites and revenge—"

"No blood has been spilled," Nendawagan cut in. "But it was our own warriors, Unitsiya and Okchanlush, who attempted to initiate such a feud. By rights, they could attack us. And then we will retaliate. No doubt we would win. And then what? What have you gained?"

"Peace is an honorable thing," someone behind her said. "But I don't think you understand a man's need to prove himself, boast of himself, recite his great deeds."

"Yes, I heard it well enough last night."

"But did you listen? Shikak is right; the young people here have few things to brag about. They cannot boast of journeying a hundred miles to plunder, or show off an old wound they received as they fought for their lives."

"No one has ever stopped them from journey a hundred miles in any direction, and they have plenty of scars from the beasts that inhabit the forest. Why must it always come down to killing someone?"

"I do not expect one such as you to understand. A man's worth is in his strength and power, his fortitude against any threat at any time. The spirit of a beast is easily placated with an offering and a fire, and we never worry about them coming into the bowl, thirsting for our blood. But men who have been wronged are not so easily placated, nor his thirst for revenge so easily satiated."

"But is it necessary to kill?"

"A man must be willing to give his life, for his pride and honor demand it," someone else said.

Nothing they were saying was new to Nendawagan. She had made this argument and asked these questions of her father many times before in private, often when new peoples arrived in Aktiya Waya and did not get along well. But in the end, everyone always settled down and went about their business, if grudgingly so. The only thing new here was that the Oceti Sakowin had, in fact, done something about their discomfort. They'd decided to leave, and they were prepared to take others with them.

Nendawagan invoked Uhnvyvgi, stripping away all noise until all that remained was the steps and breathing of her horse, as well as her own breathing. Was this sorcery truly so evil? Did it make her a witch or evil priestess? What about the rest of them? Were they all evil witches, evil spirits wielding unspeakable power over Creation?

Thinking about their predicament made her sad, and she silently prayed for her father's wisdom and safety. She didn't know what to do, if there was anything she could do. Was there anything that anyone could do, or was it really left to her father and Hoka, sitting back there in Hoka's tipi, talking?

Some of the men continued to debate the merit of returning, and a few of them floated the idea of attack. Only the idea of Yvgidahi being held hostage over it kept this from becoming more than a passing idea, though Nendawagan was forced to wonder just how effective the hostage taking would be, seeing how her father was well-versed in sorceries that the Oceti Sakowin wanted nothing to do with and could not defend against.

By that same token, no force of Oceti Sakowin warriors came chasing after them, to slaughter them while their backs were turned. Nor did any messengers join them to say how things were going.

The return to Aktiya Waya was, overall, uneventful. No one's mood or opinion had changed by the time they got back: Shikak was still lamenting his recent perceived misfortunes, Ola Achukma remained silent and thoughtful, and Nendawagan considered her own problems. She took her horse to the fields, then made for home.

The house was empty, which was fine with her. She headed for her bedroom and lay down, briefly thinking that she might fall asleep. She wished she would have as she heard footsteps enter the house.

"Nenda?" It was Popokus.

Nendawagan groaned as she got herself upright, pushing aside the curtain and nearly running into her sister, or her belly, anyway, as she was pregnant with her fifth child.

"Oh, you have returned!" her sister said, grinning and hugging her. Then she released her and grew serious. "Is Nocha all right? Lapish said you had gone to rescue him, and all we've heard otherwise is that you took off with four men, riding into the woods and conjuring for all you were worth!"

Nendawagan sighed and rubbed her face. "Of sorts, I suppose. Nocha is fine, or he was when we left."

"Where is he?"

"He's still with Hoka at the Oceti Sakowin settlement."

"Oceti Sakowin settlement?"

"It's a long story. I really hope he returns home soon and can explain everything. Before the other warriors start spreading rumors. We rode out to stop one war; I don't think we would be so lucky a second time, if the men get the thought of battle in their blood."

Her sister seemed uncertain. "Are you all right? You look...troubled."

Nendawagan waved a hand. "I'm fine. I've just been conjuring a lot lately."

"Well, Guka is in the townhouse. She'll want to know you're home safe. She spent most of the time with us, all worried about what you were getting yourself into."

"I'm fine," Nendawagan repeated.

Popokus put her hands on Nendawagan's shoulders. "Nenda, I was worried about you, too. You just took off with hardly a word! We had to get the story from Lapish! And by then, who knew where you were?

Nenda, you can't do that!"

"Do what?"

"Run off on a whim like that! What if something happened to you?"

Nendawagan made a sound of frustration as she pulled away from her sister. "Then at least something will have happened to me, and I would not be stuck here, meek and mild, worrying but unable to do anything!" She sighed and shook her head. "You sound just like Guka, you know."

"At least one of us does," Popokus said forcefully. "At least one of us has some sense to do as she's told. At least one of us is married and has children."

Nendawagan could only stare at her sister, eternally grateful when she finally turned and left, her large belly leading the way. Finally she let out a breath.

She's just pregnant, she told herself. She's just pregnant and worried. It's normal. It's natural.

All the same, she happily retreated to her bedroom and lay down to sleep.

Ontuklo Tushafa

Council and Competition

Yvgidahi not only survived his meeting with Hoka, but he even got the Oceti Sakowin chieftain to return to Aktiya Waya for further discussions and negotiations in public forum. Convincing the Oceti Sakowin and their like-minded allies to return and stay in Aktiya Waya appeared to be out of the question, but remaining on friendly terms as one people seemed to be well within the realm of possibility.

"We will be one people," Yvgidahi proclaimed, sounding as certain and as enthusiastic as Ola Achukma had ever heard him when he declared such a thing. "One people, but two villages. Each village shall have its council, and it shall have a representative on the greater, national council between us."

There was surprisingly little resistance to the idea, Ola Achukma thought, and he found himself conflicted. Shouldn't people be upset over this division? Shouldn't they wish to stay and keep everyone together? Of course, why would they, when they could hardly stand each other and so drove this exodus in the first place?

All the same, he was expecting a little more fight, and he was disappointed that he seemed to be the only one.

Was this peace, then? Dividing the people as they wished, according to their will, rather than forcing them to try and cooperate?

Why could some people get along, and not others? How was it that he could have Ashagi for a friend, and others who were not Chahta, and be fine, and yet there were those like Unitsiya who could hardly stand to look upon those who were not Aniyvwiya?

This division did not appear to run along such lines, but rather between those who did and did not wish to use the sorceries. What a foolish thing, Ola Achukma thought. Should they also cast out those who did not wish to ride horses? What about those who had opposed the irrigation system? Fourteen homes now had individual reservoirs, and more were being added every summer; should the rest of them find somewhere else to live?

"When will this national council meet?" someone asked.

"In the summer," Hoka answered. "When all festivals converge. Then we will celebrate, and have much music and dancing and feasting, and we will discuss national matters."

"And there will be tournaments," Yvgidahi added. "Tournaments of strength and courage and skill. Of hunting and wrestling and endurance and riding and other exciting events, that men may compete and win and boast of themselves."

It was almost as if he had heard the discussion they'd had on the road, Ola Achukma thought. Of course, he might expect that Nendawagan had brought up the subject with him, and this was his response to it. But would it be enough?

"And when will this festival take place?" someone else inquired.

"I will return to my village," Hoka said. "And I will gather those who wish to come, to dance and feast and compete. In ten days' time, we will return. Those who currently live in Aktiya Waya, who wish to leave and join us where no sorceries will be used, that will be the time, when we depart after the festivities."

Once again, there was far less resistance than Ola Achukma might have hoped.

He easily recalled the settlement, how small it had seemed, hardly more than a camp. Was that perception about to be reversed, where the settlement was now the thriving city and Aktiya Waya little more than a camp, a mostly deserted former city with only a few lonely residents?

"Who shall be on this national council?" Utsonadi inquired, his disposition both displeased and a bit puzzled. "Shall the same people who make decisions for a single village also make decisions for the entire nation?"

"There will be four on the council," Yvgidahi said. "One of the leaders from each village council, a priest, and one chosen by the people who may come from any village, any people, for any reason that the people decide he is a worthy leader for the nation. He does not even have to be on a village council."

Hoka picked up the thought. "Yvgidahi and myself shall comprise two of these four. The priests of both villages will convene to determine who among them shall be on the national council."

"And the fourth?" Tsisgwaya inquired.

"Is up to the people. At the summer festival, anyone who wishes to be considered may make themselves known and compete in whatever tournaments they believe will portray them as a capable leader. Upon the conclusion of the festival, that leader will be selected, and then we shall convene the first meeting of the national council."

There was a fair amount of excitement in the air, and as Yvgidahi and Hoka explained things, Ola Achukma was able to breathe again. It didn't sound as horrible as he had been fearing. This was not the end of things, and it sounded as though war had been avoided, turned into friendship instead. The summer festival would be the determining factor, he thought, and there seemed to be precious little time to prepare. Even the priests looked a bit bewildered, perhaps annoyed, that they were being asked to choose someone and given such a short deadline, forcing them to rush the spirits.

He looked around, hoping to spot Nendawagan. How much of this was her idea? True, Yvgidahi had been back hardly a day before calling this meeting, but she seemed to be the kind of woman who could get her point across quickly and make her desires and ideas known. He did not see her, but this did not surprise him. He stood in a tangle of people and could only see Yvgidahi when the tall man in front of him moved aside for a moment.

"How long do we have to prepare?" someone wondered.

"Expect ten days," Hoka answered, "for I do not use the sorceries to get me from place to place."

His expression, what Ola Achukma could see of it, was joking, but his tone was less so. Whether the jab had been a more generalized disdain for the sorceries or an intentional remark aimed at Yvgidahi was unclear. Whatever the case, Yvgidahi did not react to it, instead saying, "Another hunt will be swiftly organized, and we will need help organizing the events."

"My people will also bring food to share," Hoka threw in, as if trying to erase his previous icy remark.

Naturally, with everyone gathered in one spot like they were, it was easy to name the tasks and find someone to rise to the occasion. Mostly it was clearing areas to use for some of the tournaments, like the wrestling tournament or the archery tournament. A couple of men were chosen to determine a course for a footrace. And there were other jobs to do as well. By the end, everyone had at least one assignment.

Ola Achukma had been, he believed, deliberately not chosen to go out hunting. That was fine with him, honestly. He wasn't keen on straying too far from Aktiya Waya at the moment. Maybe, if the festival went well and the people remained at peace, then he would feel better about venturing out. For now, he was content with his role in building targets for the archery tournament.

He wouldn't say he wasn't still a tad uneasy, but after the meeting, the worst of his fears had been assuaged, and he left the townhouse feeling more confident than he had when he walked in.

He spotted Nendawagan also leaving, and he moved to intercept and walk beside her.

"How much of that came from you?" he wondered.

"Some," she said, grinning. "I wanted to come up with an idea to create a challenge, a friendly challenge, and give everyone a chance to compete and boast of themselves."

"Hopefully without killing each other?"

"That's the idea."

"They're not coming back, though. Aktiya Waya may end up being smaller than their settlement by the end of this."

"I don't think so," Nendawagan said. "Truthfully, I'm more worried that there will be accusations of cheating because of the sorceries."

He hadn't thought about that.

"But, maybe everyone will be in such good spirits and having a good time and glad to have this reprieve that...it won't come up."

Ola Achukma shrugged helplessly. "I guess. Maybe."

She sighed and shook her head, still grinning. "I'm sorry. You looked happy when you approached, and I'm afraid I've ruined your mood." She looked at him. "Do you expect to compete?"

"I expect so. Maybe in the footrace."

"You're not much into the wrestling, are you?"

"I've done it. I've practiced. I'm good at it."

"So what's the problem?"

He shrugged. "I just don't find it as fun or interesting as the footrace."

She nodded. "I see. What about the archery, since you're building the targets?"

"Of course. I have to make sure they work."

She grinned. "Well all right then." She stopped and faced him. "Seeing how we both have a lot of work to do over the next ten days, I expect I'll see you at the tournament."

She departed down the street, disappearing into a certain house, Ola Achukma staring after her dumbly.

After a moment, he shook his head, turned and navigated the streets back to his own home, nearly running into his mother when he stepped inside.

"Oh, there you are," she said, shielding his little brother.

"Were you worried for me?" he wondered.

"No, but I lost track of you after the meeting. Then I saw you talking to a girl." She grinned as he looked away shyly. "Who was she, I didn't get a good look?"

"It was Nendawagan."

"Nendawagan? Yvgidahi's daughter? The one who went with you to the settlement?" Her expression was puzzled, her tone difficult to determine.

"Yes, her."

"Is everything all right? Is there something more to this settlement or this...I don't know that I would call it an alliance necessarily, but...?"

Ola Achukma glanced at the baby in his mother's arms, hardly able to believe that it was his brother. He had nothing in common with the one year old. Apushi looked back at him with enormous eyes and reached for him. He thought of Evan and Priscilla, wondered what they would be like if they were still alive.

"Ola?" his mother prompted.

He looked at her. "No, everything is fine. She was just asking if I planned to compete in the tournaments at the festival."

"Do you?"

"Of course. I'll do the footrace and the archery. I might do the wrestling, I'm not sure."

"And are you trying to show off to anyone?"

"You mean like Nendawagan?"

His mother shrugged. "She's one option, I suppose, since I imagine she'll be staying here in Aktiya Waya."

Ola Achukma nodded. "She is quite talented in the sorceries; I don't think she would be well-received among the Oceti Sakowin."

"But she is still...Ayvwiya."

"Her mother is Lenape. And anyway, I don't see how it matters. We're one people. We live here together. We're holding a festival in ten days to celebrate that fact. And I'm going to compete, and I'm...I'm going to show off. I'm going to win. At least the footrace."

His mother sighed.

"Sashki, look at Apushi," Ola Achukma said. "He was born here, in Aktiya Waya. He never knew Aki. He never knew Evan or Priscilla."

"Aifoli and Pishuk," his mother said quietly.

"He never knew them. He never walked the Trail, never knew the hardships. Don't burden him with something he knows nothing about and can only hurt him. It does no one any good for him to see differences where they do not exist."

"And what happens when he is treated differently?"

"He won't be. If we don't allow it."

She still seemed uncertain, but their conversation was cut short by the arrival of Chilita.

"You'll be marking the course for the footrace, then," Ishki said, deliberately hiding her face from her husband until she could compose her features.

"Yes, with a couple others," Chilita confirmed. He looked at Ola Achukma. "And you're building the targets for the archery tournament. Good for you. Do you think you'll need help?"

"I should be fine," Ola Achukma answered. "I'm helping Ihya gather the material for the padding that will stop the arrows. Tsusdayi is the one building the frames, and he knows Galo'ohndiha ale Agi'a well enough to keep things together."

"Maybe you should help Tsusdayi and learn Galo'ondiha ale Agi'a for yourself."

"If I am able to, once I finish with Ihya."

His mother nodded. "Yes, helping the elders always takes priority."

Chilita echoed this as he took Apushi in his large hands and admired his son. Ola Achukma stood there awkwardly for a moment until Chilita moved off a couple steps and he could retreat to his room.

Had Ki ever looked at him like that, held and admired him like that? Ola Achukma liked to imagine that he had, and had done so also with Evan and Priscilla.

Make no mistake, he liked Chilita. He was a good man, a good hunter, and a good husband for his mother who had been lonely and depressed for several years after their arrival in Aktiya Waya. They had some good times together. But he would never be Ki.

The following morning, all of Aktiya Waya was abuzz with activity as everyone launched into his duties for the festival. To Ola Achukma, it looked like an ant hill when it starts to rain, all the ants scattering about and running around wildly. Even he was not immune to the fervor as he made his way through the streets and stopped at Ihya's home.

Ihya lived with his eldest daughter and her family. They, too, were quite busy, hurriedly finishing breakfast so as to get out to the fields, telling Ola Achukma to wait outside.

From his glimpse into their home, he'd seen Ihya, moving slowly, as content as you please, in no rush to go anywhere or do anything, the only exception to the clamor in the rest of the village.

Once Ihya's daughter's family was out of the house, running off to see to their mission, Ola Achukma let himself in and sat down at the table where Ihya was just finishing his meal and considering the cup of water in his hand.

For a long moment, they sat in silence, the click of utensils the only sound to be heard. Then Ihya sighed contentedly and leaned back in his seat, still considering his drink.

"You know what I could really go for?" the elder said.

"What?" Ola Achukma wondered.

"Coffee. A hot cup of coffee."

Ola Achukma blinked. "What?"

"Come now, Ola, you're from the Old Land. Surely you must have heard of coffee."

"I remember I didn't like it. Too bitter. And crunchy."

Ihya chuckled. "You're not supposed to eat the grounds, child."

"I know that." Ola Achukma shifted in his seat. "But I thought most peoples condemned coffee?"

The elder waved a hand. "Years and years ago, yes. Foolishness, I say. I found it rather invigorating. And every so often, I find myself craving it."

"Perhaps if there are to be future expeditions to the Old Land, some could be procured."

"Oh, naturally. And this has been done, too. But the last expedition was last year, and it did not produce any coffee." Ihya leaned toward Ola Achukma who leaned in to hear him speak. "Do you happen to know how to conjure Galohisdi?"

Ola Achukma grinned. "No, I don't. I'm sorry."

The old man made a frustrated sound. "Of course. So then that means we have to walk to the place where we expect to find padding for these archery targets."

"I'm afraid so."

Ihya sighed and stood, pushing back his chair and grabbing his staff. "Well then, we may as well get started. For as fast as I move these days, we'll need the full ten days to gather enough padding. How many targets did you say would be made?"

"Um...a lot. And I happen to know that some of the hair from the tsuyoniyvgi manes and any leftover wool from the sheep will also be used."

"It's a start, anyway."

The elder led the way out of the house and shuffled along through the streets, Ola Achukma at his side.

"Tsusdayi is building the frames," Ola Achukma began conversationally. "Chilita suggested that, if I have time, after the padding, I should talk to him about Galo'ondiha ale Agi'a."

Ihya stole a glance at him, but otherwise kept his gaze fixed on where he intended to take his next step. "Your father taught you many languages, didn't he?"

Ola Achukma hesitated for half a breath. Then, "Yes, he did."

"You use them a lot here in Aktiya Waya, don't you?"

"There are a lot of peoples here. Some don't like the idea of using the language of a banned people in order to communicate, and they only speak English if they must."

Ihya made a sound. "I have seen this as well." He paused and turned to face him. "You know what I think?"

"Clearly not."

"I think you should be the formal announcer for the festival. The official interpreter."

Ola Achukma shrugged. "I have no problem with that."

"But more than that, I think you should be the one to blend the languages."

"What?"

"The people don't want to speak English, and I don't blame them. But we can't rightly choose one language over another. Being one people does not mean favoring one over another, it means taking the best of everyone and making something new."

"What if someone doesn't want to give up something that may not be the best, but isn't bad, either?"

"Then that, too, becomes part of the new people. The important thing is to weed out the bad, the ugliness. It will not be an easy process. Indeed, there are many individuals who are still going through this process within themselves."

"Do you really think it's possible?"

Ihya gave him a look. "We won't know until we try, will we?"

He turned and continued shuffling along, his staff making hollow thuds on the stone. "Of course, these targets won't stuff themselves, either. Come on, then."

Because the targets were going to be riddled with arrows, they couldn't use the best materials, but neither could the targets fall apart on impact. The leather they gathered was tough and already damaged, usually from improper tanning. Another layer of bad leather would diffuse most of the force, but there was still a need for thick padding.

The first day, after gathering an armload of leather, Ola Achukma and Ihya retreated to the elder's home to lay out all the damaged hides and figure out how to sew them together to make bags for the padding.

"We can't have a seam on the face where the arrows are supposed to penetrate," Ola Achukma said. "If an arrow hits it wrong, it may not stick."

"Of course it will!" Ihya snapped. "Arrows penetrate thick hides all the time; it's why we still need padding. Besides, it's not about whose arrow goes through the target, but who is most accurate!"

"But if the arrow bounces off—"

"It won't bounce off. If the arrows bounces off, it's because the draw wasn't very strong to begin with. Honestly, Ola Achukma, have you never used a bow before?"

Ola Achukma knew well to respect his elders, and he'd always admired Ihya from afar during meetings or at festivals or other functions. Now the old man was starting to wear on his nerves a little. He could not well leave the elder to do the sewing, either, as his fingers were too bent and arthritic to hold a needle or weave the sinew. But now that they were at odds, Ihya didn't want to leave him alone to gather more leather or padding, in case Ola Achukma "sewed the pieces wrong and didn't make a good bag."

It was a long few days, and Ola Achukma found himself wishing, more than once, that he understood the conjuring of Time. The ability Nendawagan had used to see them to her father quickly had been conjuring Fast Time, where they moved faster than everything else. He wished for the opposite, conjuring Slow Time, that he might pass by the days quickly and not have to put up with Ihya's constant fretting over the bags.

Thankfully, by the fifth day, once most of the bags were sewn, Ihya took it upon himself to go out and find padding. This came in the form of bits of leftover wool, tsuyoniyvgi hair, woven horsehair, and bundles of grass, leaves, and small twigs, with a core of bone just to ensure that the arrow was stopped before it ripped through the bag.

But then, it wasn't as simple as just filling the bags. No, there was an art to it.

"Wrap the bone in the horsehair," Ola Achukma said. "It will stop the arrow, protect the bone, and catch anything that splinters off."

Ihya waved a hand. "Line the bag with the horsehair and back it with twigs so the arrow doesn't reach the bone at all!"

"The arrow should stick well in the padding so there's no confusion."

"That's what the painted target is for, isn't it?"

"Yes, but the farther it goes in, the better the archer feels about his shot."

The old man chuckled at that. "Yes, he does. It works the same way in love, too."

Ihya winked at him, and the sudden innuendo threw off Ola Achukma's line of thought so he could no longer be upset with the old man. Instead, Ola Achukma sighed and leaned back in the chair, an empty bag between his knees. "What are we supposed to do, then?"

"We can arrange the bags according to how we see fit," Ihya suggested.

Ola Achukma gave him a look. "You know we can't do that. If the bags aren't made roughly the same, then any of them could be defective, and it wouldn't go over well for the competitors. Someone could be accused of cheating or rigging the competition."

"Each of these materials is good," Ihya said. "We just have to figure out how to utilize them most effectively. What are the strengths of each? Surely we wouldn't expect this old wool to have much stopping power."

"No, not really. But it is quite sticky and becomes gnarled easily." Ola Achukma shifted position. "We could use that to wrap the bone and catch splinters."

The old man nodded. "We could. And the tsuyoniyvgi hair could simply be filler."

"We can use the grasses and leaves for the outermost layer followed by a layer of small twigs. The grasses will provide give so that the arrows can sink in, and the twigs will stop them. A layer of woven horsehair will provide a barrier between that and the bone, keep everything wrapped tight."

Ihya kept nodding. "We could do that, too."

Ola Achukma glanced at the old man. "Using the strengths of each people in order to craft a strong, effective, unified nation."

The elder shrugged and put up his hands. "However you wish to interpret it; I'm just here to build targets for an archery competition."

"Right. Sure you are."

But Ihya was already twisting grasses together and lining one of the bags. "Don't just sit there, child, start wrapping those bones in wool and hair, stick them here in the center of the bag."

The seventh day was spent sewing up the bags. As Ola Achukma completed his task, he sent the bag over to Ihya who painted targets on them. There were seven painted targets of varying sizes, all roughly the same across each bag. This task went over rather smoothly and was completed in a day.

Looking at the bags, stuffed full of grass, leaves, twigs, horsehair, wool, and some bones, one might not have expected them to be terribly heavy. For Ola Achukma, they were little effort to heft onto his shoulders and carry, but Ihya could barely shuffle them across the stone, never mind attempt to lift them for any length of time.

Still, the old man went with him to deliver the bags, in multiple trips, to the field which had been cleared for archery. Tsusdayi had five of the seven frames completed, and was working on the sixth. He directed Ola Achukma on how to string up the bags from each frame, leaning the last two against the fifth frame.

"Well, it looks like you young pups have this rather well taken care of," Ihya said. "I'll leave you to help Tsusdayi, then. Maybe he can teach you a thing or two."

Ola Achukma thanked him and went to Tsusdayi who was just driving a wooden peg through a couple of rough-hewn beams, Galo'ondiha ale Agi'a keeping them in place where once it might have taken three men to lift and hold them.

"The bags look good," Tsusdayi observed. "And it looks like you and Ihya are getting along better." He grinned. "He seems meek and mild, and then you start to work with him and realize that he can be quite stubborn and opinionated. Then you realize that he was just trying to teach you a lesson. Do I have that about right?"

"That's exactly what happened," Ola Achukma said. "He gave me a lot to think about."

"That's good. That's what he's supposed to do."

Tsusdayi made a motion, and Ola Achukma handed him a tool. "Do you intend to compete?"

"Of course!" the advisor said. "I would not build these frames if I did not intend to test them in some way. What about you? What are you competing in?"

"The footrace is my first choice. And I would like to do the archery as well."

"What about the wrestling?"

"Everyone else seems to want to compete in the wrestling. I'm afraid I would get lost in the shuffle."

Tsusdayi finished securing the beam and released his hold on Galo'ondiha ale Agi'a. Everything stayed exactly where it was. Satisfied, he descended his ladder and directed Ola Achukma to string up another bag.

"Nonsense!" the advisor said, speaking to his previous comment.

"You may fear being unknown within the competition, but you will certainly be known if you stay out of it."

"If I know I'm not going to win, or even be a great contender, why bother?"

"It's not just about winning. You need to test yourself, challenge yourself. Why is it that you lost? Where was your misstep? What was your error? How do you correct it? It's the same in archery. Why did your arrow go off course? Was it the wind? Was it your draw, your aim? Even the footrace involves this kind of strategy. How is your breathing? How is your gait? How do you conserve energy without sacrificing speed?" Tsusdayi nodded. "I think this festival and the tournaments will be good for you. Good for everyone." He gathered his tools and set them off to the side. "Many of these things, I learned when I was half your age. You who came here as a refugee, even the children who were born here but have seen no troubles, they are learning these things later and later. It will only disadvantage them."

Ola Achukma didn't know how to respond to that.

"Come on, then," Tsusdayi said, making a motion. "I assume you're here as much for the sorceries as just the physical labor. Let's get this last frame built."

The wood had already been gathered and the beams shaved. Despite the ubiquitous loathing of the white men of the Old Lands, some of the tools they used were from the Old Land, pilfered during an expedition. Mining for metals was a slow labor in the caves, and not undertaken with any enthusiasm when it became necessary, and so far, no one had been able to find any great deposits of good metals.

Was this what Ihya meant when he spoke of taking all the best parts of a people and using them to build something new? Ola Achukma debated this as he listened to Tsusdayi.

"Galo'ondiha ale Agi'a is more than what it sounds like," the advisor said. "It is more than simply picking something up or setting it down. It is about attraction." He picked up a rock, showed it off, then let it fall from his hands. "The rock is attracted to the ground. If it were to rain, the water penetrates the ground, seeps deep into the earth, until it finds more water, such as the river, for that is what it is attracted to. Galo'ondiha ale Agi'a is about changing this attraction, diverting it, even suspending it." He shifted his stance. "Do you know how to conjure Time?"

Ola Achukma shook his head. "No. I only know Touch, and I've only just begun."

"Very well, then, I will conjure for you."

He picked up the rock again. Before he released it, he conjured Time around the two of them. He dropped the rock, and it fell in slow motion.

"I want you to feel all the way around the rock," Tsusdayi ordered. "You will feel the forces, the attraction between the rock and the ground."

Ola Achukma did as he asked, cupping his hands around the rock, getting as close as he could and then moving outward. He felt above the rock, below it, knelt and touched the ground. Tsusdayi eased up on his conjuring of Time a little, enough for Ola Achukma to sweep his hands under the rock several times as it fell. When the rock hit the ground, the advisor ceased conjuring.

"Did you feel the attraction?" the advisor inquired.

"I think so," Ola Achukma offered. He'd felt something; he just wasn't sure what. "And yet, I know that if I had put my hand out, the rock would have fallen into my hand."

"Are we not made of earth, this tangible thing? And imbued with the forces of nature, overseen by fire?"

"Is that why fire can overpower the sorceries?"

"Fire was appointed to guide mankind. The sorceries are powerful, yes, but if the Creator wills, they are useless. Fire is the balance to keep them in check among men."

The advisor looked like he wanted to say something more, but refrained.

"What is it?" Ola Achukma asked.

Tsusdayi gave him a look. "I was going to say that, you wouldn't know this, of course, for you are not only Choctaw, but you were raised Christian."

"What does that have to do with Galo'ondiha ale Agi'a?"

"You don't have the same foundation that many here do."

"But I'm learning. It may be that I have to be taught in a different way. Perhaps I listen in a slightly different language."

The advisor shrugged. "I'm not saying you're not capable. I'm just pointing out a small disadvantage. I'm sure you'll get it, with more practice."

"What disadvantage is it to be Chahta, or Christian?"

"Because you are not Ayvwiya, you were not raised in our beliefs. You do not have the same connection to the sorceries that we do."

Ola Achukma shifted his stance. "Have you considered that maybe this is why the Oceti Sakowin are leaving, and why some are following them? Maybe that's why people fear the sorceries?"

"Why is that?"

"Because you degrade them, make them out to be too stupid to understand the sorceries and so elevate yourselves."

Tsusdayi shrugged again. "It was given to us first. And I would think you would be grateful that we rescued you. You and the other peoples."

"That doesn't mean you own us. Why can't you be grateful that it was white men who gave the sorceries to you? Are you so ungrateful to them that you had to run away and take their gifts with you? By that logic, why didn't you conform to them?" Ola Achukma pressed harder. "Either treat it as a tool that can be used equally among all peoples, or magic that belongs to a select few."

"No one has ever said that you were not allowed to learn."

"Maybe not, but if the sorceries came from the very people you despise, why do you go around touting them as something you can grasp but I cannot? I am half-white, which means, perhaps, that I am the one better suited to the sorceries."

The advisor raised a brow, then took a step back, turned, and indicated the beams for the target frame. "Well then, you should have no problem using Galo'ondiha ale Agi'a to lift and place these beams so that I can fasten them together."

Ola Achukma found himself sweating suddenly and silently cursing his stupid mouth. All the same, there was no way he could back down, and he tried to face the beams with confidence. He found himself wishing to conjure Time, to buy himself a moment to think and figure out what he was doing, what he was supposed to do.

The beams were attracted to the ground, earth to earth. Somehow, he had to break that bond. But it wasn't enough just to break it, for nothing could be alone. He had to give them something else to be attracted to.

He touched the beams, wondering if Touch might help him understand the attraction and how to reverse it. It was more difficult, trying to pick out the attraction of the beams, compared to the rock. The rock had been in motion, whereas the beams were already touching the ground, already part of it. But if he could use Touch and figure out where one stopped and the other started...

He felt the forces binding the beams and the ground together. He even managed to separate them enough that the very end of one of the beams started to lift. Tsusdayi watched with a hawk-like gaze, saying nothing.

But the forces were different than Ola Achukma had ever expected or imagined, and he was unable to overcome them to the point where he could lift, place, and hold the beams as the Ayvwiya advisor demanded. Finally, with sweat dripping off the end of his nose, he gave up and let the forces return to their natural state. He stumbled back a step, as though he had tried to physically lift the beams and failed.

"Not bad," the advisor said stiffly.

"I felt the forces," Ola Achukma said, breathing heavily and wiping his face. "It wasn't just the beams and the ground, but there was a connection. To me, to the rocks and the mountains, to the bowl, the whole earth."

"Yes. There are such connections. You would know this if you knew any traditions, whether Aniyvwiya, chagga, or others, anything but Christian. But, seeing how you are unable to do as I have asked, you can be of no further help to me. You might as well find something else to do, something that doesn't require the use of anything more difficult than Touch."

In perhaps his smartest move of the day, Ola Achukma left before his mouth could get him in trouble again. Although, his feelings about running into Ihya again were rather mixed. But the old man appeared to be in a good mood, and he happily ushered him into his home.

"I had an idea," Ihya said excitedly.

Ola Achukma took an even breath. "What's that?"

"You remember how we spoke of you being the official interpreter for the festival? And how you should figure out a way to blend the languages into one?"

"Yes."

The elder bade him sit and wait while he retrieved something. It turned out to be a smooth leather carrier with pressed sheets of paper. The paper contained letters from a language Ola Achukma had never seen before.

"A few years ago, an expedition to the Old Land brought this back," Ihya said. "An Ayvwiya named Sequoyah developed a written language for the people."

Ola Achukma looked over the strange markings. Some looked very much like English letters, others were completely new. "Why wasn't this brought up in public forum?"

"Yvgidahi did not want to appear domineering with the Aniyvwiya language, and the others, myself included, thought it unnecessary. How many books do we have here, really? What would be the purpose, except to, as Yvgidahi said, assert Aniyvwiya superiority, to which he is venomously opposed?"

"You want me to take these letters and transcribe a new language that I'm supposed to concoct out of all the languages here? Ihya, I don't even know where to begin. I don't know what I'm doing. Where are you coming up with these ideas, and why are you putting them on me?"

"Because you are a peacemaker."

Ola Achukma scoffed and shook his head. "Not today I wasn't.

Tsusdayi certainly wouldn't agree with you." He recounted the recent exchange.

Ihya frowned but did not seem overly disturbed by it. "Simply speaking words is not violence, nor is the attempt at diagnosing a disease evil. And I believe you were on the right path. This tension, this lack of peace, it is not a disease, it is a symptom. It does no good to chase down symptoms here and there as they flare up, if one does not also aim for the root of the problem. Giving medicine for the symptom of pain will not set a broken bone. And setting a bone is painful, but necessary for healing."

"I said foolish things, though. Yvgidahi is not unkind toward others. Neither are you. There are many good Aniyvwiya in Aktiya Waya, or else there would be no other peoples here. And if I am to promote this unity, I cannot still blame Aniyvwiya or anyone else, nor think in those terms. Shall I say that Nendawagan was a good Ayvwiya or Lenape for helping us? It doesn't matter, because she was being a good...we still don't even have an agreed-upon name for our singular people." Ola Achukma shook his head. "And I'm supposed to come up with a spoken and written language?"

"I am not saying that it must be done tomorrow, or that it is a tournament in this festival of competitive sports," the old man chuckled. "Give it thought. Give it time. Think about the languages, how they work, how they interact in everyone's daily lives. Introduce it slowly and let it evolve naturally. Don't make it about you and your project. Let everyone have a say in it."

Ola Achukma considered this for a moment. Finally he nodded. "I think I understand what you're saying. But I also think we need to get through the festival first. If we can survive that, we may have a chance."

The elder nodded. "Of course. One thing at a time."

"But why me?"

"Why not you? Yvgidahi is the leader chosen for political affairs, but if a leader has no followers, it does not matter what he decrees. Real change, real unification must come from within a person, from within the people. Believe it or not, many people here do wish for such peace and unity, even Unitsiya and Okchanlush. But not everyone knows how to best go about it, and sometimes, our efforts prove more fatal to the cause."

"And you think I know how to best go about it?"

"I think you are the best one for the job."

"Why?"

"Quite honestly, because your father was white. Your father was an enemy. And if two enemies can come together in peace and produce a child as upstanding as yourself, the rest of us may have a chance as well."

Ola Achukma blinked. "Surely I can't be the only one whose father was white. Or who has white background."

Ihya shook his head. "No, but you are the only one who admits to it and the only one who still holds to part of that life. Yet you are loyal to Aktiya Waya and the principles it espouses. You cannot overcome something you do not acknowledge exists."

"You think the white men are the enemy then, that they must be overcome?"

"If the white men are the enemy, when they are not even here, how much greater is the disdain for those who believe their neighbors are an enemy?"

Ola Achukma took and breath and let it out slowly. "It's a lot to think about."

"It may seem like a burden, but, believe it or not, there are many who will help you shoulder it, once you begin this quest for peace." The old man put a wrinkled hand on his shoulder. "Go now and think about what I have said. Take this with you." He handed him the manuscript. "Remember, this is not one of the festival tournaments; you are not required to complete it in a day, or even a moon, nor are you expected to do it all and be the best. Start small, see where it leads. Do not build an irrigation system that must be precise, simply undam the river and let it flow where it will."

The elder's calm demeanor helped to calm Ola Achukma's racing heart as he left the home, feeling very conspicuous, as if everyone in Aktiya Waya, and all the way to the Oceti Sakowin settlement had heard their conversation, or perhaps knew about it before he did. But no one said anything to him about it, and he returned home.

No one was home when he arrived, and he felt a little less guilty about opening up the manuscript to study the letters. An accompanying document explained how the graph was to be read, and the sounds each symbol produced, saying that it was a syllabary, not an alphabet. With exception of six letters, each letter represented a syllable, a consonant and a vowel sound.

Well, that's not going to work, Ola Achukma thought. He wasn't even sure how it was supposed to work for the Chalakki language, given that they, too, had consonant clusters. Maybe this was just an early draft that someone had gotten their hands on.

That was fine. He wasn't going to translate Chalakki, he was going to translate everything.

How was he going to translate everything? There were close to a dozen languages in use around Aktiya Waya, even if only used by one or two families. Cherokee, Choctaw, Chickasaw, Seminole, Dakota, Lakota, Navajo, Pueblo, Apache, Ojibwa, plus a few others he probably forgot.

He leaned back in his chair, staring at the manuscript which mocked him. How was he supposed to do this, and how was it going to bring peace?

He startled as the leather hide over the doorway was pushed aside, and he hurriedly swept everything off the table into his arms, again wishing he could conjure Time so as to do everything in only the blink of an eye that this intruder wouldn't see his project.

Somehow, he managed to gather everything, cross the small room to push aside the curtain that led to his room, throw the bundle onto his bed, and make it look like nothing had happened, turning just into time see it was Chilita walking in.

"I saw the targets out there," Chilita began conversationally. "They look good."

"Yeah, Ihya and I worked together on them," Ola Achukma replied.

"I'm sure they'll be perfect for the competition." Chilita disappeared into the room he shared with his wife and young son.

Ola Achukma did not say anything to that, simply left the house and walked through the village, trying to look busy. Somehow, Ihya expected him to be an interpreter for the festival, too. Once again, it all came back to language. He knew half a dozen, including English and Chahta, but what was he supposed to do for the southwestern people? Were the Navajo simply going to be excluded, have to figure things out on their own?

Whatever Ihya said, he was going to have to come up with something before the festival, some way of conveying what was going on, the rules of each tournament.

Later that night, once his mother and stepfather had gone to bed, Ola Achukma stayed up, squinting by the light of the fire—intentionally burning low because of the summer heat—trying to come up with something. Even just coming up with a name for each event was confounding him. Just trying to reconcile Cherokee and Choctaw was proving difficult, and somehow it also had to make sense to everyone else. Some words were similar, and sometimes he might finagle some syllables together, but he still wasn't sure. Would people understand what he was trying to do? What happened if he ended up favoring one language a little too much? This wasn't even trying to wrangle in the languages he didn't know.

After what felt like a day and a half of no production, Ola Achukma gathered his things and headed to his bed. He was not tired, for his mind still raced with hundreds of possibilities for just one word, never mind more, never mind an entire fabricated language. Sometimes, when he thought he had a great idea, it would slip away from him, like a fish through his fingers, and he finally fell asleep feeling no better about his monumental task than when he'd started, regardless of any confidence Ihya had in him. And he found that his biggest fear at that moment, was disappointing the old man.

Pàke Chaasch

Festival

There were never so many people in a village as when it came time to feed them, Nendawagan thought, and she watched the Oceti Sakowin entourage enter the bowl like a flood. Surely there had only been forty or so who had left Aktiya Waya, and even if a few more had gone with them the other day, why did it seem as though there were not forty, but four hundred people entering the bowl now? The whole of the settlement must have come, for she saw many children among them.

Like most of the women, she had spent the last ten days preparing the food. She had been in the group preparing the meat, taking the carcasses just as fast as the hunters returned with them, skinning the carcass, slicing the meat, then separating it into piles for jerking, smoking, or light aging and marinading. Once the meat was processed—suddenly it didn't seem as though they would be able to feed five hundred people for seven days—the hides from the carcasses were fleshed and tanned, some with the fur and some without. Many of the smaller hides were ready for use even before the festival, and they disappeared just as quickly. Other, larger hides, would cure more slowly over the course of the festivities. Likely they, too, would vanish, commandeered by anyone who needed a piece of fur or leather quickly.

Often these pieces went to the drummers and dancers as they prepared for the opening ceremonies. A drum needed a new skin, a piece of regalia needed a quick repair or last-minute adornment.

The ceremonies were to take place that evening, with the songs and dances of each people, to welcome them. Nendawagan also happened to know, through her father only, that there was to be a drumming and dancing competition each night during dinner. One representative from each of the peoples would be a judge, but each was not permitted to judge his own drummers or dancers, to try and keep things fair. Like the rest of the tournaments, some would be eliminated each day until the final round.

The first two days of the festival were to be practice, when everyone would have a chance to become accustomed to the grounds and what was expected in each competition. Wrestlers were free to wrestle and test their opponents before the match. Archers could shoot at the targets and learn the wind currents in the bowl. Racers could explore the course and take note of the landscape. Drummers and dancers could refine their songs and routines.

Starting the third day, elimination began. For as anxious as Nendawagan was about watching the horde of Oceti Sakowin enter the bowl, that was nothing compared to how she expected to feel in a couple of days, when light-hearted practice turned into something worth fighting over.

For her part, though, she had elected to not compete—and the women did have their own competitions, different from the men. But she decided to use her father's reasoning, for why he had refrained from entering himself as a competitor. This was to bring peace to those who were struggling with it, and he did not need to disrupt things by showing off. If he won, it could start accusations of cheating. If he lost, it could start accusations of cheating. Therefore, he would not participate. This time.

"They could still make accusations of cheating," Nendawagan had pointed out. "This whole fiasco stems from the sorceries. How would it be if an Oceti Sakowin were to accuse someone of using the sorceries to cheat?"

"Even among those who disdain the sorceries and wish to leave, many have minor talents and can distinguish the use of the sorceries," her father replied. "They will be ready to accuse a competitor, even as those who embrace the sorceries will be ready to defend. Knowing that your competitor has the same ability to distinguish, I don't expect there will be many false accusations."

"It only takes one to bring this whole thing down, Nocha."

"Then it shall be so. But you can't give up on something because something bad could happen. And in fact, being aware of the possibility makes it more likely that you can defend against it. But either way, you can't give in to fear or uncertainties, for there will always be something to go wrong."

He intended it as a reassurance, but Nendawagan felt it slipping away as the last of the visiting competitors filtered into the bowl and spread out along the grounds. Some inspected the clearing marked for wrestling. Others studied the target bags for archery. Still some went to walk the race course.

There was a time when Nendawagan might have looked upon the sight and marveled at it with Popokus at her side. But her sister was busy with her new baby, a daughter born only days ago. She probably wouldn't even notice the festival going on.

So Nendawagan was left to marvel by herself, trying to find some sort of joyous, child-like wonder at everything going on, and not let the anxiety and dread of adult experience get in the way. Already, looking down at the people milling about, the children were the most oblivious to the seriousness of the situation. Some of them did not understand why their friends were leaving them, and they were happy to be together, if only for this short time. Those who were still children, typically twelve and under, would not be officially competing, but there was still plenty of wrestling and racing among them, and a couple had their bows and were shooting wild arrows into their own homemade targets.

It had been many years since she was a child, though she hardly looked it, and she found that she wasn't sure just what to think about it. She should be getting of an age to almost be an elder; at the very least, she would be nearly past child-bearing age, and still she had none of her own!

She started down the slope from the cavern and made her way toward the grounds. Maybe this would be a good thing. Even if there were some minor arguments and setbacks, it was still a chance for socializing and showing off.

Looking around at the hundreds of people concentrated around the tournament grounds, there was, in spite of the heat, a certain air of infatuation. Young men who were not presently practicing their skills were bragging about them to the young women. The young women whispered among themselves, pointing to this or that competitor. Meanwhile, the men who were already married were trying to show off to their wives and prove that they were still a good catch, far better than the young whelps.

She stopped to watch some of the men at the archery field. A couple were older teenagers, but most were older men appearing in their thirties to fifties.

"What do you think?"

Nendawagan turned to see a young man, maybe twenty-five or so, standing beside her. She knew he was Aniyvwiya, but his name eluded her at the moment.

"What do I think about what?" she asked.

"About them. My competition." He gestured toward the archers.

She grinned as she realized where this was going. "Well, they look skilled enough. Are you?"

"Of course I am. I brought plenty of meat for you to prepare for this festival. Does that not prove a skilled arm?"

Now that he said it, she thought he did look familiar for such a reason. But then, she'd been so busy preparing the meat that everyone and everything else had been either a blur or an obstacle, and sometimes both.

She shrugged and gave him a coy look. "I only prepared the meat. I know not how you took down the animal. Perhaps you did not strike so true as you would have me believe, and instead had to chase down each one as it bled out."

He met her look with one of his own. "Is that so? Well then, I suppose I will just have to show you how great I am."

"You expect to win, then?"

He laughed. "Is there a reason I shouldn't?"

"You seem very confident."

"I am. I trust in my arm, and I trust in my bow. My arrows will strike true. And I will show you that I took down the animals in one strike."

She grinned. "Well then, I guess I'll just have to watch, won't I?"

He seemed pleased with her answer and her apparent support, and he moved on, vanishing into the crowd. Off to find other women to woo and get them to admire him? She didn't know. Actually, Nendawagan found herself a bit flustered by the whole thing, if only because it had caught her off guard, and she knew well that it was only the beginning. There would be plenty of men hoping to turn her eye, or turn any eye, depending on how well they did.

Indeed, it was not the last time she was approached that day by a young man trying to get her attention and brag about himself. Sometimes it was just straight bragging, with varying mixtures of confidence and cockiness. Other times, those she figured were more intent on winning her affections specifically, she was given a gift, usually no more than a flower or carved wooden decoration.

Not long before the opening ceremonies were set to begin, she returned home to drop off these gifts so she did not lose them in the excitement. To her surprise, her mother was also home, sitting at the table with some needles before her.

"I would have expected you to be helping with the food," Nendawagan said. "Is everything all right?"

Her mother nodded. "Oh, yes. I was helping Popokus fix a strap so she could take Kschipasques—" Her new daughter. "—with her to the festival."

"Oh."

"The question, though, is why you're here."

Nendawagan showed her mother the collection of gifts she'd received. "I've been a bit overwhelmed."

Her mother gave her a look. "It wouldn't be bad, you know. To consider one of the young men here. They're going to be showing off; the least you can do is pay them some mind."

"I never said I wouldn't. He would just have to be exceptional."

165

Now her mother's expression turned cheeky. "When you find the one you like, everything he does is exceptional at first, no matter how mundane."

Nendawagan raised a brow. "You no longer find Nocha exceptional, then?"

Her mother laughed. "Eventually, we all turn out to be human. But then we are faced with a choice, whether we will continue to love, or chase ever-elusive perfection." She put away the needles still left out on the table, stood, and smoothed her dress, saying, "But for the moment, we should get down to the opening ceremonies."

Nendawagan quickly took her treasures to her room, then joined her mother to walk to the grounds. They were the last ones to arrive, it seemed, and it was easy to get lost in the crowd.

The opening ceremonies took place in the dancing grounds, a spot east of the cavern that had been dedicated to its purpose since the first Aniyvwiya refugees made this place their home. A fence had been erected to show the boundaries of the circle, and the drummers sat in a smaller inner circle. Yvgidahi, Hoka, and several others stood on a platform on the east side of the circle.

"Welcome, everyone!" her father greeted.

To Nendawagan's relief, everyone seemed to be in good spirits and happy to be there, and they watched him with cheerful attention. She also noticed how one of the people on the platform was Ola Achukma, and he appeared to be acting as an interpreter. She was not close enough to quite make out his words; he did not project his voice or command attention like her father did. She caught maybe one in five words, though she couldn't be sure which language he was speaking anyway. When she thought she might understand a word, it was gone.

Well, it was no matter. She understood her father well enough. He welcomed and thanked everyone for coming, then looked to the priests to bless them.

This was the first test, Nendawagan thought. There had been great consternation from the beginning, when the first non-Aniyvwiya had been introduced to Aktiya Waya. Which spirits did they pray to, and whose ancestors would hear them? She could feel the first crackles of tension pricking the air as the first priest stepped up to pray.

The tension never went away, but it never erupted either, and Nendawagan was able to release her held breath when the prayers were finished. Everything had been kept as generic as possible. The Creator, the ancestors, the spirits, nothing except the animals being specifically named as witness to the tournaments about to take place.

Her father got up to speak once more. She knew he had plenty to say; she'd heard him rehearsing quietly and thinking aloud many times over the last ten days. But whatever it was that he wanted to say now, he evidently saw something in the crowd that made him be a bit more succinct than he'd planned, turning to Hoka who also had a few words to give, proclaiming peace between the two villages and reaffirming Yvgidahi's belief that they were all one people now. Again.

Only the first beat of the drums really dissolved the tension, rapped out even before Hoka had finished speaking. Talk was nice and all, but the people were here for sport and spectacle. Let them settle their differences in their own way, and forget about droll politics for a while. Nendawagan didn't blame them, and even she found herself greatly enthused by the dancers as they made their way into the circle.

Everyone was permitted to drum, sing, and dance in their own way, and this included the regalia. Nendawagan was treated to a grand variety of visual art in every piece the dancers wore, arranged in ways she had never seen before. She found her eyes drawn to each dancer like a mother dragging a child by the hand. She couldn't stand to look away from one person, yet she had to look at the next.

It was a dazzling display, and as far as she was concerned, it could have gone on for the whole festival and she would not have tired of it. She might have been dancing herself if not for the fact that she'd spent so much time preparing the food that she'd had no time to fix up her own regalia, dusty from years of telling herself that she would get around to mending and adding to it. Watching the dancers now only added to her shame, and she resolved that she would get on that chore and have it finished before the next festival.

The dancing finished up, and her father got up to speak again. Looking around at the crowd, Nendawagan could almost believe that they were a single, unified people. There was neither frown nor hostile eye to be seen anywhere on anyone. Not a child was crying or fussing, but everyone was mesmerized by the spectacle before them.

No one in Yvgidahi's household had been sure how the idea of a drumming and dancing competition would be taken, least of all, Yvgidahi himself. Seeing how well the opening dances had been received, Nendawagan could see her father looked much more at ease and confidently brought up the idea.

The reaction was startling, akin to what Nendawagan had always imagined to be a cacophony of war whoops as a party prepared to leave for battle, except this was in excitement, or that's what she told herself. The competitive spirit was alive and well among the people, and now it permeated all things, even the drumming and dancing.

"Then so it shall be!" Yvgidahi declared mightily. "We shall count tonight and tomorrow as practice, and then the competition will begin!"

The plan had been for everyone to be dismissed for dinner and the evening routine, whatever it was for a man. Instead, a great majority of the crowd demanded more drumming and dancing, and the dancers themselves were vying for one last routine, now that they knew there was a competition to be won.

Yvgidahi let them have it. More to the point, he didn't have much of a choice because it appeared as though his control over the situation was tenuous at best. Nendawagan couldn't decide whether this was a good or bad sign. A good sign, because the people needed this kind of release and were eager to best their competitors. A bad sign, because if there was too much competition and too little friendly socializing to smooth out the rough edges of failure, well, they weren't using children's arrows for the archery tournament, say it that way.

Sudden fatigue washed over her, but it was only just sunset. She yawned once, then slipped out of the crowd and headed for home. She was alone. Her father would be at the grounds for a while yet. He might even sleep there. Her mother she wasn't sure, but she wasn't worried.

She sat down at the table and reached for Atsvstdi to illuminate the house without having to add wood to the fire. If there was any downside to the cavern, it was that the sun could bake the rocks and turn the village into an oven during the height of summer, with no breeze for even a mild reprieve. But she had the ability to capture the glow of the embers and amplify them, and she spread out the flowers, as well as the wood and bone carvings.

She did not remember fully who had given her which gift, and she felt bad for it. She tried to brush it off a little, saying that the festival was going to be full of gifts and showing off, and if she was really intent on someone, she would remember him.

She leaned back in her chair and stared at the gifts. She'd never been opposed to marriage, but maybe she'd been taking her longer life for granted, trading relief and caution for apathy and disinterest. She was her parents' oldest child and the only one unmarried, not even looking for a husband. It had been easier to put off when her sister was by her side, but she was gone, too, now. Her nieces and nephews were starting to get married. And where did that leave her?

Maybe she should hang around the tournaments a bit during practice, see if anyone caught her eye that she wanted to root for in competition. She sighed and gathered up the gifts before retreating to bed. She didn't know why she waited. She didn't know why she bothered. She didn't know what she wanted. Was this how the men felt, living so securely in Aktiya Waya that there was no way to prove themselves beyond meager existence?

Maybe they all needed this festival and its tournaments, she thought, resting her head on her pillow.

The following morning was a lot less hectic than she'd been anticipating, but then, most of her fears had been quelled with how well received the opening ceremonies had been. She was still alone in the house, her parents nowhere to be seen.

She made her way out of the cavern into the light of dawn toward the tournament grounds, noting how few people were up and about. The campground where Hoka and his visitors were staying was fairly quiet also. There must have been more than one extra dance last night, Nendawagan figured.

Still, there were a couple competitors out in the fields, four or five shooting at targets, half a dozen wrestling in the sand pit. It was impossible to say how many might have been out walking or running the race course.

She found her parents at the dancing grounds. It appeared as though her father had indeed slept there on the grounds. Her mother, meanwhile, was busy preparing to set out the food which would be available to the people as they meandered here and there during the festivities.

"Did you sleep well?" her mother asked, not looking at her as she arranged some plates of cut vegetables.

"Fine," Nendawagan answered. "Did you sleep at all?"

Her mother grinned, still not looking at her. "Some. More than your father, anyway."

Her father, twenty feet away, was sitting on a step, looking like he was fighting sleep.

"Didn't he used to brag about being able to stay up all night and a day and a night and another day?" Nendawagan wondered, smiling.

"Your father isn't as young as he once was, and it's been a long time since he's had to stay up for a night and a day and a night and another day. I know the council meetings can feel that long sometimes, but they're not, not really."

"Ah." She nodded dramatically.

"Are you going to watch any of the tournaments?" her mother wondered, finally looking at her. "I know you weren't sure about competing yourself."

"I was thinking about watching a couple, yes. I don't think I'll compete, though."

"I see. Well, if you go down there now, you might be able to spot a fine young man and have more than a short conversation."

"I've already been down there. Most people are still asleep."

"And that should tell you something about the men who are awake and ready to face the day."

"Like Nocha?"

Her mother gave her a look. "Go down there and talk to someone."

Nendawagan took the out, returning to the archery grounds. She couldn't say what the allure was here, except she didn't have the same interest in the wrestling or racing tournaments. Wrestling might have been good for the young men to prove their strength and test their might, but if there were no wars to be fought, what was the point? Racing might have been good as a way to show one's speed and stealth through the forest, but again, what was the point? What messages had to be run?

Well, there might be a point to the speed, as her journey to catch up to her father had proven, but even that had been accomplished on horseback with the aid of sorceries.

But there was skill and practicality to be had with the bow and arrow, and these were the men and boys she watched.

"These are the men to watch," an older woman a few paces from her said. "Even if they did stay up late last night, they're showing their commitment."

"And if they didn't stay up late last night, they're showing their self-control," her friend standing beside her agreed. "There was a time when dancing was done in reverence, because it meant something. It nourished the soul. It pleased the spirits and honored the ancestors."

"Didn't men compete, to prove themselves in battle and show off to each other and their families, to win their place as a leader among the people?" Nendawagan inquired coolly.

"What's to prove anymore?" the first woman scoffed. "We have leaders, but where are we going? Where are they leading us? No offense to your father—he's a good man—but what are we doing here?"

"You don't enjoy the peace Aktiya Waya has given us? The safety for our children?"

"What children?" The second woman raised a brow at her and she felt her face burn hot. "What shall they do? What is their purpose? How shall we honor the spirits and our ancestors? Are we not meant to be warriors? Why else shall our boys compete here?"

"I haven't heard of too many people volunteering to return to the Old Land," Nendawagan pointed out. "And there are plenty of problems there."

"Bah!" The first woman said, waving a hand. "Politics. Talk. And trickery. Not like the battles of old, when men would sing of their bravery." She sniffed. "My grandfather was a great man, a warrior and a leader in his time who stole dozens of horses and killed many men." She sighed. "My teenage grandson has never seen battle, never tasted blood, never taken a scalp, and he thinks he is going to compete in a footrace to impress a girl."

Nendawagan crept away from the argument, and it appeared as though the old women were growing weary of speaking to her as well. Truthfully, she wasn't sure what to make of it, and they weren't the only two with such misgivings.

She didn't understand how people could argue in favor of war and killing. Glancing at the wrestlers, she wondered why simple superiority of strength and skills was not enough; why was it necessary for one man to kill another? Why was the presentation of a scalp and spoils the crowning achievement of a warrior? For every scalp that a man presented to a girl, another girl was weeping that her beloved had lost his.

Looking around, Nendawagan wondered if the festival would do any real good. If a man believed himself cheated of a victory, would he indeed go after the man who bested him? And do what? Was this festival only delaying the inevitable?

Her father had said that if the people had indeed divided between the sorcerers in Aktiya Waya and the normal people in the plains, fear would eventually overcome the people of the plains and they would seek to attack the sorcerers. Would this festival really be enough to quell that fear? One false accusation of treachery, whether malicious or not, one misuse of the sorceries, whether malicious or not, and the river could run red and feed the Sacred Wolf its first blood in countless ages.

She made a few laps of the grounds, trying to collect her scattered thoughts, chastising herself for getting so worked up over terrible things that hadn't happened yet. More people were out and about, and all appeared to be going well. There was friendly banter, but no yelling. There was boasting of self and demeaning of competition, but no real threats or fighting. All in all, everyone appeared to be having a good time.

She returned to the archery grounds where enough people had now gathered that even if the two old women were still hanging around, there was little chance of happenstance conversation now.

For those who were not competing in the various tournaments, there was another game they played: gambling. This first day, the actual bets were minute, if they were made at all. But there was much discussion, almost entirely among the men, about the odds of this or that competitor. Much ado was made over the straight winning or losing of a competitor, but there were other, more finely-tuned bets taking place as well, whether a runner would win by many lengths or just a nose, whether an archer would use one type of arrow or another, whether a wrestler would have clear victories or only the barest of success.

Nendawagan listened in on these conversations, tried to figure out who the favorites were. She knew most of them, and several times she almost spoke up on behalf of one competitor or another who was not favored highly by the betters. But she refrained. It was not her place to get involved.

Because it was only practice, the competitors meandered here and there as they desired, and many retreated to their homes or tents as the heat of the day grew oppressive. While the gambling talk continued, there were no prizes to be won, and most competitors wished to save their best for when it mattered most.

Nendawagan made her way to the river. After much deliberation and changing of plans, the holding tank for the new irrigation system had been converted into a series of dams, the nearby landscape reworked over several years into a kind of terraced garden. Of course, with the heat, few paid attention to the garden and instead immersed themselves in the ponds created by the dams. Nendawagan sat on the bank and put her feet in, mildly stunned by the chill but pleased with the fast relief. She might have been able to use Udilegv'i ale Uhyvtsa, but because hot and cold had to be kept in balance, it was a challenge to find somewhere for the heat to go.

Once she was cooled, she made her way back home. The deep reaches of the cavern were still cool, but the front half was quite warm, and her home was no exception.

Again she was the only one home, but she was not dead tired this time and instead picked up a bit of leather work to occupy her. It occurred to her, not long after, that no one had approached her with a gift today. A dozen or so admirers yesterday when the plains people arrived, and not a single man turned her way since. Had she somehow repulsed them by the manner in which she accepted the gifts? Had she simply been forgotten? If a man was intent on living in the plains without the sorceries, had he backed off once he realized who she was?

The situation troubled her more than she expected it would, and she paused in her work. Maybe the problem was with her. Maybe today she was supposed to approach those men who had given her gifts whom she'd found interesting. If that was the case, then she needed to get back out there and start making pleasant conversation before the day ended.

First she had to remember which gifts had come from whom. A few she remembered, but what if she'd forgotten someone important?

Well, she supposed, if they were that important, either she would remember them, or they weren't that important to begin with.

All the same, she had to get moving. Setting aside her leather work, she grabbed a necklace, a couple bracelets, and a few other nice adornments, then collected the gifts she had been given the previous day.

It was not quite time for the evening dances, but there was a lull in the activity as practice wound down, not that there was much activity to begin with, in all honesty. Nendawagan tried to decide whether it was a good thing, that there weren't fights or threats or anything similar, or bad, that there wasn't more excitement. Of course, if she didn't know how to act and what was expected of her over the course of this festival, others probably felt similarly.

She decided to simply make a few rounds through Aktiya Waya and then through the visitors' camp. She kept her gifts in plain sight as much as possible and tried to catch the eye of some of the young men. Some she remembered from the gift giving, though she could not recall exactly which gift came from whom. But she played shy and tried to entice a conversation with glances, gestures, and a few times where she intentionally made herself available for approach.

One of the young men took her up on her offer, meandering over as casually as he could manage.

"I'm not only good with a carving knife, you know," he began conversationally. "My nimble fingers are deft with a bow, too."

"Oh, so you're in the archery tournament," Nendawagan said. "I was watching some of the practices earlier this morning."

"I know. I saw you watching, so I went to grab my bow, but when I got to the grounds and was able to practice shooting, you were gone."

"Really? Will you be practicing again tomorrow?"

"I expect so, but maybe not as much. I'm also in the wrestling tournament."

She grinned coyly. "Think you're strong, do you?"

He mirrored her smile. "Well, we're going to find out, aren't we?" He gestured to the many gifts she'd received. "Looks like I have quite a bit of competition."

"Looks like it." She turned. "I'll see you at practice, then."

"Or will I see you? Are you competing at all?"

She paused. "No, but I did help prepare the food. So think of me when you take some."

It was not the most awkward thing she'd ever said in her life, nor the strangest departure she'd had from a conversation, but given the circumstances, she thought it was pretty high up there, and she walked away hoping he didn't see how she was kicking herself for it.

Although the dancing that night was still considered practice, it got the attention of a final round, and there was plenty of gambling talk going on. Nendawagan stayed out of the way, instead serving food with her mother. She saw the young man once when he came by, but there were so many people crowding the table, neither could say much more than a brief greeting. If her mother noticed, which was unlikely anyway, she said nothing of it.

The following morning, Nendawagan was up early again. This time, the competitors seemed to have remembered themselves at the dance the night before and not overdone it, and more were out and about in practice. It also appeared, to her eyes, that there was far more seriousness about them. After one day of comradery and general bragging and lackadaisical showing off, now it was time to pay mind to the actual competition at hand, the spoils and bragging rights to be won. More eligible girls and women were out and about as well, many with gifts and tokens.

Nendawagan found herself wondering if the young man she'd spoken with had given tokens to other girls. She wasn't sure how she felt about the possibility of having competition of her own. She had plenty of tokens, but she wasn't competing. How was she supposed to show off? She was not a stranger, certainly; everyone knew she was Yvgidahi's daughter. Were their affections purely political, then? After all, was she even capable of looking after herself or a family, seeing how she was fifty years old and never entertained the thought of marriage before?

Self-doubt crept into her mind, though she tried to shove it aside. Popokus was only a couple years younger and had waited many years to marry as well. Why should she suddenly be seen as old and decrepit when she still looked so youthful?

The answer came when she spotted one of her nephews practicing in the wrestling grounds, a lanky little boy filling out to be a strong young man. He might not win the tournament, but he would be a formidable opponent nonetheless.

Nendawagan sighed and moved on, heading for the finish line of the footrace. She wasn't especially interested in the footrace, but it was something to watch, anyway. Some walked the course, their eyes scanning the landscape, the ground, the undergrowth, the trees and plants, the rocks. Others were out at a steady jog, some talking to friends in groups, others focused only on their mission to win.

She should have entered in one of the women's tournaments. Skinning and preparing a carcass, well, she'd had plenty of practice. Taking a leather hide and making a pair of plain moccasins, she could do that. Even the dancing, though her regalia did need some mending. Instead, she was only a spectator, watching others compete to make themselves stand out but doing nothing for herself. She'd always told herself it was because she did not want to attract too much attention to herself and so embarrass her father. But was perhaps her lack of flair and attention embarrassing him, too?

Well, there was no time like the present to change, she figured. She might not be able to do much beyond watch the young men in the tournaments, but once the festival was over and everyone had chosen their residence and position on the sorceries, then she would know who the sympathetic men would be and she could make herself more available to them, should they come calling.

Yes, that sounded like a very good plan, she thought, turning away from the footrace and going back to the wrestling grounds to watch for the young man. She wished she could remember his name.

She watched him practice, and he caught her watching. They did not speak to each other, either at that time or afterwards.

She would not say that she felt the tingle of green love and childish infatuation—and she had felt that before, in years past, so she knew what such a thing felt like—but there was some exciting about watching the men and seeing them show off. It almost made her feel important, feel special in some way. Truthfully, she felt powerful. They could wrestle each other until their skin rubbed raw, shoot arrows until their shoulders turned to stone, and they could run until their legs fell off, but she held the final key.

Well, her and dozens of other women. She'd heard a story once about a woman in the Old Land who had come to love the game more than finding love. For years she strung along various men, devising ever more difficult and creative tests, always proclaiming her love and future children to the one who mastered these tests yet always finding a way to avoid making good on her promises. Then one day she found herself old, nearly past childbearing age, and no man would look her way, for they all knew the game and knew it was impossible for them to win.

According to her mother, that woman had been forced to settle for a man so old he died making love to her shortly after their wedding, and the child she bore died only a few years into life. By then, she could have no more children.

Fortunately for Nendawagan, she had not lost her beauty, nor was she in danger of losing her ability to have children in the near future. All the same, she couldn't be so vain or selfish. True, she didn't expect to be married by the end of the festival, but maybe a prospect or two wouldn't hurt.

She hadn't seen Popokus at the festival at all, but she supposed that was to be expected. With everyone down watching the tournaments, it might give her a chance to find some peace and quiet and sleep a bit in between caring for a new baby on top of all her other children.

Although the tournaments would begin in the morning for the rest of the events, that night was the first night of competition for the dancing and drumming, and everyone was in attendance. Nendawagan was late to arrive and couldn't get close enough to see what was going on, though she could certainly hear it.

For as much as her father wanted to bring everyone together as a single people, Nendawagan couldn't help but wonder if something might be lost because of it, if they were truly blended into one. Pink was a beautiful color, but if everything were pink, they would miss out on the stark boldness of red, or the purity of white. Blending yellow and blue would diminish the brightness of the sun and the beauty of a blue sky, but then, without blending them a little, they would miss out on luscious green grass. She was happy to hear her father's language and songs, as well as her mother's, and she found the songs of the other peoples unique and intriguing. What would happen if all of these colors mixed? Was there a way to blend them into something spectacular without losing what made each beautiful to begin with?

Perhaps she was being fanciful. She'd once heard such thoughts called "the paradoxical idealism of women." A woman wanted her sons to be brave and strong, and her daughters to marry brave and strong men. But she also wished for peace. But peace and good times do not beget brave, strong men.

And here we are, she thought.

Like the rest of the tournaments, the judges were made up of a representative of each of the peoples, but a representative was not allowed to judge his own people. She understood the thought behind it—couldn't come up with anything better herself—but it still seemed to be that there were ways that the smaller groups could be unfairly judged.

But that wasn't for her to say as the current song stopped, the drums cutting out sharply after a final, majestic thump, and the crowd began cheering or booing as skill and prejudice dictated.

It was the Oceti Sakowin who had danced, and their judgment appeared to be largely favorable, to the delight of at least half the crowd.

How did someone judge the dancing of another people? Nendawagan wondered. When one's own culture demanded certain beats, steps, rhythms, and so on, how did he judge another culture against his own, or how did he set aside his own culture to judge one he did not understand? Was it straight aesthetic, the sharpness of the steps and precision with which they danced to the drumbeat? Was it the way the regalia may dazzle and accent the dance? Was there any cultural significance of the regalia as it related to the dance, and how did that factor in?

The Oceti Sakowin dancers were dismissed. The next group she could not see and, judging by the single drum and single voice, could only conclude it was one of the smaller peoples, the western peoples of the Old Land. It was vastly different from what she was accustomed to, and she wondered whether this single, small voice would be trampled out by the majority of other peoples present.

She managed to wiggle her way through the crowd just enough to get glimpses of the dancers. It looked like a single family, an older son with a powerful arm and strong voice on the drum, while his parents and siblings made their way around the circle. The western peoples had a love for turquoise, something not yet found on Hlohi, and Nendawagan was willing to bet that, assuming the turquoise was not as common as clay in the Old Land where they were from, this family had been very wealthy among their own. They did not speak more than four words of English between them, so it was impossible to say just what their story was.

Their song and dance was surprisingly well-received, and Nendawagan knew a moment of hope. Perhaps peace was possible, if people could see the beauty in others, that it wasn't all about violence and domination. They were a single people, and they had to work together.

There had been some debate over whether the larger peoples shouldn't be allowed to have several groups participate. In the interest of keeping things fair and just seeing whether this tournament was going to work at all, it was decided that, at least this time, each people would only be allowed one group, one chance at advancing to the next night of competition. The Oceti Sakowin tried to skirt the rule by claiming distinction between the Eastern and Western Dakota as well as the Lakota, but when it came down to it, they decided that they wouldn't have good enough numbers for each group and so decided to consolidate their groups.

The Cherokee, the Choctaw, the Navajo, the Seminole, and the Dakota all advanced. The Lenape, the Apache, and the Iroquois were all eliminated. The Iroquois threw a fit, but apparently decided that they were better suited for victory in the wrestling tournament anyway.

The crowds did not disperse right away after the judging was done, instead freely mingling, congratulating those who were advancing, comforting or ridiculing those who had been eliminated. Nendawagan did not see or hear anything to make her truly afraid that a disagreement could turn into something worse, and she returned home feeling good about the day's events.

Her mother arrived home shortly after her, but they were both surprised when Yvgidahi appeared not long after them.

"I would have thought you would be out with the others half the night," her mother said lightly.

"Ah, I need to rest and be ready for the tournaments tomorrow," he replied. "Practice is good to have fun, but things really begin to matter tomorrow."

"You're not a judge," Nendawagan said.

"No, but I want to be there and see everything. And I don't want to fall asleep in the middle of it."

"Are you looking for something in particular?"

"Peace," he told her. "And hope. That this endeavor is not in vain and we can truly become one people."

Nendawagan nodded and excused herself to bed. She was still wide awake from the excitement, and she lay there staring at the ceiling for a long time, wondering. She wondered about the tournament as a whole and each of the events. She wondered about the people and who would leave with Hoka when it was all over. She wondered about the young men who had given her gifts and spoken to her, if any of them would be victorious—or even just halfway decent—in their events. The next four days were going to be long, she knew. She just hoped the trouble was worth it.

Chakkali Tushafa

Tournament

There was so much going on in the festival that Ola Achukma wasn't sure what he should pay attention to first, and this wasn't even considering his own projects. And yet, when he thought about it, he couldn't figure out why he was so overwhelmed. The Oceti Sakowin had come to Aktiya Waya, as promised, apparently bringing everyone with them, down to the smallest babe. There had been opening ceremonies with the surprise addition of the dancing and drumming competitions. Then there were the two days of practice.

Perhaps his nervousness came from his role as interpreter. For the sake of the festival, he'd chosen to do everything straight arrow the first night, for the opening ceremonies. After that, he'd decided to try and weasel in a few of his invented words, see how people would respond, if at all. Would they recognize this word or that word, so close to their own yet just off? Or would they assume it was some other people's word? Would they think him an idiot, that he couldn't manage it? Would he get any credit for trying, considering how many languages were present, some that he was entirely unfamiliar with?

Yvgidahi did not say anything about it to him, nor did Ihya. This bothered him the most, he thought, leaving the house and making for the race course in the early morning light. He wished for feedback, to let him know whether to continue on or change his approach.

Well, he supposed, Yvgidahi and the others had more pressing matters to attend to than a teenage boy's fumbling with language. Today was the first day of real competition, when competitors could be eliminated for poor performance. It was expected that not everyone would advance to the next round, but who wanted to admit to being so poor as to not last through even a single day?

At the start of the race course, Ola Achukma, arriving with some thirty other men and boys and still with more to come, sized up his competition. They averaged between thirteen and thirty-five years old. Thirteen was the youngest allowed to compete in the festival tournaments, though there were several younger boys there, perhaps to cheer on their brothers and fathers. There were also a few men of slightly more age, the eldest appearing somewhere around fifty winters.

There were few rules associated with the race. Stay on the course, no cutting corners or taking shortcuts, and no intentional sabotage of the other runners. Ola Achukma happened to know that some of the twelve year old boys, were posted as lookouts at various points along the course.

There was one last rule, one that applied to all of the tournaments: no use of sorceries. For the race, the primary temptation would be to conjure Time. The runner himself would continue to move at his own pace, but he would condense Time so that it would appear as though he ran faster.

This would be the point of contention, Ola Achukma knew, if there were any questions about the racers. After all, who would want to admit to being so poor a man as to lose out on the first round of competition? And what if he failed in the first round at all three sports, if he were participating in all three?

Well, there was nothing he was going to do about it. He was showing promise in Touch, and he thought he was getting a hang of Galo'ondiha ale Agi'a, but he had virtually no experience with conjuring Time. On the other hand, if someone thought him a threat, they might conjure Time around him, then accuse him of—

No. He shook his head as if he might clear it. He couldn't allow himself to become so paranoid. He was here to run a race and prove himself. Prove himself to whom, he did not know, but prove himself.

Maybe he was just nervous because it was the first event, the first elimination. And who wanted to be so poor of a competitor that he couldn't even last past the morning?

Few were worried about the judging at the finish line, for it was whoever crossed first that was the winner. Of the sixty-two runners, the last twelve would be eliminated. It was the part in between the start and the finish that made people nervous, hence the spotters.

Ola Achukma met with the official judge to let him know he had arrived, then took his place in the starting ring, a roped off area big enough to contain the sixty-two runners and let them strut and show off to the girls, make promises about being the fastest runner in the world. The course itself, at least to start, was enough to allow about ten men abreast, depending on their size. Having walked the course, Ola Achukma knew that there were some places where that breadth narrowed considerably so that it was little better than single-file, and there was one stretch toward the end that was a large open meadow, perfect for passing at the last moment.

He spied his mother for just a moment, mixed up in the crowd. He also spied a couple of girls he'd tried and failed to talk to the last couple of days. He managed to make eye contact, and he saw one whisper to another, pointing at him.

Then the call went up for runners to be ready. The runners tore themselves away from their girls and wives, and the crowd quieted just enough for the judge to make his way to the starting line, where the roped off ring gave way to the course which was marked with brightly-dyed horsehair.

"Get ready!" the judge called.

Some competitors got in low stances, others bounced on their toes. Ola Achukma took a breath and let it out slowly, forcing himself to relax.

"Go!"

Instantly, five boys, about thirteen or fourteen years old, shot out at a dead sprint, clearing the first fifty yards of open course and disappearing into the trees just as the bulk of the group was moving. Ola Achukma heard one of the older men, about forty years old, say, "They'll be puking before they get to the first hill."

Ola Achukma fell into the middle of the group and let it carry him along into the trees, snaking this way and that, making the first turn up the first hill, dirt giving way to gravel and then to hard stone. The trail narrowed and the shouldering and shoving began. Ten men abreast turned to eight, then five, then three.

At the first peak—by no means the top of the first hill, but close enough—they did indeed find two of the sprinting boys. One had slowed to a walk, pale and gasping for air, and the other was puking up his breakfast. Ola Achukma slipped by them, skittered down the slope on the other side, then started up the trail to the top of the first hill where a third boy was also looking quite ill as he crawled along.

The course itself started just outside the bowl of Aktiya Waya and moved west, the first hill peaking about a quarter of the way up the wolf's tail where it then dipped low, only to rise again before leveling off along a ridge for a time, then turning sharply to the south and dropping headlong into the forest to twist and turn its way through the trees and the slopes before returning to the finish line.

The fourth sprinting boy had given up halfway up the second hill, his face streaked with tears from the vomit he'd left some distance back, and he stumbled along. Ola Achukma said nothing to him, instead glancing at the spotter, hiding in a bush, looking like he wanted to help the sick competitor but knowing he couldn't unless he chose to forfeit the race.

He wasn't one of the best runners, but as they again sorted themselves out on the ridge, preparing for the plunge into the trees, Ola Achukma found himself at least in the top twenty, and he was confident that, short of a haphazard fall or some sorcery mischief, he would not be eliminated today. Up ahead, he spied the fifth sprinting boy just dropping off the ridge and speeding into the trees. Unlike his companions, he did not appear ill or hindered in any way by his explosive start to the race, except that maybe he had been a little too quick too soon.

Ola Achukma was glad that the race was the first event of the day, for the ridge was terribly exposed. The sun was just barely over the jagged horizon, but the heat was noticeable, even now. He had little desire to run this course over hot rocks in the afternoon, feeling the light and heat reflected off the mountainside just beside him. Even with the archery and the wrestling, there was a chance for water between matches, but out here, there was nothing. There was the start, the finish, and what they did in between was their own business.

He reached the horsehair marker and turned south, carefully dropping down a few ledges before hitting dirt and leaves and racing into the trees. The exhilaration was wonderful, though he knew he had to be careful lest he trip and fall and hurt himself. Looking off to the side, another competitor had done just that. He was scraped up from a tumble, but what had really stopped him was his ankle bone sticking out of his foot which was twisted quite the wrong way. One spotter was giving him water, and Ola Achukma stared just long enough to see that another had gone to fetch a healer, a woman who carried a bag of supplies for just such an occasion.

He passed them by.

The course swung hugely to the east, the slope making a rhythmic gait difficult to maintain, and he passed another runner who was older and favoring a knee.

The course was less obvious now, the horsehair markers more of a general guideline or a suggestion, placed here and there on low limbs. Finally the trail leveled out and Ola Achukma saw the meadow up ahead with a dozen men crossing it. It would be his last chance to overtake more than one at a time.

As soon as his legs brushed the tall grass, he pushed himself, trying to imitate the sprint the boys had done at the beginning, but without the puking. A few surprise brambles tore at him, but he forced himself not to stumble or lose speed. He passed only one racer in the meadow, but he'd caught up to the group at large.

Up ahead, he could hear the din of activity, and it only grew louder as they approached the finish line. By the time he saw them through the trees, the sound had changed, and he knew the first runner had crossed. He'd never imagined that he would be the fastest, but it was a little disheartening all the same.

The exact placement of runners was unimportant, with exception of the clear winner and the twelve lagging at the end, which included four of the sprinting boys and the one who put his ankle through his foot. For Ola Achukma, he came in the group of eight that basically all crossed at the same time, ranging from fourth to eleventh place. But he wasn't last, and that was all that mattered.

They crossed the finish line, exhausted and sweaty, slowing their pace and wandering off in different directions to meet their families, the girls they were trying to impress, or just get water. Ola Achukma took water as it was handed to him, seeing afterwards that it was Chilita who had given it to him.

"You did well," he praised. "You did well enough to advance to the last day, even."

"Yes, well..." Ola Achukma breathed, "I have to do it again tomorrow and the day after that in order to get there."

"I'm sure you'll be fine. You're still young."

They watched the last of the racers straggle in. The older man who had been favoring his knee managed to edge his way into the next race, but not by much. Looking at him, Ola Achukma briefly wondered if the man was going to forfeit his position to the man who had come in only steps behind him and didn't have a bad knee. But the older man had his pride, and he was going to keep it.

"At least you get a rest now," Chilita was saying as they turned away from the race. "The wrestling is next, followed by archery."

Ola Achukma said nothing to that, just followed his stepfather to the wrestling ring where he was competing. Obviously his stepfather was already married, and there was a short reprieve between events so competitors could find a moment to eat, drink, and rest before potentially going straight into their next competition.

Or to talk to girls, which is what he should have been doing. He should have gone to find those girls who had been whispering and pointing at him. He probably still could. He wasn't obligated to watch his stepfather compete or bring him water; his mother should be doing that.

After a moment or two of batting it back and forth, he got up from where he'd collapsed into the grass and set about searching for the girls he'd seen at the starting ring. He hoped they weren't planning on leaving with Hoka and the others. He rather liked the sorceries.

He paused in his search. Maybe he should wait until after the Oceti Sakowin had left and see which girls didn't mind his use of sorceries. That seemed logical.

He returned to the wrestling ring where the matches were just being announced. For the sake of time, four would be going at once, moderated by judges, switching out just as soon as a match ended.

Ola Achukma found his mother in the crowd, and she was searching for her husband to see which ring he would be in. She spotted him as he was entering, and naturally it was the one directly across from where they were standing.

It didn't take a genius to figure out that the boys would have little chance against the more experienced men, but they competed anyway. Chilita was paired with a fifteen year old boy. Ola Achukma suspected that his stepfather allowed the boy to get in a few moves just to boost his confidence, but he still won with ease once he decided he was going to, slamming the boy hard into the dirt.

With the number of competitors in the wrestling, each competitor only wrestled once the first day. The second day they would wrestle twice. Then once on the third day. Then as many times as needed on the final day until there was a clear victor.

When Chilita climbed out of the ring, Ola Achukma and his mother were there to meet him. Apushi was handed off to Ola Achukma while their mother tended to Chilita who'd hardly broken a sweat except for the growing heat of the day.

"Why did they pair you with such a young boy?" she asked. "It was hardly a challenge for you."

Chilita took the water she offered, and she took Apushi back from Ola Achukma. "I think they just wanted to weed out the weakest of us first, that way we're not sitting around all day on the final day."

"Wouldn't it have been better to arrange things by age?"

"And in the end, you would have a fourteen year old wrestle a forty year old?" Chilita shook his head and took another drink. "No, it's better this way. It teaches the boys." He looked at Ola Achukma. "What did you learn, from watching?"

"I notice that most of the boys go for the shoulders, but the men go for the hips."

"Exactly. The arms and hands cause problems, but in order to topple a mountain, you must remove its base. The hips, the knees, even the ankles if you can manage it. But the hips provide a solid grip, and you don't have to compromise yourself to reach."

Ola Achukma nodded. Before he could say anything, there came the first cry of foul play from the ring.

A skinny seventeen year old was on the ground, leaning back on his elbows. Ola Achukma could not say what people he was from, but it was one that didn't speak English well. The sentences were a mix of his own language interspersed with wretched attempts at English, but the only clear word was "sorceries." He looked up at his opponent, a bear of an Ojibwa perhaps forty years or so, as he yelled and pointed.

Ola Achukma's mother put a hand on his shoulder and whispered, "You're the interpreter. Go out there."

"I don't know what he's saying," Ola Achukma protested.

"Maybe, but your presence might help calm things down."

She nudged him and he reluctantly entered the ring, sliding past the other matches which had stalled. Gingerly he approached the teenager still on the ground. He didn't look terribly injured, just a bit dusty, but he was quite angry, yelling at his opponent and the judges who had gathered.

"Hi," Ola Achukma began awkwardly, squatting beside the young man.

The young man stopped yelling long enough to realize he was there, studying him and evidently trying to ascertain his intentions.

"Ola Achukma," he introduced. "I'm the interpreter. Sort of." He repeated. "Ola Achukma. Chahta."

The young man spit. "Chagga." Well, he knew what that meant apparently. Still, he relented. "Hospoa, Hopi."

"Hopi?"

"Hopi Pueblo."

He didn't know that language, hardly even a guess for the pleasantries. Still, Ola Achukma tried to appear pleasant as he asked, "You speak English? English?"

Hospoa searched his face, then answered, "No. English. Me. No. English." He sighed, then pointed at his opponent again. "Sorceries."

"Sorceries," Ola Achukma echoed.

"Sorceries. He..." The young man looked terribly distressed at the lack of communication. He picked up a small rock nearby, tossed it in the air and let it fall, then pointed at himself. "Sorceries." He repeated his action with the rock, then gripped Ola Achukma's wrist in a terrible grip.

"What's he saying?" one judge asked.

"He's saying that you—" He looked at the Ojibwa man. "Used the Galo'ondiha ale Agi'a sorcery on him, to keep him in place and stop him from moving."

"That's impossible!" the Ojibwa man protested. "If he could not move, then how did I beat him?"

It was a fair question, one that Ola Achukma poorly tried to relay. Whether it was a mistranslation or a false accusation to begin with, Hospoa scrambled to his feet, looking like he was spoiling for another fight, for real this time. He faced the Ojibwa man with fire in his eyes, then finally turned and stormed off, yelling in his own language and not caring who heard.

"No one saw any evidence of sorceries," the judge offered uselessly. "Misko, you are the winner of the match."

It felt like a long time before Ola Achukma was able to move and leave the ring, and the matches resumed only gradually, with much whispering from the gathered crowd.

And so it begins, Ola Achukma thought. *The accusations of sorceries and cheating. Will this festival last? Will this tentative peace survive?*

"You did well," his mother said, not looking at him but keeping her gaze firmly fixed on the matches.

"I barely did anything," he told her.

"How many people were out there just now?" Chilita inquired on his other side.

Ola Achukma blinked and shook his head. "I don't know...a dozen?"

Chilita grinned. "No, I mean, how many different peoples. There's you the Chahta, the Ojibwa man, the Pueblo man, the Cherokee judge. It doesn't matter so much that the dispute was not resolved, for not all disputes can be. What matters more is that you worked together to try and solve it. At least three of you did."

"But he accused the Ojibwa man of cheating, of using the sorceries."

"Cheating is cheating, no matter how you do it. Whether you took a shortcut through the forest during the footrace or the man used sorceries, it's still dishonest."

"But the sorceries are a skill not everyone has."

"It is only knowledge, Ola. Everyone is welcome to this knowledge. Just like knowledge of a shortcut."

"The sorceries are good, though. A tool. A shortcut is, well, a shortcut."

"And under normal circumstances, no one cares what path you take through the forest to reach your destination. That shortcut is also merely a tool. Under normal circumstances. But here, everyone wants to compete at the same level with only raw skill. Therefore, it does not matter whether everyone knows of the shortcut or everyone knows the sorceries, because it is dishonest to the sport."

Ola Achukma mulled this over and finally nodded. "I understand."

"Good. Why don't you get something to eat before the archery competition?"

He wandered off, leaving his mother and stepfather to watch the rest of the wrestling. He understood what Chilita was trying to tell him, but he couldn't help but feel that he should have done something more. Maybe he should make more of an effort to learn the lesser languages of Aktiya Waya. He might have better luck incorporating them into this cockamamie plan Ihya seemed to want him to accomplish.

He got a small snack, then returned home to grab his bow before making his way to the archery field. Seven targets, all lined up. Seven archers at a time would be given three arrows. Only the top three in each round would continue. There were over one hundred competitors in this tournament, so the cuts had to be a little brutal in order to find a winner in just four days. An old man might not be fast, and he might not have the strength and endurance to wrestle another man, but if he still had a good arm and a true eye, he could still win glory for himself.

Ola Achukma glanced around at those who were already present. Some had just come from wrestling and were sweaty and exhausted; some were bragging about how great they had been in their respective matches. Others inspected their bows for the dozenth time that day. Still some inspected the arrows, their expressions saying that they were looking for any cause of cheating: a split shaft, poor fletching, improper fletching, tampered arrowheads, anything at all. Still a few were not inspecting the arrows so much as watching those who were inspecting the arrows to make sure they weren't tampering. And still a few more inspected the targets, whether for tampering or to make sure they would hold up for four more days Ola Achukma did not know.

The cheating accusations were far more subtle here than at the wrestling tournament, though his attention was taken more by the bags, and the thought that they should have made a few more. They had made seven plus another seven for the final two rounds, and Ola Achukma had made two more extra bags, just in case. Looking at them now, he figured he should have made another seven. He debated whether it wouldn't be possible to make more tonight. Would he have time? Would there be some accusation of cheating if he made new bags, if some archers had new bags and some didn't?

He elected to say nothing about it and see what happened. Worst case scenario, they could paint targets on the frames themselves and shoot at the frames.

When the wrestling was finished, the judges made their way to the archery fields. There was no rhyme or reason to which archers went first, just whoever got out there first to make a round. There was some strategy to this, Ola Achukma figured. If there seemed to be an easy field, comprised of younger boys, a man could have an easy shot at moving to the next round. But wait too long, and you could be stuck with a field of seasoned archers and no chance of advancement.

Naturally the younger boys, the thirteen and fourteen year olds, wanted to go first, to prove themselves and, perhaps as a matter of strategy, guarantee a spot in the next round. A couple of the older young men, around twenty or so, took advantage of this to sweep a field, and Ola Achukma saw plenty of disapproving looks from the rest of the competitors, no matter their people.

He waited until the field was comprised of competitors his own age before going out, heart hammering. The footrace was easy; anxiety could be channeled through the body and produce more speed. Here it would only cause his arm to quiver and his hand to shake.

He took three arrows and stabbed two of them in the ground beside him.

"Center target!" the judge called in both English and Cherokee. A younger boy went to the center bag and pointed to the appropriate target.

The competitors drew their arrows and aimed for the center target on the bag, some fifty yards off. It was the largest target, and only one of the competitors missed, though not by much. Once all had loosed their first arrow and the boys at the end of the field had steadied the bags, the judge called, "Top left target!"

The young boy went out again, pointed to the target, and dashed back toward the judge. Then the competitors loosed their arrows.

There were five targets painted on the bags. With only three arrows, an archer had to be ready for anything. There was only the slightest breeze in the bowl, just enough to keep the air from becoming sticky and stale, but over a fifty yard field, it could make a big difference. Ola Achukma was pleased to see his second arrow struck the target, although just barely.

"Bottom left target!" the judge called.

This target was much smaller, and Ola Achukma would say that it was only luck, or perhaps a passing breeze, that allowed his arrow to strike as well as it did, about half in and half out of the painted circle. Two competitors missed the bag completely, coming up short, and two more missed the painted target.

Ola Achukma let out a breath as he was confirmed to advance to the next round the following day. The boys at the end of the field gathered the arrows and he stepped away from the ground marker so another could take his place.

"You did wonderful!" his mother said when he found her.

"I didn't think I was going to make the last one," he admitted.

"Well you did, and that's all that matters. You'll be competing again in both of your events tomorrow!"

He nodded and said nothing more. They turned to watch the rest of the tournament, especially Chilita as he joined a field around his own age. He had some trouble, only just eeking out the next competitor to be able to advance. When he returned to them, he did not look happy with himself.

"You made it," his wife offered hopefully.

"Only because the other man struck his finger on his string and tweaked his arrow. Otherwise I would have been outdone," Chilita scowled.

"You don't know that."

Chilita did not look convinced but said nothing more.

At least neither of them were knocked out in the first round, Ola Achukma thought. That had to count for something. He didn't know what, but something.

That evening, they watched the next round of singing and drumming competition, pleased that the Chahta were advancing to the next round.

The following morning, Ola Achukma was up early again and heading for the race course. It didn't seem much different than the day before, for they'd only eliminated twelve runners. The remaining fifty seemed to have expanded to fill their space in the starting ring. Today the field would be cut nearly in half, eliminating the slowest twenty runners. The next day would whittle it down to fifteen for the final race.

Ola Achukma wasn't too fazed from the run yesterday, not like some of the older runners who looked like they might be favoring a sore knee or aching hips, but even he knew that he was not invincible. He would start to really feel it, maybe as soon as tomorrow.

Today there were no stupid boys to dash off at a dead sprint as soon as the start was called. Ola Achukma wondered if that had simply been the arrogance of younger boys, or if it had been a plot by the fastest boy to eliminate his friends by challenging them to a foolish competition he knew he could win. Today that boy remained at the head of the pack, keeping several paces between himself and the next man.

Again Ola Achukma elected to remain within the general mob, only pushing when they got to the narrow parts of the first hill. When they got back into the open, jogging along the ridge, he noted that several others started crowding him. A couple pushed ahead, edging him out just before they dropped off the ridge and went speeding down the slope into the trees.

Not wishing to put his ankle through his foot like the poor soul the previous day, Ola Achukma was a little more careful about his descent, and it cost him several spots. He was able to make up a few places once they reached the meadow, but as they darted into the trees again, he was feeling very precarious in his position. Up ahead he could hear the people cheering for the first returning runners, and he knew there were plenty between them and him. He didn't think there were thirty ahead of him, but the irrational part of him said there were.

He was number twenty, or thereabouts, just edging into the next round. As he was standing there, cooling down and trying to catch his breath, he happened to notice he was standing near Yvgidahi and Adahi. He was close enough to hear their conversation as they watched the runners come in.

"Remember when we were younger, and we had to run from Itsa'ti all the way to the Lower Towns?" Yvgidahi was saying.

"Oh, when we went to intercept Saloli?" Adahi wondered.

Yvgidahi nodded. "Vv. Day and night, just running. We stopped once when we finally found Saloli and had to treat with him, but then, just running. All the way to Nagutsi' and then even farther to Taliwa."

"You remember better than I do."

"No, I just have the Book I read every once in a while."

"And what do you look for?"

"I look at what was written about my brother, the guidance Gvnagadoga gave him, see if I can't find some wisdom for myself in these times."

Adahi scoffed. "Well, for starters, we might try running the boys more. You speak of running day and night—I remember it, too—and here we're teaching them...what? Ten miles is difficult? And it's mostly flat, too. Comparatively speaking."

"Vv, but where shall they run to?" Yvgidahi countered. "We were running to save our people. This is only sport."

Ola Achukma turned away and left the finish area, pushing into the crowd. Ten miles wasn't the most difficult run he'd ever done, and a good portion of it was downhill, but he couldn't imagine running day and night, scrambling over mountains, with stakes far higher than personal glory.

He'd only ever heard of the Book, this thing that Yvgidahi kept squirreled away in his home. Supposedly it was an account of the life of himself and his brother in the Old Land, how they helped to save the people and bring them to Aktiya Waya. Supposedly it had simply appeared one day with no explanation whatsoever. Opinions were divided over it, about along the same lines as opinions of the sorceries. Was it a good thing, meant to help them and guide their way? Was it yet another remnant of a hated people without whom they somehow could not survive?

Truthfully, Ola Achukma wished to read the Book, but he dare not say so aloud, and he was too unsure of himself and paltry in his sorcery abilities to feel right about asking. Maybe once he learned more, he would ask.

He found his mother at the wrestling ring where some of the runners were already migrating. There were two rounds today, to cull the field a little more. Chilita was up early in one of the first four rounds going simultaneously. Unlike the previous day, his opponent was no young boy trying to impress a girl, but a man of about his own size and strength, and it was a terrible challenge. Several times Chilita went to a knee, but he managed to come back and get his opponent on the ground.

The second round was no easier, Ola Achukma thought, watching his stepfather face the large Ojibwa man who had been accused of cheating the previous day. He was older than Chilita, yes, with gray peppering his hair, but this did not diminish his physique in any way, except to make him look that much more formidable.

Chilita put up a good fight, no one could deny that, and their match became the spectacle with several side bets being made. He used his smaller size to his advantage, and he knew enough about leverage that he was able to make the man go to a knee on four separate occasions. He just didn't have enough to get the man to go down all the way, and he was summarily eliminated from competition.

"You fought well, my friend," the Ojibwa man said, releasing Chilita and offering a hand.

"And you," Chilita said, taking it and getting to his feet.

They clasped wrists before Chilita made his way out of the ring, his posture proud, his expression sullen.

"You did well," Ola Achukma's mother told him, handing him some water.

"I was eliminated," Chilita stated, sitting down. "How does that look to my wife who now has to look upon all the stronger men? And what does it teach my sons that I am only a mediocre man who is stronger than half and weaker than half?"

"It teaches me that in order to win, I shall have to wrestle bears, for men are too easy," Ola Achukma told him.

Chilita grinned and took a drink of water. "Maybe. So then, once this festival is over, we shall have to find you some bears to wrestle."

With the wrestling over and Chilita eliminated, they headed over to the archery field where Ola Achukma managed to stay in play, but only because there was finally an instance where cheating via sorcery was proven. One of the archers had figured out how to use Galo'ondiha ale Agi'a in order to overcome the breeze and guide his arrow to the target.

He was immediately eliminated, and his name was spread among all the competitors and all the spectators that he was a cheater and not to be trusted.

Only by his elimination was Ola Achukma pushed up into the field of winners and allowed to compete the next day.

"I'm going to be eliminated tomorrow," he lamented to his mother as they headed to the dancing grounds. "In the archery. I'm only continuing because of a technicality."

"Don't say that," she scolded him. "Anyone can have a bad day."

"They're taking the field down to fourteen tomorrow. A lot of people will have to have a bad day for me to get in."

"If you tell yourself you're going to fail, then you will," Chilita told him. "Just like archery, you hit what you're aiming for. Aim for success, and you will get success."

It was a nice sentiment, but much harder to put into practice. But Ola Achukma did not say this out loud, merely nodded and carried on.

He could still brag about it, he supposed. He'd made it to the semi-final round in the archery tournament. Technicality or not, that was an accomplishment. There had to be some girl out there who would be impressed with it. Not everyone could be expected to win; it was literally impossible.

If there was any consolation, it was that the Chahta dancers and drummers also advanced to the final round, to compete against the Cherokee and the Seminole.

The next day, the fifth day of the festival and the third day of competition, Ola Achukma managed to advance to the final race, though he really couldn't say how, except, perhaps, the others were feeling it a little more than he was. His legs were hurting even before he made it to the ridge, and he couldn't keep a steady breathing rhythm going, not like on the first day.

But for as proud as his mother was over his accomplishment, he couldn't help but notice the disapproval from some of the elders, all of them from the Old Land. It wasn't that he himself had advanced and someone else had not, but they feared for the future. Those in Aktiya

Waya were soft, they said. Even those originally from the Old Land were now soft (those who had been eliminated even more so!) because of oppression from the white men as well as the comforts Aktiya Waya afforded them. What would their ancestors think if they could see them?

It was not an encouraging thought, but there was nothing he could do except carry on as he was.

As he expected, he was soundly eliminated in the archery semi-finals, and no amount of bending the rules was going to get him in, not unless everyone else was proven to have used sorcery or cheated in some other way.

It wasn't that he did poorly, either, really. He hit the bag every time, and he hit the target every time. But by this round, that just wasn't enough. Precision was key, and when one person could not be judged as being more precise than another, the judges went by who had loosed his arrow first, as this meant that he had a faster, sharper eye. Ola Achukma was not the most precise of the group, nor the fastest, and he was sixth of the seven archers in the round.

"Maybe later you can redeem yourself by hunting down something for dinner," his mother told him.

"I will do that," Chilita said. "I think he needs to rest before the final race tomorrow." He gave Ola Achukma a look. "I can see that you are tired, and your legs are sore."

Ola Achukma wanted to accept the offer and let Chilita go out, but, remembering the disapproval of the elders, shook his head. "No. I'll go. I'll just have to be so precise that I do not need to chase anything."

He hurried off before they could object, not that he expected they would. He was basically a man now, and he couldn't be babysat like a child. He had to provide for his family. In truth, he probably should have spent more time looking for a few girls to impress. Catch their eye, give them tokens, try to show off that he was a good man and a good match.

It wasn't too late for that, he supposed. Unlike the first day of competition, where plenty of aspiring young men were humiliated in front of their girls by being knocked out in the first round, he had something to brag about. He was one of the finalists in the footrace.

Against those who were older than him, against those who were younger than him, against those who were considered more talented than him, against those who had come from the Old Land and boasted great physical superiority over him, he was a finalist.

And he had at least made it to the archery semi-finals. That had to count for something, right? He didn't have to mention that it had been a technicality that got him there.

He got a couple of rabbits for dinner, gutting them in the forest and taking them home for his mother to skin.

"It's too bad you didn't enter into the women's competition," Chilita commented. "You dress that rabbit faster than any woman I know."

"You know many women and watch them dress rabbits, do you?" Her tone was teasing.

Ola Achukma left the house. He wanted to find a wife of his own, but he didn't need to watch them.

He went to watch the dancers instead, and then he watched as a rather displeased crowd was told that the Cherokee dancers were the winners of the competition. Despite the Cherokee judge not being allowed to participate in his people's judging, and no proof of sorcery use (though how that would help, Ola Achukma did not know), there were accusations of cheating as well as rigging.

Ola Achukma backed out of the crowd, but continued to observe, and he found himself whispering a prayer.

"Please, God, don't let this peace fall apart before it's even been built."

He wondered if anyone heard him, and he wasn't thinking of spiritual eavesdroppers. Any spirituality outside of the accepted ancestral practices was suspect at best, and whispering a prayer to the God of their tormentors was not a way to calm down an angry mob.

The good news was that, ultimately, nothing became of it, at least not that night. There was plenty of yelling, talking over each other, and a majority of the crowd left greatly displeased. From what Ola Achukma could gather, in tidbits of conversation as everyone returned to their tents or homes, it wasn't so much that the people wanted the

Seminole or the Choctaw to win, as they just wanted the Cherokee to lose. They wanted the ruling class of people to be knocked off their horse.

But they were supposed to be one people, Ola Achukma silently lamented. The festival was supposed to be a way of pitting man against man as equals. And yet, every night they gathered to show off their differences and strut their individual feathers. Had it really been a good idea? Sure, it had been meant as a way for each people to show off the best, most creative, most spiritual parts of themselves, but had it really done so? Or had it only brought out the envy and hatred of the rest of them?

The following morning, the final day of competition, Ola Achukma was awake early and heading to the race course. In previous days, the spectators had been family, close friends, a few interested girls, and obsessive gamblers making bets. Others might wander in and out of the crowd as they were curious or had the time.

On the final day, it seemed as though there were some unwritten rule that attendance was mandatory. Everyone seemed to be there, and Ola Achukma found himself truly nervous for the first time. He was tired. He was sore. The elders already looked disapproving for it. How would it be if he came in last? Even if this was the final race, he couldn't come in last.

Once everyone was gathered in and the racers indicated that they were ready, the judges bade them go to the starting line.

Just one more race, Ola Achukma told himself. This is the last time you have to come to the starting line. The last time you have to run this course.

"Go!" the judge yelled.

There were no sprinters here. Indeed, the start of the race was rather mundane. They were all feeling it. The elders were disappointed because of it. Ola Achukma tried to take this knowledge and use it to push himself, tell himself to be better and not give in to fatigue. Yvgidahi and Adahi had run day and night over hills and through valleys because they had a mission, a danger to confront.

But there was no mission here, nothing beyond a footrace among men. There was no danger to be found, except perhaps at the end if someone dared to challenge and accuse another of cheating.

His motivation cooled, Ola Achukma remained in the middle of the pack, again pushing only when the course narrowed in the hills, and again through the meadow for the final push.

He finished fifth, two steps behind fourth, but still not the winner. A Dakota man took the honor of first place, and he launched into a grand speech about how he was as fast as the wind and as strong as the buffalo. Ola Achukma had never seen a buffalo, not a live one, anyway.

There was much cheering and congratulating, and quite a bit of arguing as bets were collected or refused to be given up. Ola Achukma glanced at the elders, the council, trying to guess their thoughts. Most were happy to congratulate the runners, but the rest just continued to stare with that sullen, disapproving silence. When he finally made eye contact with one of them, the whole brooding lot stood and departed the finish line.

We came to Aktiya Waya to live and keep our traditions alive. We put on this festival in order to foster peace. Are the two really mutually exclusive?

Pàke Tèlën

One People

To the casual observer or passively interested spectator, one might have said that the festival and the tournaments was a smashing success. A few arguments here and there, but that was to be expected.

For Nendawagan, her father, and others who had made a point of being involved at the higher level of organizing the event, even without competing, that success was questionable at best, and wishful thinking at worst. There were many accusations of sorcery use, and when some turned out to be true, it only drove a wedge between her father's people and Hoka's people. And Nendawagan hated to think of the people in such terms when the festival was supposed to bring about peace and understanding.

This wasn't even considering the debacle that was the dancing competition. She'd thought it was the one competition that would go smoothly, once she saw the excitement of the first night. Perhaps she'd been a wishful thinking fool. The rage she'd witnessed when the Cherokee dancers were announced as the winners was stunning, something she never anticipated. She'd watched Dakota men cheer for the Navajo dancers. An Ojibwa man volunteered to drum for the Iroquois dancers when their drummer was injured in wrestling. And suddenly the crowd of spectators turned and became what could have been a violent war party.

"It wasn't that they wanted this people or that people to win," her father explained later once they were safely home. "They just wanted the Cherokee to lose."

"But why?" Nendawagan wondered, tears streaking down her cheeks though she did not cry. "If we are supposed to be one, unified people, then—"

"Yes. But it is not about equal freedom and equal opportunity, but equal pain and punishment as well. If one man strikes another man, it is not enough for the first to promise to not do it again and treat the second man fairly for the rest of his life. The second man wants the first man to know his original pain."

"But we don't treat others unfairly. We have tried to be accommodating. You and Hoka could have been killed because of a lie, and we could be at war today. Yet here we are, enjoying a great festival and many tournaments. I have no argument with anyone here, for I have not treated anyone unfairly—"

"Perception, Nendawagan," Yvgidahi interrupted. "If a man thinks he has been treated unfairly, he will react accordingly. It does not matter what was, only what he thinks was."

Nendawagan searched her father's face. "Then we need to make people think this was a good idea. We need to make them think that things went well, exactly as intended. We need to make them think that nothing bad happened."

"No," her father cut in. "You can change a man's mind, but you cannot change the truth. We cannot lie and say nothing bad happened, for there were wrongs committed. This is known. But you are right, that we must make people believe that this was a good thing, and that we are leaving on happy and peaceful terms. This is the goal of the closing ceremonies."

"I don't envy you."

"Few do, I think. But that is all right. You worry about other things, like all the young men who came to call on you during this festival."

Nendawagan blushed.

"And another thing," he went on. "You can't go around looking sullen and anxious. It was understandable the first day or two because we did not know how things would work out. And I saw you lighten up a bit as the festival went on. But now you need to be happy. If I am telling people that the festival was a great success, my family cannot assume a posture that says otherwise. If I appear dishonest, then this whole festival was dishonest, and we won't get Hoka and his people back again easily."

"Then they are still leaving."

Her father sighed. "The festival was not about convincing Hoka and the others to stay. It was about convincing them to remain peaceful with us because of it, and attempt to forge an alliance."

"An alliance against whom? Against what?"

"Ourselves."

She wanted to ask more questions, but knew it would be pointless. She may have had a keen interest in politics, and she may have been involved more than most women, if only because of her father, but she was still a woman. Unless she was part of the women's council, she could do little to sway things.

"Don't worry, Nenda," her father said gently. "You are the reason we are having this festival and not sending out war parties. That fact is not lost on anyone who matters. There may have been arguments and disagreements. And, yes, there may have been instances of cheating and sorcery use, but it is simply life. Good life. Now then, keep your chin up, and be happy that it went well."

Nendawagan sighed but nodded. "To make men think that this was a good idea."

Her father's expression was gentle. "Because it was."

She retired to bed shortly thereafter, but lay awake for a good portion of the night, wondering. Was it really a success? Had this incident been a fluke?

The winner of the footrace was a Dakota man, and no one protested.

The winner of the wrestling tournament was an Ojibwa man, and no one had any problems.

The winner of the archery tournament was a Choctaw man, and no one batted an eye.

Among the women tournaments, a Cherokee won the carcass dressing competition, but more than three-quarters of the competitors had been Cherokee, so it was difficult to determine the mood of the rest.

Was it really as her father had said? Did the others really not care who won, as long as the Cherokee lost? What about the half-bloods and mixed-breeds, like her? If she had entered a competition and won, would she be hailed as a Cherokee or Lenape victor? She considered Ola Achukma, whose father was white though he'd been adopted by Chilita as his own son. Would anyone have been upset if the boy had won a tournament; she knew he'd made it to the final footrace. Would he have been a Choctaw or a white victor?

When the time came for the closing ceremonies, Nendawagan didn't know what to expect. It was supposed to be similar to the opening ceremonies, where all the peoples drummed and sang their songs and sent out their dancers in flashy regalia. How would things change now that the Cherokee dancers had won that competition? Would they be scorned? Would it matter? Would people cheer and simply wish for it to be over?

Nendawagan had watched the end of the first footrace and witnessed a man—too far back to make it to the next round but determined to finish anyway—sprinting toward the finish line, only to trip over his own feet and fall. He wasn't injured beyond a few scrapes, and he picked himself up so he could trudge across the finish line like a whipped puppy, dusty, bloody, and humiliated. She had an image in her mind of the festival doing something similar now. Things had gone so well. Had they tripped up right at the very end? Would they simply bow their heads and meekly accept that the festival had happened and now they needed to go their separate ways?

As she approached the grounds, she had to remind herself constantly to keep her chin up and look like she was having a good time. She had to honor her father and not call him a liar, whether in word or posture. He wanted everyone to have happy memories of the festival and tournaments and encourage peace.

Looking around as the people gathered, the atmosphere was fairly positive, she thought, and she was glad to see people freely mingling. Women laughed. Men bragged of their standings in the various tournaments or promised to outdo one another next time.

Nendawagan found herself heartened at the thought, that people were already planning for another festival and tournament. If they could encourage such thoughts, then victory or defeat could be found in the wrestling ring and not on the battlefield.

Not everyone was happy, certainly. A few angry patrons did not even make it to the ceremonies, instead preferring to pack up their things so they could leave just as soon as possible. She spotted a man, Navajo or Pueblo she wasn't sure, who had been ousted in wrestling and accused his opponent of cheating. The accusation was dismissed, but he didn't look like he was ready to forgive the ruling just yet. It probably didn't help that the man he'd accused had gone on to win the wrestling tournament.

And there were a few other disgruntled competitors, or wives of competitors, glaring at the gathering from afar. Nendawagan told herself to pay them no mind, but it had taken only two men to try and start a war between the peoples. There were certainly more than two angry competitors.

But there are plenty of happy competitors or families of competitors, she told herself. This was a good idea. Look and act like this was a good idea.

She turned her gaze from the angry people and pressed into the crowd. She congratulated the competitors, male and female, and talked to some of the twelve year old boys, promising them a chance to win their names in the tournament next year.

"Will there be a tournament next year?" one boy asked, as if she hadn't just said that very thing.

"Of course there will," she told him, trying to sound sure of herself. "How else are you going to compete and impress girls?"

The boy made a face at the mention of impressing a girl. Nendawagan laughed, mussed his hair, and moved on.

There was plenty of that, too, she saw. Eligible young men and women now mingling, talking, laughing, blushing, getting to know one another, their parents also speaking and trying to work out whether it was a suitable match.

She spied several of the young men who had approached her at various times throughout the festival. A few were talking to other girls.

A couple shied away, knowing they had done poorly in their events.

The last one she spotted did not get a chance to speak to her even if he had wanted to, for at that moment, the drums started up. All attention turned to the dancing grounds as the final ceremonies began. Nendawagan's heart lurched into her throat, and she hoped her smile was convincing to those around her.

The head dancers from all the groups formed a line across the circle to lead the cleansing walk, joined by the priests, elders, and various council members, including Hoka and his council. Once they had completed a lap of the circle, the dancers joined them, entering the circle in the order in which they succeeded in the tournament.

The Cherokee went first, and Nendawagan noted that there was a bit of indignation among the spectators. They wanted to get excited for the ceremonies and honor their leaders, but they couldn't forget what happened the other night at the competition.

Nendawagan breathed a sigh of relief when excitement won out. Maybe it was the people accepting the ruling and deciding to be happy— unlikely—or the appearance of the Seminole dancers, who had taken second place. Whatever the case, the moment of tension passed, and the people were happy again.

With that fear alleviated, Nendawagan found she could more easily project the joy her father expected of her as the leaders of the group stopped at the east point so all the dancers could file in uninterrupted. When this was done, there was almost no room left so that there appeared to be no beginning or end to the circle except the presence of the eagle staff held by the head priest. They made another lap of the circle. The crowd was going wild with the same innocent energy they'd had during the opening ceremonies.

The circle completed, the leaders began filing out, the priests and councils and dancers with them, like a snake uncoiling itself. There was a length of time of simple excited conversation from the crowd. Nendawagan watched her father take his place on the overseeing platform, Hoka and others with him.

They did not speak immediately, however, instead sitting back to relax and watch as each group got one last chance to perform and show off. Again they started with those who had been eliminated first.

When they reached the Cherokee dancers, there was far less hesitation, but Nendawagan could sense it was still there. It would have been strange for the people to suddenly stop cheering, but it was just a bit more reserved, she thought, an obligation rather than true goodwill.

But there was no violence, and that was all that mattered. Nendawagan wasn't sure what else her father had planned for the closing ceremonies, as far as dancing went, but for the moment, it was put on hold so he and the other leaders could stand and speak. Ola Achukma joined them to interpret as best he could.

Yvgidahi welcomed everyone back and thanked them for being patient and willing to help one another.

"I know it came as a swift surprise," he said, "like a storm that boils suddenly on the horizon. And we had to choose how we were going to respond. Would we abandon our brothers and fend, selfishly, only for ourselves? Or would we tie our fate with the fate of others, understanding that we are but one part of a greater whole?

"Being a greater whole does not mean that we are all the same. Shall everyone be an eye upon this body? Then how shall we hear? Shall everyone be a hand? Then how shall we walk and move forward? Everyone has a part to play, but it is not the same part. We all have our strengths and weaknesses. And we must work together, to bolster our strengths and cover our weaknesses."

He looked out at the crowd, deliberately making eye contact. "No one here would stab himself in the belly and claim that he is stronger for it. No one here would cut off his hand and claim to be better with the bow, or cut off his foot and claim to be a better runner. We are here now. We are. Together. As one people.

"I cannot command everyone here to like each other, any more than I can command the sun to rise or set. Indeed, it is an impossible thing. Even among our own families, we have our differences and arguments. But just because I have an argument with my wife does not mean I send her away. Or that a disagreement among council members means that it is a failed endeavor. No, we work together, we work through it in order to return to harmony. That is what we must do."

He paused, as if searching for the right words. "But even as we recognize that we are one people, one body with different parts and different roles, we also recognize that the ear is far from the foot. The eye is not attached to the hand.

"Hoka, the Oceti Sakowin, and others of you, have decided that the use of sorceries is not appropriate for you. That is all right. One does not use a shovel with his feet or his teeth, and the hands wish no ill will upon them because of it. We all have our tasks, our role to play. We cannot all be a hand."

He glanced at Hoka who had stood up beside him. "While it saddens me to see you depart, know that we are not your enemies, and we wish no evil upon you."

Hoka dipped his head graciously. "Thank you, Yvgidahi." He looked out at the people at large. "We are one people. We may not like it, we may not have wished for this when we were children or young men, but it is what we have become, as a caterpillar changes into a butterfly. But what we cannot become is a cancer that eats at the flesh of this tender young body.

"Let it be known, then, that we are one people, but two clans. Aktiya Waya will be Wolf Clan, guarded by the Sacred Wolf. The people of Anpa O Wicanh'pi will be Deer Clan, as we live on the vast plains."

He paused to let the people whisper among themselves. Truthfully, it was more than a whisper, but Nendawagan heard no yelling or shouts of outrage. Probably people were too stunned and trying to figure out what this meant. The clans were everything. Daily life revolved around one's clan. The clans were absolutely critical in the planning of marriages.

"Let it also be known," Hoka went on, "that each clan shall look after itself, as it has been. But if any man should strike another, whether within his own clan or another, he will be dealt with as a cancer upon the body. Only a cancer harms the body. For a hand to damage the body to which it is attached, it harms only itself."

By now, the stunned whispers were growing into something more. Questions and confusion abounded.

"How shall we marry, with only two clans?" one young man asked.

"Who shall be the keepers of children, of herbs and healing?" another woman wondered.

"Who will be our elders and storytellers?" a third man inquired.

"What about our people and families in the Old Land?" a fourth asked.

But for all the questions, neither Hoka nor Yvgidahi gave any direct answers at that moment.

"Each clan will have its own council," Hoka went on, quieting the crowd. "And it will self-govern as it sees fit. All members will conduct themselves according to the rules of the clan. As it has been. There shall also be a council of the people. Once a year, at this great festival, that council will meet to discuss issues. Hunts. Exploration. Things regarding the whole people."

"Does that include bringing more and more people here, or does 'Wolf Clan' get to decide for us?" a disgruntled man near Nendawagan grumbled.

There were a few more minor points, but then Hoka informed them that there would be clan council meetings in order to address specific questions.

The questions and confusion probably could have gone on all day, which was probably why they made the announcement first, Nendawagan figured. It was easier to move on and distract the people by presenting the winners of the various tournaments.

A Dakota man called Matho was the winner of the footrace, and there was much ado over his presentation from Hoka's group. Was it just pride on the part of the newly-formed Deer Clan, or did loyalty remain firmly along Oceti Sakowin lines? Well, of course the Oceti Sakowin would be proud of him. Nendawagan would never believe that such loyalties could be reforged at the command of another.

The Ojibwa man, called Miskwaadesii informally and Misko by his friends, was the winner of the wrestling tournament, and it was no wonder how. Nendawagan knew he'd been accused of cheating, but she couldn't figure out why. A man of his size would have no need to cheat. If he hadn't already been married, she knew there would be no shortage of women looking at him. Even though he was married, she still spied a few women trying to catch his eye.

A Choctaw known as Luksi won the archery tournament. Unlike Matho who was somewhat slender, or Miskwaadesii who was more bear than man, Luksi did not appear to have any especially defining qualities except, maybe, strong arms and tight muscles across the shoulders. Nendawagan found herself staring and wondering if he was already married.

The men were spared no praise from those gathered. They did not receive any physical awards or commendations, but their names and faces were well-known. Any apprehension over the clan and council announcements was forgotten for the time being.

The men were given seats of honor on the platform and another dance was done. Actually, three dances were done, one from the people of each man. Was that antithetical to the proclamation of the new people and the new clans? Nendawagan thought so, but she had no say in how things were done.

When those dances were finished, the winners of the women's tournaments were also presented. It seemed to Nendawagan that there was no reduction in cheering because they were Cherokee, and she perceived no ill will toward the dancers when they appeared to honor the winners.

The winners were presented one more time to even greater fanfare, then dismissed. Three more dances were done, and then it was time for the final feast.

The tournament winners were crowded by friends, family, and adoring fans. Matho was happy to entertain any and all female marriage prospects, and he seemed as much a charmer as any of the girls who fawned over him. Miskwaadesii made sure to keep his wife close in order to ward off some of these girls, but his disposition said he was no stranger to such attention, and he had no problems boasting of his wrestling prowess and other significant exploits.

Luksi was apparently not married, for he did not mind the attention he received, though he was less comfortable with it than Miskwaadesii. Nendawagan tried not to stare, did not want to linger like some of the girls, but she did want to speak to him. She skirted the edge of his attention, trying to ascertain whether he was staying in Aktiya Waya or leaving with Hoka. That would have a profound impact on her level of interest.

At several points during the festival, when she thought about looking at one man or another, she'd told herself to wait and see who stayed and who left with Hoka. Looking at the young men like Luksi, who had girls looking at them and who were looking at girls, she found herself a little annoyed, even jealous. Did no one look her way? Apart from those young men who had simply cast wide nets, did no one look at her specifically? Had no one competed in order to impress her specifically?

Annoyed, Nendawagan suffered through the rest of the night with a forced smile, congratulating the winners and the other competitors who had been edged out by them.

"Did you enjoy it?"

She turned to see Popokus approaching, her smile more genuine.

"What?" Nendawagan asked dumbly.

"The festival, the tournament, all of it," her sister said. "Did you enjoy it? I know I haven't been around much for it, but I liked what I saw."

Nendawagan gave her sister a look. "You're already married, Popokus. You can't be looking at these young men."

Her sister laughed. "I know. I might have been looking for a man for you if I knew what you liked."

She sighed. "I'd like a man who was staying here. What good would it do for me to get to know someone here, only to watch him leave Aktiya Waya tomorrow?"

Popokus conceded the point. "Well, that is true. But think of it this way: that road goes both ways. Maybe some of the young men were holding back because they didn't know which girls were staying either."

Nendawagan gave her a look. "I'm Yvgidahi's daughter. Why wouldn't I stay?"

Her sister shrugged casually. "According to Guka, you acquired quite a collection of tokens."

"Many of them boys just hoping to get noticed at all, hardly anything serious. Others looking elsewhere now."

Popokus sighed, clearly unsure what to say. Then she brightened. "Well, it's good to see you taking it seriously now. I'm sure Guka will be happy to hear that you're finally looking for a man."

She wandered off to speak to someone else. Nendawagan watched her go. Had her sister come to her of her own volition, or had their mother had a part in it? More to the point, was she serious about looking for a man? She'd collected tokens, talked to at least a couple of the young men, and she wouldn't deny the jealousy she felt when she saw some of them with other girls. Was she serious, then? After decades of general apathy toward the subject, was she ready to be serious about it?

The festivities lasted long into the night, and it was nearly dawn before she returned home with her mother. If her mother could sense her frustration with how things had turned out, she evidently thought it best to wait until they'd both had a good night's sleep. That was fine. Nendawagan didn't want to have another discussion about finding a husband, especially since she wasn't entirely sure her sister had been innocent about their conversation earlier.

She returned to her collection of tokens. Some she'd already discarded, whether because the boy was too young or because she'd learned he intended to leave Aktiya Waya and forsake the sorceries. She discarded a few more now, tossing them into the fire. Mostly these had been the young men who had barely looked her way, or not at all, at the closing ceremonies. If they couldn't be bothered to follow up on their own gifts—not for meekness, as their jovial mood and conversations with other girls had proven—then they didn't deserve the honor of her interest.

That left two tokens, neither of whom she could remember their bearers. One was a buck deer carved from wood, the detail rather exquisite. The other was a tanned rabbit's ear with bone beads woven inside. She could close her eyes and recall receiving the gifts. She could recall speaking to the young men. But their faces eluded her. One might expect that she would remember the giver of the rabbit ear, for it was the only one she received, but perhaps she'd been too enamored with the gift to remember the giver. She felt shame over that one.

Whoever it was who'd given it to her, he'd gone to a lot of trouble to decorate it with beads. And, being unique, maybe he hoped it would make him stand out. Of course, a lot of work went into carved the little wooden deer, too.

Nendawagan found herself oddly distressed, and she wasn't sure how to feel about that. Normally she just came home and went straight to bed. Oh, she'd had a few fleeting fancies over the years over this or that boy, but now she was genuinely concerned. And she felt terribly guilty over many things. Not remembering the young men. Favoring the rabbit ear over the buck. Favoring the buck over the rabbit ear. What did she do now? What if these young men were leaving tomorrow?

She went to the middle room and sat down at the table. Her mother was asleep and, not two breaths after sitting down, her father walked in the door. In the dim firelight mixed with the faint light of dawn, he looked exhausted but hopeful.

"I didn't expect you to be awake," he said, sitting down himself.

"I didn't expect so either," she admitted.

"What do you have there?"

She showed him the tokens and explained her dilemma, watching as her father's expression turned amused.

"I don't know what's happening to me," Nendawagan told him. "I wanted to stop the war, yes. I wanted peace, I still do. But where did this —?"

"You're growing up is all," her father said, grinning. "The sorceries slow our aging quite a bit, but we still age. We still mature. You have simply matured and outgrown your stubbornness to remain single, at the same time you might have if you had not embraced the sorceries and aged naturally."

Nendawagan blinked. "But...Popokus and Moskimus and—"

"They had the instinct and desire in them from an earlier age. That's all it is." He was still smiling. "We do not teach sorceries to the children because they are unprepared to handle it physically, emotionally, or spiritually. And because mothers wish for their children to grow up someday. How should it be for a six year old child to be six years old for ten years?" Even Nendawagan smiled at that. "When a child becomes an adult, that is when they may choose. But that doesn't mean they stop maturing, or that where they stop aging is where they stop learning or growing or becoming who they are meant to be."

"Why am I so late, though? I have nieces and nephews who will be getting married in the next few years."

"I don't know. It is simply how things are. Maybe because you are also more open-minded than some, and there was great animosity among the people when you were a child. They simply weren't ready for you yet. But now, with you stopping the war and bringing about this festival and this change for the people, maybe now it is."

Nendawagan blushed and smiled. "Wado, Nocha."

"And maybe there is some merit to the young men being able to show off to you in a way that isn't violent."

She blushed harder and he grinned. They sidled off to bed after that, and Nendawagan found that she was able to sleep soundly.

Because of the length of the closing ceremonies and everything else, most everyone ended up sleeping in until about midday, so when Nendawagan finally got up and around and made her way to the slope outside the cave, she was able to watch Hoka and the others pack up their camping tents and gather at the path into and out of the bowl.

This did not bother her so much as seeing how many from Aktiya Waya were joining them. She knew that not everyone liked the sorceries or approved of them, but she had kind of hoped that even if someone didn't use the sorceries that he might be able to live side-by-side with those who did.

Apparently she thought wrong. Now that Hoka had broken open that door of life without sorceries and without those who used them, a good number of people were walking through, walking away. If they'd ever had any misgivings about how to potentially house new refugees from the Old Land, well, that problem seemed to have been miraculously solved. She wasn't the best with numbers, but if she had to hazard a guess, she might say that Aktiya Waya's population was about to drop to around a hundred, nearly a fifth of what it had been only a few moons ago.

"Your father was telling me about your kindled interest in men and marriage," her mother said, walking up beside her.

"Looking at this—" She gestured to the great mass of people migrating toward the passage into and out of the bowl. "—there won't be any men left for me to take an interest in."

"Oh, of course there will. Do you think everyone who is going away is staying away?"

"That's why they're leaving, isn't it?"

Her mother gave her a look, one that said she really ought to know better. "A child leaves because his parents make him. This is expected. A young woman goes because her family is leaving, because she is unmarried and cannot stay here on her own. A young man goes because his family will need protection on the road and provision in the new settlement, which, if you are correct, is about to grow tenfold from what it was. It will need help to build up successfully. Others may be going only to ensure their safety and will return once the people are delivered to their new home. The elders go to ensure social and cultural stability; whatever happened here, in this festival, will fade and the people will need guidance to avoid division and bloodshed.

"But a young woman down there reciprocated a token from a young man here. She will expect him to continue his advances, even if it means journeying many days and miles to prove his dedication. Because he lives here, among the sorceries, she will have to return with him.

And a young man down there fancies a girl here, but, as I said, he needs to protect his mother and sisters first. Once they are settled, he will return to woo his intended lover and join her when she is ready for him.

"Similarly, an elder who has spent his life in Aktiya Waya may return to be buried with his family and establish himself in the vast sky among the others who have gone before us here."

Nendawagan sighed. It all sounded so very logical. Why hadn't she thought of that?

"It is not as hopeless as it may seem," her mother continued. "Instead, you should be glad that so many are willing to go and help those who are leaving. If we are one people now, then we must be willing to assist our people, wherever they may go, whatever their needs are." She put a hand on her daughter's shoulder. "Give it a moon or two. Some will return."

Nendawagan was still uncertain, but she nodded and went down the slope, making for the crop fields to help with the day's work. With so many people leaving, the crop fields suddenly looked comically large for such a small population. With so many women leaving, the amount of work each of the remaining women had to do increased dramatically. Considering the heat of the day, no one was enthusiastic, or even mildly agreeable.

Elsewhere in the bowl, the men worked to clean up everything from the festival. The targets were taken down, the bags riddled with holes and leaking stuffing. The frames were disassembled and put to other uses. The crude fencing erected for the wrestling tournament and the starting ring of the footrace was moved to the animal pens, sectioning off an area for a couple expectant mares. The dyed horsehair markers for the race course were gathered and given to women for use in some project or another. The extra tables and other erections for the dancing grounds were also disassembled or moved for other uses. They wouldn't have to seat five hundred people in one place anymore, only a hundred or so.

By the end of the day, the bowl within the protection of the Sacred

Wolf looked exactly as it had only a moon before, just a little emptier perhaps. Nendawagan was saddened by this. For an apprehensive as she had been about it, for all the shenanigans, for all the uncertainty, she had, overall, really enjoyed it. It felt like the first truly unified thing they'd done in a very long time, perhaps ever. No one had to pretend to be interested in the festivals, ceremonies, and rituals of another people. It was every man trying to prove himself as himself. A single man, not a people, won the footrace. A single man, not a people, won the wrestling. A single man, not a people, won the archery. Yes, there was the incident with the dancers, but overall it had been good. A good thing.

She told herself this repeatedly throughout the next moon, as she walked empty streets in the village. It was a good thing. A good thing. There were no more arguments, no more fighting, no more subtle hostility. Everyone had their personal space now and could breathe and have their own opinions about the sorceries without being cramped in such close quarters. But they were also close enough that if one or the other needed help, it was only a few days away.

But what help would Wolf Clan need of Deer Clan? What help would they need that the sorceries could not provide? How did they keep from drifting apart, other than a single yearly festival? Her father was right. The generations of Deer Clan would age and die, and Wolf Clan would live on. What stories would be told about them? What legends or paranoia would they come up with? Had they only delayed the inevitable?

Nendawagan took a breath and told herself not to get too far ahead of herself. For the moment, there was peace, and she ought to be grateful.

She breathed another sigh of relief a little over a moon later when the first people started returning from Deer Clan. Some had indeed gone as protectors, to ensure that the people were not picked off while homes were built and the village secured. Others had gone as carpenters, to fashion the poles that Deer Clan used to support their tent-like homes. Still some had gone as hunters, to bring in enough meat to feed the exploding population as well as enough furs and leather to cover the tipis.

But in the end, they were Wolf Clan, and they returned to Aktiya Waya. Not all of them used the sorceries to any great degree, or even any lesser degree, but they had no problems living with those who did.

"How will things change?" Nendawagan asked of her father one evening. "Are we still going to make expeditions to the Old Land and bring people here? Are we simply going to send people to Deer Clan if they decide they don't want the sorceries?"

Yvgidahi sighed. "For the time being, at least through the winter, maybe even all of next year, we are going to suspend expeditions to the Old Land. We need to figure out exactly how this is going to work. You're right, not everyone is going to embrace the sorceries. But Deer Clan is large; most villages do not survive well beyond five hundred people. But in order to maintain cohesiveness as a single people, we can't simply bring a bunch of people here and hope that they respect our ways. We don't even have those ways firmly established yet; there are still many divisions."

Nendawagan searched her father's face. "Do you think it was a bad idea, then? To bring a bunch of refugees here?"

He shook his head. "No. It is never wrong to help those in need. I think we erred when we simply expected people to accept what was going on and live life in peace as we know it, without understanding where they are coming from or what their customs, traditions, and experiences may be. For some, the change was minimal, and they accepted it better. For others, well, we cannot simply drop people into a new world and expect them to just go along with it."

She nodded. "I understand."

"There is no singular fault, and no singular answer. We just have to trust that things will work out for the best."

"What about all the people who are suffering in the Old Land? You obviously hear more news than I do, and everything I've heard isn't good."

Her father sighed and shook his head. "You're right. It's not good. But we have to learn from our past mistakes. We survived this encounter with dissent, among Hoka and the others, but we cannot make the same mistake twice." He smiled and put a hand on her shoulder. "Don't worry. We will not be idle this next year. With a little luck and a little providence, we will be able to save more people through proper planning than a foolish scramble."

Nendawagan considered this and finally assented.

"Now then," he continued, "say no more about it. There is nothing to be gained by worrying."

She hesitated but nodded. "I understand."

"Good. Now tell me about this boy you're looking at."

Nendawagan raised a brow. "What boy?"

He shrugged. "You tell me."

"Nocha, there isn't a boy."

"No? That's not what your mother said." He looked at Mesim who gave him a look. "She told me you were looking at a boy, though she wasn't sure which one."

Nendawagan sighed dramatically but couldn't help but smile. "There isn't a boy. I may have been looking a bit during the festival, but I wanted to wait and see who was leaving with Hoka. Then some of them decided to stay away a little longer, either because they are staying with Hoka or because they have not returned yet."

Her father nodded. "I see. And who was the boy you were watching who left?"

Reluctantly, she retrieved the rabbit ear token from her room. "I don't remember who gave it to me, and that's part of the problem."

Yvgidahi took the rabbit ear from her and examined it, saying, "Well, I can tell you he was not Ayvwiya." He handed the ear back to her. "Tsisdu is a trickster, and a rather dishonest one at that."

Nendawagan studied the ear, the soft fur and the beads woven inside. Without looking at her father, she asked, "If the Aniyvwiya considered the rabbit a trickster, and the people this boy was from did not think the same, what do our new people think? What stories should the elders tell the children about the rabbit?"

Her father shifted uncomfortably and asked, "What do you think of the rabbit?"

She shrugged. "He is a small, fast, furry animal who eats leaves and grasses and likes to burrow. And he is particularly tasty when added to a thick stew."

He laughed. "Yes. He is all those things. And from these things, does it matter whether he is a trickster?"

"It must, if it let you know that this suitor was not Aniyvwiya, for he did not believe the same thing about the rabbit as you do. Who would wish to give a girl a token of trickery and dishonesty?"

She could see her words compelled her father to thoughtfulness, for he did not answer or speak for a long time, long enough that she grew tired and announced that she was retiring to bed. No one stopped her.

Would the rabbit be a trickster, or not, among the new people? The eagle seemed to be the ubiquitous ruler, but what about other animals? What about the animals of Hlohi that were not found in the Old Land? Tsuyoniyvgi were likened to deer, except there were also common whitetail deer in the forest, brought over from the Old Land. And what about the animals that did not have such clear-cut counterparts? What would their stories be? What was their role in the world?

If they were to be truly unified, they needed a common thread, a common history, a common heritage. But men were proud. As her sister had asked so long ago, who were they to tell one people that their story was acceptable and tell another people that their story was not? Why should the rabbit remain the trickster? Why should it change?

More importantly, who was going to tell these stories? Her father had said that when the Aniyvwiya first arrived in Aktiya Waya, his brother who had been a priest with exceptional insight, declared the site so old that not even ghosts walked here anymore; all that remained was the Sacred Wolf. But he had also said that there were other Great Ones around this world. Could they learn anything about these Great Ones, their songs and stories? The priests had pieced together a little bit, from ancient relics left in the homes, but they needed more.

But who would be the ones to make up these stories? Who would be the ones to tell them? Who wanted to pass off a fiction as the truth?

Someone who wants to save the people, Nendawagan decided.

Someone who sees peace as the greatest goal. Someone who is also a man.

She thought of Ola Achukma. He'd risked a lot by accusing the older warriors of treachery, and he had done so in the name of peace. He'd also worked hard at the festival, acting as an interpreter as best he could, dealing with languages and people he barely knew. And he had done well in the footrace, too.

Nendawagan sighed. He was a good boy, but still, only a boy. Despite her appearance, she was quite a bit older than him. Perhaps, as he learned the sorceries, this would not matter in the future, but for now, he was still only just sixteen or seventeen. Maybe in a few years, if she hadn't found someone else. Or if he hadn't found someone else. The thought gave her pause as she considered the tokens, the young men, wondering if the fault had been hers for not finding even a single potential suitor during the festival. Her excuse about waiting to see who left with Hoka felt terribly petty now.

She wanted to figure out who had given her the rabbit ear, but it would be terribly embarrassing to go around and ask. Such an elaborate, thoughtful gift; why couldn't she remember who had given it to her? No, she would have to find out some other way. Maybe she could observe young men as they gave out tokens, or young women as they made adornments and decorations, see who used rabbit ears in such a way. It would be a start, anyway. Or maybe her father would ask around to find out who his daughter's secret admirer might be.

She fell asleep that night with visions of rabbits dancing through her head.

Awahachoffa Tushafa

Migration

Ola Achukma watched Apushi pretend to hunt a stuffed rabbit, sneaking up on it with his stick, then leaping on top of it and clubbing it to death. The older brother happened to know that Chilita was planning on giving Apushi his first small bow in the next few days, "just as soon as the ice breaks in the pond."

Ola Achukma was glad to see his brother growing up. He was glad to see his enthusiasm for hunting and exploring. The young child simply accepted the world into which he was born, believing that everything he saw was how everything had always been and how it was supposed to be. The older brother's worry, then, was reserved more for himself.

As soon as the ice and glass proclaimed twilight, Ola Achukma took Apushi by the hand and led him to the townhouse, handing him off to their mother and waiting for the meeting to start.

"What news?" Yvgidahi asked the returning expedition.

"As bad and worse than we feared," Unitsiya reported. "There is no negotiating, there is no compromise, there is no chance for peace. The Aniyvwiya, the Creek, the Seminole, many others, all being forced to move. Move or die. There is no other option for them."

Ola Achukma found his mind unwelcomingly flooded with memories of his childhood. The rocky road, the storms, the river crossing, the starvation, the cold. He looked at Apushi, glad that his little brother would never have to know such horrors.

"Last time, they offered citizenship and other things, other ways," someone said, eliciting hesitant murmurs of agreement.

The warrior shook his head. "Move or die. No contracts, no citizenship. All peoples are being moved en mass. Hundreds, thousands at a time."

The first time was only a test, Ola Achukma thought, to see how much of a fight we would give. And we didn't. It is just as the elders said it would be.

"When do they expect to start moving the people?" Gokhos inquired.

"The end of summer."

That turned the murmurs into an uproar as everyone tried to voice his opinion at once.

"Are they trying to kill the people?!" someone demanded as the volume slowly died down.

Yvgidahi answered, with a casual nod and shrug, "Yes."

His simple reply prompted another round of angry shouting which no one tried to quell immediately. Then, once the blind fury abated, it turned into blurry, mismatched opinions of how the situation should be rectified. Some wanted to go to war themselves, others wanted to quietly arm the people of the Old Land but stay out of it.

"What do the skiagvsta and elders of the Old Land say about this?" someone wondered, the first rational voice to make itself known.

"There are no skiagvsta," Unitsiya said flatly. "There are no skiagvsta, no uku. The Aniyvwiya, and all the others, they are nearly unrecognizable from what they once were. They do not keep the old customs and traditions, do not speak the language or sing the songs. The only thing separating them from the Americans is their skin color and parentage, and it is for this reason that they are being moved."

"And they accept this removal from their ancestral lands?" another man asked.

"Many protest, but what can they do? A few have arms, but they are being stripped of those as well. Others see it as a chance to settle in new lands and live how they want."

"They promised the same thing fifteen years ago!" someone piped up, half a breath before Ola Achukma could say something similar. "They promised freedom and sovereignty fifteen years ago, or even longer, and they have yet to honor that agreement!"

Shouts of agreement.

"Who cares?!" someone said, bringing the whole gathering under a heavy blanket of uncertain silence.

The voice belonged to, of all people, Adahi, and even Yvgidahi was stunned into silence by, not only his outburst, but his words. The advisor looked around the room a moment before speaking again, his words deliberate.

"When we first came here to Aktiya Waya, we were just hoping for survival. We brought the elders, women, and children, to preserve the people and preserve our future. That's all we wanted. In time, we opened our doors to others, those brought low by conquest and war. To preserve the people and preserve our ways. Maybe my language was different from your language, maybe my songs were different from your songs, but we were all one conquered people, even if we had many years of uncertainty and infighting. In the last seven years, since the War That Was Not, we are finally becoming one people, the people Yvgidahi imagined we would be.

"We are not the same people who came here long ago. We are not the same people who came here fifteen years ago. If we brought in any one of our ancestors from five hundred years ago, they would be as foreign to us as we would be to them. And we are still very close to our ancestral ways. We have worked hard to preserve our traditions, even if we have had to alter them in the name of peace. And never have we allowed a white man to join us, or impose his will on us.

"If the people of the Old Land are simply Americans with dark skin and undesirable relatives, and if we bring them here, are we not allowing the white men to dictate how we as a people live and change? Every culture our ancestors saw, they assimilated or accommodated. And they assimilated and accommodated their way to Aktiya Waya, and the western lands of the Old Land. Who assimilates into us?

"Every time we bring people here, even as soon as fifteen years ago, it has been harder and harder for those people to assimilate because they are further and further removed from their ancestors. You know my words to be true. How much harder will it be now? What if something more happens in another fifteen years? Or fifty?"

Adahi paused, but no one dared to do more than breathe evenly. Then, "They are not the people they once were, whether they are Aniyvwiya, Chahta, Lenape, or anyone else. But neither are we the same people. We do not go to the Old Land to take part in their council meetings, to decide where to hunt and where to raid. We have not consulted the Old Land for anything in decades. We have been here for several generations now. We are our own people. I think we ought to act like it."

The silence stretched on so long, the only reason Ola Achukma did not fear spontaneous deafness was the crackle of the fire in the middle of the room.

It was Yvgidahi who spoke first. "You are proposing we abandon the Old Land entirely?"

Adahi met his gaze. "I am."

There was another long, uncomfortable silence, and it seemed to be that everyone might decide to just leave, Ola Achukma thought. Oh, the idea had come and gone as reports from the Old Land came and went, most often with bad and worse news, but never had it been given such a strong, steady voice and a well-versed argument. And from Adahi of all people. The look that the advisor got from the skiagvsta was not one Ola Achukma could describe well except, perhaps, betrayal.

Finally Yvgidahi shook his head. "I don't think that would be a wise idea. Distant relatives or not, they are our brothers, our blood. And they are in distress."

"The Americans oppress their own," someone in the crowd said. "They oppress their slaves. Should we free a multitude of slaves because one of them might have a great-grandfather who was one of our people?"

"The justification they give for treating the people this way is the same reason we must save them."

"Should we free the slaves, then?" someone else echoed. "If we are one people, and we are separate from the Old Land, how do we choose which people to save? If the Aniyvwiya and the Chahta and the Ojibwa are all being mistreated, how shall we say to one, 'we will save you,' and say to the other, 'we will not save you' ? Before, we were rescuing our actual relatives, and the peoples we came from and still identified as. If you want us to be one people, we have to include others and gain their strengths, but we also have to give up something. If the peoples of the Old Land are just like their oppressors, the people who have done nothing but take and take and take, why should we include them?"

Yvgidahi did not get a chance to speak before someone else added, "Should we go back to the Old Land, scour the whole world, and bring every oppressed people here? Do we intend to save everyone? Every history is built on one people conquering another. How far back shall we go to find those who have been wronged? We have something good here, finally. You want us to be different, then let us be different. Let us remain separate."

The look on the skiagvsta's face said that he had not expected this kind of response. And yet, it appeared to be a unified response. A few objected to the isolationist proposal, but they were few and far between. Nevertheless, Yvgidahi did not give up.

"I cannot in good conscience simply shut the door on them," he said firmly. "And I will not." He went on before the crowd could get too loud. "That does not mean that I intend to bring everyone here. Yes, if I could help everyone, I would, but I do not want to make the same mistakes as in the past. I made mistakes. I admit it. But that doesn't mean that we stop trying. It is not wrong to want to help. It is not wrong to help. We just have to be careful about it.

"We will continue sending expeditions to the Old Land. Not more than five men, and not more than one wolf moon at a time, with another wolf moon between the excursions, unless there is a true emergency for our people, such as capture."

"And what are we doing, then? What are we looking for?" someone asked.

"True need. I refuse to believe that everyone in the Old Land has simply given up. There may be some few who do keep to the old ways, whatever they are."

Unitsiya shifted his stance. "Yvgidahi, know that I mean this with all respect, but if those few do truly exist, would it not be better to let them remain and hope that they might rekindle the fire in future generations? And if they don't rekindle this fire, would it not be better to let them walk on in their own lands, the last of us to die in the Old Lands and walk with those ancestors?"

The silence that followed was not so long or suffocating as before, and Yvgidahi replied, "That may be so, but we have never forced anyone to come here, nor to stay. No one here is a prisoner. I believe it should be their choice, but they cannot make such a choice if they do not know one exists."

No one argued with that.

"The returning team will also choose the men for the next team, so that they have time to prepare," the skiagvsta went on. "A man may go as many times as he wishes, but I would recommend resting and allowing others to go. Fresh eyes may see and fresh ears may hear something that was not seen or heard before. And it would provide an opportunity for the young men to prove themselves, if they so desire. Without the focus on fighting or rescuing others, the teams would not require such seasoned members."

That thought was enough to get Ola Achukma's attention at least, though his excitement was tempered by horrible memories still circulating through his mind.

"When should the next team leave?" someone wondered.

"Unitsiya's team has only just returned. As it has been decided, there will be a moon of rest."

"Are you volunteering for the next expedition?" Unitsiya asked, his tone bordering on sarcastic.

The person who'd spoken up went suddenly silent and shrank back as if trying to hide behind the people around him. But it was Ola Achukma who raised his hand and said, "I'll volunteer."

He could feel his mother's eyes instantly on him, but before she could speak, Yvgidahi gestured toward him. "Very good. Thank you." He looked at Unitsiya. "Now you need only to find a few more within the next moon."

It wasn't until the next morning after Chilita went out that Ola Achukma's mother confronted him.

"Why are you volunteering to go back? Don't you remember what happened?" she asked, already upset.

"Of course I do," he told her.

"And the way they're talking, it sounds like things are even worse! What if something happens to you?"

"Like what? Sashki, I know the sorceries—"

"Yes, but you are well-versed in Touch, in the sorceries of the senses. It's why you make such a good healer. Galohisdi is not Touch!"

"No, but I know how to do it. It may not be the fastest escape, not like Unitsiya and others, but I can escape if I had to." He sighed. "Sashki, the worst they can do is kill me."

"In a foreign land!"

He blinked, stunned by her words and unsure whether to be heartened or disheartened. His mother took an deep, even breath, and put her hands on his shoulders. "Ola, why do you want to go back there? There is nothing for you there. My family is long gone. Our home is long gone. Even if it weren't, the white men are taking it away anyway. And above all, your father is gone. All that awaits you in the Old Land is misery and loneliness and death."

Ola Achukma chose his words carefully. "Maybe that's true. Maybe it's even worse than that, I don't know. But I have to go. I have to see."

"See what?"

"I have to see..." He let out a breath. "I have to see that it's all real. I have to see that the Old Land is real and not just a dream." He went on before she could speak. "I need to see it for myself. I want to know that all these terrible memories are real, but also that they are only memories. I don't want all of my earliest memories to be lies, and I don't want to live in fear of that place. And...I want to know that Aki was real."

His mother gave him a look. "Of course he was real. You're here. You're his son."

"Yes, but I need to know. I don't expect you to understand, but this is what I am doing. Besides, they may need a healer with them."

After a long moment, she nodded. "All right. I can see I'm not going to talk you out of it. And maybe things really aren't as bad as Unitsiya says. Maybe we won't have to go to war."

Ola Achukma breathed a quiet sigh of relief as his mother assented and turned her attention to Apushi who had watched their conversation with wide eyes.

He wasn't a full healer, not yet. Only the very oldest residents of Aktiya Waya were considered full healers, for it had taken them many, many years to decipher the qualities of each plant in the area and how it could help or harm a person. Even then, some plants still held unknown mysteries. Ola Achukma had suggested that these mysteries developed because of the blending of the native Hlohi plants with the plants they had brought from the Old Land many decades ago.

There was one plant in particular that initially was believed to have failed in cultivation on Hlohi, the seeing fruit which Yvgidahi proclaimed to be a method of speaking to the spirits, or at least to his brother who was trapped in the spirit world of the Old Land. But, after some time, it was found that an unassuming and somewhat stunted sapling was indeed the tree that bore this fruit, although its mystical properties were still of some debate. Yvgidahi claimed that in order for the fruit to assume mystical properties, the seed had to be planted in the body of one taken by a Raven Mocker; in his day, it had been his grandmother. Unfortunately, or perhaps fortunately, no one in Aktiya Waya had been taken by a Raven Mocker, so there was no way to test this theory.

He went to this tree now and studied it, the buds just peeking out from the twigs. It was a stunted, almost deformed tree, but here it was. Maybe it wasn't the right climate. Maybe it was a different fruit tree that had been mistaken for this seeing fruit. Maybe it had taken on properties of surrounding trees and vegetation and this was the grotesque result. Maybe it was a combination of all three, plus other factors.

Ola Achukma wondered at the tree and its fruit, still many moons away. What if he were to take one of the fruits with him, later in the year? What if the reason no one saw the spirits and the ancestors here was because there were so few? The Old Land was said to be filled with spirits, and there were many ancestors there from countless generations. Maybe he could speak to Yvgidahi's brother. Maybe he could speak to Ki.

He mulled this over for a while, for many days as he prepared to go to the Old Land. It would not be until the end of summer at least, when the fruit was ripe, so he had time to consider it. He would see how things stood in the Old Land before making his decision. He wondered if the displacement of the people also displaced the spirits or the ancestors, and how they would respond.

Okchanlush was the leader of the expedition, and the group of five departed for the Old Land just as soon as the half moon came and went.

Once they recovered from the harrowing experience of Galohisdi—which he was assured never really improved—Ola Achukma was initially stunned by the change in weather. Aktiya Waya had finally broken out of winter's icy grasp and heading confidently into spring and summer. Suddenly he found himself surrounded by golden leaves and buffeted by a breeze that said, in no uncertain terms, summer is ended.

They were just within the treeline on a hill overlooking a small town about a mile or so away.

"Where are we?" Ola Achukma asked dumbly.

"Cherokee country," Okchanlush answered distastefully. "But the Americans call this North Carolina."

"Cherokee country? I thought we weren't supposed to play favorites?"

"We're not. We're making rounds, most vulnerable to least." The group started down the slope toward the town, and Okchanlush continued talking. "The Cherokee are disorganized. People proclaim themselves leaders and claim to speak for the people when they do not, and they have the highest population of half-breeds, which makes their loyalty notoriously difficult to assume, although the Americans label them all foreigners and traitors anyway.

"On the other hand, to the north, the Shawano have gathered dozens of peoples together to form a confederacy and have stayed the American northern advancement for the time being."

"Is it a war?"

"Not yet, but this whole fiasco has also called into question the Negroes and the slave industry. There is no reason not to think this will not end without a war first. Now then, you remember what we've discussed?"

Ola Achukma nodded. "I'm only here to observe."

"Exactly."

They reached the town where they were greeted by several people, three men and a woman. Only because of fading childhood memories did Ola Achukma not recoil at the sight of the cotton clothing, spectacles, and other amenities which were distinctly white, things he had lived without for fifteen years or more.

The reports were right, he thought. The people were Cherokee in skin only. Apple Indians, as they were sneeringly called, as he had been called on occasion when he'd first arrived in Aktiya Waya. Had they had light skin—and some of them did—he never would have known the difference between an American town and this Cherokee town. He saw children in cotton clothing, leading goats, petting a cat, carrying books to and from a building that looked like a school. A small stand sold newspapers.

"Welcome, Okchanlush," one of the welcoming party greeted. He was a man of about fifty years, silver starting to disrupt his short black hair and beard. He wore cotton clothing like the rest of them, including a pair of spectacles, and he carried a pocket watch.

"Robert," Okchanlush greeted.

"Did you just call him Robert?" Ola Achukma blurted.

It was likely to be the first of many blunders over the course of their visit.

"It is my name," the man explained before Okchanlush could speak. "It is the one my father and mother gave me." Now he looked at

Okchanlush. "Am I correct to assume that he is new here?"

"He came to us when he was a child," Okchanlush said. "Many years ago."

"My father was John Aberdeen," Ola Achukma said, seemingly unable to keep his mouth shut, despite being told that he was to stay relatively silent during the journey.

"Aberdeen?" Robert questioned, his eyebrows shooting to his hairline. Even the others in the party appeared to recognize the name. "The peacemaker?"

"That's right."

The middle-aged man nodded thoughtfully. "One of the last politicians anyone ever had respect for, because he respected us. He sent you to Aktiya Waya, then, before he died?"

Ola Achukma shook his head. "No. He wasn't around to defend my mother and me, so we had to go west. We were rescued on the Trail."

Robert made a disapproving sound. "Yes. The first bloody Trail of Tears." He nodded gravely. "And another one is coming."

"How are things?" Okchanlush asked directly.

Robert made a motion and they began walking, heading through town toward a building that looked very much like a town hall.

"Not good," the town leader said. "Lawless, in fact. We cannot testify in a court of law, so we cannot accuse anyone of the crimes they commit against us. Roving bands of bandits and lawless thugs, they ride into our lands in the night, break into our homes, steal our livestock, rape our women, kill our men, kidnap our children, burn the whole place down, and we can't do a thing about it. Every so often, if it's not the bandits, the government sends soldiers to search our homes and businesses to make sure we aren't arming ourselves. We can't even hunt because it requires firearms."

"What about bows and arrows?" Ola Achukma asked.

One of the other men in the welcoming party laughed. "Easy for you to say. Assuming it was not confiscated as a weapon just as readily as rifles and pistols, few here even know how to use a bow effectively, and no one knows how to make them. Traders don't bring them, and we aren't permitted to buy them either."

"What about your white-skinned people?"

Okchanlush looked ready with a sharp reply, but Robert burst out laughing. Okchanlush settled for a look, and Ola Achukma felt his cheeks and ears burn. They reached the town hall building and paused.

Robert sighed and, still smiling, said, "Ah, child. You have been pampered by self-rule and no outsiders telling you what to do." He opened the door. "We have no such luxuries here. The government claims to not care about us or our affairs. 'Govern yourselves' they tell us. But as soon as we do, they say we are not governing right, that we are planning to attack them. We must be disarmed and removed. Oh, they pretend to be our friends, tell us that we will be free in the west. We can do as we please in the west. But we are not fooled."

"Do you have any friends or allies?" Okchanlush inquired as they entered a small room that appeared to be an office or study of some kind, though it was nowhere near as regal and well-stocked as Aki's had been.

The third man of the group spoke now as they sat down. "Depends on how you define 'friends' and 'allies.' If you are talking about people who sympathize and think that this is an atrocity waiting to happen, then yes, we have many friends and allies. We have friends across the entire state, the whole country, maybe even the whole damn world. If you are talking about people who not only believe it is wrong but are willing to put themselves, their careers and maybe even their lives on the line with us, well, that's a different story."

"Many of the soldiers who come to search our homes tell us that they disagree with the orders," Robert continued, "and I believe that the vast majority are speaking truly. But they carry out the orders anyway. They say that it's to protect us. If they intentionally overlook things, let us keep our guns and—" He chuckled. "—our bows, and whatever else the government says we are not allowed to have, then not only will we hang, but they will, too, and nothing will have been gained. 'Just comply,' they tell us. 'Go along with it and wait for it all to be over.' But because we do not fight back on the small things, telling ourselves that they are merely small things, they start pushing with bigger things which we cannot defend against."

Okchanlush frowned and glanced at the woman. "And you?"

"Unlike before, the people are not willing to go west to appease government demands and hope things get better," the woman said calmly. "The Choctaw showed us what a horrible idea that was. From everyone I have talked to in every town I have visited, every single person, even mothers with young children, even the children themselves, are willing to die before being forced west. They take no rations or blankets from the soldiers when they come, and they stand firm in their beliefs."

"They say that, until the soldiers bring bullets, not blankets," Dagki growled. "A mountain may stand firm against wind and rain, but when the pickaxes and the dynamite come..."

"We're not leaving," the second man said shortly. "Everyone has decided this. Ask them yourselves if you must. We will not be moved west, nor will we run to Aktiya Waya like a bunch of cowards."

"You already have people in the west," Ashagi said. "Are they not well-established?"

"Yes, and some of them want us to move west as well, so that they can get more land tracts from the government," Robert said. "Because they are stupid enough to believe that the government will keep their word this time. How many past treaties have said, 'This agreement will stand until the end of time' and then they were broken ten years later? What reason do we have to trust them now?" He shifted in his seat and sighed. "And what does your council think of all this? Watching all of this from the safety of another island...you're all just that much better than us, aren't you? What does Yvgidahi say?"

"We've had our fair share of strife," Okchanlush said diplomatically. "We're only here to observe and extend an invitation."

"An invitation? Well, look at you. Sitting up there on your high mountain, watching us like ants, criticizing us because we do this thing or don't do that thing, and now you extend an invitation to us. How noble of you."

"Robert..." the third man muttered.

"If you want to stay here and die, that's your business," Okchanlush told him, standing. The rest of the group followed suit, Ola Achukma the last to get upright. "Or if you want to move west. But do not despise our leader his kindness and willingness to help you. Once upon a time, he was one of you. Once upon a time, you were Aniyvwiya like him."

Now Robert stood. "You watch yourself. You know whose home you're in."

Okchanlush did not back down. "Yes, but for how long? According to you, it could be stripped from you at any time. Or burned down, once you are killed, your wife raped, your children kidnapped."

Robert's facade did not last long, and there was a weariness to his bones that Ola Achukma did not normally see except in the oldest of elders; even Ihya did not look so tired most days. Robert asked, "How long do you expect to stay?"

"We'll be here only a day or two," Okchanlush replied. "Then we'll move on to the other peoples, see what they have to say."

"More of the same, I'm afraid," the woman told him. "We can admit, we are the weakest of peoples now, and if we are willing to die, the rest are also willing to fight."

The visiting group turned to leave, but Robert called to them once more. "And a suggestion for you, if you're going to be doing a lot of traveling while you're here." He made a vague gesture. "Find some new clothes, something to help you blend in. Any white man catches you dressed like that, he'll skin you alive and be rewarded for it. I'm not saying that new clothes will keep you safe—you're obviously still Indians —but you won't look like such a damn war party. You might actually get people to talk to you first before they try and kill you."

Ola Achukma found himself glad that he was not the leader of the expedition, for he had no idea what to say to that. Indeed, even Okchanlush made no more noise than a disapproving grunt before leaving the study and departing the town hall building, the rest of the group following, the town leaders staring at them the whole way.

Only once they were a fair distance from the town hall building did Okchanlush put an arm out to stop Ola Achukma.

"Do you understand what the word 'observe' means?" he asked.

"I'm sorry," Ola Achukma said.

"That's not an acceptable answer. Do you know what the word means or have you forgotten in your quest to conjure up a universal language for our people?"

Ola Achukma sighed. "I haven't forgotten. I'm sorry for speaking out of turn."

"Curiosity isn't a bad thing," Ashagi said, coming to his rescue. "The more the peoples drift away from the old ways, the more curious I am about them, too. The more I wonder how they are able to call themselves, in this case, Cherokee." He went on before Okchanlush could protest. "We're not here to fight their wars for them. We're not here to negotiate treaties or other political dealings. We're not here to tell them that what they're doing is right or wrong, regardless of Robert's apparent assessment. We ourselves are here to observe and report and offer an invitation. We can't make them accept it."

"What the Americans are doing is wrong. And maybe it was wrong for the Cherokee to adopt so many white ways to the point that they can barely be distinguished," Dagki continued. "But who are we to be critical of them when we have our own history of, as you say, strife? How many would chastise us for taking in so many peoples and doing what we have done?"

"Then why bother offering the invitation?" Okchanlush demanded. "If they can't live like Cherokee among the whites, and they can't live like Aniyvwiya among us, then all we're doing is offering a slower death to a diseased animal. Either they will assimilate into the Americans, or they will assimilate into us. Either way, they are dying." He spread his arms. "Maybe their best option is to move west. And as Martha said, they are the weakest of the peoples. It's not going to get any better among any of the others."

He wasn't wrong. Where Robert and the Cherokee had advised them to procure cotton clothing in order to blend in, their normal clothing was welcomed among other peoples who told them that the Cherokee were Indians by American decree only, not because they contributed anything to the cause of fighting them. The farther north they went, whether by foot, horse, an occasional Good Samaritan, or Galohisdi, the more they were welcomed as they were and the more staunchly their invitation was turned down. By the time they reached the Shawano Confederacy, Ola Achukma was wondering if Okchanlush wouldn't abandon Aktiya Waya to fight for the Old Land. They had come to offer safety and peace to the peoples; would they instead be returning to make the case for war?

Ashagi was the most comfortable in the north, but even he was leery of the Shawano themselves. The Comanche of the North, he called them, although their sights were presently set on their white adversary. For as proud as they were of their history, and as committed as they were to staying in their own land and continuing to observe the old ways, Ola Achukma noticed that they still used white names and lived in houses fashioned after those used by white settlers.

The proclaimed leader of this particular area of the confederacy was a man called Kevin White Fire, and they met with him and his council in his home in the state of Pennsylvania.

"The Americans stopped advancing north when they realized there was less of a fight in the south," White Fire told them, leaning back in his chair. "Better weather, too."

He was about thirty years old, but his hair was stark white. Had been since his birth, he said, a sign of a prophet. He proclaimed himself to be an able horseman, a good hunter, a good angler, and "a damn fine husband and father."

"I am going to assume that you have no interest in going to Aktiya Waya, then, and giving up this advantage," Okchanlush stated, his tone suggesting that he wasn't going to argue with the man one bit.

"You assume correctly," White Fire said, nodding. He poured himself a glass of liquor. "Fifteen years ago, the white men moved the Choctaw, part of the Cherokee, a few others. Told them to go west to new lands, be a sovereign nation!" He shook his head and took a drink. "What horseshit. Some people believed it, others didn't and were forced to move anyway. Now look at them. Oh, there's a few towns doing just fine, sure—you Choctaw made out the best, I hear—but the rest? Squalor. Poverty. No dignity, no pride, just dependence on the American government, as they wanted."

The man poured himself another drink which he downed just as fast. "Well, we're not going to be them. We're going to stay right here, thank you very much. We made our own pacts, our own treaties. We formed this confederacy and we are going to hold the line. No one is leaving, and no one is running away."

And that was that.

"Now, if any of you ever wanted to come back and join us," White Fire went on, "we'd be happy to have you." He gestured to Okchanlush. "You seem pretty capable."

Ola Achukma half-expected Okchanlush to take him up on his offer. In the end, the man replied, "Thank you for the offer, but we have to decline."

"So, what, the Krydik are declaring themselves to be Pacifist spectators?"

"The what?" Ashagi wondered.

White Fire waved a hand. "That's what they're calling you, you know. Krydik. Because you're just so damned critical of all of us here in the 'Old Land' as you so pompously call it. You look down from your safe mountaintop and criticize everything we do. We fight, it's a lost cause and we should run away to join you. We flee, we're all going to die unless we run away to join you."

Okchanlush opened his mouth, likely with a harsh retort, but White Fire again waved his hand and said, "We've made our position known. Return to your mountaintop and let the rest of us fight our wars how we will."

After a moment of tense glaring, Okchanlush stormed out of the room. Ashagi and the others followed a second or two later. Only Ola Achukma remained.

"And what do you want?" White Fire asked lazily. "You're Choctaw, aren't you? Like him?"

"We're not trying to fight your wars or tell you what to do," Ola

Achukma said. "We are only giving you a chance to save the most vulnerable among you. Your elders, your women and children."

The man leaned forward in his seat. "Did you ever hear about the Cherokee last stand?" He went on before Ola Achukma could answer, standing and moving around the desk. "After Fort Prince George, the British were hellbent on burning down the Cherokee villages. So they did. Village after village, turning them to ash. The heroes of the day, Aganstata and Mankiller, they decided to save the most vulnerable." He paused, leaned back on the desk and folded his arms. "Now, whatever you believe about the magic that got them to Aktiya Waya, I don't care. Point is, they found and settled this fabled city of safety. They sent the elders, women, and children there to be safe and preserve the people.

"The British continued to burn and pillage, always finding empty villages because there was no one to occupy them nor resist the soldiers' advance, and finally they set their sights on Chota, the capital city of the nation at the time. Aganstata and the others fought valiantly, but they lost in the end.

"But, they thought, there is still Aktiya Waya. The people have been preserved! One day they will come back and save us!" White Fire shook his head. "They never did. The Cherokee lost their land, lost their leaders, lost everything that made them Cherokee. Meanwhile, those in Aktiya Waya continued to espouse safety and a land of plenty—which it may be, I don't know—and they extended this offer of safety to others: the Lenape, the Choctaw, and others. Save yourselves and preserve your people, they said. But over time, the peoples became less distinct. Maybe there was fighting. Maybe there was intermarrying. But in the end, there are no Cherokee, no Choctaw, no Lenape, no Iroquois or anyone else you claim to have saved. The only thing that remains are critics, and the Krydik people."

He shifted his stance. "So, yes, we could go to Aktiya Waya and save our physical bodies. Maybe we could contribute a few songs and dances, some interesting vocabulary words, maybe a new recipe for stew to your great city. But we would lose our people, our identity. We would be preserving nothing."

White Fire turned and took another drink, then looked back at Ola Achukma. "I was born Shawano. I was raised Shawano. I will fight and die for the Shawano. And no one will be critical of me for it."

Ola Achukma frowned and looked around the room. "Looks pretty white to me. And I had an American father."

He did not wait to see or hear White Fire's reaction, just quietly left the room and joined the others who were waiting outside.

"Did you win him to our cause, peacemaker?" Okchanlush asked sarcastically.

Ola Achukma shook his head. "No. I didn't expect to."

"I would have been surprised if you had."

"What now?"

"Now we go home," Ashagi answered before Okchanlush could made another snide comment. "We've surveyed the situation, made our offer to everyone we could. It's been almost a wolf moon since we left, so we have to get back. There is nothing more we can do."

It felt terribly like giving up, Ola Achukma thought. Forty days gone by, and it felt as though they had nothing to show for it. No one was willing to leave. Not one. The smallest child, the sickest elder, the most destitute woman, they were all willing to stay behind and die, if that's what it took. Some were polite about declining the offer, but most were rather prickly about it, and he couldn't understand why. No one was going to force them to go to Aktiya Waya. If they did go and wanted to come back, no one was going to stop them.

They returned to Aktiya Waya empty-handed, meeting Yvgidahi and the village council in the townhouse. Joining them was Ndiyili who had been chosen at last year's festival as the fourth member of the national council. He had been a teenager like Ola Achukma when he left with Hoka and the others, but since returned to Aktiya Waya to be with his beloved whom he soon married. It was not required for the national council to be present for the expedition's report, but he still harbored some mistrust of Yvgidahi and the others and wanted to hear the reports for himself.

Yvgidahi remained on the national council also, as did Hoka. The priest of the national council also resided with Deer Clan.

Between Okchanlush and Ashagi, the group made their report. Not a single person was willing to come to Aktiya Waya. Not only that, but there was a bit of hostility toward them, the expedition, for even extending the invitation.

"All these years, all these festivals, not to mention Ola Achukma's grand efforts at unifying our languages," Okchanlush said, gesturing briefly toward him, "and we never were able to come up with a name to call ourselves. Well, the peoples of the Old Land have done it for us. They call us Krydik, because they believe we are too critical of the affairs of the Old Land."

Yvgidahi frowned deeply. "Is it their own pride, then, that stops them from accepting our invitation?"

"Whatever their reasoning, we can't just kidnap them," Ashagi said. "If they want to stay, we have no right to force them to leave, else we become the very thing they are fighting against."

There looked to be a thousand things going through the skiagvsta's mind at once, Ola Achukma thought. But whatever those things were, they never made it past his lips. Instead, he said, "Thank you for the report. Go home, now. I'm sure your wives and families have missed you." As the expedition turned to leave, he added, "Ola Achukma, please stay."

Ola Achukma's heart jumped in his chest as he turned back to face Yvgidahi who dismissed the rest of the council, assuring them that it was personal only.

"Yes?" Ola Achukma wondered dumbly as the last of the council left the townhouse.

For a long moment, Yvgidahi just stared at him, his gaze equal parts concerned and amused. Finally, "So, how was it, returning to the Old Land?"

Ola Achukma paused and chose his words carefully. "It was interesting. There was so much familiarity, but I felt as though I looked at it from the outside."

Yvgidahi nodded thoughtfully. "I understand. I remember, after losing my brother, it was five years before I returned to the Old Land. Things were so different."

"With respect, why are you asking me this?"

The skiagvsta did not answer for a long while. Just as Ola Achukma opened his mouth to apologize for giving offense, Yvgidahi answered, "Since your time, when the Choctaw were forcibly moved and you were rescued, there have been fewer and fewer expeditions, fewer and fewer rescues. Now, it seems, no one wishes to come here. Their reasons are their own, whether we agree with them or not.

"But that also means that there will be fewer and fewer people who remember the Old Land, who truly remember it. Yes, Okchanlush may lead expeditions, but he was born here in Aktiya Waya. He doesn't have the same connection to the Old Land and the old ways that his parents do.

"Furthermore, the stories are changing. We never had fables of the tsuyoniyvgi in the Old Land because there are no tsuyoniyvgi in the Old Land. But now parents and elders tell stories of them with the same authority that they speak of the deer or the rabbit. This process is only expedited as people adopt and evolve this blended language you've been developing."

"It seemed like a logical thing, and I thought it would—" Ola Achukma began.

Yvgidahi laughed. "No need to apologize, Ola Achukma. I know Ihya put you up to it." He grew serious again. "And unless we wanted to remain divided and at each other's throats, it is a logical progression of our people. With this proclamation by the peoples of the Old Land, branding us Krydik, I fear that we have been forcibly separated from our old ways. The only direction left to go is forward."

Ola Achukma studied the skiagvsta. Yvgidahi was easily ninety or a hundred years old, yet he normally looked half that. In the light of the fire in the townhouse, he looked far older.

"What are you trying to say?" Ola Achukma asked.

It was another moment before Yvgidahi answered, "It's not been brought up publicly yet, though the village council and national council have discussed it amongst ourselves. We expect to make the official announcement at the next festival."

"What announcement? And what part am I to play?"

"Some of the people of Deer Clan are unhappy with their living arrangements, most notably the old southwestern peoples, the Navajo, Apache, Pueblo, and so on. A group of riders traveled east and found another abandoned village, very much like Aktiya Waya, set into some cliffs by a great ocean. Similarly, there is a particular group of people here, most of them elders but some not, who wish to congregate and make tales of our people here, establish a new history, a new heritage."

"Erase the history of Aktiya Waya and the Old Land?" Ola Achukma questioned.

"In a sense, yes. They have been speaking of such things for years, but I was always opposed to it, believing that we could maintain ourselves and our connection to the Old Land. But if the reports from the Old Land are honest, and we are being cast off, now may be the time. With the embracing of your language and the new stories of the tsuyoniyvgi and others, I don't expect there will be much trouble. At the next festival, I and Hoka and the national council will announce that, starting next spring, we will begin the formation of Eagle Clan, there at the cliffs."

"But—"

"We are a new people, Ola Achukma. You and I, even if we were to continue to call ourselves Ayvwiya and Chahta, I fear that we are the last. More and more children are being born here, being born Krydik. Your brother, for instance. If they are, if he is to understand what it means to be Krydik, you and I must give up some of ourselves."

Ola Achukma considered this. "Not everyone is going to like that."

"No, they're not. And I understand. If you had asked me to do this fifty, sixty, eighty years ago, I would have called you absolutely mad, maybe even killed you. But that is why I want you to help. I want you to go with those who leave, go with Eagle Clan. Develop this language, create the new stories, and bring them back to the rest of us."

There was a certain feeling that Ola Achukma got then, like he was being asked to commit suicide so that his family would have something to eat.

"Your Book," he began slowly. "Do you still have it?"

Yvgidahi blinked. "I do, yes. Why?"

"Can I read it? I don't know how, but I think it might help me in this task."

The skiagvsta was silent for a long moment. Ola Achukma got another feeling, that Yvgidahi protected that Book like Ola Achukma protected his Bible. No one else cherished it like he did, and some people would happily burn it if given half a chance.

At last Yvgidahi nodded. "All right. You can read it, but please keep it safe."

"I will. I promise."

Pàke Tèlën òk Nischa

Spirited

It took four years, but Nendawagan had finally gotten around to fixing up her dance regalia, and she had danced in the festival every year since. She had competed in other events, too, sometimes. The men had added horse racing and horse combat events, and the women had begun showing particular crops: the largest gourd, the most strangely-shaped gourd, the largest ear of corn. No one knew how it started, but about halfway through spring, a woman would lay claim to a particular plant of a particular crop. She would be the sole caretaker of that plant. Then, when the festival came about, she would show off that plant, competing against the other women to show she was a better caretaker. The winner of a particular crop event would be in charge of overseeing the next year's crop. Two years ago, Mesim had won the gourd event, and the next year was in charge of overseeing the crop of gourds, using the seeds from her prize gourd as the first planting.

Other women went out to pick flowers and arrange them in exquisite bouquets to be judged, or use them to decorate their daughters, trying to get them more noticed by the young men.

The simple feeding of the masses had turned into another of the women's competitions, a cooking contest. If there were any truly dangerous events, that was the one. Oh, a man might hurt himself in his events—injured in wrestling, trampled by his horse—but there was nothing more dangerous than telling one woman that another woman cooked better than her.

It was the only contest of real contention that year that Nendawagan noticed. In the years since the first festival and the War That Was Not, there did seem to emerge a sort of bonding. Men no longer spent their years, when not hunting, idly sitting by, waiting for something to happen. He went out and worked to improve himself for next year's competitions, or, if he was older, helped the young men improve their own sports.

This was not to say there was not still some confusion and some disagreement over how things were, but Nendawagan no longer felt the need to look over her shoulder, wondering if someone might attack in order to spite either her father, the council, or Aktiya Waya in general.

It helped when there got to be a certain number of intermarriages between what once were separate peoples. No one wished harm upon his children or grandchildren, and no one wished strife between brothers on account of nieces, nephews, aunts, or uncles. The families were too intermixed to hold onto old hatred.

As for Nendawagan, she had considered several young men over the years. A couple were unwilling to use the sorceries, nor live among those who did. One had indeed caught her eye a few years back, and they'd managed to keep the courtship going over the course of the year, intending to be married at the conclusion of the next festival. At the next festival, her beloved had fallen off his horse in one of the events and broken his neck. Only because he died instantly was he unable to be saved by the healers.

Neither her mother, nor her father, nor any of her siblings, had made any mention since about her finding a husband. For this, she had been immensely grateful. As she looked around at all the people gathered, all the competitors, all the families, she wondered if she might look at another man again. Not now, of course, for the competition was over. Tokens had been given, promises spoken, gifts exchanged, plans made. Young women strutted about in the gifts of affection their men gave them: flowers and feathers and jewelry and all manner of adornments. In about a month, the young men would bring them meat, to prove he was as good as he had bragged about at the festival and ensure the engagement.

This wasn't to say that engagements didn't happen outside the festival, but it was certainly the most common time.

Nendawagan wondered how things would change once her father made the announcement. Would things be better, if the peoples were not only allowed to go where it pleased them, but finally embrace the idea of staying on Hlohi? The people always told stories, and she knew that some were invented, perhaps haphazardly, for the delight of children, but this would be intentionally inventing a new history for the people, fully committing to this new life, this new place, and taking on the identity of the Krydik.

She'd laughed when he father first told her about the name, and the reasoning behind it. Then she realized that he had been serious. The peoples of the Old Land weren't fond of the people of Hlohi, called them cowards and other, less pleasant, names. They'd just taken the most ironic one and branded them with it.

That was fine, she thought. She didn't mind being a Krydik. It gave her an identity, rather than just the mixed-blood daughter of an Ayvwiya father and Lenape mother. That didn't mean everyone shared her feelings.

As had become custom, once the grand entry of the closing ceremonies was complete, her father stood to announce all of the important decisions the national council had made for the year, including the establishment of Eagle Clan, to the east of Deer Clan, nestled in oceanside cliffs.

There was not so much outrage at the announcement as simple confusion from those who had been completely oblivious to the affairs of Deer Clan, which basically meant a majority of Wolf Clan. A few from Deer Clan looked a bit surprised, as if they'd expected greater opposition to their wishes, but otherwise, it seemed as though the people had already made the decision and had merely awaited blessing from the national council to proceed. Whether or not they would have proceeded with the new village anyway, in spite of anything the national council said, Nendawagan did not know.

She remained silent on the matter, hoping to convey a certain neutrality with her posture.

"Several from Wolf Clan will travel with the Eagle Clan villagers in order to ensure they reach their destination and are able to make it their home," her father was saying.

They would be gone a long time. According to her father, the abandoned village was easily seven days' travel from Aktiya Waya for a single man or small group. If these new villagers were also of the mindset that they wished nothing to do with the sorceries, well, they weren't going to want to use them to travel to their new home.

But the establishment of Eagle Clan went over much more smoothly than the debacle with Deer Clan and Hoka's defection. Now it seemed a logical thing to do, if for no other reason than Deer Clan was simply becoming too big. Nendawagan had heard that a few families had broken off and gone to settle half a day from the main village.

They were growing and spreading out, Nendawagan thought. They were doing as people did.

People also turned against one another, sometimes over the stupidest of reasons.

At least the ocean provided a natural barrier. If they were to establish a new village or a new clan within the next ten years, it would have to be in any of the other three directions, and according to a few adventurous explorers, Aktiya Waya was at the southern edge of a very long, very wide mountain range that, according to them, stretched on for at least forever to the north and a fair distance to the west. To the east, it ended very abruptly at the ocean, "as if someone had taken a knife to them and sheared them away to make room for the ocean."

With the announcement made, her father then introduced the national council for the next year. It hadn't changed; people were happy with their governance.

After the serious matters were taken care of, there was more dancing, more singing, more eating, more fun. Nendawagan knew her father would be sleeping at the grounds that night, and her mother might be as well, depending on how long the food lasted. So she left the ceremonies on her own time at her own pace and headed home.

As she walked, she spied someone else also going home. Well, there were a few of those, mostly mothers with children, but this appeared to be a sole figure. She quickened her pace and discovered it was a young man. Getting closer, she saw it was not just any young man, but Ola Achukma. He did not appear to slog, as though tired or drunk on fermented fruit juice, but walked purposefully for a man heading home after a party.

She called a greeting and matched his pace.

"Is something wrong?" she wondered. "You seem to be in a bit of a hurry."

"I'm heading out with the others to the Eagle Clan village tomorrow," he explained hastily. "I need to pack a few more things."

"Why are you going?"

"Your father wants me to help interpret, for the finer parts of the language that the people haven't quite gotten." He said this with a certain tone of dismay, as if her father had his heart in the right place but still missed the big picture. "He also wants me to record the stories the elders tell, so that we can bring everyone together under the same history, the same stories, the same...heritage. As Krydik."

Nendawagan nodded. "I see." She paused. "It makes sense, I suppose. Having a common language, even if it does sound somewhat distorted at times, it does help."

"It sounds distorted coming from us," Ola Achukma said, "but there are young children who are learning it as their own. The elders tell them stories that they will claim as their own. We just need to make sure things are smoothed out and consistent among the clans. Otherwise, we run the risk of becoming separated and turning on each other."

"I agree. I wish you well."

He said nothing to that, and they parted ways, each to his own home.

Nendawagan considered his words that night as she lay in bed, and she thought about them some more when she woke the next morning. The festivities had, as expected, gone late, and those who were leaving were slow to pack up. Pleasantries were exchanged with those who were staying, friendships solidified for another year, promises made, vows renewed, and she watched them leave.

Only when they were gone did her father return home.

"How long will the helpers be gone?" she asked.

He looked like he hadn't gotten much sleep the night before and was a bit slow to answer. "Most will be gone for a moon or so. They have to walk there normally, as the new Eagle Clan villagers do not especially want the sorceries, but the return trip should be easier. Adahi is more than proficient in Galohisdi.

"Adahi is going? He's on the village council."

"The village council will survive without him for a little while," Yvgidahi said, amused.

Nendawagan shifted her stance. "You said that most will be gone for a moon. I assume the rest are going only as protection on the road?"

"A few, yes. Others will be gone a little longer." He yawned. "But, given your persistence in this question and the look on your face, you have someone or something specific in mind."

"Ola Achukma said that he is going to teach the language and record stories."

"That's right. It might take a bit longer than a moon or two. Why? Wolf Clan has learned and adapted the language very well, as has most of Deer Clan. But the rest of Deer Clan, now going to become Eagle Clan, has not. We have to make sure they have a good grasp of the language so we can keep communication open, so we can understand each other."

"So we don't become separate," Nendawagan stated.

Her father nodded. "That's right. Some people don't like the sorceries. That's fine. Some people don't want to live in this environment or that environment. I understand. But we must remain one people. If we become separate, if hostilities flare up...we can't have that. If someone wants to fight, he can return to the Old Land. We can't risk our security that we have here. The best way to resolve a problem is to communicate. We can't communicate if we don't understand each other, if we don't understand the problem."

She thought about this for a long moment. Then, "May I go with them?"

Now he blinked. "You?"

"Yes."

"Why?"

"I want to help." She went on before her father could speak. "Moskimus is already going; I can stay with him. Please, I don't intend to remain with Eagle Clan, but I want to be of use."

Her father looked uncertain, his gaze flickering once or twice to her mother who had been silent so far. Finally he nodded. "All right. It might do you some good, too, I think. If we have no enemies, what reason do we have to not travel and see what lies beyond the bowl? You'll be traveling in a group with many strong men—and you are not helpless yourself—you'll be fine."

Nendawagan could not see her mother's expression behind her, but she could feel the disapproval. There was allowing her oldest daughter to leave Aktiya Waya, and then there was encouraging it.

Yvgidahi gave her a look. "Well? What are you waiting for? They've already gone! Go, grab a horse, catch up to them! They shouldn't be hard to find."

Suddenly motivated, she scrambled up from the table and left the house, unable to suppress a smile. She hurried to the horse pen where Hitguttit was checking on the horses and adjusting his routine based on how many were left after the festival, and how many mares had likely been bred when the Deer Clan competitors had brought their stallions to compete. Whatever his method or technique, he wasn't happy about, not only being interrupted, but having to alter his apparent method because she, too, needed a horse.

"You're not running off to war again, are you?" he asked distastefully.

She took an even breath. "Honestly, Hitguttit, that was years ago, and I've barely ridden since. No, I'm going with them, to Eagle Clan."

He grunted. "Well, they've only just left, so at least you won't have to kill a horse to reach them."

She gave him a look and he reluctantly picked a mare for her to use. The mare was such a light red as to be almost pink in color, with an undercoat of pale yellow and patches of white, with a particularly large patch across her rump.

"She's a bit spirited," the horse tender told her as he tied the knot around the horse's nose and put the reins over her neck. "She's got a way she likes to do things. Kind of like her rider, I think."

He spread a blanket on the mare's back and took her to a carved stump used for easy mounting. Nendawagan hiked her dress a bit and got on, taking the reins from Hitguttit.

"Does she have a name?" she asked.

"Well, not as such, but she's been compared to Utsonadi enough times that it seems to work to get her attention."

Nendawagan wasn't sure how she felt about that, but she didn't argue. HItguttit guided her out of the pen, keeping the rest of the horses away.

Once out of the pen, it was an easy, and rather exhilarating, gallop across the open fields toward the pass in and out of the bowl. Once she reached the rockier ground, she tried to slow her mare, but Utsonadi wasn't having it, and the horse's weight and will easily overpowered Nendawagan. Once the horse was free, she was free.

They hit the rockier ground at full speed, the horse leaning and turning into the slope so far, Nendawagan feared she might fall off. She squeezed the horse tight with every muscle in her legs, knuckles white around the rope reins. Facing the downward slope, the horse eased up only a little bit, leaning back so as to not fall forward, but it was a treacherous skid down the hill. Even when the pass was well and wide, the horse never slowed.

Nendawagan wasn't actually sure if she managed to breathe during that time, or if she did, if she said any helpful prayers. She kept her eyes firmly fixed on the space between Utsonadi's ears, pinpointing the exact spot where rock turned to dirt once again.

If she thought the dirt was going to slow the horse in any way, she was sorely mistaken. The dirt was firm ground, and the mare was happy to have it. The only consolation, then, was that she turned left, to the east, as desired, though again, she made a dangerously tilted turn, nearly brushing Nendawagan off against a rock.

Then the ground leveled off, and Utsonadi bolted again. Nendawagan felt the horse's powerful muscles flexing beneath her, the stout spine occasionally jabbing her in unexpected and unwanted places.

The trail turned south again and continued downward. Nendawagan had long since stopped trying to rein in her mount, figuring it a less dangerous option to just let the horse run. Instead, she tried to find hope in the fact that the group could not be moving that fast, so it wouldn't be long before they reached them. What she would do if Utsonadi didn't stop at the group, but decided to just run forever, she did not know, but by then, maybe others would see her plight and come to help her.

Carefully, she put a hand to Utsonadi's neck and gently tried to use Touch. Maybe she could figure out what her horse was after that she felt the need to run so.

She wasn't a skilled horseman like many of the men, certainly not as great as Hitguttit, but she was able to discern that her horse was panicked and desired the comfort of a specific companion who had been taken by the group. She was even able to see a distorted memory of this companion, an older mare of such a dark red so as to be nearly black.

Nendawagan tried to pass calming thoughts to the horse, that they would surely catch up to the group and there was no need to go crashing recklessly through the trees, but Utsonadi paid her no mind.

She'd no sooner ceased such efforts than she saw the group just ahead. Her horse slowed just enough to let out a shrill whinny and charge forward again.

Only when they reached people did Utsonadi slow from a gallop to a trot, falling in at the tail end of the group, to the glares of many whom she'd almost run into, and finally slowing to a walk.

Nendawagan let out a breath and tried not to gasp for air. As it was, she had to conjure Time just so she could wipe her face so no one could see her crying and shaking. Only when she had composed herself did she cease her conjuring and look around at the group.

As expected, absolutely nothing about the group had changed since they'd left only a short time before. Most people were riding, although a few did walk. She didn't even see the dark red mare that Utsonadi had been so intent to find.

As if sensing her thoughts, Utsonadi nipped at the rumps and shoulders of the surrounding horses and moved out of her position, toward the outer line of the group, and attempted a trot. Annoyed, Nendawagan pulled hard on the reins. Utsonadi snorted, threw her head, and did several high-steps in place, pawing at the ground and turning in a circle.

Then they were moving, though not by free will. Nendawagan looked and saw Moskimus beside her, gently slipping another rope around the mare's neck and leading her, plodding sullenly, back to the group.

"Need some help, big sister?" he chuckled.

Nendawagan glowered at him, which only made him laugh.

"When Hitguttit said she was spirited, I was hoping that wasn't synonymous with dangerous," she said, sounding and feeling very much like a pouting child.

"Well, there is that," Moskimus admitted, cooling his laughter. "Hitguttit just wanted to be sure you got a lively horse who can run for many days at a time to stop a war, and not fall over dead upon return."

"Mosk, that was years ago."

"All the man does is take care of the horses; he doesn't have other pursuits to distract him from any wrongs done to them, no matter how long ago."

Nendawagan huffed irritably, then said, "I Touched her, and she's looking for an older mare, dark red so she looks almost black."

"Only when she thinks she can get away with it."

"What do you mean?"

"You're not the most experienced rider. A good one, but not the most experienced." He indicated the mare. "She knows that. She knows she can get away with stuff, so she does. She bows to Hitguttit; she's bowing to me. You? Not so much."

She sighed again. As if to reinforce the point, Utsonadi snorted and shook her head. The horse did not attempt to run, though she occasionally nipped at the other horses if they got too close.

"Do you want to trade?" Moskimus offered. "Lalhan is pretty docile, comparatively speaking."

Nendawagan ground her teeth but finally agreed. They moved off the trail a few paces and traded mounts, Moskimus moving his packs from Lalhan to Utsonadi. Then they returned to the group.

"So what are you doing out here, Nenda?" Moskimus finally inquired. "Obviously you're not here to stop a war."

"I'm going to Eagle Clan," she answered. At his look, she clarified, "To help out."

He frowned but nodded. "I see. And I assume Nocha approves? We don't need him riding up on us."

"Of course he approves."

She could see her brother had doubts, but he did not voice them aloud. Instead, he said, "And I expect you will want to stay with me, seeing how I'm your brother."

"That's one idea, yes."

He gave her a look, but unless he wanted to try and turn her away, all he could do was agree. "All right, fine. Well, we have to stop at Deer Clan to drop them off, and so the new Eagle Clan residents can pick up any belongings they might have left behind and say their goodbyes."

"I understand."

"How long do you plan to stay? I am coming only for protection on the road, and, depending on how things look at the abandoned village, initial protection and maybe some construction work."

Nendawagan blinked. Moskimus was her only relative here. If he left and returned to Aktiya Waya, who would she stay with? She could stay with a family, yes, but many of them were leaving to get away from the sorceries; would any of them open their homes to one of the sorcerers?

"I guess I hadn't really considered it that much," she admitted, blushing. "I just wanted to come and help."

He waved a hand. "We'll figure it out when we get there. We haven't even seen the village yet."

"Who has?"

He nodded toward a group of Deer Clan riders some distance ahead, most of them experienced men in their thirties or early forties. "They were the ones who found it. They say the village is set in the ground, for the cliffs are very windy. On land, they are surrounded by enormous pines, at least five hundred feet tall, and beyond that, to the north, are the mountains. Supposedly, the land comes to a rather sudden stop, as if they had been sheared off in order to make room for the ocean."

"I remember hearing something similar. But didn't the southwestern peoples live in the sides of cliffs? I always thought they would be more suited to Aktiya Waya."

"Oh, they loved Aktiya Waya, no doubt about it. They just don't like the sorceries."

"They probably don't like us coming to help them, either."

Moskimus made a sound. "That point might be debated. We'll see how many are going, see how they feel about it when we get there. We still don't know what we're going to find."

Nendawagan raised a brow and made a gesture toward the riders. "You mean they didn't say?"

"Not to any of us. My guess, they didn't want us sorcerers butting in and making plans on how things should be. They want to do it themselves, but they can't just turn away protection on the road, or a helping hand."

"So they are happy to have help; they just don't want us to use to sorceries to do it."

"That's right. And I can't say I don't understand. Some of us have grown so used to the sorceries that we use them for the most mundane things. Using Galo'ondiha ale Agi'a to move a tree out of our path? Understandable. Using it to bring something to us that we are too lazy to retrieve ourselves because it would be an inconvenience to move from our place of comfort? A dream in olden times, perhaps, but far less of a gift now that we have it."

Nendawagan studied her brother. "Do you resent the sorceries?"

He shook his head. "No. They have helped us in many ways. They saved the people from terrible troubles. And they have many uses still. I am simply stating that I understand why some have the feelings they do." He lowered his voice and switched to the Lenape language. "But between you and me—Nocha told me this, but he didn't want it public yet—Adahi isn't coming back."

"What? Nocha told me that he was only staying for a moon or two."

Moskimus shrugged. "That's the official story so far, but he is going to stay."

"Why?"

"Personal issues, Nocha says. Adahi has never felt right about what happened to father's brother, and he's spent the last sixty years ingratiating himself to Nocha because of it, except he doesn't feel right about that either. So he is going to Eagle Clan where he will forsake the sorceries and take a new wife."

"But he is greatly proficient in the sorceries, uses them extensively. It will be years before he ages unto death."

Moskimus shrugged. "It's his choice."

She considered this but said nothing more about it. She'd always thought of Adahi as her father's best friend, an uncle of sorts. Had it all been a lie? Had it all been some kind of penance on his part? Nendawagan had read her father's Book, knew the circumstances of Anagalisgi's death. Even now, many years later and understanding the sorceries, she could not fathom a way to have changed things. According to Anagalisgi, everything was exactly as it should have been. Why should Adahi harbor such guilt over that for so long?

The trek to Deer Clan was rather uneventful. Even the fiercest of creatures was unlikely to attack a group so large, Moskimus explained. Perhaps at first, when people were new to Hlohi and the animals did not know what to make of them, but in the seventy or so years since, humans had established themselves as hunters and warriors rather than prey. They were not tsuyoniyvgi to run away in fear at the first sign of danger.

The last time Nendawagan had seen Anpa O Wicanh'pi—truly, the only time—it had been little more than a few tipis hastily erected by a small group of defectors and defended by an even smaller group of warriors, led by a single older man and a couple of advisors.

These days, the village had grown considerably, and that wasn't even considering how big it must have been before the Eagle Clan defectors removed evidence of their stay. There were now around forty tipis clustered together in the plains, a massive swath of land trampled to dirt by constant use. A huge wall, perhaps three or four feet high, built entirely of tsuyoniyvgi antlers and their sharp, thorny points protected the village and nearby crop fields while still providing a relatively clear line of sight to the land beyond. Inside the wall, dwellings looked more permanent, with more life and decoration among them. The tipi used by Hoka and his village council was the second-most decorated tipi, after the one used by the priests. The council tipi sported fine furs, long chains of beads, and mighty clusters of tsuyoniyvgi antlers. The priestly tipi was decorated with painted bones and feathers, an eagle likeness at the top.

For those who were returning to stay, friends and family—most of them elders and children—came to greet them and inquire how they had done at the festival. Some deeds were greatly boasted of, others quietly admitted to. Depending on how a competitor did, mostly the men, engagements were either sealed or broken among families, priests consulted as to an auspicious day for a wedding. For those already married, husbands gave their wives bouquets of mountain wildflowers or healing herbs. They gave their children seasoned jerky made from the meat of mountain animals. And other gifts were exchanged as a trading market had also popped up during the festival a few years back.

"I wonder," Nendawagan began, "what do you think it would be like to move the festival here next year?"

She and Moskimus and others who were ready to go to Eagle Clan simply stayed on their horses and waited for the rest of them to be ready, packing up forgotten belongings and saying goodbye to friends and family.

"It would be different," her brother said evenly. "It might be nice to not have to worry about all the grounds preparations for once."

"Or the food preparation," she agreed. "And if Eagle Clan is successful, we could rotate to their area, too."

Her brother nodded absently. "Well, that will be something to discuss with Yvgidahi when we return. Right now, we need to accomplish this task before we take on any others."

She couldn't deny that, and she let the matter drop.

Packing up proved to be more difficult than anticipated for those traveling to the new village, and it was soon determined that it would be smarter to stay the night and start fresh in the morning.

"How far to the new village?" Nendawagan wondered. She sat around a fire with her brother, Adahi, and a few others from Aktiya Waya.

"For a small group, four days, or so I'm told," Adahi answered. "With this group, and considering this delay, I would say six days."

Nendawagan almost asked if they really couldn't just use Galohisdi, or at least conjure Time just a little bit. She knew the arguments almost instantly. What was the hurry? If she was in such a rush, she shouldn't have come. They were leaving because they didn't want to use the sorceries, so they weren't going to use the sorceries to leave. Well, that wasn't quite true, but it sounded nice in her head.

She also almost said something about Adahi leaving permanently. She hadn't seen him pack up for the trip, though she'd thought his packs a little bigger and fuller than those who were going for only a short stay, to assist the new settlers. She saw nothing about his demeanor or in his voice that hinted at his plan to stay. Could Moskimus have been mistaken? No, not on something like this. And he'd gotten the news from Nocha. Nocha wouldn't make that kind of mistake.

Still, she said nothing about it, and the evening passed normally.

It was midmorning before they were actually on the road, though, truly, there was no road, not yet. There were a few trails that either hunters or game used to cross the plains or return to the forest, but only those from Deer Clan really knew how to find and follow those trails. Judging from conversation around her, once they reached the forest again, northeast of the plains, all roads and trails stopped. From there, they would have only the guidance of those who had discovered the village.

"You look deep in thought, Nenda," Moskimus said. "What are you planning now?"

"I am wondering about the people who used to live here," she told him. "What were they like? Our Deer Clan lives how they did in the Old Land, yet now two of our three clans will occupy villages that were once inhabited. Seeing how this new village is still very close to the mountains, it might stand to reason that it falls under the protection of the Sacred Wolf. What about Deer Clan? There are supposed to be other Sacred Ones throughout the world. Where are they? What are they? What realms do they protect? Has anyone ever gone to look for them?"

Her brother chuckled. "Nenda, I think that if you were to find a husband, the first thing you would ask him to do would be to take you out into the world so you could search out these other Sacred Ones."

"Is it so wrong to want to know?"

He shook his head. "Of course not. Curiosity is not a bad thing. I will not say that I have not wondered these things also from time to time. Maybe someday we will learn these things. Maybe there will be artifacts in this new village for you to investigate. But once again, one task at a time, and sometimes, you must choose what you want to do. Do you want to make all these suggestions and improvements to the festival, or do you want to go out into the world and explore it?"

"Why can't I do both? The sorceries can take me out into the world and bring me back."

Her brother made a broad gesture. "Then do so. No one is stopping you, although I might have to, just so I don't have to explain to Nocha that I allowed and even encouraged you to leave."

Nendawagan huffed irritably.

"I think," Moskimus went on, "you don't want to just explore the world, but you want someone else to see it, too. You want everyone to see it, to share in the wonder and awe."

She sighed. "I want too much, Mosk. I want to do so much, see so much, experience so much, and I want to do it all at once."

"You want to build and be part of the world you see in your mind, and you want everyone else to see this dream as well." He nodded. "Problem is, not everyone shares your ideals. I think you might have to stick with just one person."

"Who, though?"

Her brother raised a brow, a certain smirk on his face. "The one who brought you out here. The whole reason you decided to ride a fiery, spirited mare. The only other person who has the same deep yearning for peace and knowledge that you do, and who Nocha approves of."

Nendawagan felt her ears and cheeks burn red even as Moskimus said, still smirking, "Ola Achukma."

"He's a boy."

"You're a girl. Sounds like a match to me."

He was laughing even as she punched him in the arm. "Please, Nenda, everyone can see it. As for your remark about him being a boy —"

"Mosk, I was there when we rescued him from the Old Land. He was an eight year old boy."

"And now he's a twenty-something year old young man. He's learning the sorceries. I can see that his aging has slowed. Your actual ages matter little compared to your relative ages. He's a handsome young man, you're a beautiful young woman. You are both invested in the festival, you both value peace, and you are both thirsty for knowledge. Yes, he's here to do all the things he's supposed to do, but I guarantee that he will be studying artifacts just as much as you."

Nendawagan couldn't stop blushing, and she hated herself for it. She couldn't say Moskimus was entirely wrong, either. He'd always been there, Ola Achukma, always skirting her peripheral vision. She'd always dismissed him for a number of reasons, most of them having to do with age and how she'd known him when he was but a child. Of course, other women knew their husbands when they were but children, but the aging and the age dynamic was slightly different in this case. She couldn't bring herself to do it, even as she couldn't give a reason why she shouldn't.

Her brother said nothing more on the subject, though she could see that he wanted to. She gave him a look, he grinned mischievously, and they rode in silence.

The landscape remained very much the same that first day they set out, nothing but grass as far as the eye could see, interspersed only occasionally by a scrubby tree. She spotted a herd of tsuyoniyvgi once, knowing this only because she knew what their antlers looked like, and common sense saying that bushes did not bob in the grass like a leaf on water.

It wasn't until late the next day that the landscape began to really change. Distant hills got closer, the grass became shorter, a little more scraggly, and there were a few more bushes and ferns intermixed, as well as trees. With this change, their guides declared it a suitable time and place to stop and camp, which they did.

There were about two hundred people total traveling to this new village, about fifty of them acting as protectors or helpers only, like Moskimus and Nendawagan. Certainly Eagle Clan would have a larger beginning population than Deer Clan had. Many of them were the old southwestern peoples. Around the campfires, Nendawagan heard an assortment of languages, some of them from the Old Land, and some of them mixing with the new unified language.

She saw Ola Achukma going around to each of the campfires, talking to the people, apparently attempting to strike up amiable conversation. Sometimes he appeared successful, sometimes not.

"You like him," Moskimus teased, leaning in close.

Nendawagan swatted her little brother away. "Oh, honestly, Mosk, you're not eight years old."

"Neither is he."

She opened her mouth for a tart reply, then finally closed it and settled for a scowl. Her brother just grinned and went back to whatever he'd been doing.

And then, just like that, they were out of the grasslands. The trees got thicker, the grass turned into brush and undergrowth, and the road turned into a trail and finally vanished. They were now completely at the mercy of their guides.

Their guides never lacked confidence in their trek, Nendawagan thought. They never appeared uncertain about their path, never argued about which way to go. It was as though they had made the journey a thousand times and were now returning to their childhood homes. It was comforting, she supposed, to have such good guides; it relieved a lot of stress on those traveling.

On the other hand, if they were heading toward ocean cliffs at the end of the island, there wasn't really any way they could miss such a thing. The plains were vast, and it would be easy to miss a settlement. They wouldn't be able to accidentally walk by a large shoreline.

They always kept the mountains on their left, though as the days wore on, they slowly drifted farther and farther away. Nendawagan wanted to ask about it, but the guides still seemed to sure of themselves. The trees turned from oak into pine and grew taller, stretching upwards so that they appeared to touch the clouds. The undergrowth thinned until there was virtually nothing left, and their trail became clear.

On the sixth day, a little after breakfast, once they'd begun riding again, Nendawagan heard a great noise, like thunder and wind through the trees. Looking up, the pines were as still and rigid as the mountains. She was not the only one who heard this, and eventually, an answer to her unspoken question reached her ears.

It was the roar and foam of the ocean. They were very close now. They had to pay attention so they didn't go wandering off a cliff. This was easier said than done, as the dull plodding of the group suddenly got a spring in its step, and everyone wanted to be the first to behold their new home. Nendawagan was just excited to be traveling and seeing new things. She'd never actually seen an ocean before, never beheld water that touched the sky. She'd only ever seen a lake once, and it had been little more than a pond according to those she'd been with.

By the afternoon, she spied the end of the trees with vast sunlight and blue sky beyond. The group surged forward, eagerness overriding their better judgment and the warnings of their guides. Nendawagan nudged her horse into a trot and skirted the outer edge of the group.

When the undergrowth had thinned, the wind became far more apparent. Breaking through the trees, Nendawagan was blasted in the face with the chill wind of reality. She squeezed her eyes shut and jerked her hand on the reins to stop Lalhan who'd apparently had the same idea.

The wind died down for a moment, and she opened her eyes.

There was still a good five hundred feet of ground, barren except for a bit of scrubby grass, up to the last fifty feet which was entirely rock. It was here that Nendawagan dismounted, walking carefully to the edge, stopping a few feet but having little fear, for the wind was violent and kept her from falling.

It was exactly as the guides had described. Water so vast that it touched the sky, the sunlight glittering brilliantly off the waves. To her right, smooth cliffs and open ground, a gentle slope into the horizon and an even gentler, barely perceptible curve to the east. To her left, more cliffs, these ones jagged and rough, the ground moving sharply up and down in the mountains which ended abruptly, peaks and valley sheared off to make room for water. She spied a few waterfalls, massive amounts of water flowing down from the mountains and tumbling hundreds of feet into the ocean below.

The rest of the group was celebrating their arrival in their new village, wherever it was. All Nendawagan knew was that she wanted to see more.

Awahtochchina Tushafa

Eagle Clan

The cliffs were the easiest thing to find. The village, not so much.

Ola Achukma broke out into the open only to be buffeted by violent wind, and he remembered wondering why anyone wanted to live here. Had they missed the village? Was it hidden in the forest? Of course, everyone wanted to see the cliffs and the ocean and everything, but when they were done sight-seeing, he really would have preferred to see the village.

According to the guides, they had ended up a tad north of where they actually needed to be. So, once people were done ogling the great expanse of water—what they could see of it through squinted eyes—the group melted back into the trees for mild protection and headed south.

Ola Achukma kept his eyes out for stone structures, built from cliff and mountain rock. He looked around for wooden buildings, made of the abundant pine. He looked around for anything that might indicate civilization of some form: pottery, bones, carvings, anything at all. When the guides finally called for a stop, his only thought was: we're lost. The guides have no idea where we are.

But, in fact, they did.

Whoever had lived in the area before, they did seem to be intelligent. They built their entire village into the ground itself. Enormous square holes, about eight to ten feet deep, perhaps one hundred by one hundred feet wide, dug or carved from the earth, with squat homes built inside. There were twelve holes in all, and it looked like another had been started but never completed before whatever catastrophe wiped out the former occupants. The holes were arranged in a four-by-three grid pattern, and only the holes closest to the forest had access steps crudely chipped away.

Horses were tied to trees and the people slowly began filtering into the abandoned village. As soon as Ola Achukma stepped below the lip of the hole, the wind ceased. His face was windburned, but at least he could hear again.

Tunnels between the holes kept the village connected, and small gutters and a slightly sloped floor ensured any rainwater was carried away from the homes and back into the ocean.

Like Aktiya Waya, there was nothing living in the village except for a bit of lichen and a few small animals that ran away just as soon as the people approached. Peeking in this house or that one, Ola Achukma found stone tables and chairs, very much like the homes in Aktiya Waya, some bits of pottery or old tools, even a few bone fragments that appeared to have turned to stone as well. Like the first discovery of Aktiya Waya, as detailed in Yvgidahi's Book, even the ghosts were long gone from this place.

It was the same all throughout the village, though only Ola Achukma seemed interested, archaeologically speaking. Elsewhere, the new residents of the village were claiming houses, quickly sweeping out the dust, cobwebs, and broken pieces of a former civilization, and setting up their own: laying out rugs, hanging up furs for temporary doors, and figuring out what to do about food.

He was going to have to claim one of these homes for himself, he knew. He was here to ensure the language took hold and new stories were created. That wasn't something that was going to happen in a few days; he would be here for a while.

Well, it was only him, so he didn't need a lot of space. He found a small home in a southern hole, laying claim to it by his belongings, then sitting in the old stone chair that probably hadn't been used in generations and gnawing on a bit of jerky he'd brought.

He would have to go out and find some wood for a fire. Then he— they would have to figure out what to do about the horses. They couldn't just leave them tied to the trees, but there was precious little for them to eat, not to mention the wind. Leaving his new home, Ola

Achukma found that most had agreed to simply bring the horses into one of the holes at least for the night. They would discuss their options later at the first council meeting of the new village.

One of their guides, and now chosen leader of Eagle Clan, was a man called Dilkis Bizhi. It was no surprise that he selected the other guides to be his advisors on the village council. The priest was a man named Il. Once everyone had claimed a home and brought in their horses, Il gathered everyone to the largest of the structures, clearly meant for large gatherings, and lit the sacred fire, praying blessings over the village, its people, and all generations to come.

When the ceremony was complete, hunters and foragers were dispatched to find food for a feast, and the village council had its first meeting.

Ola Achukma returned home to continue laying out his belongings and exploring his new dwelling. There wasn't much to see, really. It consisted of only two small rooms, one little more than a closet to give privacy to a bed. Other than the table and chair, he'd found a few bits of old pottery, the bowl and part of a shaft of a broken spoon, and plenty of dust.

Thinking about it, he realized that this would be his first time away from his mother. Oh, he'd gone out on hunts and such before, but here, now, this home was his. He was responsible for the cooking and cleaning and maintenance and everything else. If something went undone, his mother or stepfather wouldn't be there to get on him about it. He didn't have a wife to see to anything either. He was entirely on his own.

It was an odd sensation, one that led him out of his house, if only because he had a hard time thinking of it as his.

In his musings, he nearly bumped into someone who was carrying a bucket full of bits and pieces of stuff.

"Got anything?" the man wondered.

"Anything of what?" Ola Achukma asked dumbly.

"Nendawagan wanted to collect all the bits and pieces of whatever we found in the village. I think she wants to examine them." He waved a hand. "I don't care. If she wants them, she can have them."

Ola Achukma blinked. "Oh. Well...here, why don't you give me the bucket? I'll take it to her."

The man surrendered the bucket easily. Ola Achukma returned to his house to collect his pieces, then went out in search of Yvgidahi's daughter.

The northwest corner hole had been set aside for those who were only in the village temporarily. Anyone who had come with the intention of helping to build new homes would be leaving quite soon, perhaps after the feast the council had ordered. Those who had come for the protection of the village until they were able to sort themselves out, they might be around a few more days, but it wouldn't take long for things to settle into a new normal.

So it was that Ola Achukma had little trouble finding Nendawagan. First, because he knew which section she would be in; second, because other people had brought buckets of things. He saw her brother there with her, looking a bit exasperated by the collection but saying nothing about it.

"You've got quite a collection," Ola Achukma observed as he handed over his bucket.

She looked at him, grinned, then looked away. "I want to know if the people who lived here were very similar to those who used to live in Aktiya Waya. If they are, why choose to build in the ground here and not go a little farther north to carve into another hill? Certainly a mountain would be of greater protection than these burrows."

He shrugged. "I would not presume to know the thoughts of men now long dead."

"Yes, but it's a wonderful puzzle, isn't it? Something to think about, to agonize over, even as you know you'll never have the answers."

He watched her as she sorted the pieces into several piles. One looked like pottery, another utensils, and another and another. "How long are you planning to stay? There's not much need for construction, obviously. Protection seems to be taken care of as well."

Now she looked a bit distressed as she paused in her sorting. "I know." She continued her work. "But I'm going to learn as much as I can anyway while I'm here."

Ola Achukma wanted to say more, but he wasn't sure what. He was only a breath away from asking her to come over to his house...for what purpose? He didn't know. So she could study it? What did his house have that anyone else's didn't? Besides, how could he ask such a thing with her brother standing right there? He might get the wrong idea.

In the end, he stayed silent, maybe mumbling a farewell before slinking off back to his house.

He saw her again at the feast the following night, though he could see that she appeared very uncomfortable in her surroundings. He watched as she would approach someone and strike up a conversation, but a few exchanges in, it would taper off until the other party excused themselves. After a bit, Ola Achukma took a breath, gathered his courage, and walked up to her.

"Enjoying yourself?" he asked, trying to sound casual.

"The food is good," she replied evasively.

"It is, but it's not the measure of one's happiness to be here."

She huffed. "You're right. I feel like I'm the only one who cares about the people who lived here before. Everyone else just wants to throw away the broken bits like trash. I want to study them, to know what the people might have been like."

"Why is that?"

"How they lived can tell us more about the area, for one. The village is literally set beneath the surface. The reason is because it's obviously very windy. I found a few fishhooks made of bone in the buckets of stuff, which means there must be some good fishing nearby. And like I said before, because of the similarity between here and Aktiya Waya, I think they may have been of the same tribe."

Ola Achukma nodded thoughtfully. "What about the pottery?"

Nendawagan sighed. "I would imagine that the people before had healers of some form, and they probably kept some of their medicines in jars. Those medicines might prove useful in knowing what kind of foraging is available here."

"But anything like that is long rotted away."

"The plants are rotted, but the pottery is still discolored."

"And how will you distinguish between one green plant and another?"

She gave him a look. "It's not a perfect plan, only an idea."

He nodded and looked around, spying her brother across the room, watching them. While there was a certain brotherly sternness about his gaze, Ola Achukma thought there was a bit of amusement as well.

"And what else have you found?" he wondered.

She shrugged. "The usual tools, utensils, everything we have that's familiar."

"Any evidence of what happened to them?"

She shook her head. "Not a thing. No bones to say they died here. No disturbance to say they were driven from here. No evidence of any writing or other graphic accounts, no drawings or paintings. Maybe there's a mass grave a stone's throw from the tree line, but it's been so long that everything would be erased by now." She sighed and folded her arms. "Nothing but the Sacred Ones."

"According to your father's brother, in the Book, we know the Sacred Ones were protectors," Ola Achukma offered. When she snapped her head to look at him, he added, "Your father let me borrow it. I suppose I should give it to you so you can return it to him when you return home."

She studied him for a long moment. Finally, rather than make a scene about him having the Book, she calmed down, nodded, and said, "Yes. The Sacred Ones were the protectors of the people before. But what could they not protect against?" She frowned. "I remember my father saying that, for several years after settling Aktiya Waya, the priests prayed to the Sacred Wolf, observed rituals, feasts, offerings, fasting, everything they knew of, trying to commune with her."

"What were they hoping for?"

"Anything. Confirmation of blessing, that they were allowed to be in Aktiya Waya. A rebuke, to tell them to leave. A story, to tell them of the people before, warn them against whatever evil had befallen them. But other than Anagalisgi's message that the Sacred Wolf had waited a long time for them—which they took as a sign of acceptance—they got nothing else. Eventually, they stopped trying so hard, figuring that if the wolf wanted to talk to them, she knew where they were."

Ola Achukma nodded and let out a breath. "And here I am, staying here, with Eagle Clan, trying to get them to invent new stories in a new language for a new people."

"You don't want to?"

He paused and considered his words. "I want the people to be unified. I want them to have peace. But do we really need to sacrifice our individual identities for it?"

Nendawagan shifted her stance. "Do you remember the first festival of tournaments? How happy everyone was to have such an event, to be able to compete?"

"Of course. It's the same way now."

She shook her head. "It's not. The feeling maybe, but it's not the same as it was then. The first night of dancing, everyone wanted to prove the dances of his own people. The Cherokee did Cherokee dances. The Lenape did Lenape. A couple years later, the Seminole group did a Navajo dance."

"I remember," Ola Achukma said. "The Navajo didn't know whether to be awed or irate."

She nodded. "The Seminole had studied them carefully and decided that they could do the Navajo dance better than the Navajo."

"They did, if I remember right."

"Yes. And for a couple years afterwards, the peoples no longer did their own dances, but each other's. Now, those dances are no longer the dance of a people, but a dance itself. The Navajo dance. The Cherokee dance. The Chickasaw dance. All treated the same as the Bear dance, or the Crow dance, or the Butterfly dance. We never lost such things; we learned to share."

Ola Achukma frowned. "I wished it worked so well with language."

"Why shouldn't it?"

"How could it? We can't have six different words for the same thing."

"Nuance, Ola," she told him. "If it's one thing I learned about English, it's that nuance is everything. How does an English speaker say that something is big?"

"He says 'big.' "

"Or large. Huge. Massive. Enormous. Grand. There are probably more words like that I don't know. And my father says that many of these words are taken from other languages, yet they are used just as well by those who speak English."

Ola Achukma considered this. "Well, I suppose I have heard some of the children—"

"The children will be your best bet for the language," Nendawagan cut in. "They don't know any better. They will make their own associations. It won't happen overnight."

"I know. Still, Ihya tasked me with this years ago. I feel like I've made no progress. And trying to make a written language from it, too?"

Nendawagan gave him a small smile and put a hand on his shoulder. "It will happen. It took seventy years to get this far. What's a few more decades? I'm told that word means a group of ten years."

He sighed. "It does. I get your point." He looked around. "Still, I wish there were more we could definitively learn about the people before. Maybe that would spark some interest and get things moving."

She nodded. "Me too."

He looked at her. "How long do you expect to be here?"

Now she faltered. "Moskimus thinks we'll be leaving in the next few days. Nothing major has come up, but we only just got here. He wants to give it a few more days, let the initial excitement die down a little."

"Makes sense. What are you going to do until then? Sift through buckets of broken pottery?"

She shrugged. "I suppose. It's all I can do."

Ola Achukma shuffled uncomfortably. "Well..."

"Well what?"

"If your brother were to approve of it, perhaps you could go out into the surrounding area and look for some more evidence of the people before. The mass grave you were talking about, or something else. I could go with you and protect you; we don't know what creatures are out in the forest here."

Her expression turned mischievous. "And I could help by foraging for plants and herbs to help the women and healers here stock their stores."

He made a gesture. "Of course. That would be most considerate of you."

She grinned. "Well, I'll see what Mosk thinks." She made as if to run across the room and beg her brother to let her go—as if she were the younger sibling—but then she stopped, turned, and asked, "Do you happen to have a lead on where to begin the search?"

"Well, we ended up north of the village on our way in, and I didn't notice anything especially interesting that way. Maybe we'll have to start south."

"Assuming the weather cooperates."

He made a gesture of assent and she moved off.

He didn't want to stick around to watch their conversation. He didn't want to stare. He couldn't look away. His only saving grace was that Moskimus was already enthralled with another conversation with some other young men. Nendawagan, not wishing to pester him like a child, but apparently unable to continue the discussion with Ola Achukma, wandered off to speak to someone else, looking much lighter on her feet and having more success in engaging others.

He returned home that evening with his stomach in knots and went to bed the same way. Had that actually happened? What had he agreed to? How would Moskimus take his offer? How would Yvgidahi receive it when the two returned to Aktiya Waya?

The following morning, after being directed to a small pool where everyone was getting their daily water, Ola Achukma sat in his house, nibbling on the last of his provisions, contemplating his next move. He would have to go out and hunt now. That was fine; it would just take a little extra time to learn the landscape, find the game, and hopefully not get lost on the way out or the way back. After that, he should probably talk to the elders, assuming he could. The elders tended to be the most resistant to the concept of a unified language. Through younger, more knowledgeable interpreters, some declared themselves too old to learn such things, and others declared the idea a tragedy and a suicide they would not partake in.

Ola Achukma wouldn't say he didn't understand, but it was also very frustrating to him and his efforts. If only he—

His thoughts were cut short as someone knocked on the stone beside his doorway, and Nendawagan's voice could be heard.

"Ola Achukma?"

Swallowing his food hard, he stood and went to push aside the fur he'd hastily hung as a sort of door.

"Nendawagan, good morning," he greeted formally.

"Moskimus thought the foraging was a great idea," she said, a sparkle in her eye. "There are a few more women waiting outside the village. We just need our protector."

Ola Achukma felt the blood rush to his face, and he stumbled over himself to get ready. It shouldn't have been as big a deal as he made it, but he felt terribly unprepared and slow to follow her through the connecting tunnels and out of the village.

There was a group of five women waiting for them, two of them with younger daughters. The wind was still that day, no more than a breezy puff. Everyone was grateful for this. Not only did it make it easier to hear each other and any danger lurking about, but it was easier to gather leaves when they weren't at risk of blowing about. Even so, all the baskets that the women brought came with secured tops, just in case.

A few of the women seemed to perceive that Ola Achukma was there for more than simple protection, and while their expressions betrayed this knowledge, none of them said anything about it.

"I believe you suggested we try south?" Nendawagan said.

Ola Achukma felt his ears and cheeks burn as he glanced at the other women who now caught on to something more than just a simple foraging expedition.

"Yes," he said. "South."

They started that way, ducking into the treeline and detouring around the spot where large trees were being cut and hauled back toward the village. Some were being used to build more of a wind block on the cliff side of the village. Others were being used to build a wall around the spot where the crops would be planted. Still more were used for just firewood as well as clearing an area which they hoped would grow grass for the horses.

"I'll be sad to leave this," Nendawagan commented once they were past the work area and came to a spot where the women began to fan out, looking for anything to forage.

"Why is that?" Ola Achukma wondered.

She shrugged. "It's all so...exciting. So new. I'm watching the people grow."

"Meanwhile, you have to return to life as usual in Aktiya Waya?" He raised a brow.

She huffed. "Yeah. Life as usual."

"It can't all be new and exciting. Sometimes mundane is good."

"Easy for you to say. You get to stay here."

"I have to come up with a language, convince a bunch of cranky elders to learn it, use it, and teach it, and I have to come up with new stories to establish ourselves here on Hlohi, completely erasing the existence of the Old Land from the minds of people who think it's better not to remember."

She frowned. "Well, I suppose that isn't the most envious of tasks."

He had a sharp reply, then bit it back at the last minute. The women were out here to forage, and he was here to protect them. Nendawagan seemed to sense his reluctance to speak, nodded once, then adjusted her basket on her arm and excused herself to go searching.

Watching the women inspect various plants was not the most exciting thing to do, especially when they bypassed a good number of them. Maybe it was too early or too late for harvest; maybe the plants were useless or even harmful. Whatever the reason, the expedition was not looking promising. But there had to be something of use; the people who had come before had made a living here somehow.

He made a short trek deeper into the forest, looking for anything that might be sneaking up on them. With the tall pines and sparse undergrowth, it was an excuse only. He saw plenty of birds high above, watched a burrowing animal scurry into its den at the base of a tree, but otherwise saw nothing of interest. Had the landscape looked different a thousand years ago?

He headed back toward the cliffs, verifying the women were in no danger, then walked into the open, grateful for the calm day. There were a few clouds floating along in the sky, but it made it easier to look at the water, anyway. It appeared a bit gray today, he thought, not like the brilliant, glittering blue that had greeted them when they first arrived.

Ducking back into the forest to check on the women, he returned to the cliffs and went south a distance. He didn't know what he was looking for, or how he would know if he found it. How did a people leave behind such a pristinely-kept village, yet no evidence of themselves? What was it that caused them to die out? The Book said something about wars and great catastrophes, but that was hardly an answer. Was there anything they, the new residents, needed to know about? Some danger?

Ola Achukma was busy looking out over the water and entirely unprepared for the ground to suddenly not be there under his feet. He fell, most ungracefully, into the earth, darkness quickly enveloping him as he tumbled head over heel down a hard rock slope, reaching out and vainly searching for something to grab onto to stop himself.

A solid rock wall stopped him before he stopped himself, and for a long moment, the most he could do was cough, breathe, and be grateful for life. Gradually, he got himself untangled, thankful he didn't have any broken bones, and looked around for which way was up. He spotted it, little more than a dot of light, a good hundred feet up and maybe five hundred feet away. Between him and the exit, the hard stone he'd bruised himself on.

But there was light coming from somewhere else as well, off to his left. Glancing at the exit, Ola Achukma turned toward the new light source. He reached for his knife, found it exactly where it should have been. He felt his bow, inwardly cringing at how loose it felt, as if the wood itself had cracked, which it probably had.

He didn't hear anything, though, and he didn't think anyone or anything would have been able to sleep through the noise he made in his fall. Cautiously, he followed the light source.

The slope continued ever downward, following what he believed to be the cliff line, though it was hardly consistent. There were many spots where the rock face had opened up as if to provide windows.

The wall to his right vanished suddenly, and in the gloom he could make out a large cavern, though little else besides another passageway on the opposite side. He went to this, stepping lightly so as not to make noise, and continued down the passage.

A short slope down, a sharp turn right, a sharp turn back left, another trek down, and he came to the end, where the passage again opened up into a large cavern. This time, however, the left wall also fell away, and Ola Achukma found himself not ten feet above the froth of the ocean. With the cavern illuminated, he could see where the water could rise about halfway in.

But he also saw something else. Grinning, he turned and started back the way he came, only gradually coming to the realization that even as the passages sloped downward toward the ocean, now he was going to have to climb all the way back up. At the same time, he had no choice because he saw no other way out, and he didn't expect to grow wings any time soon.

He returned to the foraging women, who had apparently abandoned their foraging and instead become a search party. When they spotted him, they rushed to him like a bunch of mothering hens, fussing over his bruises and scrapes.

"We thought something awful happened to you!" they told him.

"Were you attacked?" one asked.

"Your bow is broken!" another observed.

"I'm fine," he assured them. "Just made an accidental discovery."

He looked at Nendawagan as he said it. The rest of the women didn't seem to catch on, insisting that he return to the village and get cleaned up, but he saw the curiosity in her eyes.

As they walked back to the village, she fell in beside him.

"What did you find?" she wondered.

"Maybe more clues about the people who lived here," he answered.

He could see the thought thrilled her, but what could they do about it now?

Seeing him returning all bruised and scraped put the rest of the village on high alert, even after Ola Achukma assured them it was his own fault for not watching where he was going. All women and children were called back, and the men only paid half attention to their work, keeping an eye out for any more dangers. Even if Nendawagan had been able to convince her brother to let her go out with Ola Achukma before, he would never agree to it now.

It wasn't until the next day that she visited him again. He, now feeling his injuries, was less enthusiastic about going out.

"Come on," she goaded. "I told Mosk that I would be going out foraging again, since we had to cut it short for you yesterday. He thinks I'll be going out with the other women. Take me to see whatever it is you found!"

"I'm sore," he whined. "And I'll be dead if your brother finds out what we're doing."

She gave him a look. "No, you won't. Come on, Ola. I don't get to go out alone very often, never mind alone with a man who isn't a relative. You know no one else here cares about such discoveries, and short of us being husband and wife, we'll never be able to explore. Don't be selfish and keep this to yourself!"

Ola Achukma sighed but finally relented. "All right. Just promise to be careful. If I get hurt, people think I've been attacked. But if you get hurt—"

"I'll tell them that they should have seen what I did to whatever attacked us."

He couldn't help but chuckle at that as he nodded and grabbed his knife. "Well, my bow really did get broken. I suppose that as long as I gather some wood to make a new one, I can have a productive excuse, too."

Nendawagan grinned and lightly departed his house. It still took him a bit longer to get ready, for he had to search out someone who would lend him a bow for the day for protection and hunting. On top of that, he might not have broken anything, but he was pretty sure that even his bones had bruises.

He met up with Nendawagan outside the village, past all the construction work. She had her basket and was doing a bit of foraging. On seeing him, she abandoned whatever plant she was examining and followed him.

"I found it on accident yesterday," he said. "Let's find it on purpose today. It's a long way down."

"Down?" she questioned.

He chose not to elaborate, instead fixing his gaze on his immediate surroundings and scanning the ground for the opening. It wasn't an especially big hole, but one misstep was clearly all it took.

They found it quickly, and on purpose. It was the first time Ola Achukma had seen Nendawagan falter with fear, even as he went down a fair distance and told her it was safe to proceed. After a moment of consideration, she took one step, then another, then committed to the darkness and stayed hard on his heels.

A moment later, the passageway lit up. He paused and looked around.

"It's just me," she said behind him. "You haven't learned Atsvstdi?"

He felt his ears burn. "It's not my strongest ability. I really prefer Touch."

"Well, at least now we can see where we're going."

He said nothing to that as he turned and continued on.

Unlike before, the passageways were not only brighter, but far more interesting. The stone was carved and, in some places, painted. Nendawagan stopped numerous times to marvel at them. In the passageways, they appeared to be more shapes and designs and earthen things: the sun, the sky, the ocean, trees, and so on.

Then they broke into the first large cavern, and were struck by the sheer magnitude of artistry. Many of the paintings around waist level and lower were faded and covered in lichen, but everything above that was crisp and beautiful, the paintings almost tragically lifelike. These showed animals in great herds, including some Ola Achukma could not identify. There were other creatures, too, birds and fish, and whole landscapes as if painting a map of the area. Another large painting on the west wall initially looked like many line designs, until Nendawagan theorized it could be a map of a larger cave network.

"But one thing I've noticed," she said, slowly moving back to the center of the cavern, looking up at the many drawings, including the smaller etchings on the stalactites and stalagmites, "I don't see any people."

Ola Achukma started scanning the paintings for himself. Nendawagan continued speaking.

"You see the many animals here, some which we don't even know what they are. And here they run, they fly, they swim, they fight. But I don't see anything that might show what the people before looked like. Or how they lived. Over here looks like a map of the cliffs. See, these are the mountains, this is the marker where the entrance is to this cavern, and that would make this the village. But nothing about the villagers."

"That is strange," Ola Achukma agreed, though his attention was more focused on her, and the posture she struck when thinking hard. He was thinking hard, too, though not the same kind of hard.

She meandered off to the next passageway, the one that led to the ocean. By now, the tide had gone out completely, and they were a good twenty-five to thirty feet above the waves. Her attention was quickly taken by the decoration. First it had been carved, then painted, and there was evidence of organic things having been inlaid with the paint but now rotted away.

"It's the sun, and many animals below it," she observed. "But the animals are running away because something is coming down from the sky."

Ola Achukma shifted his stance. "Or maybe the sun is sending these things to the ground." He gave her a look when she glanced at him. "Sounds like a good story to me. The Creator loved to make stars, but he made too many; there was no more room in the sky for anything else. So he sent some of the stars down to the earth and they became the many creatures we see. Then he took a portion of the sun, his favorite star, and made men."

Nendawagan raised a brow and considered this. "Hiding the truth inside a story. Almost."

"Almost."

She grinned. "I like it." She looked around, then out at the ocean, the expanse of water stretching on forever until it touched the sky. "Thank you for bringing me here and showing me this."

"Consider it a token of affection. One you may have to show your brother and...take back to your father and mother?"

Now she looked at him, as stunned as he'd ever seen her. Then a huge grin spread across her face. "It's more than anything I could have asked for from anyone. But you will still have to bring something to present, a deer or something else large from the area, something to show Mosk besides a cave full of carvings and paintings."

He shrugged. "Well, you are supposed to be foraging, are you not? In the time that you will have to make up, I think I can find something to hunt."

She laughed, and they headed back up the passageway, through the large cavern, to the winding passageway. By the time they broke the surface, Nendawagan appeared a bit winded, but Ola Achukma was quite sore, if only because of his bruises from the previous day. How in the world was he going to hunt anything? Well, if he could find or make a good blind, all he needed was a little patience.

A few steps from the hole, Nendawagan turned to him. "I won't tell Mosk anything until you return with an animal. Then it will be like a double gift!"

Ola Achukma agreed and they parted ways, her to continue her foraging charade, him to find something to present to her brother so he could verify the proposal to their father. What had he gotten himself into?

He headed into the forest and managed to find enough brush to build a decent blind. The movements of the animals were not well-known yet, but if the paintings were any indication, they had to be around here somewhere. But then, Yvgidahi and many of the original Aktiya Waya settlers said that the landscape had changed drastically since their arrival, maybe because of their arrival. Who knew how things had changed since the disappearance of the old people?

But he rather liked his story. Yes, the Creator made too many stars, so he turned some of those stars into men and animals. Hiding the truth inside a story. Wasn't that how it always went?

He thought of Ki's Bible, hidden away in his home, and he knew a moment of shame and betrayal. His father had believed every word of that Book, and Ola Achukma did, too, he supposed, or at least most of it. Was it right, then, to help a people invent a lie in order to make them more comfortable? There was a verse in there somewhere that talked about people having itching ears and listening to false teachers because it made them feel good, not because it helped them. Was he about to become that false teacher?

What about peace, though? The people were finally coming together. There was still some resistance, some growing pains, a few arguments and dissenting opinions, but it was nothing unfamiliar.

On the other hand, Jesus said he did not come to bring peace, but a sword. Did that mean that Ki had been in the wrong? Was his peacemaking an error? Had his death been punishment for it? Ola Achukma did not want to believe that, because that meant that everything he himself was doing, to unite the people in language and stories, was also wrong.

His musings helped to pass the time, and he very nearly passed up a large animal because of it. He couldn't put a name to it, for he had never seen it before, but if he could bring it down with one arrow, well, that would impress Nendawagan and her family, right?

Carefully, he nocked an arrow and drew the string quietly to his ear, trying to size up the creature for a weakness other than the eyes which were quite small. A bear, perhaps, if he had to compare it to an animal from the Old Land, except this bear had spikes jutting out from its spine, shoulders, and hips, and its head fanned out on top and was smooth like a plate, its ears protected by this plated fan.

If I miss, this is going to hurt, Ola Achukma thought. And he released his arrow.

The thing made a wretched sound as it died, snarling, screaming, writhing in pain. Ola Achukma was sure the whole village was going to come running to see what was wrong.

When the thing finally stopped twitching, and nothing came tearing through the woods to investigate the commotion, he emerged from his hiding spot and went to dress the animal. It was a terrible endeavor, trying to maneuver around the spikes and get under the fanning head plate, all of which appeared to be part of its skeleton. He decided, perhaps against his better judgment, to show off the beast to everyone in the village before presenting it to Moskimus and Nendawagan, to show the others and warn them of not only how dangerous the beast was, but how difficult it was to dress. It was not an ideal hunting animal.

Being sore from the previous day did not help matters either as he dragged it behind him. If nothing else, being the first to hunt an animal of this kind, it would make an impression on Nendawagan and her family. It would have to. He didn't know how much more he could do today, and they would likely be leaving soon.

He was spotted long before he reached the village, and half a dozen men came to help him drag the carcass while a dozen women came to ogle at it. By the time they descended into the first hole, more had joined them, and Nendawagan and Moskimus were waiting inside. With a mixture of relief and reluctance, Ola Achukma dropped the carcass before them.

"I brought more, as a demonstration of my abilities and my love," he said, looking back and forth between them. "Just in case the earlier excursion was not enough."

Nendawagan's eyes shone, and Moskimus looked at the carcass. "What is it?"

Ola Achukma shrugged wearily. "I don't know. Big. Ferocious. Tough to kill and even tougher to skin."

Not a few warriors were already prodding the thing with sticks, as if afraid it would suddenly come roaring back to life. But, seeing what was going on, what Ola Achukma was proposing, no one said anything, instead waiting for Moskimus to speak.

At last the warrior nodded and looked at Ola Achukma. "We'll have to cook it up quickly then, and sample it at your feast of engagement to my sister."

The crowd erupted into whoops and cheers, and the carcass—meat, fur, skeleton and all—was taken away to the townhouse for blessing and preparation. Ola Achukma just stood there, stunned, unsure what he was feeling, unsure what was appropriate to feel.

Sensing this, Moskimus smiled and said, "Walk with me."

The two of them left the village and went out walking along the cliffs, occasionally blinded when the sun poked through the clouds and bounced off the water.

"Nenda told me what you did for her earlier," Moskimus began, "taking her to see caves with paintings and carvings."

Ola Achukma said nothing, but he felt the blood rush to his face and ears.

"For a long time, Nocha and Guka thought she would never marry, and they despaired over it. Then you came along, a young man with many curious and unusual questions, as well as a unique background. Nocha took a liking to you immediately, and even more when you favored peace and took on many tasks and roles to that end, even before Hoka's defection. After the first festival, he gathered all of his sons and instructed us that if you should ever win over Nenda and ask for her as your wife, to grant it."

For a brief moment, Ola Achukma wondered if it would be possible to survive jumping off the cliff. He wasn't sure his face could feel any hotter.

"What about her other fiance?" he finally managed to get out.

"They liked him, too," Moskimus said, shrugging. "He was a good man, and it was very promising to know that she was finally considering the prospect of marriage and family. After his untimely death, Nocha suspected it was because you were the spirits' intended suitor instead."

"If that's the case, I really didn't mean to kill him." Ola Achukma went on before Moskimus could speak. "On the other hand, if even I am not the spirits' intended suitor, perhaps I should stay away from these cliffs."

Moskimus laughed. "Perhaps so, but I think that will be unnecessary."

"But why?" Ola Achukma wondered. "Men and women marry and divorce all the time, and I don't know of many stories where the spirits intervened so...forcefully in a relationship."

"You'll have to ask a priest for those answers, but I think even they may be in the dark about it."

It wasn't the most comforting thing to hear, but it was both relieving and puzzling to think that Nendawagan's family had been eyeing him as a suitor for years. Why hadn't they said anything? Well, he knew why. He had to be the one to initiate, to ask. If he couldn't get up the courage to talk to a woman he loved, how was he going to have the courage to do anything else?

They returned to the village. Nendawagan spent the day preparing the meat and fur he'd brought back, and he spent the day wondering what in the world he was getting himself into. It was one thing to consider marriage, and that was frightening enough. It was quite another to consider that it could be a divinely appointed marriage. What did that mean? What were they supposed to do or accomplish? Did Nendawagan know about this, or even suspect it? Was her whole family in on it? How did that change her feelings toward the man she was supposed to have married a couple years ago? Did she feel responsible for his death?

At their engagement feast, it was determined that they would be married at the conclusion of the next festival, the same way her previous engagement was supposed to have ended. Neither of them said a word about it, instead choosing to enjoy the party as the first engagement in the new village. Of course, she would be leaving in another day or two, back to Aktiya Waya, and he wouldn't see her again until the festival, but that was all right, he decided. It would give him some time to figure out how marriage was supposed to work, and where marriage and fate intersected.

Pàke Tèlën òk Newo

Preparation

The whole ride back to Aktiya Waya, Nendawagan felt as though any time she opened her mouth, she talked too much or she was going to talk too much. Yet she also knew that she spoke far less on this trip than any so far; her brother told her so.

"Did you know he was going to do this?" she asked.

"Honestly, Nenda, everyone in the family has been waiting for this for years," Moskimus told her, eyes glittering with amusement.

"For what? For marriage, or for him?"

"Well...for him."

She blinked and gave her brother a look. "Yes, but...I was engaged a few years ago."

Her brother looked both uncertain and guilty. "We always liked Ola Achukma better, but you can't force a horse to eat, no matter how good the grass."

She raised a brow. "So now I'm grass? Or a horse?"

Moskimus cleared his throat and blushed hard, sweat breaking out at his hairline. "What I mean is, if Ola Achukma couldn't be bothered to make a move, then...that is, even if you're facing the right direction, you'll never go anywhere if you don't go anywhere. I mean—"

"Mosk, you sound like you're trying to propose to me," Nendawagan laughed. "Does this mean that when we return, that Nocha and Guka will already have everything all planned out?"

Her brother shrugged. "They had things planned out for your last wedding, too. I'm sure it won't take much to bring it all back together. Besides, many preparations will already be taken care of with the festival."

Nendawagan nodded, unsure how to take that. She enjoyed the

festival, but she didn't know what to think about her wedding being the final event as it were. There was no competition here, except it might make other girls jealous that their weddings were not so lavish or public. That in itself could cause problems. Similarly, she didn't want to be put on display as some kind of political pawn, her father showing off that different peoples could make peace and children. She didn't want to be a statement. But what other choice did she have? And, on the other hand, she wouldn't say she wasn't tempted to make it an even bigger event and not only show off such a large, public wedding, but really rub it in the faces of everyone else. Her father was doing this for her. The people were doing this for her.

She brooded on this as they traveled. One of the things that had been agreed upon at the Eagle Clan meeting was that any use of Galohisdi, short of a true emergency, would be stalled until at least one day's travel from the village. The sorceries were still contentious, though only about five percent of the Eagle Clan residents had even minor training in them, but all could agree that Galohisdi was best reserved for use away from the people.

"Where do you suppose we'll live?" Nendawagan wondered. "Wolf Clan is clearly more accepting of the sorceries, and it would make sense to stay closer to our families. But we have found so much more evidence of the old people around Eagle Clan, and I want to know if there's more."

"If there is, I'm sure Ola Achukma will find it, and I don't doubt that he would show you," Moskimus answered wistfully, sounding a bit disinterested. "But it would be better to stay close to your family. And his."

She let out a breath but said nothing more about it. She wanted to know. She wanted to learn. She wanted to explore. Now that they had found more evidence of the people before, more than just a piece of pottery and a bone shard, she had to find more. She wanted to go out and find the other Sacred Ones, see if any of them could shed light on the fate of those who had lived in the villages before.

Would Ola Achukma do that for her? Would he agree to such a

monumental undertaking? He was also intrigued by the people before, had found the first cave, and yet, he also seemed duty- or honor-bound to stay in the villages among the people and continue his quest for peace. The problem was that it wasn't a bad thing. In fact, it was very, very noble, and she loved him for it. But maybe just a little exploration? There had to be more out there somewhere.

"Do you think that the people of the Old Land will forget the old ways?" she asked suddenly.

Moskimus seemed caught off-guard by the question. "What do you mean?"

"It used to be that we could save some people, because they wanted to be saved. Now they chase us away, call us names, and they are nothing like us although we share a common ancestry. Some even look like us still, but they're...not us."

Her brother frowned. "I don't know. It certainly looks that way."

"What does that make them, then?"

"Lost, I suppose."

"Do you think there is any way to reach them? To bring them back?"

"Back to what? Even we are not who we once were. You and I are evidence of that, children of Cherokee and Lenape, born far away from the Old Land and knowing little to nothing of its horrors. Nocha and Guka are not who they once were either. We're Krydik now."

"Yes, but we are the combined fire that is slowly dying in the hearts of the men, women, and children we abandoned. We can't let it go out."

Moskimus brought his horse to a halt, and Nendawagan did the same.

"What do you want to do, Nenda?" her brother asked, sounding more exasperated than angry. "We've had this discussion a thousand times, in public, in private, long and short, heated and cool. What do you want? Horses and grass, Nenda, we can't save someone who doesn't want to be saved. Do you want us to just start kidnapping people and bringing them here, force them to live like us?"

"It's no different than—"

"Exactly. It's no different. They are living their lives as they have known them—"

"But it's not who they are!"

"And who are they?" He put up a hand before she could speak. "No. Stop. We are not having this discussion—again. I'm tired of it. I'm tired of hearing about it from Nocha, from the council, from you, from everyone. If someone asks for help, I will help them. But if they are going to curse me, spit on me, drive me out of their home, I have no reason to think I will be treated any differently by forcing them to come here." She opened her mouth, but he kept talking. "We're not conquerors, Nenda. We're not conquerors, we're not soldiers, we're not heroes, we're not saviors. We are Krydik. We live on Hlohi, in the village of Aktiya Waya. The Creator made too many stars, so he sent them to the earth to become men and beasts. That is how things will be from now on."

He nudged his horse forward, not bothering to check and see if she followed.

Nendawagan had a hundred replies all vying for space on her tongue. In the end, she said none of them. She watched her brother move away from her for a long moment before giving her mount a gentle kick and trotting back alongside him.

The sun slowly went down. Only when it was just about to disappear below the horizon did Moskimus open Galohisdi, putting them just outside the entrance to the bowl.

The horses didn't much like the doorways opened in midair, and Moskimus' testy mount almost didn't go through except for a little nudge from Nendawagan's horse. Truthfully, she didn't enjoy it either, and the stress and pressure from walking through Galohisdi almost knocked her off her mount.

Then it was over and they were through. Moskimus called a greeting to the sentries, and passed by unharmed.

"I think," he said cordially, "it may be best to wait until morning before making the announcement to Nocha and Guka. Unless you have no interest in sleeping tonight?"

Nendawagan gave her brother a look, then finally managed a small smile. "You're probably right."

They returned their horses to Hitguttit and made their way up the slope to the stone village.

"I wonder why we never found such paintings and carvings in Aktiya Waya?" she wondered aloud. "And I know that there are plenty of caves in the area that have been explored."

Her brother sighed as if conceding something. "Explored for useful things, obsidian and metals and the like. As far as I know, you and Ola Achukma are the only ones who go looking for paintings and carvings. Maybe you'll have to do a little looking yourself and compare your findings with his at the next festival."

She rather liked that prospect, but there was no time to entertain such a thought. For one, it was late and she was getting tired. She said her goodbyes to her brother and they parted ways, each to his own home.

Her mother was still awake when she walked in the house.

"Oh, you're back," Mesim stated. "Is Mosk back, too?"

Nendawagan nodded and yawned. "Yes. There was little work to be done in the new village."

"That's what some of the others were saying. How is it?"

After a moment, Nendawagan just waved a hand. "I'll tell you in the morning when Nocha is awake, too."

Her mother looked uncertain, but nodded and wished her good night.

Truth be told, Nendawagan didn't sleep much that night. She hadn't slept much the night before either, but that didn't seem to make a difference. She was far too excited, going over all the possibilities in her mind. Moskimus had already told her that their parents would approve of the match, but still her mind said there was a chance that they would reject it once she told them. Or perhaps Moskimus had already told them and they were just going along. But that didn't make sense because he wouldn't have had a chance to tell them; they returned via Galohisdi and then went their separate ways.

And how would Ola Achukma react? He had seemed a bit nervous about the whole thing, although, from other engagements Nendawagan had seen—including her late, fateful fiance—that wasn't uncommon. But what would he think when he learned that he'd always been the preferred suitor, if only he'd had the courage years ago? On the other hand, years ago he didn't have the ancient caves to show her as part of his gift to her. That alone put him above and beyond what any other hopeful suitor could do to catch her eye. On the more practical side of things, he'd also brought down a great monstrosity of a beast that no one had ever seen before.

What would the other girls say, those who were waiting for a good match? Popokus had been quite the envy of all with her engagement party, and such occasions were becoming more and more common as the years went by, the young men now seemingly obligated to bring two gifts, one to adorn a girl in pretty things and one to feed the entire village. And this after having to prove himself in the festival tournaments. Would the young men now be obligated to take his hopeful bride to ancient caves full of magic and wonder and history of a bygone era?

Nendawagan smiled to herself and at last found sleep. It didn't last long, however, and she found herself waking up long before anyone else. She lay abed for a while, thinking about how she wanted to tell her parents the news. Did she want to be direct, the first words out of her mouth? Did she want to lead into it? What if Moskimus really had told them already and they were just playing along, to see how she was going to react and tell them?

She pulled herself out of bed and meandered into the main room, adding a log to the fire just to keep the coals alive and warm up some water for tea. She definitely needed some to calm her nerves.

The last time she'd been engaged, everyone had been there to see it, so there was no secret to it. This time, she had to tell them. If she didn't, well, if not Moskimus, then definitely his wife would make sure everyone knew by the end of the day, and that was her being slow.

Her father was the first to wake, ambling out to the table and accepting a cup of tea as she offered one to him.

"I take it things went well in Eagle Clan?" he asked evenly.

Nendawagan nodded, her heart pounding as she sipped at her own tea. "Yes. Not much work needed to be done. Although, a new animal was discovered." She described it as best she could.

"I see," her father mused.

"It was Ola Achukma who found it. He went out hunting and found it. He says it was quite aggressive."

"Judging by the description, I would say so. But he's a fine hunter. He would have to be, to take it down as quickly and as soundly as he did."

She blushed and tried to cover it up with another drink of tea. "Yes, he is. He is also quite the treasure hunter."

Now her father raised a brow and looked curious. "Oh?"

Nendawagan told him about the caves, the carvings and the paintings. Yvgidahi listened intently, saying nothing until she was finished. Before he could speak, Mesim emerged from her slumber and sleepily made her way to the fire to pour some tea for herself.

"This looks like an earnest conversation," she observed sleepily. "Has something happened?"

"It sounds as if Ola Achukma has found much evidence of the people who came before us," Yvgidahi told her.

"Is that all?"

"And he asked me to marry him," Nendawagan blurted.

She couldn't be sure if one of them hadn't conjured Time in order to process the news more quickly, but then the dam burst and there was laughter all around. Her mother got to her first, squeezing her hard and babbling something about how happy she was. Then her father gave her a gentler hug and told her that he was also very happy for her.

It was only then that they pretended to be interested in the caves Ola Achukma had shown her, even as Nendawagan knew they just wanted the details of the proposal, details Moskimus would not be able to give them when they pestered him later. Whether or not they actually cared enough to remember anything she told them about the caves—including the invented story the two of them had come up with, about the Creator and the stars—she did not know; she was just happy to be able to relate an entire tale to someone without them making some excuse to leave.

She again had to mention the new creature Ola Achukma had found, and the feast that had followed its capture. Yvgidahi casually mentioned that while that was nice, Eagle Clan was also only just starting out. Wolf Clan would show her a proper feast.

"How will that be, Nocha, when my betrothed isn't even here?" Nendawagan asked, grinning.

"I will ride to him," he answered certainly. "I will use Galohisdi to get close to Eagle Clan, then retrieve him for a proper feast of engagement. We will also talk, he and I, man to man. After the feast, then I will also take him back to Eagle Clan to continue his work."

She raised a brow. "Nocha, Moskimus told me that you had a standing order that if Ola Achukma ever came asking, to give him your blessing. Don't scare him off now that he's done just that."

Her father chuckled. "Don't worry, Nenda. I will not try to dissuade him, or you, either. It is a talk that all fathers must have with their daughters' suitors. I did the same with Simaquon before he married Popokus."

"I remember."

"If he runs off, it is his own fault. But I do not believe myself so poor of a judge of character that I would give my blessing to a coward."

Nendawagan wasn't sure how to take that, but she found herself smiling anyway. Her father left the house, now intent on his mission to bring Ola Achukma back for the engagement feast.

Her mother took over from there, sweeping her away back to her room to fuss over what to wear for the feast. It was slowly becoming customary for girls to parade themselves in the adornments their betrothed had given them, a way to show off to other girls, married or not. Ola Achukma had given her no such adornments beyond what might have been a couple of rings which had been sifted from the buckets of stuff people had swept out of their new homes, and it was difficult to wear the wonder and awe she had felt standing in the cave.

Nendawagan considered the cave the greater gift, but her mother would not have it and despaired that her husband had been too eager to give his blessing.

"And you can't very well wear the adornments from your last engagement," Mesim fretted woefully.

"Of course not, Guka, they were buried with him," Nendawagan said.

"Well then, I suppose the only thing left is to see what I have. Come on."

So they made their way over to the bedroom her parents shared. Her mother did not adorn herself in such grandeur anymore, except on rare special occasions, but that did not mean that she hadn't kept every bit of jewelry and other pretty adornment her husband had ever given her in their sixty years of marriage. She was a bit like a rodent in that manner, Nendawagan supposed, and not a blind one either. Among the treasures were jewels from the Old Land, gems that hadn't seen the light of day in over a decade.

"At least this way no one will know that they're mine that I'm loaning to you," Mesim muttered, standing Nendawagan in the middle of the room and spending the better part of the day simply dressing her up in the various ornaments.

"Do you think Nocha will have Ola take him out to find another one of the strange creatures, to kill it and bring it back for the feast?" Nendawagan wondered aloud.

"I expect something like that might happen," her mother answered wistfully. "Was it very good?"

"A bit tough, I think, although the broth from the bones was quite delicious."

"Perhaps it was an old animal, then. You'll have to compare it, if they do find another one to bring back."

It was three days before her father returned, which was about the same time it took Nendawagan's mother to come up with an outfit she deemed worthy of the engagement feast, having lamented the entire time that Ola Achukma should have gotten her something of some beauty to add to it. Dusty caves and pretty paintings were nice and all, but part of this feast was all about showing off that the two of them would work out well together. No one could doubt Nendawagan's cooking, but what about him? Sure, he could provide well enough for himself, but what about a wife and children?

"Guka, if you didn't like him, you could have said something," Nendawagan told her over tea the night before the feast.

Her mother gave her a look and sighed. "Many years ago, I took my vows as a Moravian. I gave up many of the old ways, including being head of the household. Yes, others think it very strange and call it a relic of the Old Land, but seeing how it affects no one but our family, and it has done us no harm, I've seen no reason to forsake a holy vow."

"You still believe in the God of the Old Land, then?"

"I do. And I believe him to be the God of Hlohi as well. He is the Creator and above all the spirits of both places."

Nendawagan shifted in her seat. "Ola Achukma still carries a Bible with him, from his father from the Old Land."

Mesim raised a brow. "Does he? Well, I remember he had one when he first came here. I would have thought it destroyed by now."

"He keeps it with him at all times, so it doesn't get destroyed." Nendawagan added quickly, "If he is capable of keeping that hidden and safe, even with all his duties with the festival, the elders, and now Eagle Clan, I think he can provide for anyone and anything."

Her mother gave her a look but said nothing more about it.

The following morning was spent getting ready for the feast. Her mother went to oversee the food, sending word back that another one of the strange creatures had been hunted and brought back. Meanwhile, Popokus was set to the task of helping Nendawagan get all dressed up for it, all according to their mother's wishes spelled out in no uncertain terms on paper in the basket where the appropriate adornments had been separated.

"Well, with any luck, this one will turn out better than the last one," Popokus said, laying out each piece of jewelry.

"Honestly, that's the first thing out of your mouth?" Nendawagan asked, stricken by how precisely she sounded like their mother.

Her sister blushed. "Sorry. I just meant...I didn't expect it to happen so soon."

"What to happen so soon?"

"You finding another man. I mean, considering how long it took you to find the first, well, I mean, I had half a dozen children before that. I thought for sure it would be another ten years or more." She giggled. "So what made you change your mind?"

"About what?"

"Come on, Nenda, you're not this clueless. About Ola Achukma! Everyone has seen it for years. You are so much alike. Oh, you always said it was because of the age difference, that you knew him when he was a child. Or the sorceries, that you were so much more advanced. Sure, things have probably changed a little in the last few years, but what happened that suddenly he went from a good friend to your fiance?"

"I told you about the caves."

Popokus gave her a look. "Caves? Really, Nenda? I thought you were being funny." She glanced at the necklace in her hands. "On the other hand, considering you have to wear Guka's jewelry to your own engagement feast..."

"He's knowledgeable, Popokus. And curious. And he knows that I am, too. He didn't have to show me the caves. He could have taken the elders or the healers or the priests, or he could have just ignored them entirely like everyone else does. But he wanted to explore, and he knew I would want to see them, too. He's more thoughtful than just trying to show me off as a pretty flower."

"But you are a pretty flower. I don't know why you don't want to show it off every once in a while."

"I do show it off. And a lot of people notice. A lot of young men notice. But he is the only one who has noticed something beyond that and gave me the gift to match."

Her sister raised a brow. "Sounds like quite the intervention, then, that you didn't marry the last one."

Nendawagan frowned. Then, "I guess so."

She tried not to dwell on it. The event had been devastating enough without stopping to consider whether she could have been responsible for his death. But then, why would the spirits go to such extremes to ensure it never happened? Why not simply inform the priests that it had been a poor match and let everyone go on their way?

Popokus was quick to pick up on her discomfort and steered the conversation toward other things, such as how much she was looking forward to trying the new meat.

"It may not be as exotic as a hog," Nendawagan told her, "but Ola Achukma was the first person to hunt one, and now two!"

Indeed, just stepping out of the house, they were greeted with the smell of something delicious wafting through the air. New meat or not, Nendawagan could not say that her mother was inflexible when it came to trying new things with new foods, and this occasion demanded the finest she could give.

Already the townhouse was full of people. As Nendawagan entered—Popokus ensuring that everyone knew she had arrived—she couldn't help but wonder what everyone was thinking. Did they pity her, that she was going through this again? Were they excited? Were they just here for the food? A thousand thoughts swirled through her mind as she made nice with everyone.

Those thoughts stopped when she spotted Ola Achukma just arriving. She almost didn't recognize him. Normally very scholarly, he was more apt to carry around papers, brushes, and inkwells, keeping only a small knife for general use. Now he was presented as a great hunter and warrior, carrying a bow, quiver of arrows, multiple knives, and wearing hard leather armor. It was almost comical, really, yet she found it wildly attractive. He wasn't just the meek and mild little boy she'd met in this very townhouse all those years ago. He was a man now, a grown man of many skills and talents and gifts, and he wanted to impress her with those gifts in the same way she wanted to be part of those gifts.

Nendawagan was jerked from her musings at a nudge from

Popokus, whose smug expression suddenly annoyed her. She shrugged off her sister and made her way over to her fiance.

"You made it," she began lamely.

"Yes, your father came and got me," he replied, looking equally as uncomfortable.

"And you brought another one of those beasts."

"In Eagle Clan, we've already taken to calling them deinlato." At her apparent confused look, he clarified, "It's something like 'sharp bear.' "

"Another one of your linguistic renderings?" Nendawagan guessed.

Ola Achukma shook his head. "I had nothing to do with it. We returned from the hunt, and apparently that was what some of the children and boys just becoming men decided it should be called. No one objected, so now we have deinlato."

"I remember the skeleton from the first animal. Is that really what a bear looks like in the Old Land?"

"Not really, but it was the closest association that could be made, I suppose."

Before either could say more, a couple of guests approached, wishing them well and making small talk. Gradually more and more people surrounded them until the two of them were effectively separated, though no less the center of attention. Much ado was made over the meat, how good he was to bring it and how good she was to prepare it.

All this to say that the guests were hungry and wanted to eat, but could not until the two of them had taken the first strips of meat. Nendawagan would not say she was not hungry, and the meat, the deinlato, did smell mighty fine. She also knew it was probably the only chance she was going to get to eat that night. She and Ola Achukma would take the first pieces of meat, and this would allow the guests to eat. Everyone would be occupied for about two minutes, then, as they ate of the new meat and gossiped about it. Then things would turn back to the engaged couple and she would have no further time to herself for such things.

And this was exactly how it happened. Ola Achukma made a grand showing of cutting off two great strips of meat for himself and her. Then they stood back while the guests were given their portions, directed by Mesim, and sent away to eat. It tasted as good as it smelled, Nendawagan thought, much better than the last one; perhaps it had been an old animal last time. Then, once everyone had gotten over the novelty of the meat, they returned to the happy couple, flocking over them like vultures.

The whole point of the feast was to get everyone in the two families acquainted, including close friends, and letting everyone know that this was a good idea. Or that was what was said, anyway. It wasn't as though everyone didn't already know each other, or, as Popokus suggested, that Nendawagan and Ola Achukma were good for one another. The secondary reason, then, was simply to have a good time and eat lots of food. Nendawagan had yet to come up with a reason this was a bad thing, though it just seemed more exhausting when she was the center of attention and expectations. Despite being around sixty years old—still looking no older than twenty-five—and not one to normally shy away from the social or political scene, there were some in attendance who acted as though she'd just come strolling into town only the night before, asking her the dumbest questions and giving her the weirdest advice.

Looking at Ola Achukma, he seemed to be in a similar predicament. Nendawagan watched as one older man made a motion as if drawing the string on a bow, narrating the whole time though she could not hear the words. It seemed to be a very long and involved lecture. When she was able to catch her fiance's eye, he blushed, made a helpless motion, and absently nodded at something the older man said as he released his invisible arrow.

Nendawagan jumped as someone put a hand on her shoulder, but it was only another older woman with a bit of advice.

"When he comes to you at night, you don't have to enjoy it," she said bluntly. "In fact, after a couple years, you probably won't. But don't let him know that."

Nendawagan just stared at the old woman and could only come up with, "What?"

"Your mother has explained things to you, right?"

She blinked. "Of course she has."

"Well, has she explained that it won't always be rutted bliss like the animals?"

Nendawagan had no idea how to respond, but the woman saved her from having to come up with a reply by continuing, "Well it won't be. Rarely it will be. But if you really get tired of it—and you must know that he never will—then get pregnant and have a baby. That's one good way to keep him off you for a few moons."

Suddenly the reason for the woman having fourteen children was apparent, Nendawagan thought, and it wasn't just for Old Land tradition. On the other hand, it couldn't be all bad, right? Popokus never said anything about— well, Popokus was the ideal daughter. She would do anything their mother told them was good to do without a thought or complaint. Even Moskimus was not so adherent to their father's teachings.

She looked at Ola Achukma again, ensnared in another droll conversation with a new group of men and looking just as excited as the last time. Nendawagan found herself smiling foolishly. They were different, the two of them, neither of them quite fully of or in the worlds into which they had been born or now resided. They would find their own way, forge their own path. Their road would take them to great places. They would discover many things, learn stories and songs and histories which had not been known for countless ages. They would make Hlohi and the Krydik people fuller and richer for it. It was not just about preserving their identity, but forging something anew, something unique, something that could never have been conceived of in the Old Land. They had a grand opportunity to do something never done before, and Nendawagan quietly vowed that she would not let the opportunity go to waste.

Of course, such things were easy to dream about when staring at one's fiance while standing in the middle of a great party that revolved entirely around them. But once the festivities wound down, the day of the wedding was set, the food was eaten or taken away, and people began to disperse, such dreams became as more of a flight of fancy, waking from a good dream but knowing that there were real chores that had to be done.

She saw him briefly, afterwards, still covered in leather and weaponry, and she made sure to commit the image to mind before they said their farewells and he departed back to Eagle Clan for the year. He promised to note any major discoveries, including more caves, and maybe he would sneak back every so often in order to fetch her and show her these discoveries.

Then he was gone, and Nendawagan felt a kind of loneliness and longing she hadn't felt before. She didn't know what to do with it, and so quietly made her way back home.

For about the first moon after the engagement feast, Nendawagan drifted, as if in a dream. She almost felt as though she were already married, but then grew as confused as an elder when she couldn't figure out where her husband had gone. Then she would question whether the engagement had happened at all, and only her mother's eagerness over the wedding told her with all certainty that it had.

"You should enter as many events as possible at the festival," Mesim told her decisively over the winter. "Some of them I know you will win easily, but it doesn't hurt to have your name out there as much as possible."

"Guka, I'm already getting married," Nendawagan told her. "How much more shall I present myself?"

"You should show your new husband that you have not been idle while he's been away. You should dance; it will give you an opportunity to dress up for him again and show yourself off. Entering the cooking competitions will show him that he is marrying the best cook in Aktiya Waya—there are two ways to a man's heart, Nenda, and food is one of them. If you lay claim to some of the various plants, you can show that you are a good cultivator, both of plants and, eventually, children."

"Children are not gourds, Guka."

"Maybe not, but the principle is the same. And collecting

wildflowers and herbs shows your resourcefulness, not to mention that beauty aspect again."

"Shall I enter one of the horse events as well and show off that I can ride a wild mount?" Nendawagan asked cheekily.

"And put the men to shame? Of course not." Her mother said it so sternly, she had a hard time determining how playful she was being. "But the clothing and beading competitions will give you a chance to show off your other homemaking skills."

"Are you sure this is all really necessary? Ola Achukma has already chosen me, already done many things for me, asked me to marry him—"

"Ola Achukma is taking a chance on you just as much as you are taking a chance on him. Don't expect to change someone or be changed just because you live in the same house together." Mesim gave her a pointed look. "You must show him what you are capable of. Normally this could be done throughout the year as you see each other in town; you could adorn yourself or make some food for him or mend his clothes. But he is away now until the festival. You cannot let that time go to waste." She shifted position. "In a year, what do you expect him to be doing, hm? Sitting around? Trapping a rabbit here and there? No. You hope that he is preparing himself. And how would you feel if you learned that he decided to do nothing for the festival?"

Nendawagan sighed, bored of the conversation, but answered, "I wouldn't appreciate it."

"Exactly."

"But didn't you say that eventually we all turn out to be human?"

Finally Mesim blinked. "Well, there is a certain mundane aspect to things, yes. Ours is a bit different because of your father's position as skiagvsta, but even then there is a bit of rote boredom involved." She shifted again. "But the festival cannot be a ten-day spectacle if work is not put into it for more than just those ten days. We cannot conjure corn out of thin air to enter into competition; it must still be planted, nurtured, and harvested. The same goes for anything, even marriage."

"And what is the harvest of marriage?" Nendawagan asked.

Her mother gave her a mischievous look. "If I told you what to look for, you would never find it."

Nendawagan pondered her mother's riddle for most of the winter. Any time she thought she might start to understand, her mother would inform her that she wouldn't even begin to comprehend the question until at least five years of marriage.

Then spring came, as it always did, and such musings were set aside in favor of work in the fields. Nendawagan found herself wondering how Eagle Clan had fared over the winter, and what they were doing for spring crop planting. Did they have a tilled field? The ground had seemed very rocky. And with the wind, they would need some kind of protective wall so the cornstalks didn't break.

She also began to hope that Ola Achukma might return with some news of a great discovery he'd made. Maybe some new caves. Maybe some great artifact. Maybe some long-lost living relative of the ancient people! All right, that last one might be a bit far-fetched, seeing how it had been confirmed on numerous occasions that there were no other people on Hlohi. But still, it was fun to think about.

But her fiance did not return with such news. At first, Nendawagan was quick to make excuses to herself. After all, whatever work had to be done in Aktiya Waya, they had to do even more because it was a new village. Even Ola Achukma and his brilliant mind couldn't get out of chores, and even he had to eat occasionally. Then, once that was done, he would have more time to explore.

Then came the lull after the initial tilling and planting, and Nendawagan waited and hoped. Had he found anything? When would he come and get her to show her? Would he have any gifts to bring her when he came for the festival?

He never showed. The excuses quickly turned to annoyance. Hadn't he found something? If he could find such grand caves by accident, why couldn't he find anything intentionally? Didn't he know how to search? What other great chores or obligations did he have, really? Didn't he care? Wasn't he curious?

The anger did not last long before it was replaced by guilt over feeling such things, then despair that something terrible may have happened. Maybe he had found something, but the cave collapsed or he was washed out to sea. Maybe he'd been injured. Maybe he'd been beset by illness.

Meanwhile, Nendawagan found herself wrapped up in all of the women's events for the upcoming festival. She wasn't sure how it happened, though she knew her mother had a hand in it somehow. Maybe she was trying to help Nendawagan show off, as she'd talked about over winter, or maybe she was trying to keep her busy so her thoughts didn't get carried away so. Her efforts failed on that front.

Summer wore on, the days grew hotter, and soon the lands were being cleared, cleaned, and prepared for the festival. The course for the footrace was soon marked with dyed horsehair. Frames and targets were constructed for the archery tournament. In one open space, the wrestling rings were marked off, and in another open space, one of the horse event fences was being moved. Elsewhere, the dancing grounds were being cleaned up, more seating arrangements made, more shelters built. The food area was also set up, and down from that, a small pop-up market.

It was all very exciting, and while Nendawagan was happy to see everything come together once again, there was also a part of her that was sick with dread. She was happy to be married, but the last time things had all come together like this, her fiance had died. Just days before their wedding, he had perished. She liked to think that her union with Ola Achukma was ordained and blessed by the spirits, but the last one had been, too, or so the priests had said. If that was the case, had the spirits been powerless to save her fiance? Or had she truly been responsible for his death in some way?

The activity surrounding the festival did not give her much time to dwell on such things, which was probably a good thing. Besides, if she allowed herself to become too distracted, then she was only going to make a fool of herself in all of these events she was part of. She would trip over her regalia or burn the food or do some other foolish thing. Yes, it would get everyone's attention and let everyone know she was there, but that wasn't how she wanted to be remembered.

The morning arrived at last, when Nendawagan was awake before the sun and waiting on the slope for the arrival of the other villages. A few of the more ambitious competitors had trickled in over the last few days, but now was when the bulk of the people showed up. In the pre-dawn light, she couldn't make out much, and she didn't want to invoke Atsvstdi and disturb those who were still sleeping. But as the sky lightened, she saw the mass of people pinched at the pass but fanning out inside the bowl.

She might have hoped that there would be some sign, some way to tell where Ola Achukma was amid the mass of people—a sunbeam breaking through the clouds, for instance—but none came. Well, she wasn't going to wait any longer for him to come to her. She was going to find her fiance, and, with luck, by the end of the festival, marry him.

Awahtalhlapi Tushafa

Celebration

Ola Achukma didn't remember much about the festival itself, except, perhaps, for the number of times Nendawagan was announced as a finalist or winner for the women's events. Carcass dressing, sewing, beading, cooking, every time he turned around he heard her name being announced in accordance with advancement or triumph. Meanwhile, he only placed sixth in the footrace, made it to the semi-finals in the archery and horse racing, and didn't even make it that far in the rest of the events.

With his dismal competition record that year, he half-expected Nendawagan to change her mind about him. All of the event winners, save one, were unmarried, eligible, and highly desirable. And there he stood, a mediocre competitor who was more concerned with history and writing and "intangible things that put no food on the table and no babies in women's bellies" as his detractors frequently informed him.

At the closing ceremonies, it was announced that the next year's festival would be hosted by Deer Clan, and there would be a ball tournament added because of the extra open space the plains afforded. Ola Achukma noted that someone on one of the councils was likely to approach him and ask about the feasibility of Eagle Clan hosting the festival one year.

And then, just as if it had been planned, Yvgidahi stood and announced the imminent wedding of his daughter to Ola Achukma.

Only a scant handful of people in the entire nation didn't know about their engagement, and only another handful didn't know that it was supposed to take place at the end of the festival. Ola Achukma was not one of these ignorant people, but he still couldn't say he didn't feel a little caught off-guard by the announcement. Suddenly the whole thing became very real, and he was at the center of it with a bride whom he'd lost in the crowd.

He'd hardly moved two steps through the crowd before his mother found him, smiling from ear to ear though looking as harried as he felt.

"We have a few moments at least," she said hastily. "The priests have to get in place, and some room has to be made. Chilita has gone to get your things." She paused, huffed a sigh, and looked up at him. She put her hands on his face. "Oh, my son. I'm so happy for you. Your father would be proud of you, too. I know it."

He put his hands over hers. "Thank you."

Chilita returned then, bearing Ola Achukma's bow, a couple knives, and some leather pieces, the same as he'd worn to the engagement feast. Behind Chilita came Apushi, struggling to keep up, pushing his way between people, too small to be noticed well in the crowd but too big to weave through their legs like he used to.

Ola Achukma felt terribly slow and cumbersome, as if he were holding up the entire engagement, though he knew it was foolish. Even the priests weren't ready yet, and he still couldn't spot Nendawagan.

A number of new wedding traditions had sprung up over the years as more and more people arrived and some of them intermixed. One thing just about everyone could agree on these days was that no two weddings were the same, and sometimes they were as different as sky and earth.

Just the event and location of this wedding was testament to that, Ola Achukma thought. The festival allowed for some details to be covered, but otherwise the whole thing had been planned out by their mothers. He'd been briefed a little on what was expected of him, but Chilita had always told him to relax and repeat whatever the priest said, and always answer any questions with "I do" or "I will."

He'd read about Yvgidahi's first wife and their wedding in the Book and thought it all very nice. He remembered some Christian weddings from the Old Land and also thought them very nice. He remembered his mother's wedding to Chilita and thought that very nice.

What happened at the festival did not very much resemble any of those events.

First, a group of men and a group of women danced around the circle in their own time, one to an old Cherokee song, one to an old Choctaw song. When they were finished, Ola Achukma was escorted into the circle where he finally met up with Nendawagan who looked just as embarrassed though less perplexed by the whole thing. Then came a third song, led by both dancing groups. The song itself was new, one that had developed in Eagle Clan over the last year and deemed to be the first truly Krydik song as it was sung entirely in their new language. Ola Achukma wasn't sure if it was appropriate or expected of them to dance, but he couldn't not at least step out a rhythm to the drumbeat.

When the song and dance was complete, the dancers left the circle to the east, the gap being filled by several priests who faced Ola Achukma and Nendawagan still within the circle, spectators all around.

"Ola Achukma, son of Fichik Lukoli, and Nendawagan, daughter of Mesim, you are here today to present yourselves as husband and wife before the spirits, the people, and each other," the head priest said.

"Yes," Nendawagan said confidently.

Ola Achukma might have muttered something of the affirmative. Now that they were standing still, he was able to really look at Nendawagan and take her in. He'd seen her at some point that day, and while she was beautiful, she had looked the way she did most days. Somehow, between that time and now, standing here for their wedding, she'd managed to clothe herself in the colors and fragrance of autumn as though lit up by a sunrise and bathed in clouds.

"Take then this binding and seal yourselves," the priest said, his tone suggesting that things were at a close and something was expected of the couple which Ola Achukma missed entirely. He felt the end of a rope being pushed into his hand, but he didn't know what he was supposed to do with it. In the space of about two heartbeats, he racked his brain for any wedding custom he knew of that involved rope, but he couldn't bring anything to mind.

Nendawagan evidently knew what was going on. She also had one end of the rope, and she danced away playfully. A game? In the middle of a wedding ceremony? Which people had this come from? He liked games, sure, but maybe he should have paid a bit more attention to what was going on, or else someone should have explained to him that this was going to happen.

If he had any saving grace, it was that no one could call him out for being improper, for no one quite knew what "proper" was. Whether he was playing the game correctly or being facetious in some fashion—trying to wrap either himself or Nendawagan in the rope—no one, least of all himself, could say for sure.

But they must have done something right. After a playful dance around the circle, Nendawagan at last seemed to allow herself to be twirled up in the rope, the last length going around him as well. He took her end of the rope, she took his, and, as if directed by some outside force, they kissed. There was much cheering and hollering and the drums started up again. How the drummers and singers had sneaked into the circle, he did not know, but the first dance belonged to him and her.

They disentangled themselves from the rope and, with each having an end, they made yet another circle, wrapping in and out of the rope in a strange dalliance that surprisingly tripped up no one, least of all Ola Achukma.

After that dance, the priest proclaimed them man and wife, to another grand round of cheering and hollering. Then the dancers returned, there was another dance which he and Nendawagan were obligated to participate in before finally being allowed to leave.

They were given the seats of honor at the feast table. Mesim presented Ola Achukma with a finely arranged plate of vegetables, nuts, herbs, and other forage which Nendawagan had taken charge of herself. Ola Achukma's mother then presented Nendawagan with a fine choice cut of cured meat from an animal he'd hunted.

Only after all of that food had been consumed were they finally given water—in a two-spouted cup, no less—and something resembling free reign over their own party.

"Can someone please explain what has just happened?" he asked, grinning foolishly.

Nendawagan was also smiling, though she just appeared more beautiful for it. "Well, I don't know, but I think we're married now. I can't be entirely sure because I've never seen a wedding like that."

"You looked like you knew exactly what to do."

She laughed. "Oh, I had no idea. I knew what my mother told me, but putting words into practice is much harder than it looks."

"And I didn't even get that benefit."

The wedding had already started late in the day on account of the festival closing ceremonies, but it would be dawn before the last of the attendees would sleep; that was just a given, probably the only universal tradition at the wedding, Ola Achukma thought.

As for the two of them, once they had eaten their fill and greeted as many guests as they could stand, the new husband and wife slipped away from the party where Ola Achukma opened Galohisdi directly into his home with Eagle Clan.

"Won't the people be upset?" Nendawagan wondered.

"Only if they're in my house to see it," he told her.

Unfortunately, the terrible trip through the doorway killed any mood either of them were in, and between the late hour and the festivities, the best they could do for the time being was crawl into his bed and try to sleep it off.

It was midday before Ola Achukma woke. He'd spent the last year wondering what it would be like to wake up next to someone, and yet he found himself confused because it was the day after his wedding and he woke up alone.

His confusion was prolonged when he went out to the kitchen area and still could not find his new bride, though a fire had been started and water gathered, and some vegetables were in the middle of preparation on the table.

He turned as the door skin was pushed aside and Nendawagan walked in, bearing more firewood.

"Running a bit low?" she asked, grinning and depositing part of the load in his empty wood box and the other part directly into the fire.

"Well, I had to leave some heavy chores to do in order to impress my wife," he answered, hoping he sounded more convincing than he felt. Truthfully, he may have forgotten, being so wrapped up in, well, wrapping up. He cleared his throat. "We really haven't had much of a chance to discuss where we were going to live."

She raised a brow as she returned to the vegetables. "Well we couldn't stay in Aktiya Waya with my parents or yours, and it would be poor taste to have just stolen away into one of the empty homes."

"Yes, but, as you just pointed out, both my parents and yours live in Aktiya Waya. I can finish things up here in a moon or less, and we can return if you want. After all, you also pointed out that Eagle Clan isn't exactly friendly toward the sorceries. We can get away with it for a few days while the people return from the festival, but after that..."

Now she looked at him, her expression impossible to read though he might have detected a hint of distress. "But this is where we've found the most evidence of the people who came before. We should investigate it further."

"I've visited the caves plenty of times in the last year. I've gone out on short expeditions in all directions looking for more, even hauling a canoe down through those tunnels to the ocean at high tide, to see if there might be other caves or access points. I've found nothing. It's just as Anagalisgi said; the people have been gone for so long that even their ghosts no longer walk these lands. And that apparently includes everything else they left behind."

"How does a people leave behind these villages but nothing else?" Nendawagan challenged.

Ola Achukma shrugged. "I don't know, but the land reclaims its own. Stone just takes a little longer than wood."

She huffed. "Those paintings looked nearly fresh—those above the water line, anyway. There must be something we can learn."

"Well, studying them, whatever people were here before us, they didn't look like us."

"I don't know about that. What if they had some religious reason for not painting themselves? A show of vanity?"

"Maybe. Or what if they didn't look like us? We have no bones to tell us what they may have even remotely looked like."

Nendawagan frowned. "All right, well, what about those line paintings? We thought they might have been maps, of the area, of other cave networks—"

"The landscape has changed since then, I think," Ola Achukma cut in. "I was able to plot some points based on major features, but the variance of the land in between is too great. The one possible cave I did manage to track down, the entrance has been long since blocked."

"Did you try Galo'ondiha ale Agi'a?"

"It's not as simple as a single large boulder, or many small boulders filling in a hole. The entire ground collapsed in on itself. We would have to move the entire land itself in order to get in, assuming it is one of those networks."

He could see the displeasure mounting on her face, and he found himself afraid that it would carry throughout the day and ruin the night as well. His eagerness to use Galohisdi and get home had stricken his chances of love last night; he didn't want anything to ruin his chances a second night in a row.

He elected not to say anything more about it. Maybe it would give her time to think about it and come up with an idea. Maybe it would give her time to think of other things, like the wedding night that didn't happen.

She also said nothing more about it, but even he could see she was constantly thinking about it. After breakfast, he suggested they go out and gather firewood. As she had proven earlier, it was a task that needed to be done, though he wouldn't say he wasn't hoping for a little more than that once they were well away from the village.

Her ideas of going and getting firewood, however, drifted less toward him and more toward the cave.

"You can't find firewood where there are no trees," he told her, dragging the wood sled behind him out of the tree line, toward where she stood staring at the opening in the ground.

"There has to be something more," she said, not looking at him.

He knew where this was going. Reluctantly, he dropped the rope of the sled and went to her, taking her hand and saying, "All right. Let's go look."

That brightened her mood more than he thought it should have, but he wasn't arguing. If he could satisfy her curiosity now, he might have a better chance of satisfying his curiosity later in bed.

The carvings and paintings had not changed since his last visit, some three or four moons ago, though they looked even more lifelike with her expert use of Atsvstdi.

"Where is the cave you found?" she asked, looking at the painted lines. "Which map?"

He let out an even breath. They were never going to complete their firewood chore. It was just as well that the sorceries made it so they didn't have to eat much, but he felt his other hopes slowly draining.

Nevertheless, he pointed out the particular map—assuming they even were maps—he had used to deduce the collapsed cave's location.

"So then what are these?" she wondered, using a stick to indicate other markers. Some were X's, other were O's, and others were shapes they had no name for.

"I don't know. I tried to trace them, track them, look for anything unusual. I couldn't find anything." He went on before she could say more. "If it makes you feel better, I copied the maps the best I could. They're sitting at home. You can look at them later."

"Are they very good maps?" she asked, still looking up.

He blinked. "I copied them as best I could. They might be more accurate than these, just by accident. Or they could be worse. But the fact that there isn't much to find either way..." He shifted his stance. "You want me to take you to the collapsed cave."

"I want to see the map and I want to see the cave and I want to orient myself and—"

"All right, all right," he sighed. "But can we please get the firewood back home first? I don't want to leave the wood sled out."

That much she agreed to at least, and they departed the cave where he grabbed the wood sled and headed for home.

Day one of marriage, and his mind was reeling. He'd gone out and done things at the suggestion of friends, the orders of the council, and other such situations, but having a wife was a whole new experience. He didn't know what to make of it. He didn't know how to react. On the one hand, it wasn't as though he had a rigid lifestyle that demanded some constant attention or a hefty schedule. On the other hand, he felt as though he'd been riding a horse, then someone jumped on the horse with him, wrested the reins, and changed direction. And he'd fully known and even anticipated such a thing happening.

He'd known married life would be different. He'd seen it in his mother after marrying Chilita, and he'd experienced it as a child. He remembered much of the ribbing that other betrothed men got from their peers, and he took care not to foolishly assume that such things would not apply to him. But to actually experience it?

As promised, he showed Nendawagan to the collapsed cave. As expected, there was nothing either of them could do about it. They returned home as the sun was going down. Ola Achukma could see his wife was frustrated, but also tired from the day's adventures.

He knew a moment of something like pity. He'd taken his position for granted. He could have explored the caves every day if he had so chosen. She had only her dreams and imagination. Now that she had a chance to see everything again, why wouldn't she want to take it? Give it a few days, he reasoned, and things would settle down.

Of course, he only wanted things to settle down as far as her boorish insistence on cave exploration went. As for other matters, well, he didn't want it to settle down before it ever really got going, and he hoped that lovemaking would improve over time. It felt good, yes, but it was all very strange. At the very least, it kept his mind occupied for the next day when Nendawagan wanted to go out again. She could analyze the caves and the paintings, and he could analyze...other things.

Ola Achukma had hoped that his wife—and it was very strange to think of her in such terms—might calm down from her frenzy after a few days. Had the weather been so accommodating, this might have been the case. Instead, after that first day or two of exploration, there was a string of storms that swept through the area. If it wasn't the storms themselves keeping everyone inside the village—the wind going over the village, but the rain testing the drainage system—then it was the pine trees that came down because of the wind. Nothing was truly damaged, but no one was going to let that much wood go to waste.

By the time all the trees were processed, everyone had more than enough firewood to last the season, and all of the younger boys got brand new bows with which to practice and make their first kills.

But whether it was being cooped up inside or something about the storm itself which sparked an idea, just as soon as things were cleaned up and back to normal, Nendawagan wanted to go out again.

Make no mistake, her enthusiasm rekindled his enthusiasm, and he was slowly reminded why he had asked her to marry him in the first place. They were both intellectual and curious. He was hard-pressed to find anyone even mildly interested in the caves and the people before, and the elders had tired of his speculations, constantly reminding him that he was there to help invent stories, not dig up ancient, irrelevant truths. With Nendawagan, they could speculate and bounce ideas off each other and tell stories about the people that could have been startlingly accurate or laughably misguided.

It was during a stretch of decent weather that he finally agreed to again haul a canoe through the tunnels to the tide and take Nendawagan up and down the cliffs, looking for more caves.

"Do you suppose the people before might have kept watercraft in that large cavern, so they didn't have to haul it up and down the passages?" she wondered aloud.

"Considering that's what I'm going to do if you plan to go out more than this one trip, I can't imagine they wouldn't," Ola Achukma commented. "That's assuming they even went to sea. If they wanted to fish, well, they could just as easily do so from the ledge or wait for the tide."

"So if it was such a chore, then it wouldn't be done haphazardly," she mused. "They wouldn't want to just dillydally around the cliffs looking for clams when the forage is better and easier up top. Assuming they did go to sea, it would be for long distances."

He nodded. "I think there were peoples from the Old Land who are like that. Entire peoples who move from island to island, spending days or weeks on the open water, navigating only by the stars."

"Is there so much water in the Old Land?"

"Aki showed me a map once. There are huge oceans where it takes over a moon to cross, and that's using very large, fast ships."

For a moment, Nendawagan was silent, perhaps trying to imagine such large oceans and so much water. Ola Achukma would admit that, even having lived in the Old Land for the first few years of his life, his memories of that time were limited and fading, and even he felt as though such knowledge came more from a dream than reality. Only his one trip back to the Old Land even assured him that it hadn't been a dream. That, and Ki's Bible.

"I don't think the people before were a seafaring people," Nendawagan decided suddenly. "The difficulty getting down here, and how needless it would be. Fishing from the ledge would produce far more than coming all this way for a few clams."

"It's also a lot more dangerous to try and navigate these currents than to just walk up top," Ola Achukma added. "Even if this is an ocean and the destination can only be reached by boat, would you want to bring pregnant women and elders down through those caves?"

Nendawagan shook her head. "No. And there are no paintings in the caves that are even close to such a thing. Paintings of fish, but no boats, no crossings, nothing."

As disappointing as it was to not find any caves or other landmarks of interest, there was also something deeply satisfying about being able to say something almost concrete about the people before. They weren't seafaring people. They didn't make much use of boats. If they wanted fish, they could stand on the ledge or wait for the tide, but otherwise, their interests ended at the shoreline.

"Why use the caves then?" she wondered as they hauled the canoe out of the water and maneuvered it into the big cavern, making sure to keep it above the tide line.

"What do you mean?" Ola Achukma asked.

"We come down here and there are carvings and paintings and everything else. We've just established that the difficulty of getting down here would preclude regular, if any, ocean travel."

"All right?"

"Ola, the village is entirely bare. Sure, a cup or a spoon or a bone shard, but the stone is bare. There isn't a chisel mark or streak of paint to be found anywhere. Paint may have washed away, but carvings? Don't you find that a bit strange? Why would you come all the way down here to paint when you have bare rock just two steps from your front door?"

He looked around. "You have a point."

But it was not a mystery that they were going to solve that day. They returned home where Nendawagan set about making dinner. Sorceries or not, trying to paddle around against the currents at the bottom of the cliffs was not an easy or light chore, no matter how calm the weather. Just another reason the people before probably didn't take to sea.

"So if they weren't seafaring people, why build a village so close to the cliffs?" he found himself asking. "The wind is brutal. Why not build farther inland?"

"The wind is just as bad there," Nendawagan said, stirring the pot. "At least out here, we don't have to worry about trees dropping on people."

There was that. "If they had the ability to dig into solid rock like this, they probably could have cut down a few trees and kept a place clear. Why build here at all? A day's travel, maybe two, better protection, better forage. It just doesn't make sense why you would have to build—" He lightly slapped his hand on the table. "—right here."

His wife grinned and made a girlish giggle. "Maybe it's not about the sea, but the wind. What if the people could fly and they needed the wind currents?"

He gave her a look but couldn't stop a smile from breaking out on his face as well. "Ah, well, that solves everything, doesn't it?"

"You should tell the council at once," she said with mock seriousness, ladling out a bowl of soup for him, then sitting down with a bowl of her own. "The people who lived here before us could fly. Therefore, we should all sprout wings in order to take advantage of everything this land has to offer."

Ola Achukma laughed. "Ah yes. That would go over well. No doubt they would tell us some story from the Old Land about a hunter who made a deal with a buzzard and sprouted wings."

"Then they would remind us that there are no such buzzards here," Nendawagan finished.

Ola Achukma chuckled a bit more, took a bite of soup, swallowed, and sighed. "But really, what are we doing?"

She gave him another look. "What do you mean?"

"We're taking away from the people. We're taking away their history, their lineage, everything."

She shook her head. "We're not taking away, we're adding to." She went on before he could speak. "Nocha told me stories of the Old Land, and even though I am a woman, I listened to the reports from those who went back. People go to war over stories. Maybe it's religious, maybe it's political, but it's always over a story." She made a gesture. "Look at children. One claims his brother hit him. His brother says he hit him first. Stories. One is true, the other is false, and only those telling the story know for sure." She sighed. "Some stories are harmless, intended to delight. Others are good lessons. But some stories are harmful when set against others. It's those stories we need to smooth over. We're Krydik now, Ola. You're not Choctaw anymore, and I am not the daughter of a Cherokee and a Lenape. Krydik. And as Krydik, we have our own history, our own heritage."

"But what if we're wrong?" Ola Achukma wondered. "What if we're all just walking lockstep, hand-in-hand into hell?"

"Referring to the hell in your father's Bible?"

"I don't know. Maybe."

Nendawagan frowned. "Stories, Ola. Stories that people go to war over."

"But what if it's true? What is more important, truth or peace? How do you choose between war and lies?"

"How do you know what you're going to war over is the truth?"

Ola Achukma opened his mouth but could only sigh. "I'm sorry, I've ruined this whole meal."

She shook her head. "No, it's all right. It's just the two of us. But I wouldn't bring it up to the elders or the council."

He scoffed but couldn't deny it and hurriedly took a bite of soup.

The thought did not go away, though it did settle into the back recesses of his mind. He found himself grateful for his wife's enthusiasm in deciphering the paintings from the people before. Together they made several more copies of the various maps, then went out and tried to make maps of the area around the village, even camping for several days in order to get a wider spread. But neither one of them was a cartographer, and it was impossible to say whether their lack of success came from missing treasure or bad directions.

"If everything they left behind in their own village turned to dust, why shouldn't anything else?" Ola Achukma said, trying to calm down a rather upset wife as she paced in front of the fire. "Even the bones were gone."

"Yes, but what about the caves?" Nendawagan asked, not for the first time that evening. "There must be more caves. And those caves will likely have more paintings and carvings. You found one, but it was collapsed. Why shouldn't there be others?"

He couldn't argue that point, but he didn't know what to say or suggest. A year they'd been at this. Other than their initial conclusions that the people before were not a seafaring people, any progress seemed to have ground to a halt. And for as interesting as it was to go out and look, and as fun as it was to speculate, Ola Achukma was beginning to wonder what it was all for. They were the only two who cared. Even if they did find some fabled cave with the entire history of the people before written out for them, who were they going to tell? Who would care? And even if someone did care, what then? It wasn't going to bring the people before back. Other than the villages, the people before had left nothing of real use behind, so it wasn't as though they would be uncovering some hidden knowledge.

It was a depressing thought. He did not say any of this out loud to Nendawagan, but he could see she was probably thinking something similar.

"We've done everything we can think of," he told her, finally coaxing her to sit down and talk about it. "Maybe if we take a break from it for a little while, we can start fresh and find something we've missed because we've looked through it so often."

She sighed, looking defeated. "Maybe."

"The festival is coming up soon. Why don't we focus on that? Deer Clan is hosting it this year, so it should be interesting."

This new line of thought brought some life back to her at least. "And the ball tournament. That should be something to watch. Like the dancers, each clan produces one team."

"Yes, but there are three clans. How will that work?"

She waved a hand. "I don't know. I don't make the rules, and I'm not playing."

Ola Achukma chuckled humorlessly. "Neither am I. I don't think Eagle Clan would want me on their team. They don't even like it when I walk by the field when they practice. I think I'll stick to the footrace."

Nendawagan nodded. "Well, after sweeping the field last year in just about every women's event, I think I'll back off this year entirely."

He gave her a look. "Why? You won fair and square. If any of the others don't like it, they'll have to fight you for it."

She shook her head. "No..." She hesitated. "My mother admitted to rigging at least a few of the competitions."

"What?"

"She wanted to get my name out there so everyone would know my name, hear my name, and know that you were marrying a good woman."

Ola Achukma blinked, trying to process the information. "And you didn't say anything?"

"I didn't know until afterwards, late into the wedding, when she pulled me aside. By then...it no longer mattered, and it's bad luck to start a fight, especially with a family member, at a wedding. After that, we came here and just...haven't really left. With all the work we've been doing with the people before, well, I just let it go. Figured I wouldn't compete this year anyway."

"Why did she do it, though? Did she think I wouldn't marry you unless you won everything?"

His wife shrugged. "I don't know. I was so mad that I just...didn't say anything. Not to her, not to anyone. I didn't want to start something and incur bad luck right on our wedding day."

He let out a breath. "Well, I can't fault you for that." He paused awkwardly. "What about your father?"

She shook her head. "Nothing to do with anything. She assured me of that much at least."

Ola Achukma took a measured breath. "If anyone else found out about this in the last year, we could be walking into a snake pit in Deer Clan."

"Which is why I don't intend to compete," Nendawagan said evenly. "You can stick to your footrace. It's hard to rig those unless someone intentionally runs slow or sets up some kind of trap."

He nodded. "I guess I'll stick to that, then. Maybe I'll try one of the horse events. A man may cheat, but the animal only knows what it knows."

"Agreed." She frowned. "I'm sorry I never told you. It just hasn't seemed important in the middle of all our other work."

He took her hands in his. "Just promise me you had nothing to do with it."

"That I can and will promise."

"Then there is nothing for you to apologize for."

She seemed uncertain. "Promise me something, then. If we get to the festival and no one knows anything—"

"Don't bring it up," he finished. "I won't. It would only cause problems."

It didn't make him feel any better about the situation, though. Packing up to go to the festival and watching other families do the same, he felt conspicuous, as if everyone knew about the cheating and the shame but never said a word. Maybe it was his own guilt. And why should he feel guilty? He'd had absolutely no part in the charade. Knowing that Nendawagan knew, well, she claimed to have no part in it and he could find no reason that she ought to be held accountable for anything. It also wouldn't be the first time that a mother went out of her way to bolster her daughter's image in front of a prospective suitor or even her betrothed.

Perhaps what bothered him the most was that Mesim had once been a Moravian, and she had made it known on several occasions that she had never given up on that vow. That meant she was still bound by the words of the Bible. The Bible had some rather stern words about liars and cheats. Even without the Bible, decent society had stern words about lying and cheating. Bolstering Nendawagan's image was one thing, but to rig festival games? The festival had been started as a means to peace and unity. Cheating would not help anything.

Well, he supposed, the only thing left to do was wait and see what happened at this year's festival. Maybe no one would know about the cheating. If they did know, maybe they wouldn't hold it against Nendawagan. Maybe the love of the games would hold off any serious conflict. After all, there were always accusations of cheating, some that could be proven and some that could not. After a year, who could say for sure?

He was still a bit uneasy about going to the festival, but when the day came for Eagle Clan to depart, they were right there with the rest of them. No one said anything about cheating, and four days after setting out, they arrived in Deer Clan.

The plains had been transformed into a massive complex. In the center were the dancing grounds, with space enough for everyone and everything to relax comfortably and dance freely. To the east were the camping grounds for visitors, including the provided feast food, and it was here that Ola Achukma and Nendawagan pitched their tent. To the south were the common events, those that didn't take a lot of room: wrestling, the women's events, and so on. To the west was the Deer Clan village. To the north were sectioned off huge swaths of land for the events requiring more room: the footrace, the archery, the horse events, and the new ball game tournament.

It looked far more planned out than what Wolf Clan could come up with, but then, Deer Clan had no shortage of space to sprawl out as needed.

Nendawagan giggled as she looked around. "I can't remember a time when I didn't have to help set up for the festival or prepare myself for it in some way. It's kind of nice."

Ola Achukma nodded. "Yes, but what if they decide to ask Eagle Clan to host it next year?"

She frowned. "Eagle Clan is still very new and still getting established. Do you think they could handle it? Where would everyone camp? Where would the events be held?"

He conceded the point, and the two of them departed to find their respective families. Nendawagan had no trouble finding her parents, he saw, but it took some searching to locate his mother.

"I was wondering if you were going to come," she said, embracing him. "Seeing how you are obviously so busy being a married man that you can't even come home for a visit."

Ola Achukma felt his blood burn hot. "I'm sorry, Sashki. Things have been a bit busy."

She gave him a cheeky look. "Do I have grandchildren on the way yet?"

His face burned hotter. "Well, no, not that I've been made aware of."

His mother frowned. "I see. Well, considering how long it took her just to get married, what's a few more decades for grandchildren, hm?"

"Sashki..." Ola Achukma pinched the bridge of his nose. "Is Chilita here?"

"Yes, he is. He's showing Apushi around the camp. Your brother is so excited to be here."

"Why shouldn't he be? It's his first time out of the bowl, isn't it?"

"He's accompanied me sometimes when I go out foraging, but otherwise yes, this is his first time out of the bowl."

It wasn't hard to find his stepfather and little brother; they were watching the horse tenders as they sorted the horses between those used just for travel, and those that would be used in the events. There seemed to be more order to it than that, but as Ola Achukma was not a horse tender, he did not concern himself with it.

"So, is he going to be your squire?" he asked, going to stand beside Chilita.

"Who's going to do what?" his stepfather wondered.

"Apushi. Is he going to squire for you?"

"What's a squire?"

Again, Ola Achukma blushed. "Sorry. From the Old Land. A squire helps someone with their horse and any horse combat."

Now Chilita laughed, though his expression said he still had no idea what he was talking about. He patted Apushi's head. "No, no. I'm not doing any of the horse events this year. Are you?"

Ola Achukma shook his head. "No. Footrace and archery for me."

"You should do the horse race."

"Maybe next year."

Chilita nodded and they watched as a large gray stallion trotted past, intent on a mare and frustrated with the tenders trying to move him elsewhere.

"I will be joining the ball tournament, though," Chilita stated.

"What kind of game is it?" Ola Achukma wondered.

"Well, it's supposed to come from the old Anishinaabek, though several other peoples had similar variations of the game, which is why it was chosen. You have a ball, and everyone on the team has a stick with a net on the end. You keep the ball in that net and you pass the ball from man to man in this stick. And you throw it in another net, guarded by the opposing team, in order to score."

"Sounds fascinating."

"We'll give it a try anyway. If it doesn't go well, we can say it was just practice."

The three of them meandered over to the field where the tournament was to take place, and they watched as a couple young men practiced tossing the ball back and forth to each other using the sticks with nets.

"I wonder if those would work so well for fishing," Ola Achukma said. "Just scoop the fish right out of the water."

Chilita laughed. "Maybe afterwards we will have to see."

The days seemed to last far longer on the plains than they did the mountains or the cliffs, owing to the open expanse of land and sky that there was nothing to obscure the sun as it set. So where it might have been near-dark in Eagle Clan when Ola Achukma returned to the tent, in Deer Clan the sun was still resting above the horizon, casting everything in a fiery orange glow.

Nendawagan was already back, cooking up a bit of meat and some vegetables. Neither of them were very hungry, apparently, for they ate little of either, instead mostly drinking tea, swapping stories from their parents, and watching the shadows grow long.

"I have an idea of what I'd like to do after the festival," Nendawagan stated just as Ola Achukma was about to suggest they turn in for the night.

"And what's that?" he wondered. "Does it have more to do with the people before?"

"Yes. I feel like we're not making much progress in Eagle Clan. We've solved a few minor mysteries, but there is so much that's missing."

"So...you want to return to Aktiya Waya and do some cave hunting there?"

She shrugged and took a drink of tea. "That was my backup plan."

"Then what's your main plan? I don't think you'll find too many caves here on the plains."

"I'm not necessarily talking about caves. I'm talking about the Sacred Ones."

For a long moment, he could only stare at her. Then, "What do you mean?"

"In my father's Book, it talks about other Sacred Ones, including one to the south. I want to find it and see if there is anything there."

Ola Achukma shifted in his seat. "Nenda, we don't even know if they would be the same people. There could be different people for every Sacred One."

"And how exciting would that be?!" She grinned, eyes sparkling like starlight. "Ola, there is so much out there to know and explore and see. We have the sorceries to get us where we need to go, to defend ourselves, to make this possible!"

He balked. "And you just expect it to be the two of us, alone, in the wilderness, not knowing where we're going or what we're looking for, for an unknown length of time?"

She didn't seem pleased by his rebuttal. She said nothing more about it, just got quiet except for a polite suggestion that they head to bed; the first day of the festival, even if it was practice, was still a big day. She might not be competing, but he was, and he didn't want to waste any time, did he? The day turned very hot very quickly on the plains, and he didn't want to be running in the heat of the day, did he?

He took the hint and followed her to bed, knowing that he wasn't going to get anything that night and kicking himself for it. Maybe he should have played along with her fantasy; at least that way he could have gotten some and staved off the argument until morning when they might be a little more prepared for it.

But that was neither here nor there. There would be no grandchildren made this night. He sighed. Lying beside Nendawagan, he used Touch and, very gently, probed within her. Nothing. He sighed again. Nope. No grandchildren.

He drifted off into an uneasy sleep.

Pàke Tèlën òk Kwëtash

Wanderlust

"Eventually, we all turn out to be human."

This was the advice her mother had given her. Eventually, she would realize that her husband wasn't perfect. If she displayed any kind of wisdom, she would realize that she wasn't perfect either, and they would grow together, stronger because of it.

Nendawagan had been prepared to accept this reality. She learned, very quickly in fact, that her husband was, as her mother said, human, and therefore, imperfect. He slept weird, sometimes crowding her nearly off the bed. He had a bad habit of leaving things lying around. The things he did organize, he organized in a way she didn't like. He didn't always pick up on her cues, when she wanted to talk and have a lengthy, in-depth conversation versus a mere bantering of words, although he never missed her cues when she was ready for love. Sometimes he got pushy on the point when she wasn't especially interested in love.

There had been mild ups and downs and a minor argument or two. This was to be expected, and Nendawagan held onto that notion with a certain begrudging whenever she and her husband disagreed. Eventually the rain would pass, and they would move on. It was just how things were. It was different in practice than listening to her mother, but things turned out fine in the end.

Most often, their thoughts would turn back to the people before, the caves, the paintings, the carvings, the theories, anything they had learned so far, no matter how minute. They were both frustrated about the lack of information, the seemingly disconnected pieces and dead ends, but they still tried to learn and make things fit.

Why couldn't the people before have left more behind? What was the story for why they hadn't? When their own people, or the ones from the Old Land, anyway, had artifacts from countless generations ago, what was it that made this land so barren? Curiosity aside, if there was some unknown danger here, it would be good to know about it. They'd made up a story about the Creator making too many stars, and yet Nendawagan couldn't help but wonder if their tale of fancy was based on a history of devastation.

But with nothing new turning up where they were, they would have to expand their search. The only way she could think to do that was by investigating what she knew, or what she'd been told was out there. There was another Sacred One out there somewhere. Maybe it would be a different people before that they would find, but if the same catastrophe wiped out every man upon this island no matter his allegiance, it still bore some investigation.

She had hoped that Ola Achukma would have jumped on the idea with some enthusiasm. He had been the one to find the Eagle Clan caves initially, and he had made numerous copies of the maps, gone exploring. This whole time, he had seemed just as invested in the idea as she was.

Why, then, was he so hesitant about searching for the other Sacred Ones? If they were merely two people alone in the wilderness, she could understand. She might not have even proposed the idea. But they had the sorceries at their beck and call. If they really wanted to, they could go out and explore, pick a direction and go as far as possible, mark it in some way, then use Galohisdi to return to their own home at night. In the morning, use Galohisdi again to return to the place they had marked and continue on. This wasn't even counting the advantages they had if they got into trouble with predators or other hazards.

The festival allowed for too little and too much time to think. Too little, because Nendawagan was often out visiting with family and friends from Aktiya Waya and watching her husband practice or compete, depending on the day. Too much, because her thoughts always wandered back to a single topic, a single goal. Now that she had been refused, she wanted nothing more than what she had been denied.

She tried not to bring it up during the festival, so that Ola Achukma would not be distracted in his events. She also did not bring it up to anyone else. The only one who might be remotely sympathetic to her was her father. Well, even if he didn't have many duties concerning the festival, it still wouldn't be enough. Her father would listen to her, offer some advice, give out a few warnings, maybe tell a story about something from the Old Land, and nothing would change. Not that she expected it to, from him. He couldn't order Ola Achukma to take her to the Sacred Ones.

So she watched the festival, smiled, made small talk, enjoyed the fact that she didn't have to work or cater to visitors because this time, she was a visitor. But always her thoughts went to the Sacred One, rumored to be somewhere in the south. How far south, she did not know. Perhaps she should read her father's Book again to see if there were clearer directions she simply did not recall.

Ola Achukma's events had ended for the day—with him advancing in both—but he was out doing other things, so she took the time to seek out her father. She was more surprised to be able to speak to him amid everything else he was doing, but then, he, too, was primarily a visitor this year.

"Nenda, what can I do for you?" he greeted as she approached.

She got closer so she did not have to raise her voice and alert others. "Nocha, do you still have your Book?"

This unexpected conversation starter saw him mentally stumble, but he answered, "Yes, it's back home. Why?"

"When the festival is over, can I borrow it? I wish to read it."

"That is usually what one is expected to do with a book, but why? You've read it several times."

She hoped her grin was convincing. "Well, Ola Achukma does good work, but you will notice that there are very few books circulating among our people."

Whether Yvgidahi genuinely believed her or simply accepted her answer because he was distracted by other things was unclear, but he nodded anyway and replied, "That much is true. It is hard to set a written language when the spoken one is still tumultuous."

"Build a boat in a storm."

"Exactly. Although I hear that some of the new stories are being written down and kept with the national council."

She nodded. "That is true."

"He's a good man, your husband," her father stated. "Dedicated to the people."

Nendawagan felt her face burn hot, and she hoped her father didn't notice, or dismissed it as the embarrassment of a new wife. "Yes, well, his dedication is not making books fall from the sky. May I borrow yours?"

"Of course you can. You may borrow it any time you wish."

She thanked him and left him to his duties before her tongue betrayed her true intentions. Instead, she sought out Moskimus who was just finishing up one of the horse events, handing his mount off to one of the tenders. He was dusty and sweaty but grinning hugely. He spotted her and, after accepting the praise of his wife and children for his apparent advancement, motioned for her to follow him to the river where he waded in to rinse himself off.

"I didn't see Ola Achukma out there," he observed.

"He decided not to do many events this year," she told him.

"Ah, I see. I understand." He shrugged and immersed himself in the chilly water, then slogged his way out. "What can I do for you, little sister?"

"Please, Mosk, I'm the eldest child."

"But I'm taller and the first one to marry."

She gave him a look, but changed the subject. "How far from Aktiya Waya have you been? How many days, what direction? Have you seen anything interesting?"

Like her father, the unexpected question gave him pause. Finally, "I rode west, once, with a group of hunters. We were told to both hunt and explore the land."

"What did you find? About the land, I mean?"

He shrugged. "Nothing especially important. The mountains

continue on for a long time. Eventually, we got tired of looking at them, so we turned south. The land remained hilly for quite some time."

"What about the plains?"

Moskimus looked around. "Well, I guess you could say this is the western part of the plains. Or maybe the northern, depending on the land around Eagle Clan. But we never found plains on our ride. The hills eventually leveled off, somewhat, but we never left the forest. There was more water, more rivers and lakes, but overall, nothing of interest. Why do you ask?"

Nendawagan barked a laugh, knowing this answer would be far less convincing than the one she'd given her father. "I wanted to know if there were other landscapes available for other people, other villages."

"Is there trouble in Eagle Clan? Disagreements and such?" her brother asked.

She shook her head. "No, not really. But if there were to be such disagreements, it would be better to be proactive about it, wouldn't it? Instead of having a problem and then searching to fix it, have a solution ready to offer."

The look he gave her said he wasn't entirely convinced, but he couldn't deny her line of thought either. When he at last assented, she made some excuse to leave and wished him luck in his other events.

Well, at least that gave her some ideas, though it frustrated her that the only direction that remained a mystery was north. Anyone who had gone exploring simply said that the mountains never really stopped, so they turned around and came back.

According to Ola Achukma, there were mountains in the Old Land, bigger than the ones her father had come from. Some of the mountains were so big, the trees could not grow on them and they remained barren and rocky. These mountains stretched for many thousands of miles north to south. But there was land beyond those mountains to the west, and an ocean, too.

Perhaps, then, they were just exploring the wrong direction.

Nendawagan considered returning to Aktiya Waya herself to grab her father's Book, if for no other reason than to occupy herself during the festival. It was hard to focus on other conversations when all she could think about was an adventure no one else seemed to care about.

Finally, the fifth or sixth day of the festival, she did break down and use Galohisdi to return to Aktiya Waya, momentarily stunned at how empty it appeared. The horse pens were mostly empty, and the crop fields stood idle. A few people had stayed behind to tend to minor chores while the majority were away, but the bowl was nearly deserted, and Nendawagan had an odd sense of déjà vú.

Is this how things appeared when my father first set foot in this place? she wondered. No, there would have been much less. No horses, no pens, no crops. She tried to picture such a thing, but the mental image was incomplete. She looked around. What would be left of us if we were to suddenly disappear?

The horses would either go wild or die, and the pens would rot. The crops might survive, dropping seeds where they stood, but the refinement and preparation would be lost so that they grew anywhere and everywhere they could. Or perhaps the horses would eat them before they had a chance to regrow. Everything material would rot away.

She found herself stepping quietly, almost tiptoeing, through the streets, unsure why she felt like she was doing something wrong. Her father had given her permission to take the Book. Maybe because she'd intended to do so afterwards, but instead was doing it now, like eating dessert before dinner. It was going to happen; it was just occurring in the wrong order.

As expected, no one was home. She slipped into her parents' bedroom and had little trouble finding the Book, tucked away in a wooden box with other valuables.

The Book itself was rather unusual. Unlike Ola Achukma's Bible which was bound in leather, her father's Book seemed to be held between two pieces of wood which were then wrapped in tight-fitting cloth. Over this was another, very large paper featuring a most unusual image, in that it did not appear to be painted. There were no layers to the colors painted on the paper, and it was smooth, almost soft like velvet. She had no word for how the image got there, nor how the depicted wolves could appear so lifelike, as though their likeness had been perfectly captured in a single moment in time.

The lettering was foreign, but not unusual. Printing, it was called in the Old Land. Letters cast in metal, dipped in ink, and rolled onto paper. The precision with which this was done in this particular Book was astounding, though, the same precision that brought the wolves on the cover to life. As a little girl, Nendawagan had always enjoyed looking at the wolves. Now, thinking about it more logically, it frightened her just a little. What sorcery was wielded to make such an artifact? She could think of no ability that she possessed that would allow for such a creation.

She placed the Book in her satchel and left the house, navigating the empty streets with ease, a bit spooked by the emptiness.

If I saw that my people were dying, or if I knew that death was imminent, what would I do? she thought. *Well, if I knew that I was going to die by staying where I was, I'd probably take my chances anywhere else; it couldn't be much worse.*

Maybe the reason the villages had been so empty was because the people before had simply packed up and left. Death was coming, and they were going to try and outrun it.

It made sense. After all, hadn't her father's people done the exact same thing? Hadn't that been the mission of Aktiya Waya for the longest time? Death was coming for the people of the Old Land, so they packed up and moved to Aktiya Waya. Anything left behind would rot, but there would be no bones or large relics.

If that were true, she thought as she emerged into the sunlight, then even if they did find the other Sacred Ones and other villages, there would be nothing of interest. Obviously the people before hadn't survived whatever they had tried to outrun, and a single man would rot away in the wilderness with none to mourn him.

She paused and considered the Book in her bag, the reason she had wanted it. Was it worth it? And why was she having such doubts? She knew the people before hadn't survived. What, then, was she looking for? As Ola Achukma had asked, what good did it do to learn about them? Curiosity was nice and all, and having the cave so close to the Eagle Clan village was certainly an adventure, but to actively pursue this fantasy into the wilderness? That was entirely different.

She kept the Book but returned to the festival with far less enthusiasm than when she'd left. Ola Achukma was not in the tent, so Nendawagan simply lay down to read quietly for a while.

As much as she told herself she was only interested in the part where the band of desperate warriors first discovered Aktiya Waya, she found herself going back farther and farther in the Book until she decided to just start from the beginning. In a way, it helped her to get to know her father. She'd always known him as a level-headed mediator, so it was interesting to read about him as being a hot-blooded young man who wanted to be the warrior everyone else made him out to be.

Nendawagan looked up from the Book when she heard the tent flap rustle; it was Ola Achukma. The sky outside was orange, but the sunlight would be gone soon, she knew.

Her husband looked ready to say something, then spied the Book in her hands and instead said, "I didn't realize your father carried that around with him."

She shook her head and closed the Book. "He doesn't. I asked if I could borrow it after the festival, and he said yes. I got bored, so I retrieved it early."

"Looking for directions to the other Sacred Ones?" His tone was difficult to judge.

"I was, but then I ended up starting from the beginning. I'll get there eventually."

He sighed. "Why are you so insistent on this?"

"Why are you so resistant to it?" she countered.

He paused and looked like he was searching for the right words. "I admit, I'm curious. Exploring the cave is fun, and trying to work out the maps has a certain appeal. But the people are gone, Nenda. In both places where we have discovered evidence of their existence, virtually nothing has been found, which gives me little hope for anywhere else.

Yes, the paintings are interesting, but they have imparted nothing of real value. They have warned us of no dangers, shown us no new technologies, nothing."

"Nothing we've been able to decipher," Nendawagan cut in. "What if that great sun carving is a warning of some kind, and we just can't decipher it?"

"We've been here for seventy, eighty years? If such a danger were common, I think we would have found it by now. If it's uncommon, or rare, or even a one-time event, what do you expect to do?"

"Why don't you want to pursue this?" she asked. "What are you afraid of? We have the sorceries to defend us from danger." She explained her idea about returning home every night, though his expression remained stubbornly neutral. "There is no reason we can't do this except that you don't want to. I want to know why."

"What purpose does it serve?" Ola Achukma asked, his voice tense. "I was sent to Eagle Clan to solidify the use of the new language and introduce stories to bind all the people together, so that we are one people."

"Yes, but you're not going to do that single-handedly. The people have to be allowed to come together in their own way, too. You've built the fences, now let the horses mingle."

He blinked as if unable to comprehend the analogy.

"At what point would you agree to go searching?" Nendawagan asked calmly. "What goal are you trying to reach?"

He sighed, any harsh resistance fading. "I want to actually feel like one people. I want to be able to say I am Krydik, just like everyone else here." He continued before she could speak. "Your parents were from separate peoples, so you know what it's like to be a mixed-blood. Your parents tell you everything is fine, but you see the looks, you hear the whispers. I got the same thing when I was a child. I got it when I came here. Oh no, his father was the dreaded white man. Even though my father was dead and many people here have never even seen a white man. I want to be able to walk through any village, amid any crowd, and not feel ostracized because of that."

Nendawagan stared at him for a long moment, unsure what to say or do. After a moment, Ola Achukma just shook his head, sat down, and rustled around in a bag for a bit of jerky which he tore into with some undo ferocity.

"You're right that I do understand what it's like to be a mixed-blood," she said at last. "I was only a few years old when Wolf Clan started to really bring non-Cherokees to Aktiya Waya. They'd done so a handful at a time, here and there as it was convenient, such as my mother and the Moravians, but this was the first intentional, large-scale rescue of a non-Cherokee people. It was a hard sell for everyone, and some were still against it, but it happened anyway.

"Once the initial shock and recovery period wore off, there were disagreements immediately. I think you can guess what some of them were. And as a little girl, I didn't understand why they were fighting. We had food, water, shelter, peace. What more did people want? Who was this 'us' and 'them'? Why was I supposed to like or dislike 'them'? I never understood." She paused. "The troubles that arose after you came are, really, very mild compared to the earlier years."

Ola Achukma stared at the jerky in his hand, sighed, swallowed what he had, then put the rest away and rubbed his face. "My father, Aki, John Aberdeen, was a diplomat. An ambassador. A peacemaker. The different tribes almost went to war over who got to adopt him as their own because they all loved him so much. He could walk into a room about to explode into violence and everything would just calm down, and people would talk. He just had that effect on people."

"And you wish you could do the same."

He nodded sullenly. "Instead, what do I have? A floundering language and a handful of stories, trying to overwrite the people rather than unite them."

She went to sit beside him, leaning on his shoulder. "Are you Krydik?"

"What do you mean?"

"Are you Krydik? Are you a Krydik man?"

He shrugged helplessly. "I don't know."

"How would you know if you were? If you were to return to the Old Land and introduce yourself as a man of the Krydik nation, what is it that you want other people to see? What sets you apart? What are your stories and songs? What is your history? What are your dances, who are your spirits and ancestors? What is your food? What is your art?"

Her attempt at encouragement seemed to have the opposite effect.

She went on, "If it took forty years to get from where we were when I was a child, to where we were when you arrived, things aren't going to be solved in a year, no matter how perfect your language or how convincing the stories."

"And even if it took another twenty years, the people before will still be just as dead and their remnants will still be just as empty," he pointed out cynically.

She gave him a look, then softened. "Or are you afraid that if we were to leave and be gone for a while, that the people would change? Then we would be the strangers, returning to a new people with a new language and a new history."

He did not reply, but his posture spoke more.

"Why don't we split the difference, then? We have Galohisdi. We can spend a few days out searching, and then a few days back home."

He still resisted. "What is your goal, then, with this? What do you hope to accomplish? What are you trying to reach?"

Truthfully, she didn't have a particularly good answer other than, "I'm just curious. I just want to know."

"The pursuit of knowledge is endless, my father used to say, and will never be satisfied."

"The same could be said for the pursuit of peace."

At long last, he nodded. "It would seem logical, then, to, as you said, split the difference." He sighed. "If we have these great sorceries that can move mountains, why do we limit them to pebbles?"

Nendawagan grinned. Before she could say anything, he said, "But not until after the festival has concluded and we've returned home."

She considered this for a moment, then nodded. "I can agree to that."

"And I want a plan for where we're going, where we might search. I don't want to just wander around haphazardly in the wilderness hoping to fall into another hole."

She laughed but agreed. "I'll keep reading, then, and see if there are any clearer directions than simply 'south.' "

Her husband had the look of a man who isn't entirely certain what he's just agreed to. It was a similar expression and posture as when he'd both asked to marry her, and when they'd actually gotten married. Seeing how he hadn't expressed any regret over the first two occasions, Nendawagan was determined to make sure he didn't regret this adventure now.

Reading the Book, she came across something that she'd always dismissed before. Yes, she knew about the Sacred One to the south, but there was mention of another Sacred One of the plains. Was it referring to these plains that Deer Clan called home? She didn't recall ever seeing or hearing about any large formations or structures.

The following day, nearing the end of the festival, she found herself standing next to a Deer Clan woman who was watching the wrestling tournament with only mild interest.

Nendawagan looked around dramatically. "So much grass. Does it ever end?"

The woman, appearing not older then forty years, chuckled. "It must, for it gives way to whatever you call home. Those infernal mountains or rocky cliffs."

Well, there was that. "But where does it all go? Where does it end? There is nothing out there but the grassy horizon."

The woman merely grinned but said nothing more. Three more women or younger teenage boys gave her similar responses. It was a more seasoned warrior who finally gave her something more.

"It's not all flat plains," he said. "I went out with my sons one day and followed the river southeast for about six days. There's a gorge, a massive canyon that has been scooped out of the earth like an animal raking its claws over the land."

"Did you explore this canyon at all?"

He shook his head. "Too dangerous. The waterfall was high and narrow, and the walls of the canyon were very smooth, worn by the wind."

Nendawagan nodded slowly. "Was there anything beyond the canyon? Forest, mountains?"

He shrugged. "We turned east for another day, followed the ridge as much as we dared. There may have been more to the south, hills and trees, but we stayed on the north grassy side."

She did not ask more about it, though she was glad to have something more concrete. Even Ola Achukma looked a little more at ease when she told him of her findings that night.

"If we follow the river, we're sure to come to the canyon," she said. "We can use Galo'ondiha ale Agi'a to get to the bottom of the canyon and explore. Who knows? There might be more ruins down there."

Her husband nodded thoughtfully. "I've also been thinking that maybe I should bring some supplies with me to make maps. The maps from the people before might have worked well for them, but things seem to have changed since they've been gone."

"A good idea," Nendawagan agreed. "Did your father teach you much about cartography?"

Now Ola Achukma shook his head. "No. He said that most of the tribes were not greatly literate in such things, the concept of taking the living world and making it flat, beyond simple sketches in the dirt. He said he was going to the people as they were, so he learned how they did things before trying to teach them new, better things. Cartography was never really a priority."

"I see."

He shrugged. "Anyway, it's really just for our reference, I think. I don't know that too many people here would be so enthusiastic. We're the only ones curious enough to go anywhere."

"Yes, but if we find interesting places, interesting things, others may want to see them, and they'll need a guide to get there."

"First we need to find interesting places."

Nendawagan scowled at him but could not deny the point.

"So then," she began stiffly, "the question then becomes, do we really want to go all the way back to Eagle Clan once the festival is over, or do we want to simply start from here and follow the river southeast to the canyon?"

Ola Achukma faltered as he searched for words to formulate an answer. Finally, "It would be the smart thing to do, to start from here. Otherwise we're just wasting time. We'll need this tent, and we have basic supplies if anything comes up."

"Why don't we start from here, follow the river and find the canyon first?" Nendawagan suggested.

He nodded. "Then we can go home to Eagle Clan for a few days, like we talked about. And, depending on what we find at the canyon, we can make a plan for how to proceed."

She nodded and grinned, greatly pleased with herself. "And who knows? Maybe there will be more stories there for you to bring back."

"Maybe, but let's just find the canyon first."

That she could agree to. Counting corn before it's harvested and all that.

There were only two days left in the festival, the finals and then the closing ceremonies. Ola Achukma had, once again, made it to the finals in the footrace, but there was one Deer Clan man he just couldn't beat. No matter how much he pushed himself, how long he stretched his stride, how much he huffed and puffed, the Deer Clan man bounded over the course like, well, a deer, smoothly crossing the finish line and appearing no worse for wear. Every single spotter confirmed that there was no sorcery used; he was just that talented.

All the same, second place wasn't bad, and Nendawagan found herself smirking at all the young women who eyed the finalists. Ola Achukma was already taken, and he belonged to her. She brought him some water and sat down beside him.

"Some years I can't stand him," Ola Achukma puffed as he guzzled the water. "All the years I've spent running up and down mountains, you would think flat ground would prove no challenge."

"This is the closest you've ever come to winning," Nendawagan told him. "Maybe next year will be your year."

"He's won every single year, ever since the first festival," he continued. "Is that even possible?"

She sighed but didn't have time to speak before he was at it again.

"He was never especially talented in the sorceries, so I wouldn't expect him to be able to come up with some underhanded tactic to cheat and get away with it. But that also means that his aging hasn't slowed much, if at all. Granted, he was young when he started, but there's no way he can keep it up for too much longer."

"And when he does finally stumble, you will be there to fill the empty void in the winner's circle," Nendawagan cut in. She pushed the water toward him again. "Until then, be happy that you not only got second, but that you don't have to deal with a bunch of ogling girls."

He took a drink and said nothing to that. After another minute or two, he stood and she followed.

"I'm going to talk to some of the Deer Clan men," he announced, "see if I can't find out any more about the canyon. Why don't you start packing up so we can be ready to leave just as soon as closing ceremonies are finished?"

She agreed, and they parted ways.

Truthfully, there wasn't much to pack up; they'd brought so little with them. They did not eat regularly because of the sorceries, nor did they have children to feed and entertain. She did return her father's Book, though with the chaos surrounding the closing ceremonies and cleaning up the festival, it was impossible to gain an audience with him for such a trivial matter. She found her mother instead and let her know what was going on.

Her mother did not appear impressed.

"Honestly, Nenda," she said. "I understand that marriage can be a new, exciting adventure, and you want to be able to do things that you couldn't while living with us as a single woman, but really! Am I ever going to get grandchildren from you, or are you just going to while away your time in frivolous, selfish pursuits?"

"Guka, you have a whole hoard of grandchildren. And great-grandchildren! Besides, I have time. I have the sorceries."

Her mother scoffed and waved a hand dismissively. She went on, "And there's no telling what we'll find in the canyon. Maybe we'll discover something that will benefit the people. Would that be selfish?"

"For what purpose?" Mesim sighed. "Why do you insist on doing this to me?"

"Doing what to you?"

"Embarrassing me! You've always been a problem child. I've indulged you, humored you. I told myself it was because you grew up in a mixed world."

"And now we're searching for ways to bring us together and make us a single people," Nendawagan protested.

"By digging up old bones? Oh, wait, we haven't even found that much."

"By looking for stories. For history. A history of the people before that we can call our own."

Her mother still did not look impressed.

"And if something were to happen to you, then what? I have no grandchildren from you."

Nendawagan sighed, unsure how to continue the argument, if she even wanted to. Her mother quickly made that decision, however, turning and leaving, muttering unsavory things under her breath.

The festival could not have ended too soon, in Nendawagan's opinion, though she seemed to be the only one who held such sentiments. Everyone else had a great time, and there was much talk about how well things went, holding the festival in the plains and having the ball tournament. Some called for the festival to be moved to the plains permanently. Others suggested rotating it between the clans, meaning Eagle Clan would host it next. Nendawagan breathed a sigh of relief when the clan council stated most emphatically that Eagle Clan was not ready to host such a large event. Maybe the year after.

The thought of leaving and going to search for the canyon and the possibility of finding another Sacred One kept Nendawagan on edge throughout the closing ceremonies. She wanted to go. She wanted to. If they were in Aktiya Waya, she might have been able to at least slip away back home, but here they were guests and had to remain attentive.

And then it was over. Like a dam bursting, Nendawagan could breathe again, and she all but ran to the spot where their things were packed up, just waiting to be situated on a horse. She gathered the packs and went to find Ola Achukma who was just leading their horses out of the pen. The packs were arranged, and they mounted, turning their horses south rather than north.

"Ready?" Ola Achukma asked, and it was unclear exactly who he was speaking to, her or himself.

Nevertheless, she assented, and they made their way against the current of people, slowly nosing their horses forward. A few made joking remarks about it, others gave them looks. A few called out farewells and various encouragements about the festival.

Just getting out of the village and away from the people seemed to take half the day, and Nendawagan felt as though they had wasted far too much time.

"Do you think I should conjure Time?" she asked abruptly, once everything was finally behind them. "We may find the canyon faster and have some time to explore before—"

"I thought our first objective was just finding the canyon?" Ola Achukma interrupted.

She felt her face burn hot. "Well...yes, I suppose it was. Is."

"Why don't you want on the conjuring until we get there? Otherwise we could spend a spectacular amount of time getting ourselves lost."

Her face burned hotter and she wordlessly agreed.

She didn't think much about it until the next day, waking up beside her husband, that they were alone. There was no village, no group, no convoy. Once they got past the heart of the plains where Deer Clan called home and regularly patrolled, they wouldn't have much, if any, help to call on if something happened. There was no warrior patrol around every rock and, well, blade of grass. There were no other villages this direction. Her father would not hear her call. They had only each other and the sorceries.

She brooded on this for most of the day as they followed a small creek which they were told would lead to the main river they were to follow.

Ola Achukma, for his part, spent his day looking deep in thought, studying the river, the landscape, the sky. When she asked him about it, he said that he was equal parts looking for danger and planning out how to draw everything for his map. He would probably have to make several maps, he said. One to show everything in relation to each other, and one to show more localized directions.

"Are all half-bloods so...white?" she asked awkwardly.

He gave her an offended look. "What do you mean?"

"Your mother was Choctaw, and your father was white. You spent a lot of time among the different tribes of the Old Land. And yet, even for living here most of your life, many of the ideas you present are still very...white. Is it just something you're born with, then? This writing and cartography and other things?"

Her husband blinked, his expression bewildered and offended and suspicious and annoyed and sad and hurt all at the same time. "Are you saying you don't think I should make the maps?"

"I'm just wondering why no one else seems so inclined toward such things."

"You are, and you have no white blood in you."

She blushed. "Well, maybe."

Now he relaxed. "I think it's a matter of necessity. If you don't need something, you probably don't think about it. I have no need to fly, so I don't think of ways to make it happen. We have no need to eat dirt, so you don't try to come up with recipes to make it palatable."

"We don't need to find these Sacred Ones, so why are we going?"

"We need to go in order to satisfy your curiosity. I need to make sure your curiosity is satisfied so I can sleep in my own bed at night."

He grinned as he said it, and Nendawagan matched him, blushing. "Maybe. But I still can't figure out why no one else seems to care."

Ola Achukma sighed. "I don't know. They have their own worries, I suppose. Those who don't use the sorceries have cares that we can afford to ignore for a while, like hunger and constant food. Most of those who do use the sorceries have children and families to think about."

Nendawagan frowned. "My mother is angry with me that I haven't given her any grandchildren yet."

"We can fix that, you know."

She gave him a look. "She called me selfish."

Her husband faltered, searched for his words. "If not for the sorceries, I would be inclined to agree. But the ability to extend one's life...I don't know that too many people know how to handle it. In themselves or others."

"In the Old Land, I would be expected to marry and have many children. And maybe I would. I don't know how things would be if I lived there and knew nothing of any of this."

"In the Old Land, there is war and famine and plague and many other terrible things. Having children ensured the survival of your family and people," Ola Achukma pointed out. "Here, outside of tragic accidents, we have no such fears. We have the freedom to live our lives at our own pace without worrying whether enough people will survive to continue our traditions."

She considered this and couldn't help but agree. True, she did feel anxious about being out in the wilderness all alone—well, with her husband—but her fears were purely directed toward wild animals. She did not fear enemy warriors slaughtering them in the night or taking her away as a prize. Even injury and disease were mostly minor annoyances anymore. Anything that did happen, well, given half a breath, they had the sorceries at their disposal.

The creek flowed smoothly into the river, and they continued their journey southeast. They got as close to the river as they dared. It was at its lowest point now, which meant the surrounding landscape was marshy, sucking mud. Ola Achukma did take the opportunity once to kill and butcher a tsuyoniyvgi that had indeed gotten stuck in a mud pit. At least then they would have ample food for the journey, though almost all of it would go to others when they returned home.

On the sixth day after the creek turned into the river, they found the canyon. They'd had an inkling that they were close because the wind patterns had shifted the day before. Then they crested a small rise and paused.

Nendawagan had never actually seen a canyon before, barely knew what it was as a concept. Now it was seared into her mind as the river suddenly fell, disappearing below the ground. As the warrior had described, it was as though great claws had scored the earth, tearing through tender flesh and exposing smooth muscle beneath. Even from their vantage point, it was impossible to say how far the claw marks extended, and the earth that had been removed appeared to be piled in the distance as hills and maybe even more mountains.

"Wow," Ola Achukma murmured.

"That's a lot to explore," Nendawagan stated. "Do you think there's a Sacred One down there?"

"Only one way to find out." He nosed his horse forward. "Come on. Let's get a closer look."

She grinned. "What about going home first?"

He called over his shoulder, "I want to see if it's feasible to take the horses down there. If it's not, then we don't need to bring them back with us."

She gave him a look, though he couldn't see. Likely excuse.

Awahotoklo Tushafa

Escape and Plan

True to the warrior's word, the canyon walls were worn smooth. They were dangerously smooth, in fact. There was no possible way a man could safely scale the walls, and there was no good path to navigate a horse. Galo'ondiha ale Agi'a would be the only way. This was no problem for a man, but horses were less keen on being arbitrarily removed from solid ground and suspended in the air.

And anyway, they'd fulfilled their first primary objective. They'd found the canyon. Now that they'd been here, it would be easier to use Galohisdi to get back and forth. This didn't make it any more pleasant, however, to return home, and, after listening to a heated lecture from the horse tender at Eagle Clan about putting horses through such stress, they spent the rest of the day and all night in bed. Though once they were awake and functioning again, even Nendawagan was willing to agree to a few days of rest before using Galohisdi again to return to the canyon.

"Do you think there might be a better path somewhere else along the canyon?" Nendawagan wondered, the day before they had planned to return.

"The Deer Clan warriors didn't say anything about it," Ola Achukma answered.

"Yes, but were they looking? Did they look everywhere?"

"I'm sure if we use Galo'ondiha ale Agi'a to get down, if there is an easy path, we'll find it no matter which direction we approach from."

She considered this, then silently agreed.

Part of him still wondered whether it had been a good idea to go along with her whims to find the Sacred Ones and see if there weren't more clues about the people before. Was he curious? Yes. But part of him had a sneaking suspicion that this was going to be akin to a lifelong endeavor. Short of finding a suspicious, specifically-detailed, written history, they would never know everything about the people before, which would only fuel the desire for more knowledge about them. Would that pursuit cloud out all other needs and desires? Would it become even more of an obsession than it appeared now?

It was a bit like the pursuit of peace, he thought. A horizon always within sight but always out of reach. A nod. A handshake. An agreement. The laying down of arms. But as one fire was put out, two more sprang to life. And still they marched on, pursuing peace ever more, John Aberdeen taking his wife and children here and there, always so close to finally sealing that one pact that would make everything "better."

Ola Achukma quietly considered this. He had work to do here, among the people. Was his struggle for peace more or less productive than his wife's desire for knowledge? What was his goal? What did he hope to accomplish? At what point did he consider his work "finished"? Maybe the same time that she declared her curiosity satisfied.

But they had made an agreement and a plan, and he was willing to stick to it for the time being. A few days exploring the canyon and searching for the Sacred Ones, and a few days back home so he could continue his work. Although, his work seemed to have gotten away from him, and not in the way he had hoped.

Aside from the usual resistance and accusations that he was trying to introduce too many "white" ideas to the people who were trying to get away from the white men and their ideas, he'd also begun noticing people whispering behind his back when he was out and about in the village.

He ignored it, for the most part. Most people were smart enough to stop talking or look away when he turned toward them. Others were not so smart, or else they were trying to pick a fight.

It seemed to be the latter group who found him out gathering wood the evening before he and Nendawagan were supposed to return to the canyon. Their jeers and jibes were intentionally loud, and when he finally turned to face them, one hand on the wood sled rope, the group of six surrounded him.

"Can I help you?" Ola Achukma asked levelly.

"Where are you going with that wood?" one man asked.

"Home."

"Yeah? Why?"

"Because we need heat and a way to cook our food, same as you."

Now one of the men behind him spoke. Ola Achukma turned slightly, but didn't like the idea of turning his back on any of them. "Same as us? It's the height of summer, barely a need for a spark to keep us warm. And don't your sorceries keep you well-fed?"

"We still have to eat sometimes," Ola Achukma offered lamely.

"Why did you bring your sorceries here? Why are you here?" someone else demanded. "Don't you know we came here to get away from such devilry?"

"I didn't come here to teach you the sorceries. I came here to keep you as part of the people, to learn the language and the stories and—"

"And everything the white men brought us in the Old Land, right before they murdered our families and burned our villages," the first man said, stepping forward menacingly.

"I am not going to kill anyone," Ola Achukma insisted. "I am trying to keep us united so we don't kill each other."

"And only you can do that. Our white savior, here to educate us and make our lives better."

"I am one of you. I am Krydik, the same as you."

Whatever the first man was going to say, he never got a chance before Ola Achukma was suddenly struck from behind. He had little skill in conjuring Time, so he could not slow things down to understand what was going on. The next thing he knew, he was on the ground, staring up at a sky that was much darker than he thought it had been previously, and his body hurt quite a bit more than when he'd started out.

Slowly he pulled himself to a sitting position. The trees around him moved and spun, and he let his forehead rest on his knees until he could think straight. After a moment, he put a hand to the back of his head where he'd been struck. He found blood and dirt matting his hair. In a moment of clarity, he was able to use Touch to investigate the wound further. There was a minor depression in his skull, but otherwise he seemed to be all right. At the very least, he might be able to get back to the village to have someone with a clearer head look at him.

He lifted his head and looked around, letting his gaze focus on various things for a long while before moving to the next object. The wood sled and everything in it was gone, but that seemed a minor thing compared to his own plight.

Maybe he could...

As soon as he tried to invoke Galo'ondiha ale Agi'a, trying to effortlessly lift himself so he wouldn't have to stumble all the way back home, he was hit with another, more severe headache such that he found himself retching with nothing to give.

He didn't know how much time had passed before he came back to his senses, but he knew he was not in the same place he had been. Somehow, he'd both blacked out and gotten himself to move. Ahead, he saw the village, safely set below ground level to avoid the wind which was beginning to pick up, whipping over the cliff's edge like a slap to the face.

Later on, and sometimes even in the moment, he would remember nothing about how he got home, stumbling around in the growing dark, assisted by kind yet faceless people for the last hundred feet.

When he did manage to crawl back to lucidity, it was the middle of the day and his head was beating like a drum. For a long time, the throbbing was all that mattered. At some point, he was able to set that aside long enough to realize he was not in his own bed. In fact, it didn't appear that he was in his own home. He should be seeing a stone ceiling, not the stretched leather of a tent.

Gradually, he clawed his way to a sitting position, grateful that the pain in his head did not turn into nausea. Taking a breath, he crawled out of the tent.

All around him rose great stone walls a hundred feet high, or perhaps more. Wavy layers of rock, ranging in color from nearly white to bronze to pale dawn red, ran in smooth parallel lines, punctuated only occasionally by a new path or small cave. Musical notes greeted his ears as the wind whistled through the canyon, sweeping past him and driving away any lingering heat.

He also did not see his wife. Glancing at how well the camp site was set up, with the tent and a small fire and a few small comforts, he figured it was safe to say that he was not the one who had done it. He didn't even know how he got here.

Then he was left with the decision whether to go and look for her. On the one hand, he wanted to know what happened. On the other hand, what if something happened to her? It didn't have to be as terrible as what he had been through, but what if she got hurt exploring this canyon? A loose rock, a botched Galo'ondiha ale Agi'a, even a wild animal.

Ten steps away from camp and he was on his knees, unable to see straight. He forced himself upright but only managed another three steps before he had to sit down.

"Ola?"

His sigh of relief took him to the ground, but he didn't care. Footsteps rushed toward him and then he was looking at his wife's anxious expression.

"Ola, are you all right? How do you feel?" she demanded.

He managed to lift a hand and found hers.

"I'm fine now, knowing that you're all right," he told her.

Now her expression turned unreadable, but she helped him back to the campsite. She tried to make him lie down in the tent again, but when he refused, she agreed to let him sit by the fire.

"What happened?" he wondered.

"I could ask you the same thing," she replied. "I was out on an errand and returned home to find everything had been stolen or broken, the whole house ransacked. While I'm looking over everything, someone starts shouting that there's been an attack. Then you didn't come home. We're just about to go out and look for you, when the next thing I know, someone's brought you back to me, nearly unconscious. I ask if anyone else has been attacked and needs help, no one knows anything." She paused and took a breath. "Somehow it turns into a group of men is looking for us specifically, so I decide to grab you and bring us here."

Ola Achukma wanted to nod, didn't dare. Instead he asked, "Why here? Why not go to Aktiya Waya?"

Nendawagan blushed. "Honestly, my first thought was that there was no way that anyone could get down here except for Galo'ondiha ale Agi'a, and even if someone in Eagle Clan does have some skills, I doubt they'd want to try them out here."

"Agreed." He stretched a leg in front of him, keeping his gaze fixed on a single point.

She shifted position. "What happened to you, though?"

He shrugged, still staring at the fixed point. "I was out gathering wood. I know I was surrounded. There were five of them, I think. Maybe six. Or...eight? I don't even know, and I can't remember who they were." He told her what he did remember, which was precious little. "Then I wake up here."

She nodded. "Well, I was able to use Touch and heal you some, but I was nervous about making it worse. How do you feel?"

"My head hurts, but I'm sitting here talk to you, aren't I?"

She gave him a look, then relaxed and sighed. "What are we going to do? I saved what I could, but we can't return to Eagle Clan."

"Why not? I may not remember who hit me, but now that I know it's escalated to this, I won't let it get that far again."

"And what are you going to do, kill them?"

"Not kill them, unless it comes to that. Maybe I'll just knock them on the head a little."

"What about being a peacemaker?"

He shifted uncomfortably and deliberately stared into the fire. "Did you find my Bible?"

Nendawagan opened her mouth, but it was a long time before she relented and admitted, "No."

"And I didn't have it with me when I went to get wood. Even if I had, I guarantee they would have taken it from me. It's gone." Angrily, he tossed a stick into the fire. "The last tangible memory of Aki is gone."

Silence lingered over them.

"No, it's not."

After a moment, he took a breath and looked at her. "What do you mean?"

She scooted closer to him. "The last tangible memory of your father isn't gone. It's right here."

He sighed. "I have a headache. Explain it to me."

"You are a tangible memory of your father. Your father and everything he stood for. Peace, unity, all of it. You can't say he was never attacked or degraded for his views."

Ola Achukma made a sound but assented. "He did come home with a black eye or split lip a few times. Almost every time, it came from his own people."

"And still he worked for peace."

Grudgingly, he agreed. "And still he worked for peace." He huffed a sigh. "At the very least, I'd still like to know who it was."

"I would, too. But why don't we give it a few days? For one, your head needs to heal."

"A little Time conjuring should help with that, but I agree that we should wait a few days before returning." He sighed again. "I guess this means we'll be exploring the canyon."

"We were already planning on doing that," she reminded him.

He agreed wordlessly and said no more. His thoughts were more focused on the loss of Ki's Bible. His notes, his underlines, his personal commentary, the strings and ribbons he used as bookmarks, even just the wear on the pages where his fingers had settled comfortably into the dirty grooves. All of it was gone now, destroyed in a fit of rage by faceless illiterates.

He made an excuse to lie down in the tent, yet he lay awake, wondering, brooding, planning and feeling guilty for it. He should be a peacemaker like his father, a living memory as his wife had said. He wanted to strangle the men who did this. And, not only had they attacked him, but there was every chance that if Nendawagan had been home that she would have been attacked as well. He could forgive them for attacking him, but no one got away with touching his wife.

His dizziness and fatigue drove him to sleep before his hurt and anger could drive him to do something stupid, like go back and start demanding answers, or worse.

He knew he woke up some time in the night, but quickly drifted off again. When he did finally wake for the day, the light was still dim, but he crawled out of the tent to the fire Nendawagan had stoked. It took him a moment to realize that his head didn't hurt anymore. Well, it did, but he no longer felt as though he were being clubbed repeatedly; everything had settled into a dull, almost forgettable din right in the spot where he'd been struck. Putting his hand gently to the wound site, he found the barest of depression in his skull, which he actually couldn't be certain hadn't been there before, but no blood or split tissue whatsoever.

He jerked his hand away when something appeared in his peripheral vision, but it was only Nendawagan.

"Are you feeling better?" she asked, grinning as she sat beside him.

"Much better. You conjured Time to heal the wound faster, I assume?"

"I did. I also used Touch to try and put things back the way they were."

He made a show of feeling the wound again and assuring her all was well. He loved to see the light in her eyes as he praised her, and he found himself again smoldering silently. How close had they really come to danger, to death? What if his attackers had succeeded in their attempts to kill him? What if they had gotten to her? Would they have killed her, too? How would Yvgidahi have responded? Had his survival and their escape prevented a war? Or only delayed it?

He hated the implications of that line of thought. Had their purpose, their plan for peace and unity among peoples in a new land, crumbled already, in less than a hundred years? How did this happen? Some of those who had been alive in that time were still alive, still youthful even. Some of the rescued peoples had been on Hlohi for less than ten years, so it wasn't as though they could have suddenly forgotten what made them flee in the first place. He could remember the Trail, and he had been a child; surely adult memory did not wane that fast. Were they not educating their children, then? Did they not tell them stories of such hardships and rescue, the obstacles they'd had to overcome?

Or had Yvgidahi and the others made things a bit too easy? With no external, unifying threat, they were now free to indulge in their petty disagreements. Except those disagreements had become far more than petty. He wasn't the easiest target to pick, and others would not be so fortunate to have such a skilled wife for healing. How he wished he could remember the men who attacked him! Then he might be able to investigate and see whether it was a rogue group of malcontents, or if the feeling was rife throughout Eagle Clan and somehow he'd missed it in all his running around in dark caves.

"Your expression says you're troubled," Nendawagan said quietly, sipping at a cup of tea. She went on before he could speak. "I can guess; you don't have to explain it to me. But I still think it's a bad idea to return right now. Why don't we explore this canyon a little, just like we planned?"

Despite his mind latching onto the philosophical line of thought, he managed to agree to the plan. A piece of jerky distracted him long enough to stand up and consider his surroundings.

The camp was situated in the middle of the canyon floor, but a stone arch overhead obscured them from most lines of sight from the lip of the canyon. The floor was mostly flat, smooth stone, with an occasional scrub bush struggling to find sunlight, or a few small boulders that looked like they had been sitting so long they'd melted back into the ground. The path stretched out as far as the eye could see in either direction, with only minor variation.

"I took the liberty of using Galo'ondiha ale Agi'a to lift myself above the canyon and observe it like a bird," Nendawagan stated.

"What?!" Ola Achukma blurted, cutting her off. "What if you had fallen?!"

"I know how to use it," she defended. "It really wasn't that hard, although I've discovered I'm a little afraid of heights."

"Or maybe you're afraid of heights when you don't have solid ground below you."

"Relax—"

"Relax? Nenda, I was beaten, almost killed. There's no reason to think that whoever did it wouldn't have attacked you if you had been home. Now you tell me that you're using Galo'ondiha ale Agi'a to fly, with no one around to help if—"

"I didn't fly," she said sternly. "I just went straight up and straight back down again. It's not difficult."

"Don't do it again!" he snapped. "Not unless someone is around to help."

Her look was as stony as the canyon walls, but she assented, saying levelly, "Fine." She took a breath. "I understand what you're saying. Let's go explore this canyon."

He nodded stiffly and turned toward the tent. "Do you think we should pack everything up?"

She shook her head. "If we pick one direction today, we can do the other direction tomorrow."

He knelt and grabbed the pack he had made up for the trip. It, too, had been ransacked. Nendawagan kept talking.

"I salvaged what I could. Most of the paper was spared, but only one container of ink survived to any real usefulness."

He frowned as he discovered her words were true. Ki's Bible had also been in the pack, but it was conspicuously missing. He knew another flare of anger, but forced himself not to act on it as he closed up the bag and stood, shouldering the strap.

"It'll work for now," he said. "I guess I should be grateful I have anything to work with at all."

"If you want, maybe we can go to Aktiya Waya and—"

"No. It's fine. Besides, I need the practice. I've never done my own cartography before, so I don't know what I'll need. That won't help at all, if we go for supplies."

She nodded. "All right. Well then, which direction do we want to try first?"

He looked back and forth, trying to judge. Finally he sighed and asked, "How does it look to a bird?"

Her liked the light in her eyes, but he didn't like the feeling that he'd just surrendered something. Pride? Dignity? He didn't know. His head didn't hurt, but he was still very confused.

"There are five canyons, really, or maybe five branches. The waterfall feeds the northernmost canyon, but the river flows through that one and the next south canyon. The middle canyon looks the shortest—"

"Which one are we in?"

"We're in the southernmost canyon, more east than west. It looked like the safest spot, in case you were still out of sorts when you woke up."

He nodded. "Well, I guess if we're more east than west, let's try east first and see what we can find, see how this is going to go."

"How does your head feel?" she asked.

"It feels fine. And if it doesn't, we can come back." He started out, and she easily kept pace. He glanced at her. "But I never asked about you. Are you all right? Were you hurt at all? Did anyone touch you"

"No one touched me," she assured him. "And I'm fine."

"What about your head? Using Galohisdi to escape is bad enough, but then you had to get me and everything else, it couldn't have been easy."

"It wasn't, and I slept almost as long as you did. But I'm fine now, same as you."

He nodded uncertainly and let out a breath. "How do we explain what happened? We know that not everyone likes the sorceries, and we don't flaunt them. We barely use them outside our own home."

"I don't know," Nendawagan admitted. "I wish I did. But maybe we can focus on this canyon? What do you need to help you make your maps?"

He stopped and rummaged in his pack. Half a second later, he paused and let his arms drop. "Do you think it's a good idea?"

"The maps?"

"Maybe I'm remembering something, or maybe it's just something from another day, but...is this cartography too white?"

She shifted her stance and folded her arms. "What kind of question is that?"

He searched for words. "I've been accused multiple times of bringing white ideas to the people, and no one wants white ideas. Is this too white? Even if I made perfect maps, would people even use them? Would they take them and burn them just to make a point? It's one thing to hit me over the head for having too many white ideas. What happens when they decide that I myself am too white?"

"That's nonsense."

"It's not and you know it," he stated sharply. "Aki's Bible harmed no one. It was an object. Most people didn't even know it existed. But to those who did, it was a menace, a relic of a people they hated. They don't even have to look upon white people anymore, but their hatred is so great, they have to destroy everything that even remotely reminds them of white people. Right now, it's only ideas. How long before they come after people? I had a white father, everyone knows it. They'll come after me for it. What about the people who were rescued who used to live like whites? My mother, for marrying a white man? Anyone else, because they lived in a white house in the Old Land? Had livestock?"

"Ola, stop, you're scaring me," Nendawagan whimpered.

"Then they'll come after those with the sorceries, because a couple of white men taught the people the sorceries—never mind that it was to save them. And the sorcerers will have two options: they roll over and allow themselves to be murdered, or they defend themselves. Inevitably, someone will die. That will be the excuse anyone needs to hate the sorceries, hate the sorcerers, hate those who hate the sorcerers, and we are plunged back into the same wars our parents fled from!"

"Then what do you suggest?" Tears were streaming down her cheeks and she took deliberate breaths. "What do we do? Kill them preemptively? Strike them down and validate every fear they have of us?"

He let out a breath, his frustration hampered by his guilt of putting her through such misery when they were supposed to be exploring as they had planned. Finally he said, "We have to send them back."

"Send them back? To the Old Land?"

"Yes."

"Ola, you've heard the reports. They'll die!"

"Then they should be grateful for what they have here!" he snapped. "We have no one to compete against except each other. There is no famine, there are no shortages. This is a great land of plenty. What reason is there for this?! At most, for the entire nation, we have eight hundred people, maybe nine. No one else on this whole island, and here we are, the first fugitives of our own people, through no fault of our own." He took an even breath, trying to calm the situation so he didn't have to see her cry. "We don't have to kill them. But if anyone can't accept the way things are, they can go back. Forcefully. We extended a hand of peace and prosperity, and this is how we are repaid. We should repay in kind."

"What happened to making peace, turning the other cheek?"

He took another breath, keeping his voice low. "You don't want to kill them. Fine. I don't either. They're frightened, and, comparatively, they're pretty powerless. But I don't want to be killed because of their ignorance and fear. I don't want you to die for their ignorance and fear."

She blinked and wiped her face, nodding emphatically. "I know, I know. I just...I'm scared, Ola. I don't understand how this could happen. All the stories that my father told me...the things I remember growing up...yes, there were problems, but it felt so simple. And then the War That Was Not and how you stopped it...and we now have this grand festival every year because of it. I really thought it would fix things."

He took her face in his hands. "You fixed one problem. But if there are no real problems to be solved, a man will get bored. When he gets bored, he will look for some relief. If he can't find that relief, it creates a new problem. Men like to fix things, solve problems. If he can't solve the problem, he looks for someone to blame."

She searched his face. "You think life on Hlohi is too easy?"

He let his hands drop to his sides. "I don't know. Maybe. We don't have to worry much about food. Or shelter. Or land. Or even disease, really, with the way the healers can use Touch—and I don't know a single person, no matter how antagonistic he is to the sorceries, who would protest the use of Touch if it meant healing an ailment or fixing a bone in mere moments versus days or weeks or months. So we look to other things to occupy our time."

Nendawagan shrugged. "The festival worked for a while." She wiped her face again, composed once more. "But why the attack? Why this sudden outburst of fear?"

"I don't know," Ola Achukma admitted. "If I had any memory of who my attackers were, I might be able to guess."

She nodded, then took his hand and they continued walking. "My father once said, 'Hate is a weed. It can spring up anywhere, even the most unlikely of places. But it always has a root, a source from which it derives the nourishment to grow.' "

He frowned. "My father once said that hate is a disease. It takes only one person to infect thousands. If it is not treated swiftly, many will die from it, one way or another."

"Did your father happen to mention the cure for this disease? Love, I expect?"

Ola Achukma shook his head. "No, not love. Knowledge and wisdom. You don't have to like someone to get along with him; you just have to understand his motives."

Her expression turned confused. "But we understand the motives of your attackers just fine. Fear."

"Yes, but why? What is it that causes them to fear? Why did they hold such disdain for an object? Why go after books and paper and ink? If they were afraid of me and me alone, they would have come after me, killed me, and been done with it. But they are afraid of an idea. White men and white ideas. I would be willing to bet that at least one of my attackers had never seen a white man. He was afraid because the others told him to be. Why?"

"Tracing the sickness infecting thousands...back to the one who started it," she deduced.

"Exactly." He shook his head. "But I just...I just can't remember."

"Maybe if you stopped trying so hard, it will come back to you naturally," Nendawagan suggested. "Why don't you focus more on drawing these maps of yours? We may need them to find our way back to the camp."

He glanced behind them where the tent sat, unassuming, not five hundred feet away. Up ahead, the canyon remained almost straight, curving slightly to the north in the distance, he thought. "I don't think we're going to run into too many problems with that."

But he did need to consider his maps. He vaguely remembered some of the maps his father consulted when he was a child, and Aki's Bible had had a few loose maps stuffed in the pages—maps of Israel and Babylonia and Assyria other places in the Ancient East—though how those maps had come to be, and how they were so precise, he had no clue. He thought of the maps in the caves, then decided that maybe they weren't the most reliable source.

"Maybe we should just use Galo'ondiha ale Agi'a, fly above the canyon like birds, and I can draw the map from that," he sighed, after stopping several times to think about how to draw his map, how and where to position everything so that it fit on the paper.

"Oh, now you want to use it?" Nendawagan teased.

"I only said you shouldn't use it alone, when no one is there to help if something happens. I didn't forbid you from using it at all."

Her expression was somewhere between a tease and a smirk. "Maybe, but then how would you document some of these formations in the walls, the small tunnels and caves?"

He had no idea, and the task seemed to grow larger and larger with each step, each tunnel and small cave they passed, each one whistling out a different note as the wind rushed by.

"Do you know," Nendawagan began, "that clouds are very wet?"

"Wet?" Ola Achukma wondered.

"Yes. We've always called it fog in Aktiya Waya, but I'm wondering if perhaps fog isn't a cloud that has fallen out of the sky."

"You touched a cloud, then?"

"When I used Galo'ondiha ale Agi'a to survey the canyon, yes. I had to go high into the clouds. The lower ones were wet. When I went higher, because I was curious, I found that some were made of ice."

"Ice?" Ola Achukma looked up through the narrow gap of the canyon walls to a few white clouds floating lazily, far overhead. "But winter isn't for a few more months."

Nendawagan shrugged. "I don't understand it either. Maybe if we return to Aktiya Waya, we shall have to study the fog when it forms."

He groaned and rubbed his face. "Something new for you to study to satisfy your curiosity."

She giggled. "Oh, of course. But at least that would be a little closer to home."

He raised a brow. "Why don't we finish this investigation first?"

She could agree to that and they kept walking.

It didn't take long to reach the end of the canyon. Ola Achukma stood at the bottom of the wall and craned his neck as far as he could, bending back until he could see the top. Near the top, there was a sloped formation that might have served as the beginning of a path into the canyon, but the end of the slope was still very high up, and there did not appear to be any other paths.

"Did you happen to see any way in and out of here, other than Galo'ondiha ale Agi'a?" he wondered, touching the smooth canyon wall.

Nendawagan hesitated. "There might have been a path, in the lower north and middle canyons, but I couldn't say for sure. I only looked briefly."

He nodded and brought out the map he'd drawn so far. Well, to say he'd "drawn" a "map" would be an overstatement, he thought. It was more of a doodle comprised of only a few haphazard lines. How did he convey the intricacies of this place? There was a cave a few hundred feet back that might have actually been a tunnel. There was a bizarre, almost unnatural, cluster of grooves in the stone near the top of the wall not far from their camp. If it was unusual, if the people before, or maybe even the Sacred Ones, had made those grooves, they must hold some significance.

Frustrated, he drew what he could, making small marks to denote the approximate location of the tunnel and the grooves and several other features of interest and potential importance.

They returned to the camp and kept going in the other direction. There was very little of interest, as far as plants and animals. A scraggly bush, a small rodent. There were more arches here, shading their trek, and he tried to draw those into the map. The ground sloped upward ever so slightly, but then a groove began to form. Twisting this way and that, it almost appeared to be a dry river bed. Nendawagan said as much.

"Maybe the river used to flow into this canyon then," Ola Achukma suggested. "I wonder what caused it to go dry and divert to the north canyon?"

The ground never managed more than a gentle incline, although the arches became more frequent until they became tunnels. Finally it opened up into a large clearing, the gentle riverbed dropping off into a jagged, rocky bowl where a waterfall pool may have been innumerable years prior. The canyon walls here were smooth where the water had once flowed swiftly over the lip, but the surrounding area was more rocky, with enough handholds that Ola Achukma was able to climb a fair distance with little hesitation. He carefully used Galo'ondiha ale Agi'a to return himself to his wife's side, standing on the edge of the bowl looking contemplative.

"What do you think?" he wondered.

"If there used to be water here, where did it go?" she mused. "There is no path at the other end of the canyon; was this all full of water once?"

"There was that one cave we saw that might have been a tunnel."

She didn't look convinced, but he didn't have an answer either. He again got out his map and scribbled more lines, noting the tunnels, the arches, the bowl, and the spot where the water had once flowed. He looked up, back toward the tunnel.

"What do you think is up there?"

Nendawagan followed his gaze, then glanced at him. "Want to find out?"

This time she initiated Galo'ondiha ale Agi'a and carried them up to the top of the tunnels and arches. Now they were only about forty feet from the top of the canyon. But it was not this proximity that captured their attention, the need to look for a more viable way in and out of the canyon.

Rather, they were taken by the presence of more paintings and carvings. But unlike the art in the cave, these paintings somehow had the ability to appear and disappear with each breath of wind and glimmer of the sun as it also appeared and disappeared with the clouds. When there were clouds and no wind, the rock was as dull and bare as the rest of the canyon. When the sun shone, the images appeared as glittering paintings, as though infused with specks of gold or silver dust. But when the wind touched them...

Ola Achukma rubbed his eyes several times as the images seemed to lift off the rock face and even move. An animal that may have been a tsuyoniyvgi appeared in the sunshine, its great antler rack shimmering brilliantly, and then rose on the breath of the wind, its legs seeming to move as though it were bounding away.

Glancing at Nendawagan, Ola Achukma saw she was smiling and wiping away tears.

"It's beautiful," she whispered, and he understood her more by the movement of her lips than her words. "How does it...?"

"I don't know," he answered uselessly, mesmerized himself by the floating images.

Even after the wind died down for a moment and the sun fled behind a cloud, Ola Achukma was still dizzy from the experience. After a minute or two, when the sun returned, he turned his back on the north wall so he could think straight. Nendawagan followed suit, still wiping her eyes.

"Do you think the other paintings in the cave would do such a thing if they ever saw the sun?" she wondered.

"I think if the people before had wanted to produce such paintings near Eagle Clan, they would have some other way," Ola Achukma suggested, though his resolve was still a bit weak.

"Do you think there are other places like this?"

"I don't know why there wouldn't be."

With the next gust of wind, Nendawagan grabbed his hand and they raced along the top of the tunnel, using Galo'ondiha ale Agi'a to leap across the nearby arches, all in the midst of painted tsuyoniyvgi and other animals, alive and racing beside them. When the arches started getting narrower and farther apart, the paintings disappeared and the animals ceased to run. The two of them paused on the last arch and looked back. Even being this close to the last of the art, it was practically nonexistent once they were out of the area.

"Probably why we didn't see it from the ground," he murmured.

Still he made great remarks about the art on his map, and they returned to camp talking excitedly.

"Do you think these are the same people?" Nendawagan wondered, sitting down and stoking the fire which had burned down to coals. "With art this beautiful, I can't imagine why the cliff-dwelling people wouldn't want to learn the technique."

"I think it might be more productive to compare the art itself," Ola Achukma suggested. "You and I might use the same paints and materials, but you are much better at drawing than I am."

She considered this for a moment, then nodded. "Understandable. Do you think we'll find more in the other canyons?"

He grinned and reclined, leaning on his elbows. "I think what we found today was only a sample."

The thought excited her, and her excitement sparked a different kind of excitement in him. With no one around, they made love there in the open.

Despite Nendawagan's conjuring of Time to allow for more exploration, the sun had retreated from the canyon floor and the heat evaporated quickly. They lay together beside the fire, saying nothing.

It had been a good day, Ola Achukma decided. Their discovery proved promising and it gave some direction to their studies. And yet, as the sky turned a multitude of colors and finally faded to black, shadows darkened his thoughts as well. How long would they stay out here? What was waiting for them back home? Even if they found something immeasurably spectacular out here, some great proof of the people before and their civilization, would anyone care? Thinking about the amazing paintings they'd seen, how the tsuyoniyvgi had run with them through the canyon, was such beauty destined for destruction if those like his attackers deemed them to be evil sorceries?

He shifted position ever so slightly, mindful of his wife who had fallen asleep. His first and foremost job was to keep her safe. But if things spiraled out of control among the people, between the sorcerers and those who hated them, would they return only to find chaos and destruction? Would he and Nendawagan be left as the veritable Adam and Eve? What then?

He shook his head and scoffed quietly. Such foolish thoughts. But then, looking around at the silent canyon walls and the dry river bed, whoever had made those living paintings had probably had similar thoughts. Now look at them.

Pàke Tèlën òk Chaasch

History and Archaeology

Early the following morning, when it was just light enough to see by, they packed up and moved their camp to the second south canyon, trying to stay as close to the middle as possible. They explored the east half in the morning and the west half in the afternoon, Nendawagan conjuring Time to give them as much time to explore as possible in the canyon's short days.

There were far fewer arches in this canyon and no tunnels save for one that did indeed connect both south canyons. They found none of the magical paintings in the second canyon and returned to camp a bit disheartened. Or Nendawagan felt a bit disheartened. Or maybe more than a bit.

"Which canyon do we want to search tomorrow?" Ola Achukma asked conversationally as they sat by the fire, occasionally opening small Galohisdi to grab firewood from some unknown place.

"I figured we were just going to move to the middle canyon," she replied, confused. "Did you have a different idea?"

"You said the middle canyon is small, and the northern canyon was the longest. Why don't we search that one? We might have more luck searching by the river."

Nendawagan nodded, though she wasn't entirely convinced. "Do you think the river moved before or after the people before disappeared? Did the people cause the river to move, or did the river moving have something to do with their disappearance?" She went on before her husband could speak. "We can get in and out of here just fine because of the sorceries, but what about those who don't have them? I brought you here for safety, but..."

She trailed off, trying to bring her words together and figure out what she intended to say. New ideas, new concepts, and she was fresh out of new words.

"If the people before had paint that could lift itself off the rock face, dance before our eyes and run with the wind, I don't think they had too many problems getting in and out of this place," Ola Achukma said, grinning. "Besides—" He gestured around. "—there may have been rope ladders or wooden stairs long ago. Such things would have rotted away by now."

She shrugged. "That is true."

They fell asleep in their own time and were moving again in the morning. This time they searched the northernmost canyon, the river rushing through the red dirt, twisting here and there like a snake.

"Do you think Deer Clan comes this way often?" Nendawagan wondered once they'd pitched the tent and set off west, downriver.

"Even if they do, I don't think they'll pay mind to us," Ola Achukma assured her. "We're so far down, they wouldn't think us more than a couple of animals."

"Easy prey targets, don't you think?"

He paused and hesitated. Then, "You may have a point." He shrugged and his steps became lively again. "But then they would have to come all the way down here, plus haul everything all the way back up. And on top of that, you'll be conjuring Time, right?"

"Yes, but not so intensely that everything else stands still. That's difficult to do, and I still want to do some searching myself."

"Even so, we'll have plenty of time to spy them on the ridge if they do come this way."

Nevertheless, they stuck close to the wall and kept a watchful eye on the opposite ridge, just in case. They never saw or heard anyone, and Nendawagan wondered if her caution might not be a bit foolish. Ola Achukma was right; it was too much hassle to try and get down here to claim a prize. Even if the hunters were in a sporting mood, the odds of being able to hit a target at this distance were extreme. Even if the arrow did strike, how likely was it to be a lethal hit? It might strike the arm or the leg, at which time they would undoubtedly run. So either the hunter would have to climb all the way down to go after his prey, or he would have to live with the shame of possibly having missed his target and the loss of an arrow.

But the ridge remained empty, as did the canyon.

Then, with the east end coming within sight, just as Nendawagan was ready to give up on that direction, Ola Achukma stopped, grabbed her arm, and pointed.

It was only the faintest of shimmers, perhaps a trick of the eye in the effulgent sunlight. Only because she had seen the other paintings did she know what to look for, and understand when she found it. It was about twenty feet off the ground, the shadows only just touching the feet of the running animals. Had she not been conjuring Time, the shadows would have already obscured them.

There was no archway or other platform to stand on to observe the art, but Galo'ondiha ale Agi'a worked just as well for the time being. Once there, Nendawagan saw that the animals started a short distance back, a little closer to the ground—about ten feet up—and as they continued east, they wound their way up and around. The river disappeared into a small lake and a tunnel at the end of the canyon, and the animals kept running up the walls, vanishing at the midpoint, almost directly above the tunnel.

She slowly released Galo'ondiha ale Agi'a, and they safely touched ground, gazes still fixed on the end of the river.

"What do you think?" Ola Achukma asked, his grin mischievous. "Do you think we should explore the tunnel?"

"Or maybe that's where the paintings end because the sun doesn't touch the south wall," Nendawagan suggested. She shifted her stance and folded her arms. "On the other hand, what's the harm?"

They approached the lake, skirting the canyon wall and fighting for balance on wet rocks, using Galo'ondiha ale Agi'a to carry them across a line of stepping stones as close to the tunnel as they could manage. The rushing river foamed and frothed hardly a foot below where they crouched, swirling into the tunnel darkness.

"I don't see any paths inside," Nendawagan said, peering closely and almost shouting over the noise of the river, "and I can't swim."

"I sort of can, but I wouldn't want to go in this," her husband mused, running his tongue over his teeth. "And I don't see a path inside either."

Carefully they made their way back to safety, stopping at the far end of the lake to continue to stare at the tunnel. After a while, neither of them having any ideas, they decided to return to camp and explore the west end of the canyon, as originally planned. They found nothing quite as exciting as the paintings—although a few bits of pottery gave Nendawagan hope that there was more to the area than met the eye, as the paintings had already quite proven.

The following day they searched the second north canyon, following the minor branch of the river to the east, hoping for a better find. Again, they found paintings on the north side. Again, the river poured into a small lake—this one more of a large pond—before boring into the canyon and vanishing. Again the adventurous couple approached, looking for a path inside.

"I don't see anything," Nendawagan sighed. She looked up at the high walls. "How did the people before get around?"

"Maybe they really could fly," Ola Achukma suggested.

"Why would a flying people want to leave so much of their art underground, though? And to live underground or in mountainsides? Birds may touch the ground looking for food, but they still nest in the trees."

"I don't know, and there aren't too many of them around to ask."

They returned to the camp. Their search of the west end of the canyon proved fruitless, which only served to frustrate them.

"Only one canyon left," Ola Achukma stated. "And unless we find something, I can't imagine it will take us long to search it."

Nendawagan just grunted her acknowledgment.

"What do we want to do after that? Do we want to return to Eagle Clan?"

She hesitated. Then, "I think we've been gone long enough that any anger toward us has cooled, at least enough to get anything we have left and leave, if that's the best course of action."

"We should return to Aktiya Waya," he said. "I should hope they have more tolerance for sorcery."

He clearly intended it as humorous, but she could not enjoy it. Instead she asked, "And then what?"

"What do you mean?"

"Anything you don't have with you is probably destroyed by now, so I would say your work in Eagle Clan is finished. And unless the small canyon holds anything of significant value, we're really no closer to answering any questions about the people before." She shook her head and sighed. "Even my plans and ideas sound foolish now. Learning more. Satisfying curiosity." She scoffed.

She could feel her husband's concerned gaze.

"What are you saying?" he wondered. "You don't want to know?"

"I do, but I never will. No one will."

"Maybe, but how does that translate into abandoning the pursuit? Nenda, you are a very intelligent woman, very curious." She wondered if he felt as awkward as he sounded. "It's what I love about you. You want to know. You have to understand. You want to make things better. You're not content to simply sit down and live your mother's life."

She spit a laugh and glanced at him. "Well, you're right about that."

"And if you're not going to live her life, well...honestly, what other options do you have?"

She met his gaze and managed a small smile. "The ones I decide. With you." She shifted position. "If there is a Sacred One near Eagle Clan, we've missed it. If there is a Sacred One near Deer Clan, maybe in this canyon, we either missed it or haven't found it yet. But there is a Sacred One for Wolf Clan. We can continue searching there."

"Exactly," Ola Achukma said. She could hear the relief in his voice. "But first, we should rule out anything in the middle canyon."

It didn't seem like too much to ask. They could do some exploring in the morning, then return to Aktiya Waya in the afternoon. It wouldn't take long to find an empty home to move into, although she still wondered whether they shouldn't stop by Eagle Clan briefly, just to see if anything was left. But after six days, seven days, however long it had been, even if anything had been left, it had probably already been taken. If anyone did care to keep their stuff safe, probably they would think to take it to Aktiya Waya.

She could hope, but she decided that it was safer to assume that everything had been destroyed. Actually, she felt worse for her husband, losing so much of his work to which he'd dedicated years of his life.

Neither one of them slept well that night, and they were on the move even before the sun was up, navigating the canyon walls by the light of a gray dawn. This helped them only so much, however, and it was a tense descent into the small middle canyon which was also narrower than the others, or maybe the dark just made it seem that way. They stayed as close to the wall as they could, electing to make camp on the west end, where the center might have been had it been as long as the other canyons.

They didn't bother pitching the tent or starting a fire, knowing their expedition would be short-lived. They simply dropped their things off and headed east.

"Do you think it would be better to wait until the sun is higher in the sky, that we might see any more paintings?" Nendawagan wondered.

Ola Achukma shook his head. "The paintings are beautiful, but they've shown us little of interest."

"Not necessarily. If you think about the paintings in the caves, they depicted different images in different locations. The tunnels had shapes and designs, and the caverns depicted animals and larger scenes. And we still don't know the meaning of the large image in the lower cavern by the water."

"All we've found here, though, are animals. Maybe the canyons are little more than a gallery, someplace where the artists of the people before could show off their talents."

By the time they reached the east end of the canyon, the sun had come up and was slowly filtering down into the dark gorge. They both looked up, expecting to find animals or paintings of any kind. There was nothing. Nendawagan could not hide her disappointment as they turned back west, still looking up as the sun illuminated more and more of the canyon wall.

"Nenda, look!"

Nendawagan stopped suddenly, ripping her gaze from the ridge toward where Ola Achukma was pointing. Then she was laughing, though she could not decide whether it was from joy or fear.

There, in the west wall, not twenty steps from where they'd abandoned their stuff, was a great carving. It appeared as something the warriors called zukatopa. Her father had once called it a snake, but it was not like the snakes from the Old Land, he said. Zukatopa had four large eyes, flared out so they could see in front of and beside them. A broad snout hid five fangs, two on either side and one poisonous dagger in the center. The center fang was set just back from the rest of the teeth. When the beast struck, it used its side fangs to hold its prey while the center tooth injected its poison. The tooth remained lodged in the victim, but the zukatopa would just grow another in a few days. Zukatopa poison was not usually fatal for the warriors or their horses if treated swiftly, but it could be a real threat when out on long missions.

Only the head was carved in the canyon wall, its mouth and five fangs bared menacingly, daring all challengers to approach the tunnel of its mouth, gaping wide at almost twenty-five feet high. Nendawagan had never seen a real zukatopa, so she could only speculate as to what the rest of the beast looked like. Given the head, though, she wasn't sure she really wanted to know.

"What do you think?" Ola Achukma asked, grinning. "Do you think this might be the Sacred One of the Plains?"

Nendawagan laughed again. "It might be."

"Ask and you shall receive." He shifted his stance. "I think we might have to explore it a bit."

"What if it eats us?"

"I think if it wanted to do that, it would have gobbled us up as soon as we landed here and laid our stuff out before it."

She couldn't deny that, but she still let him take the lead, approaching the beast with a certain kind of awe. Was this how her father had felt upon seeing the Sacred Wolf?

The zukatopa did not chomp down on them once they were under its fangs, or make any movement at all, though a breeze from inside the creature gave them pause.

"What do you think?" Ola Achukma asked, his grin becoming permeated by nervousness. "Shall we continue?"

Nendawagan took a breath and nodded, again waiting for him to make the first move. She glanced back only once, past the fangs into the canyon, where their stuff sat undisturbed.

Once they were well into the beast's throat, where the precision carving gave way to more natural stone and they were forced to use Atsvstdi to navigate, the height of the tunnel diminished rapidly until Ola Achukma could put his hands up and touch the ceiling. Nendawagan wondered if maybe there was nothing inside, that they would soon hit a dead end and that would be the end of their adventure as they slowly descended into the earth.

Nothing could have been further from the truth. All at once, the tunnel ended, everything opening up into a large cavern, another tunnel directly across from them. With Atsvstdi fading and their eyes straining in the darkness, Nendawagan spied what might have been some kind of fire pit in the middle of the room. Indeed it was, and Ola Achukma wasted no time in lighting a fire, the wood inside long dead and catching easily.

Flames roared to life, and the cavern paintings with them. They were not so spectacular as the ones that danced in sunlight, but as Nendawagan tried to take it all in at once, it was easily the most beautiful sight in the world.

The cavern was a naturally disfigured shape, but it was obvious that large swaths of rock had been chiseled away to flatten particular areas for painting. These chiseled areas depicted great scenes like the one found in the lower cavern at Eagle Clan. Suns, moons, stars, and grand creatures she had no name for, all locked in an eternal dalliance of which she could not begin to understand the significance. Around these areas were carvings of animals, some painted some not. Everywhere else were elaborate designs and shapes, interspersed occasionally by animals.

"Still no people," Ola Achukma observed, walking around to each chiseled wall and running his hand over the ancient paint. "But definitely a similar style to the cliff paintings."

"Similar, but not the same," Nendawagan mused. "The animals in the cliff paintings were shapes unto themselves. Lines, shapes, merely arranged so that you could tell it was an animal. But if you look, these animals have eyes and teeth. This one has darker lines like it has fur."

Her husband nodded. "You're right. And here, this looks like a river with fish." He brushed the fish with his fingertips. "These fish have scales." He glanced back at her. "Would you say the cliff paintings are older, then?"

"Maybe. We become more skilled in our craft as we age. Not to mention the dancing paintings outside. Why, you seem hesitant?"

He frowned and stood back from the wall. "The cliff paintings were simple shapes, yes, but they were proportional. The animals had proper head and body sizes, even if they were less detailed. These..." He gestured. "If that's a tsuyoniyvgi, the legs are far too long." He pointed elsewhere. "If that's supposed to be an homage to zukatopa, the head is ridiculously large. These are more detailed, but these remind me more of a child's drawing."

Nendawagan looked around. "Maybe. You think it's possible that these were a different people?"

"Possible? Sure."

They spent a fair amount of time staring at the walls, but Nendawagan didn't feel as though she made much progress in learning anything. At last Ola Achukma suggested they continue on, deeper into the belly of the zukatopa.

Her fear now gone, Nendawagan confidently followed her husband into the tunnel. He'd grabbed a stick from the fire, and Nendawagan used this to fuel Atsvstdi and illuminate their path.

This tunnel was not so small as the first, and they could both breathe a little easier, continuing a steady, if slight, descent. The wind was stronger here, and Nendawagan found herself wondering if this stone serpent weren't actually breathing in some way. They continued on, Atsvstdi quickly failing in its usefulness as the stick burned out with no more convenient fire pits in sight.

"The cliff people could apparently fly, and these underground people could apparently see in the dark," Ola Achukma commented as if knowing her thoughts. "I wonder what the southern people could do?"

Their progress slowed once Atsvstdi became useless, but there did not seem to be any danger lurking about. Only by the change in the acoustics did they know they had emerged from the tunnel into another cavern. This one felt bigger than the last, with a definitive wind current.

"Can you relight the stick?" Nendawagan asked. "Just enough to grab some light and see about more fire pits?"

A moment later, she heard the scraping of flint on stone. Scrape, scrape, scrape, spark, spark, spark. The stick did not burst into flame like she'd been hoping, but the nub of charcoal managed to hold the fire long enough for her to capture the light and use Atsvstdi. In her dim sphere of influence, she spied a fire pit and pointed it out.

"It's empty," Ola Achukma reported, the disappointment very much in evidence. He rubbed the pit with his hand and his expression changed. He shook his head. "It's coated in something sticky." He examined the pit more. "And there's a trough here. No, it's a track. It's like the irrigation system in Aktiya Waya, but it's all covered in this resin."

"Is it the same wood?" Nendawagan wondered.

Her husband shook his head. "It's not wood. It's metal."

"Metal?"

He sniffed his fingers. "And it smells different. Foul, but not rotten."

He motioned her over and took the weak torch from her hand. Setting the lit end in the pit had an immediate reaction, and they both leapt back as flames exploded into existence, then began racing away from them, licking the metal frame hungrily. It snaked away from them into the darkness of a cavern that was far bigger than anything Nendawagan would have imagined.

In the light which was fast increasing, she saw dozens of homes on multiple levels, very much like the ones in Aktiya Waya. The fire made a straight shot for a great stone pillar and began snaking its way up and around, bringing not only light, but also heat to the cavern. When it reached the ceiling, the fire disappeared. A moment later, large protrusions from the ceiling lit up, like giant hanging lanterns, the fire spider-webbing across the ceiling. And still the fire licked its way around the room. It reached five more stone pillars. It was slower to move down the spiral tracks, but when it did, it again raced along the ground, revealing five more tracks spread out from the city, fire pits at the end of each one. All in all, the cavern was easily a hundred times the size of Aktiya Waya with thousands of homes arranged just so around the pillars.

"This is...incredible," Nendawagan breathed, grinning.

"We're going to need a bigger map," Ola Achukma agreed.

"Where do we even start?"

"Anywhere, I think. It's all new."

There were three distinct levels to the underground city, with a vast assortment of in-between levels as well. Stepping away from the entrance toward the city was both exhilarating and terrifying. She was excited by the discovery, and yet it felt like walking into a city of ghosts. This big of a city, there should be some kind of activity. Conversation, laughing, crying, working, running, anything. But the whole cavern was empty, devoid of life and even the spirits. She could not explain it, but now she thought she understood what her late uncle had meant when he said that everything happened so long ago that even the spirits had given up their presence.

The streets were empty, many homes barren. If there was any indication of history here, it came in the form of broken stone. Edges and corners broken, a few homes cracked in half. There were more bones here than Wolf and Eagle Clan combined, many of them broken.

"I think I know what the people before looked like," Ola Achukma said suddenly.

Nendawagan looked up from where she examined a bone. Her husband had disappeared around a corner, but she followed his voice.

She found him crouching in front of a pile of bones. Most of them had deteriorated, but there was no mistaking the formation of a skull. He turned one over in his hands.

"I think they looked like us," he stated, not looking at her. "Judging by the damage, I'd say a battle was fought here."

She nodded. "There's damage everywhere. Anything disposable is long gone, but the rocks still speak."

"Something terrible happened here." Ola Achukma stood. "I want to know what."

"Is that wise?" Nendawagan asked. "To disturb the dead?"

"We're already living in their homes in two other locations. If they were going to get angry about it, I think they would have done so by now." He made a gesture. "Besides, there's nothing left. There are no spirits here to disturb."

She knew that, but that didn't mean it didn't still feel wrong. "Where do you suggest we start, then?"

Her husband hesitated, looked around, as if trying to take everything in all at once and describe it very simply. Finally, "Where are we? I mean, where are we really? We were told, your father and the other original refugees, that this place, Hlohi, was uninhabited. Once, maybe, but no more. Furthermore, Galohisdi was the only way in and out; their pursuers would never be able to get here."

Nendawagan shrugged. "Yes, it's in the Book."

Ola Achukma ran a hand through his hair. "How did the people before get here? Who were they? How did Andrew and Nathan know to bring your father here? Could they have brought the people before also, long ago?"

"Ola, I don't know what you want me to say; I don't have those answers."

"No, but I think I know who might."

"You want to seek out Andrew and Nathan? We don't even know

where they are."

"I'd be willing to bet they're in the Old Land somewhere." He looked around. "But first I want to look around this place a little more, see what else we can find. There's no rain or weather down here, so I think we'll find a lot more here than anywhere else."

"Do you think we should split up? There's a lot of ground to cover down here."

He considered that for a moment, then nodded. "That sounds smart. I don't think we'll lose each other, really." He went on, "I'm going to start on the outside and try to map this place."

Nendawagan dipped her head. "All right, I'll start around here."

If either of them thought the place was big before, once Ola Achukma had disappeared—clambering over a stone wall to try and get back to the outer edge to begin his drawing—and she could no longer hear him, the place got a whole lot bigger. She looked around at the size and sheer number of buildings, suddenly lost as to where to begin, though one place really would have been as good as any other.

Without thinking, she invoked Galo'ondiha ale Agi'a, trying for a bird's eye view. Or maybe a bat's eye view?

From above in the light of the fire, she saw the six stone pillars seemed to mark the center of certain districts; homes were intelligently arranged on the levels around each one as terrain demanded. More homes then filled in the gaps, haphazardly creating various streets and alleys and binding the various districts together like too much glue. There was a certain beauty to the precision of the districts, yet it appeared marred by everything in between.

Nendawagan spied her husband moving along the outer wall, head down as he considered his maps. Feeling better about the task at hand, she slowly released Galo'ondiha ale Agi'a and landed safely on the ground.

She approached one of the pillars, using the houses to shield her eyes from the glare of the fire. Some of the buildings, those making up the districts, looked like they had been carved from the cave itself, as if the floor might have once been higher than it presently was. The rest of the buildings, the ones that were stuck here and there like glue, they were built individually, one stone on top of another. But why were they so haphazard? Aktiya Waya had also been carved out from the mountain, yet there was nothing haphazard about it. The cliff village of Eagle Clan was carved out with stunning precision, the extra quarry discarded no one knew where. Why keep this stone here? And why use it to ruin the precision of the rest of the layout?

There were more bones to be found, as well as more skull piles. Some were animals, but there were enough human skulls to make her wonder. Simple fascination with her father's Book was quickly turning into suspicious curiosity. Not against her father, but Nathan and Andrew, maybe even the Book, too.

The dimness of the cave made it so she lost all sense of direction, but she discovered that one district was different from the others. It had no haphazard houses, and the houses that were there were bigger than the rest, with many rooms. One in particular stood out as a very large building, and it had a wall around it. There was only one point of entry that she could see.

She approached cautiously, unsure what to expect, unsure whether she should feel foolish for having such feelings. But this was the only building that made her question whether all the spirits were truly gone, whether this place really was uninhabited.

The walls could not have been more than fifteen feet tall from the outside, but as she entered through a gate that no longer existed, they seemed to stretch all the way to the ceiling. The light from the fire could not penetrate here, but she spotted several places where fire may have burned, unconnected to the rest of the system.

She used Atsvstdi to guide her way as she walked into the building. Not ten steps in, she discovered a large pile of bones. There were not just skulls here, but whole skeletons. Assuming each head had a body, twenty skeletons lay a tangled heap. All flesh was rotted to dust, all clothing eaten away by time.

"The spirits are long gone," Nendawagan whispered, feeling a chill creep up her arms.

She turned away and hurried through the first door she saw. There were more skeletons here, one to four in every room in the building, twenty-two rooms across three floors in all.

Perhaps the most interesting thing she found was in a back room on the first floor. Judging by certain marks, she might have guessed there used to be a wall or a door or some other partition, likely made of wood or some other material that was now rotted. A skeleton lay there, its size suggesting an adult, its position suggesting the person had been curled up. Flesh was gone, clothing absent, but there lay a metal object within the skeleton, delicate finger bones still keeping hold.

Nendawagan reached for it, then pulled back, reached again, pulled back. She did this several more times before finally snatching it out of the bones and retreating across the room, half-expecting the skeleton to rise and give chase. It did not, and the whole building remained eerily silent.

Still she waited until she was well away from the building, outside the walls, and back in the city before examining her find. To her eyes, it appeared merely as a chunk of metal. It was not quite straight, but not quite L-shaped either. One arm was longer than the other, two prongs twisted into a spiral. At the outside junction of the arms was a cluster of four prongs, twisted into a spherical shape. Turning the object this way and that, something fell out of the sphere. Kneeling in the dirt, she found tiny shards of glass, collectively no bigger than her thumb nail.

"Ola?!" she called, hoping her cry sounded more curious rather than fearful. She would not say she was not wary of this place now, her enthusiasm and curiosity certainly tempered, but she didn't need him getting worried and thinking she was hurt.

"Nenda?!" he called back.

The echoes made it impossible to determine precise location, but she used Galo'ondiha ale Agi'a to lift herself above the city where, with some creative use of Atsvstdi to be able to see heat in addition to light, she was able to pick out her husband's location and see herself safely there.

"Ola, I found something," she said, releasing the sorcery and running the last ten steps toward her husband.

She nearly shoved the metal piece into his hands, almost causing him to drop his maps.

"What is it?" he wondered, juggling everything.

"I don't know," she admitted, pouring the glass shards into his other hand. "I was hoping maybe it resembled something from the Old Land."

He shook his head. "No, not really."

"Not really?"

"Well, I mean, if you removed this sphere and made these prongs solid and added a hammer and a trigger, it might resemble a pistol I suppose. But that's a bit of a stretch, I think. It could just as easily be a tool."

Nendawagan shook her head and described the scene in the large building. "Even if it was a tool to begin with, that person was relying on it to be a weapon."

"Seems a bit unreliable in that regard, then," Ola Achukma mused. He handed it back to her. "But it does make me want to find and question Nathan and Andrew."

She nodded. "Agreed. Curiosity is one thing. Knowledge is another. But what happened here...what happened everywhere, that's something else entirely." She paused. "I wonder...that painting in the cave, where the sun and stars are coming down to the world...what if it wasn't the Creator making things, what if it was the Creator destroying them? The animals were spared, for they had done no wrong, but all evidence of men was wiped out. What if we were more accurate in our storytelling than we thought, just opposite of what we expected?"

Ola Achukma grunted. "Well, I don't think I want to correct them just yet, not until we figure out this mystery." He huffed a sigh. "That brings up the next question. This is clearly the Sacred One of the Plains." He gave her a serious look. "Do we dare tell Deer Clan about this place?"

Nendawagan's hesitation was apparently her negative opinion which he immediately agreed with.

"After what happened in Eagle Clan, we can't risk one clan becoming so much more powerful than the rest, not until we know what's going on."

"But Deer Clan is comprised of Oceti Sakowin and—"

"Yes, they are skilled in open combat, but, using the tunnels, this place is easily defended."

She glanced at the metal piece still in his hands. "Obviously not."

"We don't know what happened here. But we can't risk it happening again." He nodded emphatically and handed the piece back to her. "Besides, as of right now, we still need Galo'ondiha ale Agi'a to get into the canyon. Wolf Clan is happily settled, and I don't think we have to worry about the others in that regard."

Nendawagan nodded. "How is your map coming?"

He turned his paper so she could see it. "I've got the outer wall mapped pretty well, I think. There are more tunnels here, here, and here, but I didn't explore them. Here are the six pillars. I kind of started the outlines of the streets, and this is the big building where you said you found all the bodies."

"It looks good."

"It's a start." He put his things back in his bag. "But this thing you found, plus everything else, it's only going to consume me the more I think about it, and even more if I try to not think about it." He looked at her. "We should return to Aktiya Waya. If nothing else, we should let your family know you're all right."

"And yours, too. Your mother must be worried sick," Nendawagan cut in.

"And mine, yes. Then I'm going to go to the Old Land, try to find Nathan and Andrew."

"What should I do in the meantime?"

His expression faltered and he blinked, as if he hadn't considered her role. Finally he said, "We'll see what your family has to say."

They ended up exploring two tunnels to dead ends before finally finding the one that took them back to the head of the Sacred Zukatopa. The day had long since vanished and only the stars gave them any clue where the canyon walls ended. They hastily pitched the tent just as something to keep off any sudden rain, but it proved to be unnecessary.

In the morning, Galohisdi took them out of the canyon straight back to Aktiya Waya. It was not an official rule, but it was considered polite to limit Galohisdi inside the bowl, for the safety of others, so they landed right in the pass and walked the rest of the way. In the early dawn light, only a few people were out and about. Some of the horses looked up as they passed by, but otherwise their arrival was unremarked.

"Go see your mother," Nendawagan told her husband. "If she doesn't know about the attack—"

"Don't tell her," Ola Achukma finished. "I know. You do the same."

They parted ways.

Nendawagan found her mother just waking, but her father was nowhere to be seen. As soon as Mesim saw her eldest daughter, she let out a shrill cry and rushed to embrace her.

"I guess you heard," Nendawagan gasped.

Her mother released her and took her head in her hands. "By the stars, Nenda, are you all right? Where's Ola Achukma? Did they kill him? Where have you been?!"

"Ola's fine, he's gone to see his mother."

"Oh, she'll be so relieved. What happened?"

"What have you been told?"

Her mother took a breath and seemed to remember herself. "Some days ago, a rider came to Aktiya Waya. There was an attack. Eagle Clan had turned. Specifically, the Apache people. They're driving off, attacking, even killing anyone who uses the sorceries or even sympathizes with those who do."

Nendawagan took an even breath. "I see. But there aren't very many Apache, are there? A dozen, at most?"

"Well, they're the instigators, but by no means the only ones who feel this way apparently." Mesim rubbed her eyes. "But what happened to you? Why didn't you return sooner?"

So she gave her mother an abbreviated version of events, all the while trying to figure out what was going on. She finished by asking, "Where's Nocha?"

"He's taken the council and some warriors and gone to Deer Clan to collect more of the same. Then they ride to Eagle Clan."

"Are they going to kill them, the Apache and their supporters?"

Her mother shrugged helplessly. "I don't know what their plans are; your father doesn't discuss such matters with me. He was hard-pressed to bring it to public forum except that he wanted people to understand that he wasn't doing this lightly. He could be seen as breaking his peace promise, and he didn't want to risk more trouble from others."

Nendawagan turned, but her mother grabbed her arm. "Nenda, don't. It's not your place."

"But we can't—"

"It's over, Nenda. First blood has been drawn. War is here. Now, if your father and the others can convince the Apache to leave peacefully and return to the Old Land, I'm sure they'll be happy to do so. But if they don't stop this here and now, it will only get worse, and we will be just as we were in the Old Land. Peace comes at a price, Nenda. Sometimes it's the blood price."

An odd sensation came over her then as she looked at her mother. She could not describe it except as a feeling of mutual respect as well as a unique kind of courage, and she knew then that she had severely underestimated her mother for many years.

She left the house as calmly as she could manage but still hurried to find her husband. She did not run into him in the street, so she headed to his mother's house.

Fichik Lukoli looked more frazzled than her own mother, but her attention was also distracted by Apushi, Ola Achukma's brother nearly fifteen years his junior.

"Oh, hello, Nendawagan," she said wistfully, not looking at her and immediately saying something to her younger son.

"Did Ola Achukma come to see you?" Nendawagan wondered.

The woman's look said it all, but she answered, "He told me what happened. I expect your mother explained things to you also?"

"She did."

"He's gone to try and catch them. Galohisdi, Adahnesagi'a, I don't know, but I don't think he'll make it."

"Why not?"

"They left many days ago, and I doubt Yvgidahi is going to sit idly by and ride like a common man while people are being murdered. If the Apache are killing people just for having the sorceries, well, that's good incentive to use them. But what do I know of war?"

"We're not at war yet," Nendawagan protested weakly.

"Not yet," Fichik Lukoli echoed. "We will be, though, if they don't end this swiftly."

Nendawagan shook her head. "I don't understand why, though."

Her mother-in-law straightened and abandoned whatever task she'd been idling on in order to give her full attention. "Many years ago, I was married to a peacemaker, Ola's father, John Aberdeen. He negotiated many treaties, settled many disputes large and small. But for as much peace as he made, I think I learned more about war.

"Men like power, Nendawagan. They like control. They don't like feeling helpless against the winds of fate. What your father has done is taken a bunch of powerless people, moved them to a new land, and rendered them just as powerless."

"They can learn the sorceries—"

"And become just like you. In the same way that they could have bought White lands, worn White clothes, gotten White citizenship, owned slaves like a White man, and lived like a White man. They could have lived, but only in a manner approved by those in control."

"Then they don't have to learn—"

"And they will watch as these sorcerer gods do not eat, do not sleep, do not age. The sorcerer gods go on adventures to distant lands at a whim, discovering trinkets from long-dead civilizations. Meanwhile they toil and labor with animals and crops and children." She went on before Nendawagan could speak. "You can argue all you want, Nenda. A man is wise in his own eyes, and he will find every excuse to nurture his anger once it has taken hold."

Abichakkali Tushafa

Bad News

Seeing Yvgidahi, the council, and a small band of warriors riding up the trail toward Aktiya Waya told Ola Achukma that he was far too late, and he reined in his horse on the rocky slope. Yvgidahi's expression confirmed his fears.

"Is Nendawagan safe?" the skiagvsta asked calmly, sounding tired.

"She's fine," Ola Achukma said dumbly. "What happened?"

"We could have used a peacemaker," someone behind Yvgidahi answered. "But as it turns out, the sorceries make peace just fine on their own."

"You killed them, then?"

"Some were willing to return," Yvgidahi sighed. "Some were not."

With that, the skiagvsta nudged his horse forward, around Ola Achukma, and carried on up the trail to the pass. Ola Achukma could only watch them go. There were two dozen in all, and it wasn't until he finally decided to follow, about three horse-lengths behind, that he realized that every single one of them were seasoned warriors from the Old Land.

No one said anything the whole ride back, which, in truth, was not very far. Had Ola Achukma sat down to have a bite to eat like his mother had suggested, he never would have made it to his horse to ride after the warriors. So he tagged along like a child. The difference was, a child would see that the adults were upset and he would not understand why. Ola Achukma did understand. He just didn't know what to do about it.

The return to the bowl was unremarked at first, and they were able to turn their horses out without much fanfare. Once they reached the cavern entrance, though, a cry went up and people appeared from every side street and shadow, asking questions and demanding answers. Ola Achukma stayed back, not wanting to get caught up in a campaign he had not been part of. Still he was close enough to hear Yvgidahi say that the warriors were going to first purify themselves, then hold a private meeting before opening it up to the public.

The crowd dispersed, and Ola Achukma headed off to find Nendawagan. He checked her parents' home first, but her mother informed him she'd already left.

"Presumably to find you," Mesim told him. "I thought you might have ridden off to try and stop them."

"I tried," he admitted. "I barely made it out of the pass before I saw them coming back."

"They've returned?"

He related what her husband had announced, then took his leave. His next stop was his mother's house, where he found her and his wife sitting at the table talking.

"Now will you have that bite to eat?" his mother asked pointedly.

He sighed, but nodded and took a seat. A moment later, his mother put a bowl of soup in front of him. He glanced at her. "Did you know they were nearly back?"

"I suspected as much," she replied. "Are they going to hold a meeting?"

Nendawagan's gaze was burning a hole in his side as he answered, "Not immediately. They have to purify first."

It was an acceptable answer and an acceptable course of action, but that didn't make the wait any easier. He decided to play it safe and simply say that the group hadn't said anything to him. He knew that if he even hinted at the possibility that the warriors had killed anyone, Nendawagan would have a fit and he would have no answers to give. Better to let Yvgidahi explain things, and then she could gnaw on his arm about it.

When he was finished eating, he and Nendawagan went out to find an empty home to settle into. It was strange to consider that everything they carried was everything they owned. Almost instinctively, he went looking for several items which no longer existed, Ki's Bible among them. He hadn't had the courage to tell his mother that the Bible was gone. He just let her revel in the fact that he was alive and well and back in Aktiya Waya among friends.

"How long will they purify?" Ola Achukma wondered, turning to his wife.

She blinked and shifted her stance. "I don't know. This is the first time anyone has ever had to do wartime purification here. In my father's Book, I think it says seven days."

"Seven days?! It takes that long to ride from here to Eagle Clan!"

"Ola, I don't know for sure. But if they have time to do such a thing, obviously they don't perceive any immediate threat to the village, right?"

There was that. He sat down. It was not the chair he was used to, the one in Eagle Clan where he had learned the grooves of the stone and the cushion that covered it and knew how to sit. This one was cold, hard, unfamiliar, and it chafed. He supposed he could learn to get used to it, get comfortable and make it his own, but he didn't want to.

"We're safe now," Nendawagan said, finding another chair to sit in. "We can rest here for a bit. I know you want to go to the Old Land and find Nathan and Andrew, but the dead aren't going anywhere."

"Maybe," Ola Achukma said, "but if whatever killed the people before is still out there, we should know about it before it comes back and finds us fighting amongst ourselves."

She gave him a look. "Ola, the people have been here for decades. If something wanted to kill all of us, you think it might not have done so by now?"

"The people have always been small, isolated. Only in the last ten years or so have we really expanded, grown, spread out, and now gone to war." He added quickly, "Or something very close to it. We might attract attention."

Her look persisted. "What, nine hundred people in this one small area of the island? Ola, the battles described in the Book are huge and nearly incredible except for the witnesses who were there. Two or three times as many men on a single side of the conflict, with many thousands more in other places. If we were truly going to attract attention from anything out there, I think we would have to cause more of a ruckus than a few minor disputes and almost-violent encounters."

Ola Achukma decided to let the matter drop before he let on about what really happened in Eagle Clan, but it was a long seven days.

Late at night, once Nendawagan had fallen asleep beside him, he would get up, go to the mouth of the cave, and look out across the bowl. He would stare at the Sacred Wolf, at the pass where her nose almost touched the tip of her tail. Such an imposing creature, massive and majestic, yet even she failed to protect those who had come before. And the serpent, safe and hidden in the depths of the earth where no man could ordinarily go, gutted and ruined, choking on the bones of those left behind. If they did go out again looking for more Sacred Ones, what would they find? Was it really a good idea?

On the other hand, what if he was wrong? What if there was no threat anymore? After a people had been driven from a place, it was only logical that the conquerors should seek to settle in that same area. That was actively playing out in the Old Land. But everywhere they went, there was nothing to be found. Perhaps such a thing had happened, but then something else happened to the conquerors and they were now gone, divine justice destroying them just as they had destroyed the people before.

If that were true, then, there was no reason to run off so swiftly to the Old Land looking for answers, and he was agonizing over nothing.

If it weren't true, though, he had every reason to leave as soon as possible.

Truthfully, he probably could have just asked Nendawagan or someone else proficient in Galohisdi to send him back. He could ask around and look for Nathan and Andrew the old-fashioned way; he was not entirely ignorant of their customs, though he might be a little young in his perceptions. But he did kind of want to ask Yvgidahi for guidance. It was only proper, after all.

So he waited. They both waited. Yvgidahi and his warriors

remained isolated during their purification, and the priests would not speak of them either except to say that they were well.

If they had hoped to simply observe old rituals and move on, they were sorely mistaken. Going years without needing such extensive purification and rituals reminding them of war, the people were only made more aware of what such rituals meant. The people became uneasy, and there were plenty of whispers and questions over what really happened in Eagle Clan. No one from Eagle Clan had come back to attack, true, but neither were there any visits, or word of any kind. No one wanted to go out to Eagle Clan for fear of what they might find. Ola Achukma would not say that he was not affected by it also, but he made sure to keep himself under control lest he give away what he knew.

When the warriors did finally emerge from their purification, they spent another three days in private conference with those on the council who remained behind, the priests, and the elders.

"Has he said anything to your mother?" Ola Achukma asked of his wife. It was the third evening of deliberation. The rumors going around Aktiya Waya were fierce and, oftentimes, contradictory.

"No, but, knowing him and seeing him briefly the other night, I don't think it's actually that bad," she told him. "I've seen a lot of things frustrate him over the years. He's not taking this as personally as he's taken other problems." She nodded as if the emphasize the point and reassure herself. "I think he's tired from it and whatever political implications there are, but I don't think anything really bad happened." She shrugged. "Maybe he was able to convince the naysayers to return to the Old Land, spread their lies and hatred there."

Ola Achukma nodded stiffly. "Maybe."

He wanted to believe her, but Yvgidahi himself said that not everyone who was violent had agreed to return to the Old Land. There was only one way such a confrontation could end.

The following morning, there came the announcement that the private meeting had ended and the warriors were ready to convene a public meeting, to begin at twilight as per usual. Nendawagan appeared to be almost back to normal, as though no time at all had passed since leaving Wolf Clan to join him in Eagle Clan. Even the attack seemed to have faded from memory a bit, though she sometimes faltered if she happened to be looking for something that had been destroyed.

As for him, he'd finally had to tell his mother that Ki's Bible was gone. If he'd ever questioned whether his mother still held some fondness for her late husband, her silent tears were proof enough. She didn't say anything other than to thank him and ask him to leave. He'd left the house, but lingered outside a moment longer when he heard her soft weeping.

Gathering in the townhouse for the meeting, all thoughts were centered on the warriors and the situation with Eagle Clan. There was plenty of whispering, several rumors still circulating through the crowd until Yvgidahi called for quiet.

"Thank you for being here," he began. "We realize the last ten days have been unusual and uncertain. We know that there are some rumors going around, like leaves on a river. But if there are too many leaves, they pile up, constrict the flow of water that is truth, and make it so the truth cannot be seen." He looked around at the crowd. "Now, then, we will clear away the leaves."

He and the other warriors shifted their positions until they were more comfortable, which only made Ola Achukma uneasy.

"At the last full moon, a group of warriors from Eagle Clan— preferring to be identified by their Old Land affiliations—decided to attack others in Eagle Clan who were known to use the sorceries, and also those who supported those who used the sorceries. Several people were attacked, their homes destroyed, including my oldest daughter and her husband."

This news was not unknown, for Ola Achukma had spoken of his ordeal, but there was a greater reaction to it than he was comfortable with. Some of it was shock, others were outraged.

"These warriors conducted this attack intending it to be a warning as well as a declaration of separation." Yvgidahi shook his head. "We could not let this stand. We have worked too hard, suffered too much, accomplished too much, to let ourselves be consumed by this madness. And so, as you know, I and these warriors here—" He gestured to the men to his right and left. "—rode to meet these separatists, to lance the boil before it became infected and spread throughout our entire body.

"The offer we made them was simple: they could stand down and return peacefully to the Old Land, to the lives they had always known, or they would be executed." He went on before the murmuring got too loud. "Such poisonous thoughts could not be permitted to remain among us, or else the sickness would return." He shook his head. "We are not without mercy, but we could not abide such treachery, that any man or woman should fear for himself or his family because he is friends with the wrong person, or because his child plays together with the child of a sorcerer. We are not barbarians. We also could not risk their safety by retaliation from the families of those who were attacked—"

"Clan justice has always been our way!" someone spoke up, gaining instant support from several around him. "We deal with our own matters!"

"And Clan justice has been dispensed," Yvgidahi said harshly. "Wolf Clan has retaliated against Eagle Clan. There were thirteen traitors in all. Nine chose to return to the Old Land. We wish them well. The other four were thrown from the cliffs."

Ola Achukma noted Nendawagan's sudden change in posture, though she said nothing.

"The matter has been dealt with," her father went on. "It is settled."

"Why not kill them all and declare it a failed experiment?" someone else asked. "Clearly the sorceries are dividing us, so why not expel or execute those who will not use them? If time, separation, and ignorance breed fear—and none of these were in great supply when these men rebelled—then why not make it mandatory to learn? If the sorceries are what make us unique from the Old Land, why not embrace it?"

And the same old cycle of arguments began again, Ola Achukma thought, sighing inwardly. He could almost recite them from memory, though he wouldn't be worried until he started dreaming of them. Beside him, Nendawagan had a similar disposition, though she appeared to still be processing the information that the warriors had executed four of the attackers. It wasn't that it wasn't warranted, but it was the first of its kind on Hlohi. Things were different now.

The two of them left the meeting once it became clear that the discussion was not moving away from the old arguments.

"I don't understand," Nendawagan said before they were even in the door. "His body language...I thought for sure things went well. I never imagined that it could come to that and..."

"Maybe he wasn't the one who did it," Ola Achukma offered lamely. "If there was a fight, things could get complicated and confusing. Maybe he was busy overseeing the others who were returning to the Old Land."

She looked uncertain. "I suppose, but it just...it doesn't make sense."

"What doesn't make sense? We were attacked. It sounds like others were also attacked. Your father and some others went to try and offer them a peaceful solution. Some accepted, others didn't. What were they supposed to do, just turn around and leave? As your father said, it's a poison that could not be allowed to stay."

"I know you're right, but I can't...comprehend it." She huffed a sigh. "I can't comprehend it, and yet I would be lying if I didn't admit that I kind of wish I could have at least slapped one of them. Maybe knocked some sense into him."

Ola Achukma laughed. "Well, it's a little late for that now."

She grunted something he chose to interpret as an agreement, then said, "Tomorrow I will go visit him and ask for more details."

He had no problem with that, and in fact he accompanied her, for he still wanted to ask about the possibility of returning to the Old Land to find Nathan and Andrew.

Yvgidahi was sympathetic toward his daughter, but caught off-guard by Ola Achukma's request, and he initially refused.

"We just sent nine disgruntled villagers back to the Old Land. Now you want to return? Yes, it may be for your own purposes, but if any of them catch you, they may think you're looking for revenge on them, which I promised would not happen if they return. If they were to attack again, there will be no warriors around to protect you. Your wife either.”

“Then I will avoid them,” Ola Achukma said simply. “The Old Land is a big place.”

“You’re not wrong there, which brings me to the next point. I don’t know where Nathan and Andrew are or might be or even if they are still alive. How do you propose to begin that search? And why do you need to find them?”

After more than ten days of not being able to truly relate their tale and findings, Ola Achukma and Nendawagan erupted into an avalanche of incoherent, disorderly babble that quickly overwhelmed him. Only once Mesim had fetched everyone some water and a bite to eat were they able to get their thoughts together and form a more organized recollection. Ola Achukma showed Yvgidahi the strange metal object and the glass shards.

“Is it from the Old Land?” Ola Achukma wondered.

Yvgidahi’s brows furrowed, but he shook his head and handed the pieces back. “If it is, it’s not anything I’ve ever seen.” He frowned and leaned back in his seat. “The bones of men, you say?”

“Men, women,” Nendawagan confirmed. Then she shifted position, her disposition turning puzzled. “But no children.” She shook her head, then nodded. Ola Achukma glanced at his father-in-law for some help in interpreting the gesture, but got nothing. “Yes, the whole place was peculiarly absent of the bones of children.”

“Slaves, then,” Ola Achukma stated.

“No,” Yvgidahi murmured, then immediately assented slightly. “Well, yes, perhaps, but for as idealistic as we may be, for the size of the conflict that must have gone on, children are an inevitable casualty. Their absence is rather conspicuous.” He sighed heavily. “But it is not an adventure which I am free to join at the moment. We have more important matters to attend to.”

“If this thing is still a threat—”

“What thing? We don’t know who or what these people faced.” Yvgidahi continued before Ola Achukma could speak. “In sixty, seventy, eighty years, I couldn't tell you if Nathan and Andrew are dead or alive, or where they might be hiding. After how many hundreds or thousands of years, we have the same information on whatever threat killed those people. If it or they are still out there, it clearly has the ability to decimate a people. We are having the same problem internally. One of them is a threat that I can see and deal with."

"I understand," Ola Achukma said. "I was only asking for some information, some advice, looking for a direction. I wasn't implying that you come with me."

Now his father-in-law just raised a brow. "So your entire plan is to just go to the Old Land—by yourself, entirely alone—for an undetermined length of time, asking random strangers if they have ever heard of Nathan and Andrew, and, if they have, where they might be?" He went on, "And this is assuming there aren't more people named Nathan and Andrew. I don't know if you know this, but white men enjoy naming their children after other relatives, producing an inordinate number of men and women with the same name in the same family."

"I do know that," Ola Achukma said through gritted teeth. "I know that very well. You forget that I am originally from the Old Land—"

"You came here as a child of eight. I would be willing to bet that you no longer remember your father's face, nor the home where you lived, or anything pertinent to the situation."

"—and I have been on missions to the Old Land."

"Ah, yes, that was how many years ago now?"

"Are you going to forbid me from going?"

The tension hung in the air like thick fog, and everyone deliberately took a drink of water.

"I cannot forbid you to go," Yvgidahi said levelly. "I merely question your methods. I don't want you to do something foolish and stupid and get yourself killed, thereby widowing your wife, my daughter. And before either of you say anything, I do forbid you from going, Nenda."

"But, Nocha—" she began.

"You are too important. To him, to me, to this clan, to the people.

Things were bad when he was rescued as a child. Things were worse when he returned from that mission some years ago. We have no reason to believe that it has improved in any way since then. If he wants to be a hero, he can go on this quest. But I will not see my daughter raped and murdered at the hands of savages."

The fog solidified into ice. Ola Achukma and Nendawagan paid respect to her mother and offered a grudging goodbye to her father before leaving. Neither said a word until they arrived back home.

"That did not go as expected," Ola Achukma sighed, slumping into a chair. "I don't know what I was hoping would happen, but that wasn't it."

"Agreed," Nendawagan murmured. "I've seen things get to him before, but this was...something new."

He shook his head. "Not new. Old. Aktiya Waya, Hlohi itself, this is all new. Unifying the people is new. Going to war, having to kill attackers and exile dissenters, that's all old. Old events from an Old Land he left behind a long time ago."

"And you just asked him for more information about it and informed him that you were planning on going there."

"Exactly. Not the smartest thing I've done today."

"He is right, though. It's not safe, and you don't know where to start."

Ola Achukma rubbed his eyes. "Nathan and Andrew were clearly friends of the Cherokee. I imagine they got along with other peoples, too. Right now in the Old Land, the people are being persecuted, moved, even killed. They're rallying together, and they need all the help they can get. If Nathan and Andrew are alive, and if they are still in the United States, I can't imagine they're not helping in some way. Maybe they're not teaching sorceries, but information and supplies are just as valuable. Someone has to know something." He drummed his fingers on the table. "Maybe I can talk to Kevin White Fire, see what he knows."

"How long do you intend to stay, then?" Nendawagan wondered. "Will you wander forever, looking for these men?"

He stood and put his hands on her shoulders. "Of course not. I don't think it would take that long, to confirm whether they're there or not."

"And if you do find them?"

"Once I've located them, I will show them the pieces we found, ask them what they know about it, about the people before and what happened to them. Their answers will determine my next course of action."

She looked uncertain, but he was entirely unprepared for what she said next.

"I just don't want you to be gone so long that you miss the birth of our first child."

He felt his knees give out and he heard Nendawagan make an unnatural sound.

"Oh, jeez, don't make me carry you, too," she growled as she guided him back into the chair.

Once safely seated, he reached out to her with Touch. She put her hand on top of his as he probed deeper. There in her belly, only about the size of a mustard seed, was a tiny human being. His mind went blank as he suddenly reconsidered his role in life. In an odd sort of way, he no longer felt like the "end." He was going to continue on. His father was going to continue on. There was life, and he'd helped to make it.

"Are you all right?" Nendawagan asked.

He realized he was grinning dumbly. Finally he laughed, stood, and kissed her.

"This is wonderful news," he said. "I thought you were worried that the sorceries meant you could not have children?"

"Well, after Popokus started lining them up like dolls, I asked her what she did. Finally I decided to try it."

"Whatever it is, it seems to have worked." He kissed her again.

Suddenly he found himself doubting whether it was a good idea to go to the Old Land. He just found out he was going to be a father. And he wanted to run off on some fool's errand looking for two men in a wide world, two men he didn't even know for sure if they were alive or would be able to help? Yvgidahi appeared to be well in the right on this one, and he felt foolish for arguing about it.

Then his thoughts returned to the underground city and the piles of bones, the bodies Nendawagan said she found in the large building. Something had killed all those people, and until he could definitively say that it was no longer a threat to the people—and now, his unborn child—he couldn't let himself relax.

"Have you told anyone else?" he asked at last.

She shook her head, eyes shining. "No, you're the first. I was planning on announcing it earlier when we went to see my parents, but..."

He cleared his throat. "Sorry."

"Well, what's done is done. I'll just have to tell them tomorrow or the next day, once things have calmed down."

They did, however, go to see his family and celebrate together. Ola Achukma fully expected his mother to weep with joy, and for Apushi to be happy even if he didn't fully understand why, but he was quite unprepared for the slap on the back and hearty congratulations from Chilita.

This was promptly followed by a frenzy of cooking and other preparations to set up a grand feast for the five of them—or, "the six of them," as his wife and mother cheekily put it, as if conspiring together. When a few neighbors came to investigate the sudden party, more food was produced for them as well.

It didn't take long for word to get around that something was going on, and it was inevitable that Yvgidahi and Mesim would investigate. It was poor practice for the host or focus of the party to be upset during the festivities, and it was terrible etiquette to be the one to upset them, so Ola Achukma had more hope for a civil conversation that evening.

By the time he was able to fight his way over to Yvgidahi—the party having spilled out of his mother's house into the street— Nendawagan had already broken the news and her parents were giving her many congratulations.

"I never thought I would see the day!" Mesim cried, clapping her hands together. "Maybe I did do something right with you."

"Of course you did, Guka," Nendawagan told her. "It just took a little longer. Mosk and the boys were the early season corn, Popokus was the mid-season corn, and I am the late season corn."

Her mother laughed and the two of them stepped away to converse between themselves.

Yvgidahi turned his gaze to Ola Achukma.

"Does it change your mind any?" the skiagvsta asked.

"About going to the Old Land?" Ola Achukma hesitated. "It gave me pause, that's for sure. But I would never forgive myself if whatever killed those people was still out there and could come after us, and I did nothing to try and stop it, or figure out a way to save us."

"What if you can't find Nathan and Andrew? What if they have no answers to give?"

"Then at least I can say I tried. I need to do that much." He went on before his father-in-law could speak. "It may be that there is nothing to find. It may be exactly as you say, that there is nothing out there anymore. If that is the case, then I am merely a fool. But if there is something out there, and I do nothing, then I am a coward."

Yvgidahi took an even breath and appeared to consider his words. After a long moment, he nodded. "You have the right of it." He made a small motion and the two of them stepped aside. "Come to speak to me tomorrow in the townhouse. If you are intent on returning to the Old Land for this mission of yours, you may as well do some other work for us, too."

Ola Achukma agreed, then swiftly returned to the festivities, easily slipping back into an ecstatic mood. Later that night, holding Nendawagan close to him in bed, he couldn't help but feel a certain sense of accomplishment, as if he'd really, truly done something. More than just delivering messages, more than just talk and planning parties, more than discovering lost civilizations even, he had done something bigger than himself. They had made life.

He Touched his wife again, felt her warm body, then pressed deeper until he found their tiny unborn child. So small and yet so obviously human. To think of how much the sorceries had been able to teach them about the human body, and yet he was still so in awe of its conception and growth! He had to protect it. Had to protect her.

He fell asleep feeling more like a man than he had ever felt in his life, and for just a moment before he drifted off, he might have even said that he felt like Ki.

Morning came too soon in his opinion, and he was slow to be ready. Other than speaking to Yvgidahi, he had no engagements, but he still felt woefully sluggish, as though he were somehow missing out on some errand of activity.

Whatever it was, it clearly wasn't important enough to warrant any space in his mind, and once he got himself freshened up a bit—making sure to hold his wife close, kiss her, and promise them the world and stars—he headed out.

His first stop was just going outside to see the sunshine. Aktiya Waya was well-protected, yes, but living in a cave could be dreary at times. He recalled a fleeting, childish memory, how he hated it when his mother threw open the doors and pushed aside the curtains in the house, letting in all the sunlight and interrupting his sleep. Now he wished he could have just a sliver of sunlight coming through the windows in the morning.

He found himself staring again at the Sacred Wolf, the river flowing into her mouth and providing nourishment for her. What out there could be so powerful as to defeat her?

His elation from the night before effectively crushed, he turned back toward the town and made his way to the townhouse. Yvgidahi was only a few steps ahead of him, and the skiagvsta motioned for him to join in a conference with the rest of the council.

"The last couple seasons, we've debated sending small scouting missions to the Old Land again," Yvgidahi began. "In the event that things here did indeed escalate, was there anywhere we could send such dissenters where they might have a chance at surviving?"

"Did you find such a place?" Ola Achukma wondered.

"We never sent any scouts. Too risky, for them and us. If our supporters found out, they might accuse us of trying to bring even more ingrates to Hlohi. If the dissenters found out, they might accuse us of something similar but more akin to kidnapping, enslavement. Either that, or that we were going to start making the dissenters 'disappear' in the dead of night. Who knows the mind of a madman? But now, since you wish to embark on this crazy mission of yours, it may be the perfect excuse."

"What do you want me to do? Find new lands in the Old Land for the dissenters? That's what the Trail was all about, and they were much less kind about it."

Yvgidahi shook his head and shifted his stance. "No, nothing so extreme, although if you do happen to find such a place, by all means, let us know."

"What we really need is information," one of the other members said. "What is the state of things there?"

"If it's anything like the last time I was there a few years ago...it probably hasn't gotten any better," Ola Achukma cut in. "Even I am not hesitant to admit that white men's wars are terribly lengthy, most often padded with words and papers and flowery, meaningless gifts. We may do such things in peace, but for them, their wars are fought on paper as much as the ground."

"Which will hopefully buy you some time," another councilman stated. He grinned. "Assuming your new child isn't motivation enough to return quickly."

Ola Achukma couldn't help but return the smile as his ears burned hot with embarrassment. He coughed to cover it up and asked, "What, specifically, are you looking for?"

"Not all who returned to the Old Land went because they were fearful," Yvgidahi said. "Some were merely patient and went in order to protect their families. Even those who were killed sent their wives and children with the others."

"You think they might retaliate."

"Yes."

"How, though? They hate the sorceries, their whole attack was intended to kill the sorcerers and any who supported us. Without

Galohisdi—"

"It has grown beyond that now. The sorceries are a thing, an idea that they hate. But now they have the faces of the sorcerers who killed four of their brothers and sent them back to the Old Land on threat of death. If they intend to stick to the old ways no matter the cost, revenge killing is not out of the realm of possibility. They may have to form a temporary alliance with a sorcerer to use Galohisdi to get them back here."

"Were any of those you sent back proficient in Galohisdi to do such a thing? If they did not support the sorceries, then how—?"

"Never underestimate what a man will do to get what he wants," a councilman said gravely. "If he wants to kill someone, he will find a way to make it happen."

Ola Achukma nodded once. "That is all well and good, but why ask me to do this? They already tried to kill me once. I can't imagine they would be overly willing to speak to me now."

"You don't have to make friends with them," Yvgidahi told him. "You don't have to kill them either. All we want is for you to keep an eye on them and tell us if they are planning some kind of feasible attack."

He didn't see how this could possibly work, but he needed to get back to the Old Land somehow. He could use Galohisdi just fine around Hlohi, jumping around the villages. Traveling to the Old Land was something else entirely.

"It would be unwise to go now," another councilman said, evidently trying to lighten the mood a little. "Those who were sent back will need to reorient themselves to the Old Land and anything that may have changed—"

"And that's another thing," Yvgidahi interrupted. "We need to know what's changed, if things are any better for those who were moved. The last time a group went out, the Aniyvwiya were still fighting their removal. See if they won and by what means. If they did lose and were forced to leave their lands, see if they have truly fared better in new lands or if they are suffering even more."

"Are we planning on rescuing more people?" Ola Achukma wondered.

"I fear that would be a bad idea. But if the people of the Old Land are doing well, more here may very well wish to leave. We will not stop them."

"And if the people are suffering? You say we cannot or will not accept more refugees, but if those you just sent back go to those suffering people and tell them of the good things we have here—great natural treasures guarded only by a handful of greedy, evil sorcerers—we may have a problem on our hands if anyone is proficient at all in Galohisdi."

"Which is why you need to ascertain their intentions and capabilities."

Ola Achukma let out a breath. "What if, instead of bringing people here, we sent supplies there? We shouldn't turn a blind eye to suffering, but if their presence is only going to cause strife, why not help them where they are? We do the same thing here."

"Because we know the people here, and here we are the people," a third councilman said, his tone suggesting that the matter had been decided and closed long ago. "The people back in the Old Land are lost, confused, and demoralized. They have no foundation, no purpose. They have lost the old ways. They have become lazy and dependent. It does not matter whether they are dependent on the United States or on us, they are still dependent. Feeding that mentality is an atrocity, disgraceful to us and shameful to them. And they cannot become independent until they figure out who they are."

"But you don't want to bring them here to remind them?"

"We've tried that. We've been trying for many years and you see what it's gotten us. And that was when some people still had a sense of pride in themselves and a willingness to become new."

Ola Achukma turned to face the man head-on. "But in order for someone to want to become Krydik, they must leave behind their individual identity which you say is essential to them in the Old Land where they are suffering not by choice."

"Politics is a terrible game, Ola Achukma," Yvgidahi said, getting between them. "It's even worse when you've been playing the game far past its enjoyment, realizing that there is no end to it. We bring the people here, you've seen what happens. We leave them there, they risk becoming dependent and lifeless. We give them supplies, they are but livestock who need tending. We give them heritage, we not only lose our own people back to them—a minor inconvenience, I think—but as they flourish, those who broke them down originally in order to move them take notice and come after them again. Only the next time, the solution will be far more permanent." He nodded slowly. "That is the beast that awaits them in the Old Land. I don't know what killed those people in the underground city, but that is the fate that awaits the people of the Old Land, no matter what they do."

"You propose isolation then," Ola Achukma stated.

"It would seem to be our best option."

"It has worked well for us the last few years," a councilman said. "With exception of this group of dissenters, we've had no problems. We haven't had to worry about finding or building homes for refugees. We haven't had to worry about supplying the needs of women and children while they adapt. With your help in building this new language, communication has improved and I think that is why some people have relaxed. New people would not understand, and it takes so long to teach them.

"And of course for every single family we bring, they see this land of plenty and wish to bring their mothers and fathers, sisters and brothers, large families. It is impossible to import whole nations and still maintain our own identity." At Ola Achukma's look, he added gently, "This is not to say that we will never help anyone again, or that we might not make an occasional exception. But just as the peoples of the Old Land are trying to fight for themselves and their sovereignty, so we must fight for our own, or be destroyed."

"Wait a moon," Yvgidahi advised. "Make whatever preparations you deem necessary, consider a plan of action. When you are ready, simply let me know and I will send you to the Old Land myself. Maybe there is a way I can get you close to where Nathan and Andrew might be, assuming they live."

There was nothing more to be said or done. It sounded as though the council had made up its mind long ago. Ola Achukma would not say he didn't understand or that their arguments did not have merit. He just hated how it made him feel. If trying to rescue someone from drowning ended up with both people dead, was anything really accomplished? The attempted rescuer might be honored as a hero, or scorned as a fool; either way, he was still dead. But how could he just stand by and watch a drowning man suffer? How could he close his eyes and pretend not to see? How could he close his ears to the panicked cries for help and choking until it all went silent and the only thing left to do was fish the corpse from the water?

Peace, a horizon always within sight but always out of reach, Ola Achukma thought. And politics seemed to be the distance in between.

Pàke Nishinxke

Worse News

Nendawagan might have been more accepting of Ola Achukma leaving for the Old Land if he had done it right away once he spoke to her father. Having him stay put for another month while he planned and prepared only annoyed her and made her want to force him to stay.

Oh, he'd explained things to her, what the council expected him to do, perhaps as payment for letting him go at all, but it didn't make her feel any better about it. He was trying to be polite, and now they were treating him like some kind of lackey, as if he owed them something. Preposterous! If anything, they owed him a favor or three. Why not let him go if wanted to? If she had known it was going to be this complicated, she would have sent him herself. She should have sent him herself. Then he wouldn't have to worry about spying on those who'd just left, who'd been happy to leave. Even if they hadn't been happy to leave and hated those in Aktiya Waya, what would be the point of coming back for revenge?

She was more interested in politics than some women, and even she found it exhausting sometimes. Or maybe that was the pregnancy talking. It was getting hard to tell some days.

The day after Ola Achukma left for the Old Land, she went to visit her parents, mostly so she could speak to her father. It was almost nighttime, and Mesim was just making some tea.

"Ola told me what you're having him do," Nendawagan began, sitting down at the table. "Spying on those you just exiled."

"Exiled?" Yvgidahi wondered. "Returned. They didn't want to be here."

"They did want to be here."

"Well, quite frankly, so do I. But I'm not going to stand there and let them slit my throat and take my scalp just so they can sleep at night."

"They want to be safe. They want to feel safe!"

Her father took a level breath. "It is one of the duties of any uku or skiagvsta to ensure the safety and security of the people he is responsible for. But he cannot act on every foolish whim. A bear is a threat and should be dealt with. But should I exile one person because another is fearful of him? Would you have had me resign instead and take all of us back to the Old Land?"

"Well, no, but—"

"You're smarter than this, Nenda, and the only reason I'm even entertaining this conversation is because I remember how irrational your mother could be when she was pregnant."

"I—"

"I can't please everyone. Believe me when I say I am doing this to keep you safe. To keep everyone here safe. And to keep those who were sent back safe. The peace is held together for now, but what would happen if they did decide to return for revenge? You think I would be able to keep the warriors among us from going back and killing in their own retaliation, for their own honor?" He sighed and took a drink of his tea. "Nendawagan, you have been a blessedly sheltered child. You've never had to truly worry about life and death, whether your children will live to see adulthood, or even adolescence. In the Old Land, you would have said goodbye to Ola Achukma half a dozen times now, every spring as he goes out on raids or other expeditions. You would not have the luxury of exploring on a whim."

"But we don't live in that world, Nocha. We don't live in the Old Land," Nendawagan pleaded.

"You're right. We don't. I'm trying to keep it that way. We want to be free to live our lives the way we wish. Well sometimes, people have a problem with how other people are living, even if they are causing no harm. What do we do then?" He went on before she could speak. "I'll hear no more of this from you. Your husband is out doing his work, and you ought to be preparing to step into your role as a mother. You have different responsibilities now. When you were a little girl, we let you play with the boys, but eventually, you had to become a woman. This is no different."

Nendawagan looked to her mother for support, knowing full well she wouldn't get any. Her mother had been telling her this for decades, why stop now?

After a long moment, she just nodded and said, "Yes, Nocha."

She left her parents' house and went home, trying to keep her head high and back straight. They meant well. She knew they did. But it was so infuriating! She didn't even know who to blame, or if there was anyone to blame. And even if there were, what was she going to do about it? Her father wasn't wrong. How could people be so stupid and insensitive? If someone was living peacefully, not bothering anyone, leave them alone.

She sat down quietly, telling herself not to get upset. She remembered her mother when she was pregnant, and she remembered her sister. She wasn't going to be in her right mind sometimes. She had to maintain control.

What, then, was their excuse? The attackers were not pregnant, to have such insane thoughts. Ola Achukma had once said that it was a man's need to be physical and show off and prove himself. Was daily life not struggle enough? Was victory at the festival no longer an appealing goal? What was it that drove them to such fear, manifesting as violence that resulted in at least four deaths?

And, really, what was she going to do about it now? They were out of Eagle Clan and the attackers had been dealt with. Ola Achukma was in the Old Land working on his mission. And some side work for the council. Unless she wanted to go charging into the Old Land, putting herself and her child at risk, the most she could do, as her father said, was prepare herself to be a mother.

The thought was daunting, and the stress only gave her a headache. She lay down, thoughts swirling. Suddenly it all seemed like so much. How had her mother done it? As a child, it was simply the way things were, the way things had always been. Guka and Nocha, her and, eventually, her siblings. It just was. Now she was on the other side of things, when everything changed.

Her mother had been born to one people, left them to devote herself to another people, was attacked and left for dead, rescued and taken to live with yet another people, married, had children, now having grandchildren and great-grandchildren. How did she manage it all so well? More to the point, why couldn't she, Nendawagan, handle her own, comparatively minor, changes with such grace?

Maybe it really was the pregnancy talking. She needed to rein in her thoughts before they ran away. She needed to remain in control of herself. For the life of her, she couldn't imagine why some women desired ten or more children. To go through this for so long, so many times? Did it get easier each time? Maybe, once they knew what to expect. But all the same, why?

She fell asleep, feeling rather uneasy. She physically knew what was going on, but somehow she just couldn't get a handle on it. And she had to suffer for how many moons?

By morning, nothing had changed. She wouldn't say she wasn't disappointed, but somehow she felt calmer about the whole thing. Ola Achukma was gone for a while, and she just had to carry on. It wouldn't be difficult. It wouldn't be any different than any other day. Everything in Aktiya Waya was the same as it had been for decades. Tend the crops, tend the horses, tend the children, enjoy the day, make busy with some housework.

The cave isn't collapsing, she told herself. There are no bands of warriors trying to get into the pass. You're making everything bigger than it needs to be.

Most homes had individual water reserves now, but in the heat of summer, much of it had depleted, and she was forced to go to the communal pool which was also quite low. They would probably make it to fall when the rains came again. She hoped so because she didn't like having to go all the way to the river.

Soon enough she would have a child in tow when she did all these things. It would be like when she was younger and she would have to watch her little brothers while their mother did chores. Was that why some women had so many, so the older could take care of the younger and free up her hands? How different things seemed when she was the mother of the bunch, and not even a mother yet!

She returned home with the water, nearly dropping the buckets when she opened the door and found Ola Achukma standing there. He looked rather tired, his direction and posture suggesting he was heading to bed.

"Ola," Nendawagan stated.

He turned.

"What are you doing here? I thought you were in the Old Land? Is everything all right?"

He nodded and yawned. "Fine, except I have not found an adequate place to sleep. It's night in the Old Land now, so I thought I might as well come home to sleep well. And it allows me to practice Galohisdhi, which you know I am not very good at."

To her eyes, he looked ready to fall over. She wanted to say so many things, but the best she could do was a wordless nod and a gesture for him to go to bed, which he did gratefully.

She decided not to tell her father about her husband's return, instead contenting herself with some minor housework and going through Ola Achukma's things, making sure everything was in order. Well, even if he hadn't found a decent place the sleep, he did not appear to have been involved in any fights. His bag was still pristine, and nothing appeared to have been stolen.

Just past midday, he emerged from the bedroom and sat down at the table.

"I need to get back," he sighed, still sounding a bit sleepy.

"Have you accomplished anything so far?" Nendawagan asked quickly.

He chuckled. "I've been gone for two days. Your father managed to get me close to a city called Charleston, but I was soon accused of being a runaway slave and had to flee quickly into the surrounding wood."

"What are you going to do?"

"Scout the area a bit, see if I can't use the sorceries and try to get some attention from Andrew and Nathan."

"How will you do that? Won't it also attract the attention of their soldiers?"

He shrugged. "It might, but I have to do something."

"What happened to looking for Kevin White Fire?"

"I will, if Charleston doesn't produce any results. I don't want to be running around here and there with no real direction."

She nodded. "Do you need food, water, anything before you go? Will you come back again?"

"Water would be nice. As for coming back, I do need to practice with Galohisdi more. I have the luxury of time and familiarity right now, but if I find myself in trouble, I may need a hasty exit."

She handed him a cup of water. "Well, don't hurt yourself. We don't know what happens to someone if a doorway closes on them partway through, but I can't imagine it's anything good."

"You think it might lead to another island? Adahi has some experience with it, though in the Book it sounded like the Old Land, but he was invisible."

"I don't know, but I know my father has said to never bring it up to him. Whatever the case, it took the sacrifice of Anagalisgi to save him."

Ola Achukma nodded. "That is true, and I don't want to have to ask anyone to sacrifice themselves for me if I don't have to."

With that, he finished off his water and stood. Nendawagan handed him his bag, then stood back while he conjured Galohisdi. A doorway, with no physical sides or top, yet there in front of her eyes was another world. The trees were strange, known to her only because of her singular trip to the Old Land many years previous. It was just dawn in the Old Land, the shadows stretching long. As her husband stepped through, his shadow also appeared.

Then the doorway shut and he was gone. Vanished to another island without ever leaving their home.

She waited a few days before telling her father of the encounter. As expected, he barraged her with questions she could not answer. She knew only what her husband had told her, nothing more. While she did hope that he would continue to visit, at least so the months didn't feel so lonely, he hadn't said anything about when he might return next.

"Well, at least he is able to return in an emergency," Yvgidahi mused.

"Of course he is," Nendawagan told him. "Why did you think otherwise?"

Her father gave her a look. "Few of the sorcerers know how to use Galohisdi, and fewer still have a reason to. Ola Achukma is talented in Touch, not so much anything else that I've seen."

"He knows how to conjure Time."

"Knowing how to do something and doing it skillfully are two different things." He went on before she could speak. "Your husband is a healer and a peacemaker. Quite frankly, his skill in Touch is more valuable than anything else."

The look on her father's face said he knew exactly where Nendawagan would take the conversation. She knew it, and he knew she knew it.

"Then why send him back to the Old Land on what could turn into a violent encounter?" she asked, trying to remain polite. "He was already almost captured once."

His expression hardened. "We've already been through this, Nenda. I'll not allow myself to be goaded into another argument."

He left it at that, speaking to her no more that evening. Her mother was cordial, but eventually she saw herself out, heading home, wishing and praying Ola Achukma would be there for another visit. Even if he had already passed out in bed, she just wanted to see him.

He wasn't there.

She irrationally cried herself into a kind of stupor that bordered on sleep, her second-to-last ounce of will still hoping for her husband to appear, her last ounce of will telling her that she was being stupid and childish and she needed to compose herself. When she finally sat up, wiped her face, looked around, and thought a little, she felt even more foolish. She was worried about her husband, yes, but she was safe, the village was fine, nothing was happening. She was just alone in her home crying like the baby she was going to be birthing in a few moons. She couldn't have that.

She thought of the stories her parents had told her and her siblings when they were growing up. They said that they, the children, should be very thankful for the way things were, that they knew their parents well. In the Old Land, after the fields were cleared in the spring, the men would leave home to go hunting and raiding and do other exploits. They might be gone a moon at a time or even the whole summer, sometimes into fall, not returning until the frosts came. Sometimes the women would go out on shorter trips, most often to visit relatives in nearby villages. So for both Yvgidahi and Mesim to be home with their children every day and every night, leaving for no more than ten days on a large game drive, it was something truly amazing. And—at least at the time, when there was only one village—everyone lived in the same place, so there were no treacherous journeys to visit relatives. Even so, they had Galohisdi if they wished to go somewhere quickly.

She thought of a phrase she'd heard an elder use once. "What we perceive as a miracle, our children perceive as simply the way things are, and our grandchildren perceive as the way things must be." Considering the history and heritage of her parents and their ancient peoples, she herself was the odd one out. She was the one living a fantastically different life. She had everything her ancestors dreamed of. And she knew it. She had only to listen to her parents and the others from the Old Land, read the Book, and she understood that her life was very easy.

She just didn't understand why others hated her for it. They could have it, too; the door had been open for years. Were some people really so addicted to fear and anger that they were incapable of seeing and accepting what they claimed to desire most?

Sitting there in the dim light, Nendawagan rubbed her face and yawned. Were these even her thoughts, or was this the pregnancy talking? Speaking to other pregnant women, they'd always seemed pretty normal. Even Popokus had managed fairly well. Was this everything they were holding back? Or was she just overreacting to the sudden poor timing of her husband's departure? Did it ever get any easier?

She lay back on the bed and closed her eyes. Oh, Ola, where are you? I hope you find Nathan and Andrew soon so you can put that artifact to rest. I hope you find that the exiles are living comfortably in the Old Land with no thoughts of returning so that you can ease my father's fears. Then you can return home and celebrate the birth of our first child.

Many years ago, using Touch, the healers had been able to decipher tiny particles within each person. More than just their whole bodies, each particle itself was them, a sequence that was uniquely theirs. But, among that, men as a whole had a unique particle. Everyone had what the healers called an X particle. Women had two of them. But men were missing a leg on their second X particle, leaving only a Y. This, the healers said, was proof that men needed women in order to be complete, that the women gave men their "extra particle" in another way, so that the men could then provide the women with children.

So it was that, if an expectant mother so wished, a healer could examine the particles of the unborn child and search for either the X or Y particle.

Nendawagan thought about it for a while. She didn't know if she wanted to know. What would Ola Achukma think? Would he want to know? Was it possible to know this early? Why wouldn't it be?

At some point she simply fell asleep, and that was perfectly fine with her.

It was almost a moon before Ola Achukma visited again. Like before, his first and foremost thought was sleep, though not before mentioning that he wanted to speak to Yvgidahi and the others before he went back.

Later on, at twilight, the men met in the townhouse. Nendawagan might have been forced out of the private meeting, but she volunteered to bring them food and water as required. As she was leaving to fetch a pitcher of water, she heard her father say something to the effect of, "It's better that she'll hear it for herself; this way neither I nor her husband will have to try and answer her obsessive questions or else cast her aside in the matter, knowing that she will not accept such an outcome."

One of the other men made some comment about the presence of a pregnant woman at the meeting, but she was already too far away to hear the response. It must have been favorable for her, for she was not asked to leave upon her return. She did notice that some of them looked uneasy, but no one said anything to her face. Not wishing to jeopardize her position, she simply hung back and waited to be summoned for food or water.

"I was able to track down Kevin White Fire again," Ola Achukma began. "The news isn't good."

"Their petition failed, then," someone said.

"More than that. The Cherokee are being moved west, just as the Chahta were some years ago. Little food, little shelter, and they're being forced into the same area. Other groups are being moved as well, just like last time. Even the northern peoples are being moved, though they have some relief as the territory is quite inhospitable in the winter months and the soldiers do not wish to travel in such conditions."

"Is there anyone left in the original lands?" another man asked.

"Unlike last time, there are fewer options for anyone who wishes to stay. Options for citizenship are reserved for the few and well-connected. There were reportedly some skirmishes early on, but now it seems as though the government simply sends in their army. Twenty men surrounded a farm, just to move a widow and her children. Another dozen or so kidnapped an elderly man in the middle of the night from his hunting cabin where he'd retreated so he might die in his ancestral lands."

This was met with a number of whispered curses upon the soldiers.

"Is there any good news to be had?" Yvgidahi asked, his voice tense.

"Maybe." Ola Achukma shrugged. "Only rumors. Grumblings."

"What are they?"

"It's not only our peoples who are moving. The United States is expanding rapidly. Many whites are also heading west into new territories, new states." He put up a hand as one of the men prepared to protest. "There is great political divide over how this should be done, what rules must be in place, how the government shall rule the people so far away. The divide is breeding some discontent."

"So what?" someone asked. "What do we care if the white men do not like their white leaders?"

"Kevin White Fire believes that there is too much momentum for the government to call the people back out of the west. The demand from the people is too great; they want to move out of the cities, they want land, they want to farm. That dam has already burst."

"And swept our peoples downstream with it!"

"Yes. The United States government cannot call them back, but they cannot make everyone happy. There are whispers of secession, splitting the land. The people of what they call New England has spoken of it, and there are fancies of the Pacific territories doing something similar."

"Dividing the land between one group of white people and another group of white people," someone scoffed. "How does that help our peoples?"

"Now wait a minute," a fourth man interrupted. "What are we talking about here? I thought we had agreed that we are Krydik. The Krydik people of the island of Hlohi. This is our land, this is our way of life. The people of the Old Land told us in no uncertain terms that they don't like us and they don't want us interfering."

Yvgidahi sighed but nodded. "You have the right of it. We cannot simply swoop in and force ourselves into a conflict where we are not wanted. It is nonsensical to fight and die for people who hate us. Even if we were to assist them and we did win land and rights for them, we could not stay to ensure such an arrangement stands. We could not do it when our peoples had ten times the numbers and weapons and the enemy was a fraction of its size." He sighed again and stared into the fire. "We cannot interfere in such a way. We cannot." Who he was trying to convince was anyone's guess. He looked at Ola Achukma. "Were you able to find those we exiled?"

"I did a passive search on my own and could not find them," Ola Achukma answered. "I asked around and gave their description to Kevin White Fire, but he's heard nothing about any exiles from Aktiya Waya. He was surprised to hear of such a thing, actually."

"Did you tell him anything of what happened?" one of the councilmen demanded.

"Only that we take insults to our hospitality very seriously, but we are not without mercy. He accepted the answer and no one has spoken of it since."

"Good," Yvgidahi murmured. "We're already disliked by those in the Old Land; we don't need to be perceived as a foolish laughingstock as well."

"What do we do now, then?" another councilman asked. "We've just reaffirmed that we will not interfere, and without news from those in exile, we can only conclude that they are either unable or unwilling to bring some sort of retribution against us. That's all well and good, yes, but now what? Shall we seal ourselves off once more and call a permanent end to these Old Land crusades?"

For a long moment there was silence. Yvgidahi made a motion, and Nendawagan brought the platter of food and water. The men took their fill, and she retreated back to her spot.

"The white men are crossing the land in droves," Ola Achukma stated warily. "Not just adventurers or explorers or traders or a few quiet farmers. Not just groups hoping to get from one coast to the other. They are planting themselves in the wilderness and building towns and cities. There is no way to stop them at this point, short of a miracle."

Yvgidahi took a drink of water. "Is that your honest opinion? Is this how things are going to be?"

"I do believe so, yes."

Nendawagan watched as her father shifted position several times and called for a refill on his water. Finally he said, "Then it is for that reason I believe we should continue information expeditions to the Old Land."

"Why?" someone asked.

"It is one thing to be lied to and removed from your home. But land is not infinite, nor is human patience. The people will run out of land, or they will perceive it so. Once this tide begins to swell and there is nowhere for it to go, they will turn on each other. They will look for someone to blame. Native peoples are the easiest target. They have been moved once. Now they are being moved again. The third time, it will not be simple removal they seek, but execution. Perhaps when that time comes, some of the people will have a sudden change of heart about us. We should keep our doors open to that possibility."

"More refugees? Yvgidahi, we just exiled nine people, killed four, because they refused to adapt. A man may say anything to spare his life. But what shall we do if another situation arises? How many people shall we take in? A dozen? A hundred? A thousand?"

"Then we should start planning early. We must be ready to receive people who are like us only in appearance and ancestry, but they themselves are hopeless. We must educate them, and we must be ready to educate them. This is our land, and the people who come here must conform to our ways. We will also teach everyone the basics of the sorceries. It cannot be made a taboo to be feared. They do not have to use it in their lives if they do not wish to, but they cannot fear those who do."

"How shall this be accomplished then?" someone else asked, his tone venomous.

"We will discuss such things in a formal meeting," Yvgidahi told him. "We'll need the others on board with this."

The dismissal was not a cheery one, but it was a welcome relief. Nendawagan put away the remaining supplies and walked home with Ola Achukma in silence.

"Do you have to leave right away?" she asked when they walked inside.

"I should be getting back. Kevin is expecting me to help him today. Tomorrow. Whatever time it is."

Nendawagan sighed. "All right, fine. You should hold to your obligations. But before you go, do you at least want to know whether we're having a girl or a boy?"

That gave him pause. Then, "Do you know? Have you Touched—?"

"No, I haven't. I wasn't sure I wanted to. I thought I would leave it up to you, since you're going to be away for a while."

He made a sound that he did when she pushed a decision onto him that he didn't want to make but no one else could. He ran his tongue over his teeth, chewed on the inside of his lip, paced around the room a few times. At first it was amusing, but it quickly became annoying. Just as she was about to speak, he said, "All right. Yes. Yes, I want to know."

She grinned and held her hand out to him. He took it and she pressed both their hands to her belly. Using Touch, they felt first her, then their child, growing bigger every day. Although they could not physically see it, Touch gave them a clear mental picture of tiny hands and feet with even tinier fingers, a little thumb so close to a little mouth one might have been excused for believing it was already sucking. They went deeper, marveling at how quickly the child developed, the simultaneous division and multiplication of cells. And still they went deeper, searching for the particles.

Everyone had an X, two arms and two legs. But there they also discovered the Y.

"A boy," Ola Achukma said, grinning hugely. "It's a boy!"

Nendawagan matched his smile. "See now? You'll have to return so you can see your firstborn son introduced to the world."

The revelation was enough to get him to stay a little while longer, most of the time spent simply marveling at the fact that their first child would be a son. Several times he approached her, Touching their child as if to reassure himself that what they'd found was true.

"How am I going to explain this to everyone?" he wondered, making another lap of the house. "No one in the Old Land can do as we do; they'll never understand it."

"Then let them wonder," she told him. "Tell them anything you want, it doesn't matter. If they believe in the sorceries, let it be sorcery. If they don't believe, then no answer will satisfy. Just continue with your mission and come back as fast as you can. I don't like these short visits."

As he pulled her close, she could feel his excitement, not only in his tight muscles but also his taut bow. He wanted her, but now that her pregnancy was known, they would not couple again until after their child was born. This wasn't to say that he couldn't be satisfied in other ways, and he returned to the Old Land a very happy man, she thought.

Once again, she was left alone. She knew a moment of jealousy, that her husband was out on missions and having adventures. She wanted to have adventures, too. Exploring the caves near Eagle Clan had been fun. Exploring the canyons, discovering the surreal paintings and the underground city was beyond her imagination. She wanted to go back and look some more. Now that the initial shock was wearing off, she kind of wanted to explore a little more, see what else she could find. Maybe Ola Achukma could work on his maps some more.

Now that she thought about it, maybe she ought to make up a list of things to bring back from the Old Land. Paper was a rather convenient commodity. Not enough people used it to warrant making it themselves, but it was in just enough demand from those who did to maybe see about a bit of trade. But only with the native peoples of the Old Land, of course, those like Kevin White Fire. And there were a few other things that might come in handy. Obsidian was excellent for making a sharp blade, but there were a few families who had cast iron pots and pans from the Old Land which were far superior to the more crude copper and tin pans—themselves terribly old and in poor shape since mining was not an enjoyed chore and the copper was limited, to say nothing of the effort needed to shape the metal into useful objects.

Maybe that could be their excuse, Nendawagan thought. They weren't secret information-gathering missions, but rather trading expeditions. Yes, that sounded good. It wasn't a bunch of sorcerers come to inspect a land before attempting to conquer it; it was simply a different people come to trade their unique wares. It allowed them to keep a passive eye on things without being aggressive in their work, and trade was a respected affair between all peoples.

She wanted to bring the idea to her father right away, see if she couldn't influence his meeting with the council and direct them away from the war path. At the same time, she was perhaps already too involved in things. She'd been rebuked enough times to know when to stand down.

Maybe she would suggest the idea to Ola Achukma the next time he came home and he could present it to the council. He was already the current intermediary, so why not? Maybe arrangements could be made with Kevin White Fire and any other peoples willing to pursue peace.

She debated the merits of her idea, but her musings gave way to worry as two full wolf moons passed with no word from her husband. He did not visit for any length of time, nor did he leave any messages as if he had come and gone quickly with no time to speak to anyone. She told herself not to worry, but lately her attention span was short and her emotional stability even shakier. This wasn't to say she was a wreck, but even she knew she did not feel or act like herself some days.

Only when there had been no word for three moons did she confront her father, irrationally demanding to know whether he had been hiding contact with Ola Achukma.

"Why would I do something like that?" Yvgidahi wondered, everything about him projecting confusion. "More to the point, why would he do something like that?"

"I don't know, maybe so I don't get overly emotional and overbearing?" she suggested, only partially aware that she sounded absolutely ludicrous by now. "Maybe because he knows that if he sees me, he'll want to Touch our child and that will make it so he doesn't want to return and so he forfeits his mission to find Nathan and Andrew?"

"While that may be mildly true, I don't think you're giving him enough credit. Everything he's doing is, in his mind, to protect you and your child and the rest of us. We can argue over whether those fears are truthful and grounded, but the point is that his motive is pure."

"Then where is he? Why hasn't he contacted us? It would be one thing if he didn't have the sorceries, but he's already proven that he can use Galohisdi to get back and forth. At what point do we send someone after him?" She huffed and shook her head. "Someone should have gone with him. Something could have happened and we might never know. Maybe something did, but White Fire has no idea how to contact us!"

That, at least, gave her father pause. After a long moment, he took an even breath and said slowly, "You have a point that we may have to figure out some better means of communication—"

"And we can't send people out alone!"

He put up a hand. "—and maybe we shouldn't send people out alone. But we cannot assume the worst. Yes, Ola Achukma has demonstrated that he is capable of Galohisdi, to come and go as needed. I would expect that if he were in trouble, he would flee. He is smart enough to know that no baseless mission is worth his life."

Nendawagan blinked. "You don't think he's onto something? What about what we found in the underground city?"

"I don't know what you found. You don't know what you found. He doesn't know what you found. I understand that your discovery may be shocking and something terrible may have happened, but we have no reason to fear unknown, outside dangers from who knows how many eons ago. Our greater concern should be the threats we do know about and do suspect, like those who fear the sorceries, fear us, and may try to harm us. Harm you." He said "you" but gestured to her swollen belly. He continued before she could protest. "I understand your concern. I do. I would be lying if I said I wasn't thinking something similar, that we should make contact. But please, let the council handle it. You need to be focusing on yourself and your child right now."

He was right, but she still didn't have to like it. Still, he would hear no more about it from her, and she could see that his patience with her was thin, and that only because he knew she wasn't entirely in her right mind.

She loved her unborn child, and she couldn't help but feel a bit foolish for waiting so long to have children. However, she also decided that she did not like being pregnant. She didn't like not feeling in control of herself. She could understand how physical changes had to happen, but did she have to lose her mind in the process? How had Popokus dealt with it? What about their mother? Or maybe they had simply embraced it as part of who they were now.

Sleep did not come easy that night or the night after. She wanted to ask her father for word, but she could already imagine the answer. If it wasn't a simple, "No, there has been no word," then it would probably be some story about the Old Land. The men would leave in the spring after clearing the crop fields. They would go on long hunts, minor raids, and major battles. They would travel hundreds of miles over the course of many moons, not returning until the fall or even the frost in the worst of cases. The women would have no idea of the fate of their husbands, fathers, brothers, and sons all summer. There would be no word of their success, failure, or death, until such time as they returned. If successful, their whooping and cheering could be heard half a day away, and they would come back to the village with songs to sing and grand stories to tell. The best spoils would be given to the elders, the best stories to the children and younger warriors.

But if they were unsuccessful, their return would be silent, and all would know their shame and dishonor. Women would come running to see which men had returned and which had not. And the woman who did not count her husband among them would weep, not only for his death, but also for the hope that she had kept in her heart for so long that was now entirely dead. She would scream and cry and tear at the earth with her fingers.

Nendawagan wanted news, but there was no such word in the Old Land. There was no way to know, not without sending more than one person at a time. Of course, Ola Achukma going alone was a bit irregular, but even so. If things were as he had said three moons ago, that there was division among the white people and resentment from the rest, did that not spell danger? Or had he relied on Kevin White Fire and his people to stay safe?

She wanted to go look for him herself. She knew it was a foolish idea. She wanted to beg her father to send someone after him. He'd already said he'd begun to consider such a thing.

Indeed, not two days later, Yvgidahi politely informed her that he had sent someone after Ola Achukma, if for no other news than he was alive and well or he was not. His last known location was with Kevin White Fire, so the search should not take long.

She had thought such a move would calm her down, and it did initially. But when a day passed, and then two, and then five, with no news, her anxiety increased to levels she'd never considered possible except that she was pregnant. Had something happened to the messenger? Had something happened to Kevin White Fire? Had they all been removed, forced onto the Trail? That was well and good, but where was her husband? Why did he not use Galohisdi to return home?

Had one of the exiles caught them perhaps? Just because they didn't like the sorceries didn't mean they didn't have a little training; maybe they knew of a way to stop them from using Galohisdi to flee.

She shook her head. No. That was far-fetched, even for her addled mind. Realizing this, she was able to get a handle on her thoughts, though her emotions still ranged from terrified worry to near-crippling anxiety. She also knew that she projected these worries for all to see, and she had to believe that her father would not ignore her if any news did come back, for good or ill.

And actually, it was the messenger who found her first. Or perhaps she found him. It was a chance meeting, she running into him while he was on his way to the townhouse to speak with the council, and she cornered him—quite literally.

"Just tell me one thing," she said harshly, putting one hand on the walls on either side of the man. "Is my husband alive? Is he well?"

"That's two things," the man told her smartly. "And I'm meeting with the council about it."

"You will tell me of my husband. Whatever adventures he's having, he can tell me himself, assuming he can. Is he alive at least?"

He hesitated, then finally nodded. "Yes. He's alive. He's a bit scattered, but he is alive and well."

She dipped her head. "Thank you. That's all I wanted to know."

Before she could step back, he pushed past her, making for the townhouse. Breathing a sigh of relief and wiping away a few anxious tears, Nendawagan went about her day.

Pokkoli Toklo Akucha Achaffa Tushafa

Good News

Kevin White Fire and his men were not overly enthusiastic about seeing Ola Achukma again, but they decided they liked him better than anyone else the Krydik might have sent. They didn't much care about his personal mission to find Nathan and Andrew; in fact, many berated him for it and repeatedly told him how impossible it was going to be. When he grudgingly informed them about his secondary objective, finding and tracking the exiles, he was met with uproarious laughter.

"I'm serious," he insisted.

"I'm sure you are," Kevin said, still chuckling. "But let me tell you something. This is going to play out one of two ways: first, you're going to find them because they won't be able to keep their mouths shut about how they were treated by you Krydik bastards, and they'll find plenty of sympathizers, but they won't be able to do anything; second, you're not going to find them because they don't want to admit such defeat and look like fools and cowards that they chose exile over death."

"Seems like a lot of people are choosing that route," Ola Achukma commented dryly.

"And no one wants to admit to choosing it. They want to believe that they are forced."

"Some people have children. Would you orphan hundreds or thousands of children for a future they probably wouldn't see?"

"They don't see it anyway. You think the children are safe? That's one of the first things they do, take the children. Take them away, send them to a white family while the adults are sent west. Not all of them, of course, but enough to make a point to those who try to resist."

"What?" Ola Achukma shook his head as if he might somehow better understand the man's words.

White Fire nodded gravely. "Tell me now that they're courageous for meekly submitting to their captors."

"But why...? I mean, we could help them—"

"Help them how? Your sorceries couldn't save your people a century ago, and they won't save the people now. And I'd be willing to bet that your council isn't keen on the idea of letting everyone come and settle in your lands, right? No, of course not. Not if you're exiling people already."

"They attacked us," Ola Achukma cut in. "People are welcome to come and live peacefully."

The man was nonplussed. "As I said, you don't want us there, and we don't really want you here. Out of simple racial courtesy I'm letting you stay here as a base of operations for your search for your two white men, provided you don't bring them here if you do miraculously conjure them out of thin air."

"Believe me, I won't."

"Good. Then we have an understanding."

Ola Achukma was ready to further conversation and try to convince White Fire to be a little more open to alternative ideas, but the man was evidently done for the time being and wandered off.

The "racial courtesy" the man spoke of was limited to a bed to sleep in as well as breakfast and dinner, and those only if he did a few chores around the house or went hunting to help supplement the food supply. Many people wouldn't do business with injuns, either out of force from the government or true spite, trying to force them west by other means.

It made it harder for Ola Achukma to get around, even in the north. He wasn't as likely to be accused of being a runaway slave, but there were plenty of signs—and plenty more gestures—indicating which businesses were for white Americans only. More to the point, some were only open to whites "of the non-Irish variety."

It was just like Hlohi, he thought, making his way toward a city called Boston. They might look similar, with the appropriately fair skin and fine hair, but they weren't the same enough to be equal. Looking at the free blacks and those of mixed parentage, then looking at himself, he wondered what it was all really for.

Eventually he did find a business that would allow him. It was a tavern, populated almost exclusively by those not permitted in other taverns. He fit in and found many smiles toward him, but knew he was unlikely to find Nathan and Andrew in such an establishment.

As he sat down at the bar, feeling very conspicuous, he noticed a sign on the back wall.

"Alcohol open to all, beds for freedmen and whites only."

The barkeep ambled over to him. "What for ya?"

"I take it that Natives are not permitted beds here?" Ola Achukma asked politely, nodding toward the sign.

The man made an odd motion with his head. "He can read. He can't understand. That's what the sign says, don't it? We serve all kinds in here, but we don't need fleas in the beds. Bad for business."

"I don't have fleas, sir."

"I don't care. The sign says what the sign says and them's the rules. Now either you order something right now or you can get the hell out of here and start packing west. Got it?"

Ola Achukma sighed but agreed to a bowl of soup. He had only a few bits which White Fire had given him in the event he grabbed something and forgot that currency was in use in the Old Land. But the soup was good and he was hoping someone might have some information on Nathan and Andrew. Although, with the size of Boston, there were probably a dozen or more Nathans and Andrews running around. How could he be sure that he and a potential informant were talking about the same men?

The barkeep returned with the bowl of soup, saying, "Only because I'm impressed with your ability to read did I not piss in it."

Ola Achukma tried not to react, but he couldn't help but sniff the liquid just in case. The barkeep chuckled. "Only foolin', son. I promise, I only spit in it."

Sighing, he took a bite so he didn't have to say anything right away.

The soup was good, he would admit that, and he happily scraped as much as he could, using a torn piece of bread to sop up the last. The barkeep returned to him once more.

"He has manners, too. Sometimes your kind like to lick the bowl."

"Which kind would that be?" Ola Achukma asked pointedly. "My Choctaw mother, or my American father?"

"Mixed mutt, eh? At least you got it half right."

"I'm looking for a couple of men—"

"Oh, now he's trackin' like a real injun. Put your ear to the ground, boy, you might find something."

That earned a chorus of hoots from a few nearby drunks, and the barkeep meandered away, though not before taking Ola Achukma's money and telling him to get lost.

Well, it had been a nice break from the mundane, anyway. Ola Achukma relinquished his seat to the next alcohol-seeking patron and made for the door. As he approached, ready to leave, a man at the table nearest the door waved him over.

There were two men at the table, neither one appearing out of the ordinary in present company.

"You're looking for someone?" the waving man asked. Both men looked to be of mixed parentage, but this man had the darker skin. "Hard for injuns to track people in the city. I know, I understand. The urban jungle is a different beast. Maybe we can help."

Figuring he didn't have much to lose, and that Nathan and Andrew could use the sorceries far better than he could if trouble arose, Ola Achukma reluctantly nodded. "Yes. Two men. Nathan Wilde and Andrew O'Dell. Quite frankly, I don't even know if they're in Boston, or even in America."

The man frowned and made a disapproving noise. "Mm, well, that does make it a tad more difficult, don't it? What do you know of these men? What do you want with them?"

"I've never actually met them before. I'm trying to find them on behalf of the people of Hlohi."

"Never heard of them people."

"No, I expect you wouldn't have. We're only a small group."

The man shrugged.

The second man asked, "You know what these men even look like?"

Ola Achukma gave them a description, the best he could recall from the Book. Andrew had black hair and a thick black beard. Nathan was more slight, clean-shaven, with brown hair.

"Sounds about like half the men in this city," the second man said, half-chuckling, half-scoffing. "But the name O'Dell pegs the one as an Irishman at least. Good chance the other is as well. Not too many people want to willingly associate with us pariahs."

"Do you think you can help me or not?" Ola Achukma asked.

"We can keep an eye out, an ear to the ground as it were," the first man said. Noting Ola Achukma's look, he sighed and said, "No offense to you. An expression, isn't it? Anyway, come back in a week. We'll let you know if we turned something up."

"And what do you expect for payment?"

"A round of drinks will do nicely."

Ola Achukma had his doubts, but he wasn't going to argue. He managed a thank you and left the tavern, grateful for the somewhat fresh air. Boston smelled funny. The people were strange. Even when Ki was still alive and they lived here in America, they spent so much time in the wilderness and among the various native peoples that white life never factored into their daily lives the way it did here. Even when he returned with the scouting party some years ago, they'd spent time in small towns and settlements that were a little more open and free. City life felt so restrictive and yet so energetic, like too much water rushing through a too narrow channel.

He returned to Kevin White Fire's home and told him of what had transpired in the tavern over dinner. The man appeared neither surprised nor intrigued.

"They're as likely to help you find the men as bring more friends of their own to beat and rob you," he stated bluntly. "Lot of ruffians in places like that."

"You count yourself as a fearsome savage, then?" Ola Achukma asked pointedly. "Because that's where you would have to go if you wanted to partake in alcohol and other activities."

White Fire laughed. " 'Partake in alcohol and other activities.' God, listen to you." He shook his head, still grinning. "We were fearsome warriors once, because our way of life demanded it. It was a noble calling. It was who we were." He made a noise that was something like a sigh. "When you take away a man's identity, he will fight to take it back. The problem is that if he does not win, he becomes no better than a beast."

And that was how the conversation ended.

Even though the man said to return in a week, Ola Achukma went back to the tavern every night just in case. On the seventh night, as promised, the two men were back. After Ola Achukma bought them each a few drinks, they agreed to talk.

"Well, with your vague descriptions and everything, we can't guarantee that the Nathan and Andrew we found are the ones you're looking for," the second man said, his demeanor saying he wasn't drunk yet but he was close to it. "But we did catch wind of a couple of gents down just south of New York City."

"That's it?" Ola Achukma wondered.

"What more do you want? You didn't give us a lot to go on, but if these are your fellas, it's enough to find someone down there who has more information. Now what do you say to a last round as a proper thank you?"

He didn't want to. He thought about refusing. He wondered what Ki would do in such a situation. If what the men said was true, and if they had done any work on his behalf, then he owed them something— because three rounds of drinks just wasn't enough apparently. On the other hand, they could have just made something up in order to get free drinks.

Against his better judgment, he agreed to the drinks. The men thanked him heartily enough, and he departed.

He'd never been to New York before, though he'd heard plenty of stories about it. Kevin White Fire did not hold it in especially high opinion, but that was to be expected. The man only asked for the courtesy of knowing when Ola Achukma planned to leave, that way he knew his disappearance was intentional. Ola Achukma wanted to ask him to clarify what he meant, except he already had a good idea.

Not wanting to stay in White Fire's cheery presence, as well as the Old Land, longer than he had to, he left the next day for New York. He had never been there, and so refrained from attempting Galohisdi, but he got as close as he could and started walking. Truthfully, he would have much preferred to ride a horse, but he didn't need to attract attention to himself and be accused of being a horse thief or, again, a runaway slave.

It gave him a lot of time to think about things, and he found himself with mixed feelings over his return. Other than the general uncertainty of whether this was all for a ghost story, he wondered what Ki would say or do if he were still alive. If he had lived, would they have had to leave on the Trail? Would they have ever even heard of Aktiya Waya, much less gone there to stay? Would the council and others have allowed Ki to live there because he was Ola Achukma's father, or excluded him because he was white, regardless of any cultural or diplomatic standing he had?

Politics could be confusing at times. How was he going to explain this to his son? How could anyone tell an innocent child to hate others, just based on factors they could not control? How would he explain that they, the Krydik, were hated because of factors beyond their control? The questions were simple enough; the answers, less so.

Other than the storm in his mind, the trip to New York was uneventful, for which he was grateful. The sight of New York City was about the most excitement he thought he could handle. And he thought Boston was big!

He recalled the times when Ki left home to go to Washington City and meet with the politicians. Ola Achukma had always envisioned a very big city—which, to his mind, only vaguely resembled Boston. New York was astounding. Was Washington even bigger? It seemed like it would have to be if it was the primary city of the entire nation. And this was a very big nation. As much as he wanted to go home, he also wanted to see as much as possible, drink his fill while he had the chance.

He didn't want to admit to being lackadaisical, but he couldn't not explore New York City, at least a little bit. There was just so much to see, and he couldn't take it all in from a distance. He figured that as long as he continued south, he would be all right. The city couldn't go on forever, right?

So many people and buildings and businesses and several open markets. Everywhere he looked, there was something to see, something to capture his attention. With his attention frequently distracted, he was also often yelled at by various carriage drivers and other mounted pedestrians. To that end, he also stepped in more than one pile left behind by the horses. Street scrapers ran to and fro, trying to keep things cleaned up, but to little effect. He stumbled into a few people, earning some shoves and accusations of being drunk, and he hurriedly moved away.

Pretty soon, he was lost. He'd tried to keep to a single direction, but the twisting streets, numerous alleys and shortcuts, and being bumped around by vivacious crowds had completely unraveled his sense of direction. He looked up, the sky a haze from the smoky chimneys, unable to see the sun. Looking at the people and buildings around him, he was able to discern enough shadow to determine east and west, and he adjusted appropriately.

When large buildings finally gave way to smaller buildings, then more open land, and finally to the outlying farming community, Ola Achukma stopped and looked around. How far south were Nathan and Andrew? Were they here, in the immediate vicinity? A day or two away? Well, he supposed he could always ask.

His first few attempts to speak to someone were met with silence and subtle or not-so-subtle hostility. Only when he finally approached a lad of about thirteen years was he able to have a conversation.

"I'm looking for a couple of men, supposed to live south of New York City. Nathan Wilde and Andrew O'Dell. Are they near here?"

The boy, who looked respectable enough though evidently shirking chores, shrugged. "I know a couple fellas by that name. What's it to ya?"

"I just need to find them and talk to them. They helped my father-in-law once."

The boy chewed on the inside of his cheek, picked at a bit of dirt under his nails. He squirmed a little, made a sort of half-shrugging motion, then straightened. "Well, it sounds like them, I guess. Mr. O'Dell is kinda scary, but they both seem to like helping people, 'specially non-Americans."

"What do you mean?"

"Paddies, niggers, squaws, they seem to think everyone needs to be equal and free."

Ola Achukma raised a brow. "And what do you think?"

Another shrug. "I ain't had no trouble with paddies, and most niggers is harder workers than any white man round here."

"And...squaws?"

"I'm talking to you, aren't I?"

Ola Achukma sighed. "Where does Mr. O'Dell live?"

He got directions to a small farm southwest of the city, right on the edge of some land being clearcut for apparent agricultural expansion. The house was small to average, quiet for the moment; the chicken coop ten feet from the back door looked almost of equal size with all manner of fowl cackling and screeching about something. A dirty creek ran through the area, a dug out pond home to a dozen or more ducks and geese. A well-kept garden sat idle, and out in the field, three large horses grazed contentedly.

There was no one in sight as Ola Achukma crept around the house, trying to look in windows without looking like a burglar. His attempt was in vain as he came around the corner only to be met by the barrel of a shotgun. He startled and fell backwards, throwing his hands up and shouting, "I'm not armed! I mean no harm!"

The man was quite large, tough and sturdy from farm work. His shirt was dusty and his pants had a small tear in them above the knee. His hair was clean under the straw hat, but it still stuck out, thick and black like his beard.

"Who the hell are you and what are you doing sneaking around my house?" he demanded.

"M-my name is Ola Achukma," Ola Achukma stammered. "Are you Andrew O'Dell?"

"Depends on who's asking." The shotgun remained pointed at him.

"Are you the man who once helped Yvgidahi and his brother Anagalisgi escape to Hlohi?"

The change was profound as the man relaxed completely and finally lowered the gun. After a second of consideration, he held out a hand and helped Ola Achukma to his feet.

"All right, you said enough to get my attention. How do you know about all that?" Andrew asked.

"Well, sir, I'm Yvgidahi's son-in-law."

"Really? Good for you. Good for him, too, I guess. Honestly, I knew him only through his brother. But that doesn't explain why you're here now. Has something happened on Hlohi?"

"It's a long story," Ola Achukma told him. "Is Nathan Wilde also nearby?"

"Aye, he's a few miles down the road, part of the expansion expedition. Twat doesn't do much by way of labor, but he is organized and keeps them on schedule." Andrew shrugged. "But, I imagine he'll want to hear some kind of update. We know how things turned out here, but we never really heard anything about those who left." He shouldered his shotgun and started toward the road, Ola Achukma in tow.

"We know quite a bit about the Old Land," Ola Achukma said.

"Old Land?" He thought a moment. "Appropriate, I guess. And you must know something; you speak English very well."

"Well, truth be told, I'm from here. Well, not here. My mother was Chahta. My father was John Aberdeen—"

"Aberdeen? The diplomat?"

"That's right."

"We heard him and his family died of illness."

"He did, as did my brother and sister. After they died, my mother and I were forced west. On the journey, some scouts from Aktiya Waya came and rescued a handful of us. We've lived there ever since. Well, I did go to live with Eagle Clan for a while—"

"Hold your horses, kid, it sounds like you've got a lot to tell, and I'll be damned if I have to listen to it twice."

Their four-mile trek into the thinning woodland was uneventful, though they had to stay off the main trail to allow for a multitude of teams dragging logs.

"Do your horses help drag logs like this?" Ola Achukma wondered as a team trotted swiftly by.

Andrew shook his head. "No. They could, easily, but I won't let the foreman abuse my boys like that; they're too valuable, too loyal."

"I thought you said Nathan was in charge?"

"I said he keeps them organized. He's the one who makes plans for the foreman to tell the laborers what to do, where and what to cut."

They came upon the camp as they were settling in for the night, pots and pans over open fires, coffee and ale being passed around with some liberality. Most of the tents were small, crude, easy to pitch and pack up at a moment's notice. The one they approached, however, looked a little more important than that.

Andrew did not bother with formality as he let himself in. Ola Achukma followed meekly behind.

"Andrew!"

The man was indeed smaller than Andrew, with fine brown hair and nicer clothes compared to the men outside. He was clean-shaven and his overall demeanor spoke of being more well-mannered.

"Nathan," Andrew murmured, helping himself to a chair.

"I wasn't expecting any company tonight," Nathan said, hastily snatching up a pot and some cups. "Who's your friend?"

"This is..." Andrew stopped and looked at Ola Achukma who was just sitting down. "What was your name again?"

"Ola Achukma," he said politely.

"Olachukma, son-in-law of the great Yvgidahi from Hlohi."

Nathan nearly spilled the cup he had just finished pouring, but he managed to get it safely into Andrew's hands. He stared at Ola Achukma for a long moment before pouring the second cup for him and a third for himself.

"Yvgidahi," he stated. "That's someone I haven't thought about for a long time."

Ola Achukma studied the liquid in his cup. It smelled like heaven, if he could say such a thing, but when he tried it, it was tragically bitter. He set it back on the table, determined to forget about it.

"So, the residents of—what did you call it? Hlohi?—still live, do they?" Nathan said, raising his cup in a half-toast. "Good, glad to hear it. Glad to know that our efforts so long ago were not entirely in vain like they are here today." He scoffed and shook his head. "At least you don't have to face any of the horrors going on right now."

"You mean like the Cherokee Trail of Tears, or the Choctaw Trail of Tears that I was rescued from?" Ola Achukma wondered, not unkindly.

"Ah, so you have seen them." Nathan took a drink. "Otherwise, how are things on Hlohi?"

He decided to start with the good things. The people were thriving, with many families, many children. They'd done some rescue operations in the past, which was how he'd been introduced and inducted into the Krydik, and they'd expanded out into two more villages. Every summer they had a huge festival with many sports tournaments. Not only that, but he'd been one of the ones to help found and plan the festival. He'd also come up with a combined, universal language for everyone to use, including a written language. On top of that, he'd discovered some ancient caves and helped to develop a more grounded mythos for the people, a way to explain things and erase the troubles of the past.

"You've been busy, then," Nathan commented. "Yvgidahi is lucky to have you for a son-in-law. What's your wife's name?"

"Nendawagan. Her mother was a Lenape Moravian."

The slender man nodded thoughtfully. "I remember hearing about them, some years ago." He thought a moment. "Maybe more than a few years, a few decades maybe. Anyway, good for you. Children?"

"Our first is on the way."

"Good for you, congratulations. Glad to hear things are going well." Nathan laughed humorlessly. "If you are from here, if you really are John Aberdeen's boy, well, you know how things have been going on this side of things. Just as well you're inventing new stories because I don't know that you would ever be able to return to the Old Land, as you call it."

"Some have. Recently, a few did, and not under very good circumstances."

At some point in his recitation of the good things on Hlohi, Ola Achukma had decided that if he could avoid it, he wouldn't point out the bad things. He wasn't keen on sharing their bad news with everyone. Mostly because then everyone would have an idea on how to fix things without actually understanding the problem they were trying to fix, and without having to suffer the consequences of their own ideas.

But here it was. He tried to minimize it as much as possible, saying only that there were nine individuals who had been exiled, who didn't especially like the sorceries, and who might try to figure out some kind of revenge. It was likely to be ineffective, but if such a thing ever crossed their ears, let them know if possible.

"Well, we'll help out however we can, if we do hear something," Andrew said, "but we've got our own problems to worry about. You know about the removals, but the rest of us aren't having a much better time of it."

"I've heard passing rumors of secession and war, but it seems to be just disgruntled tavern talk," Ola Achukma said.

"No, not anymore. We're not at the breaking point yet, but it's coming."

"All the same, searching for your antagonizing exiles might prove a relief from our own madness," Nathan postulated. "Take our minds off our own problems for a while."

"Maybe," Ola Achukma cut in, "but that's not actually why I came to find you."

"Oh? Then why did you? Not that we're complaining about this lovely visit, but it does seem a tad bit suspect."

He grabbed his bag and rifled through it until he found the metal piece and shards of glass. He laid them out on the table.

"I told you that we found caves with many paintings. This is true. To the southeast is a cluster of canyons which are also painted. In one of these canyons is another Sacred One, with a tunnel leading to an underground city ten or even a hundred times the size of Aktiya Waya. It's abandoned, but not empty. Hundreds, maybe thousands of skeletons or parts of skeletons, human in all appearance, all with some kind of terrible trauma, some with weapons nearby. My wife found this one, and it seemed to be the most complete and least degraded." He indicated the piece on the table. "It's obviously not ours. It's also the only real relic that we've been able to find from the people before.

"I would be amazed if as many as six people cared about this find. And maybe it's just something from the people before and there is nothing to it. But the fact that we have found nothing—and I mean nothing, besides some cave paintings—anywhere makes me wonder more about what happened to the people before and whether there isn't something still out there."

He didn't miss how Nathan and Andrew studied the piece, though neither moved to touch it. There was a certain recognition there that made Ola Achukma nervous.

"You found only human skeletons, you said?" Andrew inquired, finally taking the metal piece in hand.

"We believe so. There were piles of skulls, a few whole skeletons, plenty of other miscellany scattered about, but all the shapes and sizes suggested human."

The man with the bushy beard made a guttural sound of disapproval.

"If you want, I can show you the underground city," Ola Achukma offered. "No one is there; it's almost impossible to get to without the sorceries."

"That might be best," Andrew said, turning the piece over in his hands before handing it off to Nathan. "If this is what I think it is, your fears may not be unfounded."

That was the last thing Ola Achukma wanted to hear. He honestly didn't want to be vindicated. He wanted to be told that he was wrong, silly and childish for being so paranoid, so he could quietly sneak back home and spend time with Nendawagan and await the joyous arrival of their first child.

The two men debated for a moment over whether it would be better to go now or wait until morning. It was decided that sooner was best.

Ola Achukma was able to direct Galohisdi to the Sacred One in the canyon, but it was Andrew and Nathan lending their strength that saw them safely through.

It was about midmorning, and the large serpent head still yawned in greeting. Ola Achukma took the lead and started into the mouth, down the throat, and finally into the tunnels. All the while, Andrew and Nathan were having a muffled, guarded, not-quite-a-conversation comprised almost entirely of sentence starters, such as, "Now who would...?", "Why would they...?", "Did they really...?" and the like. Each of them had a lantern, but someone used Atsvstdi to light their way even more as they picked their way deeper into the earth.

Whatever oil fed the fires in the underground city had long since burned out, and Ola Achukma had no idea where to find more, at least, in such quantity as to light up an entire city. The only light in the cavern now was their augmented lantern light, though their steps still echoed eerily in the distant darkness.

Ola Achukma led them toward the large, walled building, but they stopped several times to investigate piles of bones. He watched while the white men picked through them. If they used any sorceries, he could not say which ones.

"Human," Nathan stated, standing and brushing his hands on his jacket. "All human."

"Not just any humans either," Andrew growled. He looked at the metal piece which he'd held since leaving the logging camp. "Tacagans."

"Tacagans?" Ola Achukma echoed, clueless. "Where are they from?

Who are they? What people?"

"That's just it. They're Tacagans," Andrew said, turning to face him. "They fancy themselves as being superior to all other human beings."

"Doesn't everyone think that about their people from time to time?"

"Well, yes, except these humans think it all the time, and they have gone to great lengths to establish their superiority."

"So they're from Europe somewhere?"

Nathan and Andrew glanced at each other. It was Nathan who said, "Every human—actually, every living thing in the universe is made up of teeny tiny particles. You have what you can see, and then—"

"Like the particles that told my wife and I that our first child is going to be a boy?" Ola Achukma interrupted.

"Exactly," Nathan told him, "but even smaller than that. It hasn't been discovered on Earth yet, but in more advanced communities, it's called DNA. It's what makes people who they are, their looks, their personality, the framework for experience to color in."

"All right."

"The 'sorceries' as you call them, can alter some of your DNA, to a very limited degree and, most often, only temporarily."

"Yes, we know. Touch and Feel are very widely used. We don't change ourselves, though, for that is a terribly cruel deception."

"But you know what I'm talking about." The man seemed surprised by this. "Well, the Tacagans have figured out how to make these changes permanent, and they can do it from the moment of conception."

"Why would they do that?"

"Because they don't want to be merely human," Andrew said bluntly. "They want to be better than us, above us. They want to be separate."

"What does that have to do with any of this?" Ola Achukma gestured around the empty city.

"The Tacagans are originally from Earth, the Old Land," Nathan continued. "Like you, they left for greener pastures. Unlike you, they did it voluntarily, for the sole purpose of advancing themselves, advancing technologically, and becoming, as stated, more than mere human beings. And they have done it. They travel through the stars, through outer space. They have the capability to do things I wouldn't believe if I didn't see it for myself.

"A long time ago—no one knows exactly when, and the Tacagans won't say—the Tacagans attempted to colonize a planet, a moon to be specific. Problem was, the moon was already inhabited. Peace didn't work out—"

"So they tried to force the people to bend to their will," Ola Achukma stated coldly.

"Yes. All that is really known to outsiders of the conflict is that both sides lost. They not only lost, but they were annihilated. Mutually-assured destruction."

"And you think this...?" Ola Achukma looked around.

"This weapon is Tacagan in origin," Andrew said, indicating the metal piece. "It's an older weapon—and with it, we might be able to narrow down when this massacre took place—but it is theirs. You have to understand, the Tacagans are so stuck up, they don't even really like to leave their home planet for long periods of time. They don't have much of a need. But this place would be within reasonable distance to attempt to colonize. We don't know what brought them here in the first place—possibly resource excavation—or why they haven't returned since."

Ola Achukma looked at the metal weapon, then at the pile of bones. "Are my people in danger?"

Andrew and Nathan glanced at each other again.

"We don't know," Andrew admitted. "I wouldn't expect so. If the Tacagans were really that worried about this place, they could have returned at any point. I mean, it's only been...we don't know how long. Long enough for flesh to rot and ghosts to depart. Long enough for them to declare this place a lost cause."

"We can certainly look into it," Nathan cut in. "We wouldn't want to tell you to relax, only to discover later that they know you're here and aren't happy about it."

"Or they may not know, but your snooping alerts them to us," Ola

Achukma pointed out.

The men faltered, and Nathan eeked out something like an agreement.

"The good news," Andrew said, "is that if you were looking for some impending doom, it isn't here. There is no army marching toward your village."

"That is good to hear, and I will be happy to pass it along. But what should I tell my people?"

"Anything you want," Nathan said, shrugging. "There is no danger now. We can't promise that there never will be. It might be that we slip up and alert them to your presence. It might be that they won't make a move for a thousand years. We can't say for sure. The Tacagans aren't very chatty with their 'less-evolved' kin."

"Less-evolved?" Ola Achukma wondered.

Nathan waved a hand. "Bestial. Animalistic. Doesn't matter, really. They don't like us."

Ola Achukma nodded slowly. "The inhabitants they were fighting, trying to colonize...who were they?"

"Quite frankly, you know more than us on that front," Andrew told him. "The first and last that anyone knows about them is this conflict where they were destroyed."

"They must have been human-like at least." Ola Achukma vaguely gestured around. "For a mutually destructive conflict, there seem to be only human bones here."

"Maybe," Nathan agreed. "And maybe we'll find out more as we dig into this. Maybe we won't. But if we do come across something that we believe will be of importance to you, such as an impending attack by the Tacagans, we will let you know. Otherwise, it sounds like you have other things to attend to with your people and your wife."

Ola Achukma felt the blood rush to his face as he meekly agreed. He looked around again. "One thing bothers me about this, though."

"What's that?"

"There were people here once, and they were great enough to build or carve cities into mountains and underground, and they utilized paints that we have never encountered before. Clearly they were a well-established people. But the only great weapons we have found are these...Tacagan pieces. You identified it yourself. But there is nothing else here of similar type. If the Tacagans are so great at exploration and these other inventions that you say you cannot comprehend except that you have seen them, then what power and technology did the people here possess in order to effect their mutual destruction?"

Nathan and Andrew glanced at each other, suddenly uneasy.

"And where did it all go?" he finished, looking up into the ceiling darkness.

A long moment passed in the not-so-empty cave.

"If there was ever any doubt that you were Aberdeen's kid, it's gone now," Nathan commented.

"Did you know my father?" Ola Achukma wondered, looking at him.

"I didn't know him personally, but I knew several people who did. He was quite popular among those who agreed with him, and there were plenty who did. Just not enough to elevate his voice above the din of naysayers who didn't like him quite so well."

"What did they say about him?"

"I assume you mean his supporters."

"I mean everyone, even those who didn't like him."

Nathan shrugged. "Well, one man's virtue is another man's vice. Supporters said he was determined, opponents said he was stubborn. Supporters said he was bold, opponents said he had a mouth begging for a fist."

Ola Achukma frowned. "I never knew him like that. I always saw him as the one who was kind and soft-spoken, 'able to bring God and the Devil to the table to talk' as a preacher once put it."

"And I'm sure he was," Nathan said, grinning. "That was how he mediated disputes and negotiated treaties with lesser men. But when it came to persuading obstinate politicians, well, humility only gets you so far. He had to be strong, bold, and he had to be willing to make some enemies."

"Sometimes, as a child, I wondered, if Aki were alive, would we have been forced to go west?"

"In one way or another, I imagine. It may have been a bit more comfortable than the Trail, but some politicians with enough clout probably would have pulled enough of the right strings to send your father—and the rest of you—out west to 'negotiate treaties' or some other excuse just to get him away from Washington, away from them."

Ola Achukma nodded. "I suspected as much, now that I am older and understand the ways of the world, or I try to."

"Word of advice," Andrew said, stepping up and clapping his shoulder. "Don't. It makes more sense when you don't try to make it make sense." He went on before Ola Achukma or Nathan could speak. "And in the meantime, why don't you go back to your wife and child, and we'll work on this Tacagan problem, eh?"

For as spooky as the cave was, Ola Achukma was still fascinated by it. He wanted to stay a bit longer and look around some more, but he wouldn't say he didn't want to go home and sleep beside his wife again. Was this how the warriors of old felt when they had been gone all summer and were now faced with the prospect of returning home?

They made their way out of the cave, through the tunnels, back into the canyon where the long shadows obscured any paintings or other interesting features. The three of them turned to face the Zukatopa and its five fangs.

"Perhaps it was not advanced technology that killed the people and the Tacagans," Ola Achukma stated. "Perhaps the Sacred Ones came to the defense of their people, but perhaps they were too late."

Nathan spit a chuckle and tried to cover it up with a cough. "Well, that would be one way to defeat a Tacagan: straight religion and magic." He cleared his throat awkwardly.

Ola Achukma wished the two men well, and the pair departed back to the Old Land via Galohisdi. Once they were safely out of the way, he also used Galohisdi to send himself back home. Having done this a couple times now, it was becoming more familiar, though only marginally easier. He stumbled his way to bed and crawled under the blanket, closing his eyes until his head stopped swimming.

When he opened his eyes, he found Nendawagan beside him. She was heavily pregnant, nearly due. Just how long had he been gone? Had it really taken so long to find just two men?

She kissed him, bringing him back to the present moment.

"Just passing through?" she asked.

"No," he told her. "I found what I was looking for, and I'm home to stay."

"And after all this time, are we in terrible danger?"

He shook his head, mindful of a lingering throb in his temple. "No."

At least, not yet.

Pàke Nishinxke òk Nisha

Priorities

They named him Galiliga. It was a Cherokee word meaning "happy" or "thankful" which was exactly how they both felt upon seeing their firstborn son. And it was a fun word to say, happy in its own way.

Nendawagan had held many tiny newborns over the years, whether it was her siblings or her nieces and nephews, but there was something special about it being her own child, her own flesh and blood whom she'd nurtured in her belly. He was all scrunched and wrinkly with hair so long it probably could have been styled and tied back as he was being dried off and cleaned up. His blue eyes were a stark contrast to his dark skin as he stared at her, trying to figure out what was going and what this new existence was.

She was trying to figure it out, too. She loved this little thing in her arms, but she wasn't quite sure what to do with it. Any other occasion, she held the squirming infant, cooed over it, then handed it off to the next woman to do the same. When watching over other children, she would give them food, play with them, then hand them back to the parents at the appropriate time. This thing here, now, was hers. Now the roles were reversed and she handed him off to her mother and sister and other interested women to ogle over.

Afterwards, she took him out to the river where they were both immersed in the water for cleansing. Seven times each, and then they returned home where Ola Achukma had just returned and was anxiously waiting.

"Here he is," Nendawagan told him.

Her husband moved with the flexibility of a cat but the size of a horse, and she found herself unsure whether she even wanted to give him the infant who was nearly asleep in her arms. He looked terribly nervous and he took the child as though he were a baby bird with a broken wing.

"Is this it?" Ola Achukma asked dumbly. "Is it him?"

"Of course it's him, who else would it be?" Nendawagan wondered, unsure if she should laugh or sigh.

Ola Achukma just looked confused and a little afraid, staring at the brand new sleeping infant in his hands.

"Did you expect something more?" she prompted. "This isn't the first baby you've seen. What about when your little brother was born?"

"Yes, but even my little brother was not my responsibility. He was my brother, not my son. Our mother took care of us, and I was old enough to be doing other things, making myself a man." He shook his head. "I don't know what I was expecting. Something more, maybe?"

"Like what? He doesn't walk or talk yet. He sleeps, he cries, he feeds, and he learns. That's all."

She thought her husband looked a little disappointed at the thought, so she added, "Now you must decide what you are going to teach him and how. And know that he will always be watching. Everything you do, everything everyone does, he will see and learn from. If he ever asks you about it one day, you will have to explain it to him, why you did or didn't do something."

Now her husband went pale. "Oh."

"You think a few years will be enough time for you to figure something out?" she teased.

"Um, well, maybe?" He gave her a look. "Did you want more?"

She burst into laughter. "Not right now. No, don't worry about that. Focus on our one child here and now. It's not as scary as you think it is, I promise."

She didn't know where her authority was coming from on such a thing, but it seemed a correct thing to say. She rescued her husband from the clutches of the newborn infant and set about heating water for tea.

Over the next moon or so, she wondered what sorcery use would do to a baby. She did not expect the infant to use sorceries, naturally, but what if she used them on him? Would he grow up faster? Slower? She'd refrained from sorcery use while pregnant out of caution, but now she was curious again. But curiosity about paintings and caves and extinct peoples was one thing and only put herself and maybe her husband in harm's way. This was something entirely different, and watching her firstborn roll around and want to explore the world around him, she knew she couldn't do any foolhardy experiments on him, no matter how curious she might be.

She chastised herself for even thinking such a thing. How terrible was she that she would even consider experimenting on her son?

On the other hand, what if she discovered something truly helpful, something that would help parents in the future?

Or what if she didn't? In fact, what if she discovered something devastating? What if she killed her son, looking for some fabled miracle to a problem she wasn't sure existed?

No. She couldn't do it. There really wasn't anything wrong with him, so there was nothing that needed to be fixed. He was a baby, for goodness' sake. He didn't know any better; he relied on his parents for everything. The priests had divined that he would be a warrior, so it was their job as parents to encourage him on this path. Neither she nor Ola Achukma had any problem with this responsibility. It could be exhausting at times, yes, and it only got worse as the infant started to crawl and then walk and then use his newfound powers to disappear and get into trouble, but he was their son, their responsibility, and she wasn't going to jeopardize that for selfish curiosity.

This wasn't to say that Nendawagan wasn't still a bit selfish. Once Galiliga started really walking and running, she often encouraged him to follow his father around, do what he did, learn how to be a man—and leave her alone. Then she would breathe a sigh of relief and relish a moment of quiet solitude before going to see her mother or sister.

"It is nice to have a moment of peace and quiet," her mother told her, bouncing a great-grandchild on a knee and stopping only long enough to take a drink of tea, "but it starts to grow on you, having children around, the noise, the joy, the unconditional love and admiration they have for you."

"That comes from grandchildren, Guka, not children," Nendawagan said. "At least, that's what you once told Nocha."

"And how do you expect to have grandchildren if you don't have children? Nieces and nephews are well and good by themselves, but it's special when they're your own."

"Please, Guka, Galiliga is only four years old. He won't be having children of his own for a while yet."

Her mother waved a hand. "No, of course not. But what about you? When are you having more? Surely you want Galiliga to have brothers and sisters he can play and bond with. It's such a shame that Ola Achukma and Apushi aren't closer, but they can hardly be blamed, given their age difference."

"We've talked about it," Nendawagan said evasively. "If it happens it happens."

"Please, Nenda, I'm not stupid. Popokus told me all about what it takes for a woman sorcerer to conceive. Having to Feel your woman parts, force them to release as they are supposed to, trying to get the timing right for a man's seed to implant in them."

"Guka, please."

"Isn't that what you had to do? You're lucky, knowing all that. I had just assumed I had to wait until the effects of the sorceries wore off. Your generation knows a lot more than mine did about the sorceries. It's not for lack of knowledge that you don't have children."

Nendawagan rolled her eyes. "Is there nothing I can do to please you? First, you just wanted me to look at a man. Then you wanted me to get married. Then you wanted me to have children. Now you want me to have more. When will I have done enough?"

Her mother blinked, apparently caught off-guard. Then, "I just want you to have a full, productive, fulfilling life."

"I do, Guka. I do. I'm just doing it at my own pace. I don't need to hurry, not like you were accustomed to. I mean, I'm sixty years old but I barely look twenty. We're safe here, Guka. We can take our time."

Even living in relative safety for sixty years, her mother still didn't seem to grasp the concept as she waved her hand again. "I'm just trying to look out for my grandchildren. Galiliga really should have brothers and sisters. He should understand that he won't always be the center of attention in the house, and he ought to help look after the others, as any good man should."

Her mother wasn't wrong, she just didn't understand, Nendawagan thought. And there was no good way to make her understand. They didn't have to worry, they didn't have to hurry. They had numerous stories of fictional peoples who lived good lives of ease and comfort, yet the Krydik seemed incapable of realizing it for themselves.

She wouldn't say that they hadn't talked about having more children. Ola Achukma brought it up more than once, and he did it more and more as he took Galiliga out to show him the world and their way of life. He was a good father, she thought. Not perfect, but good. When she considered her motives for delaying having more children, she couldn't help but feel terribly selfish.

At last she relented, and less than a year later, a second son was born to them. Him they named Tsona, a rendition of Ola Achukma's father's name. He was also divined to be a peacemaker. Nendawagan didn't think her husband could be any happier, but apparently he could.

So it wasn't hard to tell when his mood suddenly changed. Late one night, as she sat up trying to soothe a fussy four moon old baby, she heard a rustling and started inwardly crying because she didn't want a fussy five year old bothering her either. But it was only her husband. At first she might have dared to hope he would offer to take Tsona for a short while, perhaps conjure Time for her so she could get in a nap. He did no such thing, and, in her haze of fatigue, she noticed he wasn't just taking a brisk evening stroll either.

"Something wrong?" she asked softly, fighting a yawn.

"I'm..." If he had any excuses, he chose to discard them. "I'm supposed to meet Nathan and Andrew. Day and night are a little off between here and there, so—"

"Nathan and Andrew? From the Old Land? Whatever for? I thought you settled all that years ago?"

"They said they would look into some things."

"And five years later they're just getting around to it?"

"I don't know. That's what I'm going to find out."

She shifted position, mindful of the baby that was finally quieting. "When did they contact you?"

"A few days ago."

"Were you going to tell me?"

He shrugged. "If they discovered a problem, I planned to tell at least your father and the council. I'm sure they would call a meeting."

She stood, Tsona finally dozing in her arms. "What about me?"

"You're taking care of the children. I didn't want to worry you." He faltered. "I also didn't want to lie to you."

She took an even breath, swaying her hips to keep herself awake as much as soothe the child to sleep. "Well, I appreciate that. But why not tell me?"

"You're taking care of the children," Ola Achukma repeated. "They are your priority. My priority is to protect them and you. I'm going to meet with Nathan and Andrew and see if I have to do just that."

Evidently satisfied with his own logic, he turned away from her, conjured Galohisdi with great effort, and vanished.

Of course, it was daytime in the Old Land, and the momentary blink of light only roused Tsona to crying again. Nendawagan sighed and started making slow laps around the room. She was just finishing the second lap when Galiliga toddled out to her, asking for water and begging to be picked up. Groaning, she sat down again and let the small child scramble onto her lap.

"Why is brother crying?" Galiliga wondered.

Nendawagan was too tired to come up with an answer, but her son didn't seem to notice as he touched Tsona's shoulders and looked at his wrinkled, crying face. When Tsona finally opened his eyes to take a breath, he saw Galiliga and immediately quieted. A moment later, the baby smiled and giggled, reaching up toward his brother.

"Can I hold him?" Galiliga asked.

Carefully, she shifted everything around until she was holding Galiliga who was holding Tsona who was smiling and playing with his brother's face. This was the last thing she remembered before falling asleep.

She startled at a hand on her shoulder and momentarily panicked as she realized her children were gone. As she started to stand, Ola Achukma gently pushed her back down, then he grabbed a chair for himself.

"They're sleeping now, don't worry," he told her. "You should be, too. In bed."

He stood and held out a hand to her which she took with some relief. The house was quiet and it was still dark, everything outside perfectly still.

Ola Achukma was gone again when she woke to Tsona's crying. It wasn't until after the babe was on her breast that she noticed Galiliga had disappeared as well, probably to run after his father. She felt better than she had when she passed out the night before, but she was still too tired to give much worried thought to where either of them might be. If she'd had any fears, they were soon assuaged with the return of her husband and older son.

"Were you able to get any sleep?" he asked, half a second before Galiliga bowled into her legs with something resembling a hug before running off again.

"Some," she sighed. "You?"

"A bit, though, more than you, I think."

"What did Nathan and Andrew have to say? Were you out speaking to my father just now?"

He nodded. "I was. As for Nathan and Andrew, well, it's a bit of a story."

She sat down. "Five years ago you said there was no trouble, nothing to worry about. What's changed?"

"I said they were going to look into some things, and they have." He dodged an energetic five year old and grabbed a chair of his own to sit in. "The weapon we found belonged to a people called Tacagans. Once, they were like our people, human, living in the Old Land. They broke away and settled on a new island."

"This island?"

"No. A different one." He put up a hand. "I know. How many islands are there? According to Nathan and Andrew, plenty. Anyway, where we were more or less forced to leave the Old Land, the Tacagans left intentionally. They no longer wished to be human. They settled on a new island and eventually made their way here, seeking to expand. But there were already people here."

"The people before. Who were they?"

"The stories are unclear. Some say they were human. Others say they were talking animals such as we have in our stories. Still some say they were celestial beings of smoke and lightning."

Nendawagan shook her head. "They must have been men or animals of some form. What man, even with an army, could stand against such powerful celestial spirits?"

"I don't know," Ola Achukma admitted. "I only know what they told me."

"The people before were obviously lost. What of the Tacagans?"

"They still live on their island. They still desire to be more than human."

She ran her tongue over her teeth. "Perhaps they came to the people before who truly were celestial beings, desiring to know their secrets, and were denied. Perhaps that is what started the war. But still, how could they overcome them so terribly?"

"We may never know. All Nathan and Andrew could find was that the Tacagans declared it a lost cause and left this island. In fact, they consider it such a failure that they've worked to erase it. Even if they know we're here, they may not know the significance of this place or the people before or anything at all. We are just meager humans on another island, no threat to them."

Nendawagan breathed a sigh of relief, but it was cut short as Galiliga made another wild pass through the house. Ola Achukma finally stuck his arms out and swooped the small child into the air. Galiliga laughed hysterically as Ola Achukma growled and swung him upside down a few times before sweeping him out of the house. She could still hear them romping and playing, and she smiled.

A few minutes later, Ola Achukma returned. He plopped back down in his chair, saying, "I sent him to see Popokus and her kids."

She nodded, but her smile faded quickly. "So if there is no threat to us from the Tacagans, why did you first bring this apparent non-issue to my father?"

"The Tacagans do not appear to be a threat, but there is more trouble brewing in the Old Land. I just happened to be there when the scout group returned with their report."

"Is there ever not trouble there? What makes this different? More removals?"

"Not so much removals as voluntary departures. A lot of the peoples are heading south."

"Whatever for?"

"The last scouting group says that some of the southern United States are talking about seceding."

"Seceding?"

"Leaving the country. Splitting the nation in two."

"What does that have to do with the peoples? Will they be occupying the southern nation?"

"The southern leaders have promised to recognize them as sovereign entities."

She raised a brow. "You mean the same way the leaders promised that to your people and my father's people and everyone else they wanted to kindly send away to die?"

He faltered only a little, but pressed on in his line of thought. "I know it's hard to believe, but they might be honest about it this time. These men are not leaders of any significance; for them to speak this way is dangerous, even among their own kind. But speak they have. They have also recognized the chiefs of the peoples and drawn up maps showing the proposed sovereign lands."

She shifted position. "When is this to take place?"

"As anyone who spends any time in Old Land politics knows, things are very slow moving, and there are more issues at stake than just our ancestral peoples. It could be ten years or twenty."

"Oh." She couldn't help but feel a little deflated by the thought. She looked at Tsona, sleeping in her arms. He might be ten years old, about ready to become a man. He might be twenty years old, already a man and perhaps courting a woman. Galiliga? He might have children of his own by that time. She looked at her husband. "What other issues are there?"

"Slavery, and freedom of conscience," he answered. "The North wants to get rid of slavery, but their economy is dependent on cheap, slave-made goods. They also want all states to obey a single government. Meanwhile, the South wants to keep slaves and let each state, each man live according to his own conscience."

Nendawagan shook her head. "What's the problem? Our ancestors had slaves, and they lived according to the rules of the clan and the people as a whole, and each man lived according to his conscience."

"Does a slave live according to his conscience? Shall one clan proclaim a man free, and another clan claim him as a slave?" He went on, "But if one man's freedom causes another ninety-nine to suffer, should he be denied? If a man is allowed to live free and demand fair compensation the same as any other man, what happens to those who can no longer give him any compensation, never mind what might be considered fair?" He shrugged. "I can't answer these questions. And they are not my problems to solve. Your father is more interested in what the different nations intend to do."

"What do they intend to do?"

Ola Achukma shifted uncomfortably. "Considering Kevin White Fire voluntarily left the north to meet with some of these southern leaders, most of them have already sided with the South, in secret if not public. They're just waiting to see what the polite side of politics will yield before making any drastic moves."

"What about the Cherokee, the Choctaw, all of them?"

"They prefer the southern leaders, but even they are not unified in the decision."

"But it will still take ten or twenty years for anything to come to fruition?"

He shrugged. "That's politics for you. My father accomplished many things when going between our Native nations, but virtually nothing when it came to the United States government."

She frowned. "That's too bad. What does my father think?"

"He's going to call a special session of the national council, to let them know what's happening and get their input. Best case scenario, everyone accepts all terms, the nations of the Old Land are recognized and granted sovereignty, and all is well again. Worst case scenario, there is war. Because one group of people doesn't like how another group lives and wants to forcibly change it, even though they are dependent on the way things are."

Nendawagan shook her head. "I don't...I don't know what to think. And where do we come into this? More refugees?"

"Refugees, if things erupt into war. If they remain peaceful and chiefs and lands are recognized and honored, some people here might want to return. Or maybe we open up to more regular contact and trade with the people of the Old Land, once we don't have to fight the United States government anymore."

She stood slowly, trying not to disturb Tsona. "I guess only time will tell."

For as much as she or anyone complained or joked about how slow politics in the Old Land moved, sometimes Krydik politics could be just as slow. Even once the national council was convened, they spent a good ten days in closed session. Then they left and the village council was in private session for another ten days.

Nendawagan sometimes visited her parents just to check on her father and maybe get some news, but if he wasn't sleeping, he was usually in session. When the private sessions ended, he didn't have much to say, at least not to her.

"There is so much that isn't known, it's hard to make a decision," he told her, sounding worn out from the whole thing. "If there will be no war, there will be no need to prepare for refugees. If there will be war, we must not only decide our position about it, but we must also consider whether the peoples of the Old Land want us to get involved."

"Why wouldn't they?"

"Why would they? It's not as if they don't know we're here. Since we've been sending scouting parties back on a more regular basis, it's not as though they can't contact us. It's a matter of will and differences of opinion. If this is true, and if the southern leaders are honest and do intend to give the nations sovereignty, why would the peoples abandon that to come here, to start over and have to assimilate into yet another new people?"

She opened her mouth but couldn't come up with a good rebuttal. Finally she asked, "Do you think we live too comfortably?"

Her father frowned, as if he did not wish to contemplate any more complex ideas at the moment. After a moment, he sighed and answered, "I think we have a lot of luxuries and a lot of privileges that most people of the Old Land only whisper about as if they are fantastical stories of heaven or other places unattainable in this life. And I think some of our problems stem from the fact that while we may have whispered about such easy lives, we never considered how we would have to change in order to accommodate our luxury; we just assumed that our luxuries would always accommodate us."

"So what do you think of this fabled war that is supposed to be coming in ten or twenty years?"

He shrugged. "The people of the Old Land, native and white, seem to think it is inevitable. Not imminent, just inevitable. From our vantage, well, we don't exactly have people pounding on our doors begging to come in, so it seems much less significant."

"Is that what the other council members think?"

"By and large, yes. We've always been here, we'll always be here. If they don't ask for help, then it is their own fault for whatever happens."

Nendawagan shifted her stance. "That sounds so...callous, though. If two men get into a fight and the smaller is obviously losing, to the point where he may be killed, why shouldn't we intervene?"

"Sometimes it is a matter of honor. Better to die an honorable warrior than live as a coward."

"Would that not make everyone here a coward? Would that not make you a coward?" She shook her head. "I refuse to believe that."

He chuckled. "Well, I thank you for your vote of confidence, though I'm afraid it won't mean much if indeed this unfolds as they are predicting." He shrugged again and sighed. "But no matter what, it's still some years away, plenty of time for anything to happen." He gave her a look. "And your husband and I don't want you getting too wrapped up in this. Your priorities should be focused on your children, not a war on another island."

She blinked. "Didn't Ola Achukma tell you of his findings from Nathan and Andrew?"

"Five years ago, there was nothing to worry about. Five years later, there is still nothing to worry about. I appreciate the caution, and your curiosity and love of exploration has always been a shining light in this village, but eventually we must consider what is really important in life, what we are fighting for, if we fight. We don't fight for old caves and underground cities; we fight for what is here, now, right in front of us. Don't ever lose sight of that."

His tone said that the discussion was over. To emphasize the point, he retired to bed, ignoring even his wife who turned and gave Nendawagan a look.

"What?" Nendawagan asked.

"You know what," her mother stated.

"I'm only trying to get a feel for things."

"You're getting involved in things that don't concern you."

"Don't concern me? If war were to break out today, I would be concerned for my husband because he may want to help in some way, use Touch to bind up the wounded. If war breaks out in ten years, Galiliga would be old enough and unsettled enough that he might want to go fight and prove himself in some way. If war breaks out in twenty years, Tsona might be there beside him. Yes, I think this does concern me."

Her mother's expression said she hadn't quite considered it that way, and she backed down from the argument. Frustrated, Nendawagan headed home.

Almost no one outside of her, Ola Achukma, her father, the council, and the scouting groups even knew that there were such problems in the Old Land, and it seemed as though, at least for a little while, the Krydik had finally achieved internal peace. Those who used the sorceries regularly lived in Aktiya Waya and were called Wolf Clan. The Deer Clan village of Anpa O Wicanh'pi tolerated minimal use of the sorceries and generally preferred to live on the plains. Eagle Clan used no sorceries and lived in their cliffside village of Lehogyed. The unified language Ola Achukma had developed was growing and becoming far more common, and being able to be understood calmed a lot of tensions between the peoples.

Festivals came and went, the variety of tournaments determined by the landscape of the host village, which helped to keep things interesting. Popokus eventually coordinated a sort of children's activity, for those who were too young to compete but too old and energetic to simply stand and watch the tournaments for days on end. A grand event, Nendawagan thought, that had come about because her husband had desired to prevent a war.

As she watched Galiliga, now eight years old, who was watching Ola Achukma in the archery tournament that year, she couldn't help but wonder if such a miracle couldn't be pulled off again, this time for the Old Land. Maybe the people of the Old Land needed a similar tournament, a way to prove themselves better without having to kill each other.

Except their problems did not stem from boredom and searching for problems where none existed. Their problems seemed to be more ideological, economical, political, and the people did not seem to believe that the same divine providence which could guide a man's weapons to favor a winning army could also guide a man's playing sticks and favor a winning sports team.

Then the round was over, her husband advancing to the next day, and all conscious thoughts of war in a far away land vanished from her mind.

"You made it!" Galiliga cried as his father exited the arena.

"I did," Ola Achukma said, handing his bow off to the child who took it with glittering eyes. His own expression said he was unsure just how he'd made it, but he wasn't going to argue.

Tsona, now almost four years old, put his hands up, whimpering and begging to be picked up, which Ola Achukma obliged.

And for a while, one could almost be forgiven for thinking that life was perfect on Hlohi.

This illusion was shattered twice on the same day, but for very different reasons. It was at the festival a few years later, the morning of the first day of real competition.

Nendawagan had hoped to put things off just a little longer, revel just a little more in her two sons being so young and innocent and totally dependent on her. But even that dream had begun to fade as Galiliga finally reached the point of becoming a man, not only in physique but also in his first year of competition. He wanted to impress a girl.

That was only the first crack in the ice, for it was also the day Nendawagan confirmed she was pregnant. Upon polling the men of the house, only Tsona, now eight years old, wanted to know the sex ahead of time.

So it was that even as Nendawagan would have to prepare for another tiny babe, she was also having to prepare herself for Galiliga taking his place as a man.

"How did you feel when your mother announced she was pregnant with Apushi?" she asked her husband as they lay together in bed that night. "You were about Galiliga's age, weren't you?"

"I was happy for my mother," he answered simply. "She'd been so sad for so many years after the deaths of Aki and Evan and Priscilla. Marrying Chilita and having another child brought life back into her."

"But you and Apushi have never been very close, have you? I mean, he's married with children of his own now and you don't relate quite like brothers, I think."

He shrugged. "I was still trying to figure out life here on Hlohi, and, like Galiliga, I was a little more preoccupied with showing off and impressing girls."

"Oh were you?"

"Must have worked because here you are."

She stifled a snicker. "Ah, yes, of course. To think that's where it all started, when I saw a gangly thirteen year old boy running around the field looking at all the different insects. That's when I knew I was going to marry him in ten years."

"That was all it took? Here I thought it was my willingness to stop a war, or maybe my work in trying to unite the peoples and the language and the stories and everything else."

She sighed dramatically, rolling over and going to sleep.

For as big a day as it had been, and for as chaotic as the festival could be, things did not, in fact, change overnight. Galiliga, against the advice of most everyone, participated in five different events and advanced in none of them. His dismay was palpable long after the festival was over, up until the arrival of his first baby sister.

They named her Netami, and she became the instant favorite in the family. There was nothing that she wouldn't smile or laugh at. According to Mesim, she looked exactly like Nendawagan at that age, no matter what age it was, whether she was a suckling infant, a clumsy toddler, or an energetic child. Even Ola Achukma agreed that Netami was the spitting image of her mother. Even Galiliga and Tsona did not look so much like him or like each other. Nendawagan simply took it as a compliment that she was still as cute and beautiful as a child, no matter how ugly she felt some days just from sheer stress of trying to keep up with her children.

Most days, she was happy to step back and let life happen. Most days, she could almost believe that this was how things had always been. The Krydik had always been here, had always had these traditions. Their ancestors were buried in sacred places and the stars were theirs, too. Most days, she didn't question any of it and she let herself believe these lies.

Because inevitably, the truth would come back to remind everyone of its existence, remind everyone that this was not how things had always been and there was always the possibility that things could change again.

Nendawagan knew of it before most, because Ola Achukma had happened to overhear a bit of conversation between the council and a returning scouting group. Having them give reports was nothing new, for the scouting groups had been going out regularly over the last couple decades. But, according to Ola Achukma, this was the first time they had confirmed that war was happening. It was not just disgruntled rumors, not just a nebulous threat, but a new reality in the Old Land.

Despite only hearing a snippet of conversation, Galiliga and Tsona demanded to know everything their father had heard. Galiliga was some twenty years or so now, a man grown, Tsona a few years behind though only in number.

"I'm sure we'll hear more about it when the council calls a public meeting," Ola Achukma told them.

They sat together for a light dinner they only rarely shared because of their proficiency in the sorceries.

"When will that be?" Tsona wondered.

"I don't know. Obviously not tonight. Tomorrow, maybe? The next day? They may wish to convene the national council first."

Galiliga made an exasperated sound. "They've only been discussing this war for as long as I've been alive. Why wouldn't they have a plan by now?"

"And what do you hope this plan will be?" Nendawagan questioned. "What do you think you'll be doing from here?"

"From here?" He raised a brow. "Nothing. We need to go there."

"And do what?"

"I don't know. Fight, maybe? Help the people?"

"Which people?" Ola Achukma asked. "We have no stake in the white man's war. You want to help the native peoples, our ancestral peoples? Half of them don't like us but they tolerate us because we offer help. The other half don't like us and would attack as soon as look at us."

Tsona shifted position. "Then why have we kept watch on the Old Land like we have? Why were we raised with knowledge of the Old

Land? Why not just let us live here and believe that we are all that exist, all that matter? If the Old Land doesn't matter, why does the council treat it like it does?"

Nendawagan sighed and glanced at Netami, but the little six year old girl ate quietly, giving her mother a look as if echoing the question.

"I don't know," Ola Achukma answered. He shrugged. "I don't. It's been a discussion that's gone round and round in circles since before you were born."

"The council claims to lead the people, but how can they if they do not see themselves as Krydik?" Galiliga pressed.

"You will not disrespect the council," Nendawagan told them coldly.

"The council disrespects us," her older son shot back. "How much loyalty can they really hold toward us when they keep one eye out on their old lives in the Old Land as if things will go back to the way they were?"

"Just a moment ago you sounded excited to go to the Old Land and fight," Ola Achukma stated.

"I don't know," Galiliga snapped. "I don't know. Listening to the council in their meetings, I don't think they know either. I think their judgment is too cloudy. By the time they make a decision, the war will be over, and we will be stuck listening to them discuss refugees, maybe bring over a dozen or so, and then go back to the fretting and waiting."

"And what would you do?" Nendawagan asked. "If Yvgidahi were to walk in here right now and ask for your sagely advice, what would you tell him?"

"I would tell him to declare us as the Krydik. I would tell him to stop sending random men and teenagers who are bored and need something to do back to the Old Land to walk around and listen to idle gossip. I would tell him to send real envoys, of peace or war, with real warriors or real diplomats, and make us known. Maybe the other people don't like us because they see us as leaderless and directionless and we are not worth taking seriously because they have problems and we don't. And while they fight for what seems to be a lost cause, we occasionally drop in to pour salt in their wounds and offer to clean up the blood left behind and whisk away those they fight for until there is nothing left."

Tsona's posture and expression backed up his brother's words, and even Netami appeared to be in agreement. Nendawagan looked at Ola Achukma who deliberately stared at his food, picking at it but not eating.

The silence stretched long, at least until they were all done eating, or at least done pretending to be interested in the food. Nendawagan tapped Netami and motioned for her to help clear the table and manage cleanup. That motion broke the men out of their steely trance as Ola Achukma stood and motioned for Galiliga and Tsona to follow him outside.

"Are brothers in trouble?" Netami asked, her large brown eyes wondering if she would also be in trouble.

"I don't think so," Nendawagan said, trying to be reassuring. "I think Nocha is taking them to see Yvgidahi."

"Why?"

"Because they said some very bold, very powerful words. But you shouldn't say such bold and powerful words unless you are willing to follow them with action."

"So Tsitsa is making sure Galiliga and Tsona are putting actions to their words?"

Nendawagan sighed. "Tsitsa" was something of a childish conglomeration to refer to one's father. It had just appeared one day and now most all the children used it, along with "Tsitsi" to refer to their mothers. She nodded. "That's right."

"And what they were saying about the council," Netami went on, her expression thoughtful, "words don't mean very much, do they?"

"Words can do some amazing things. They can make you feel such incredible emotions that you cannot describe in a single word or phrase. But they have no power by themselves. It's what you do in reaction to those words that make them powerful or not."

She did not expect the little girl to understand, but she looked like she was trying to.

Ola Achukma returned not much later, alone.

"Where are the boys?" Nendawagan wondered.

"Well, I took them to see Yvgidahi and told them to tell him everything they told us," he replied, a bit smug in her opinion. "They were a little wormy about it at first, but once they started talking, I let them have the discussion."

"Do you think that was a good idea? I mean, for my father and all? I know he's been under a lot of stress."

Her husband shrugged. "Honestly, Nenda, the boys have a point. Aktiya Waya alone has been around for a hundred years now, and we still can't make a decision on who we are and what our purpose is, what our relationship is to the Old Land, mostly because almost everyone on the councils are from the Old Land." He went on before she could speak. "I'm not saying that they don't need a bit of tact when expressing their frustrations, but their sentiments are not unknown among their peers."

Nendawagan sighed and folded her arms. "I can't say I don't understand either." She frowned. "Do you think we should interfere over there?"

"I think we should make a decision and stick to it. Do we interfere, or do we not? What policy should we set forth as the basis for future decisions? That way if news does reach us of terrible things happening in the Old Land, we don't have to take twenty years to discuss it. We know whether we will face it or not, when we will consider it a threat or not. Having that issue resolved, that purpose and the knowledge of how we will react, will go a long way in establishing who we are as Krydik, something that really should have been done even before I got here."

"You're not wrong. When this village was first discovered—or perhaps 'rediscovered' I should say—the only thought was survival. But once the people were settled down, once the war was over, no one gave any more thought to the priorities of the people as a whole, and everything spiraled out into this mess."

He nodded. "Let's just hope that we get things straightened out quickly, before we find ourselves facing our own civil war."

Pokkoli Toklo Akucha Tuchina Tushafa

Division

Ola Achukma couldn't say he didn't understand his sons' frustrations; he shared many of them, and he had had similar inner monologues over the years as he struggled to bring the people together to find common ground and lay the foundation of a new nation. The problem was, where his generation or those in his position had absorbed enough of all sides to be sympathetic to all, Galiliga, Tsona, even Netami, they were, as they said, one hundred years removed from the problems that the council didn't seem to realize they'd solved. And everyone in the Old Land knew those problems had been solved, so it wasn't for lack of knowledge or opportunity that they remained behind in what appeared to be a hopeless situation.

In all reality, there was no one person, no singular entity to blame for their predicament. Indeed, they had never faced anything like this before, in that, the original chiefs, the original skiagvsta and uku, were still alive. One hundred years after helping to lead the people to Aktiya Waya, Yvgidahi was still leading the people. Ola Achukma remembered his father sometimes quoting the wisdom of dead men and wondering what they would do or say in certain situations. The Krydik had that opportunity, to have their legendary leaders walk among them for years to come. But was that ability actually harming them?

Galiliga and Tsona were gone far longer than he might have expected for a simple meeting. Either Yvgidahi truly took their words to heart and they had a long conversation with the council about their thoughts, or else the boys had wandered off to do other things as well. Galiliga was eyeing a girl, Ola Achukma knew, so maybe he'd gone to woo her in some way.

The pair was out all evening. By nightfall, Netami was already asleep, and Nendawagan was just getting ready to join her. Ola Achukma was determined to wait up for the boys, and they did eventually return, evidently not expecting anyone to be awake when they got back.

"Had a long discussion with Yvgidahi, did you?" Ola Achukma asked. "I didn't see you at all afterwards, even around town."

The boys got a certain look when they were embarrassed, something that Nendawagan said they inherited directly from their father. It was Galiliga who answered, "We talked some, and then we went hunting."

"Oh? And what did you find?"

"Not much."

Ola Achukma raised a brow but did not pursue the matter. Instead he asked, "What did Yvgidahi have to say?"

"Nothing we didn't expect," Tsona said, his voice tinged with acid. "He valued our concerns. We were not the only ones to express such thoughts. The councils, both here and nationally, had been considering such things for a while now. Any tangible suggestions we might have could be brought up at the public meeting and would be given equal weight."

Again, Ola Achukma found himself feeling just as frustrated as his sons, but he couldn't allow himself to feed their brewing anger. The problem was, he didn't need to; any of the other young men would do it just as easily and more willingly.

"Is there going to be a meeting?" he inquired instead.

The boys shrugged and moved past him, Tsona saying, "Don't know."

"What do you mean you don't know?"

"Might be tomorrow, might be the next day, might be ten days from now. Whenever the council can get together and make up its mind and decide that it needs to make up its mind."

"I share your frustrations, but you should not disrespect the council so. Yvgidahi led the people here on the Great Migration—"

"One hundred years ago," Galiliga interrupted. "And what since? You got the festival of tournaments started and running, brought the people together, and then what?"

"Then I married your mother and had you," Ola Achukma said coldly. "I've spent my life trying to keep the people together, keep you safe."

"Well. Here we are. Safe and sound."

With that, the boys turned and headed off to bed. He watched them go, making no move to stop them. After a moment, he joined his wife in bed. He tried not to disturb her, but she was apparently already awake.

"My nieces and nephews and their children are the same way," she murmured quietly.

"Get enough of them together and it could get ugly," he agreed, sighing. "But where would the battle lines fall? Twenty-five years ago, people were afraid of the sorceries and those who used them. Other than a few disgruntled people here and there, nothing has come of it. But what would happen if the young people rebelled against the council? It's more than just a handful of people to be dealt with or sent back to the Old Land."

"I don't know, but it wouldn't be good. It would be like the War That Was Not, except this would be a real war, and, as you said, it's not just one or two or ten people."

"Maybe we should send warriors to the Old Land to fight in their war, just to let the young men blow off some steam."

"You would send Galiliga and Tsona to the Old Land to potentially die just because they're frustrated men?"

"I'm saying that if we don't allow it, they'll find a way to make it happen anyway, and it will easily be a more dangerous endeavor because they're trying to hide it from us as well as accomplish whatever they think they need to accomplish."

Nendawagan sighed. "I'm not saying you're wrong, I just don't want you to be right."

"Believe me, I don't either. But maybe the council will make a decision to not interfere in the affairs of the Old Land. At least that would put an end to some of the complaints, that we have no direction as a people."

"Yes, but it does nothing to alleviate the frustration of the young men. Once you set your mind to something, it's very difficult to break."

He chuckled. "Well, you're not wrong."

It took four days for the council to call a meeting, but by that time, most of the young people, specifically the men, had already made their decision on what they wanted to do. Galiliga and Tsona had not discussed it with Ola Achukma, certainly not with Nendawagan, but he could see that they were ready to go to war. They wanted to fight, to prove themselves, to show off and do the things their ancestors had done before they had retired to a remote island with nothing to do but bicker over the minutia of festivals and tournaments.

As they gathered in the townhouse for the meeting, Ola Achukma saw, perhaps for the first time, how old Yvgidahi appeared. For the longest time, he had looked no more than forty-five, maybe fifty on the most stressful days, but always with a mixed air of youthful confidence and seasoned experience.

Tonight, Ola Achukma saw the lines on his face, the graying of his hair, the tinge of arthritis in his joints. Had he stopped using the sorceries, or was age finally catching up with him? The sorceries only slowed aging; they did not stop it completely.

Perhaps the worst part was his look of defeat. He still walked with a certain air of leadership and authority, but his expression said he knew that he was already outnumbered. Maybe not by the council, but if an angry crowd got their heads together and agreed that they wanted to do something, no soft words of persuasion would tell them otherwise.

Ola Achukma already knew how this would go. Yvgidahi would delay as much as possible, tell a story or two, ask someone else to tell a story. Probably they would be terrible stories of the fires of the Old Lands, whole villages burned to the ground with people trapped in their homes to die, and other woes meant to discourage the young men from seeking out the war path.

The problem, Ola Achukma thought, was actually already outlined in the Book. They had the ability to not only fight, but run away to safety. They did have the ability to get food and water when needed, bind their wounds with better care than what might be mustered in the field. And there was nothing the enemy could do about it, not without the sorceries.

And the excuse for war was as plain as day. Yvgidahi and the others would recount the most horrific tales to try and dissuade the young men, but it would have the opposite effect. The young men would want the revenge that their ancestors never sought or never achieved, even avenging those who had more recently been forced off their lands. And they could do it from the comfort and safety of Aktiya Waya.

This was not going to go well. Looking at his wife as they took their places in the townhouse, she had also reached this conclusion. She looked away and he followed her gaze to where Galiliga and Tsona were speaking with other young men whose expressions and postures said the group was largely in agreement and clearly unhappy.

"Do you think we didn't do enough to teach them about peace?" Nendawagan wondered.

Ola Achukma shook his head. "No. I think we didn't do enough to teach them about war."

Sadly, it was a subject about which they, too, were sorely ignorant. Perhaps they had merely taken for granted the trust and obedience of children, that it would magically carry through from cradle to grave, generation to generation. But, like children, these green young men desired something they'd never had, and they desired it all the more because their elders forbade it.

Neither Yvgidahi nor anyone else on the council was in any hurry to start the meeting as they stood along the wall, draped in shadow, simply observing the crowd. Were they assessing the futility of trying to calm down an angry mob? Were they simply gathering their nerve, knowing that any answer would displease half of those in attendance?

Yvgidahi led the way, and the council took their seats. The crowd quieted down, but there were no passive onlookers this night. The priests blessed the place and the people, and the pipe was lit and handed first to Yvgidahi.

"We are here," he began deliberately, "to discuss some matters of great importance."

Now begins the delay, Ola Achukma thought.

"Only children and fools are unaware of the plight of our brothers and sisters in the Old Land. Many here and in the other villages are witnesses to the atrocities committed upon them or their families, and still more of you are the children of these witnesses, growing up hearing these tragic tales. Some of these crimes happened ten years ago, some twenty or fifty or even a hundred years before this meeting here tonight.

"These crimes, and the tales we tell concerning them, are like seeds planted in the mind. Not only are they seeds, but they are, in fact, magical seeds, for they may grow and bear one of two very different fruits. The first fruit is peace. It is healthy and nutritious, not only for the individual, but for his family and his community. A man grows this fruit when he helps his neighbor in a game drive and divides the meat fairly. He harvests this fruit when he helps to build or repair the irrigation system so an elder may have water. He serves this fruit to his family when he chooses to forgive an offense his wife or children may have committed against him. He offers this fruit to his community when he disciplines his children so they may understand the proper way to live.

"But there is another fruit that this seed may bear, and that is war. This fruit gives the illusion of health and nutrition at first, but always turns out to be poison. A man grows this fruit when he dwells on the wrongs others have done to him. He harvests this fruit when he takes what is not his or when he strikes his brother. He serves this fruit to his family when he is cruel to his children and does not respect the life his wife gives. He forces this fruit on his community when he raves about wrongdoing and engages in rumors and gossip with the intent of bringing shame upon others and sowing discord.

"The man who merely receives these fruits is not to blame for their effects, any more than one man who bumps into another is not to blame if he was pushed. It is only a consequence. But we must recognize these consequences, recognize this poison is among us. Once we admit that we have been poisoned, that it is indeed poison and not nutrition, then we may accept an antidote and begin to heal."

He looked around at the gathered crowd, intentionally making eye contact with certain individuals. Galiliga and Tsona were among them, Ola Achukma noticed.

"This does not mean, however, that everything is a mere accident. For a seed to grow, it must be nurtured. It is those who nurture this hatred and fear who are responsible for the poison in our community. If a man dies by poison, it is the one who gave it to him who is responsible. If a mother does not stop her child from eating a fruit she knows to be poisonous, she is the one at fault.

"Regrettably, I know not where this poisonous fruit has come from, who has brought it here to our people. I know how the seeds were planted, but he who nurtured them to grow into vile thorns is yet unknown and may never be revealed." Yvgidahi paused and did another sweep of the room. "But I have an idea. Ignorance. If knowledge is simply a seed, then the water that feeds it must be either Experience or Ignorance. Anyone here who desires war is not only ignorant of war, he is also ignorant of peace, the tranquility and the prosperity that we have, that we ought to be grateful for and work to uphold. You live in peace but are ignorant of it. You do not recognize its worth and so desire war, thinking that it is the greater thing, the greater path.

"We have heard little but bad news from the Old Land. Few here have any endearing experiences. The Old Land has been at war since before even the first settlers came here. Ignorance turns a blind eye and deaf ear to these tales, believing that this is different somehow. It is, in the sense that we cannot turn back from this. Once we send our young men to war in a land they have never seen and know nothing about, fighting for a people who have already claimed to disown and even hate them, there are then no more limits on what may be done in our future of warfare.

"We may have our reasons and our excuses and our justifications, and they may seem noble at the time. But once this precedent is set, will you be able to look at your children and grandchildren and explain it to them? Will you be able to explain why you chose to go? Will you be able to explain to yourself why they chose to go and fight in a new war, in a land they have never seen and know nothing about for an ungrateful people? We stand at this door. Once it is open, it cannot be closed easily, and your future children will also have the ability to walk through."

Whether or not Yvgidahi intended to end his speech there or merely take a moment to pause and let it sink in, the silence was long enough for someone in the crowd—Ola Achukma was only thankful it was not one of his sons—to speak out of turn.

"You say that Ignorance has brought this upon us," he began. "Then why has the council made such an effort of keeping watch over the Old Land? Why should we be distant guardians to peoples we evidently have no intention of protecting in their time of need, knowing that we have the ability to do so? Years ago, there was great controversy of bringing too many new peoples here and merely reigniting the old conflicts, and it was decided to remain isolated, or so we thought.

"We are like an animal who has lost his mate to another of his kind—not even that, but willingly let her go, pushed her, even, to him!—only to skulk about in the shadows, resentful of the fact that his mate is gone but doing nothing to get her back despite himself being the stronger, better animal. How long shall we torture ourselves so?

"We would not be here if not for the evils of the Old Land. If there is anywhere we may place blame, it is there. But now we hear that the peoples of the Old Land—whether or not we associate with them, we are still descended from them—they have a chance to be free once more, be rid of their captors. How can we not avail ourselves of the opportunity for both revenge and liberation?!"

Those around him more than murmured their agreement. Ola Achukma thought the council looked a bit distressed over it, but Yvgidahi maintained his composure as he calmly stood to meet his opponent.

"Gvnagadoga is dead," he stated. "Long dead." He moved slowly around the room. "His children are dead. Likely his grandchildren are, too, or they may be very old. Aganstata, Atagulkalu, Major Grant,

General Forbes, and others whose names I have long forgotten, they are all dead. We will be avenging ourselves against no one."

"That may be true for you, but some of us have more recent grievances." Now Ola Achukma saw the challenger, a man who called himself Nvya. He was about forty years of age, rescued from one of the many removals, but the sorceries had made it so he looked no more than thirty. He moved to the forefront of the group of disgruntled men, stopped, considered, then went to meet Yvgidahi face-to-face. "One might even be forgiven for thinking that if your people hadn't bowed, my people wouldn't be here." He let that hang there for a moment, appearing to savor the subtle reaction from the crowd. He went on, "We have a chance to ensure our grandchildren cannot say the same about us."

He turned to address the crowd. "Our peoples, whoever they were, wherever they came from, they were all united in that they were warriors. They did not shy away from a fight. They fought to prove themselves, to make their names known, and to keep their families safe. Boys were given a bow just as soon as they could draw a string. Men young and old would travel hundreds of miles and spend an entire summer searching for that one trophy to impress the woman he loved. Women would spend the winter repairing a warrior's clothing, sewing charms into it to keep him safe the next year.

"And what have we become since then? A boy does not receive a bow until he is able to compete in some festival of tournaments? He travels, only once or twice a summer, no more than a few days, to hunt wayward game? And then what?"

He paused and nodded slowly. "I will not deny that our women, our life givers, have thrived in Aktiya Waya and the other villages. It is safe here, and they are free to blossom as a flower in a bed with no weeds. But to what end? Why should they make warriors clothing and sew charms when there is no reason to fear? Why should they bend their backs for us when we do little work, little more than clear the fields once in the spring? What need do they have for us except to give them children?" He suddenly raised his voice. "And what need do we have for children when we may live long lives and rarely fear sickness or tragedy? But with no children, what is the purpose of a woman? What is the purpose of a man? What is the purpose of life if we have little need for anything?"

Ola Achukma wouldn't say he didn't understand what Nvya was saying, but he did wonder how much of the man's preaching his sons agreed with. What did the man and his friends talk about that resonated more deeply than the teachings of one's parents and elders?

Nvya faced Yvgidahi who was still puffing on the pipe. "We have lost our way as a people because every man and woman here has lost their purpose, or they are about to. We have lost our love for life because we have lost our fear of death."

Yvgidahi looked thoughtful for a moment before replying, "When a man believes he has no reason to fear, he becomes careless, even reckless."

"Careless, because he has no cares here. He fears not illness, nor broken bone, nor poisonous plant, nor any animal. Reckless, because he is bored."

"No one forces you to use the sorceries. I am sure that those of Eagle Clan or Deer Clan would have different views on the matter, as they do need to hunt and cultivate to survive."

"If that is how it shall be, then that is how it shall be," Nvya stated. "And if so, we should cast off all thought of the Old Land. The peoples, their troubles, their wars. And we should cast aside the sorceries as well. They served their purpose, to preserve the people. Now we must live without them, or we shall surely die because of them.

"But if we wish to hang on to the Old Land, we cannot do it as mere sheep or bystanders. We have the ability to help. We are in the strongest position to do so. All we need is the willingness."

"Which you seem to have in abundance," Yvgidahi mused, shifting his stance and puffing on the pipe.

"Tell me, Yvgidahi, what would you have me tell my son? What should I tell him his purpose is, what he should strive to become? Should his only goal be to clear stones from the field in the spring and hold contests once a year? What will he tell his grandchildren when he is old? What will he have accomplished? What will his legacy be? What will he have contributed to the greatness of our people?"

"We have irrigation now. When we arrived, we had none, and everyone had to trek to the river to fetch water for the day. Now every home has its own reservoir, that it may be gotten at leisure. Through discovery, we have also begun to implement a lighting system, that we do not need to dwell in darkness like bats, using small torches in the middle of the day." He went on before Nvya could speak. "Food. Shelter. Clothing. These basic means of survival have been taken care of. How many winters did you listen to your belly rumble with hunger, and you wondered where your next meal would come from? How often did you pull a threadbare coat around your shoulders, wondering if anyone had anything at all to patch the holes, wondering whether it would be better to go without gloves or socks just so you could repair a hole in your shirt? What activities did you wish you had the time and energy to do, if only you did not have to labor in the most menial of tasks, all for a handful of grain? Now is the time of growth and improvement of our people, the ideas and inventions of—"

"If we wanted to live like white men, we would have stayed with the white men!" someone shouted from the crowd.

Any more clever arguments or beautiful oration Yvgidahi had prepared fell apart then. It was not that he lost control of himself, but he lost control of those gathered.

With that single statement, the dam burst, and everyone began talking over each other. Ola Achukma noticed how much of the din was people recounting grand, heroic tales of their ancestors who fought in this battle or stole a horse from that white man and got away with it. All the tales of their idols, tales they would never be able to live up to if they stayed in meek and mild Aktiya Waya, only participating in a festival of tournaments once a year.

He glanced at his wife who wore an expression of dismal certainty. The opposition had won. They were going to war. All that remained was for the council to declare it so.

But would they? And what would happen if they refused?

Nothing the council said or did could quell the shouting. Fortunately, it only remained at shouting and never escalated into anything physical. It was a bit pathetic, Ola Achukma thought, that he should be worried about such a thing. Everything he remembered about the Old Land and the peoples there said that such meetings, although they could get heated, never got so raucous or blatantly disrespectful. For a long moment, Ola Achukma found himself wondering if he had failed to stop this, or if he had perhaps caused it.

"We cannot simply rush over there and start killing people!"

It was unclear just who had spoken, but it finally got things back under control. Gradually the crowd quieted, heroic tales fading into disgruntled silence and impatient expectations. Nvya looked particularly annoyed, but he did not say anything, giving Yvgidahi a chance to speak once more.

"If it is the will of the young men to fight, regardless of the advice and desires of your elders, parents, children, women, and everyone who cares about you, then they will fight." He spoke grudgingly, though rather than attempting to contain anger, he looked to be containing a kind of tremendous heartbreak. "But we cannot simply watch you run off and die senselessly. The white men have a certain way of waging war, which must be understood and respected. Certainly the peoples know their land better than you do." His word choice was not lost on anyone. "A scouting group must be sent first, to acquire names and locations and—"

"No," Nvya butted in. He stepped forward again, out of the crowd. "No more diplomacy. No more scouts. No more stalling so you can try to persuade or guilt us into abandoning our cause. You fret like a woman, yet even I know that the skiagvsta used to be in charge of matters of war. The scouts have already said that the war has started. Talk will do no one any good now. Right now, they need our help."

"What if they don't want your help?" one of the council members inquired innocently.

"Why wouldn't they want it?" He went on before anyone could

answer. "This is why we are in such a predicament. Because there is no formal diplomacy anywhere. Our leaders never go anywhere; they send scouting parties, listen to reports, and hold endless meetings with no action! Well, no longer. I am taking charge of this expedition." He turned to address the group. "Any man who wishes to fight will go with me to the Old Land. Take ten days to prepare yourselves, purify yourselves, and make ready whatever supplies you may need." He looked back at Yvgidahi. "No more talking. No more negotiating. Now...now we pick up our hatchets and fight."

There was nothing more to be done. Yvgidahi had lost. Perhaps he had lost even before the meeting had begun, though it was impossible to say just where the point of no return had been crossed.

With a whoop and a great sweep of his arm, Nvya left the townhouse, taking with him virtually all of the men of fighting age, a small group of boys not quite ready to fight, a good portion of the older men, and even a gathering of women. All that remained was a handful of young men, the council, some elders, and the women and young children.

For a long while, they stood or sat in silence, each trying to process what had just happened, what was about to happen. Could it be just a bad dream? Was there anything that could be done?

Finally, Yvgidahi sighed, took the pipe out of his mouth, and dumped the plug most unceremoniously into the fire, saying, "I suppose there is nothing left to say at this point. Nvya seems to be the one in charge of the expedition, and all other matters are rather insignificant in light of these developments. Good night."

He left the townhouse. Beside Ola Achukma, Nendawagan leapt to her feet but did not otherwise move or say anything. What was there to say?

The two of them left silently, though they had the same idea to go visit Yvgidahi at home where Mesim was just pouring him a cup of tea. If the man had looked old and tired at the beginning of the meeting, by now he'd easily added another ten or twenty years. His gaze was distant, posture that of utter defeat. Ola Achukma did not blame him.

The man did not acknowledge them right away, even when they sat down at the table.

"Nocha, I—" Nendawagan began.

"Tsitsa," Yvgidahi murmured. "That's how the children are saying it now, isn't it? Tsitsa. Almost familiar, but yet it slips one's comprehension if he doesn't understand why the word is the way it is."

"I don't understand."

"I failed, Nenda. One hundred years to make things right, make things perfect. And I failed." His brows furrowed and he studied his tea. "Should we not have rescued so many different peoples? Should we have truly cut ourselves off? Should we have never come here in the first place? Should we have done something different when—"

"Humanity is not beyond saving," Ola Achukma cut in, "but we can't do it ourselves."

Yvgidahi smiled and scoffed lightly as he took a drink. "Yes, I forgot you were raised in a white man's religion. Still threading some of those tenants through this new unified people, are you?"

Ola Achukma took a breath and chose his words carefully. "Nvya is right about a few things. Men crave purpose. He wants to know that between the time he wakes up and when he sleeps, he will have done something worthwhile. You are correct that we are prosperous here. When we did isolate ourselves, we could only sharpen our iron on each other. Because we were going nowhere, not really. We were trying to build something without even knowing what we were building or how we would know when we were finished."

"And every time we brought people from the Old Land, refugees who had nothing but bad news and no possessions or families, it only reminded those here of their anger and desire for revenge."

"And when we didn't, we had people who were so afraid of us and the sorceries that they were willing to start a war."

"Then we should have gotten rid of the sorceries, forbade them until they faded from existence."

Ola Achukma gave his father-in-law a look. "If not the sorceries, it would have been something else. As the people grew and expanded and founded new villages, as the people grew apart, it would be only a matter of time before something happened. We would have prevented nothing, only delayed the inevitable."

Yvgidahi now gave him a look that said he wasn't helping matters.

"War is not what we want, but it what is going to happen," Ola Achukma stated. "Nvya and a fairly large portion of the village—and probably other villages, too, if he sends word and gathers the men there— are going to the Old Land to fight. We can't abandon them there."

"What do you suggest?" Yvgidahi asked, the question more sarcastic than serious. "Are you here to declare yourself a leader as well?"

"I will if I have to. But we can't abandon them or else they will resent us when they return, which will only cause more problems. I'm not saying that everyone must be forced to fight or go against his own conscience, but we must prepare ourselves as well. We must be prepared to receive and treat wounded, repair weapons, and send food and other supplies." He paused. "If this is what unites the people, our defense of the Old Land and the restoration of its peoples, then so be it."

He watched his wife's father slowly come back to life, the spark of ideas kindling into flame once more. He shifted position, sitting more upright in his seat. "We could act as the active war camp, where the men come and go, where the wounded are treated. If we can get Deer Clan to agree to it, they could supply meat."

"Eagle Clan can be in charge of weapons," Ola Achukma said. "The stone of the cliffs may not be obsidian, but it is sharp enough to scrape a fine edge."

Yvgidahi nodded, then hesitated, faltering in his renewed confidence. "I want you to speak to Nvya and see what you can coordinate regarding this. I don't think he'll listen to me, no matter how great the ideas."

"Agreed."

"Nenda and I will speak to the women's council and coordinate the women," Mesim announced. "We will ensure the food is prepared and ready to go, and oversee care of the wounded."

"I will also act as liaison between the Old Land and Hlohi," Ola

Achukma offered. "Nvya has stoked the flames of passion in the men, and none of them will want to be relegated to something as lowly as a mere messenger. And none of the boys are trained in Galohisdi. I have no desire to fight, but I can carry messages, reports, and—" He glanced at Nendawagan. "—keep an eye on our sons." He looked back at Yvgidahi. "I'm not as talented as Nendawagan when it comes to Galohisdi, but I can do it."

Yvgidahi nodded. "I know you can. It will allow Nvya to keep control of the forces going to the Old Land, and I can manage things here. You will be the messenger between us, as you are now."

Ola Achukma wasn't sure whether to feel proud or embarrassed, and he set off to find Nvya feeling a mixture of both. It took a lot longer than he thought necessary to find the man, as he seemed to be giving every one of his supporters a personal pep talk and listening to the heroic stories which had been shouted down in the chaos of the meeting. When he was finally able to get Nvya's attention, the man was not overly enthusiastic to see him, but he motioned for him to follow anyway.

"So, Yvgidahi's little pet," Nvya began, grinning and clearly not intimidated by his new walking companion. "Are you here to plead with me to give peace a chance? Just one more talk will do it. Just the right string of words. Just the right intonation. Just the right something and everything will be solved."

"I have no such illusions," Ola Achukma informed him. "My father was a professional diplomat. All he did was talk and negotiate. Even he was not successful all of the time."

"One is forced to wonder how things may have turned out if he had been more or less successful in his attempts." Nvya stopped short and turned sharply to face him. "What do you want? Ten days may seem like a long time, but there is a lot to get done. What does Yvgidahi want? That is who sent you, isn't it?"

"I come with a proposal. You're right, Yvgidahi did send me, but he didn't think you would be in any kind of mood to listen to him."

"Indeed I'm not, and I'm only affording you a margin of respect at the moment, which could change based on this proposal of yours. Let's hear it."

"You want war. You want to fight. But it's not as simple as wrestling in the tournaments or going out on a game drive. There is a lot more that goes into directing hundreds or thousands of men. You're going to need help, and not the fighting kind."

Nvya raised a brow, folded his arms, and shifted his stance. "I'm listening."

Ola Achukma laid out the plan, using Wolf Clan as the war camp, Deer Clan as the supply camp, and Eagle Clan as the weapon camp. He also detailed how Mesim and Nendawagan would coordinate the women. He had no idea how they were actually going to pull it off, but he figured it wouldn't be for him to know, and Nvya wouldn't be keeping track of such details.

"Yvgidahi still opposes the war and the fighting," he finished, "but he will not abandon you to fate."

Nvya considered this for a long time, standing there in the middle of the street. Finally he nodded. "I understand. And it's good to have the support of the people. What will you be doing, exactly?"

"I will be the messenger between the Old Land and Hlohi, between you and Yvgidahi." He laid out his reasoning.

"You have valid points." Nvya clapped Ola Achukma on the shoulder. "And I am glad to have you on our side."

What other side would I be on? He almost asked the question but refrained at the last moment, instead agreeing and leaving Nvya to go about his tour. Ola Achukma watched him go, garnering greetings, backslaps, wrist grabs, and other accolades as he made his way down the street and disappeared around a corner.

Ola Achukma returned to the home of his in-laws who were quietly engaged in discussion. Yvgidahi looked up.

"And?"

"He accepts the proposal." Ola Achukma sat down. "He didn't say much more than that; he's a bit busy being a celebrity."

"That's fine," Mesim said curtly. "He can lead the men into war and we will not interfere. As if we could. We will just be here waiting to receive the consequences of their decisions."

"Our sons are going with him," Nendawagan informed her mother. "So are my brothers, your sons. And some of their sons as well. We will all have to deal with the consequences of their decisions."

"It may not be so bad," Yvgidahi said, though he hardly sounded convinced by his own words. "The white men never did like the native peoples and our way of doing war. The French found it useful at first, but it didn't win them their war. I would be willing to bet that most of our men will be given minor tasks."

"Or they may be sent directly into the line of fire as a human shield for the white men," Mesim told him.

No one said anything to that, and Ola Achukma and Nendawagan soon departed for home, both of them exhausted from the evening's events. They stopped by Popokus' house to pick up Netami, then went home where Galiliga and Tsona were already packing.

Nendawagan ignored her sons and instead herded Netami along to get ready for bed. Ola Achukma turned to the boys. Men. Both were well over twenty years of age, though they only just looked it.

"If you want, we will leave your house," Galiliga began after a moment of awkward silence. "We will stay in the Old Land while the war is going on, and when we return, we will find homes of our own. And wives as well."

"We are not asking or telling you to leave," Ola Achukma said. "But you would do well to make amends to your mother before you go." As they turned as if to go after her, he added, "Not now. It's been a long night."

"Nvya said you had a plan," Tsona stated. "He said that you were going to coordinate efforts here, to receive the wounded and ensure we got supplies."

"That's right. I myself will be the messenger between here and there. At least then I might be able to keep an eye on you."

"We'll be watching out for each other, don't worry," Galiliga said.

"Your mother will always worry about you. So will I."

The boys nodded, and the elder son sighed. "Do you really think this is a bad idea?"

Ola Achukma hesitated and sat down at the table. His sons slowly followed. "My father, your grandfather, was a mediator. A diplomat. He talked to a lot of different peoples, negotiated a lot of different disputes. He was very good at what he did, but he wasn't always successful. I've told you this before. And one thing he taught me was to always strive for peace. As a child, this is a simple enough concept. As an adult, it is far more difficult to discern what peace even is, never mind how to obtain it. If we want peace here, it seems we must unite under the banner of war. If we had forsaken the war, Nvya and his most faithful followers would only harbor resentment against us. He would have done so if we allowed him to go but did nothing here to support him."

"Sometimes there are no good answers," Galiliga said, shrugging.

"You're right. There aren't. And I have come to the conclusion that peace is like the horizon, always within sight, but always out of reach. This does not mean that we never travel, never make decisions. Rather, we must simply learn to appreciate the beauty it holds, the sunrises and sunsets, the vast forests and grand mountains. And when we cannot see the horizon, cannot see peace, when we are surrounded on all sides, in that moment, the only thing we can do...is look up." He intentionally met both his sons' gazes. "Keep one eye on each other, and one eye on your surroundings. When you see the horizon, run toward it as fast as you can."

Pàke Nishinxke òk Newa

War Camp

Nendawagan did not want to go the meeting, as if by not going that she could somehow prevent what inevitably happened. It might not have been so bad, except this time her sons were in full agreement with Nvya and against Yvgidahi and the council. Her boys wanted to go to war. They wanted to fight. They wanted to kill.

How could she have gotten such men when her husband was so calm and patient and peaceful? Tsona had even been divined as a peacemaker; where had he gone astray? She'd watched him grow up and, other than the usual frustrating awkwardness that all boys experienced as they became men, he'd always been kind and gentle. He had never been disposed toward violence until now. What had changed? It felt so odd.

Or, perhaps, they were the odd ones. When it seemed as though the entirety of humanity was defined and shaped by war and violence, their oasis was something of a marvel. Maybe they should have isolated themselves earlier on rather than refreshing the grievances with each new batch of refugees.

But whatever could have been or should have been, it no longer mattered. Nvya had effectively usurped Yvgidahi as the war leader and taken eighty percent of the people with him. If Ola Achukma managed to prove himself as a decent liaison, then they might hope to have a voice of reason in the realm of authority, but the hope was slim.

At least by the following morning, most of the shock had worn off and she could focus a little more on preparing herself and her family. If Eagle Clan agreed to help with weaponry—sharpening the hatchets and arrowheads, crafting arrows and so on—then at least she knew that her boys would be able to defend themselves. And even if Eagle Clan refused, Galiliga was more than adept at sharpening his blades, and Tsona could fashion arrows faster than anyone else. Ola Achukma was well skilled also, and he had a way with the horses, a method of Touch to communicate what he wanted so the horse understood.

She repeated these things to herself throughout the day, trying to convince herself that everything would be all right. Her boys were skilled. Her boys were smart. Her boys were skilled. Her boys were smart. The peoples of the Old Land didn't even like the Krydik, didn't want much to do with them. They would refuse the help and send the warriors home after some self-righteous lecture.

She sighed. And if words could persuade Nvya to turn his path, it would have already been done. No. He would not tolerate refusal. If he would not be integrated into the army of the Old Land, he would direct his men himself, lead the charge himself. Maybe some of the less enthusiastic followers would return home, but a majority seemed ready to follow Nvya anywhere.

Revenge was a terrible thing, Nendawagan mused. It could drive a man to madness unlike anything else in the world. According to scout reports, the Cherokee had recently banned the practice of clan retaliation. What was once acceptable retaliation for a wrongdoing was now a crime all its own.

It had not been well-received among the Cherokee, and Yvgidahi also attempting to forbid this war must have seemed like an echo of that to Nvya. Whatever wrongs had been committed against him would not be avenged; there would be no justice except for what he made himself.

But what revenge did her sons seek? Who or what were they avenging? All of their family was here; there was no separation. They had never even seen a white man, much less been mistreated by one. Were they really going to war over offenses that were decades old? Did they somehow believe that they were going to right the wrongs that had been done to their father forty years ago? Were they going to avenge the death of their grandfather's brother over a hundred years ago?

She wanted to ask but was afraid of the answer. What if it wasn't about revenge? Was if they truly just enjoyed the thought of violence? She couldn't bear to think of her sons in such a way.

It was then that she decided that Aktiya Waya had never been destined to succeed, not in the way her father envisioned, isolation or not. Human nature always had the final say. They might try to curb it, to direct it, but it would never be anything other than what it was. Even a small river, if persistent, could eat away at the strongest mountain, and people were nothing if not persistent.

It didn't make her feel better about the situation, but at least it was something to help her make sense of what was going on. Like anyone who had been born and raised in Aktiya Waya, she'd never had to prepare for war. She didn't know what it entailed, what they would need. Food, weapons, medicine, fine, but how did it all come together, really? There were maybe twelve hundred people total between the three villages, and it was still a chore to get them coordinated for the festivals. How could a man direct an army of tens of thousands? How did he feed and supply them?

She did not know whether it was comforting or chilling to think that some of Nvya's closest friends, who were quickly becoming his advisors, did know some of the answers to such questions, and they were happy to direct anyone who needed help.

Nendawagan was more than willing to let her mother be in charge of coordinating the food while she just took orders and carried out assigned tasks, Netami faithfully at her side.

"Tsitsi, where are Galiliga and Tsona going?" the young girl wondered as they made their way through town.

"They're going to the Old Land," Nendawagan answered. "You know that."

"Yes, but where? Tsitsa says the Old Land is a big place with a lot of people."

"I don't know exactly where. You would have to ask them."

"They won't tell me."

Nendawagan smiled to herself. "Then I wouldn't worry about it."

"But you do worry about it. You worry about them." Netami gave her mother a look. "Tsitsi, what is war?"

Now Nendawagan sighed and knelt to look her daughter in the eye. "I've never seen war, so I don't know exactly." She frowned. "You know how your brothers like to talk about game drives, how they get on their horses and take down animals while running very, very fast?" Netami nodded. "War...I think it's kind of like that. Except instead of animals, they hunt other men. And the other men are also trying to hunt them."

"To kill them."

"That's right."

"Why?"

"Revenge, sweetling. Getting back at someone for doing something bad to you."

The girl just looked puzzled. "What did these other men do?"

Nendawagan wiped a tear from her own eye. "They stole, dear one. They took land and animals. They killed some people, then sent the rest away to die."

"The removals, like what happened to Tsitsa."

"That's right."

"Are they going to get the land and animals back? Will we be moving to the Old Land when it's all over with, if we win?"

"I highly doubt it. But the people they stole from might go back."

"People like Nvya."

"Yes."

The expression on Netami's face said she was struggling to work through it all. "What if we don't win?"

Nendawagan shook her head. "I don't know. I've never seen war. I've never had to do any of this before."

"Oh. Well, I think you're doing a good job."

She grinned and stood. "Thanks. So are you. You're being a good little helper. Come on, let's get these chores taken care of."

Through the time of preparation, Nendawagan learned quite a bit about war, mostly that it wasn't just about opposing sides trying to kill each other. There were a lot of logistics involved, too. In fact, she came to the conclusion that war was actually only about five percent fighting and ninety-five percent logistics. Going from here to there, moving things, moving people, making sure everyone knew basically what was going on.

In a way, it actually gave her hope and helped her to calm down a bit. Her sons would be just fine. They would be marching here and there on their horses, moving supplies, setting up shelters, distributing food, and doing other small tasks. Their actual time in danger would be minimal, if at all. Sometimes there was something to be said for being hated, and the peoples of the Old Land might not want to share the victory with the Krydik. They might intentionally keep the Krydik out of battle and try to humiliate them with menial labor.

While that thought eased her fears about her sons being injured or killed in war, it also sparked a sense of indignation, a small anger that the peoples who had been trodden on, humiliated, beaten, even enslaved or killed, would turn up their noses at an ally in their fight for freedom, especially when some of that help came from their own people who just happened to live in a different land! The Krydik might live peacefully, but they could still fight for a just cause!

Did that mean she supported the war? Looking around at Aktiya Waya, all the people running to and fro in a frenzy not seen even in the most chaotic of festivals, and considering her place in the middle of this chaos, she thought she might have to admit that she did. At least a little, under certain terms. She did not approve of the killing, however. She couldn't. Why couldn't the United States government just accept that not everyone wanted to be like them, live like them? Why couldn't they recognize that some people wanted to live their own way? There was no reason they couldn't still be friends or allies. Was subjugation really necessary?

At the same time, it was also a bit exciting. It was something new, something different. Kind of like when the festival came around and it was their turn to host, there was so much energy and anticipation. It was a change from the mundane, and people really got into it. And, if she really wanted to admit it, something deep in her blood and bone found this uniquely right. There was a nobility and rightness about this that called to her, bade her dive deep and breathe in the traditions of her ancestors. Yet this warred—no pun intended—with her sense that the murder part was wrong.

She didn't talk to her sons much during the preparation period, and she felt terribly guilty for it. She should say something to them, encourage them, let them know that she loved them and just wanted them to come home alive. They could keep their tales of glory; she just wanted them. But she didn't know what to say. Enjoy yourselves? Do well? What kind of words were those coming from a mother? That was what she told them when they went on hunts, a noble task to provide meat for the people. But going out to kill other men?

Still, she didn't want them to leave thinking that she was angry with them. Annoyed, disappointed, maybe, but not angry, and she wished no ill upon them, or any of those who followed Nvya out of sheer frustration. She had to say or do something, but she didn't know what, and she asked her husband about it while they lay in bed two days before the men were supposed to leave.

"It would mean a lot to them," Ola Achukma said. "They have expressed some confusion over your distance."

"Why are they confused?" she asked. "They know I don't approve of the war and killing."

"No, but they are your sons, and as much as they seek pride and glory and approval from me, they also need to know that you support them, too."

"Yes, but—"

"Nenda, how many times have you disapproved of something I have done, but when confronted in public, you stand by me? Not because you approve either, but because you know that you, as my wife, must support me?" When she sighed, he said, "It's the same way with the boys. Galiliga and Tsona are about to leave and risk their lives for something they've only been told about second- and third-hand, something that integrates perfectly with their own feelings of frustration. They are trapped animals straining against their bonds. They just want to know that you will still support them once they've broken free."

"Ola, they're my sons. I carried them in my womb and nursed them at my breast. I know their victories and defeats and triumphs and embarrassments. Of course I will always love and support them."

Ola Achukma chuckled softly. "Well, as I've told you often enough, men do not always understand the minds of women. And I have missed enough of your hints to make you mad on plenty of occasions. You have to tell them explicitly."

She sighed and shifted uncomfortably. "I will."

"We're expecting Eagle Clan to arrive today with the extra weapons, assuming they want to be punctual and not wait until the last moment. You should talk to Galiliga and Tsona before then, otherwise their minds will only be on the weapons and what they will be doing with them."

His statement broke the moment, but Nendawagan tried to keep a level head as she said, "Well, even if Eagle Clan doesn't arrive until after you've all left, we've worked out a supply line that will get them to you regardless."

"Yes, but as the festival has proven many times, plans are only perfect on paper."

They lay there for a short time longer before admitting defeat and rising to meet the day. Galiliga and Tsona were already out on their own errands. Nvya had some special morning routine for all the fighting men, trying to prepare them for fighting in a foreign war. It wasn't like fighting in the wars of old, and seeing how a majority of the volunteers had not encountered anything more violent than an occasional grouchy animal or difficult wrestling opponent at the festival, well, they would need a lot of preparation on that front.

Ola Achukma, in his role as messenger and liaison, did not attend these morning rituals. Rather, he was occupied with ensuring the other clans knew what was going on, which was how he knew Eagle Clan was supposed to arrive, again, assuming they wanted to be punctual. They were reportedly quite enthusiastic about the proclamation of war, and some had even swallowed their pride and allowed themselves to use Galohisdi to get to Aktiya Waya as quick as possible. For those who remained behind, however, and elected to do things the old way, well, there was a fluid perception of time. This perception was endemic to the peoples, but sometimes there was something to be said for having a deadline and meeting it. The war had already started without them; they didn't need it to end without them, too.

Nendawagan went about the morning chores as usual, trying to stay as close to the fighting men as possible, though she still remained at a fair distance so she would not be thought of as trying to get someone's attention. Her boys were men grown who were out to prove themselves. As much as she wanted to speak to them and express her love and support, she didn't need to embarrass them here.

She thought about what she would say, agonized over it, even. Stay safe? They were going to war, for goodness' sake; plus they already lived in a safe haven. Do well? She didn't want to encourage killing and violence, especially when it was at someone else's behest. Be well? Hardly a problem, given their use of Touch and ability to identify and heal disease. Stay warm? Maybe, though all reports said that they would be in the southern, warmer area of the Old Land.

By the time the morning rituals were completed and she had a chance to speak to her sons, she'd gone over a dozen or more halting, awkward speeches, most of which faded into rambling obscurity. She wasn't an orator like her father or other leaders; she did not know hundreds of flowery analogies or dozens of grand stories to weave into an endless fountain of wisdom. Out of the corner of her eye, she saw her sons head back into the cave, into town, and she let them go.

Early in the afternoon, Eagle Clan showed up, those who had elected to travel the old-fashioned way, anyway. They used horses to carry the many loads of weapons they'd brought with them. It took four horses alone to carry all the arrows they'd fashioned, plus another horse to carry the spare arrowheads. Most warriors already had their own bows, but more had been made just in case. Other weapons included spears, blowguns, and clubs. The clubs were a bit more crude than the ones the men might make themselves over the course of a month—rounding every edge and oiling it just so—but for the time given, they would work.

The women had no part in the distribution of weapons, so Nendawagan watched from a distance. Nvya handled everything, meeting the people from Eagle Clan, inspecting the weapons, then broadly dividing them among his closest friends so they could better distribute them to the volunteers. Every man must have gotten a hundred arrows, if not more. Nendawagan found herself wondering if Eagle Clan hadn't relented just a little and conjured Time in order to craft so many so quickly. Or perhaps they had supplemented from their own stores.

She couldn't imagine needing so many arrows. How many men had to die before an army commander decided to turn back? In the Old Land, her father said, in the old times, a man could be stripped of all his war titles and standing if he lost too many men in battle. Even losing one man was cause to question his leadership, and losing three or five or more could even be grounds for banishment, if only temporary.

Apparently the white men did not believe in this philosophy. Even Ola Achukma commented multiple times that they would fight until ninety percent of their forces were dead or dying. Sometimes they would fight to the last man.

Nendawagan couldn't decide if this was noble or foolish. Then she wondered, if they were going to fight a white man's war, if her sons might not be ordered to do the same, and if they truly would. Would they really fight and die for white men? Could the white men be trusted to keep their word and honor the rights of the native peoples?

She didn't know much about war; that much was obvious. But she did understand a little about politics. There was no such thing as a free horse. Assuming that the Confederates did win the war, and assuming they did honor their agreement to acknowledge the sovereignty of the native peoples, what would they ask for in return? What would they want? An alliance, to come to their aid in future wars? Food, supplies, other goods?

She didn't like how cynical she sounded, even to herself, and she silently chastised herself for it. She should be figuring out a good time to speak to her sons, and a good way to convey what she wanted to say, even if she wasn't quite sure what that was. Let the men handle the logistics of war. If the weapons convoy was any indication, they were more than adequately prepared to fight.

While the men were busy with the weapons, she returned to the open slope where her charge had been delivered many days ago. Deer Clan had hunted down an entire herd of tsuyoniyvgi. The meat was curing into jerky, and she joined the other women who were gathering some of the midseason corn to dry and mash. They would form the mashed corn into small, hard biscuits which could be soaked in water and eaten. Or, as the men liked to joke, tied to the end of a stick and used as a makeshift club.

She found her mother teaching Netami how to properly form the biscuits for drying, and she joined them.

"If the sorceries make it so we don't feel very hungry, why are we making so much food?" the little girl was asking. "Why do we grow so much food?"

"Well, the horses still need to eat," Mesim replied gently. "And children need to eat, too; you're not using the sorceries yet. And fighting is hard work, a difficult job. Sorceries or not, the men will have to eat more than they do here."

"And not all the men going to fight are skilled in the sorceries," Nendawagan added. "They don't feel the sorceries' effects as strongly as we do, so they will have to eat more as well."

"Like Eagle Clan."

"That's right."

Netami shifted position, staring intently at the mash in her hands which she formed into little biscuits and set aside. "What happens if all the Eagle Clan warriors die?"

Nendawagan raised a brow. "What do you mean? Why only Eagle Clan?"

"They don't use the sorceries. What happens if they get sick? Or if they're hurt? They can't use the sorceries to heal themselves, and they don't want others helping them with the sorceries either."

Nendawagan glanced at her mother over the child's head. Mesim did not appear to have anything to offer.

"Then it will be a sad day in Eagle Clan," she answered finally. "But I don't think they will all die. They're strong. They're fast. They know how to fight. Some may die, but I doubt all of them will."

"And," Mesim interjected, "while they may claim they want no help from the sorceries now, things can change when you are far from home and facing death. Dying for the cause of the people is a noble thing. Dying from sickness while you are cold and alone in a foreign wilderness is less enticing."

"Oh," Netami stated, still staring at her hands as she formed biscuits and set them aside. "Do you think some of them will stay in the Old Land if we win? I don't think they like it here."

Nendawagan nodded. "Some of them might, yes. They were unable to fight for their lands before, when they were only small groups, but now that they are united and fighting together, they might have a chance."

"And then what?"

"Then...they go home. Everyone goes home. To live peacefully, how they want, how their ancestors lived, where their ancestors lived."

"What about us?"

"We continue to do and live how we always have."

"So we wouldn't go back to live in the Old Land?"

"No, we wouldn't."

"What about Galiliga and Tsona?"

Nendawagan shifted and said, "I don't think they would want to go back either."

"Then why are they going?"

"To help. Just like you or I might help someone who asks. Not because it benefits us, but because it's the right thing to do. Like helping Humi with these biscuits so you can also help your brothers."

Netami nodded thoughtfully and mercifully changed the subject.

"Will there be a lot of weddings when they come back? Tsututa says that when warriors come back, they give gifts to pretty girls and then there are a lot of weddings."

Both Nendawagan and Mesim laughed, and it was Mesim who answered, "Well, that is true, and I imagine that there would be something like that happening when the men return, yes."

"Would I get married?"

"Why would you get married?" Nendawagan wondered, still smiling.

The girl shrugged. "I don't know. What if Galiliga brings me something nice?"

"Child, you can't marry your own brother," Mesim told her. "You have to marry outside your clan."

"Oh."

"Besides, you are much too young to get married," Nendawagan said. "You've not even had your first blood."

Netami remained deep in thought about the whole thing as they continued to take the mash as it was delivered and form thousands of small biscuits which were then laid out to dry until they were little more than rocks. Once that was done, they were distributed among the warriors. Nendawagan herself took a couple rations to her sons that evening once they had returned home.

"Thank you," each replied cordially, taking the biscuits from her as if from a stranger.

"Galiliga," she said. "Tsona." She hesitated. "Sit down a moment."

They did so obediently, and she also found a seat.

"I've not intended to be so distant from you," she began. "Nor have I intended to convey any offense." That was about as far as she'd gotten in any of her silent speeches before floundering in a mishmash of platitudes, begging, and emotional wantonness. Taking a breath, she continued, "Please understand, like you, I grew up in Aktiya Waya. I grew up in relative peace, but I heard the stories of what happened to those in the Old Land. And I was thankful for the peace and safety Aktiya Waya afforded, even if we were not always peaceful.

"I'm not saying you are not grateful. I think you are. And I think you are taking things to the next logical step. You want to help others. That is a good thing. That is a very good thing. And it is your duty as men to protect others." She sighed. "I guess I never appreciated that sometimes, maybe, violence is not only an acceptable answer, but the right one, even the best one. It is how we have come to be here, in Aktiya Waya. Now we must bring Aktiya Waya to others."

It sounded bad, even to her. Pathetic, nonsensical, even cowardly.

"It is our duty to protect others," Galiliga echoed. He met her gaze. "But it is your duty to care for others, to protect them in your own way, as a woman, the bringer of life. We've never lost sight of that. We simply wish to protect the life that was given to us, that was given to the peoples of the Old Land that others wish to steal away."

She nodded, willing herself not to break down in tears. "I know. I still don't want you to go. I still want you to stay. But I understand what you're doing."

She embraced each of them in turn, whispering, "Promise me you'll look after each other."

"We will," Tsona promised.

She left the house after that, if only to get away for a moment and compose herself. Maybe it wasn't the grand oration one might expect from her father, but it had settled everything, and she no longer felt as though she were a bad mother for sending her sons off without being on good terms.

Still she lay awake that night, knowing that they were going to leave anyway. Was this how Diwedalohi felt each spring as she sent Yvgidahi out to hunt and raid and war? Certainly the Book was more exciting from the brothers' points of view, but what about those left behind? What about the mothers and wives who watched their men leave to go to war, to fight the Anigilisi? The stories and legends never mentioned them.

She would be alone. Most of the women in Aktiya Waya would be left alone, with exception of the very old and those with young children. But she would be alone. Popokus would be alone. They might have to move back in with their parents for the duration of the war, just to support each other. How did their ancestors ever manage this?

Her anxiety and imagination kept her awake most of the night, and she didn't know whether or not it was a relief when she discovered Ola Achukma was just as anxious, though slightly less restless.

"A long time ago," he murmured, "I wondered what might have happened to us if my father had lived. Would we still have been forced to go west?" There was a long pause. "For a long time, I was almost certain that we wouldn't have. Oh, the government would try all manner of excuses to be rid of him, but in the end, we wouldn't leave with the rest of them. We would continue to live as we always had, sometimes in our own home, sometimes among the various peoples. But the mission would always be the same. Our lives would always be the same."

"All children think life is fixed to the way it was when they became aware of it," Nendawagan told him.

"Maybe. But I continued to think that even as a young man and for a while as an adult. I was and am not ungrateful that I'm here, and I understand the events leading to it, but I still thought that if Aki hadn't died, we would still be living basically as we were."

"Now you think otherwise."

"Yes."

"What changed?"

"This war, my understanding of politics, and my understanding of my father. He was a diplomat, charged with bringing peace. The removals, from the very beginning, were conjured and based on deceit and treachery, the evil intentions of evil men. Aki always taught us that we should abstain from violence and pray for God's deliverance. But all the prayer in the world means nothing if there is no action behind it. David did not kill Goliath with flowery words and tired reverences. It requires action.

"The removals were not conjured out of thin air. They were not a means, they were an end. It began with fear, demonization, demoralization, disarming, and then the soldiers came. And almost no one fought back. Because they couldn't. Because they didn't want to.

"My father would have gone west because he was not strong enough to stand against the tide as a single man, and neither was anyone else. Strong in spirit and solid in his faith, but he had no willpower to take up the stone and slay the beast that demanded our blood."

Nendawagan remained silent, unsure how she should feel. Ola Achukma had always idolized his late father. Was he starting to give up on that dream?

"I have to do better than that," he went on. "Faith is good, as a strong arm is good. But if a man has a strong arm and never uses it for action, for more than showing off, his family will go hungry. How can I teach peace to my sons, knowing that such a coveted thing does not happen on its own? Even Yvgidahi was forced to make a choice when it came to those who threatened the peace we have."

"You have always said that peace is like the horizon, always within sight but never within reach," Nendawagan reminded him.

He shook his head and shifted position. "No. Peace is a possession. A small one, fragile, easily lost by our own carelessness. But it can also be stolen. And just as we may fend off a thief who comes to steal our food and furs, so we must also fend off the armies who come to steal it from entire nations of people."

In the dim light of the low fire in the main room, Nendawagan could just barely make out her husband's features. "What, then, is peace? Silence is something that disappears as soon as you say its name. Does peace also disappear as soon as you take up a knife to defend it?"

"I don't know," Ola Achukma admitted. "But I suspect that this war is going to teach me many more lessons I have never before considered."

"Agreed," she sighed reluctantly.

Somehow, the discussion helped to ease her anxious heart and mind, and she was able to find something that resembled sleep. She still felt terrible when she finally woke up, but her thoughts no longer raced, and she calmly made a large breakfast for her men.

There had been some disagreement among the priests over the purification of the warriors, especially concerning traditional fasting.

Because of the sorceries, going seven days without food was hardly a challenge. Instead, they decided, there would be seven days of eating, three large meals a day of a variety of foods, taking in the strength of the earth and all it had to offer.

It was fairly reminisce of having to cook for her sons when they were teenagers. Judging by the way they ate this last morning, she wondered if they weren't still teenagers. And that went for Ola Achukma, too.

"Are you leaving us today?" Netami asked, looking at her brothers.

"Yes, we are," Galiliga told her. "But we'll be back."

"When?"

"Once we've driven back the white men and free the peoples of the Old Land," Tsona answered.

"How long will that take?"

"With luck, not long at all."

As soon as breakfast was finished, everyone gathered in the townhouse. Many of the women looked the same way Nendawagan felt, and she wondered if anyone had slept well. Nvya and his friends, who were now appointed officers, huddled together conspiratorially, while Yvgidahi and the council did the same only ten feet away. Would there be fighting even before the warriors left?

Once everyone had gathered, Nvya called for quiet and began to speak. It was nothing Nendawagan hadn't heard from him in the last ten days. They were going to do a good work, to free the peoples of the Old Land and make their ancestors proud. They were walking the old way, as their ancestors had done for countless generations.

Nendawagan wanted to say or do something, anything. One last hug for her sons, a last kiss for her husband. But they were too intent on the speech and what they were about to do. Even as she thought it, Galohisdi opened there in the townhouse. Nvya went through first, followed by his top officer. After that, certain groups of men began to go through, all in order, without a break or hesitation, as if they had rehearsed this in their morning rituals.

As Galiliga and Tsona began to move, she instinctively reached out for them, but they were too fast and soon out of range. Her heart twisted at that moment, and her gaze misted over. Did they have to go? Did they really have to go? Who would see to them? They weren't even married; they had no children. What if something happened?

She watched Moskimus and the rest of her brothers leave, and even many of their sons who were old enough. These boys she had loved and even cared for since infancy, now going to fight and possibly die in a foreign land. Off to one side, near the council, Nendawagan saw her mother fighting for composure as she watched son after son after son disappear.

Then Ola Achukma moved, and Nendawagan lurched after him. She grabbed his hand and he turned. She could see the longing in his gaze, that look that said he was doing his best to be the voice of wisdom and sanity in a realm of chaos. If he thought he could stay, he would, his expression said. But there was no other choice. He had to go, or he would never forgive himself.

She opened her mouth to say something. Anything. The best she could manage was a choked goodbye and some squeaked out profession of love. Her husband spoke no words, but she saw the reciprocation. He squeezed her hand, and she let go. Then he vanished through the doorway to the Old Land.

She glanced down at Netami. Tears were streaming down the girl's cheeks, but she stood there, absolutely rigid, staring into the void where the men were disappearing. She sniffed hard and wiped her nose.

"They're going off to do a great thing," Nendawagan said, though even she wasn't sure just whom she was speaking to. "They'll be gone for a little while, but then they'll be back. You'll see. Until then, we have to be strong and make do on our own. There's still plenty of work to do. We can't be idle while they're away."

No one was listening, certainly not her daughter, but she didn't care. She took a breath and blinked rapidly to clear her vision. Other women were not so composed. The only ones who seemed to bear the burden with any sort of dignity were those who were newest to Aktiya Waya, those who still held some memories—even if just stories—of the old ways, when such departures were the norm. Nendawagan felt foolish, even cowardly. So many had fled to Aktiya Waya to protect the old ways, but it seemed as though they had lost them all the same.

When it appeared all the men had gone, all but one of the officers also crossed. A moment later, Nvya reappeared.

"If any still wish to join us, this may be your last good opportunity," he said, looking around, trying to look strong and bold despite the nauseating effects of Galohisdi.

Only about half a dozen of the fighting age men of Wolf Clan had declined to join the party. One was the youngest of four boys and claimed he did not wish to leave his mother without a son, but the rest were staunchly opposed for one reason or another. Some didn't like the war, others didn't like Nvya. Whatever their reasons, they weren't abandoning them now, and they stood there staring at Nvya with brooding gazes.

If the man was offended by their refusal, he did not show it. He turned as Yvgidahi approached.

"Come to wish us well?" Nvya asked, his tone impossible to judge.

"I'm coming with you," Yvgidahi announced.

"No!"

The outburst came from Mesim, but Nendawagan couldn't be sure she hadn't had a part in it, too. For a long moment, the two men just stared at one another. Yvgidahi looked serious, Nvya confused.

"I don't understand," the self-styled leader admitted. "You have opposed me at all turns, now you want to join? What trap have you laid for me?"

"No trap," Yvgidahi promised sincerely. "Only the hope of a restoration of my honor, and the honor of a people I have evidently failed. What kind of skiagvsta am I if I don't even go to war with my own men?" He hesitated for only half a breath. "It may have been a century ago, but I do have experience fighting the white men. I could be useful."

Nvya continued to stare at him as though he were speaking nonsense. To Nendawagan's ears, he was. Her father was not an elderly man, true, but he wasn't the strong, youthful man he had been at the time of the Book, either. It was his time to lead, not fight.

Or perhaps that was the point. Perhaps her father would be used simply as an advisor. Like Ola Achukma, he wasn't much for fighting and bloodshed, but he had certain skills that could be beneficial to the campaign as a whole. And he did have the wisdom of age and experience to temper Nvya's more rash impulses. Hope flared in her chest.

Nvya grinned and put a hand on Yvgidahi's shoulder. "Of course. We would be glad to have you."

As the men walked through Galohisdi, the last officer with them, Nendawagan knew a moment of heartbroken pity for her mother. She had known for a short while that Ola Achukma would be leaving. He had let her know he was going, he had defined his role, and they had taken time to come to terms with it. But her mother and father had clearly not had such discussions. Yvgidahi had not told his wife his intentions; they had not lain awake in the darkness wrestling with the implications of the separation and the roles each was expected to play. He might have been planning it since the beginning, but she had only just found out. And the last thing she would remember of her husband for an unknown length of time was him simply leaving, not even a glance back to say he loved her.

Nendawagan then knew a flash of annoyed anger with her father. How could he do such a thing to his wife? How could he just leave her like that? No forewarning, no discussion, nothing but a sudden announcement and departure, leaving Mesim to weep openly in the townhouse once he was gone.

But he was right, she admitted, putting a hand on Netami and guiding her toward Mesim. He was supposed to be their leader in the affairs concerning the Old Land. This was a pretty major affair, and he had to be part of it in some fashion or risk losing all respect. He also had to be a mentor to his sons and other war virgins.

Mesim put up no resistance as Nendawagan and, a moment later, Popokus got her to her feet and helped her out of the townhouse, their daughters and young sons following. There were no dry eyes among them, but at least they could walk.

When they reached Mesim's house, Nendawagan went ahead to start hot water for tea, and Popokus and the younger girls made Mesim comfortable at the table.

"He didn't say anything to me," she said, regaining some composure. "Not a hint, not a whisper."

"He'll be all right, Guka," Nendawagan told her gently. "He's just going to help the young men, advise them. He has battle experience; they don't. They need his guidance."

She wasn't sure how much she wanted to hold onto that hope, but it eased the tension in the air. Popokus knelt before their mother, holding her hand and speaking softly. Nendawagan used Udilegv'i to bring the water to a quick boil and soon served everyone tea.

No one moved to do chores, though some of the younger children got restless and went out to look for something to do. But Nendawagan and the rest of the women stayed where they were, drinking tea, not saying much. They all slept over at Mesim's house, her daughters not wanting to go home to a cold, empty bed, uncertain if it would ever be warm again.

Pokkoli Toklo Akucha Tahlapi Tushafa

Company

Ola Achukma had never witnessed a battle, or anything more violent than an occasional fistfight or drunken brawl. He didn't know what it looked like to move thousands of men at a time through field and forest, or to supply them.

Nvya and others had spent part of the night moving the horses over to the Old Land. It was not an easy feat, and they risked theft of the animals and the supplies while unattended, but it let the horses get reacquainted with their surroundings so they were less spooky when the warriors arrived to ride them.

They came upon some large gathering of people moving through the forest, though if this was the army they were looking for, anyone might be forgiven for immediately thinking the endeavor a lost cause. Ola Achukma saw old men and even women. Some appeared drunk, others infirm or in otherwise poor health. Few had the strength or will to carry anything, though their horses looked no better. Most paid the warriors no mind, and the rest were a mixture of surprise, relief, and a tiny bit of suspicion and hostility.

"We may be going home sooner than expected," someone murmured. Nervous glances agreed.

Ola Achukma was not the most well-liked person, and some of the officers suspected him of plotting betrayal of some form, but his position was both notable and necessary. For that reason, he was in attendance for most of Nvya's meetings, or at least one of the first to hear about them.

So it was that he was present when Nvya approached a somewhat official-looking man in the camp and asked to speak to the commander or even the general himself. The man guffawed loudly, drawing the attention of everyone and everything for several miles and prompting

Ola Achukma to experience a rather unpleasant and unwanted flashback to the river crossing when he was a boy on the Trail.

"Well, if you find them, let me know," the man finally said, wiping a tear from his eye. "Just what do you suppose you've found here?"

"If this is the army, I've little hope in the cause," Nvya told him, posture rigid with anger, skin hot with embarrassment.

"Naw, this ain't the army. We're the camp followers. Got the washerwomen, the cooks, couple smiths. We're everything that makes the army possible. You're welcome, by the way."

"We're not here to wash clothes. We're here to fight. Where is the army?"

The man sighed dramatically. "Listen, we're headin' to Tennessee meet up with Thomas. Now he's putting together a legion, mostly you native folks. He's gonna hold the eastern front, or that's the plan. He'll know more'n me; he can put you to work soldierin' if that's what you want."

"It is."

"Now if you really want to make a good impression, why don't you stick with us an' escort us there? Shouldn't be more'n a few days. As you can see, we're not exactly heavily fortified. Unioners catch us, we're easy pickings, and these supplies never make it to the soldiers. Help us help you."

Nvya looked ready to refuse, but Yvgidahi murmured something to him quietly which apparently changed his mind, and he agreed to the escort. Word spread back through the warriors who quickly had the camp followers surrounded. Ola Achukma elected to remain nearer to his father-in-law than Nvya.

"Why did you come?" Ola Achukma asked in their own language. He'd been meaning to ask since he'd first spotted Yvgidahi, but never got the chance as Nvya tried to organize them and get moving. "Who am I supposed to report to in Aktiya Waya?"

"You will report to the council, as expected," Yvgidahi told him simply. "As for why I came, I am a leader. What kind of leader would I be if I did not join in the fight?"

"You've preached peace for decades, though."

"Indeed, and still I stand by peace. But one must examine what peace is and how it may be brought about. If the peoples lose this war, there will be no peace for them, only continued subjugation, violence, and death. If I did not come, it would cause division at home, which would disrupt the peace we enjoy."

"What did Mesim say about it?"

Yvgidahi was silent for a long moment before answering, "I didn't tell her. She didn't know until I departed."

Ola Achukma blinked. "Why?"

Yvgidahi grinned. "Come now, Ola Achukma, you're married. More than that, you are married to my daughter. You understand the power that women hold over us. She would have disapproved, and I, being of such weak will after a century of nonviolence, would have caved to her will. But I knew in my heart that this was the best way, and so I hid it from her." He gave him a look. "Do not think I do not hold some regrets over not telling her, or that I do not feel guilty even now. But choices must be made, and I have made mine."

Ola Achukma could not think of a reply, so he made his choice to stay silent on the matter. He looked around until he spotted his sons, some distance back on the other side of the slow-moving convoy. They appeared to take the new assignment with great seriousness, constantly looking around, assessing any and all potential threats.

"Is it strange for you, being back here?" he blurted.

Yvgidahi looked around. "A bit, yes. Even if I do not immediately recognize the area, I know well these trees, these leaves, this sky. I do not know whether I am walking into a dream, or waking from it." He glanced at Ola Achukma. "What about you?"

"Less strange, since I have been back here on at least a few occasions."

"Understandable."

"Is there anything you would wish to do or see while you're here, while you have the chance?"

Yvgidahi gave him a look. "I am just as capable of Galohisdi as you are, Ola. I have always had the chance to come back." He hesitated.

"Although, I would like to see if the tree of the seeing fruit still lives, and if the fruit is still viable. The trees of Hlohi bear fruit, but they do not appear to hold the spirits within them."

"Do you think Anagalisgi still walks these woods?"

"I do. I would like to see him, speak to him again, if I could." He looked around, giving a hard regard in all directions. "But this place is almost entirely unfamiliar. I wouldn't know where to begin my search."

"We'll find it," Ola Achukma promised. "I think we will do much exploring of this place in the near future. Something must strike a memory somewhere."

Yvgidahi did not reply.

By the end of the day, much of the staunch seriousness that had enveloped the group had worn off. They were still alert and attentive, but they were no longer stiff as old trees. Ola Achukma watched his sons joke around with others their own age who had also been born and raised in Aktiya Waya, now seeing the Old Land for the first time. Many comments were made about the white men, their pale skin and strange practices.

Nvya, meanwhile, still trying to recover from his embarrassment at approaching a meager band of camp followers rather than the army itself, was busy telling grand stories of his ancestors and other legends of war glory and promising the same for the rest of them. His officers joined in with their own tales, and even Yvgidahi offered a story or two, and their fires were rather lively places.

A couple of older white men joined Ola Achukma at his less exciting fire.

"What's that young sprat's name, boy?" one asked, jerking his head toward the group.

"What?" Ola Achukma wondered.

"Your leader, the one with the big yapper. What's 'is name?"

"Nvya."

"Nvya, eh? Well, y'all get new names when you get all signed up, I reckon. Anyway, I seen you speakin' to 'im, figure you're someone of some importance to 'im."

"Well, not really."

"Whatever the case, you do speak to'm. Tell 'im this: there's plenty of us here who's got injun blood. Some was injun raised. We hear what he's sayin' and some don't like it. We all fightin' on the same side here. Don't make enemies in a friendly camp."

Ola Achukma sighed and nodded. "I'll tell him."

"Good. You seem like a nice young lad. What's your name?"

"Ola Achukma among my people, but I was once known as Roland Aberdeen."

"Aberdeen, hm? Any relation to ol' John Aberdeen?"

Ola Achukma was ready to say that John was his father. Then he thought about it. He was well over forty years old, maybe over fifty, yet he didn't look old enough to be his own sons' father. Their brother, but not their father. Finally he settled for, "He was my grandfather."

The old man nodded solemnly. "I 'spect ol' John woulda been a Unioner, if he was still alive, but he was a good man, did good work. Lord's work. Maybe you gonna help finish it."

There was a prospect no one had ever considered before, Ola Achukma thought, that his father's work might be finished. It was a laughable thought, really, yet he found himself mulling over it for the remainder of their journey. Was he clinging to false hope, or could there be something to it?

It was four days before they reached Knoxville, Tennessee, where William Thomas had figuratively set up camp, hoping to sign up more recruits, particularly of the native kind. When an entire self-assembled, self-supplied army showed up at the tavern where he waited, and volunteered to fight, the man was more than ecstatic to receive them.

"I see you've got horses," he observed, grinning hugely. "Good-looking beasts, too. Big, healthy, and strong. They ever been to battle?"

"No," Nvya answered, "but they have been used in game drives."

"Well, some experience is better than none. Shoot, you just gave me a nice dedicated cavalry, didn't you? What you got for arms?"

"We have our bows and our knives. And our clubs."

Thomas faltered just a bit. "Uh...you got guns? Rifles, muskets, pistols? Hell, I'll take a blunderbuss."

"No, we have none of those."

Now the man sighed and shifted his stance. "Well, it's not a huge surprise, I suppose. I guess I had just hoped..." He shook his head and regained some of his former cheer. "No matter. Bodies are bodies, and you didn't come unprepared. You've still got horses, and a bow with arrows is more useful than a rifle with no bullets. And you got your mounts, too. Actually, you might be better prepared than some of the army proper, but don't tell them I said that."

"Will you take us or not?" Nvya asked pointedly.

"Hell yes, I'll take you!" Thomas snapped his fingers toward a boy of about twelve years. The boy jumped into action, digging in a bag and bringing out sheets of paper, ink, and feathers. Thomas got everything arranged just so and looked at Nvya, "I'll just need your name and where you're from."

As the old man at the campfire had predicted, they all got new "English" names. The officers did not take kindly to this, and there was a bit of a heated argument over it. Ola Achukma suspected that the only reason Nvya relented was because he wanted to see battle and win the war more than he wanted to lose face over a name. To the white men he was called Nigel Thomas, but he remained staunchly Nvya.

Yvgidahi was renamed Johann Kline and declared, "The most injun-lookin' Prussian anyone ever did see."

"And your name?" Thomas asked when Ola Achukma stepped up. A dozen men into the conscription and he looked ready for a nap.

"Roland Aberdeen."

"Oh, Lord, an injun with a name I can pronounce." He dipped his feather in the ink and began scratching away.

"It was my name as a boy," Ola Achukma told him.

"Well, it'll work for me. Welcome to the Confederate States of America, Private Aberdeen."

With his name officially registered, Ola Achukma, like the rest, was sent to a wagon out behind the tavern where he was given something that was supposed to resemble a uniform and ten cartridges for a gun he didn't have.

"Where are the guns?" he asked dumbly.

The man with the supplies shrugged. "Could be on their way, could be not. We don't have what we don't have. If you wanted one, your best bet was to bring it yourself."

Ola Achukma moved aside for the next man in line. As they entered the tavern, the men were eager and talking excitedly. As they exited, they appeared more confused, though still eager for the war to come. He intercepted his sons as they got their uniforms.

"What name did they give you, Tsitsa?" Galiliga asked, smiling. "They called me 'Logan Gray.' Tsona here is 'John Gray.' "

"I used the name my own father gave me, Roland Aberdeen," he answered. "But don't think that means you don't have to do as I tell you."

"No, of course not," Tsona laughed. "Tsitsi would never let us home again if we tried."

Ola Achukma nodded even as he wondered how Nendawagan and the women were doing. The first few days, fine, they might enjoy a brief reprieve from the men and could pretend that they were off on a game drive, maybe at the festival of tournaments even. When did the loneliness really hit?

He was not able to dwell on it for long. Just as soon as everyone was signed up and had their uniforms, Thomas was already motioning for Nvya to return to the tavern, handing out orders. Ola Achukma left his sons and hurried toward the meeting, standing in back while Thomas, Nvya, Yvgidahi, and the officers huddled around a map.

"How familiar are you boys with these hills?" Thomas asked, his tone gone from merry to serious.

"I have some familiarity," Yvgidahi offered, "but these boys, not so much."

"Well, you're going to want to get familiar real quick." Thomas marked a spot on the map. "This is Alum Cave. Got a lot of good minerals, good saltpeter in there. Union would love to take it for themselves, starve our boys of powder. I want you boys to ride up there and protect it. I'll be a few days behind, see if I can't sign up a few more local injuns to help." He put two fingers in his mouth and let out a shrill whistle. A man somewhere between the apparent ages of Nvya and Yvgidahi descended the steps from the second floor of the tavern. He was clearly of Native blood, though he carried himself like a white soldier. "This is Lieutenant Astogatoge, though you'll hear others call him John. He's from the area. He'll get you to Alum Cave and show you what it means to be a Confederate soldier. Got that?"

They had no choice but to agree. They were committed and signed Confederate soldiers. And what did that mean exactly? Well, it sounded like Astogatoge was going to show them.

It was no small task gathering everyone up, getting their horses, and starting out once more. Ola Achukma wondered if it wouldn't have been better to rest a night, but apparently that wasn't how it was done in the army.

Astogatoge took the lead on his own horse, a brilliant black stallion. He did not speak until they were out of sight of the tavern.

"It's not all bad, really," he said, and it was unclear just whom he was addressing. "The white men make it sound very stiff and serious. For their part, it is. But for us, fighting with our own people, we have a little more freedom." He went on before anyone could speak. "You all claimed to be from Aktiya Waya." He grinned. "I heard stories, you know. As a child. Even heard occasional rumors, that the warriors from Aktiya Waya returned from time to time."

"We're here now," Nvya said. "You're welcome."

But Astogatoge ignored him and looked at Yvgidahi. "My family also told stories. About a young warrior called Yvgidahi, who wielded tremendous sorceries and became immortal. Is it true? Are you the same Yvgidahi?"

Yvgidahi coughed a polite laugh. "I am the same man, yes, but as you can see, I've not been blessed with immortality, not quite."

"But you do wield great sorceries."

"Yes. We all do, to some degree."

Astogatoge grinned hugely. "Then our victory is assured!"

Yvgidahi looked uncertain. "I don't know about that. The sorceries did not stop the Anigilisi a century ago."

"A century ago we did not have the same weapons as the enemy, nor did we have an entire army at our backs. You were facing not only the British, but your own enemies as well. Even the greatest warrior will be overwhelmed eventually. Things are different now. You'll see."

The thought appeared to hearten the old warrior a bit, and he inquired, "So then, if you know so much about me, do you happen to know if there remains a tree of seeing fruit? It was from my brother, Anagalisgi."

Astogatoge considered this. "I know vaguely of what you speak, though many things have changed since you have been here, many more since the removals. I do know of certain trees that the traditional priests go to. I will ask them if I have the chance."

"It would be greatly appreciated."

"Of course."

Ola Achukma thought Nvya looked a bit annoyed, but before anyone could say anything more, Astogatoge gave the order to remain as silent as possible. They were heading into the wilderness now and didn't need to attract attention.

What few conversations were going on promptly ceased. The road remained clear for another half mile, then abruptly disappeared into the trees and up a steep slope. A few of the horses sighed and hesitated but continued on at a slight nudge. Ola Achukma kept his gaze fixed firmly ahead.

As far as enemy encounters went, their journey was uneventful. Adjusting to life in a white man's army, well, that was something a little different. Considering that Astogatoge said repeatedly that their group was a little more lax because they were wanted for a different set of skills, Ola Achukma frequently wondered how much worse things had to be for the white regiments.

Because they were all mounted, they were not forced to march. Anyone who knew anything about armies commented on what a relief this was and told everyone else to be grateful for it. They were, however, instructed to ride in formation. This took up an entire morning where Astoagtoge interviewed every single warrior and placed him in a specific position in a specific row in a specific section of their formation.

Nvya did not find this to be the best use of time or talent, despite Astoagtoge's repeated assurances that it had been tested thoroughly. These particular elements of the formation ensured the most effective use of weapons, skill, and sheer manpower to beat back an enemy attack. There was more arguing, but it ultimately came down to, if the Krydik wanted to help, they were going to have to come under someone else's direction. If anyone didn't want to take those directions, they could go home.

Grumbling ensued, but no one made any move to leave.

Compared to that, the irritation over the uniforms was pretty minor. Astogatoge promised them that if they were ever sent on scouting missions, they could wear their normal clothing, or whatever they felt would be most beneficial. But when it came to formation, lounging in camp, or especially when going into battle, they had to wear the uniforms.

"Not all of the people are for the Confederacy," he warned them severely. "Even the Cherokee are divided. Do not presume that because a man says he is your brother, that he truly is."

"Why wouldn't the people side with the ones proclaiming their sovereignty?" Nvya asked.

"Quite frankly, because that side has always lost, and every time the people are punished for it. Some believe that if they side with their captors this time, maybe their captors will be kinder to them."

"So they have embraced their chains and their servitude."

"Some have, yes. In the south and west, it is easier, for the nations are unified. Here in the east, the water is murkier. Some people have citizenship. Many are mixed-blood to some degree, and they worry over their fate should one side or the other win."

"And what do the Confederates plan to do with the peoples who sided against them?" Yvgidahi inquired.

Astogatoge shrugged. "Every man will be given a chance to declare his loyalty to the Confederacy and to whatever people he chooses within the Confederacy. Let the peoples choose to accept him or not. Let each man live how he will. But we will suffer no Union traitors. Let the behemoth devour itself and any who defend its unnatural ways. We will stand strong."

It was enough of an encouragement to see them to Alum Cave without further incident. The large rock face was exposed to the sun, and there appeared to be several caves in tight niches and tucked-in corners, a stream running just outside one entrance. The main area of activity appeared to be a broad swath of bare rock which ended abruptly and dropped a good thirty feet to a forest clearing. There was a bit of mining and excavation going on, but if this was a prime target for Union troops to attack and so smother the supply of saltpeter to the Confederate gunsmiths, Ola Achukma wondered what the lesser targets looked like.

"Any trouble?" Astogatoge inquired of the miners.

"Union movement northeast of here, but we've not been troubled," one answered. "Jer'miah thinks they might be tryin' to set up a blockade down the road, but they don't know the trails like we do. We'll get around 'em."

"Glad to hear it. We'll be camping here for a bit, make sure you aren't bothered."

"You expect the Union to want to bother us?"

"They might. You keep working well like you are, and we'll make sure it stays that way."

The miners didn't seem to mind much one way or the other.

Astogatoge led the warriors a short distance from the mine proper to a spot as clear as one might expect in the hills. There the warriors learned about how white armies made camp. Minor adjustments had to be made for the landscape, but they seemed to value their precise rows and other formations. For as much time as it took to get everything set up just so, somehow it also had to be done in such a way as to be packed up at a moment's notice. This was not an especially difficult concept for the warriors, packing up quickly and moving, but the insistence on everything else was a bit irritating.

"It's good you found Thomas, then," Astogatoge told them, noting the discomfort and annoyance. "He's been the most successful at recruiting and keeping native regiments in the east, and this will be the first all-native legion anyone has ever put together. If you had fallen in with anyone else, you'd be cutting trees, building pikes, and digging three dozen latrine pits."

"Why is Thomas in charge and not you?" Nvya questioned.

"I am in charge, in case you didn't notice," Astogatoge said smartly. "And believe it or not, Thomas is one of us, though he doesn't much look it. Native born, Native raised, Native chief."

"What?! Have the people lost their minds?"

Astogatoge gave him a look. "He's the first chief to unite the people like he has since the time of Aganstata and Atagulkalu. He's the reason most of us are here. Do well to remember that." And he moved on without another word.

Once camp was set up, everyone was free to start dinner. Ola Achukma was not particularly hungry, but it gave him something to do, something to take his mind off the events of the day. Looking around, he could see others were having similar thoughts. Were any having regrets? Were any of them making silent plans, that "If this shall or shall not happen in such a timeframe, I am going home"?

He wondered whether he shouldn't make a quick trip home, report to the council that they had been accepted into the army and were now on their first mission. It might ease some of the uncertainty among the women, to let them know that their men were alive and well and not in constant danger.

He spoke to Yvgidahi about it, and the skiagvsta agreed, though he suggested waiting until after dark so as not to cause a sort of disgruntled panic or exodus.

A few hours later, he was back in Aktiya Waya, speaking to everyone in the townhouse. It seemed strange, both for how few people were there and the fact that it was primarily women.

The relief could not have been more obvious if they had written it on their faces, to know that, essentially, nothing had happened to their men since they'd left. A lot of riding, a lot of grumbling about the white man's army, but no danger, no fighting, and no death.

On the other side of things, the men were glad to know that their women missed them but were otherwise doing well. It was a new and strange situation for everyone, but they were making their way.

It made things a little easier, a little less gloomy around camp as Astogatoge roused them early to start more formal training and assessment of their abilities. No, they didn't have guns, but the nice thing about bows was that they were silent, which would give them every advantage on an ambush.

"Aktiya Waya proves to be a blessing," Astogatoge commented, watching them fire off arrows with amazing accuracy. "Your preservation of the old ways gives us another weapon in our arsenal. Few people now can make bows so fine, or arrows so straight, never mind know how to wield them. When supplies run low, we will turn to you."

"Supplies don't seem to be overabundant to begin with," someone said dryly.

"Now you understand."

Before he could say more, there was the sound of hoofbeats, and two warriors rode toward the practice field.

"William Thomas is here," one reported. "And it seems he has already been to battle."

The dozen shooting warriors hastily turned and followed the riders back to camp where Thomas and another hundred or so men had just arrived. Some of the men were wounded, but all attention was focused on the man in ropes, lashed to Thomas' horse.

"Major Thomas," Astogatoge greeted.

"Astogatoge," Thomas said, his tone impossible to determine. He jerked on the rope. "Found this lad running around the woods like a little lost doe."

"He's a decent warrior if he managed to wound twenty of your men."

Thomas barked a laugh. "Hardly! There was a small camp of them. Scouts. Bad ones."

Astogatoge looked around at the men who rode with Thomas. "Looks like you raised another company."

"I did."

"They look white."

"They are. They'll be staying here to look after the miners."

"And the rest of us?"

Thomas handed Astogatoge a folded piece of paper. "You're to head to Powell's Valley. Seems the Union is trying to rally some forces there and march this way. Stop them."

"Sir."

With a shrill whistle, Astogatoge got the attention of the the Krydik and ordered an immediate evacuation of the area. Nvya was already leaping into action, and if any green recruit needed a lesson on how to quickly pack up a camp, the Krydik could have given him that lesson. Even Astogatoge was impressed, but there was little chance to say so before heading out, riding north. Their pace was slowed only for the safety of the horses on particular parts of the trail, but when there was an opening, they moved quickly.

Despite their enthusiastic start, Powell's Valley was several days away, and they soon fell into a comfortable, steady rhythm.

They were camped near the Tennessee-Virginia line when Astogatoge finally seemed to recognize Ola Achukma's existence and sat with him at his fire.

"So what are you doing here?" Astogatoge wondered.

"Sitting. Thinking," Ola Achukma answered.

"No. What are you doing here? Everyone else is excited for this opportunity, but you don't join in."

Ola Achukma hesitated for half a second, then replied, "My father was John Aberdeen. He was a diplomat."

"Yes, I heard stories about him. He negotiated several treaties and was widely loved by many peoples. He was your father?"

"He was. After he died, my mother and I were forced west, where we were rescued and taken to Aktiya Waya." Ola Achukma shook his head. "My father always preached peace. Always. He abhorred violence. Always peace, never violence. Vengeance belongs to the Lord, he would say. Always believe in peace. And we have had peace in Aktiya Waya for a long time. And yet my sons are here, just as eager as the rest of them, but I can't figure out why. My wife and I always taught them peace."

Astogatoge nodded. "I wonder about it, too, sometimes. But then I read stories like David and Goliath, and Jesus driving out the moneychangers. You know those stories?"

"Of course."

"Violence, yes, but always in defense of the weak and the helpless and the holy. David, defending his small nation from a much bigger, meaner one. Jesus, protecting the sanctity and purity of the temple. Neither foe would have gone quietly just because someone asked. They had to be removed by force. Here, we are protecting our home, our right to live as we see fit, opposing the Union which would see us subject to a corrupt federal government."

Ola Achukma considered this. "I suppose I never thought of it like that, not really."

"Well, it makes a difference when you are staring at war and not merely theorizing about it." Astogatoge paused. "I'm going to guess and say that you don't have Bibles in Aktiya Waya."

"No. I kept my father's Bible for many years, but it was destroyed in a bout of revenge by someone who didn't like me very much."

Astogatoge shifted position. "I'm sorry to hear that. Would you like to borrow mine for a bit?"

Ola Achukma shook his head. "Not tonight, but I thank you for the offer. Maybe another time."

"Of course. Any time."

Astogatoge stood and continued on his rounds, speaking to each cluster of men at their respective fires. Ola Achukma watched him, wondering if he shouldn't make a report to the council. He had made another brief trip the first night after they started north. Unlike the previous visit, where his message had helped to ease some of the worry, that message had done the opposite. First, the men had been just fine and not in danger. Now they were actively riding toward danger with the intent of engaging the enemy.

Ola Achukma fell asleep that night, contemplating the merits of the phrase, "No news is good news."

The following morning, they were on their way before the sun was up. They were supposed to cross into Virginia at some point during the day. Then it wouldn't be far to Powell's Valley.

Those who had been born and raised in Aktiya Waya had never heard a gunshot before, and it was they who did not react quickly enough to the sound to save themselves from the ambush.

All anyone saw was that Astogatoge suddenly collapsed, dead before he hit the ground.

All hell broke loose then, as Ola Achukma instinctively reached for his bow and looked around for his sons. He spotted them, still upright and appearing unharmed in their saddles, though their horses had spooked and become difficult to control. Up above, on the tall hills and cliffs of Baptist Gap, Union soldiers came swarming down, diving into bushes to reload their guns.

With the horses, the warriors had no chance of escaping up the slopes, though the best that Ola Achukma could tell, the Union soldiers had them pinned on three sides anyway.

"Don't let them surround you!" Yvgidahi's voice could just be heard above the din of gunshots and frightened horses. "Into the trees!"

Ola Achukma's first thought was that Hitguttit and the horse tenders were not going to be happy if all the horses were killed. Theft was bad enough, but abandoning them to be slaughtered? Unacceptable.

Still, he slid off his mount and ran for the trees. At some point, he knew he should probably try to conjure Time. But as the gunshots and yelling and whinnying all garbled together, he couldn't get himself in a position to focus and do it. He just wasn't skilled enough in that particular sorcery. No one really was; it wasn't something they used much in Aktiya Waya.

He saw hands appear in front of him, one holding a bow. As the hands struck hard against a tree, he realized they were his hands, and somehow he'd gotten to safety, relatively speaking. He squeezed his eyes shut as bark suddenly exploded beside him. Squatting low in a cluster of tangled, thorny undergrowth, he tried to get a look around and figure out what was going on.

The scattering of their group had stalled the Union forces for the moment, confused them and halted their advance. Someone, Nvya maybe, was shouting to advance, pick off the soldiers from the bushes.

Ola Achukma reached for an arrow, nocked it on his bowstring. He glanced down at himself to double-check which color uniform he was wearing. He noted that it wouldn't do much good to fire blindly into the trees where he was, but he had an excellent view of the opposite slope. If his side was anything like the other side, then the Unioners had relied solely on the element of surprise. He did not see many, certainly not as many as they had in warriors.

He picked out a blue uniform on the other side of the gap and drew the arrow to his ear.

He had only a heartbeat of notice, only the flicker of an out-of-place shadow, before the bayonet came crashing down, slicing into air where his head was but a moment before. Ola Achukma dropped awkwardly into the bush, rolling and loosing his arrow. The arrow faced virtually no resistance as the arrowhead popped easily out the back of the man's skull, the shaft burying itself all the way to the fletching right between his eyes. The bloody body fell forward onto Ola Achukma who rolled it off just in time to dodge a second Unioner as he was fleeing, four warriors giving chase.

In the cathartic shouting, a single message bubbled to the surface: the Unioners were in retreat. Chase them down and kill them.

Down in the valley, Nvya was leading the charge. Ola Achukma remained on the slope as part of the flanking team, keeping the Union soldiers in the narrows. A few warriors fired off arrows as they were running, and those who were close enough took a swing with their clubs or knives, but now the hunt was in the chase phase. A few warriors had gone back for their horses and called out warnings to get out of their way so they could ride through and trample the fleeing soldiers.

Ola Achukma watched several men go down, flattened under huge hooves. Most of the riders went ahead and circled back around, ready for another charge, but a couple kept going, eager to see what lay beyond. They disappeared around a curve in the trail.

A moment later, there came the sound of a screaming horse, and one of the riders came galloping back.

"Artillery!" he called. "Artillery!"

The warriors, caught off-guard, slowed their chase, and the riders retreated. The Union soldiers managed to break away from the warriors and the gap widened until the foretold artillery reinforcements appeared, lumbering toward them like a slow-moving bear just out of hibernation. There were only a few cannons, but the men following them were less tired than the ones who had just been chased off.

Nvya dove to the ground as the Union soldiers let loose a volley of musket fire, but it was all they were able to do.

"Attack!" Nvya bellowed, scrambling to his feet with a weapon in each hand.

No longer bothering with flanking and maneuvers, the warriors streamed out of the trees toward the Union soldiers like a massive fist. Each cannon was only fired once as the warriors descended before the Union soldiers turned to flee. But flight was not good enough, and surrender was not an option. War whoops echoed in the mountains, drowning out the moans of the dying and the screams of the fleeing. Ola Achukma, still with bow in hand, let loose three arrows before fully diving into the fray. Having come from the slopes, he was not among the leading warriors, but he did come across soldiers who did not die from their initial wounds. These he finished off with his knife or club, not wishing to waste his arrows.

Small groups of warriors continued chasing the Union soldiers who had the speed and endurance to flee, but eventually Nvya called everyone back.

"They killed Astogatoge!" he roared. "They killed our brother and leader! But we have prevailed! And this is my response to their failed attack!" He grabbed the nearest Union body, took his knife, and scalped the corpse in a single, impressive draw. "For every one of ours they killed, take two more! If any are still alive, take them prisoner as Thomas took his man prisoner!"

This course of action greatly pleased the warriors, and they set about scalping Union corpses and even a few living souls. Meanwhile, Ola Achukma went back to Astogatoge's body, staring at the blood obscuring distorted features.

"He died a warrior's death in the land of his ancestors."

Ola Achukma looked up to see Yvgidahi approaching. His uniform was torn and he had several minor wounds, but he looked younger and more alive than he had in ten years or more.

"He did," Ola Achukma said simply. He looked around. "But what about the rest? We should get them back to Aktiya Waya for proper mourning and burial."

Yvgidahi nodded. "Agreed. It is good that we have the ultimate victory to speak of, that these men did not die in vain, though I doubt their widows will see it that way."

"I will see that they understand."

"No. I will oversee their return, and I will address the people. It is my duty as skiagvsta to explain this to them, make this into a good thing. You will take word back to Thomas, tell him what has happened here. Then come and meet us in Powell's Valley."

"You intend to meet the Union forces there?"

"Those are our orders. I don't fully understand how the white army works, how it functions, and I don't always agree with it, but they must do something right, for as much destruction as they cause. We will follow orders and continue on to Powell's Valley. And you will follow my order to take word back to Major Thomas. Do you understand?"

"Yes sir."

Yvgidahi put a hand on his shoulder. "You did well. As did your sons."

Ola Achukma turned suddenly, looking around. "Galiliga, Tsona, where are they?"

Yvgidahi pointed. "Just there. They're fine."

Ola Achukma breathed a sigh of relief. "Good. All right, I'll find a horse and get back to Major Thomas."

Before he did that, he knelt and opened Astogatoge's jacket, relatively unmarred by the bullets. In one pocket, he found the man's small Bible. It was dusty and worn, and several pages were torn, but it was still readable. In the front was a faded picture of a young woman. Ola Achukma put the picture and the Bible in his own jacket, then stood and looked around for a horse.

Those that had fled after the initial gunshot scare were not difficult to locate, though they were not keen on the thought of being caught and ridden again. When he did manage to grab the reins of one, he had to use Touch in order to impart feelings of calm and trust. Even then it was a minute or two of gentle persuasion before he felt confident in getting on. The horse was a little more willing to move once it realized he was intending to ride away from the scary battlefield.

Ola Achukma wouldn't say he wasn't nervous about riding off alone, but then, he was glad to do this, rather than have to take the bodies back to Aktiya Waya and try to explain how it was a victory. Had anything been gained? Any land regained, spoils taken? The scalps might be a start, but was there anything else to boast of? Why had the rest of the men ridden off after their attackers? What was their plan?

No, he did not envy Yvgidahi or Nvya or any of those who were in charge. Though as he rode, he noticed how his hands were trembling. Over and over in his mind, he could visualize the man attacking him from behind, how close his bayonet had come to his head. Only the flicker of a shadow had saved him. Then he turned and put an arrow through the man's face, the feathered fletching seeming to explode out of his nose and eyes.

He elected not to make camp that night, and he rode as long as he could stand. He did not make a proper camp, just rolled out a blanket, nibbled on a bit of tasteless food, and stretched out for a fitful sleep.

Over and over again, he saw the shadow and the feathers in the man's face. For some reason, he also had a still image, like a picture imprinted in his mind, of him holding Astogatoge's Bible. Several times, when he woke in the night, he put his hand over the pocket where he knew the Bible lay. He thought of Ki's Bible. Finally, he sat up, brought out the Bible, and, squinting in the light of a single candle, opened up the pages.

Astogatoge's Bible was marked up, much as Aki's had been. But Astogatoge seemed to have written translation notes, circling some words, scrunching others in margins, even putting a question mark beside a few. Ola Achukma smiled to himself.

He woke up slumped over the open Bible. The candle had burned to nothing. Yawning and rubbing his eyes, he put the Bible away, rolled up his blanket, grabbed his horse, and continued on.

When he arrived back at Alum Cave, he learned that Major Thomas had just left the previous day, "gone to bring more injuns to the cause." Once he was pointed in the right direction, Ola Achukma started off again.

He didn't catch up to the Major until Knoxville, at the same tavern where he'd conscripted the Aktiya Waya company.

"Aberdeen," Thomas said, standing and evidently unsure how to receive his appearance. "Seven hells, man, you look awful. Come, sit, have a drink. Surely you could not have reached Powell's Valley already?"

Ola Achukma shook his head. "We were ambushed in Baptist Gap, a small Union force. Astogatoge is dead."

He reached in his pocket and dug out the Bible, holding it out to Thomas. Thomas ignored the Bible for the moment, instead asking, "And the company?"

"We prevailed, but not without a few casualties. Yvgidahi is overseeing the return of the bodies to Aktiya Waya. Nvya is leading the men now. Prisoners were taken, and for every one of ours they killed, we cut two more scalps."

"Scalps!" Thomas barked, turning away in disbelief. "Scalps!" He shook his head and looked at Ola Achukma. "Scalps, are you mad?!"

"It is our way. It is what was expected."

Thomas leaned over the table, lowering his voice. "You ride back to the company. Tell Nvya that he—all of them—are to release their scalps to the bodies they were taken from."

"But—"

"And shut up about it! We can't have people thinking that we scalp our enemies. It looks savage."

"It makes the enemy fear us, though. They will be less likely to attack, or attack effectively."

"No," Thomas said decisively. "No scalps. No talking about scalps. No threats of scalping. None of it. I will not have it under my command. Is that understood?"

Ola Achukma took an even breath. "I will make sure the men know."

"See that you do."

Thomas straightened and, running a hand through his hair, sighed, "Scalps. Jeez, as if I don't have enough of a political battle as it is."

Ola Achukma stood cautiously and again offered the Bible. "This was Astogatoge's Bible. I think his family would want it."

Thomas waved a hand. "Keep it, if you wish. His wife died in childbirth last winter."

Ola Achukma blinked, then nodded and replaced the Bible in his pocket. He wanted to say something, but he didn't know what he wished to accomplish. What was done was done, and there was no going back.

He left the tavern.

Pàke Nishinxke òk Kwëtash

Woman's Work

There wasn't a woman in all of Hlohi who could say she hadn't lost a relative in the year and a half of the Old Land War. For Nendawagan, she'd lost two brothers and several nephews. Galiliga had been injured once, but the power of the Touch sorceries had him healed and going back for more. According to her father who had visited once or twice, the men were in the best spirits he'd ever seen them as long-buried purpose bubbled to the surface and invigorated them.

According to Ola Achukma, who made more regular visits, it wasn't quite so simple. Yes, overall morale was quite high. The warriors had become more accustomed to how things worked in the army and what was expected of them. There was some frustration that a great majority of their time was spent guarding bridges and warehouses, though it was not without its dangers; one or two Union scouts would try to sneak past them, or they might try to set fire to a warehouse. Otherwise, they were moving from place to place on someone else's order. On the whole, it was a dull affair, but belief in the cause remained strong.

The real blow came when they did engage in battle. Thanks to Touch, none of the warriors had perished of disease, and only one or two had suffered debilitating injuries, one man losing a leg and another an arm to cannonballs and being unable to locate the limbs before being forced to evacuate the field for treatment. Even the most skilled healers were not able to regrow limbs. But when death came, as the elders said, when it rained it poured. No healer or priest could bring back the dead, and by the beginning of the Old Land year 1864, of the approximately five hundred men who left Aktiya Waya to fight, only about one hundred or so remained, and they comprised about a fifth of the remaining legion forces.

Nendawagan did not know what this meant, exactly. What she did know was that Nvya and all but one of his closest officer friends were dead, had been for about three moons now. They had all left behind wives and children. Some had lost children of their own, those who had been old enough to fight, and those widows and remaining children came together for comfort, along with all the other widows of Hlohi.

In the beginning, Ola Achukma's arrival was anticipated, for he brought news of the Old Land and all the great heroism of their warriors. Now he was only a herald of death, come to tell them that ten men had died, or twenty, or even forty-seven on one occasion. Anymore, when he appeared in the townhouse, the only question asked of him was, "How many?"

"Four today," he reported one day, "but none of ours. A couple of cocky sharpshooters decided to attack a warehouse, but our men were not guarding it at the time."

No one cared about the details, and Nendawagan and the other women who were preparing to receive the wounded breathed a sigh of relief.

"What news, then?" one of the council asked.

Ola Achukma hesitated and gave a look to everyone else to politely ask them to leave. Nendawagan did so, knowing she would get a chance to ask him about it later, which she did.

"Something is coming," he told her hesitantly. "The Confederates are not an easy dog to put down. We don't have the same numbers and weapons that the Union does, but we are holding our own."

"Why doesn't the Union leave you alone, then?" she asked. "If you wish to live peacefully, then—"

"For the same reason that Yvgidahi could not allow Hoka and Deer Clan to separate from Aktiya Waya," he cut in, sounding more tired than angry. "Pride. Fear. Both sides have legitimate reasons for their actions, but neither one can allow the other to succeed and be validated in them. One side has to do something drastic to force the situation. The problem is that only the Union has the resources to make that push."

"What do you think is going to happen?"

"I don't know, but I think it's going to be similar to what happened in your father's time. The Union is going to gather its forces and make a hard, merciless punch right into the heart of Confederate territory and burn everything to the ground in order to break us."

"What will you do?"

He shrugged. "Fight. It's what we signed up to do."

Nendawagan shook her head. "You signed up to defend the people of the Old Land, but they are not your people. It is not your land. Not anymore. There is no glory to be won. No one will appreciate you there. And if you lose, there will only be punishment."

"There may not be glory, but even I could not suffer such cowardice. We swore to defend the people, and we will do so. Not because it is convenient for us, because we have a safe place to run to, but because it is our duty and honor to do so. One day, we may need help from the Old Land, and cowardice and broken promises yield no allies."

He wasn't wrong, but it didn't stop the next words from coming out of her mouth. "So you intend to die as your father did? Alone, in a land that did not care about his ideals or the work he did for what seems to have been a lost cause?"

Ola Achukma looked utterly stunned, and Nendawagan couldn't decide how guilty she felt. They stared at each other for a long moment until he finally said, "My father died of sickness."

"And if he hadn't? Do you think he would have been that one individual who could have prevented this war in the first place?"

"No," he admitted.

"He died, and left you and your mother alone to move west in a land that hates you." She shook her head. "Don't do that to Netami. Don't do that to Galiliga and Tsona, and don't let them do that to the families they don't even have yet! How many men shall we lose? How long will the people have to wait before our young sons are grown and able to have a family? Who will be around to teach them? Please, Ola. Take this message back to those who remain: Don't abandon us here. You have gone to defend another land, but do not let your own village burn down while you are away."

He did not say anything after that beyond a brief goodbye to both her and Netami who had watched the whole exchange with wide eyes. Then he left.

Nendawagan closed her eyes and tried to breathe, but was promptly interrupted by a tap from her daughter.

"Tsitsi, what's wrong with Tsitsa?"

"What do you mean?" she asked, sitting down.

"He used to talk so much about peace, and that peace was the ultimate goal. Now he talks about honor and glory and everything else. Is peace no longer the goal?"

"Well, it's possible to have multiple goals," Nendawagan said. Then she sighed. "I think the trouble comes when they cannot all be fulfilled, when some are exclusive of each other."

Netami sat down across from her. "What do you mean?"

"Well..." Nendawagan thought a moment. "Let's say that someone was being mean to you. They weren't hurting you, but they were saying mean things, and you really couldn't do anything about it. And let's say that Galiliga happened to see it. If he spoke up about it, there could be a problem. Let's say that the mean person would turn around and hit him. That's not peaceful, is it? But it would be an honorable thing to do, for your brother to defend you. If Galiliga stayed silent and did not intervene, there might be peace, but how would it be for him to not come to your defense when you needed him to?"

There were times when Nendawagan wished her daughter wasn't growing up so fast, or that she wasn't so perceptive. Everyone said it was because she took after her mother.

"Is honor the ultimate goal then?" Netami wondered.

Nendawagan shifted position. "It's an admirable one to have. But just remember that Nvya died with honor, and now his children are fatherless. Many children on Hlohi are now fatherless because of the call of honor."

"But they died feeling as though they were fulfilling a purpose. When they were here and safe, they seemed so unhappy."

"Yes, I suppose so."

Then Netami asked a question Nendawagan wasn't prepared for. "Do you feel fulfilled, Tsitsi, helping the men like you are?"

For a moment, she was simply stunned by the question. She opened her mouth as if to answer, but then she started to think about it. Did she feel fulfilled? What was she doing differently now that she hadn't done when the men were home?

At last she answered, "I do."

"Why?" Netami inquired. "How do you know? How do you know when you're fulfilled? You still work in the fields and prepare food, except now Tsitsa and Galiliga and Tsona are gone and may not come back."

"That is very true," Nendawagan acknowledged, "and you know that not a day goes by when I don't worry about them. You know how worried I was when Galiliga was wounded. I wish the men could all come home and stay here and we could be happy, but even now, yes, I suppose you could say I am fulfilled. Because Hitsa and Hoda are out there fulfilling their purpose, and I am aiding them in it."

"Is that our purpose, then? To serve men?"

"To serve the people. In times of war, the men fight, and we supply them and bind their wounds. In times of peace, we prepare the food and keep the home, raise the children."

Netami frowned. "What if a man does not want to fight? What if a woman doesn't want to keep the home?"

Nendawagan sighed. "You ask a lot of difficult questions, child. But it's a sign of a curious mind. Sometimes we cannot pursue what we want, for it would mean the suffering of the whole people. Other times, we should listen to the voice inside ourselves that says a thing is right or wrong. You know the story of how Hitsa stood up to Yvgidahi and challenged the senior warriors, called them out on their treachery. He risked much to go against the people, against the council, or that was how it seemed at first."

She could see her daughter struggling.

"If the sorceries were given to the people to save them, to deliver them to peace, wouldn't going to war be the same as going against the will of the spirits?" Netami went on before Nendawagan could speak. "But if such things bring fulfillment, at least to the men, wouldn't that mean that the men were acting against the spirits?"

"The sorceries rescued our people, yes. Now we use the sorceries to help others."

"But everyone has said repeatedly that the people of the Old Land don't want our help. They don't like us."

"That is true. There is some contention between us, but that's where we must do what is right and honorable." Nendawagan continued before Netami could say more. "Someday you will understand. When you are an adult, when you marry and have children, when you live long enough to understand what politics is."

"Tsitsa says politics is what stands between men and peace."

Nendawagan laughed. "He's not wrong. But it is a little more complicated than that. Now then, why don't you run and see if you can't catch up to him before he leaves?"

The girl brightened at the thought and did so. Not three seconds later, she returned, Ola Achukma in tow.

"I found him hiding outside the door," she announced proudly.

Nendawagan raised a brow first at her, then at her husband. "Oh really?"

He shrugged, embarrassed. Then he bent down in front of Netami and said, "Wait for me in the townhouse. I'll see you there before I leave."

Netami bounded away, and they watched her go. After a moment, Ola Achukma looked outside to make sure she'd gone, then ducked back in, closing the door behind him.

"How much of that did you hear?" Nendawagan asked.

He replied by bringing her in close and kissing her. With a little creative conjuring of Time, they made love and no one would have ever been the wiser.

"I know it's hard," he murmured afterwards. "I don't want to be away any more than you want me to be away. And I know it's terrible, seeing the bodies come back. I see that on a scale you would not believe, men littering the battlefield like toys left out haphazardly by a careless child. But I am glad to have your support, and to know that you understand why we do this."

"Honestly, I don't," Nendawagan told him. "I don't. Not really. But I had to tell her something."

"No," Ola Achukma said, brushing a hair out of her face. "I think you do understand; you just don't want to admit it. The same way I don't want to admit to knowing what war is. There are the stories you've been told, the tales of wars both real and fantastic, and then there is the reality of it. I wish I didn't know, but I do."

She sighed but nodded.

They lay together a while longer and then for a little time after that. They could have lain there forever, Nendawagan thought. But he had a war to fight, and she had warriors to supply. Eventually, they admitted defeat, surrendering themselves to reality and all its horrors and heartbreaks.

She went with him to the townhouse where he said goodbye to Netami, promising to take her greetings to her brothers.

Then he conjured Galohisdi back to the Old Land, stepped through, and was gone.

Only Nendawagan and Netami were in any kind of genuinely good mood that day, maybe even the whole moon. Oh, the other women found their happy moments, and there were some smiles and laughter as they got used to life without the men, but there was always a bit of an undercurrent of jealousy toward Nendawagan. Her husband got to come home sometimes, whether or not he was wounded.

"Why don't the other men come home to visit sometimes?" Netami asked once, spying a distasteful gaze as they worked in the fields.

"They want to stay focused on their mission," Nendawagan told her, repeating something Ola Achukma had said about a year earlier when she had asked a similar question. "They want to work on one thing at a time tind not get distracted by worries at home. They know we're safe here, that we are protected and provided for. So, with that taken care of, they work on doing the same for the people of the Old Land."

"I heard one of the elders once say that men get cranky when they don't lie with a woman for a long time. Is that why they're so good at war, because they stay away from women for a long time?"

Nendawagan gave her daughter a look, but Netami pretended not to notice. "Did an elder say that, or one of your brothers?"

Netami blushed. "Tsona might have said something like that, too."

"Uh-huh. Don't lie to me, and don't disrespect the elders either." She sighed. "But it is a true statement, and I'm sure it has some bearing on the war."

To her relief, her daughter had no more odd questions, at least for that day. Nendawagan didn't remember her sons ever being so strange, but perhaps that was the difference between boys and girls. Girls had to know, whereas boys had to do. Or maybe she was the one overthinking things. But then, she was a woman. Like mother, like daughter, then?

As odd as it was, she clung to her fanciful thoughts for just a little while as a distraction. If something big was going to happen in the war, as Ola Achukma seemed to think, then they would hear about it, from Ola Achukma, from Yvgidahi, from someone. They would be treating the wounded that resulted from it. So as long as they didn't hear anything from the Old Land, then chances were good that nothing was happening. The men would be guarding bridges and warehouses, maybe harassing small groups of Union soldiers who tried to sneak across the border. Nothing too terrible.

Of course, one of her nephews had been killed while guarding a bridge. They had stopped a covered wagon to inspect its load. The load turned out to be smuggled soldiers. One had shot him in the face, dead instantly. The other bridge guard had been killed, too, and the smuggled soldiers got across the bridge. It didn't take long to track them down and kill every last one of them, but it didn't bring back the dead guards, including her nephew.

That line of thought didn't help her mood much, but over the course of the war, she'd learned how to carry on. She had to, for the sake of her daughter...and her mother, who was not handling the trauma half so well.

As one might expect, war was not waged in full strength during the winter. It was not even waged at half strength. It was a time for planning and plotting and gathering information, figuring out your own strengths and resources and trying to figure out how to exploit those of your enemy. Then, once the snow melted and the game started running again, your blow struck hard and true.

And did it ever.

Aktiya Waya only heard about the initial strike after the fact, but as Ola Achukma had predicted, it was a big event that could not be contained to a single day, or even a few days.

The Union was pushing hard against the Confederacy, sending every last man and cannon to bear, it seemed, and everyone in the Confederacy was being called upon to defend the land. But the Union was powerful and had the men and resources to spare that the Confederates did not.

"We have only one hundred men left," one woman wailed when the council gave an update on the situation. "Shall we become a nation of widows?"

"If the cause is lost, we should bring them home," another agreed, sounding a little more level-headed.

"We cannot give them orders," one council member said. "And they have already decided to stay until the end." He went on before the woman could speak again. "What would you have us do, kidnap them? Far be it from any of us to come between a man and his honor."

"Honor!" a third woman exclaimed. "Honor! You speak of honor! Now? After how many years of preaching peace? We speak of our families, our children! So much of ourselves was lost when we brought all of our peoples together as a single nation, but we also gained much, too, not only in culture but also understanding. If we lose an entire generation of men, we will lose everything. Who will teach our boys how to make bows and arrows and hunt and ride in a game drive? Who will train the horses? Who will train up my sons and nephews? Who will marry our daughters and give them children? Who will lead us and guide us on the council?"

Murmurs of agreement rippled through the crowd.

"As I said," the council member reiterated, "would you have us kidnap them from the field of battle?"

"Talk some sense into them at least," someone said. "Make them see that there are some things more important than honor."

Nendawagan sighed and raised her voice. "The sacrifice of honor is what drove many people here in the first place." Once she had their attention, she continued, "Surrendering saw our ancestors and our peoples removed time and again, always pushed out of their lands, farther west, farther south, farther here and farther there. On roads and trails that saw hundreds and thousands of people dead by starvation and exposure. That is not honor. That is no way to live." She went on before someone could object. "The only reason we are 'alive' as you will no doubt say, is because we got lucky. The spirits or someone else gave us an opportunity to run and save ourselves. But if they hadn't. If my late uncle had never learned the sorceries, we would be exactly where the people of the Old Land are today, having to choose between life and death. Surrender has not worked up until now."

"Fighting doesn't seem to be working either, because the Confederates are losing," one woman said.

"Maybe. But for the first time in a long time, our men are men again, fulfilling the ways of their ancestors."

"This coming from you? Whose husband and father have done nothing but preach peace and isolation for decades?" another woman challenged.

Nendawagan found her challenger and locked gazes. "And if you are the same woman now that you were before the war, then you are a fool." She let that hang there for a moment. "I have lost brothers and nephews, and at any moment I could lose my husband, my father, or my sons. I do not wish for this in any way, even in my darkest moments. But I know that right now, they are doing as they are meant to do, as they are made to do. And I am proud of them for that. I cannot ask my husband to settle down into women's work of tending home and children any more than I would expect him to ask me to go out and fight with him." She nodded and looked around. "And you may have noticed that they are not doing that. They are low on supplies, men, morale, and they may be facing total defeat. But they have never asked us to come fight with them, to bolster their numbers, or to bolster their morale by going to lie with them. Because they know that we are here doing everything we can, just as they are. We cannot expect any more or less than that."

She saw a few nods, but only a few. Mostly she was met by gazes either stony or frantic. These women just wanted their men back. She understood—truly she did—but she also understood that there was more to life than mere existence. Animals existed. They worked to see that their basic needs were met and nothing more. It was men who craved purpose, a reason to ensure that his needs were met. The problem seemed to be that the purpose of one always ran the risk of depriving the other of her purpose. Perhaps that was the reason for children.

Whatever the case, and however close she might have been to the truth, it did nothing to sway the crowd at large. If she held any sway with the council, it was only her relation to Yvgidahi and Ola Achukma. Maybe it was enough, because the council refused to budge in their position. They were not going to kidnap the men from the Old Land, nor were they going to try to persuade them to come back. The men knew where home was, and they knew how to get there. If they decided that they'd had enough, they were free to leave at any time.

This did not please the women one bit, and they continued to petition the council, ignoring the rebukes for speaking out of turn or getting more involved in the politics than was appropriate for a woman. This was a unique situation, true, but that did not mean they could completely ignore the rules of propriety. There were plenty of older men whom they could speak to and ask to bring their grievances before the council properly.

Nendawagan, having spoken her piece and knowing nothing good could come from rubbing everyone's face in it, decided to back off. She did notice, however, that Netami took it upon herself to try and explain her mother's position to other girls her age who were also struggling.

She tried to encourage them, tell them that their fathers were heroes who had fulfilled their purpose in life. Few responded to this in any positive manner, at least right away. Perhaps in time they would understand, Nendawagan thought, and made no move to silence her daughter, no matter how often the other mothers rebuked her for Netami's behavior.

It was another moon before the fruits of her speech started to make themselves known, or that was how the others framed it. If they had been heeded, and the men brought home, everything would be fine. But because the council supported her position, now they had wounded to care for.

There were only twelve wounded, but it may as well have been twelve hundred for as well as the women at large handled it.

"What's going on out there?" Nendawagan asked of one man, trying to distract him from the work she was doing.

"An attack on a supply line," he managed through gritted teeth. "One wave of soldiers to attack the line, draw our attention. A second wave ready for us when we got there."

She nodded absently, focusing on her work. He'd been shot multiple times. She used Touch first, feeling her way through his body. First she had to determine whether any of the bullets were still in his flesh; they had discovered early on that lead was poisonous. If a bullet remained lodged in the body, it would slowly kill a man, even if the wound was healed.

She did discover one, crammed into a nook between rib and spine. The easiest way to remove a bullet in soft flesh was usually just manipulating the surrounding tissue to push it back out—hardly painless, but extremely effective. When it was lodged in bone, however, things got a little more tricky and a lot more painful. It involved using the tiniest bit of Galo'ondiha ale Agi'a to dislodge the unwanted object. The sharp edges of the bullet were bad enough as it was then forced back out, but the broken bones were not easily ignored either.

Once the foreign objects were removed, it wasn't difficult to use

Matter and Time to knit flesh back together and make it so it never happened. Of course, it was still traumatic on the part of the patient, and he was given a pain-relieving tea in his half-dazed stupor, then left to recover a while.

Treating twelve men shouldn't have taken as long as it did. None of them were severely injured; all of them were awake and talking, some better than others as various treatments were performed on them. Despite looking a bit haggard overall from the rigors of war, they appeared to be in good spirits, ready to jump back into battle just as soon as they regained their faculties. A few of them did just that, even before they were fully right in the head.

Nendawagan helped with most of the men, if only because a majority of the other women couldn't seem to find their own heads, and they looked as dazed as some of the patients.

When everyone had been taken care of, she made another round, taking cups of tea which Netami had prepared and handing it out.

As the men came back to life, the women began demanding news of the others, usually a specific husband or brother or son. Nendawagan wouldn't say she didn't pester the men for news of her husband or sons, but she did not crowd around like the others.

"Most were all right," one man said. "I couldn't really see much. It's chaotic out there."

That was a common refrain. It was chaotic. There was smoke. There was debris. I was looking somewhere else. There was no reason not to believe such things, but much of the time it sounded like a ruse, a way to avoid answering tougher questions.

For as much as Nendawagan tried to keep a level head and be something of a role model for the other women, even she couldn't help but ask at last, "What news of Ola Achukma or Yvgidahi? Or my sons, Galiliga and Tsona?"

One of the men waved a hand as he used the wall to get to his feet. "Ola Achukma wasn't even there. He was on some other errand. Yvgidahi hasn't done much fighting lately; he's been working more with the commanders. The legion is sorely depleted, and the white commanders don't know how to lead a Native battalion. He's their go-between."

"And Galiliga and Tsona?"

"Fine, last I knew. They were being held in reserve, waiting for another anticipated attack in another location."

"Is it true, then?" a woman asked fearfully. "Are the Unioners winning?"

The man shook his head. "Not if we have anything to say about it. They're putting up a good fight, but so are we."

"Unioners are scared to death of us," another man agreed. "Colonel was all bent out of shape about the scalping incident a couple years back, and he still disapproves of it—when he catches us—but it sends a message."

"Now if all the other soldiers could learn to fight like us, we could have this war wrapped up in a couple months," a third man said, sipping at his tea.

Several of the others raised their cups in agreement and a few more stood, ready to go back.

Nendawagan had so many questions for them, but she knew she wouldn't get the answers she wanted. Some of the men genuinely wouldn't know or would be hard-pressed to speculate, others would not say because she was a woman. She would have to wait until her husband or father returned.

No news is good news, she reminded herself, sending seven of the men back to fight. The others would be ready soon enough. It was the younger ones who wanted to get back just as soon as possible. The older ones were a little more content to sit and wait and at least finish their tea before jumping back into the fray. They were also the ones who usually had the funny stories from the conflict, the tales that made the war seem a little less miserable.

And they did not disappoint now.

"You know, these boys like to act all tough, but there are a few ways to remind them that they're not as mighty as they perceive themselves," one began, a twinkle in his eye.

"What do you mean?" Nendawagan asked innocently.

"The boys may know all the plants here, what's good to hide in, what's good to eat, and what to avoid. Not all of them know the plants of the Old Land. That is forgivable, but failing to learn the plants is not. And the spirits have a way of reminding you of your place."

"Come on, Tsiyo, out with it," another of the calmer women begged gently, more of an obligation.

Tsiyo smirked and glanced at another man who clearly knew where the story was going. He continued, "Do you women know what poison ivy is?"

"Ola has talked about it on occasion," Nendawagan answered. "He said he touched it when he was a child and it made him very red and itchy."

The older man nodded. "Indeed, that is what it will do. Now imagine one of these young men here—let's say Ofi—is standing around the fire at night, and he is bragging about his member being larger than those of the Unioners. And another young man—Mahli, for instance—says he does not. They argue, all in good fun, of course. Later on, Ofi comes running back to camp, howling and scratching at his backside. Because he has sat in poison ivy, and now his buttocks are terribly itchy and swollen red. And Mahli teases him again, saying, 'I thought it was your front that was supposed to be bigger than the Union.' "

Most of the women, Nendawagan included, just sighed or groaned, but few were without a smile.

Their fun had, the older men finished off their tea, then stood and prepared themselves to return.

"Don't worry," one man said. "I have a feeling this war is going to be over with sooner than you think."

"We can only hope," one woman said, earning multiple nods of agreement.

Then Galohisdi was opened and the older warriors stepped through to the Old Land.

Nendawagan had once asked if the commanders—those who didn't know about Aktiya Waya or the sorceries or how any of it worked—ever noticed the warriors who went missing. Did they ever wonder about them? Did they wonder about wounds being miraculously healed?

She had been told on several occasions that the chaos of battle was often great enough that such tricks could be pulled unnoticed. If there were many wounded, it was difficult to keep track of who went where. And if a man were miraculously healed, no one was going to pause long enough to question it. If it was a small skirmish with few wounded, sometimes it was as simple as saying that a man pursued his attackers into the trees and came back when he was ready. Whatever misgivings the commanders may have had in the beginning, the warriors had proven their battle prowess more than enough times to be given a little leeway in their affairs, including the occasional scalping. If they disappeared for half an hour but came back without a scratch, all the better for the army overall.

Not knowing anything about war, Nendawagan could only accept the explanation. It wasn't as though the warriors didn't know how to get home if something went wrong anyway.

And, it appeared, something did go very wrong that day.

Nendawagan had left the townhouse after the warriors and was out doing chores when she heard the scream. Upon arriving in the townhouse, she found five women huddled over the body of a young warrior, wailing and shrieking. Nendawagan did not know the man personally, and she found herself thankful only that it was not her relation.

"What happened?" she asked the two warriors who had borne him. "There were a dozen wounded earlier, but they made it sound like things were fine." She gestured to the body which, apart from half a dozen bullet wounds which might have been healed had he been brought back earlier, appeared no worse for wear. "Why was he not brought back?"

"He was missing," one warrior answered. "When we found him, he was dead."

"Was no one able to conjure Time to look for him faster?"

The two men gave her a sneering look and did not answer. After a moment, they moved forward to pay their respects before retreating to the Old Land.

It was perhaps the only part of the war that the women had no part in, the preparation of the body and the burial. That was left solely to the priests. After an all-night vigil, the women went with one priest to the river to be cleansed, while another priest took the body to be buried and a third went to collect his possessions. His weapon of choice would be buried with him, but the rest would not. In olden times, they would be destroyed. But with a lack of men at home as well as a lack of trade, they were now being redistributed to those who needed them. Or they would be, once they knew who would be left to need such items. Until then, the priests simply collected them and kept them in a sectioned-off part of the townhouse.

Nendawagan paid her respects to the family, then left them to their mourning. A death for the simple fact that he had not been found in time. If there was more to the story, they would probably never know, and even if they did, it wouldn't bring him back.

It bothered her in ways she could not readily describe. Maybe because there would be no hero's tale for him, at least, not an honest one. If he had fallen on the field of battle with many witnesses to his grand demise, he would be a legendary figure, a role model for his orphaned children. Wandering off to die alone in the woods, even if he had done some great heroic feat, no one would know about it.

His was not the last death over the course of the Union campaign that summer, but it was perhaps the only one she might consider senseless. And as the months wore on, as Ola Achukma returned to give updates, she could see that the confidence expressed after that first skirmish was quickly waning.

"We're going to lose," Ola Achukma confessed privately to her one evening, having delivered another bad report. It was now September in the Old Land.

"What do you mean?" Nendawagan asked dumbly. "What about all the certainty you had in the beginning? What about the sorceries?"

"The sorceries are nearly useless against invisible sharpshooters, and entirely so against fire. Your father's skills are rusty at best, and the rest of us...Nenda, using the sorceries to make daily life a little more convenient is nothing compared to the power and concentration required to manipulate elements of a battlefield. I may stop one or two muskets from firing, but when a hundred men are shooting at you, I may as well save my energy."

"What about conjuring Time? What about Galohisdi, getting around the enemy?"

"You know how much strength that takes. By the time we conjure, we have little will left to fight." He went on before she could speak. "The warriors of your father's time, they probably could have won this war. Without widespread use of fire, it would be easy. But once the people settled in Aktiya Waya, we focused less on war and more on healing. Our skills lie in the realm of Touch, but Touch does no good on the battlefield."

"What about the ambush tactics, attacking them without going onto the battlefield?"

He shook his head. "We're out of time, Nenda. We're out of supplies. We're out of men. The higher commanders are trying to recruit as many as possible, rally everyone together, but supplies are short, morale is low, and the Union...the Union just has us beat. It's only a matter of time."

Nendawagan searched her husband's face for any indication that something might be salvaged, but he seemed resigned to defeat. She took an even breath. "What now, then? Are the warriors coming home?"

"No." He shook his head again. "No, we plan on standing to the end."

"What will happen to the people? They were so ready to be free, so sure it would happen this time."

"I don't know. The United States will surely punish them for their role in the rebellion, but I cannot speak to specifics. Nothing good. Yvgidahi is torn over whether we should offer them refuge, if only because we lack men."

Nendawagan sighed. "I would advise against it. They would only bring their grudges here and nurture resentment and hatred. The next time some conflict rose up in the Old Land, we would have a dozen or more like Nvya, rising with it with a mind to avenge those wrongs."

Her husband nodded. "I was thinking something similar. We got involved this time with the honest intention of helping, but we can't let ourselves get so tied up in such affairs."

"How is my father doing? He doesn't visit much, even to hold council."

"He is facing the second war that he's lost."

She shook her head. "No, this isn't his war. He followed Nvya because it was the proper thing to do."

"But he is skiagvsta; he is responsible for our part in the war, and he is responsible for every man wounded and killed."

She gave him a look. "Was he deposed from the council?"

"No, but I suspect he will be, when he returns, when this is all over."

"He did not order the men into this war. Surely he hasn't stopped anyone from returning home."

"Not at all. But it is the way of things. Someone has to take the blame. The ones who should are the ones winning this war, but there needs to be some kind of closure."

Nendawagan shook her head. "What do Galiliga and Tsona think?"

Ola Achukma's expression was gentle. "They don't blame their grandfather for the war or its failings, but they do understand the need for closure and change."

"What do you mean, 'change'?"

"There has been some talk among the men, that maybe we ought to do things a little differently. If we are not going to live in the old ways, then we should not govern in the old ways. If we do not intend to make war—indeed, we cannot, with only a hundred good fighting men—then there is no point in having a war chief. There is still some discussion over whether we ought to remained involved at all in the Old Land, but it has been readily determined that we cannot repeat what has happened here."

She stared at him for a long moment. She hadn't realized until just then how dependent she had become on the council being structured as it was, with her father as the skiagvsta. It was not only part of her identity as Krydik, having that stability, but also part of her as well, using her father to have a unique in on political discussion. Not only was she about to lose that avenue, but she was going to lose that stability as well, that relationship between her and everyone else in the village, the governing body, all of it, exchanged for something entirely new.

At the same time, if it marked a new era for the Krydik people, one of peace and relative isolation, could she really be so opposed?

"No one knows for sure what is going to happen," Ola Achukma said, sensing her discomfort. "First we have to make it through the end of this war."

She sighed. "Win or lose, it will be good to put it behind us."

He did not disagree, though he still seemed a bit sullen. Five hundred men had gone out with such hope, such confidence that this was the time and way to deliver the peoples of the Old Land who had been kicked and beaten relentlessly for over a hundred years. Those dreams were now shattered into a cold reality that bespoke of far worse punishment for the peoples even as the Krydik slunk home like dogs to lick their wounds.

Pokkoli Toklo Akucha Untuklo Tushafa

Battle of Cedar Creek

When October came, only eighty of the five hundred Krydik warriors remained. The sorceries kept disease at bay, but it did nothing to produce supplies out of thin air, or cause the enemy to retreat or surrender. Having lost so many warriors meant they now had to mix and match into any units that could be feasibly formed. Thomas was still intent on keeping his Cherokee Legion, but that dream now took second place to simply winning the war—not even winning, but surviving— and the Krydik now came under the command of Jubal Early and his Army of the Valley.

Being so mixed also made it more difficult to use the sorceries. They had to give thought to their surroundings and their peers when attempting to heal a wound using Touch. In the chaos of battle, it might be accomplished, assuming one also had some measurable skill in conjuring Time, but afterwards, it wasn't so easy. Ola Achukma still wondered at how they'd managed to smuggle the twelve wounded warriors back to Aktiya Waya for treatment.

He also wondered how they were expected to pull off any more campaigns after the month of hell they'd endured. The Shenandoah Valley was all but lost to them, with Sheridan's Union army burning everything for miles. Farm, fields, barns, mills, factories, everything that supplied the army. Losses elsewhere meant they could expect no help from the Deep South either. They were effectively pinned in position. Nothing could get to them, and they couldn't get out to anything without going through the Union.

Even the commotion of an approaching rider was met with little enthusiasm. Activity, but not enthusiasm, and there was palpable relief when it was only a Confederate scout. Whatever the scout intended to say, it probably had something to do with the ragged soldiers following not a quarter mile behind.

"Kershaw's boys," someone near Ola Achukma said.

"Because we really need more mouths to feed and hands to supply," someone else grumbled.

For as bad as the Army of the Valley felt, Kershaw's men somehow looked ten times worse. No one asked what happened, for it was plain to see. Defeat. Just defeat. Kershaw himself appeared and disappeared into the command tent to speak to Early. Ola Achukma saw Yvgidahi join them, but he himself was not invited, and he did not ask. What was there to say or do?

Still, his curiosity got the better of him, and he asked Yvgidahi about the meeting later.

"Sheridan is retreating down the Valley, and Early intends to pursue, now that Kershaw is here," the skiagvsta reported. "They think Sheridan believes us cowed, unable and unwilling to attack. If we move quickly enough, we may be able to surprise them."

"You don't sound confident," Ola Achukma noted.

"It is what must be done, if we do not wish to cower and surrender like whipped dogs. But we must surprise them, or else we will suffer tragic losses."

Ola Achukma nodded. "Is this how it felt, when you launched your final attack on the Anigilisi?"

Yvgidahi shook his head. "Back then, we were terribly overconfident. Yes, more than half our land and villages had been burned, but we were certain that it would be different that time. That time, we were close to home and we had the sorceries. Sorceries which had done little to help us because of the Anigilisi's use of fire." He sighed and looked around. "There is little fire here now, but we failed to train for anything but peace. Now, the sorceries might aid in staying alive, but little more." He frowned. "I fear that Nvya and his supporters, including your sons, may have been right all along. Maybe we did strip our people of their identity by moving them to Aktiya Waya. We were once a warrior people, fearsome to behold and devastating in battle. Now look at us."

Ola Achukma took a breath. "Peace is a priceless possession. War is how we keep hold of it."

His father-in-law managed a single, awkward laugh. "Perhaps." He let out a breath. "Perhaps." He nodded. "At any rate, be ready to move out. Early expects to be on the move by sunrise."

The message quickly spread, though its delivery was a little more heartening than simple pursuit. The word was, Sheridan had been defeated in such a place, pushed back by angry residents as he tried to burn more fields and kill livestock. Furthermore, he hadn't considered that in killing all the food, he was starving his own army, too. Now he and his army were retreating like cowards, the yellow stripes on their backs plain for all to see. They were going to pursue the sons of bitches and attack in the night.

When there was just enough light in the sky to see by, the soldiers were up and packing their things, ready to be on the move. The prospect of attacking fleeing cowards went over a little better than going to yet another battle. Only most of the soldiers had guns, and only most of them had any decent supply of cartridges. Most of the men had gotten something decent to eat, though no one had what one might consider a full belly. Even the Krydik who ate far less and had Aktiya Waya to reinforce them were feeling a bit disgruntled and hungry.

As if to reinforce their hatred for the Union, they made a point of marching through the burned area. Nothing but charred remains as far as the eye could see. Harrisonburg, Port Republic, Staunton, Waynesboro, all the crops and livestock, all the barns and mills and factories, gone.

"What kind of a man burns the crops right before harvest time, before winter?" one man growled.

"Or kills the livestock at breeding time?" another added, indicating a rotting goat corpse.

If there was any consolation, it was that the man appeared to have had the sense to spare the residents, at least their lives. That didn't mean that Sheridan was going to risk losing them to the enemy. Over a hundred young men of good physique had been beaten so their legs or arms were broken, and sometimes more than that, making them useless as soldiers. But they were, however, very good informants, and more than happy to point the army in the direction of their attackers.

The following day they were joined by another division, Major General Rosser's cavalry, freshly defeated at Tom's Brook, though they'd escaped with their spirits in tact.

Ola Achukma looked at the horses, wishing he still had his mount. His horse had been shot out from under him the previous year, and he wasn't important enough to warrant an immediate replacement. Or, as circumstances dictated, any replacement. So he had to walk with the rest of the infantry, his only advantage being that he apparently had tougher feet than most of the white men who frequently suffered infection owing to soft heels.

They did not catch up to Sheridan that day, and vigor was swiftly running low. Conversation quickly turned from attacking the Union soldiers to simply skirting around them to find somewhere to resupply and rest a little longer.

The next day, October 12, a messenger arrived with a letter from General Lee himself. After spending some time among the present Confederate generals, a few more commanders were summoned, including Yvgidahi who in turn motioned for Ola Achukma to attend but stay out of the way.

"If we are to die tomorrow, I want you to be able to tell the stories," the skiagvsta told him severely. "You will be our carrier of stories to the widows. To do this, you must know what is supposed to happen."

"If we die tomorrow, it's because things did not happen as planned," Ola Achukma stated.

"All the same. Take the stories back to the people that our names might survive."

Ola Achukma promised he would and the two of them ducked into the tent.

" '...infantry and cavalry numerically as large as you suppose.' " Early read from a letter. "General Lee intends for us to not only attack

Sheridan but crush him. However, I am not convinced that Sheridan is so weak."

"We need a distraction," one of the other generals said, "a way to lure them out of hiding without bringing assault upon ourselves."

"My people can pick some off," Yvgidahi offered.

A third general shook his head. "I doubt he would even notice. Their men are suffering just as much as ours. Disease, bullets—" He shook his head. "—one at a time won't do."

"But," Early began thoughtfully, "we may be able to use your people another way." He pointed to the map. "Sheridan is camping here at Cedar Creek. If we can line up our artillery here and shell the camp, we can draw their attention this way while your people—" He looked at Yvgidahi. "—sneak around and do some reconnaissance. Give us their numbers, their strength. When you return with the information, we can discuss how to proceed."

His role determined, Yvgidahi left the tent, Ola Achukma falling into step beside him.

"I know who I want with me," Yvgidahi was saying. "You are not one of them. Stay here until we return."

Ola Achukma slowed until he stopped, but Yvgidahi kept going, barking for this warrior or that warrior to meet with him. He called twenty in all, and that was as much as Ola Achukma knew about it. They met once more with Early that evening, and that was that. It might have been that the warriors even sneaked down to the camp that night to gather information before the chaos that the shelling would bring.

He remained in his tent for a bit, reading Astogatoge's Bible by candlelight. Funny thing, he used to read all the stories in Ki's voice. He used to know all the pauses, the intonation, the rising and falling. He still knew them, somewhat, but he no longer heard them in his father's voice. They were all his voice now.

He wished he still had Ki's Bible. He wished he could have read it to his sons the way his father used to read to him. It would have been the one thing that his boys got from their grandfather.

But that was neither here nor there. Few of the peoples were interested in the Bible or any Christian teachings, believing them to be the weapon that uprooted their ancestors and stripped away their traditional livelihoods. At this point in the war, most had settled into the idea of agreeing to disagree. If two men of different beliefs were going to die tomorrow, well, they would quickly see who was correct.

Was that peace? Ola Achukma thought bitterly, closing the Bible and tucking it in his bag. Some days he didn't know what to believe. Did any greater being see this war? Did anyone out there care? Why were the native people always on the losing side? Had they done something wrong? What could they do to improve their lot?

Or had the sorceries been that gift, that way out, and they just insisted on remaining tied to the Old Land? Perhaps the fault was solely on them.

Whatever the case, there was nothing they could do about it now except see it through to the end. If this attack on the Unioners didn't go as planned, that end might come sooner rather than later, in more than one sense.

Ola Achukma was not part of the group that rolled the artillery over hill and dale to begin shelling the Union camp the following morning, though it was still clearly heard.

"You think them Unioners really was bluffing?" a young kid no more than twenty-two asked, shining up what remained of his boots.

"I don't know," Ola Achukma replied modestly, focusing on his own project, ensuring his rifle was in good working order, though he had only a handful of cartridges.

The kid shifted position as he switched boots. "I mean, if I was a Unioner, an' I woke up to cannonfire raining holy hell down on my head, I'd want to attack. Wouldn'you? An' if I was me an' I was there, doing the firing of the cannons, an' a army came running after me, an' I knew I didn't have a lot of men to back me up, I'd turn tail and run back to where my army was. Wouldn'you?"

Ola Achukma nodded. "Probably. That's how a lot of our people waged war, back in the day. Lure the enemy after you by making him believe he has the advantage, then ambush him at a place where he is weakest."

"Yeah, just like that. Why don't they, though?"

"I don't know. I'm not there. I don't see what they see or know what they know."

His thoughts remained firmly fixed on Yvgidahi and those scouting for an advantage, and he did not breathe any sigh of relief until he saw them return to camp with those who had shelled the Union army. Ola Achukma had never held so much respect and esteem for his father-in-law until the war, and now was no different. Any time the man went out on some mission, or even a simple errand, he seemed to shed years until he was a young man again, off to win his name.

Tsona had gone with the group and he had never looked more of a man. He had a purposeful stride and a gleam in his eye that bespoke pride in himself, his people, his cause. Ola Achukma couldn't help but admire him for it. His son had a reason, had a purpose. He wished he could capture the moment and show it to the women in Aktiya Waya. Their men were real men again.

Then the moment passed. The groups dispersed. Tsona went to find his brother, and Yvgidahi retired to the command tent to converse with the other officers. Ola Achukma was not invited to the command tent, so he followed his son instead.

"What did you find out?" he asked Tsona, trying to sound a bit casual.

"They are disorganized, and not very bright," Tsona replied a bit haughtily. "They think themselves secure, that they have won the war. They leave their left side wide open."

"Could it be bait, to lure us into an easy slaughter?"

His son shook his head. "No. The men of that camp were lazy, disorganized, some were drunk. Even the commander spoke ill of their general and the idea of making defenses."

"How many men do you think?"

Tsona stopped and turned to face him. He gave a quick glance around and lowered his voice, though he was hardly disheartened as he reported, "Twenty-five thousand, even up to thirty. But they do look to have a powerful cavalry, and they have more artillery than we do."

Ola Achukma grunted. "Did Yvgidahi and the others speak much on the return?"

"Yvgidahi worries that we lost the advantage of surprise with this display, but that is all I know of such things."

"Well, I suspect we will find out more soon enough."

As long as one's definition of "soon" was somewhere in the vicinity of four days. Ola Achukma was never invited to the command tent, and Yvgidahi was tight-lipped about the details, but the raised voices and the stress on all of the commanders was very much in evidence. From what little could be gleaned, there was initially some disagreement over whether they ought to attack and take the advantage of surprise while they had it, or divert to resupply in the nearby towns.

Early gave the order to attack.

After speaking to other commanders, Yvgidahi gathered the remaining Krydik.

"You're all being assigned to Gordon's column under Atkinson," he announced. "Any who were with me to scout the camp, Atkinson wants you close to him especially. We're going to be following a little pig path to flank the camp. I will be ahead with Payne's cavalry to escort you to the area, but then we have our own task. We leave just as soon as it gets dark."

Ola Achukma glanced at the sky. It was already well into the afternoon.

Earlier in the war, when they still had food and supplies, there might have been a mad rush to hurry up and pack, stuff one last meal in one's mouth before going to potentially puke it back up on the battlefield. Now, there was little to do but find the appropriate unit, the appropriate commanders, and wait to leave.

"You think the Unioners have food in their camp?" someone wondered. "If they have more men than we do, they must have more food."

"They been takin' everything they get they hands on," someone else grumbled. "Why not food, too? I'm sure they got somethin'."

More than a few stomachs growled.

Ola Achukma spotted Colonel Atkinson speaking to Brigadier General Evans just a minute before Major General Gordon started calling for formation. He reiterated everything Yvgidahi had said, that they were the flanking unit and would be sneaking around in the mountains on a pig path in order to surprise the Unioners. They had the farthest to go, so they would be leaving first.

It was about eight o'clock when they finally left camp. Ola Achukma spotted Yvgidahi at the head of the cavalry force, riding alongside Colonel Payne. Toward the head of the infantry, near Atkinson, he also spied Tsona. Not far from him, though not as special as those who had gone scouting the Union camp, Galiliga also marched along, the spitting image of his grandfather as a young man.

The pig path was not only steep, but narrow as well, and progress slowed to a crawl as they were forced to move single file through some areas. Only when they reached the railroad did Ola Achukma dare to feel relief, but as they crossed the north fork of the Shenandoah River, he knew terrible anxiety. It was nothing new of course, for any man who claims not to be anxious before battle is either a liar or a fool, but there was a certain sense of certainty that accompanied this anxiety. This battle would determine whether the war continued, or whether the South surrendered. That was a disquieting thought.

They halted briefly to ensure that everyone had crossed safely and to scout the area for movement and location. Thick fog could disorient even those most familiar with the area, and that morning was no exception. They positioned themselves for attack, the camp before them still sound asleep.

Ola Achukma made sure to keep his sons in his sights as much as he could even as he watched Yvgidahi and the small cavalry escort break off to slide around the camp and fulfill whatever special mission they were tasked to accomplish.

"We wait until Kershaw sends those bastards in the trenches running for the hills," someone said. It might have been Atkinson, or just someone who sounded like him. Ola Achukma did not reply, just turned his attention toward where he judged Kershaw's men to be, though fog still obscured everything more than ten feet in front of him.

An unsettling silence weighed upon the landscape as the earth held its breath, waiting to drink blood and feed on corpses.

Then a sound rattled the fog, flying toward Ola Achukma like a bird fast in flight, chased by a predator. Men, running. It started as a low rumble, like thunder in the distance. Then came the piercing cries of surprise and a few strangled garbles of death.

The sudden transition from perfect stillness to chaotic movement began to stir the fog, and Ola Achukma could make out vague shapes in the distance. Men, a few dragging coats or hanging onto boots, some in only their underclothes, running blindly across the land, screaming, shouting for help.

"Ready!" Atkinson roared.

More from muscle memory than conscious thought, Ola Achukma raised his rifle.

"Aim!"

There was little to aim at, but he did so obediently.

"Fire!"

They were able to repeat this twice before Kershaw's men got too close, and they were at too great a risk of firing on their own men. When that happened, Atkinson gave the order to attack, to chase the bastards all the way back to Winchester and beyond.

Ola Achukma stood and ran into the fog. They descended on their target camp with terrible ferocity. More soldiers, most of them barely dressed beyond decency, could do little more than run. If they were lucky, they were able to grab their rifle or their coat, rarely both.

"Them natives are here!" someone screamed. "They gonna scalp us!"

There was no time for that now, but his cry gave some joy to the Krydik and other peoples who heard him. As they sent up their war whoops, it encouraged other peoples to do the same. Even some of the white men took it up, making it sound as though the entirety of the army sweeping through the camp was comprised of natives looking for scalps.

The sudden boom of a cannon interrupted the trance, and Ola Achukma dove for the ground. He was not the only one, and he and a dozen others wiggled around on the ground like worms for a minute, trying to figure out where the artillery was and which way it was pointing. A sudden explosion of dirt and gravel not twenty feet from Ola Achukma answered that question, and the men scrambled for cover.

After that, it all turned into a game of what the white men called "chicken." Who was brave enough to stand and try to shoot at those who manned the cannons, and who was smart enough to be able to time it correctly so they didn't lose their heads? It was not a fun game to play. Personally, Ola Achukma even preferred facing a cavalry force compared to artillery. At least a cavalry force still had to get within range in order to deal damage.

The shelling did not last long, for it had only intended to buy the Unioners time to grab their guns and run. There was, however, a secondary round of shelling coming from somewhere else, another camp that had heard the attack and was not presently under siege and so able to come to the aid of their fellows.

More cannonballs buried themselves in dirt, tents, and men's bodies. Then, for a brief period of time, long enough for the men to realize the pause and exploit it for about fifty yards, the shelling stopped. Peeping around a Union tent and peering through moonlit fog that was beginning to dissipate, Ola Achukma was able to make out the third column of Confederates, Wharton's men, coming on the Union's other flank, entirely unimpeded.

Amid the chaos and screams of the wounded and dying, Ola Achukma was able to make out two distinct and very different orders. The first, coming from those who had just been blindsided by Wharton's men: Retreat! Retreat! To Grover's line! Another, seemingly emanating from the same area: Hold the line! Keep the rebels back! Reform and be ready to attack!

As the Union soldiers finally found enough time to pull on their jackets and ready their guns—some soldiers still comically without pants— orders came down for the Confederate men as well. Rally at a safe distance at a certain point and be ready for a fight. The element of surprise was still on their side, but they couldn't let themselves become scattered.

Still trying to time out the cannons, Ola Achukma broke cover and retreated to where the rest of the men were again forming up. He leapt and rolled behind a rock, narrowly avoiding what might have been a fatal bullet wound.

The two sides again engaged in a game of chicken. To the north, toward the plantation, supply trains and other slow-moving or lightly-armed units were making a hasty retreat.

The Unioners were unable to hold their line forever and they eventually fell back. The plantation was abandoned and the blue coats broke and ran. At the first opportunity, the call went out for the Confederates to advance. Ola Achukma and the rest jumped out of their hiding spots and raced toward the retreating Unioners.

The farthest of the Union camps had been able to form a proper defensive line and they gave swift, deadly cover to their fleeing comrades.

A cavalry brigade burst onto the landscape, and only Yvgidahi's distinctive war whoop kept Ola Achukma and the others from aiming for either him or his horse in the foggy chaos. Rifles flashed, swords sang, and men fell. The three hundred horse escort cut down dozens or hundreds of men even as they themselves made for safety.

Ola Achukma was close enough to hear Yvgidahi's somewhat loud conversation with Early.

"Sheridan isn't here," he reported.

"What?" Early hissed, more from disbelief than being unable to hear.

"He's not in camp or the surrounding area; he wasn't with the supply chain or any of the units fleeing the manor. He's not here."

"Damn his eyes!" Early huffed. "Well then I hope his men remember him for the coward he is. We've got them on the run; I see no reason to stop now. Regroup with the others and be prepared to hit this line hard before it has a chance to solidify into something more than a nuisance."

Yvgidahi gave some sound or gesture of affirmation, then turned his mount and rode off, calling to others of the group.

The Unioners continued to flee behind the line. A few at a time, the fastest of the group, and the line held. As the bulk of the force arrived, some wounded more severely than others, the soldiers could no longer remain in decent formation. Heavy shelling was ordered, breaking them up even more, like bringing boots down upon an infestation of mice. With the men in disarray, the cavalry was given the order to charge.

Another line of Unioners broke formation and fled to yet another line, this one a little more sturdy and better able to absorb the fleeing men.

With so many men having fled and regrouped, this line proved to be a little more formidable. Eventually, Ola Achukma ran out of cartridges for his rifle. He had only a half dozen arrows which he used up in short order and to no great effect. He scavenged a few supplies off nearby bodies, even managed to control himself well enough to weakly conjure Time and run out into the middle ground and scavenge some from bodies there.

By the time he used up those cartridges, he was exhausted and not a little hungry. Looking at the line and immediate area, now finally free of fog, he saw that they did not have nearly the numbers they should have had.

"Focus, men, focus!" someone shouted.

But where were the men? Sure, some were still dutifully firing and reloading, but a great number of soldiers seemed to have disappeared.

Ola Achukma spotted a group of men breaking away from the line. He might have suspected they were also looking to scavenge cartridges, except they passed by numerous men, apparently intent on another prize. Curious, and also out of cartridges himself, he followed them.

He soon found where a good number of soldiers had gotten off to. They had returned to the Union camps to pillage whatever they could find. The greatest prize seemed to be food, although boots and clothing were a close second. Cartridges and anything battle related seemed to be the furthest from the mind.

Ola Achukma could only watch for a long moment until he spied his eldest son just leaving a tent, pawing through a bag.

"What are you doing?" Ola Achukma demanded. He snatched the bag from Galiliga's hand. "You're supposed to be fighting. The battle is that way." He pointed in a vague direction.

"We're hungry," Galiliga told him. "We're tired. We want more than a dumb creek to show for our efforts."

"If we take this 'dumb creek' then I'm sure you can loot all you want. But until it is ours, it is not yours. Where is your brother?"

"I don't know. Last I saw him, he was still fighting."

"How long ago was that?"

"I don't know."

Ola Achukma sighed and looked around. His son was not merely one of a dozen misfits shirking his duties; there were literally thousands of men, including officers, plundering the various camps. Finally he looked back at his son.

"Is this the tale you want told of you? That you abandoned your brothers—your brother—and went to take a prize that was not yours? Because everyone in Aktiya Waya, including your mother, will hear of this."

He could see the shame cross his son's face, but he didn't stick around long enough to know what Galiliga decided. He dropped the pilfered bag, scavenged a dozen cartridges, and returned to the line where the fighting had died down.

The Union had managed to regroup into a respectable line in an advantageous position, and now both sides were wondering just what to do with each other. The Confederates had held the advantage throughout the morning, but now they were on low ground and the bulk of the army was in disarray. The Union held the high ground, but they had high casualties and had just abandoned their camp and a good portion of their supplies.

Ola Achukma returned to his position just as Yvgidahi and half a dozen riders approached Early who was studying the Union line through a spyglass.

"Their cavalry is strong," Yvgidahi reported. "We're not going to break that line."

Early grunted. "And if we attempt to strike the middle, they'll fold on us." He lowered the spyglass and snapped it shut. "Like a fly trap." He frowned. "I don't care for the situation." He glanced only once at the cannoneer beside him before barking, "Cease fire!"

A few cannons belched one last ball of fire and lead, and the line fell silent.

Early turned to Gordon. "Keep an eye on those sons of bitches, but don't attack. I need to figure out where the hell our men have run off to."

Ola Achukma could only imagine what was in store for the men who were plundering the Union camp, and he elected to stay on the line instead. A few minutes later, Yvgidahi approached, dismounting but keeping an eye on the Unioners in the distance. After another minute or two, he reached into his pack and pulled out what looked like half of a peach, though it had a tougher, bumpier skin like an orange.

"How would you like to meet my brother?" Yvgidahi asked casually, using a knife to slice the fruit in half.

Only from the sight of the unusual fruit and Yvgidahi's odd question was Ola Achukma able to piece together what it was. "Is that...the seeing fruit?"

"It is." Still the skigavsta did not look at him as he offered a slice.

"You found the tree, then? When?"

Now Yvgidahi shook his head. "According to my brother, the original tree is long gone, cut down because it was believed to be fueled by witchcraft. But a root of it survived, still tethered to the body of our grandmother stolen by a Raven Mocker. I found it about a moon or so ago, the fruit just ripe." Now he looked at Ola Achukma and made a motion. "Take it. It won't hurt you, and the flavor is sweet."

Ola Achukma took the piece and popped it in his mouth. It was indeed sweet, and after many moons of bland food, he was quite unprepared for it.

Of course, he was more prepared for the taste than the things he saw. Like lifting a veil, he watched as white animals began to appear before him, spread out across the battlefield. Deer, elk, bears, wolves, lions, crows, rabbits, animals he had no name for at present. While they appeared relaxed, Ola Achukma also thought that perhaps it was their presence that maintained the uneasy ceasefire on the battlefield.

He also saw something else, something he might have missed except for its uniqueness. He saw creatures of smoke and shadow, almost identifiable as animals of sickness and death, yet ethereal in form.

"Are these the spirits your brother spoke of?" Ola Achukma asked. Immediately his head began throbbing and he felt suddenly unsteady.

"They are," a new voice answered.

Ola Achukma looked. Only by his uncanny resemblance to Yvgidahi did he know the stranger approaching them now was Anagalisgi. He looked no more than thirty years, yet his eyes and expression bespoke a man with the wisdom of someone who had seen nearly everything throughout the passage of time.

"Is this the spirit land then?" Ola Achukma blurted. "What about the souls of the men who died here today? Is there anything beyond to look forward to?"

Anagalisgi just grinned, like a parent who entertains a silly question from a child. "I am not dead, although these are spirits." He grew more serious. "Where these men have gone, I do not yet follow."

Ola Achukma glanced around at all the white spirits, intentionally avoiding the shadow spirits, as if by staring at them too long he might incur some wrath. "These spirits. There are good ones and bad ones, and it takes no amount of genius to tell which is which. But which ones fight for which side? Do we fight for evil, and that is why we are losing?"

Anagalisgi also looked around a moment. "This war...extends far beyond mere borders and laws, and there are good men and evil men on both sides. But some things simply must happen a certain way."

"But why? Why must our people suffer yet again? Is the desire for freedom and autonomy really so evil? What good is so much better that the punishment that awaits them is necessary?" Ola Achukma took a breath and tripped over several words before asking, "What is peace, Anagalisgi? Is it the horizon? Is it a possession? Is it even real, or just a made up story we tell ourselves to make it seem like there is a reason for suffering?"

"Peace is real," Anagalisgi told him calmly. "It is very real. And it is an admirable goal to strive for. But there is no goal, no virtue, which cannot be turned into an idol and so make us twisted zealots of an unholy cult. Sometimes, peace must be set aside. Sometimes, peace is evil and war is good."

"A time for everything," Ola Achukma quoted.

"Exactly."

"But if peace is merely a means, what is the end?"

The spirit man's expression was gentle. "Love is the end. And it takes many forms. Sometimes it is comforting your wife after a loss. Sometimes it is encouraging your child when he fails. Sometimes it is rebuking a leader when he does wrong. Sometimes it is coming to the aid of a people in need, and sometimes it is letting someone learn a hard lesson by themselves. Because you love someone and you want the best for them." He went on before Ola Achukma could speak. "And for every decision you make as you journey toward love, the decision whether to go right or left, to do one thing or another, each fork in the road is called wisdom. Wisdom allows you to look ahead, to know where your choices will lead."

Ola Achukma studied Anagalisgi for a long moment. "Like Solomon, then? Who asked for wisdom? And Aki always said that God is love. What, then, does that make the Author, spoken of in the Book? Is the Book heresy that should be burned?"

"And sometimes," Anagalisgi said with something like a grin, "the answers will not reveal themselves for many, many years."

"You see the future, then? Are you a prophet? What happens here today?"

The man merely dipped his head once and answered, "The end."

"The end? The end of what?"

Somewhere in the distance, or perhaps it only seemed that way, someone began shouting. Ola Achukma turned and tried to locate the source, but the sudden movement made his vision fuzzy and he couldn't see who it was. When he looked back for Anagalisgi, the man was gone. He then looked at Yvgidahi who still stood there beside his horse. He did not appear to have eaten his piece of fruit.

"Why did you give me the fruit?" Ola Achukma demanded.

"He told me to," Yvgidahi answered. "He said you needed to see him and also to hear some things. I don't know what, and I don't know why. It is not my place to know."

Ola Achukma just stared at him for a long minute, frustrated and confused and barely able to think around the pounding in his head. He hoped the commanders didn't order a charge any time soon; he would be dead for sure.

"How long has it been since you spoke to your brother?" he asked instead, squeezing his eyes shut and rubbing his face.

"The end of the Book was the last time, so many, many decades ago," Yvgidahi replied. "Then I found the tree. We have spoken at length several times since. He has been watching us ever since we've been here."

"I'm guessing he doesn't have any ability to influence the outcome of this standoff?"

The skiagvsta shook his head. "No. He has shown me the Whites and the Shadows and tried to explain things, but I was never in tune with the spirits like he was. Some of the things he speaks of, I cannot comprehend."

Ola Achukma frowned and looked across the battlefield where the Union still waited. Unseen by everyone else, the white spirits and the shadow spirits watched and waited. Shadows lurked among the men on both sides while the Whites stood in the unsettled ground, keeping the mere mortals from killing each other at the invisible behest of the Shadows. He looked around the immediate vicinity. More Shadows lurked. Several looked up at him, realized he saw them. One ran away, its form like that of a fox that had only three legs and all were broken. The other Shadows hissed at him, baring broken, smoky teeth. One appeared as a sickly dog-like creature, another as something like a mountain lion and a bear.

"Some things," Yvgidahi said slowly, cutting in on his thoughts, "I think we are not meant to see."

"I beg to differ," Ola Achukma replied, still staring at the beasts. "I think we are meant to see them, but if everyone did, the war that would inevitably follow would surely destroy us all."

Before either could say more, Early returned, heading straight for Gordon. Without a word, Yvgidahi mounted up and rode after him.

Whatever Early had said or done, it motivated the plundering soldiers to return to ranks, and they slowly rebuilt their ragged lines. A few minutes later, there was a volley of cannonfire. Ola Achukma watched a few Union soldiers scatter, making for boulders or bluffs for cover.

Then came the order to attack. Perhaps it was the seeing fruit still muddying his mind, but Ola Achukma thought the order sounded a bit hesitant, halfhearted. He could see that there were Whites and Shadows in the general area of the commanders, but they were less distinct now, fading slowly as the fruit wore off.

Nevertheless, the great column of soldiers began moving. Gripping his rifle and trying to keep his gaze focused as blurry flashes of white and black clashed in the middle of the ranks, Ola Achukma charged forward.

The Union was not so feeble as they had been only hours earlier. They did not run away; they barely gave an inch. A few men were stabbed, a few shot, but overall it seemed to be little more than a game of breaking the chain, of which the Confederates were sorely unsuccessful. There was another round of cannonfire and a few more deaths or injuries, but then came the order to withdraw.

Ola Achukma, having done little more than grapple with a man who merely happened to be in his way, happily retreated. The man spit insults and phlegm at his back, but nothing else.

As quickly as their little assault had started, it was over, and neither side had anything to really show for it. If there had been any real point to the attack, it was being discussed among the commanders and no one else.

This left the two sides of common soldiers to stare at each other. Ola Achukma wondered about his sons. He managed to pick them out at a distance. Neither one looked wounded in any fashion, although they still bore the look of men who have been chastened by their commanding officer. Well, it wasn't as though they hadn't deserved it.

He again looked toward the Union line. The Whites and Shadows were gone now, but he had no trouble imagining where they were. He wondered if he should ask Yvgidahi about the fruit, where he had found the tree. Maybe at a later time, once this battle had been decided. He couldn't imagine the Union wasn't planning some kind of attack, not after their humiliating wake up call.

The attack finally came in the afternoon. There had been a little cannonfire exchanged, an odd sharpshooter or two, but the Union forces didn't move until about four o'clock.

With all the Confederate forces finally rounded up, disciplined, and set in position, they were not as easily toppled as the Unioners evidently expected. Ola Achukma fixed his gaze on a man he knew was coming for him. No, not for him, for the man behind him and the man behind him. The Unioner planned to simply bull his way through like a wild animal, to act as the tip of an arrow that the rest of the soldiers behind him might also break through.

With only enough time for a single breath, Ola Achukma steeled himself, gripped his rifle, and brought it up with a single, barking war whoop. His rifle connected solidly with the man's chest and effectively halted at least two dozen men behind him. Thinking quickly, Ola Achukma then turned his rifle forward and fired. He watched as the first man's eye exploded in a spray of pink. But the bullet didn't stop there, instead exiting through the first man's skull, tearing through the fleshy part of the neck of the man behind him, and finally lodging itself in the face of a third man.

The maneuver gave the soldiers in the immediate vicinity pause and bought Ola Achukma enough time to duck behind his own line and find a safe spot to reload.

The Union pressed hard and they never seemed to stop. They had to have gotten reinforcements from somewhere. And the Confederates, too intent on plundering the camp, had never noticed. While the infantry kept the bulk of the forces busy, Ola Achukma saw the cavalry slowly work its way around the flanks. He had no time to contemplate this as he fired off a shot, then ducked low again to rip open his last cartridge and reload.

The cavalry joined the fight, but it was hardly at full strength. They were trying to force the Confederates to move a certain direction, but where? And why? It didn't matter, Ola Achukma knew, because the soldiers were about to oblige. Already they were falling back, each soldier giving one eye to the infantry forces ahead of him and the cavalry sneaking around the side.

Ola Achukma was not immune to the fear and panic, and he considered his options. Which way could he run? When did he want to make a break for it? Once they started running, there would be no stopping, not until the herd made it to safety.

The decision was made for him when the Union's final fist came down, another unit of cavalry bearing down on the Confederate cavalry, the last stalwart defense against any sudden surprises. The cavalry and the left flank crumbled. Men threw their rifles at their immediate opponent to buy themselves mere inches for a retreat.

Ola Achukma spotted his son Tsona running as fast as he could, but a great bay stallion was faster still, the soldier on its back leaning out with his sword to strike him down. Ola Achukma changed course to intercept, trying desperately to conjure Time but with virtually no success.

Then, it was as though time slowed down. He didn't know whether it was only his mind or if he had managed to conjure Time, but even he knew that it would not have changed what happened next.

Sword met flesh, a red stripe lancing across Tsona's back and neck. At the same time, Yvgidahi appeared—he was conjuring Time to such an extent that a river of sweat followed him. He kicked his horse to jump and the cavalrymen collided. Yvgidahi was a fearsome sight in his red war paint, gleaming war club raised, lips drawn back in a snarling whoop. The Union solider went utterly pale and dropped his sword.

Everything returned to normal as horses and riders hit the ground in a tangle of legs and broken bones, the horses screaming in pain and still trying to run away. The Union horse managed to get up and flee, the dead rider trapped by his leg in a stirrup and now plowing the ground.

But Yvgidahi's horse did not get up, nor did its rider. Ola Achukma scrambled over the dead horse and nearly wretched at the sight of his father-in-law. He'd been crushed, and only his war club gave any indication as to the identity of the rider.

Not five feet away, Tsona lay face down on the ground. Ola Achukma ran to him, but his younger son's spine had been completely severed in the neck.

He wanted to yell, he wanted to cry, he wanted to mourn, he wanted to burn everything and everyone still on the battlefield. But the problem was that he was not alone on the battlefield and the Union was still bearing down. Resistance had completely fallen away; now there was only retreat. But he couldn't just leave them here to be haphazardly buried in a mass grave. This was his son. This was his wife's father. They had fallen in battle and deserved better. Yvgidahi especially deserved more.

Taking a breath and not caring who saw, Ola Achukma conjured Galohisdi back to Aktiya Waya. He was able to use Galo'ondiha ale Agi'a to move the horse off of Yvgidahi's body and get the two into the townhouse.

He heard the shrieking even before he'd fully recovered his wits, and he knew that one of the voices was his wife. As his vision cleared, someone grabbed him by his shoulders.

"What happened?!" It was Nendawagan. "What happened here?! What happened to my son and my father?!"

"They..." Ola Achukma could not think of anything, and the best he could come up with was, "Your father died trying to save your son."

"And where were you?!"

He took a breath. "I was too late."

She shrieked again, made a lap of the townhouse, knelt beside both of them in turn, then returned to him. "And Galiliga? Where is he? Where is my other son?!"

"I...I don't know."

She pushed him away. "Find him!" she commanded. "Find my son! And bring him back to me alive! I don't care what he says or what he protests! Bring him home!"

Ola Achukma nodded slowly, still trying to process everything that was going on and inwardly grimacing at the thought of returning to the battlefield, not to mention conjuring again. He let out a breath. "The battle and the war is lost anyway. There is no point in remaining."

"Go!" Nendawagan screamed.

He nodded once and conjured Galohisdi, returning to the same spot, unsure if it was even safe. He did not die immediately upon entering the Old Land, so he counted that as a good thing. Looking around, he had no idea what was going on or who or where or anything, but he was able to spot the gray uniforms of the Confederates as they retreated. He started in that direction, then stopped and returned to Yvgidahi's horse. His bag was still fastened to the saddle. Ola Achukma grabbed it and slung it around his shoulder. Then he dug inside and fished out the last piece of seeing fruit. Hesitating only a moment, he ate it and started walking across the battlefield, white wolves at his side.

Pàke Nishinxke òk Chaasch

Aftermath

In the old days, when a woman lost her husband or her son in battle, she was expected to take a year off from everything, even caring for herself. Her mother, sisters, and daughters would tend to her every need, including bathing and dressing. During that time, the woman's job was only to mourn.

Because of the war, this was hardly feasible, and the best Nendawagan was able to manage was three days, not because the three days held any great significance, but because the rest of the men started coming home. More accurately, they crept home, like dogs with their tails between their legs. Sixty-eight of them, out of approximately five hundred, not counting the handful that had been permanently maimed.

There was very little real anger to be found, as everyone was simply exhausted. Perhaps they wished for a sorcery to go back in time, to tell themselves, tell their dead brothers not to go to war. If only they had known that it would be so devastating, and they wouldn't even taste victory in the end.

She only had to close her eyes to picture her son. The priests had done well to lay him peacefully so that his severed neck was not so obvious, but the best they could do for her father was a sheet over his mangled, crushed body, his war club and bow beside him just to mark his identity.

Ola Achukma had watched it happen. He wouldn't tell her at first, saying it wasn't something she needed to hear in detail and she should be content knowing only that they had died heroically, and her father had died trying to save her son. He held to this position for several days, at least until Galiliga returned home, looking more hollow than a rotted log. Only then did he tell the real story.

In reality, Nendawagan was not intended to hear the story. She was just getting home from another stressful walk through Aktiya Waya when certain bits of conversation caused her to stop and listen outside the door.

"He was as youthful and ferocious and determined as anyone had ever seen him," her husband was saying. "He was the warrior of old that Nvya and the others had so desired to be. In that moment, he was the embodiment of the heritage that he and the others sought to protect when they came to Aktiya Waya." There was a low voice, probably Galiliga, and then Ola Achukma continued. "He charged straight for the rider. He stood upon his saddle just a moment before they collided, and he crushed your brother's killer like a boulder rolling off the mountain. But in doing so, the impact was so great, that both horses went with them."

Nendawagan chose that moment to enter the house. Before either man could speak, she put up a hand and said, "It's all right. I heard."

The two men looked a bit guilty but made no mention of it.

"Do you think we were right to go?" Galiliga asked of his father. "We lost over eighty percent of our fighting men, half our council, and the greatest skiagvsta Aktiya Waya ever had who tried for years to warn us against such things. But we didn't listen."

"No, we didn't," Ola Achukma acknowledged. "But that doesn't mean that he was right."

"What do you mean? We went voluntarily. If things had gone any worse, we might have exterminated ourselves, not for any outside force encroaching on our lands or way of life, but for our own pride."

"And I'm not saying you're wrong. But sometimes...sometimes there is no good answer. Sometimes there is only the least bad."

"How do we stop ourselves from doing something so stupid in the future? Even with the boys and old men, we are only, maybe, two hundred. And our people only number six or seven hundred. If we get involved in anything in the next fifty years...we really will exterminate ourselves."

"The way things are is because of the way things were,"

Nendawagan said quietly. "If we want to ensure that the future is not more of the same, we must change the way things are." She poured them all a cup of tea. "My father died for and because of the old ways, and it is no lie to say that trying to stick rigidly to the old ways has caused more than a little strife over the years. Perhaps, with his death, it is time to lay those old ways to rest as well."

"And how do you propose we do that?" Galiliga asked, though there was little malice in his voice.

"I don't know," she admitted. "And I understand that some might see it as yet another loss. But at this point, we have little left to lose, I think. We must save what we have." She went on, "There are more of you who went than didn't who now have a voice in political matters. I think you should be able to come up with something."

"Maybe," Ola Achukma sighed. "but it will not be today."

That much they could agree on, and they all retired to the same fitful, dreamless sleep. Nendawagan never knew if she woke up because of her husband's tossing and turning, or if her sudden waking up caused him to toss and turn and wake up himself.

"I can still see it," he murmured into the darkness. "Every night, I watch our son die, and your father die trying to save or avenge him."

She said nothing, just put a hand on his chest, feeling his heart race.

"What was it all for?" he asked. "Did we really have to sacrifice four hundred and thirty men in the Old Land War just so we didn't lose four hundred and fifty in our own civil war on Hlohi?"

"If we had gone into civil war, we would have lost more than just fighting men," Nendawagan told him. "We would have lost our children, too, and us women would have also been in danger."

"That is true, but was this really the least bad we could hope for?" He sighed. "I spoke to your uncle, Anagalisgi."

Nendawagan got up on one elbow. "What?"

"Your father found the old tree, and the fruit was ripe."

"He is alive, then, walking with the spirits still?"

"Yes, he is. And he speaks such wisdom."

"What did he tell you?"

"Everything that I have been saying. Sometimes it is only about the least bad. And..."

"And...?" Nendawagan prompted.

Ola Achukma let out a breath. "I asked him about peace. What more did we have to do to find peace? Isolation worked for a time. Separating ourselves worked for a time. But nothing seemed to work."

"What did he say?"

"He told me that peace...peace is a tool. As war is a tool. And just as we use different methods to discipline our children, to shape their behavior so they are good people, so it is with war and peace and everything in between."

"What is the final work, then? What are we crafting with these tools?"

"When used correctly, the means point us toward love."

"How does war create love? How does killing men you've never met before, whose existence has had no impact on your life, beget love?"

"I don't know. But more than just Anagalisgi, I saw the spirits he walks with. And I saw what they are fighting as well. And I think that the war goes far beyond simply men fighting and killing each other over land or governance."

She pondered this for a moment. Then, "You said that when the tools are used correctly, they create love. What happens when they are used incorrectly? Hate?"

"I don't think so. I haven't figured that out yet, and Anagalisgi either did not know or would not say. By the time the last of the fruit began wearing off, he said only that I had discovered what I needed to and the rest would be passed on."

"To Galiliga?"

"He didn't say specifically, but it sounds logical enough. Or simply the next generation as a whole. I think few people in the next hundred years will not have an ancestor father who did not fight in the Old Land War."

"Perhaps then we will have learned, now that we are one people."

"There are too few of us left to be anything else."

"Do you think there will be a festival this year? We haven't been able to have one since you all left. Are there enough competitors now?"

"I think there will be. I think there must be. The festival is ours, and we have to keep it that way. It will be smaller, not so many tournaments, but it will happen."

Nendawagan lay back down and put her head on his shoulder. "My father was always a great leader and a great warrior. But why did Tsona have to die?"

Ola Achukma did not answer.

The following morning, Nendawagan and Netami made their now-routine trip to see Mesim. Old tradition or not, she had stopped caring for herself, so her daughters dutifully came over at certain parts of the day to cook, clean, bathe, and dress her, or just keep her company. Much of the time was spent watching her weep, or weeping with her. Sometimes she was just silent. But every so often she would say something.

"I know the men and the remaining council all get together in the townhouse to have their meetings," she whispered. "All day, every day, meetings and more meetings."

Nendawagan nodded as she braided her mother's hair. Across the room, Netami tidied some dishes.

"I keep thinking that your father is there with them, always arguing, trying to be the voice of reason, trying to impart some wisdom. He wasn't always ignored, you know, though it felt like it sometimes. I think you ignored me more than they ignored him." Nendawagan rolled her eyes though her mother couldn't see. "He always felt responsible for everything that happened here, and he always worried. I think it had to do with his being responsible for evacuating the warriors from the last battle in the Old Land, but I also think a large part of it was losing his brother. He said he never felt quite right after that, and even speaking to him in the spirit lands some years later never really lifted that burden of guilt."

Mesim turned, and Nendawagan twisted her fingers in her mother's hair to try and save her progress.

"Why did he have to go, Nenda?" Mesim wondered, tears streaming down her cheeks.

"Because he was the skiagvsta," Nendawagan told her, not for the first time. "It was expected of him. And he was always a warrior at heart." She took an even breath. "He may not have been able to save Tsona, but he did avenge him. And he saved other men in other battles."

Mesim wiped her face and turned back around. "I suppose so. But why...?" She scoffed. "Oh, I don't need to ask the question for an answer I already know. Pride. It always comes back to pride and honor."

"Love, Guka."

"How was that love?"

"We care for the men, for it is our way, our nature. And they fight to defend us, for it is their way, their nature. Those like Nvya felt as though they had been driven away and never had a chance to fight—"

"And those like Yvgidahi and Tsona?"

Nendawagan sighed. "I don't know."

The house was blessedly silent for the rest of their time together, until Popokus showed up to help with midday chores and Nendawagan and Netami departed.

Once they were a fair distance from the house, Netami asked, "Do you think things will change much, once the men are out of session?"

"I don't know. Maybe," Nendawagan answered tiredly. "Some of those from Deer Clan and Eagle Clan arrived yesterday, so I expect the meetings will continue for a while."

"Do you think Tsitsa will present my idea to them?"

"If he does, I expect he will disguise it as his own idea, or maybe Galiliga's."

"But why?"

"Because for one, you're still a child. You have had to experience many terrible things over the last couple years, but you still have a lot of growing up and maturing to do."

Netami gave her a look. "And it's because I'm a girl."

Nendawagan sighed. "Outside of the women's council, we don't get involved in politics. I was always unusual because Yvgidahi was my father, and because I wanted to be involved."

"You said that it's time to put the old ways to rest. Girls outnumber boys two to one now. And there are no wars to fight anymore, or none that anyone wants to fight. Why can't we have more of a say in things? Maybe then you won't lose any more sons."

Nendawagan took a deliberate breath and slowly let it out.

"I'm sorry, Tsitsi," Netami said in a small voice, her expression saying she knew she'd crossed a line.

She put a hand on her daughter's head. "It's all right. And maybe you're right. Maybe things would get better if we had more say in our affairs. But we should remember that it should always be for the good of the people, not just ourselves. Sometimes we have to set aside our own ambitions for the interests of the community."

Netami considered this. "How did you do it?"

"Do what?"

"How did you manage to follow all the rules, but still be yourself?"

Nendawagan laughed, she thought, for the first time since the end of the war. "Oh, child. I broke the rules plenty of times. But know that for every time that I was right and justified for doing so, there were easily two or three more times that I was not. You have to pick your battles, choose your opportunities, and always do so for the betterment of the people, not out of spite or revenge or selfish ambition."

"But how do you know what's best for the people?"

Nendawagan looked around and made a motion. "You see that baby?"

Netami looked. "Yes."

"What is that baby going to be? Good with a bow? A knife? Will he excel in stealth? Will he be a champion horseman in the festival?"

"Tsitsi, he's only a baby. We don't know yet."

"You're right, we don't. But if we love him and want him to succeed and to be a good man, he will need every opportunity and every encouragement. But he will also falter and make mistakes. Some can be corrected gently, others will require a more stern discipline."

"What does that have to do with helping the community?"

"Because a community is made up of individuals. If he is permitted to run wild, he becomes a grief to his parents, a terror to the town, maybe even a danger to other people. If we want to help the community, we have to start with the individual."

Netami blinked. "I don't understand."

Nendawagan nodded and grinned as they continued on their way. "I know. A lot of the time, it's not so simple as a baby. We are all connected in the community, and sometimes our threads get tangled in knots."

"Then you have to decide whether to use war or peace to get them untangled," the girl said, parroting her father. "Because they are tools, as long as love is the goal."

"Something like that."

"Do you think the men will open up the meeting soon?"

"I'm sure I have no idea, and don't go begging your father or brother either."

"Would I do that?"

"I know you would."

"How?"

"Because you are very much like me."

"Is that a good thing?"

Nendawagan looked down at her daughter. "You tell me."

Netami thought a moment, making dramatic gestures. Finally, "I think so. You're nice, and you like to help people. And you let people know when something isn't right."

"Thank you for that."

But Netami quickly followed up her statement with, "So why aren't you like that at home?"

Nendawagan raised a brow. "What do you mean?"

"At home you're sad sometimes, even before Tsona and Tsituta died, and you make me do a lot of the chores."

"A lot of what you have known in life has been strife, which does make me sad. I don't like it when people fight, and I don't like it when they go away. Seeing my father and your father and brothers leave, it did make me sad." Nendawagan huffed a sigh. "But as for chores, you are old enough to do chores, child, and have responsibilities. I can't let you get married without knowing how to be a wife."

Netami nodded thoughtfully. "Does this mean you're going to have a baby soon?"

Nendawagan laughed. "What makes you say that?"

"Part of being a wife is also being a mother. I can't have babies of my own yet, which means you need to have at least one more so I can have a baby to take care of."

Well, she really couldn't argue the logic. All the same, the thought of having another child after just losing one didn't feel right. She wasn't ready yet. She needed to get out from under her sadness first.

"You're not wrong," she said at last, "but I don't think I'm going to have a baby just yet."

"Oh. Is Tsitsa too tired when he gets home from the meetings?"

"All right, that's enough out of you."

"I'm just asking."

"Enough, or you'll get even more chores to do."

This wasn't to say that Nendawagan wasn't amused, and she put her daughter to work only so she could smile and be embarrassed in private for a few minutes. It was definitely different raising a girl. Considering that Netami really was very much like her, she held a new appreciation for all the grief she had once caused her own mother.

She made mention of the conversation to Ola Achukma that night, who was indeed tired from the meeting which had run very late.

"So this is Netami asking for the baby," he said, his voice amused in the darkness.

"We need to have one, that way she can practice being a mother," Nendawagan told him jokingly. "I'm doing a very good job of educating her in how to be a wife, but how is she supposed to be a good mother if she has no younger siblings to practice with?"

"I see." Nendawagan felt her husband shift position and put a hand on her hip. "Sounds like a good deal to me."

She sighed and put her hand over his to stop his caress. "Ola...it feels wrong, like we're replacing Tsona."

He withdrew his hand, and she could feel the anticipation in the air dissipate. "Nenda, nothing we do is going to bring him back. He was a man grown, even, fully capable of making his own choices. What do you think he would say if he saw you give up like this?"

"I'm not giving up, I just..."

She didn't even know.

"My mother lost two children," he said. "It took a while, but she eventually learned to love again and she had my brother. But there was so much time between us that I didn't really see him as a brother."

"And you think another child is going to have a brotherly relationship with Galiliga, who is more than twenty years old?"

"I don't know. Probably not until they are both well old enough and trained in the sorceries that they are more of an apparent age and experience. Same with Netami."

"Ola, we only just lost Tsona. I can't."

He put his hand back on her hip. "Then we won't make a baby tonight. Let's—"

She shook her head though he couldn't see and rolled away from him, saying, "I can't. Not tonight."

His disappointment was obvious, even in the dark, and she couldn't help but feel a little guilty.

She tried not to seem too sad over the following days, remembering Netami's comments, but it was difficult. Her first distraction came when the private meetings were finally opened up to the public. It was nearly two moons since the end of the war, and everyone eagerly gathered in the townhouse at twilight.

Nendawagan was hit with a wave of vertigo as she entered the stone building. She fully expected to see her father sitting in his usual spot, pipe between his teeth, in that posture he always slipped into when he was deep in thought and trying to make his opinions and reasoning known as clearly as possible. She could picture it so perfectly, she was briefly forced to wonder if she weren't hallucinating. Or maybe it had all been a dream. Maybe the body had been misidentified in some way and he'd spent the last two moons huddled in private conference.

But then, all the men who had attended the meetings would have known, including Ola Achukma, and she and her mother would not have spent so much time in mourning.

Looking around, there did not appear to be very many men at all, which was to be expected, but still a shock to see it laid bare. As Netami had said, the women outnumbered the men by a stunning margin, even counting the children.

Only two from the council had survived the war, if only because they were the older men who could not fight. Part of the private meetings, then, had simply been finding replacements for the rest. It was Ihya, as frail as a frosted flower and just as thin, who led the meeting. He could barely stand to announce the start of the meeting, and Nendawagan wondered if much of the delay in opening up the meeting had to do with his near inability to complete a sentence without becoming winded. But his mind appeared clear, perhaps the clearest of all of them.

"We have come a long way in the last one hundred years," he huffed, his voice as delicate as his body. "When the first Aniyvwiya made the Great Migration, there was much fear and uncertainty over what would become of those back home, in the Old Land. When it became clear that our stay was not as transitory as we might have hoped, we bent our backs, dug in our heels, and went to work making this place our home. While we flourished, thanks not in small part to the sorceries given to us by Anagalisgi who sacrificed himself to bring us here, those in the Old Land suffered.

"Decisions were made. We could not turn a blind eye to the suffering of others, be they Aniyvwiya or anyone else. So we brought other peoples here. Lenape. Choctaw. Even sworn enemies such as the Creek, the Sioux, the Apache, and others. Because we were prosperous and wished to be generous with our fortune. We gave others a chance to live freely, without fear of subjugation and with the ease of life that the sorceries had provided."

Ihya paused, wheezing to catch his breath. Someone brought him water which he drank gratefully and sat down. It was still another long minute before he was able to continue.

"What we failed to realize was that while we lived peacefully, others did not. Some had known only fear and subjugation, and these things were brought here as readily as elders and children. Our lives were different, our experiences were different. And just as they had been terrorized by a people with great weapons and power, so we also appeared to wield great weapons and power. Every peaceable thing we said only held echoes of broken promises and bad faith.

"There was much conflict. Some was quelled through peaceful means. Other bad energies were diverted, a rushing river channeled instead for good use. And still some issues could only be resolved with a hard line between life and death."

The elder looked around, and it was unclear whether he was nodding or if his head was simply bobbing. "Yvgidahi often called for peace, for unity, as these were the things he believed in. 'Let many different streams flow together into a mighty river,' he would say. He did what he could to make others feel welcome, feel accepted, and no one ever questioned that his love for Mesim was genuine. He truly believed that we might one day live and act as one people.

"But it is no small feat to put dreams into practice, and he enlisted the help of others to help him realize this dream. Though he often felt that for every step we took toward unity and peace, we took two steps away. We took a step forward as the festival of tournaments was born, but two steps back as a new village was established, its intent uncertain as the people were often fearful of those in Aktiya Waya. We took a step forward as a new common language was born, but two steps back as one clan elected to stay as far away from Aktiya Waya as possible, shunning nearly everything and everyone and even bringing about the first violent rebellion this place has known.

"Then word got around that the peoples of the Old Land were not only being attacked, but that if they won the fight, won the war, they had a chance to be free. Another decision had to be made. Did we turn a blind eye to both their suffering and their goal? Or did we become engaged in a war when we already had strife here?"

Ihya took up his staff and, with the help of it and two other men beside him, got to his feet. "Yvgidahi did not return often, to report on the war. But I remember once, when he did, he said to me, 'I fear that I have been wrong this entire time. I fear that my quest, my desire for peace among the people has robbed each man of the peace within himself. For in the likes of the tournaments, every man is pitted against his brother, vying for supremacy. We say that it is to redirect a man's frustrations, but I fear it only enhances them, for he has nothing outside himself to bind him to his opponent.

" 'It is for this reason,' he said, 'that our ancestor fathers were able to hold a nation of thousands together, because though he may compete against his brother, there was always the greater purpose for this competition, a struggle for survival. Lacking a greater opponent that can only be defeated through cooperation, a man finds he must prove himself in other ways. He finds that he no longer trains with his brother, but against him. For it is a man's nature to look for a problem to solve. If his brother is his only problem, he will desire to solve that problem any way he can, at the expense of all other concerns. A man does not wish to waste away to nothing, having no merit, no name or titles to speak of. If he cannot solve a problem, he will then inevitably create one.' "

The elder sat back down in a heap, though he looked displeased for it, as though he wished to give a grand oration like a much younger man.

"His words ring true, even now," he continued, huffing and puffing. "We did not become brothers because it was decreed so, or even because we had a common tongue, though that certainly helped. We became brothers because we had a purpose. Nvya showed us that purpose. He showed us who and what we are, what we could be. Our men could be warriors, fearsome warriors who would make our ancestors proud, no matter who they were. And we could use our gifts, our talents and good fortune, to help others. Because that is who we are. We are Krydik of Hlohi, great and mighty warriors with incredible power, come to help and show that the people of the Old Land were not forgotten."

He let that linger for a long time while he drank more water and fought for breath.

"And yet," he went on, everyone straining to hear him, "here we stand, with less than two hundred men—less than eighty of any good usefulness—and women and children who need taking care of. Whether Nvya was right or wrong to take the men to war, I do not know. Whether Yvgidahi was right or wrong to oppose him or go with him, I do not know. But this is the situation in which we find ourselves.

"We cannot pretend that we are who we once were. We cannot cling to the old ways as if we are people of the old ways, for we are not, nor do we all have the same idea of what the old ways are. We have no threats here, and we are blessed with wondrous prosperity, great power, and long lives. We have our own language, our own customs, our own stories, and they will only get stronger as time goes on and more children are born and raised here.

"Our purpose, as Krydik, being stewards of this great power and prosperity, will be to help others. We have preserved ourselves, we have preserved our way of life. We will help others to do the same, the peoples of the Old Land."

"Do you expect us to send our remaining men to die for them?" someone asked.

"No. Such a thing would be terribly foolish. And as it has been well proven, such endeavors rarely end well for our kind."

The other council member put a hand on Ihya's shoulder. The old man looked a bit annoyed, but finally nodded and allowed the other member to speak.

"By this time, everyone has made their choice where they wish to be," the councilman said, standing. "The peoples of the Old Land have no desire to come here. And we have no desire to leave. We—are—Krydik. We are keepers of tradition and keepers of sorcery. This is no small burden and we must bear it as one, always remembering why it is that we help others lest we forget and revert back to the hostility that has brought us to this place.

"Eagle Clan will be the keeper of stories, the tales and legends that define who we are, where we came from, why we are who and what we are. I believe you have little shortage of inspiration to draw from.

"Deer Clan will be the keeper of tradition, the way of hunting and of skinning and of crafting and of taming horses. They will be the guides for everything our ancestors did to live before the white men came.

"Bear Clan—which will be established in a certain location by a certain group—will be the keeper of the tradition of war, how a man is expected to fight, how war is waged, how it is ended.

"Wolf Clan will be the keeper of the sorceries and the gatekeepers to the Old Land. We must explore and learn everything the sorceries have to offer, that we may not be caught off-guard, floundering with half-learned skills."

At the mention of Bear Clan, murmurs had started going around the crowd. Their population had been devastated, and they were expected to establish a whole new village? Nendawagan took note of who did not partake in the whispering, for they were the most likely candidates for starting the new village.

"We will maintain the order that Yvgidahi and Hoka established, that each village, each clan have its own council, as well as a national council. The national council, along with the priests of each village, will maintain authority over the festivals, that we might all celebrate as one people, especially the festival of tournaments. They will also take matters of the Old Land into consideration.

"We do not yet know the results of the Old Land War, how the peoples have been punished. But they will be punished. We cannot send an army, but we can send brothers and sisters to bring food, water, clothing, and tend children."

He paused for a long moment, his posture suggesting that he was very uncomfortable with whatever he was going to say next. He allowed the group to whisper amongst themselves for a long moment before putting his hand up for quiet. Even then he did not speak for another long moment.

"The women among us outnumber the men to a staggering degree.

Not a single man has any regrets about the women not fighting, for such a thing is nearly incomprehensible. Our women are our mothers, our wives, the givers of life. In this way they excel. And it is the women we turn to in order to lead this effort to bring life back to our people and the people of the Old Land. The kind touch of a woman may go places where all the force of an army may stall." He hesitated. "In no way will we force you to risk yourselves or your children, and we are aware that many of you are ready to remarry and have yet more children."

His demeanor suggested he was hoping for a negative response, that the women would back down from such a task. And several did. Then there was one woman who stepped forward and said, "My children have been left without a father, and they have only one uncle left. And though I have never been to war, I know for a fact that there are many children in the Old Land who have no parents now. They will need help."

This ignited a largely positive response from the women, even Nendawagan. She was not the only woman to lose a son or a father. Up until that last fateful battle, she was probably the only one lucky enough to say that she had not lost any children. Thinking about it brought tears to her eyes, but she was able to wipe them away and compose herself. Looking at Netami, her daughter seemed to be taking it all in and working through it in her mind. Nendawagan smiled. She could almost hear what her daughter was thinking, for they were fruits of the same branch.

"For the time being," the councilman went on, "until we know for sure what the situation is, only groups of men will go to the Old Land. There will be no more than four in a group, and the assignments will last no more than a moon. These will be for information only, until such time as the villages maintain their own councils, as well as the national council, and come to an agreement as to what should be done."

He turned as if to sit and relinquish his right to speak, but first he helped Ihya to stand once more. It was a great effort on the part of the elder, and he had to catch his breath for a minute before speaking.

"We are emerging from a very dark, very chaotic time," he puffed.

"But now we have order. We have guidance. It is up to us to maintain that order. We fell out of balance with our own natures, for we have never had to understand ourselves more than we do now, for we are the only ones here to receive glory or shame. There is no one else. But it is in the stillness and the silence that we may hear the most minute sounds, the scuttle of a mouse, the scurry of a rabbit, the slither of a snake, even a leaf falling to the ground. And it is in that peace and solitude that we become balanced and find ourselves, rediscover our purpose and our strength. We must do that now if we are to survive. Take this time of rebuilding as an opportunity to learn and to grow and to balance yourself. Only once this peace is achieved can one discern the path he is to take, where it will lead. We must, as a people, choose our path wisely."

There was hardly room for dispute, and more than a few people looked chastened by his words. Nendawagan spotted her mother, appearing calm and almost clear-headed for the first time since her husband's death.

There was some more discussion over the concept of Bear Clan, where it would be located and who would be the first to live there. Other things were also discussed, but Nendawagan only listened to what she considered to be relevant to her: the role of Aktiya Waya and Wolf Clan, the role of women in the Old Land, and similar things.

"We will adjourn the council sessions for three days," one council member announced, "so that all may have time to discuss this with your own families. Then we will reconvene."

The group was slow to disperse, and Mesim approached before Nendawagan could leave with Netami.

"There was a time," she sighed, "when I would have known all of this, every discussion from every day and every night."

"And every opinion Nocha held concerning every topic," Nendawagan agreed.

"Mhm." Mesim nodded. "Sometimes he even asked for my opinion."

Nendawagan grinned. "He rarely asked for mine, but he got it anyway."

Her mother was slow to manage a small smile. "Yes. And though he often got annoyed with you for it, he did value your opinion, more than he let on. He wanted to create a safe haven for you and your sister, where you did not have to fear being attacked, nor losing your sons to senseless wars, nor being scorned for your choice of husband."

Nendawagan took her mother's hands in her own and looked her in the eye. "Nocha may be gone, but I think he did finally get the world he was hoping for."

Mesim looked around at all the small groups of people, speaking in hushed voices about the meeting that he had just transpired. "That remains to be seen, I think. Our future lies in our hands now."

Nendawagan squeezed her hands. "And we will work harder than ever to make sure it is a good one."

She thought her mother wanted to feel confident about it but was struggling. Nendawagan hoped that she herself looked more confident than she felt. Looking around, there were only a handful of people remaining in the nation who had made the original crossing. Ihya, Adahi, a few others, but almost everyone had either come later or been born on Hlohi. The stories were well known, yes, but the heroes of those stories were fast dying, along with any remaining secrets.

Popokus took Mesim home, and Nendawagan and Netami also returned to their home where Ola Achukma and Galiliga appeared to be in some heated discussion.

"I have to go," Galiliga was saying. "I can't let anyone else make my mistakes."

"Did the war teach you nothing?" Ola Achukma shot back. "Even the best plans can fall apart. There are many factors you cannot control, and the worst one is men themselves."

"I must still try. I have to. I owe it to Tsona."

"Owe what to Tsona?" Nendawagan asked. She didn't mean to say it aloud, but there it was.

Both men suddenly realized that the women had walked in, and they awkwardly shifted their stances, trying to appear nonthreatening. It was Ola Achukma who said, "Galiliga wants to go with Bear Clan."

"Whatever for?" Nendawagan wondered.

"I saw a lot of fighting. I have to help the younger boys understand, and I have to make them realize that…" He let out a breath. "I left Tsona. I left him, I lost track of him, and now he's dead. Worse, Yvgidahi died trying to save him. I don't want anyone else to suffer such a thing."

"That doesn't sound like a realistic goal," Netami stated bluntly. "Wouldn't it be better to stay here and teach them to a new brother?"

Galiliga blinked and stared at Nendawagan who blushed and said, "No, I'm not pregnant. Your sister seems to think we should have many more children, but it's not happening right now."

Her eldest son closed his eyes and breathed a sigh of relief.

"But she is right," Nendawagan went on. "As is your father. Granted, I have not seen battle, but I can't imagine that saving everyone is possible in war, and death plays no favorites."

"But it's not…fair," he said weakly. "I need to do something."

She smiled and now took her son's hands, looking up at his sullen face. "Find a woman. Get married. Have children. Be a good husband and father and help our nation grow, not only in number, but in strength and stature and honor. Be the man your grandfather was, a rock for both the people and the family. Teach your sons everything you want them to know. When Netami has sons, teach them the same. You will do more in this way than any other way. Believe me."

Her son hesitated. Then, "Is there anyone to blame? Is there any way to make it all better, to fix things?"

"I wish there were," Ola Achukma said. "I wish there had been a simple answer that might have brought back my father and my siblings, a simple method to undo our forced removal. But things are complicated, and forces beyond our comprehension move in our midst. And even if there were a single man or a single cause of those pains, removing that man or that cause would not bring back the dead."

"But it would make things balanced, wouldn't it?"

"Balanced in our own selfish view, but we don't know how far our actions stretch. If we hadn't been forced to move, if I hadn't spoken to the Aktiya Waya warriors, if I hadn't gone after Yvgidahi and his warriors, if this or that or this or that..." He shrugged. "We just don't know. We just have to do the best we can."

Galiliga frowned. Then, "I suppose there really isn't much of a reason for me to go to Bear Clan. All the men who are going fought in the war; they have their own stories and lessons to teach. And the boys here will also need instruction of some form."

"And all the women going to Bear Clan are married," Nendawagan quipped. "There would be no women for you to court. But there are plenty of girls here."

He gave her a look. "Is this the sort of thing your mother would say to you to get you to marry and have children?"

Nendawagan grinned. "I might say that I regret not doing so sooner, but then I never would have considered your father."

"Well I'm not going to wait that long," Netami declared. "I am going to marry just as soon as I can!"

"Oh, you will not," Nendawagan sighed. "You still have a lot to learn."

"About being a wife, hardly. I already know all about being a wife; I watch you every day. I even know some of the things that I would change and do better."

"Is being respectful one of those things?" Ola Achukma inquired.

Netami shrugged. "Well I do."

Galiliga folded his arms and shifted his stance. "And what is one of these things that you would do better?" He gave Nendawagan a mischievous look.

"Well for one, I'm not going to have babies ten years apart. Then there's no one to play with. And I'm going to make sure that my last baby is a boy. Girls need to know how to be mothers, so they have to take care of their baby brothers and sisters, but it does no good if the youngest is a girl because she won't have anyone to take care of. And boys don't take care of babies like girls do, so a boy can be the youngest."

"You help with Popokus' children," Nendawagan reminded her.

"I know, but it's not the same."

Nendawagan sighed and shook her head. "Oh, were that you were my mother's child; she would have doted on you."

"All I'm saying," Netami went on, "is that you two—" She pointed to Ola Achukma and then to Nendawagan. "—need to get to work and have a baby that I can take care of."

"That's enough out of you, little one," Galiliga said, sweeping Netami off her feet and slinging her over his shoulder. She protested, but he just laughed and left the house, carrying her like a sack of rocks.

Ola Achukma couldn't stop laughing, but Nendawagan just felt humiliated.

"I don't know if I want to have another child," she admitted, grinning anxiously. "One of her is bad enough; what if we had another?"

Her husband grinned and put his arms around her, rubbing his hands suggestively. "Oh, we might be able to work something out, use the sorceries to our advantage."

"You think it would work?"

He shrugged and pulled her hips close against his. "You want to find out?"

She sighed, but before he could completely shrink in defeat, she said, "Why don't we skip the baby? This time."

Pokkoli Toklo Akucha Abihchakali Tushafa

Generations

It was Wolf Clan's turn to host the festival, and the slope was abuzz with activity as everyone worked to mark the fields, set up tables and targets, and take care of all the little details that often went unnoticed by the general public, that is, unless those details did not get taken care of.

For his part, he was supposed to be helping to mark the race course. But things had changed that morning, and he found himself with a little more free time on his hands. So he crossed the slope, heading away from the main hub of activity, climbing to an area that, these days, was fairly unremarkable. Once he reached a certain spot, he sat down and looked out at all the people working on festival activities.

"Strange thing," he said aloud. "It's been three years, but somehow I still expect to see a larger gathering. Larger gathering, more activities. But for as much time as we put between us and the war, it won't make the boys grow up any faster. We're almost back to where we started, with a footrace, a wrestling tournament, an archery tournament. Hitguttit finally allowed us to host a horse event again, though it's only the race; it'll be a few more years before he'll allow equestrian combat games again. By then, Bear Clan should have something to show us.

"I keep expecting to see you down there. You always were talented with the horses, much like I was, though I didn't compete in those events much. And if it wasn't the horses, then maybe the archery, trying to impress a girl.

"Your brother managed to catch a girl's eye last year, when he took third place in wrestling. They plan to get married this year."

Ola Achukma sighed before continuing.

"She's from Bear Clan. And one of the traditions that has stuck with us through all these years, especially during the time of transition, is that men will join their wives in their wife's clan. He will always be Wolf Clan, but he will live with Bear Clan now, about four days to the southwest. The village itself is in deep forest, but they are well within range of the mountains and the plains of Deer Clan. Plus it isn't impossible to think they might not explore further and look for the Sacred One of the Desert even farther to the southwest.

"Your mother finally got Deer Clan into the canyons, showed them the moving paintings, the Sacred Zukatopa, the underground city, all of it. The priests have declared the underground city a cursed place and off-limits to everyone, but the canyon itself is fine, assuming you can get down there. Being the keepers of tradition, they're working on figuring out how to make the paint that moves. So far they've been unsuccessful.

"As for your sister, well, she's finally reached womanhood, though she lacks a great deal of maturity. She has her mother's thoughts and ideas, but very little of the tact and diplomacy that anyone else in the family possesses. Considering your mother and I, her parents, my parents, we're not entirely sure where this boisterous attitude comes from. Whatever the case, we try to counsel her, but we can only hope that it is simply something that she outgrows. Your mother says it might have to do with all us men being gone for so long that she didn't have the male guidance she needed to understand her place, what it was and why it was. I don't know.

"Speaking of us being gone, the reports from the Old Land aren't promising in the slightest. Lee surrendered and the land is officially back under Union control, though many people still swear loyalty to the Confederacy.

"Things for the native peoples have gotten worse. Living conditions, legal standing, anything they ever had to their name has been effectively stripped away. Children are being taken from their parents, placed in boarding schools of abominable conditions, or just given to white families to raise, falsely told that they were abandoned and unwanted.

"Such reports have greatly upset your mother and sister, but there is little that either of them can do about it at this point. Netami is far too young yet, and your mother, well, she has other obligations right now."

He paused for a moment and picked up a handful of dirt, letting the gritty substance slip through his fingers.

"I wonder, sometimes," he said, "about where you are, if I taught you the right things. About the spirits, about life, about God, if He exists. I've managed to keep Astogatoge's Bible safe at home; if anyone knows I have it, they've not said anything, nor tried to steal and destroy it. I know you and your brother were always resistant to such things you saw as 'too white' and the war certainly didn't help this opinion. But now I'm forced to wonder. Are you one of the spirits now, as our ancestors taught us? Are you burning in Hell because I didn't do enough to save your soul? Is there some other answer that someone has yet to reveal to us? And what of the Book and the Author?

"Your mother says I give such things too much thought. But my encounter with Anagalisgi that day on the battlefield...seeing the Whites and the Shadows, what does it all mean? He said that such things would be revealed in time, in many, many years, but it still bothers me greatly. If there is any message or warning that I may impart, I wish to know it. But perhaps it is not my message or warning to give. What, then, would be the purpose of speaking to me about it? Do you suppose there may be more to the story? There are other Books listed in the front of Yvgidahi's Book, including a second one after his; perhaps it has something to do with that. I don't know.

"I say many times that I don't know. Truly, I don't, and I wish I did. I wish I were as great an orator as Yvgidahi was, or any on the councils now. I wish I were as wise as Ihya was. I wish I were as great a listener and mediator as my father was. I feel that I will never truly measure up to any of them. I think your brother still harbors some resentment that I did not accept a position on the Wolf Clan council. I think he will try to work his way into the Bear Clan council, either to his own ends or just out of some spite for me.

"I've never sought power or prestige, and I've never felt worthy of some of the tasks the council or the elders have endowed me with, especially Yvgidahi and Ihya when they charged me with uniting the various peoples. I don't even feel that I played a significant role in such things; the war did more than I ever could.

"For the longest time, I always sought peace. Peace was what my father taught. Always peace. Peace was the goal. It was the ultimate goal, the only goal that mattered. And as I watched peace slip away from here again and again, I declared peace to be the horizon, always within sight but never within reach. Truthfully, it made me bitter and resentful, toward peace itself and toward my father who preached such an impossible task.

"It was Anagalisgi who helped me to realize that peace is merely a tool. The horizon does not change and has no meaning of itself. But a tool can become a weapon. Even peace can become a weapon. And if peace is a tool, then so is war. Seeing the Whites and the Shadows made me believe that sometimes war is the best weapon we have, and sometimes it is painfully necessary.

"At least I hope so. I can't stand the thought of you dying in vain, stabbed in the back by some coward. Because if you died in vain, then so did Yvgidahi. I couldn't live with myself if that were the case.

"I've not tried it yet, but I wonder if I returned to the Old Land and ate of the seeing fruit once more, whether I would see Yvgidahi again—and you, too—or just Anagalisgi. He implied that it was only him that walked with the spirits, and everyone else moved on to something different. I think that's why I haven't gone yet, because I don't want to give up on that hope.

"The fruit trees here are useless for speaking to the spirits. In Yvgidahi's Book, it says they have to be planted in the body of one whose heart has been stolen by a Raven Mocker. We have not had such problems, and the priests are trying to divine some other method of infusing the trees, even new saplings, with the ability to see into the spirit world. I think they could greatly benefit from Anagalisgi's wisdom."

Even as he said it, a gust of wind buffeted his face and he squinted his eyes. In the distance, he spotted a figure heading toward him.

"I know I've said much of this before," he said, wrapping up. "I guess I just wanted to make sure that everything got said before things change. But then, how does the saying go? 'The more things change, the more things stay the same'?"

He stood to meet Natachtu, one of Popokus' sons who was of an age with Netami.

"Tsitsi told me to come get you," Natachtu said simply.

Ola Achukma nodded and followed the boy down the slope, away from the mass grave. "Did she say what it was?"

"No, but I think Netami will let you know soon enough." He added, "Either that or you're going to think she's the mother."

Ola Achukma grinned. "She does seem to have this idea in her head that we need to have children for her. Nendawagan tells her to just wait a few years, get married, then she can have all the babies she wants to take care of."

Natachtu glanced back him, his expression saying that he was uncertain of the social protocol of his next statement. "Tsumi says that maybe she should go to the Old Land and help rescue some of the stolen children, see how much she likes that."

"Maybe once she's older. We don't want her to be stolen either."

The boy grunted an agreement.

The village itself was nearly empty, everyone out working on festival chores, and it was no difficult feat to navigate the streets to get home. By this time, both mother and child would have been to the river to be cleansed. When he finally opened the door to the house, he was not surprised in the least to see Netami holding the squirming bundle.

"Well, Netami, I'm glad your mother and I could accommodate you in your desire for a baby," he said, smirking.

She looked up, grinning hugely. "Tsitsi let me name him!"

Ola Achukma glanced at his wife, brow raised.

"I asked for a suggestion and happened to like it," his wife corrected.

"His name is Sabelu," Netami announced.

He nodded. "I like it, too."

Like taking a bear cub from its mother, Ola Achukma got the newborn infant away from Netami. He was still wrinkled, but clean and dry, with a toothless pink mouth and full head of black hair.

Sabelu. Shining brightly. A fitting name, Ola Achukma thought, a good omen for the days ahead. New life, new opportunities. Oh, there would be some stumbling blocks along the way, no doubt, but things just felt like they were getting better.

He handed the babe to Nendawagan, much to Netami's dismay.

"I want to hold him," the girl who was just breaking into womanhood lamented.

"Believe me," Nendawagan told her, "there will be many sleepless nights that I will happily leave to you if you want."

Suddenly Netami didn't look so sure, as if she'd just realized what she was asking for. She wasn't about to admit it, of course, instead composing herself and giving some nonverbal agreement. Nendawagan shooed her out of the house, then sat down, Sabelu dozing off after a long day.

"And I thought Popokus was bad," she sighed.

"I give her three moons before she turns into you," Ola Achukma said, sitting next to her. "Swearing off boys and children for a long, long time."

"You think? I don't know. I think she's a little more determined than that."

He shrugged. "I guess we'll just have to make sure Sabelu knows you're his mother."

Despite the infant being his fourth child, Ola Achukma couldn't help but stare at him in awe. He was so small, a tiny life brimming with potential. The following morning, they took him to the priests to have that potential divined. Would he be a great warrior? Archer? Storyteller? Rider? A small lock of hair mixed with herbs and added to the incense would show them.

"What do you see?" Ola Achukma asked impatiently.

After an uncomfortably long moment of silence, the priest answered, "History. All the stories and threads of our peoples, pouring out as from many streams into a cup too small to hold all of the water."

"A storyteller, then. A historian."

But the priest's expression was less than confident. "No. These are not the good stories of the people, such as the elders and storytellers share, such as is kept by Eagle Clan. These are not those stories. These are the rest of the stories. Sad stories, tragic tales, black rivers of the memories we wish to forget and work to erase from our minds. But none of it untrue." The priest shook his head. "He will not be a story teller. He will be a truth teller. He will be the vessel of our history and truth."

"What does that mean?" Nendawagan wondered. "Honesty is a prized virtue."

"Will he be like Anagalisgi?" Ola Achukma inquired. "Will he be like the dark seer of old?"

The priest frowned but nodded, his expression twisting into something resembling a sort of understanding. "Yes. Like the dark seer, but not of the future. He will be the dark seer of the past."

"A bad omen, then, to remind us of our failings and mistakes," another priest said, breaking his otherwise silent eavesdropping. Realizing that he'd outed himself, he approached. "We understand our shortcomings; we have just fought a war and lost many men because of it. With our long lives, memories and eyewitnesses are in no short supply." He shook his head. "Clearly this is a bad omen. Not a dark seer, but an evil witch, meant to drive us into the dark. The child should be drowned, the evil spirit cleansed from this place as well as your home."

"What?" Nendawagan gasped.

"We should not jump to conclusions," the first priest said sternly, giving the second priest a look. Looking at Nendawagan, "We will pray about it and seek the spirits. Clearly there is more to your son than meets the eye, and we should not jump to conclusions. The last thing we need is to upset the spirits by murdering one intended for us."

Ola Achukma put an arm around Nendawagan and they left the townhouse before either priest could say more to them.

"Ola..." she began as they walked away from the townhouse. "I don't even know what to think. What did they mean? What does this mean for Sabelu?"

"I don't know," he answered honestly. "But it sounds like he is a special child regardless."

"Do you really think he could be evil?" She looked down at the infant who slept soundly in her arms. "In my father's Book, it was said that lightning from the spirits struck Anagalisgi at his birth, and the woman who nursed him after the death of his mother saw something in him, even as a baby. Ola, I saw nothing at his birth, nor did anyone else. I see nothing in him now other than my own flesh and blood, my own son." Tears started streaming down her cheeks. "Please, Ola, I can't lose another son."

"We will have to wait and see what the priests say," Ola Achukma offered lamely. "It might simply be an overreaction. Anagalisgi was often scorned and ridiculed, but that didn't mean he wasn't right or that he wasn't responsible for saving the people."

She sniffed and wiped her eyes. "What does that mean for the people, then?"

"I don't understand."

"Let's say that he is evil, and we have to drown him. It is only that we have lost a son. But let's say that he is good, a truth teller and dark seer like Anagalisgi. We are the product of what happened to the people because of Anagalisgi. What will happen to the people if Sabelu is intended to walk a similar path?"

Now that she said it, Ola Achukma didn't want to consider it. What did it mean for the people if Sabelu were the new Anagalisgi? Would there be some trouble in the Old Land that they would get sucked into yet again? Would there be some trouble from the Tacagans and the people before and the underground city? Would it be an entirely new danger that they could not yet comprehend? And if they could not find refuge on Hlohi, a deserted island seemingly tailored just for them, where would they find refuge?

More to the point, would the people have enough sense to listen to whatever Sabelu had to say, rather than brushing him off or ridiculing him as the people had done to Anagalisgi? Was this a second chance for the Krydik, a chance to redeem themselves? Would there be another, real opportunity to help the people of the Old Land reclaim their respective lands? There was so much they didn't know, so much he didn't want to know or think about. They'd just gotten out of one war, why should they jump into another?

Looking at the small babe cradled in his mother's arms, Ola Achukma found that he was able to push most of his worries from his mind. Whatever the future held, Sabelu was only just one day old. He'd never held a leaf much less a bow. He could not even sit up by himself, never mind ride a horse. Anything that was to happen would come far enough in the future that they could prepare for it.

Assuming Sabelu had a future.

They headed to the festival grounds to take their minds off what had just transpired in the townhouse. Nendawagan had at least stopped crying, though her expression still conveyed great distress. The ogling of other women over the newborn babe did not appear to be helping matters. Ola Achukma wished he knew how to help, but he could hardly master his own racing thoughts.

They left the grounds early and headed home.

"I don't know what to do," Nendawagan said once they were safely alone. "Should I dote on him, only for the priests to say we must drown him? Should I ignore him, only to be told that he will be great?"

"I don't believe it will take quite that long for the priests to divine an answer," Ola Achukma told her, finally feeling confident in his words. "If the child truly is evil, he ought to be vanquished as soon as possible, days rather than months or years. But if he is good, he must be raised accordingly as soon as possible. Like Anagalisgi, he should learn to interpret his dreams and walk the right road."

She looked uncertain, but nodded and bared her breast for a now-hungry infant. Ola Achukma left her to it, returning to the grounds just in time to see Galiliga wrestle his opponent to the dirt with almost no resistance. There were cheers and reluctant bet payments. Ola Achukma intercepted his son as he left the arena.

"I thought I saw you earlier, but it was almost my turn," Galiliga said, grinning. He was sweaty and filthy but looked quite pleased with himself. "What did the priests say? Is my new little brother going to be a great warrior, or more of a storyteller?"

Ola Achukma faltered. He tripped over his words a bit before gathering his tongue and saying, "Well, neither. Or not quite."

"What do you mean? Tsitsa, you're making no sense." But Galiliga's attention was on his wife-to-be, still watching him from across the ring.

"I mean Sabelu may be an evil witch, and he may have to be drowned."

"What?" Now his son looked concerned, his head snapping toward his father. "They divined this?"

"One priest said he would be like Anagalisgi, a dark seer. Not evil, but warning of evil. Another priest said he was evil and needed to be drowned."

"What, they don't know the difference?"

"They are currently praying about it, seeking the spirits for further guidance. I don't expect it to take long. Regardless, when you see your mother, be kind to her. She's afraid of losing yet another son, this one hardly a day old."

Galiliga dipped his head. "Of course."

He still looked concerned, but the edge was shaven off at the approach of his fiancée. Ola Achukma wished them both well and departed.

One son was getting married, and the other was under threat of death for possibly being an evil witch, all in the same week. If he felt happy for the first, he felt bad for not giving the second more attention. If he felt terrible about the second, he felt worse for not showing the appropriate support and encouragement to the first. Did this really all have to happen at the same time?

Netami was delighted to compete in the women's events without her mother's help, and she had been determined to have as many entries as possible. Ola Achukma had no trouble finding her, for she was more than happy to show off her cooking and her vegetables and her crafts to anyone who would glance at them. Once Ola Achukma had shown the proper amount of adoration for her things, she, too, asked about the divination.

"What do you mean an evil witch?" Netami demanded, too loudly for Ola Achukma's taste, when he told her what the priests had said. "He can't be evil; he's hardly a day old. And he did no harm to Tsitsi when he was still inside her, or during birth. Don't evil spirits cause their mothers to languish in terrible labor, sometimes even killing them?"

"Quite frankly, I don't know, I'm not a woman," Ola Achukma sighed. "But the priests are praying to divine clearer answers. We do not want evil to live, but we also don't want to murder an innocent."

"Do you think it will take long?"

He shook his head. "No. A few days, maybe. The spirits understand the severity of the situation."

Netami nodded once and folded her arms. "He's not evil. An evil witch wouldn't allow himself to be named Sabelu."

Ola Achukma smiled. "I hope you're right."

"I am. Just like I know that Galiliga isn't likely to win the wrestling tournament this year."

"Why do you say that? He's your brother, and he's doing very well in the practice rounds so far."

"He's also too distracted by his wife."

"She's not his wife yet."

"That's my point."

Ola Achukma sighed. "I can appreciate that you are very much like your mother, but at least your mother understands discretion. Do you even know what that is?"

Netami shrugged. "I know what it is."

"Then why don't you practice it more often?"

She opened her mouth as if to reply, then apparently got distracted by someone else looking at her crafts. Ignoring her father completely, she turned and started talking to the onlooker. Ola Achukma just sighed and left the area.

Assuming things with Sabelu went smoothly, and assuming that they decided to have more children in the future, they were only going to have boys. His sister had died at a young age, but he shuddered to think what she might have become when she reached womanhood. Was it like this for all girls, or just his?

He went back to the wrestling arena and watched Galiliga some more, noting that Netami's predictions were probably going to come true. He did well, yes, but he also made several foolish mistakes that would cost him in the actual tournament.

Maybe they should add a new rule to the festival overall: All couples intending to marry within one moon of the close of the festival should instead be married before the festival begins in order to minimize distractions.

On the other hand, such a rule might cause the newly-married men to make even more mistakes.

Just thinking about it caused Ola Achukma to start thinking about how long it was going to be before he and his wife coupled again. If things with Sabelu went well, probably only a moon or so, less if she used the sorceries to heal herself from birthing. If things didn't go well, and they ended up having to drown the infant, who knew how long it would be?

He made for the townhouse, just in case the priests had received a swift answer. One look at their posture of fervent prayer told him all he needed to know, and he went home instead.

Nendawagan asked about Galiliga and Netami in the festival, but they were questions of propriety; her thoughts were clearly more focused on Sabelu, sleeping soundly in the crib in the corner. All the same, Ola Achukma told her of Galiliga's wrestling, Netami's crafts, and Netami's predictions for her brother, including the reasons.

"Were you so...boisterous as a new woman?" Ola Achukma wondered.

Nendawagan gave a shy smile. "I won't say I couldn't be so obnoxious, but I think it's different being the parent."

"Even so, she does need to be taught some discretion and respect."

She nodded. "I agree, and I've tried talking to her about it."

"Well, she still needs to learn to be respectful. Just because there is the possibility of the village councils and the women's council merging, it doesn't mean that she can fire off her every thought like an arrow."

"I will speak to her." She sighed. "Honestly, I kind of wish my parents were still alive to teach her such things. Power, responsibility, respect, discretion. I don't know that I'm any good at it."

"You must be if we've raised two brave sons already." She looked at him and he went to her, put his arms around her. "You are a good mother. Netami does need to learn, but she has a good teacher. And I'm sure Sabelu will be just as great."

She smiled though she looked like she was trying hard to dissociate from the infant, lest he be declared evil and in need of drowning.

They returned to the townhouse the next morning, but the priests were still busy praying. Ola Achukma suggested they go and watch Galiliga wrestle, or ogle appropriately at Netami's entries, but Nendawagan simply wished to stay home, in case the priests divined an answer. She wanted to know as soon as they did. The only reason she did not wait in the townhouse itself was because she could not, not while they were praying.

When Ola Achukma returned home that evening, he found Nendawagan at the table, still as a statue but for the tears in her eyes. The crib was empty and Sabelu was nowhere to be found.

"What happened?" he demanded. "Why did you not come get me?"

"They didn't take him to be drowned," she said softly. "Not yet anyway." She shifted position, several joints popping. She wiped her eyes and looked at him. "They took him to the townhouse, to pray over him and offer him up to the spirits."

"That's a good thing, isn't it?"

"I don't know. They are either going to divine his future or determine his fate."

Ola Achukma slowly let out a breath as he sat down. "They must have said something. Anything?"

She shook her head.

All were barred from the townhouse after that. No one but the priests themselves were permitted inside, this enforced by an equally-perplexed council. With this move, soon everyone knew of the infant in question and the question of his nature. It became the primary topic of discussion on the festival grounds, to the point where Ola Achukma had to withdraw and return home to escape the questions and the gossip. Even Netami and Galiliga looked exhausted from those harassing them.

"I hope they come up with an answer soon," Netami grumbled as they retired to bed. "Or else people will start to think we're all evil spirits."

"Hush, child," Nendawagan said, though her words held no malice.

Ola Achukma wouldn't say he hadn't thought something similar, but he didn't like it when such thoughts were put into words.

He didn't think anyone got much sleep that night. When he dared to approach the townhouse in the morning, he found it still off-limits.

"Has there been any news?" he asked, fighting a yawn.

"Not that we've been told," the councilman told him.

Nendawagan did not leave the house. Ola Achukma got as far as the mouth of the cave before deciding he didn't want to listen to even a shred of gossip about his son. It was the first real day of the tournaments, eliminating the slowest and weakest competitors. He might have competed, probably should have, except Nendawagan begged him not to because of how it coincided with the birth. Now he found himself longing for the distraction of running, chasing his competition on the race course.

It was midafternoon when one of the priests in training came to their house and said an answer had been divined.

They ran to the townhouse, though it felt more like a crawl, and Ola Achukma couldn't decide whether he was ready for the answer, even as he demanded to know.

"The good news is that your son is not an evil witch," the priest began. "He does not need to be drowned."

Nendawagan burst into tears as she took the infant from the priest and held him tight to her chest. Sabelu began wailing and she happily offered him her breast.

"You said that's the good news," Ola Achukma stated. "I'm guessing it's not the only news."

"It is not," the priest confirmed.

"Then he is a dark seer."

"He is, like Anagalisgi of old."

"What does that mean? How can we help him?"

"He should be trained in the priesthood as soon as possible, taught our ways. He should be encouraged to dream, to communicate with the spirits and to see signs and interpret them. Most importantly, the people must understand his gift, and they must learn to listen to him, to heed his warnings. The people in Anagalisgi's time ignored him to their own peril. We must not allow such a thing to happen again."

Ola Achukma nodded. "Agreed. Do you have any idea the things he might see, this disaster he is supposed to predict?"

"No one knows, and he has not the words to tell us yet."

"What should we do for him now?" Nendawagan asked.

"He should be placed on a special diet. Mashed corn or corn milk for every meal. Greens and herbs brewed as a tea in the morning. Once he is able to eat of it, smoked meat of a different animal each night. And of course, mother's milk as long as is appropriate. He should be wrapped only in a special cloth such as that—" He indicated the white leather wrap that swaddled the infant. "—or sleep under a similar blanket. When he is old enough, he will wear the appropriate garments of a priest in training.

"Take note of his behavior, for even babies may dream and see signs. Note when he is happy or upset, the people he is around, the animals he sees, the weather passing through. No detail is insignificant.

"When he gets older, if he ever speaks of any dreams or visions, take note of it, and have him record everything just as soon as he can write. Do not worry about the interpretation; we will take care of that instruction. But if he does provide an interpretation, make note of that as well. And be vigilant of everything going on around you, around us, the people. We must not be caught off-guard as the people of old were. We will stand strong against the tide of evil."

Ola Achukma watched as all the joy that had been drained from his wife over the last few days returned to fill her up to overflowing. More than simple happiness, there was also great determination in her posture. Sabelu had a great and marvelous destiny, but it would require the understanding and cooperation of all the people.

"Is there anything else we must know about him at this time, while he is still a baby?" Ola Achukma wondered. "Shall we use sorceries on him, or refrain from it? When should we teach him sorceries?"

"Do not use the sorceries on him," the priest said, not unkindly, "but do not hinder him if he starts to use them of his own accord. Encourage him. Train him. If he uses any sorceries you are unfamiliar with, ask him to teach you."

It was an unusual but also thrilling and terrifying to think that their son would have such command over the sorceries, even greater than Anagalisgi himself. Ola Achukma found himself wondering what Yvgidahi might say to such a thing. Then he considered the seeing fruit, and he wondered what Anagalisgi might say to such a thing. Did he know about Sabelu and his destiny? Would he have any insight?

"Would it be appropriate to rename him, then?" Nendawagan asked. "If he is to be a dark seer, Sabelu seems a bit presumptuous, don't you think?"

"No," the priest said, grinning. "No, it's perfect. You did well to name him this. Perhaps you already knew what he was to be, for he is a beacon to all."

Neither Nendawagan nor Ola Achukma corrected him, and once they were out of earshot of the townhouse, she said, "Don't say anything to Netami or it will go to her head."

"Agreed," Ola Achukma said. "Do you think she will still want to take such care of him knowing all the new rules he must follow?"

"Want to find out?"

As it turned out, for as ecstatic as Netami was to learn that her new baby brother had an exceptional destiny, she was less keen on having to adhere to all the rules that suddenly went with it. She listened patiently, but found every excuse to not have to participate, at least during the festival. Even after things had wrapped up—Galiliga taking sixth in the wrestling tournament—she still managed to weasel her way out of some of the chores.

"And to think, these are only the most basic of rules we have to follow," Nendawagan teased. "Wait until he starts walking and talking."

Netami blanched at the thought.

"It seems Sabelu's first miracle is teaching his older sister discernment and discretion," Ola Achukma commented once Netami had wandered off. "She doesn't open her mouth half as much as she used to."

"A few sleepless nights did that, I think," Nendawagan told him.

"Suddenly she's not so eager to have a bunch of babies?"

"Well, she's not begging me to have more any time soon."

Ola Achukma nodded. "She's gotten suddenly quiet about Galiliga and his new wife having a bunch of children for her to care for, too."

Nendawagan looked at Sabelu in his crib. "Not even one moon and he's already changing things."

"Yes, but how much more will he change?" Ola Achukma wondered. He briefly explained his musings, about finding the seeing fruit and talking to Anagalisgi. "You think he might have any insight?"

"I don't know," Nendawagan answered. "He seems to be relegated only to the Old Land. I don't know what he sees here."

The first step, regardless, was finding the seeing fruit. Ola Achukma went on several expeditions to the Old Land—both authorized and unauthorized—looking for the tree Yvgidahi had found. Then, once he finally found the tree, or what he believed to be the tree, he had to wait until the fruit was ripe, which was easily half a season.

By that time, Sabelu was walking and experimenting with sounds, trying to form words. And though he was a special child with a great destiny, anyone who spent any length of time with him noticed that he was a very serious child. He did not freely laugh like other babies his age, but rather he studied everything with the intent curiosity of an elder. If anything, his experimentation with language resembled an old man who has lost the ability to speak coherently, though his mind still works, and he finds himself frustratingly stalled in his attempts to communicate.

It was September 1869 in the Old Land when Ola Achukma finally plucked a ripe seeing fruit from its stem and ate of it.

He nearly pitched sideways as his equilibrium shifted. He caught himself on the tree before he went down. Every time he blinked, White animals of all kinds came more and more into focus. Finally, Anagalisgi himself appeared.

He looked not a day older from when Ola Achukma had seen him on the battlefield five years prior.

"Anagalisgi," he stated dumbly.

"Ola Achukma, welcome," Anagalisgi greeted.

Ola Achukma suddenly couldn't remember just why he'd come, and the best he could manage was, "I...I'm sorry about your brother."

Anagalisgi dipped his head once. "I thank you, but it was his time. And he knew it."

"He knew it?" Ola Achukma blinked. "You told him."

"I did."

"You couldn't have told him to be there just a little sooner? My son might still be alive!"

Anagalisgi shook his head. "He would not be. And neither would you. Which means your third son would also not be alive now."

"So you know about Sabelu," Ola Achukma said.

Anagalisgi grinned. "I like the name, it's very good. Very fitting, though it won't seem like it."

"Then you do know his future, his destiny. You know what will happen."

"I know as much as I am allowed to know, and I see things only here on Earth. I cannot see anything on Hlohi as I do not walk there."

Ola Achukma let out a breath, told himself to stay calm. He nodded slowly. "What do you see? He's been called a dark seer, likened to you but with even greater power in the sorceries. But this time the priests do not want to ignore him as they ignored you. Whatever danger is coming, they want to be ready for it." He went on before Anagalisgi could speak. "Help me to help my son to help my people. What is going to happen?"

Anagalisgi closed his eyes and did not speak for a long minute.

Finally he nodded and opened his eyes. "As I said, I do not see what happens on Hlohi. I cannot tell you what he will do there, the things he will see or say."

"But he does come here, to the Old Land?"

"He does. He comes here to escape."

"Escape? Escape what? Does it have to do with the underground city? Do others come with him?"

"He comes alone. And with you. And with his sister. And alone again."

"He makes many trips, then. Our threat comes from the Old Land."

Anagalisgi shook his head. "There no longer exists a threat to you from the Old Land, save whatever you create for yourselves."

Ola Achukma looked around. "Like the war."

"Like the war."

He looked back at Anagalisgi. "Why does Sabelu come to the Old Land? What is he escaping from? What does he do here?"

"He will learn the tools of peace and war."

"And does he use them to shape love?"

Anagalisgi made a hesitant sort of sound. "He will not be the most inspirational person, not the best role model for youngsters, but he will do good, even if the people can't see it right away."

Ola Achukma gave him a look. "What do you mean?" He shook his head and asked, "No. Is there anything I can do now, while he is young, to help him?"

Anagalisgi's expression was sympathetic. "The priests may liken him to me, but he will not walk my same path. Do something for him that was not done for me. I did not need to know this, but he will."

"What's that?"

"Teach him how to stay in the waking world."

Ola Achukma blinked. "But, if he is a seer, shouldn't he commune with the spirits?"

Anagalisgi shook his head. "He is not only a seer, he is a vessel."

"A vessel for what?"

"For the people." He went on before Ola Achukma could argue.

"Make sure he stays in the waking world. The spirits will have no trouble finding him, but he must stay in the waking world."

"How do I teach him this?"

"Teach him life. Teach him everything."

"But I don't know everything."

"Make sure he learns that, too."

"You speak in riddles and shadows."

Anagalisgi shrugged. "I know only what I am allowed to know, and in this case, I am blind in one eye."

Ola Achukma glanced at the tree, then back at Anagalisgi. "Should I bring him to see you, that you might speak to him of things I do not know?"

Anagalisgi smiled gently. "We will speak. On many occasions. Don't worry about that. But the most important thing you can do is teach him life and keep him in the waking world."

"The priests want to help him refine his dreams and interpret signs; they want him to be you."

"What they want, and what will happen, are not always the same thing. Whatever strife comes between him and them, you must remain his father, and you must teach him everything."

"And ensure he stays in the waking world."

"Yes."

Ola Achukma sighed. "I still don't understand. How am I supposed to raise a son like this? I already feel like I don't understand him, not like Galiliga and Tsona. Sometimes I think I understand Netami better."

"Just be his father," Anagalisgi said. "Everything else that you are, first you are his father."

After a long moment, Ola Achukma nodded. They could speak all day, and even if Ola Achukma did have some epiphany, Sabelu was still only a baby. Any great, mystical triumphs or failures were still years away.

He thanked Anagalisgi and returned home, repeating his conversation with Anagalisgi to Nendawagan as best he could recall. To no one's surprise, she was also a bit confused.

"Keep him in the waking world?" she wondered. "What does that mean?"

"I don't know," Ola Achukma admitted, watching Sabelu as he used the wall to stand and take a few tentative steps. "I think, perhaps, the priests may be a bit overzealous to ensure that they do not ignore Sabelu as they ignored Anagalisgi." He shrugged. "Whatever the case, our task appears to be ensuring that he stays in the waking world."

At that moment, Sabelu, attempting to walk without the help of the wall, went down on his seat. He started whimpering. Nendawagan went to him and scooped him up protectively.

"Maybe in the future," she said, bouncing the fussy child. "But right now, I think he's tired and needs to go to the sleeping world."

Ola Achukma nodded and stood aside so she could put the child down for his nap, carefully laying the white blanket over him. Sabelu still fussed a bit, not calming until Nendawagan started humming. Within moments, he was asleep.

"Do you think he dreams, even now?" Ola Achukma wondered quietly as they backed away.

"I imagine so," Nendawagan said.

"What do you think he sees?"

"I don't know. But I do know that if we're supposed to keep him in the waking world, then we shouldn't let ourselves get so distracted from it either."

"I know, but...I worry. We have the benefit of knowing things about Sabelu that your father and his people didn't know about Anagalisgi."

"Maybe so, but once again, we have to remain in the waking world, too. And right now, in the present moment, in the waking world, our son is asleep in his crib, safe and sound. Whatever evils he may see in the future, we still have to protect him from now."

Ola Achukma sighed but nodded. "I know. You're right. I know."

She took his hand and moved it around on her body provocatively. "Maybe you need a little something to keep you anchored in the waking world, too."

Well, he wasn't going to argue with that.

ᎤᎶᏃᎥ

Ulosonv

Some of the things Anagalisgi had seen concerning Sabelu had worried him in a way he hadn't known since he'd walked in the primary dimension. While he could not walk the spirit world on Hlohi the way he walked on Earth, he could still dream-walk.

He'd never dream-walked to an infant before, but he'd dream-walked to adults whose thoughts and dreams were not so coherent. This, too, worried him.

Initially he found himself in the forest on a hillside. Only when he got past the treeline did he recognize the area. There was a large clearing with a steep drop on two sides leading into the valley.

Beside him, Yawi appeared, the great white wolf's fur prickling and a low growl emanating from its throat. Anagalisgi put a hand on the wolf's shoulder.

"I don't like it either," he murmured.

At the sound of a clattering rock, he turned his gaze toward a trail that did not yet exist. Steep and rocky, a man pulled himself into the clearing. It took Anagalisgi a long moment to realize that this was Sabelu, but as a man grown. He looked very much like his father, but there was also something distinctly Yvgidahi about him. Maybe Anagalisgi was being sentimental.

He had a bow in one hand with a quiver of arrows on his hip. He looked around the clearing as though searching for something, probably game of some form.

Several things happened at once, and Anagalisgi could not quite say what came first, whether it was the snap of a twig, Yawi bursting forth to attack something, the boom of a gun, or Sabelu collapsing to the ground. As soon as everything happened, it was over. Yawi had vanished, but Sabelu remained on the ground. Anagalisgi ran to him.

Sabelu lay on his back, staring up at the sky. He did not appear injured, only confused. He looked at Anagalisgi, a man's knowledge in the body and dreams of an infant.

"What is this?" Sabelu asked.

"A dream," Anagalisgi answered, unsure just what to say or do.

Sabelu shook his head, still lying on the ground. "No. It's more than that. It's real, but not yet."

"A prophetic dream, then, showing you things to come."

He lifted his hands and stared at them, turned them over and back again. "Yes. It must be."

"I've never known someone so young to have such...vivid prophecies before. Even I did not until I was a little older."

"Do you normally speak to those as young as me?"

Anagalisgi felt his face burn hot. "Well, no, I suppose not."

Sabelu blinked. "What do I do with the prophetic dream?"

Anagalisgi let out a breath. "You're too young to communicate this to your parents. But I'm here. I will keep it for you, and I will tell them."

To his surprise, Sabelu shook his head. "No. Don't tell them. It's not on them to know, and it would do more harm than good."

Sabelu twisted, picked himself up off the ground, and faced him. "I think it's time I returned to the waking world."

Anagalisgi could only nod as he stared at his great-nephew. "Yes. I think so, too. And if at all possible, for the time being, please stay there."

ᎢᎬᏁᎢᎤᎠᏏ ᏗᎪᏍᏇᎵᏍᎩᎶᎤᎩ

Igvne'isdi Digohwelisgi

Every time I start a new *TKC* story, I know I'm going to get myself in trouble in some way. Something is going to offend someone. And that's okay. I don't think stores are going to run out of kites any time soon.

But, boy, did I run into this one or what?

This was one of the few books that I did not have a clear outline or sequence of events when I started out, and I had to reorganize and rewrite several times. I had to take what I had already established in previous books and work it into a new plot. The pieces that fell in the Old Land came together very easily. Having to create daily life on Hlohi was a whole different beast. I didn't want to just copy and paste from Itsa'ti because that wouldn't make sense, nor would it be fun, to write or read.

Only once I really looked at some of the logistics that I was facing (such as how and why Nendawagan would wait so long to get married and have children) did things really start to come together. And I think the central theme that emerged was simply human nature. At the end of *Wolf Pack* (with the added benefit of modern knowledge), we see the Aniyvwiya dropped off on Hlohi, and we know they won't be returning. We now have an isolated, homogeneous population with no real enemies to speak of and enough power to ensure that their basic survival needs are wholly met. What do they do with that? How does man react to paradise? What is the purpose of life when our most basic struggles are taken care of?

On top of that, why do some people seem unable or unwilling to let go of the past once they are delivered to paradise? What is peace? How does a society achieve long-lasting peace? What does a peaceful people do when there is rot from within?

As I said in *Wolf Pack*, I expect *The Lone Wolf* to be the most serious series of the entire *Timekeeper Chronicles*. For readers of *The Chivalrous Welshman*, you got a glimpse of Sabelu and his shining personality. You've also come to know Anagalisgi as a familiar face. And while *The Lone Wolf* may be seen as less pertinent to *TKC* than, say, *The Hands of Time*, I think *TLW* will end up being the most thorough explanation of the less physical aspect of all the wars going on in all of the other series.

I hope some of the more subtle and finely-tuned aspects of TKC start to come together for you, Reader. Because once they do, I think they're going to turn your world upside down.